"Picoult approaches the troubled (and troubling) psyche of the high school students with empathy and respect."

—*The Washington Post*

—*Entertainment Weekly*

"Every bit as gripping and moving as Picoult's previous novels, *Nineteen Minutes* will no doubt garner considerable attention for its controversial subject and twist ending."

—*Booklist*

This title is also available as an eBook

"Picoult's writing finesse shines. . . . Coupled with its illustrated counterpart, [The Tenth Circle] becomes a treat for both the mind and the eye."

—*Houston Chronicle*

"In her taut tale, Jodi Picoult deftly builds the suspense as the story moves from the aftermath of rape to more heartache. . . . [She] will make you guess until the end."

—*Pittsburgh Post Gazette*

Praise for

VANISHING ACTS

"Ms. Picoult is a solid, lively storyteller."

—*The New York Times*

"Richly textured and engaging."

—*The Boston Globe*

"The worlds Picoult creates for her characters resonate with authenticity, and the people who inhabit them are so engaging."

—*People*

Also by Jodi Picoult

The Tenth Circle
Vanishing Acts
My Sister's Keeper
Second Glance
Perfect Match
Salem Falls
Plain Truth
Keeping Faith
The Pact
Mercy
Picture Perfect
Harvesting the Heart
Songs of the Humpback Whale

Nineteen Minutes

A Novel

Jodi Picoult

ATRIA BOOKS

NEW YORK   LONDON   TORONTO   SYDNEY

ATRIA BOOKS

A Division of Simon & Schuster, Inc.
1230 Avenue of the Americas
New York, NY 10020

This book is a work of fiction. Names, characters, places, and incidents are products of the author's imagination or are used fictitiously. Any resemblance to actual events or locales or persons living or dead is entirely coincidental.

Copyright © 2007 by Jodi Picoult

This Atria Books export edition November 2007

ATRIA BOOKS and colophon are trademarks of Simon & Schuster, Inc.

For information about special discounts for bulk purchases, please contact Simon & Schuster Special Sales at 1-800-456-6798 or business@simonandschuster.com.

Manufactured in the United States of America

10 9 8 7 6 5 4 3 2

ISBN-13: 978-1-4165-4699-3
ISBN-10:   1-4165-4699-5

Acknowledgments

You know it's going to be an intriguing paragraph when I first thank the man who came to my house to teach me how to shoot a handgun in a woodpile in my own backyard: Captain Frank Moran. Thanks, too, to his colleague, Lieutenant Michael Evans, for detailed information on firearms, and to police chief Nick Giaccone for the bazillion last-minute email questions about search, seizure, and all things police-oriented. Detective Trooper Claire Demarais gets her own special kudo for being the queen of forensics and for walking Patrick through a crime scene of enormous proportion. I'm fortunate to have many friends and family who happen to also be experts in their fields, who let me share their stories, or who serve as sounding boards: Jane Picoult, Dr. David Toub, Wyatt Fox, Chris Keating, Suzanne Serat, Doug Fagen, Janine Scheiner, Conrad Farnham, Chris and Karen van Leer. Thanks to Guenther Frankenstein for his family's generous contribution to the expansion of Hanover's Howe Library and for the use of his marvelous name. Glen Libby patiently answered my questions about life at the Grafton County Jail, and Ray Fleer, the under-sheriff at the Jefferson County Sheriff's Office, provided me with materials and information about the school shooting at Columbine. Thanks to David Plaut and Jake van Leer for the *really* bad math joke; Doug Irwin for teaching me the economics of happiness; Kyle van Leer and Axel Hansen for the premise behind *Hide-n-Shriek*; Luke Hansen for the C++ program; and Ellen Irwin for the popularity chart. I'm grateful, as always, to the team at Atria Books that makes me look so much better than I truly am: Carolyn Reidy, David Brown, Alyson Maz-zarelli, Christine DuPlessis, Gary Urda, Jeanne Lee, Lisa Keim, Sarah Branham, and the indefatigable Jodi Lipper. To Judith Curr, thanks for singing my praises without stopping to take a breath. To Camille McDuffie, thank you for making me that rarest of things in publishing: a brand name. To Laura Gross, I raise a wee dram of Highland whiskey and salute you, because I can't imag-ine this business without you. To Emily Bestler, well, check out the following page. A very special nod to Judge Jennifer Sargent, without whose input the character of Alex could not have existed. And to Jennifer Sternick, my own personal prosecutor—you're one of the brightest women I've ever met, and you make work way too much fun for our own good (long live King Wah), so it's clearly your own damn fault that I keep asking you to help again and again. Thanks, as always, to my family—Kyle, Jake, and Sammy—who make sure I remember what's really important in life; and to my husband, Tim—the reason I'm the luckiest woman on earth. Lastly, I would like to thank a cadre of people who were the heart and soul of this book: the survivors of actual school shootings in America, and those who helped with the emotional aftermath: Betsy Bicknase, Denna O'Connell, Linda Liebl, and the remarkable Kevin Braun—thank you for having the courage to revisit your memories and the grace to let me borrow them. And finally, to the thousands of kids out there who are a little bit different, a little bit scared, a little bit unpopular: this one's for you.

For Emily Bestler,
the finest editor and fiercest champion
a girl could ask for, who makes sure
I put my best foot forward,
every time.
Thanks for your keen eye, your cheerleading,
and most of all, your friendship.

PART ONE

If we don't change the direction we are headed,
we will end up where we are going.

—CHINESE PROVERB

By the time you read this, I hope to be dead.

You can't undo something that's happened; you can't take back a word that's already been said out loud. You'll think about me and wish that you had been able to talk me out of this. You'll try to figure out what would have been the one right thing to say, to do. I guess I should tell you, <u>Don't blame yourself; this isn't your fault,</u> but that would be a lie. We both know that I didn't get here by myself.

You'll cry, at my funeral. You'll say it didn't have to be this way. You will act like everyone expects you to. But will you miss me?

More importantly—will I miss you?

Does either one of us really want to hear the answer to that question?

March 6, 2007

In nineteen minutes, you can mow the front lawn, color your hair, watch a third of a hockey game. In nineteen minutes, you can bake scones or get a tooth filled by a dentist; you can fold laundry for a family of five.

Nineteen minutes is how long it took the Tennessee Titans to sell out of tickets to the play-offs. It's the length of a sitcom, minus the commercials. It's the driving distance from the Vermont border to the town of Sterling, New Hampshire.

In nineteen minutes, you can order a pizza and get it delivered. You can read a story to a child or have your oil changed. You can walk a mile. You can sew a hem.

In nineteen minutes, you can stop the world, or you can just jump off it.

In nineteen minutes, you can get revenge.

As usual, Alex Cormier was running late. It took thirty-two minutes to drive from her house in Sterling to the superior court in Grafton County, New Hampshire, and that was only if she speeded through Orford. She hurried downstairs in her stockings, carrying her heels and the files she'd brought home with her over the weekend. She twisted her thick copper hair into a knot and anchored it at the base of her neck with bobby pins, transforming herself into the person she needed to be before she left her house.

Alex had been a superior court judge now for thirty-four days. She'd believed that, having proved her mettle as a district court judge for the past five years, this time around the appointment might be easier. But at forty, she was still the youngest judge in the state. She still had to fight to establish herself as a fair justice—her history as a public defender preceded her into her courtroom, and prosecutors assumed she'd side with the defense. When Alex had submitted her name years ago for the bench, it had been with the sincere desire to make sure people in this legal system were innocent until proven guilty. She just never anticipated that, as a judge, she might not be given the same benefit of the doubt.

The smell of freshly brewed coffee drew Alex into the kitchen. Her daughter was hunched over a steaming mug at the kitchen table, poring over a textbook. Josie looked exhausted—her blue eyes were bloodshot; her chestnut hair was a knotty ponytail. "Tell me you haven't been up all night," Alex said.

Josie didn't even glance up. "I haven't been up all night," she parroted.

Alex poured herself a cup of coffee and slid into the chair across from her. "Honestly?"

"You asked me to tell you something," Josie said. "You didn't ask for the truth."

Alex frowned. "You shouldn't be drinking coffee."

"And you shouldn't be smoking cigarettes."

Alex felt her face heat up. "I don't—"

"Mom," Josie sighed, "even when you open up the bathroom windows, I can still smell it on the towels." She glanced up, daring Alex to challenge her other vices.

Alex herself didn't have any other vices. She didn't have *time* for any vices. She would have liked to say that she knew with authority that Josie didn't have any vices, either, but she would only be making the same inference the rest of the world did when they met Josie: a pretty, popular, straight-A student who knew better than most the consequences of falling off the straight-and-narrow. A girl who was destined for great things. A young woman who was exactly what Alex had hoped her daughter would grow to become.

Josie had once been so proud to have a mother as a judge. Alex could remember Josie broadcasting her career to the tellers at the bank, the baggers in the grocery store, the flight attendants on planes. She'd ask Alex about her cases and her decisions. That had all changed three years ago, when Josie entered high school, and the tunnel of communication between them slowly bricked shut. Alex didn't necessarily think that Josie was hiding anything more than any other teenager, but it was different: a normal parent might metaphorically judge her child's friends, whereas Alex could do it legally.

"What's on the docket today?" Alex said.

"Unit test. What about you?"

"Arraignments," Alex replied. She squinted across the table, trying to read Josie's textbook upside down. "Chemistry?"

"Catalysts." Josie rubbed her temples. "Substances that speed up a reaction, but stay unchanged by it. Like if you've got carbon monoxide gas and hydrogen gas and you toss in zinc and chromium oxide, and . . . what's the matter?"

"Just having a little flashback of why I got a C in Orgo. Have you had breakfast?"

"Coffee," Josie said.

"Coffee doesn't count."

"It does when *you're* in a rush," Josie pointed out.

Alex weighed the costs of being even five minutes later, or getting another black mark against her in the cosmic good-parenting tally. *Shouldn't a seventeen-year-old be able to take care of herself in the morning?* Alex started pulling items out of the refrigerator: eggs, milk, bacon. "I once presided over an involuntary emergency admission at the state mental hospital for a woman who thought she was Emeril. Her husband had her committed when she put a pound of bacon in the blender and chased him around the kitchen with a knife, yelling *Bam!*"

Josie glanced up from her textbook. "For real?"

"Oh, believe me, I can't make these things up." Alex cracked an egg into a skillet. "When I asked her why she'd put a pound of bacon in the blender, she looked at me and said that she and I must just cook differently."

Josie stood up and leaned against the counter, watching her mother cook. Domesticity wasn't Alex's strong point—she didn't know how to make a pot roast but was proud to have memorized the phone numbers of every pizza place and Chinese restaurant in Sterling that offered free delivery. "Relax," Alex said dryly. "I think I can do this without setting the house on fire."

But Josie took the skillet out of her hands and laid the strips of bacon in it, like sailors bunking tightly together. "How come you dress like that?" she asked.

Alex glanced down at her skirt, blouse, and heels and frowned. "Why? Is it too Margaret Thatcher?"

"No, I mean . . . why do you bother? No one knows what you have on under your robe. You could wear, like, pajama pants. Or that sweater you have from college that's got holes in the elbows."

"Whether or not people *see* it, I'm still expected to dress . . . well, *judiciously.*"

A cloud passed over Josie's face, and she busied herself over the stove, as if Alex had somehow given the wrong answer. Alex stared at her daughter—the bitten half-moon fingernails, the freckle behind her ear, the zigzag part in her hair—and saw instead the toddler who'd wait at the babysitter's window at sundown, because she knew that was when Alex came to get her. "I've never worn pajamas to work," Alex admitted, "but I do sometimes close the door to chambers and take a nap on the floor."

A slow, surprised smile played over Josie's face. She held her mother's admission as if it were a butterfly lighting on her hand by accident: an event so startling you could not call attention to it without risking its loss. But there were miles to drive and defendants to arraign and chemical equations to interpret, and by the time Josie had set the bacon to drain on a pad of paper toweling, the moment had winged away.

"I still don't get why *I* have to eat breakfast if *you* don't," Josie muttered.

"Because you have to be a certain age to earn the right to ruin your own life." Alex pointed at the scrambled eggs Josie was mixing in the skillet. "Promise me you'll finish that?"

Josie met her gaze. "Promise."

"Then I'm headed out."

Alex grabbed her travel mug of coffee. By the time she backed her car out of the garage, her head was already focused on the decision she had to write that afternoon; the number of arraignments the clerk would have stuffed onto her docket; the motions that would have fallen like shadows across her desk between Friday afternoon and this morning. She was caught up in a world far away from home, where at that very moment her daughter scraped the scrambled eggs from the skillet into the trash can without ever taking a single bite.

Sometimes Josie thought of her life as a room with no doors and no windows. It was a sumptuous room, sure—a room half the kids in Sterling High would have given their right arm to enter—but it was also a room from which there really wasn't an escape. Either Josie was someone she didn't want to be, or she was someone who nobody wanted.

She lifted her face to the spray of the shower—water she'd made so hot it raised red welts, stole breath, steamed windows. She counted to ten, and then finally ducked away from the stream to stand naked and dripping in front of the mirror. Her face was swollen and scarlet; her hair stuck to her shoulders in thick ropes. She turned sideways, scrutinized her flat belly, and sucked it in a little. She knew what Matt saw when he looked at her, what Courtney and Maddie and Brady and Haley and Drew all saw— she just wished that she could see it, too. The problem was, when Josie looked in the mirror, she noticed what was underneath that raw skin, instead of what had been painted upon it.

She understood how she was *supposed* to look and *supposed* to act. She wore her dark hair long and straight; she dressed in Abercrombie & Fitch; she listened to Dashboard Confessional and Death Cab for Cutie. She liked feeling the eyes of other girls in the school when she sat in the cafeteria borrowing Courtney's makeup. She liked the way teachers already knew her name on the first day of class. She liked having guys stare at her when she walked down the hall with Matt's arm around her.

But there was a part of her that wondered what would

happen if she let them all in on the secret—that some mornings, it was hard to get out of bed and put on someone else's smile; that she was standing on air, a fake who laughed at all the right jokes and whispered all the right gossip and attracted the right guy, a fake who had nearly forgotten what it felt like to be *real* . . . and who, when you got right down to it, didn't want to remember, because it hurt even more than this.

There wasn't anyone to talk to. If you even *doubted* your right to be one of the privileged, popular set, then you didn't belong there. And Matt—well, he'd fallen for the Josie on the surface, like everyone else. In fairy tales, when the mask came off, the handsome prince still loved the girl, no matter what—and that alone would turn her into a princess. But high school didn't work that way. What made her a princess was hooking up with Matt. And in some weird circular logic, what made Matt hook up with her was the very fact that she was one of Sterling High's princesses.

She couldn't confide in her mother, either. *You don't stop being a judge just because you step out of the courthouse,* her mother used to say. It was why Alex Cormier never drank more than one glass of wine in public; it was why she never yelled or cried. A trial was a stupid word, considering that an attempt was never good enough: you were supposed to toe the line, period. Many of the accomplishments that Josie's mother was most proud of—Josie's grades, her looks, her acceptance into the "right" crowd— had not been achieved because Josie wanted them so badly herself, but mostly because she was afraid of falling short of perfect.

Josie wrapped a towel around herself and headed into her bedroom. She pulled a pair of jeans out of her closet and then layered two long-sleeved tees that showed off her chest. She glanced at her clock—if she wasn't going to be late, she'd have to get moving.

Before leaving her room, though, she hesitated. She sank down onto her bed and rummaged underneath the nightstand for the Ziploc sandwich bag that she'd tacked to the wooden frame. Inside was a stash of Ambien—pirated one pill at a time from her mother's prescription for insomnia, so she'd never notice. It had taken Josie nearly six months to inconspicuously gather only fifteen pills, but she figured if she washed them down with a fifth of vodka, it would do the trick. It wasn't like she had a strategy, really, to kill herself next Tuesday, or when the snow melted, or anything concrete like that. It was more like a backup plan: When the truth came out, and no one wanted to be around her anymore, it stood to reason Josie wouldn't want to be around herself either.

She tacked the pills back beneath her nightstand and headed downstairs. As she walked into the kitchen to load up her backpack, she found her chemistry textbook still wide open—and a long-stemmed red rose marking her place.

Matt was leaning against the refrigerator in the corner; he must have let himself in through the open garage door. Like always, he made her head swim with seasons—his hair was all the colors of autumn; his eyes the bright blue of a winter sky; his smile as wide as any summer sun. He was wearing a baseball hat backward, and a Sterling Varsity Hockey tee over a thermal shirt that Josie had once stolen for a full month and hidden in her underwear drawer, so that when she needed to she could breathe in the scent of him. "Are you still pissed off?" he asked.

Josie hesitated. "I wasn't the one who was mad."

Matt pushed away from the refrigerator, coming forward until he could link his arms around Josie's waist. "You know I can't help it."

A dimple blossomed in his right cheek; Josie could already feel herself softening. "It wasn't that I didn't want to see you. I really *did* have to study."

Matt pushed her hair off her face and kissed her. This was exactly why she'd told him not to come over last night—when she was with him, she felt herself evaporating. Sometimes, when he touched her, Josie imagined herself vanishing in a puff of steam.

He tasted of maple syrup, of apologies. "It's all your fault, you know," he said. "I wouldn't act as crazy if I didn't love you so much."

At that moment, Josie could not remember the pills she was hoarding in her room; she could not remember crying in the shower; she could not remember anything but what it felt like to be adored. *I'm lucky*, she told herself, the word streaming like a silver ribbon through her mind. *Lucky, lucky, lucky.*

Patrick Ducharme, the sole detective on the Sterling police force, sat on a bench on the far side of the locker room, listening to the patrol officers on the morning shift pick on a rookie with a little extra padding around the middle. "Hey, Fisher," Eddie Odenkirk said, "are you the one who's having the baby, or is it your wife?"

As the rest of the guys laughed, Patrick took pity on the kid. "It's early, Eddie," he said. "Can't you at least wait to start in until we've all had a cup of coffee?"

"I would, Captain," Eddie laughed, "but it looks like Fisher already ate all the donuts and—what the *hell* is that?"

Patrick followed Eddie's gaze downward, to his own feet. He did not, as a matter of course, change in the locker room with the patrol officers, but he'd jogged to the station this morning instead of driving, to work off too much good cooking consumed over the weekend. He'd spent Saturday and Sunday in Maine with the girl who currently held his heart—his goddaughter, a five-and-a-half-year-old named Tara Frost. Her mother, Nina, was Patrick's oldest friend, and the one love he probably would never get over, although she managed to be doing quite well without him. Over the course of the weekend, Patrick had deliberately lost ten thousand games of Candy Land, had given countless piggyback rides, had had his hair done, and—here was his cardinal mistake—had allowed Tara to put bright pink nail polish on his toes, which Patrick had forgotten to remove.

He glanced down at his feet and curled his toes under. "Chicks think it's hot," he said gruffly, as the seven men in the locker room struggled not to snicker at someone who was technically their superior. Patrick yanked his dress socks on, slipped into his loafers, and walked out, still holding his tie. *One*, he counted. *Two, three.* On cue, laughter spilled out of the locker room, following him down the hallway.

In his office, Patrick closed the door and peered at himself in the tiny mirror on the back. His black hair was still damp from his shower; his face was flushed from his run. He shimmied the knot of his tie up his neck, fashioning the noose, and then sat down at his desk.

Seventy-two emails had come in over the weekend—and usually anything more than fifty meant he wouldn't get home before 8:00 p.m. all week. He began to weed through them, adding notes to a devil's To Do list—one that never got any shorter, no matter how hard he worked.

Today, Patrick had to drive drugs down to the state lab—not a big deal, except that it was a four-hour block of his day that vanished right there. He had a rape case coming to fruition, the perp identified from a college face book and his statements transcribed and ready for the AG's office. He had a cell phone that had been nabbed out of a car by a homeless guy. He had blood results come back from the lab as a match for a break-in at a jewelry store, and a suppression hearing in superior court, and already on his desk was the first new complaint of the day—a theft of wallets in which the credit cards had been used, leaving a trail for Patrick to trace.

Being a small-town detective required Patrick to be firing on all cylinders, all the time. Unlike cops he knew who worked for city departments, where they had twenty-four hours to solve a case before it was considered cold, Patrick's job was to take everything that came across his desk—not to cherry-pick for the interesting ones. It was hard to get excited about a bad check case, or a theft that would net the perp a $200 fine when it cost the taxpayers five times that to have Patrick focus on it for a week. But every time he started thinking that his cases weren't particularly important, he'd find himself face-to-face with a victim: the hysterical mother whose wallet had been stolen; the mom-and-pop jewelry store owners who'd been robbed of their retirement income; the rattled professor who was a victim of identity theft. Hope, Patrick knew, was the exact measure of distance between himself and the person who'd come for help. If Patrick didn't get involved, if he didn't give a hundred percent, then that victim was going to be a victim forever—which was why, since Patrick had joined the Sterling police, he had managed to solve every single case.

And yet.

When Patrick was lying in his bed alone and letting his mind sew a seam across the hem of his life, he did not remember the proven successes—only the potential failures. When he walked around the perimeter of a vandalized barn or found the stolen car stripped down and dumped in the woods or handed the tissue to the sobbing girl who'd been date-raped, Patrick couldn't help but feel that he was too late. He was a detective, but he didn't *detect* anything. It fell into his lap, already broken, every time.

It was the first warm day of March, the one where you started to believe that the snow would melt sooner rather than later, and that June was truly just around the corner. Josie sat on the hood of Matt's Saab in the student parking lot, thinking that it was closer to summer than it was to the start of this school year, that in a scant three months, she would officially be a member of the senior class.

Beside her, Matt leaned against the windshield, his face tipped up to the sun. "Let's ditch school," he said. "It's too nice out to be stuck inside all day."

"If you ditch, you'll be benched."

The state championship tournament in hockey began this afternoon, and Matt played right wing. Sterling had won last year, and they had every expectation of doing it again. "You're coming to the game," Matt said, and it wasn't a question, but a statement.

"Are you going to score?"

Matt smiled wickedly and tugged her on top of him. "Don't I always?" he said, but he wasn't talking about hockey anymore, and she felt a blush rise over the collar of her scarf.

Suddenly Josie felt a rain of hail on her back. They both sat up to find Brady Pryce, a football player, walking by hand-in-hand with Haley Weaver, the homecoming queen. Haley tossed a second shower of pennies—Sterling High's way of wishing an athlete good luck. "Kick ass today, Royston," Brady called.

Their math teacher was crossing the parking lot, too,

with a worn black leather briefcase and a thermos of coffee. "Hey, Mr. McCabe," Matt called out. "How'd I do on last Friday's test?"

"Luckily, you've got other talents to fall back on, Mr. Royston," the teacher said as he reached into his pocket. He winked at Josie as he pitched the coins, pennies that fell from the sky onto her shoulders like confetti, like stars coming loose.

It figures, Alex thought as she stuffed the contents of her purse back inside. She had switched handbags and left her pass key at home, which allowed her into the employee entrance at the rear of the superior court. Although she'd pushed the buzzer a million times, no one seemed to be around to let her in.

"Goddamn," she muttered under her breath, hiking around the slush puddles so that her alligator heels wouldn't get ruined—one of the perks of parking in the back was *not* having to do this. She could cut through the clerk's office to her chambers, and if the planets were aligned, maybe even onto the bench without causing a delay in the docket.

Although the public entrance of the court had a line twenty people long, the court officers recognized Alex because, unlike the district court circuit, where you bounced from courthouse to courthouse, she would be ensconced here for six months. The officers waved her to the front of the line, but since she was carrying keys and a stainless steel travel thermos and God only knew what else in her purse, she set off the metal detectors.

The alarm was a spotlight; every eye in the lobby turned to see who'd gotten caught. Ducking her head, Alex hurried across the polished tile floor and nearly lost her footing. As she pitched forward, a squat man reached forward to steady her. "Hey, baby," he said, leering. "I like your shoes."

Without responding, Alex yanked herself out of his grasp and headed toward the clerk's office. None of the other superior court judges had to deal with this. Judge Wagner was a nice guy, but with a face that looked like a pumpkin left to rot after Halloween. Judge Gerhardt—a fellow female—had *blouses* that were older than Alex. When Alex had first come to the bench, she'd thought that being a relatively young, moderately attractive woman was a *good* thing—a vote against typecasting—but on mornings like this, she wasn't so sure.

She dumped her purse in chambers, shrugged into her robe, and took five minutes to drink her coffee and review the docket. Each case got its own file, but cases for repeat offenders were rubber-banded together, and sometimes judges wrote Post-it notes to each other inside about the case. Alex opened one and saw a picture of a stick-figure man with bars in front of his face—a signal from Judge Gerhardt that this was the offender's last chance, and that next time, he should go to jail.

She rang the buzzer to signify to the court officer that she was ready to start, and waited to hear her cue: "*All rise, the Honorable Alexandra Cormier presiding.*" Walking into a courtroom, to Alex, always felt as if she were stepping onto a stage for the first time at a Broadway opening. You knew there would be people there, you knew their gazes would all be focused on you, but that didn't prevent you from having a moment when you could not breathe, could not believe you were the one they had come to see.

Alex moved briskly behind the bench and sat down. There were seventy arraignments scheduled for that morning, and the courtroom was packed. The first defendant was called, and he shuffled past the bar with his eyes averted.

"Mr. O'Reilly," Alex said, and as the man met her gaze she recognized him as the guy from the lobby. He was clearly uncomfortable, now that he realized whom he'd been flirting with. "You're the gentleman who assisted me earlier, aren't you?"

He swallowed. "Yes, Your Honor."

"If you'd known I was the judge, Mr. O'Reilly, would you have said, 'Hey, baby, I like your shoes'?"

The defendant glanced down, weighing impropriety against honesty. "I guess so, Your Honor," he said after a moment. "Those *are* great shoes."

The entire courtroom went still, anticipating her reaction. Alex smiled broadly. "Mr. O'Reilly," she said, "I couldn't agree more."

Lacy Houghton leaned over the bed railing and put her face right in front of her sobbing patient's. "You can do this," she said firmly. "You *can* do this, and you will."

After sixteen hours of labor, they were all exhausted—Lacy, the patient, and the father-to-be, who was facing zero-hour with the dawning realization that he was superfluous, that right now, his wife wanted her midwife much more than she wanted him. "I want you to get behind Janine," Lacy told him, "and brace her back. Janine, I want you to look at me and give me another good push . . ."

The woman gritted her teeth and bore down, losing all sense of herself in the effort to create someone else. Lacy reached down to feel the baby's head, to guide it past the seal of skin and quickly loop the cord over its head without ever losing eye contact with her patient. "For the next twenty seconds, your baby is going to be the newest person on this planet," Lacy said. "Would you like to meet her?"

The answer was a pressured push. A crest of intention, a roar of purpose, a sluice of slick, purpled body that Lacy quickly lifted into the mother's arms, so that when the infant cried for the first time in this life, she would already be in a position to be comforted.

Her patient started weeping again—tears had a whole different melody, didn't they, without the pain threaded through them? The new parents bent over their baby, a closed circle. Lacy stepped back and watched. There was plenty of work left for a midwife to do even after the moment of birth, but for right now, she wanted to make eye contact with this little being. Where parents would notice a chin that looked like Aunt Marge's or a nose that resembled Grandpa's, Lacy would see instead a gaze wide with wisdom and peace—eight pounds of unadulterated possibility. Newborns reminded her of tiny Buddhas, faces full of divinity. It didn't last long, though. When Lacy saw these same infants a week later at their regular checkups, they had turned into ordinary—albeit tiny—people. That holiness, somehow, disappeared, and Lacy was always left wondering where in this world it might go.

While his mother was across town delivering the newest resident of Sterling, New Hampshire, Peter Houghton was waking up. His father knocked on the door on his way out to work—Peter's alarm clock. Downstairs, a bowl and a box of cereal would be waiting for him—his mother remembered to do that even when she got paged at two in the morning. There would be a note from her, too, telling him to have a good day at school, as if it were that simple.

Peter threw back his covers. He moved to his desk, still wearing his pajama bottoms, sat down, and logged onto the Internet.

The words on the message board were blurry. He reached for his glasses—he kept them next to his computer. After he slipped the frames on, he dropped the case onto the keyboard—and suddenly, he was seeing something he'd hoped never to see again.

Peter reached out and hit CONTROL ALT DELETE, but he could still picture it, even after the screen went blank, even after he closed his eyes, even after he started to cry.

In a town the size of Sterling, everyone knew everyone else, and always had. In some ways, this was comforting—like a great big extended family that you sometimes loved and sometimes fell out of favor with. At other times, it haunted Josie: like right now, when she was standing in the cafeteria line behind Natalie Zlenko, a dyke of the first order who, way back in second grade, had invited Josie over to play and had convinced her to pee on the front lawn like a boy. *What were you* thinking, her mother had said, when she'd come to pick her up and saw them bare-bottomed and squatting over the daffodils. Even now, a decade later, Josie couldn't look at Natalie Zlenko with her buzz cut and her ever-present SLR camera without wondering if Natalie still thought about that, too.

On Josie's other side was Courtney Ignatio, the alpha female of Sterling High. With her honey-blond hair hanging over her shoulders like a shawl made of silk and her low-rise jeans mail-ordered from Fred Segal, she'd spawned an entourage of clones. On Courtney's tray was a bottle of water and a banana. On Josie's was a platter of French fries. It was second period, and just like her mother had predicted, she was famished.

"Hey," Courtney said, loud enough for Natalie to overhear. "Can you tell the *vagitarian* to let us pass?"

Natalie's cheeks burned with color, and she flattened herself up against the sneeze guard of the salad bar so that Courtney and Josie could slip by. They paid for their food and walked across the cafeteria.

Whenever she came into the cafeteria, Josie felt like a naturalist observing different species in their natural, nonacademic habitat. There were the geeks, bent over their textbooks and laughing at math jokes nobody else even *wanted* to understand. Behind them were the art freaks, who smoked clove cigarettes on the ropes course behind the school and drew manga comics in the margins of their notes. Near the condiment bar were the skanks, who drank black coffee and waited for the bus that would take them to the technical high school three towns over for their afternoon classes; and the druggies, already strung out by nine o'clock in the morning. There were misfits, too—kids like Natalie and Angela Phlug, fringe friends by default, because nobody else would have them.

And then there was Josie's posse. They took over two tables, not because there were so many of them, but because they were larger than life: Emma, Maddie, Haley, John, Brady, Trey, Drew. Josie could remember how, when she started hanging around with this group, she'd get everyone's names confused. They were *that* interchangeable.

They all sort of looked alike, too—the boys all wearing their maroon home hockey jerseys and their hats backward, bright thatches of hair stuck through the loops at their foreheads like the start of a fire; the girls carbon copies of Courtney, by studious design. Josie slipped inconspicuously into the heart of them, because she looked like Courtney, too. Her tangle of hair had been blown glass-straight; her heels were three inches high, even though there was still snow on the ground. If she appeared the same on the outside, it was that much easier to ignore the fact that she didn't really know how she felt on the inside.

"Hey," Maddie said, as Courtney sat down beside her.

"Hey."

"Did you hear about Fiona Kierland?"

Courtney's eyes lit up; gossip was as good a catalyst as any chemical. "The one whose boobs are two different sizes?"

"No, that's Fiona the sophomore. I'm talking about Fiona the freshman."

"The one who always carries a box of tissues for her allergies?" Josie said, sliding into a seat.

"Or not," Haley said. "Guess who got sent to rehab for snorting coke."

"Get *out*."

"That's not even the whole scandal," Emma added. "Her dealer was the head of the Bible study group that meets after school."

"Oh my *God!*" Courtney said.

"*Exactly.*"

"Hey." Matt slipped into the chair beside Josie. "What took you so long?"

She turned to him. At this end of the table, the guys were rolling straw wrappers into spitballs and talking about the end of spring skiing. "How long do you think the half-pipe will stay open at Sunapee?" John asked, lobbing a spitball toward a kid one table away who had fallen asleep.

The boy had been in Josie's Sign Language elective last year. Like her, he was a junior. His arms and legs were skinny and white and splayed like a stickbug; his mouth, as he snored, was wide-open.

"You missed, loser," Drew said. "If Sunapee closes, Killington's still good. They have snow until, like, August." His spitball landed in the boy's hair.

Derek. The kid's name was Derek.

Matt glanced at Josie's French fries. "You're not going to eat *those*, are you?"

"I'm starving."

He pinched the side of her waist, a caliper and a criticism all at once. Josie looked down at the fries. Ten seconds ago, they'd looked golden brown and smelled like heaven; now all she could see was the grease that stained the paper plate.

Matt took a handful and passed the rest to Drew, who threw a spitball that landed in the sleeping boy's mouth. With a choke and a sputter, Derek startled awake.

"Sweet!" Drew high-fived John.

Derek spat into a napkin and rubbed his mouth hard. He glanced around to see who else had been watching. Josie suddenly remembered a sign from her ASL elective, almost all of which she'd forgotten the moment she'd taken the final. A closed fist moved in a circle over the heart meant *I'm sorry.*

Matt leaned over and kissed her neck. "Let's get out of here." He drew Josie to her feet and then turned to his friends. "Later," he said.

The gymnasium at Sterling High School was on the second floor, above what would have been a swimming pool if the bond issue had passed when the school was in its planning stages, and what instead became three classrooms that continually resounded with the pounding of sneakered feet and bouncing basketballs. Michael Beach and his best friend, Justin Friedman, two freshmen, sat on the sidelines of the basketball court while their Phys Ed teacher went over the mechanics of dribbling for the hundredth time. It was a wasted exercise—kids in this class were either like Noah James, already an expert, or like Michael and Justin, who were fluent in Elvish but defined *home run* as what you did after school in order to avoid getting hung up on coat hooks by your underwear. They sat cross-legged and knob-kneed, listening to the rodent's squeak of

Coach Spears's white sneakers as he hustled from one end of the court to the other.

"Ten bucks says I get picked last for a team," Justin murmured.

"I wish we could get out of class," Michael commiserated. "Maybe there'll be a fire drill."

Justin grinned. "An earthquake."

"A monsoon."

"Locusts!"

"A terrorist attack!"

Two sneakers stopped in front of them. Coach Spears glared down, his arms folded. "You two want to tell me what's so funny about basketball?"

Michael glanced at Justin, then up at the coach. "Absolutely nothing," he said.

After showering, Lacy Houghton made herself a mug of green tea and wandered peacefully through her house. When the kids had been tiny and she'd been overwhelmed by work and life, Lewis would ask her what he could do to make things better. It had been a great irony for her, given Lewis's job. A professor at Sterling College, his specialty was the economics of happiness. Yes, it was a real field of study, and yes, he was an expert. He'd taught seminars and written articles and had been interviewed on CNN about measuring the effects of pleasure and good fortune on a monetary scale—and yet he'd been at a loss when it came to figuring out what Lacy would enjoy. Did she want to go out to a nice dinner? Get a pedicure? Take a nap? When she told him what she craved, though, he could not comprehend. She'd wanted to be in her own house, with nobody else in it, and nothing pressing to do.

She opened the door to Peter's room and set her mug on the dresser so that she could make his bed. *What's the*

point, Peter would say when she dogged him to do it himself. *I just have to mess it up again in a few hours.*

For the most part, she didn't enter Peter's room unless
he was in it. Maybe that was why, at first, she felt there was
something wrong about the space, as if an integral part
were missing. At first she assumed that it was Peter's absence that made the room seem a little empty, then she realized that the computer—a steady hum, an ever-ready
green screen—had been turned off.

She tugged the sheets up and tucked in the edges; she
drew the quilt over them and fluffed the pillows. At the
threshold of Peter's bedroom she paused and smiled: the
room looked perfect.

Zoe Patterson was wondering what it was like to kiss a guy
who had braces. Not that it was a remote possibility for her
anytime in the near future, but she figured it was something she ought to consider before the moment actually
caught her off guard. In fact, she wondered what it would
be like to kiss a guy, period—even one who wasn't ortho-
dontically challenged, like her. And honestly, was there
any place better than a stupid math class to let your mind
wander?

Mr. McCabe, who thought he was the Chris Rock of algebra, was doing his daily stand-up routine. "So, two kids
are in the lunch line, when the first kid turns to his friend
and says, 'I have no money! What should I do?' And his
buddy says, '2x + 5!'"

Zoe looked up at the clock. She counted along with the
second hand until it was 9:50 on the dot and then popped
out of her seat to hand Mr. McCabe a pass. "Ah, orthodon-
tia," he read out loud. "Well, make sure he doesn't wire
your mouth shut, Ms. Patterson. So, the buddy says, '2x +
5.' A binomial. Get it? *Buy-no-meal?!*"

Zoe hefted her backpack onto her shoulders and walked out of the classroom. She had to meet her mom in front of the school at ten o'clock—parking was killer, so it would be a drive-by pickup. Mid-class, the halls were hollow and resonant; it felt like trudging through the belly of a whale. Zoe detoured into the main office to sign out on the secretary's clipboard, and then nearly mowed down a kid in her hurry to get outside.

It was warm enough to unzip her jacket and think of summer and soccer camp and what it would be like when her palate expander was finally removed. If you kissed a guy who didn't have braces, and you pressed too hard, could you cut his gums? Something told Zoe that if you made a guy bleed, you probably wouldn't be hooking up with him again. What if he had braces, too, like that blond kid from Chicago who'd just transferred and sat in front of her in English (not that she liked him or anything, although he *had* turned around to hand her back her homework paper and held on to it just a *smidgen* too long . . .)? Would they get stuck together like jammed gears and have to be taken to the emergency room at the hospital, and how totally humiliating would *that* be?

Zoe ran her tongue along the ragged metal fence posts in her mouth. Maybe she could temporarily join a convent.

She sighed and peered down the block to see whether she could make out her mom's green Explorer from the conga line of passing cars. And just about then, something exploded.

Patrick sat at a red light in his unmarked police car, waiting to turn onto the highway. Beside him, on the passenger seat, was a paper bag with a vial of cocaine inside it. The dealer they'd busted at the high school had admitted it was cocaine, and yet Patrick had to waste half his day taking it to the state lab so that someone in a white coat could tell him what he already knew. He fiddled with the volume button of the dispatch radio just in time to hear the fire department being sent to the high school for an explosion. Probably the boiler; the school was old enough for its internal structure to be falling apart. He tried to remember where the boiler was located in Sterling High, and wondered if they'd be lucky enough to come out of that kind of situation without anyone being hurt.

Shots fired . . .

The light turned green, but Patrick didn't move. The discharge of a gun in Sterling was rare enough to have him narrow his attention to the voice on the dispatch radio, waiting for an explanation.

At the high school . . . Sterling High . . .

The dispatcher's voice was getting faster, more intense. Patrick wheeled the car in a U-turn and started toward the school with his lights flashing. Other voices began to transmit in static bursts: officers stating their positions in town; the on-duty supervisor trying to coordinate manpower and calling for mutual aid from Hanover and Lebanon. Their voices knotted and tangled, blocking one another so that everything and nothing was being said at once.

Signal 1000, the dispatcher said. *Signal 1000*.

In Patrick's entire career as a detective, he'd only heard that call twice. Once was in Maine, when a deadbeat dad had taken an officer hostage. Once was in Sterling, during a potential bank robbery that turned out to be a false alarm. Signal 1000 meant that everyone, immediately, was to get off the radio and leave it free for dispatch. It meant that what they were dealing with was not routine police business.

It meant life or death.

*　　*　　*

Chaos was a constellation of students, running out of the school and trampling the injured. A boy holding a hand-made sign in an upstairs window that read HELP US. Two girls hugging each other and sobbing. Chaos was blood melting pink on the snow; it was the drip of parents that turned into a stream and then a raging river, screaming out the names of their missing children. Chaos was a TV camera in your face, not enough ambulances, not enough officers, and no plan for how to react when the world as you knew it went to pieces.

Patrick pulled halfway onto the sidewalk and grabbed his bulletproof vest from the back of the car. Already, adrenaline pulsed through him, making the edges of his vision swim and his senses more acute. He found Chief O'Rourke standing with a megaphone in the middle of the melee. "We don't know what we're dealing with yet," the chief said. "SOU's on its way."

Patrick didn't give a damn about the Special Operations Unit. By the time the SWAT team got here, a hundred more shots might be fired; a kid might be killed. He drew his gun. "I'm going in."

"The hell you are. That's not protocol."

"There is no fucking protocol for this," Patrick snapped. "You can fire me later."

As he raced up the steps to the school, he was vaguely aware of two other patrol officers bucking the chief's commands and joining him in the fray. Patrick directed them each down a different hallway, and then he himself pushed through the double doors, past students who were shoving each other in an effort to get outside. Fire alarms blared so loudly that Patrick had to strain to hear the gunshots. He grabbed the coat of a boy streaking past him. "Who is it?" he yelled. "Who's shooting?"

The kid shook his head, speechless, and wrenched away.

Patrick watched him run crazily down the hallway, open the door, burst into a rectangle of sunlight.

Students funneled around him, as if he were a stone in a river. Smoke billowed and burned his eyes. Patrick heard another staccato of gunshots, and had to restrain himself from running toward them blindly. "How many of them?" he cried as a girl ran by.

"I . . . I don't know . . ."

The boy beside her turned around and looked at Patrick, torn between offering knowledge and getting the hell out of there. "It's a kid . . . he's shooting everyone . . ."

That was enough. Patrick pushed against the tide, a salmon swimming upstream. Homework papers were scattered on the floor; shell casings rolled beneath the heels of his shoes. Ceiling tiles had been shot off, and a fine gray dust coated the broken bodies that lay twisted on the floor. Patrick ignored all of this, going against most of his training—running past doors that might hide a perp, disregarding rooms that should have been searched—instead driving forward with his weapon drawn and his heart beating through every inch of his skin. Later, he would remember other sights that he didn't have time to register right away: the heating duct covers that had been pried loose so that students could hide in the crawl space; the shoes left behind by kids who literally ran out of them; the eerie prescience of crime-scene outlines on the floor outside the biology classrooms, where students had been tracing their own bodies on butcher paper for an assignment.

He ran through hallways that seemed to circle in on each other. "*Where?*" he would bite out every time he passed a fleeing student—his only tool of navigation. He'd see sprays of blood, and students crumpled on the ground, and he did not let himself look twice. He pounded up the main stairwell, and just as he reached the top, a door cracked open. Patrick whirled, pointing his gun, as a young female teacher fell to her knees with her hands raised. Behind the white oval of her face were twelve others, featureless and frightened. Patrick could smell urine.

He lowered his gun and beckoned her toward the staircase. "Go," he commanded, but he did not stay long enough to see if they did.

Turning a corner, Patrick slipped on blood and heard another gunshot, this one loud enough to ring his ears. He swept into the open double doors of the gymnasium and scanned the handful of sprawled bodies, the basketball cart overturned and the globes resting against the far wall—but no shooter. He knew, from the overtime detail he'd taken on Friday nights to monitor high school ball games, that he'd reached the far end of Sterling High. Which meant that the shooter was either hiding somewhere here or had doubled back past him when Patrick hadn't noticed . . . and could even now have cornered him in this gym.

Patrick spun around to the entrance again to see if that was the case, and then heard another shot. He ran to a door that led out from the gym, one he hadn't noticed in his first quick visual sweep of the area. It was a locker room, tiled white on the walls and the floor. He glanced down, saw the fanned spray of blood at his feet, and edged his gun around the corner wall.

Two bodies lay unmoving at one end of the locker room. At the other, closer to Patrick, a slight boy crouched beside a bank of lockers. He wore wire-rimmed glasses, crooked on his thin face. He was shivering hard.

"Are you okay?" Patrick whispered. He did not want to speak out loud and give away his position to the shooter.

The boy only blinked at him.

"Where is he?" Patrick mouthed.

The boy pulled a pistol from beneath his thigh and held it up to his own head.

A new rush of heat surged through Patrick. "Don't fucking move," he shouted, drawing a bead on the boy. "Drop the gun or I will shoot you." Sweat broke out down his back and on his forehead, and he could feel his cupped hands shifting on the butt of the gun as he aimed, determined to lace the kid with bullets if he had to.

Patrick let his forefinger brush gently against the trigger just as the boy opened his fingers wide as a starfish. The pistol fell to the floor, skittering across the tile.

Immediately, he pounced. One of the other officers—whom Patrick hadn't even noticed following him—retrieved the boy's weapon. Patrick dropped the kid onto his stomach and cuffed him, pressing his knee hard into the boy's spine. "Are you alone? Who's with you?"

"Just me," the boy ground out.

Patrick's head was spinning and his pulse was a military tattoo, but he could vaguely hear the other officer calling this information in over the radio: *"Sterling, we have one in custody; we don't have knowledge of anyone else."*

Just as seamlessly as it had started, it was over—at least as much as something like this could be considered over. Patrick didn't know if there were booby traps or bombs in the school; he didn't know how many casualties there were; he didn't know how many wounded Dartmouth-Hitchcock Medical Center and Alice Peck Day Hospital could take; he didn't know how to go about processing a crime scene this massive. The target had been taken out, but at what irreplaceable cost? Patrick's entire body began to shake, knowing that for so many students and parents and citizens today, he had once again been too late.

He took a few steps and sank down to his knees, mostly because his legs simply gave out from underneath them, and pretended that this was intentional, that he wanted to check out the two bodies at the other end of the room. He was vaguely aware of the shooter being pushed out of the locker room by the other officer, to a waiting cruiser downstairs. He didn't turn to watch the kid go; instead he focused on the body directly in front of him.

A boy, dressed in a hockey jersey. There was a puddle of blood underneath his side, and a gunshot wound through his forehead. Patrick reached out for a baseball cap that had fallen a few feet away, with the words STERLING HOCKEY embroidered across it. He turned the brim around in his hands, an imperfect circle.

The girl lying next to him was facedown, blood spreading from beneath her temple. She was barefoot, and on her toenails was bright pink polish—just like the stuff Tara had put on Patrick. It made his heart catch. This girl, just like his goddaughter and her brother and a million other kids in this country, had gotten up today and gone to school never imagining she would be in danger. She trusted all the grown-ups and teachers and principals to keep her safe. It was why these schools, post-9/11, had teachers wearing ID all the time and doors locked during the day—the enemy was always supposed to be an outsider, not the kid who was sitting right next to you.

Suddenly, the girl shifted. "*Help . . . me . . .*"

Patrick knelt beside her. "I'm here," he said, his touch gentle as he assessed her condition. "Everything's all right." He turned her enough to see that the blood was coming from a cut on her scalp, not a gunshot wound, as he'd assumed. He ran his hands over her limbs. He kept murmuring to her, words that did not always make sense, but that let her know that she wasn't alone anymore. "What's your name, sweetheart?"

"Josie . . ." The girl started to thrash, trying to sit up.

Patrick put the bulk of his body strategically between her and the boy's—she'd be in shock already; he didn't need her to go over the edge. She touched her hand to her forehead, and when it came away oily with blood, she panicked. "What . . . *happened?*"

He should have stayed there and waited for the medics to come get her. He should have radioed for help. But *should* hardly seemed to apply anymore, and so Patrick lifted Josie into his arms. He carried her out of the locker room where she'd nearly been killed, hurried down the stairs, and pushed through the front door of the school, as if he might be able to save them both.

Seventeen Years Before

There were fourteen people sitting in front of Lacy, if you counted the fact that each of the seven women attending this prenatal class was pregnant. Some of them had come equipped with notebooks and pens, and had spent the past hour and a half writing down recommended dosages of folic acid, the names of teratogens, and suggested diets for a mother-to-be. Two had turned green in the middle of the discussion of a normal birth and had rushed to the bathroom with morning sickness—which, of course, stretched as long as the whole day, and was like saying summertime when you really meant all four seasons of the year.

She was tired. Only a week back into work after her own maternity leave, it seemed patently unfair that if she wasn't up all night with her own baby, she had to be awake delivering someone else's. Her breasts ached, an uncomfortable reminder that she had to go pump again, so that she'd have milk to leave the sitter tomorrow for Peter.

And yet, she loved her job too much to give it up entirely. She'd had the grades to get into medical school, and had considered being an OB/GYN, until she realized that she had a profound inability to sit bedside by a patient and not feel her pain. Doctors put a wall up between themselves and their patients; nurses broke it down. She switched into a program that would certify her as a nurse-midwife, that encouraged her to tap into the emotional health of a mother-to-be instead of just her symptomology. Maybe it made some of the doctors at the hospital consider her a flake, but Lacy truly believed that when you asked a patient *How do you feel?*, what was wrong wasn't nearly as important as what was right.

She reached past the plastic model of the growing fetus and lifted a bestselling pregnancy guidebook into the air. "How many of you have seen this book before?"

Seven hands lifted.

"Okay. Do not buy this book. Do not read this book. If it's already at your house, throw it out. This book will convince you that you are going to bleed out, have seizures, drop dead, or any of a hundred other things that do not happen with normal pregnancies. Believe me, the range of normal is much wider than anything these authors will tell you."

She glanced in the back, where a woman was holding her side. *Cramping?* Lacy thought. *Ectopic pregnancy?*

The woman was dressed in a black suit, her hair pulled back into a neat, low ponytail. Lacy watched her pinch her waist once again, this time pulling off a small beeper attached to her skirt. She got to her feet. "I . . . um, I'm sorry. I have to go."

"Can it wait a few minutes?" Lacy asked. "We're just about to go on a tour of the birthing pavilion."

The woman handed her the paperwork she'd been asked to fill out during this visit. "I have something more pressing to deal with," she said, and she hurried off.

"Well," Lacy said. "Maybe this is a good time for a bathroom break." As the six remaining women filed out of the room, she glanced down at the forms in her hand. *Alexandra Cormier*, she read. And she thought: *I'm going to have to watch this one.*

The last time Alex had defended Loomis Bronchetti, he had broken into three homes and stolen electronics equipment, which he then tried to fence on the streets of Enfield, New Hampshire. Although Loomis was enterprising enough to dream up this scheme, he failed to realize that in a town as small as Enfield, hot stereo equipment might raise a red flag.

Apparently, Loomis had escalated his criminal résumé last night when he and two friends decided to go after a drug dealer who didn't bring them enough pot. They got high, hog-tied the guy, and threw him in the trunk. Loomis whacked the dealer over the head with a baseball bat, cracking his skull and sending him into convulsions. When he started choking on his own blood, Loomis turned him over so that he could breathe.

"I can't believe they're charging me with assault," Loomis told Alex through the bars of the holding cell. "I saved the guy's life."

"Well," Alex said. "We might have been able to use that—if you hadn't been the one who inflicted the injury in the first place."

"You gotta plead me out for less than a year. I don't want to get sent down to the prison in Concord . . ."

"You could have been charged with attempted murder, you know."

Loomis scowled. "I was doing the cops a favor, getting a lowlife like that off the streets."

The same, Alex knew, could be said for Loomis Bronchetti, if he was convicted and sent to the state prison.

But her job was not about judging Loomis. It was about working hard, in spite of her personal opinions about a client. It was about showing one face to Loomis, and knowing she had another one masked away. It was about not letting her feelings interfere with her ability to get Loomis Bronchetti acquitted.

"Let me see what I can do," she said.

Lacy understood that all infants were different—tiny little creatures with their own quirks and habits and peeves and desires. But somehow, she'd expected that this second foray into motherhood would produce a child like her first—Joey, a golden boy who would make passersby turn their heads, stop her as she pushed the stroller to tell her what a beautiful child she had. Peter was just as beautiful, but he was definitely a more challenging baby. He'd cry, colicky, and have to be soothed by putting his car seat on the vibrating clothes dryer. He'd be nursing, and suddenly arch away from her.

It was two in the morning, and Lacy was trying to get Peter to settle back to sleep. Unlike Joey, who fell into slumber like taking a giant step off a cliff, Peter fought it every step of the way. She patted his back and rubbed small circles between his tiny shoulder blades as he hiccuped and wailed. Frankly, she felt like doing that, too. For the past two hours, she'd watched the same infomercial on Ginsu knives. She had counted the ticking stripes on the elephantine arm of the sofa until they blurred. She was so exhausted that *everything* ached. "What's the matter, little man," she sighed. "What can I do to make you happy?"

Happiness was relative, according to her husband. Although most people laughed when Lacy told them her husband's job involved putting a price on joy, it was simply what economists did—find value for the intangibles in life. Lewis's colleagues at Sterling College had presented papers on the relative push an education could provide, or universal health care, or job satisfaction. Lewis's discipline was no less important, if unorthodox. It made him a popular guest on NPR, on Larry King, at corporate seminars— somehow, number crunching seemed sexier when you began talking about the dollar amount a belly laugh was worth, or a dumb blonde joke, for that matter. Regular sex, for example, was equivalent (happinesswise) to getting a $50,000 raise. However, getting a $50,000 raise wouldn't be nearly as exciting if everyone else was getting a $50,000 raise, too. By the same token, what made you happy once might not make you happy now. Five years ago, Lacy would have given anything for a dozen roses brought home by her husband; now, if he offered her the chance to take a ten-minute nap, she would fall to the ground in paroxysms of delight.

Statistics aside, Lewis would go down in history as being the economist who'd conceived a mathematical formula for happiness: R/E, or, Reality divided by Expectations. There were two ways to be happy: improve your reality, or lower your expectations. Once, at a neighborhood dinner party, Lacy had asked him what happened if you had no expectations. You couldn't divide by zero. Did that mean if you just let yourself roll with all of life's punches, you could never be happy? In the car later that night, Lewis had accused her of trying to make him look bad.

Lacy didn't like to let herself consider whether Lewis and their family were truly happy. You'd think the man who designed the formula would have happiness figured out, but somehow, it didn't work that way. Sometimes she'd recall that old adage—the shoemaker's sons go barefoot—and she'd wonder, *What about the children of the man who knows the value of happiness?* These days, when Lewis was late at the office, working on another publication deadline, and Lacy was so exhausted she could fall asleep standing up in the hospital elevator, she tried to convince herself it was simply a phase they were stuck in: a baby boot camp that would surely transform one day into contentment and satisfaction and togetherness and all the other parameters Lewis plotted on his computer programs. After all, she had a husband who loved her and two healthy boys and a fulfilling career. Wasn't getting what you wanted all along the very definition of being happy?

She realized that—miracle of miracles—Peter had fallen asleep on her shoulder, the sweet peach of his cheek pressed against her bare skin. Tiptoeing up the stairs, she gently settled him into his crib and then glanced across the room at the bed where Joey lay. The moon fawned over him like a disciple. She wondered what Peter would be like when he was Joey's age. She wondered if you could get that lucky twice.

Alex Cormier was younger than Lacy had thought. Twenty-four, but she carried herself with enough confidence to make people think she was a decade older. "So," Lacy said, introducing herself. "How did that pressing matter turn out?"

Alex blinked at her, then remembered: the birthing pavilion tour she had slipped away from a week ago. "It was plea bargained."

"You're a lawyer, then?" Lacy said, glancing up from her notes.

"A public defender." Alex's chin came up a notch, as if she was ready for Lacy to make a deprecating comment about her affiliation with the bad guys.

"That must be awfully demanding work," Lacy said. "Does your office know you're pregnant?"

Alex shook her head. "It's not an issue," she said flatly. "I won't be taking a maternity leave."

"You might change your mind as—"

"I'm not keeping this baby," Alex announced.

Lacy sat back in her chair. "All right." It was not her place to judge a mother for the decision to give up a child. "We can talk about different options, then," Lacy said. At eleven weeks, Alex could still terminate the pregnancy if she wished.

"I was going to have an abortion," Alex said, as if she'd read Lacy's mind. "But I missed my appointment." She glanced up. "Twice."

Lacy knew you could be solidly pro-choice but unwilling or unable to make that decision for yourself—that's exactly where the choice part kicked in. "Well, then," she said, "I can give you information about adoption, if you haven't already contacted any agencies yourself." She reached into a drawer and pulled out folders—adoption agencies affiliated with a variety of religions, attorneys who specialized in private adoptions. Alex took the pamphlets and held them like a hand of playing cards. "For now, though, we can just focus on you and how you're doing."

"I'm great," Alex answered smoothly. "I'm not sick, I'm not tired." She looked at her watch. "I am, however, going to be late for an appointment."

Lacy could tell that Alex was a coper—someone who was used to being in control in all facets of her life. "It's okay to slow down when you're pregnant. Your body might need that."

"I know how to take care of myself."

"What about letting someone else do it once in a while?"

A shadow of irritation crossed over Alex's face. "Look, I don't need a therapy session. Honestly. I appreciate the concern, but—"

"Does your partner support your decision to give the baby up?" Lacy asked.

Alex turned her face away for a moment. Before Lacy could find the right words to draw her back, however, Alex did it herself. "There is no partner," she said coolly.

The last time Alex's body had taken over, had done what her mind told her not to do, she had conceived this baby. It had started innocently enough—Logan Rourke, her trial advocacy professor, calling her into his office to tell her that she commanded the courtroom with competence; Logan saying that no juror would be able to take his eyes off her— and that neither could he. Alex had thought Logan was Clarence Darrow and F. Lee Bailey and God rolled up into one. Prestige and power could make a man so attractive it took one's breath away; it turned Logan into what she'd been looking for her whole life.

She believed him when he told her he hadn't seen a student with as quick a mind as Alex in his ten years of teaching. She believed him when he told her that his marriage was over in all but name. And she believed him the night he drove her home from the campus, framed her face between his hands, and told her she was the reason he got up in the morning.

Law was a study of detail and fact, not emotion. Alex's cardinal mistake had been forgetting this when she became involved with Logan. She found herself postponing plans, waiting for his call, which sometimes came and sometimes didn't. She pretended that she did not see him flirting with the first-year law students who looked at him the way she used to. And when she got pregnant, she convinced herself that they were meant to spend the rest of their lives together.

Logan had told her to get rid of it. She'd scheduled an abortion, only to forget to write the date and time on her calendar. She rescheduled, but realized too late that her appointment conflicted with a final exam. After that, she'd gone to Logan. *It's a sign,* she'd said.

Maybe, he told her, *but it doesn't mean what you're thinking. Be reasonable,* Logan had said. *A single mother will never make it as a trial attorney. She'd have to choose between her career and this baby.*

What he really meant was that she'd have to choose between having the baby and having him.

The woman looked familiar from behind, in that way that people sometimes do when you see them out of context: your grocery clerk standing in line at the bank, your postman sitting across the aisle of the movie theater. Alex stared for another second, and then realized it was the infant throwing her off. She strode across the hallway of the courthouse toward the town clerk, where Lacy Houghton stood paying a parking ticket.

"Need a lawyer?" Alex asked.

Lacy looked up, the baby carrier balanced in the crook of her arm. It took a moment to place the face—she hadn't seen Alex since her initial visit nearly a month ago. "Oh, hello!" she said, smiling.

"What brings you to my neck of the woods?"

"Oh, I'm posting bail for my ex . . ." Lacy waited for Alex's eyes to widen, and then laughed. "Just kidding. I got a parking ticket."

Alex found herself staring down at the face of Lacy's son.

He wore a blue cap that tied underneath his chin, and his cheeks spilled over the edges of the fleece. He had a runny nose, and when he noticed Alex looking at him, he offered her a cavernous smile.

"Would you like to grab a cup of coffee?" Lacy said.

She slapped ten dollars down on top of her parking ticket and fed it through the open mouth of the payment window, then hefted the baby bucket a little higher into the crook of her arm and walked out of the court building to a Dunkin' Donuts across the street. Lacy stopped to give a ten-dollar bill to a bum sitting outside the courthouse, and Alex rolled her eyes—she'd actually seen this particular fellow heading over to the closest bar yesterday when she left work.

In the coffee shop, Alex watched Lacy effortlessly unpeel layers of clothing from her baby and lift him out of his seat onto her lap. As she talked, she draped a blanket over her shoulder and started to nurse Peter. "Is it hard?" Alex blurted out.

"Nursing?"

"Not just that," Alex said. "Everything."

"It's definitely an acquired skill." Lacy lifted the baby onto her shoulder. His booted feet kicked against her chest, as if he was already trying to put distance between them. "Compared to *your* day job, motherhood is probably a piece of cake."

It made Alex think, immediately, of Logan Rourke, who had laughed at her when she said she was taking a job with the public defender's office. *You won't last a week*, he'd told her. *You're too soft for that.*

She sometimes wondered if she was a good public defender because of skill or because she had been so determined to show Logan that he was wrong. In any case, Alex had cultivated a persona on the job, one that was there to give offenders an equal voice in the legal system, without letting clients get under her skin.

She'd already made that mistake with Logan.

"Did you get a chance to contact any of the adoption agencies?" Lacy asked.

Alex had not even taken the pamphlets she'd been given. For all she knew, they were still sitting on the counter of the examination room.

"I put in a few calls," Alex lied. She had it on her To Do list at work. It was just that something else always got in the way.

"Can I ask you a personal question?" Lacy said, and Alex nodded slowly—she did not like personal questions. "What made you decide to give the baby up?"

Had she ever really made that decision? Or had it been made *for* her?

"This isn't a good time," Alex said.

Lacy laughed. "I don't know if it's ever a good time to have a baby. Your life certainly gets turned upside down."

Alex stared at her. "I like my life right side up."

Lacy fussed with her baby's shirt for a moment. "In a way, what you and I do isn't really all that different."

"The recidivism rate is probably about the same," Alex said.

"No . . . I meant that we both see people when they're at their most raw. That's what I love about midwifery. You see how strong someone is, in the face of a really painful situation." She glanced up at Alex. "Isn't it amazing how, when you strip away everything, people are so much alike?"

Alex thought of the defendants that had paraded through her professional life. They all blurred together in her mind. But was that because, as Lacy said, we were all similar? Or was it because Alex had become an expert at not looking too closely?

She watched Lacy settle the baby on her knee. His hands smacked the table, and he made little gurgling noises. Suddenly Lacy stood up, thrusting the baby toward Alex so that she had to hold him or risk having him tumble onto the floor. "Here, hang on to Peter. I just have to run into the bathroom."

Alex panicked. *Wait,* she thought. *I don't know what I'm doing.* The baby's legs kicked, like a cartoon character who'd run off a cliff.

Awkwardly, Alex sat him down on her lap. He was heavier than she would have imagined, and his skin felt like damp velvet. "Peter," she said formally. "I'm Alex."

The baby reached for her coffee cup, and she lurched forward to push it out of reach. Peter's face pinched tight as a lime, and he started to cry.

The screams were shattering, decibel-rich, cataclysmic. "Stop," Alex begged, as people around her started to stare. She stood up, patting Peter's back the way Lacy had, wishing he would run out of steam or contract laryngitis or just simply have mercy on her utter inexperience. Alex—who always had the perfect witty comeback, who could be thrown into a hellish legal situation and land on her feet every time without even breaking a sweat—found herself completely at a loss.

She sat down and held Peter beneath his armpits. By now, he'd turned tomato-red, his skin so angry and dark that his soft fuzz of hair glowed like platinum. "Listen," she said. "I may not be what you want right now, but I'm all you've got."

On a final hiccup, the baby quieted. He stared into Alex's eyes, as if he was trying to place her.

Relieved, Alex settled him into the sling of her arm

and sat a little taller. She glanced down at the top of the baby's head, at the translucent pulse beneath his fontanelle.

When she relaxed her grip on the baby, he relaxed, too. Was it *that* easy?

Alex traced her finger over the soft spot on Peter's head. She knew the biology behind it: the plates of the skull shifted enough to make giving birth easier; they fused together by the time the baby was a toddler. It was a vulnerability we were all born with, one that literally grew into an adult's hardheadedness.

"Sorry," Lacy said, breezing back to the table. "Thanks for that."

Alex thrust the baby out toward her as if she were being burned.

The patient had been transferred from a thirty-hour home birth. A firm believer in natural medicine, she'd had limited prenatal care, no amnio, no sonograms, and yet newborns had a way of getting what they wanted and needed when it came time to arrive in the world. Lacy laid her hands on the woman's trembling belly like a faith healer. *Six pounds*, she thought, *bottom up here, head down here*. A doctor poked his head through the door. "How's it going in here?"

"Tell the intensive-care nursery we're at thirty-five weeks," she said, "but everything seems to be fine." As the doctor backed away, she settled herself between the woman's legs. "I know this has been going on for what seems like forever," she said. "But if you can work with me for just one more hour, you'll have this baby."

As she directed the woman's husband to get behind his wife, holding her upright as she began to push, Lacy felt her pager vibrate at the waistline of her sea-blue scrubs.

Who the hell could it be? She was already on call; her secretary knew she was assisting at a birth.

"Will you excuse me?" she said, leaving the labor nurse in the room to fill in while she walked to the nurses' desk and borrowed a telephone. "What's going on?" Lacy asked when her secretary picked up.

"One of your patients, insisting to see you."

"I'm a little *busy*," Lacy said pointedly.

"She said she'll wait. For however long it takes."

"Who is it?"

"Alex Cormier," the secretary replied.

Normally, Lacy would have told her secretary to have the patient see one of the other midwives in the practice. But there was still something elusive about Alex Cormier, something she couldn't put her finger on—something that wasn't quite right. "All right," Lacy said. "But tell her it might be hours."

She hung up the phone and hurried back into the birthing room, where she reached between the patient's legs to check her dilation. "Apparently, all you needed was for me to leave," she joked. "You're ten centimeters. The next time you feel like pushing . . . go to town."

Ten minutes later, Lacy delivered a three-pound baby girl. As the parents marveled over her, Lacy turned to the labor nurse, silently communicating with her eyes. Something had gone terribly wrong.

"She's so tiny," the father said. "Is there . . . is she okay?"

Lacy hesitated, because she didn't really know the answer. A *fibroid?* she wondered. All she knew for certain was that there was a lot more inside that woman than a three-pound infant. And that any moment now, her patient was going to start to bleed.

But when Lacy reached up to grab the patient's belly

and press down on her uterus, she froze. "Did anyone tell you you were having twins?"

The father went ashen. "There's two in there?"

Lacy grinned. Twins, she could handle. Twins—well, that was a bonus, not some horrible medical disaster. "Well. Only one now."

The man crouched down beside his wife and kissed her forehead, delighted. "Did you hear that, Terri? *Twins.*"

His wife did not take her eyes off her tiny newborn daughter. "That's nice," she said calmly. "But I'm not pushing a second one out."

Lacy laughed. "Oh, I think I might be able to get you to change your mind."

Forty minutes later, Lacy left the happy family—with their twin daughters—and headed down the hallway to the staff restroom, where she splashed water on her face and changed into a fresh pair of scrubs. She took the stairs up to the midwifery office and glanced at the collection of women, sitting with their arms balanced on bellies of all sizes, like moons in different stages. One rose, red-eyed and unsteady, as if she'd been pulled upright magnetically by Lacy's arrival. "Alex," she said, remembering only in that instant that she had another patient waiting. "Why don't you come with me."

She led Alex into an empty examination room and sat down across from her in a chair. At that moment Lacy noticed that Alex's sweater was on backward. It was a pale blue crewneck—you could barely even tell, except that the tag had flapped out along the curve of her neck. And it was certainly something that might happen to anyone in a rush, anyone upset . . . but probably not Alex Cormier.

"There's been bleeding," Alex said, her voice even. "Not a lot, but. Um. Some."

Taking a cue from Alex herself, Lacy kept her own response calm. "Why don't we check anyway?"

Lacy led Alex down the hallway to fetal ultrasound. She charmed a tech into letting them cut the patient line, and once she had Alex lying down on the table, she turned on the machine. She moved the transducer across Alex's abdomen. At sixteen weeks, the fetus looked like a baby—tiny, skeletal, but startlingly perfect. "Do you see that?" Lacy asked, pointing to a blinking cursor, a tiny black-and-white drumbeat. "That's the baby's heart."

Alex turned her face away, but not before Lacy saw a tear streak down her cheek. "The baby's fine," she said. "And it's perfectly normal to have some staining or spotting. It's not anything you did that caused it; there's nothing you can do to make it stop."

"I thought I was having a miscarriage."

"Once you see a normal baby, like we just did, the chance of miscarrying is less than one percent. Let me put that another way—your chance of carrying a normal baby to term is ninety-nine percent."

Alex nodded, wiping at her eyes with her sleeve. "Good."

Lacy hesitated. "It's not my place to say this, really. But for someone who doesn't want this baby, Alex, you seem awfully relieved to know she's all right."

"I don't—I can't—"

Lacy glanced at the ultrasound screen, where Alex's baby was frozen in a moment of time. "Just think about it," she said.

I already have a family, Logan Rourke said later that day when Alex told him she planned to keep the baby. *I don't need another one.*

That night, Alex had an exorcism of sorts. She filled up her Weber grill with charcoal and lit a fire, then roasted every assignment she'd turned in to Logan Rourke. She had no photos of the two of them, no sweet notes—in retrospect, she realized how careful he'd been, how easily he could be erased from her life.

This baby, she decided, would be hers alone. She sat, watching the flames, and thought of the space it would take up inside her. She imagined her organs moving aside, skin stretching. She pictured her heart shrinking, tiny as a beach stone, to make room. She did not consider whether she was having this baby to prove that she hadn't imagined her relationship with Logan Rourke, or to upset him as much as he had upset her. As any skilled trial attorney knows, you never ask the witness a question to which you do not know the answer.

Five weeks later, Lacy was no longer just Alex's midwife. She was also her confidante, her best friend, her sounding board. Although Lacy didn't normally socialize with her clients, for Alex she'd broken the rules. She told herself it was because Alex—who had now decided to keep this baby—really needed a support system, and there wasn't anyone else she felt comfortable with.

It was the only reason, Lacy decided, she'd agreed to go out with Alex's colleagues this evening. Even the prospect of a Girls' Night Out, without babies, lost its luster in this company. Lacy should have realized two back-to-back root canals would have been preferable to dinner with a bunch of lawyers. They all liked to hear themselves talk, that was clear. She let the conversation flow around her, as if she were a stone in a river, and she kept refilling her wineglass with Coke from a pitcher.

The restaurant was some Italian place with very bad red sauce and a chef who went heavy on the garlic. She wondered if, in Italy, there were American restaurants.

Alex was in the middle of a heated discussion about some trial that had gone to jury. Lacy heard terms being tossed and fielded around the table: FLSA, *Singh v. Jutla*, incentives. A florid woman sitting to Lacy's right shook her head. "It's sending a message," she said. "If you award damages for work that's illegal, you're sanctioning a company to be above the law."

Alex laughed. "Sita, I'm just going to take this moment to remind you that you're the only prosecutor at the table and there's no way in hell you're going to win this one."

"We're all biased. We need an objective observer." Sita smiled at Lacy. "What's your opinion on aliens?"

Maybe she should have paid more attention to the conversation—apparently it had taken a turn for the interesting while Lacy was woolgathering. "Well, I'm certainly not an expert, but I did finish a book a little while ago about Area 51 and the cover-up by the government. It went into specific detail about cattle mutilation—I find it very suspicious when a cow in Nevada winds up missing its kidneys and the incision doesn't show any trauma to tissue or blood loss. I had a cat once that I think was abducted by aliens. She went missing for exactly four weeks—to the minute—and when she came back, she had triangle patterns burned out on the fur on her back, sort of like a crop circle." Lacy hesitated. "But without the wheat."

Everyone at the table stared at her, silent. A woman with a pinhole of a mouth and a sleek blond bob blinked at Lacy. "We were talking about *illegal* aliens."

Lacy felt heat creep up her neck. "Oh," she said. "Right."

"Well, if you ask me," Alex said, drawing attention in her

own direction, "Lacy ought to be heading up the Department of Labor instead of Elaine Chao. She's certainly got more experience . . ."

Everyone broke up in laughter, as Lacy watched. Alex, she realized, could fit anywhere. Here, or with Lacy's family at dinner, or in a courtroom, or probably at tea with the queen. She was a chameleon.

It struck Lacy that she didn't really know what color a chameleon was before it started changing.

There was a moment at each prenatal exam when Lacy channeled her inner faith healer: laying her hands on the patient's belly and divining, just from the lay of the land, in which direction the baby lay. It always reminded her of those Halloween funhouses she took Joey to visit—you'd stick your hand behind a curtain and feel a bowl of cold spaghetti intestines, or a gelatin brain. It wasn't an exact science, but basically, there were two hard parts on a fetus: the head and the bottom. If you rocked the baby's head, it would twist on the stem of its spine. If you rocked the baby's bottom, it swayed. Moving the head moved only the head; moving the bottom moved the whole baby.

She let her hands trail over the island of Alex's belly and helped her sit up. "The good news is that the baby's doing fine," Lacy said. "The bad news is that right now, she's upside down. Breech."

Alex froze. "I'm going to need a C-section?"

"We've got eight weeks before it comes to that. There's a lot we can do to try to turn the baby beforehand."

"Like what?"

"Moxibustion." She sat down across from Lacy. "I'll give you the name of an acupuncturist. She'll take a little stick of mugwort and hold it up to your little pinky. She'll do the same thing on the other side. It won't hurt, but it'll be uncomfortably warm. Once you learn how to do it at home, if you start now chances are fairly good that the baby will turn in one to two weeks' time."

"Poking myself with a stick is going to make it flip?"

"Well, not necessarily. That's why I also want you to set an ironing board up against the couch, to make an inclined plane. You should lie on it, head down, three times a day for fifteen minutes."

"Jeez, Lacy. Are you sure you don't want me to wear a crystal, too?"

"Believe me, any of those are considerably more comfortable than having a doctor do a version to turn the baby . . . or recuperating from a C-section."

Alex folded her hands over her belly. "I don't hold much faith in old wives' tales."

Lacy shrugged. "Luckily, you're not the one who's breech."

You weren't supposed to give your clients rides to court, but in Nadya Saranoff's case, Alex had made an exception. Nadya's husband had been abusive and had left her for another woman. He wouldn't pay child support for their two boys, although he was making a decent living and Nadya's job at Subway paid $5.25 an hour. She'd complained to the state, but justice worked too slow, so she'd gone to Wal-Mart and shoplifted a pair of pants and a white shirt for her five-year-old, who was starting school the following week and who had outgrown all of his clothing.

Nadya had pled guilty. Because she couldn't afford a fine, she was given a thirty-day jail sentence deferred— which, as Alex was explaining to her now, meant that she wouldn't have to go for a year. "If you go to jail," she said, as they stood outside the ladies' room in the courthouse, "your boys are going to suffer greatly. I know you felt desperate, but there's always another option. A church. Or a Salvation Army."

Nadya wiped her eyes. "I couldn't get to the church or the Salvation Army. I haven't got a car."

Right. It was why Alex had brought her to court in the first place.

Alex steeled herself against sympathy as Nadya ducked into the bathroom. Her job had been to get Nadya a good deal, which she *had*, considering this was the woman's second shoplifting offense. The first one had been at a drugstore; she'd pinched some Children's Tylenol.

She thought of her own baby, the one who had her lying upside down on an ironing board and sticking torturous little daggers against her pinky toes every night, in the hopes that it would change position. What sort of disadvantage would it be to come into this world backward?

When ten minutes had passed and Nadya had not come out of the bathroom, Alex knocked on the door. "Nadya?" She found her client in front of the sinks, sobbing. "Nadya, what's wrong?"

Her client ducked her head, mortified. "I just got my period, and I can't afford a tampon."

Alex reached for her purse, rummaging for a quarter to feed to the dispenser on the wall. But as the cardboard tube rolled out of the machine, something inside her snapped, and she understood that although this case had been settled, it wasn't over yet. "Meet me out front," she ordered. "I'm getting the car."

She drove Nadya to Wal-Mart—the scene of her crime—and tossed three supersized Tampax boxes into a cart. "What else do you need?"

"Underwear," Nadya whispered. "That was my last pair."

Alex wheeled up and down the aisles, buying T-shirts and socks and panties and pajamas for Nadya; pants and coats and hats and gloves for her boys; boxes of Goldfish crackers and saltines and canned soup and pasta and Devil Dogs. Desperate, she did what she had to do at that moment, although it was exactly what the public defender's office counseled their lawyers not to; but she was entirely rational and aware that she had never done this for a client and never would do it again. She spent eight hundred dollars in the very store that had pressed charges against Nadya, because it was easier to fix what was wrong than to picture her own child arriving into a world Alex herself could sometimes not stomach.

The catharsis ended the moment Alex handed the cashier her credit card and heard Logan Rourke's voice in her mind. *Bleeding heart*, he'd called her.

Well. He should know.

He'd been the first to rip it to pieces.

All right, Alex thought calmly. *This is what it's like to die.*

Another contraction ripped through her, bullets strafing metal.

Two weeks ago, at her thirty-seven-week visit, Alex and Lacy had talked about pain medication. *What are your feelings about it?* Lacy had asked, and Alex had made a joke: *I think it should be imported from Canada.* She'd told Lacy she didn't plan to use pain medication, that she wanted a natural childbirth, that it couldn't possibly hurt that much.

It did.

She thought back to all those birthing classes Lacy had forced her to take—the ones where she'd been partnered with Lacy, because everyone else had a husband or boyfriend assisting them. They'd shown pictures of women in labor, women with their rubbery faces and gritted teeth, women making prehistoric noises. Alex had scoffed at this. *They are showing the worst-case scenarios*, she'd told herself. *Different people have different tolerance for pain.*

The next contraction twisted down her spine like a cobra, wrapped itself around her belly, and sank its fangs. Alex fell hard on her knees on the kitchen floor.

In her classes, she'd learned that prelabor could go on for twelve hours or more.

By then, if she wasn't dead, she'd shoot herself.

When Lacy had been a midwife in training, she'd spent months walking around with a little centimeter ruler, measuring. Now, after years on the job, she could eyeball a coffee cup and know that it was nine centimeters across, that the orange beside the phone at the nurses' station was an eight. She withdrew her fingers from between Alex's legs and snapped off the latex glove. "You're two centimeters," she said, and Alex burst into tears.

"Only two? I can't do this," Alex panted, twisting her spine to get away from the pain. She had tried to hide the discomfort behind the mask of competence that she usually wore, only to realize that in her hurry, she must have left it behind somewhere.

"I know you're disappointed," Lacy said. "But here's the thing—you're doing fine. We know that when people are fine at two centimeters they will be fine at eight, too. Let's take it one contraction at a time."

Labor was hard for everyone, Lacy knew, but especially hard for the women who had expectations and lists and plans, because it was never the way you thought it would be. In order to labor well, you had to let your body take over, instead of your mind. You revealed yourself, even the parts you had forgotten about. For someone like Alex, who was so used to being in control, this could be devastating. Success would come only at the expense of losing her cool, at the risk of turning into someone she did not want to be.

Lacy helped Alex off the bed and guided her toward the whirlpool room. She dimmed the lights, flicked on the instrumental music, and untied Alex's robe. Alex was past the point of modesty; at this moment, Lacy figured she'd disrobe in front of an entire male prison population if it meant the contractions would stop.

"In you go," Lacy said, letting Alex lean on her as she sank into the whirlpool. There was a Pavlovian response to warm water; sometimes just stepping into the tub could bring down a person's heart rate.

"Lacy," Alex gasped, "you have to promise . . ."

"Promise what?"

"You won't tell her. The baby."

Lacy reached for Alex's hand. "Tell her what?"

Alex closed her eyes and pressed her cheek against the lip of the tub. "That at first I didn't want her."

Before she could even answer, Lacy watched tension grip Alex. "Breathe through this one," she said. *Blow the pain away from you, blow it between your hands, picture it as the color red. Come up on your hands and knees. Pour yourself inward, like sand in an hourglass. Go to the beach, Alex. Lie on the sand and see how warm the sun is.*

Lie to yourself until it's true.

When you're hurting deeply, you go inward. Lacy had seen this a thousand times. Endorphins kick in—the body's natural morphine—and carry you somewhere far away, where the pain can't find you. Once, a client who'd been abused had dissociated so massively that Lacy was worried she would not be able to reach her again and bring her back in time to push. She had wound up singing to the woman in Spanish, a lullaby.

For three hours now, Alex had regained her composure, thanks to the anesthesiologist who'd given her an epidural. She'd slept for a while; she'd played hearts with Lacy. But now the baby had dropped, and she was starting to bear down. "Why is it hurting again?" she asked, her voice escalating.

"That's how an epidural works. If we dose it up, you can't push."

"I can't have a baby," Alex blurted out. "I'm not ready."

"Well," Lacy said. "Maybe we ought to talk about that."

"What was I *thinking?* Logan was right; I don't know what the hell I'm doing. I'm not a mother, I'm a lawyer. I don't have a boyfriend, I don't have a dog . . . I don't even have a houseplant I haven't killed. I'm not even sure how to put on a diaper."

"The little cartoon characters go on the front," Lacy said. She took Alex's hand and brought it down between her legs, to where the baby was crowning.

Alex jerked her hand away. "Is that . . ."

"Yeah."

"It's coming?"

"Ready or not."

Another contraction started. "Oh, Alex, I can see the eyebrows . . ." Lacy eased the baby out of the birth canal, keeping the head flexed. "I know how much it burns . . . there's her chin . . . beautiful . . ." Lacy wiped off the baby's face, suctioned the mouth. She flipped the cord over the baby's neck and looked up at her friend. "Alex," she said, "let's do this together."

Lacy guided Alex's shaking hands to cup the infant's head. "Stay like that; I'm going to push down to get the shoulder . . ."

As the baby sluiced into Alex's hands, Lacy let go. Sobbing, relieved, Alex brought the small, squirming body against her chest. As always, Lacy was taken by how *available* a newborn is—how present. She rubbed the small of the baby's back and watched the newborn's hazy blue eyes focus first on her mother. "Alex," Lacy said. "She's all yours."

Nobody wants to admit to this, but bad things will keep on happening. Maybe that's because it's all a chain, and a long time ago someone did the first bad thing, and that led someone else to do another bad thing, and so on. You know, like that game where you whisper a sentence into someone's ear, and that person whispers it to someone else, and it all comes out wrong in the end.

But then again, maybe bad things happen because it's the only way we can keep remembering what good is supposed to look like.

Hours After

Once, at a bar, Patrick's best friend, Nina, had asked what the worst thing he'd ever seen was. He'd answered truthfully—back when he was in Maine, and a guy had committed suicide by tying himself with wire to the train tracks; the train had literally cleaved him in two. There had been blood and body parts everywhere; seasoned officers reached the crime scene and started throwing up in the scrub brush. Patrick had walked away to gain his composure and found himself staring down at the man's severed head, the mouth still round with a silent scream.

That was no longer the worst thing Patrick had ever seen.

There were still students streaming out of Sterling High as teams of EMTs began canvassing the building to take care of the wounded. Dozens of kids had minor cuts and bruises from the mass exodus, scores were hyperventilating or hysterical, and even more were in shock. But Patrick's first priority was taking care of the shooting victims, who lay sprawled on the floor from the cafeteria to the gymna-

sium, a bloody trail that chronicled the shooter's movements.

The fire alarms were still ringing, and the safety sprinklers had created a running river in the hallway. Beneath
the spray, two EMTs bent over a girl who'd been shot in
the right shoulder. "Let's get her on a sled," the medic
said.

Patrick knew her, he realized, and a shudder went
through his body. She worked at the video store in town.
Last weekend, when he'd rented *Dirty Harry*, she'd told
him that he still had a late charge of $3.40. He saw her
every Friday night when he rented a DVD, but he'd never
asked her name. Why the hell hadn't he asked?

As the girl whimpered, the medic took the Sharpie
marker he was holding and wrote "9" on her forehead. "We
don't have IDs on all of the wounded," he told Patrick. "So
we've started numbering them." As the student was shifted
onto a backboard, Patrick reached across her for a yellow
plastic shock blanket—one every officer carried in the back
of his cruiser. He ripped it into quarters, glanced at the
number on the girl's forehead, and wrote a matching "9" on
one of the squares. "Leave this in her place," he instructed.
"That way we can figure out who she is later, and where
she was found."

An EMT stuck his head around the corner. "Hitch-
cock says all the beds are taken. We've got kids lined up
on the front lawn waiting, but the ambulances have nowhere to go."

"What about APD?"

"They're full, too."

"Then call Concord and tell them we've got buses coming in," Patrick ordered. From the corner of his eye he saw
an EMT he knew—an old-timer planning to retire in three
months—walk away from a body and sink into a crouch,

sobbing. Patrick grabbed the sleeve of a passing officer. "Jarvis, I need your help . . ."

"But you just assigned me to the gym, Captain."

Patrick had divided up the responding officers and the major crimes unit of the state police so that each part of the high school had its own team of first responders. Now he handed Jarvis the remaining pieces of the plastic shock blanket and a black marker. "Forget the gym. I want you to do a circuit of the whole school and check in with the EMTs. Anyone who's numbered gets a numbered blanket left in place when they're transported."

"I have one bleeding out in the girls' room," a voice called.

"I'm on it," an EMT said, picking up a bag of supplies and hurrying away.

Make sure you haven't forgotten anything, Patrick told himself. *You only get to do this once.* His head felt like it was made of glass, too heavy and too thin-walled to handle the weight of so much information. He could not be everywhere at once; he could not talk fast enough or think quickly enough to dispatch his men where they needed to be. He had no fucking idea how to process a nightmare this massive, and yet he had to pretend that he did, because everyone else was looking to him to be in charge.

The double doors of the cafeteria swung shut behind him. By now, the team working this room had assessed and transported the injured; only the bodies remained behind. The cinder-block walls were chipped where bullets had pierced or grazed them. A vending machine—glass shattered, bottles pierced—dribbled Sprite and Coke and Dasani onto the linoleum floor. One of the crime techs was photographing evidence: abandoned bookbags and purses and textbooks. He snapped each item close-up, then at a distance with a little yellow tented evidence marker to record its placement in relation to the rest of the scene. Another officer examined blood-spatter patterns. A third and a fourth were pointing to a spot in the upper right corner of the ceiling. "Captain," one of them said, "looks like we've got a video."

"Where's the recorder?"

The officer shrugged. "Principal's office?"

"Go find out," Patrick said.

He walked down the main aisle of the cafeteria. It looked, at first glance, like a science fiction movie: everyone had been in the middle of eating and chatting and joking around with friends, and then in the blink of an eye, all the humans were abducted by aliens, leaving only the artifacts behind. What would an anthropologist say about the student body of Sterling High, based on the Wonder-bread sandwiches scarred by only one bite; the tub of Cherry Bomb lip gloss with a fingerprint still skimming the surface; the salt-and-pepper composition notebooks filled with study sheets on Aztec civilization and margin notes about the current one: *I luv Zach S!!! Mr. Keifer is a Nazi!!!*

Patrick's knee bumped one of the tables, and a loose handful of grapes scattered like gasps. One bounced against the shoulder of a boy slumped over his binder, his blood soaking into the college-ruled paper. The boy's hand still held tight to his eyeglasses. Had he been cleaning them when Peter Houghton arrived for his rampage? Had he taken them off because he didn't want to see?

Patrick stepped over the bodies of two girls who lay sprawled on the floor like mirror twins, their miniskirts hiked high on their thighs and their eyes still open. Walking into the kitchen area, he surveyed the troughs of graying peas and carrots and the runny slop of chicken pot pie;

the explosion of salt and pepper packets that dotted the floor like confetti. The shiny metallic helmets of the Yoplait yogurts—strawberry and mixed berry and key lime and peach—which were still miraculously aligned in four neat rows near the cash register, an unflinching, tiny army. One worn plastic tray, with a dish of Jell-O and a napkin on it, waiting to be served the rest of the meal.

Suddenly, Patrick heard a noise. Could he have been wrong—could they *all* have missed a second shooter? Could his team be canvassing the school for survivors . . . and still be at risk themselves?

He drew his gun and crept into the bowels of the kitchen, past racks with monstrous cans of tomato sauce and green beans and processed nacho cheese, past massive rolls of plastic wrap and Sysco tinfoil, to the refrigerated room where meats and produce were stored. Patrick kicked open the door, and cold air spilled over his legs. "Freeze," he yelled, and for the briefest moment, before he remembered everything else, he nearly smiled.

A middle-aged Latina lunch lady, wearing a hair net that crawled over her forehead like a spiderweb, inched out from behind a rack of prepackaged bags of salad mix. Her hands were raised; she was shivering. "*No me tire,*" she sobbed.

Patrick lowered his weapon and took off his jacket, sliding it over the woman's shoulders. "It's over," he soothed, although he knew this was not really true. For him, for Peter Houghton, for *all* of Sterling . . . it was only just beginning.

"Let me get this straight, Mrs. Calloway," Alex said. "You are charged with driving recklessly and causing serious bodily injury while reaching down to aid a fish?"

The defendant, a fifty-four-year-old woman sporting a

bad perm and an even worse pantsuit, nodded. "That's correct, Your Honor."

Alex leaned her elbows on the bench. "I've got to hear this."

The woman looked at her attorney. "Mrs. Calloway was coming home from the pet store with a silver arowana," the lawyer said.

"That's a fifty-five-dollar tropical fish, Judge," the defendant interjected.

"The plastic bag rolled off the passenger seat and popped. Mrs. Calloway reached down for the fish and that's when . . . the unfortunate incident occurred."

"By unfortunate incident," Alex clarified, looking at her file, "you mean hitting a pedestrian."

"Yes, Your Honor."

Alex turned to the defendant. "How's the fish?"

Mrs. Calloway smiled. "Wonderful," she said. "I named it Crash."

From the corner of her eye, Alex saw a bailiff enter the courtroom and whisper to the clerk, who looked at Alex and nodded. He scrawled something on a piece of paper, and the bailiff walked it up to the bench.

Shots fired at Sterling High, she read.

Alex went still as stone. *Josie.* "Court's adjourned," she whispered, and then she ran.

John Eberhard gritted his teeth and concentrated on moving just one more inch forward. He could not see, with all the blood running down his face, and his left side was completely useless. He couldn't hear, either—his ears still rang with the blast of the gun. Still, he had managed to crawl from the upstairs hallway where Peter Houghton had shot him into an art supply room.

He thought about the practices where Coach made them skate from goal line to goal line, faster and then faster still, until the players were gasping for breath and spitting onto the ice. He thought about how, when you felt you had nothing left to give, you'd find just one iota more. He dragged himself another foot, digging his elbow against the floor.

When John reached the metal shelving that held clay and paint and beads and wire, he tried to push himself upright, but a blinding pain speared his head. Minutes later—or was it hours?—he regained consciousness. He didn't know if it was safe to check outside the closet yet. He was flat on his back, and something cold was drifting across his face. Wind. Coming through a crack in the seal of the window.

A window.

John thought of Courtney Ignatio: how she'd been sitting across from him at the cafeteria table when the glass wall behind her burst; how suddenly there had been a flower blooming in the middle of her chest, bright as a poppy. He thought of how a hundred screams, all at once, had braided into a rope of sound. He remembered teachers poking their heads out of their classrooms like gophers, and the looks on their faces when they heard the shots.

John pulled himself up on the shelves, one-handed, fighting the black buzz that told him he was going to faint again. By the time he was upright, leaning against the metal frame, he was shuddering. His vision was so blurred that when he took a can of paint and hurled it, he had to choose between two windows.

The glass shattered. Jackknifed on the ledge, he could see fire trucks and ambulances. Reporters and parents pushing at police tape. Clusters of sobbing students. Broken bodies, spaced like railroad ties on the snow. EMTs bringing out more of them.

Help, John Eberhard tried to scream, but he couldn't form the word. He couldn't form *any* words—not *Look,* not *Stop,* not even his own name.

"Hey," someone called. "There's a kid up there!"

Sobbing by now, John tried to wave, but his arm wouldn't work.

People were starting to point. "Stay put," a fireman yelled, and John tried to nod. But his body no longer belonged to him, and before he realized what had happened, that small movement pitched him out the window to land on the concrete two stories below.

Diana Leven, who had left her job as an assistant attorney general in Boston two years ago to join a department that was a little kinder and gentler, walked into the Sterling High gym and stopped beside the body of a boy who had fallen directly on the three-point line after being shot in the neck. The shoes of the crime scene techs squeaked on the shellacked floor as they took photographs and picked up shell casings, zipping them into plastic evidence bags. Directing them was Patrick Ducharme.

Diana looked around at the sheer volume of evidence—clothing, guns, blood spatter, spent rounds, dropped book-bags, lost sneakers—and realized that she was not the only one with a massive job ahead of her. "What do you know so far?"

"We think it's a sole shooter. He's in custody," Patrick said. "We don't know for sure whether anyone else was involved. The building's secure."

"How many dead?"

"Ten confirmed."

Diana nodded. "Wounded?"

"Don't know yet. We've got every ambulance in northern New Hampshire here."

"What can I do?"

Patrick turned to her. "Put on a show and get rid of the cameras."

She started to walk off, but Patrick grabbed her arm. "You want me to talk to him?"

"The shooter?"

Patrick nodded.

"It may be the only chance we have to get to him before he has a lawyer. If you think you can get away from here, do it." Diana hurried out of the gymnasium and downstairs, careful to skirt the work of the policemen and the medics. The minute she walked outside, the media attached themselves to her, their questions stinging like bees. *How many victims? What are the names of the dead? Who is the shooter?*

Why?

Diana took a deep breath and smoothed her dark hair back from her face. This was her least favorite part of the job—being the spokeswoman on camera. Although more vans would arrive as the day went on, right now it was only local New Hampshire media—affiliates for CBS and ABC and FOX. She might as well enjoy the hometown advantage while she could. "My name is Diana Leven, and I'm with the attorney general's office. We can't release any information now because there's an investigation still pending, but we promise to give you details as soon as we can. What I can tell you right now is that this morning, there was a school shooting at Sterling High. It's unclear as to who the perpetrator or perpetrators were. One person has been remanded into custody. There are no formal charges yet."

A reporter pushed her way to the front of the pack. "How many kids are dead?"

"We don't have that information yet."

"How many were hit?"

"We don't have that information yet," Diana repeated. "We'll keep you posted."

"When are charges going to be filed?" another journalist shouted.

"What can you tell the parents who want to know if their kids are okay?"

Diana pressed her mouth into a firm line and prepared to run the gauntlet. "Thank you very much," she said, not an answer at all.

Lacy had to park six blocks away from the school; that's how crowded it had become. She took off at a dead run, holding the blankets that the local radio announcers had urged people to bring for the shock victims. *I've already lost one son,* she thought. *I can't lose another.*

The last conversation she had had with Peter had been an argument. It was before he went to bed the previous night, before she'd been called into a delivery. *I asked you to take out the trash,* she had said. *Yesterday. Don't you hear me when I talk to you, Peter?*

Peter had glanced up at her over his computer screen. *What?*

What if that turned out to be the final exchange between them?

Nothing Lacy had seen in nursing school or in her work at a hospital prepared her for the sight she faced when she turned the corner. She processed it in pieces: shattered glass, fire engines, smoke. Blood, sobbing, sirens. She dropped the blankets near an ambulance and swam into a sea of confusion, bobbing along with the other parents in the hope that she might catch her lost child drifting before being overwhelmed by the tide.

There were children running across the muddy courtyard. None of them had coats on. Lacy watched one lucky mother find her daughter, and she scanned the crowd wildly, looking for Peter, aware that she didn't even know what he was wearing today.

Snippets of sound floated toward her:

. . . didn't see him . . .

. . . Mr. McCabe got shot . . .

. . . haven't found her yet . . .

. . . I thought I'd never . . .

. . . lost my cell phone when . . .

. . . Peter Houghton was . . .

Lacy spun around, her eyes focusing on the girl who was speaking—the one who'd been reunited with her mother. "Excuse me," Lacy said. "My son . . . I'm trying to find him. I heard you mention his name—Peter Houghton?"

The girl's eyes rounded, and she sidled closer to her mother. "He's the one who's shooting."

Everything around Lacy slowed—the pulse of the ambulances, the pace of the running students, the round sounds that fell from the lips of this girl. Maybe she had misheard.

She glanced up at the girl again, and immediately wished she hadn't. The girl was sobbing. Over her shoulder her mother stared at Lacy with horror, and then carefully pivoted to shield her daughter from view, as if Lacy were a basilisk—as if her very stare could turn you to stone.

There must be some mistake, please let there be a mistake, she thought, even as she looked around at th nage and felt Peter's name swell like a sob in her throat.

Woodenly, she approached the closest policeman. "I'm looking for my son," Lacy said.

"Lady, you're not the only one. We're doing our best to—"

Lacy took a deep breath, aware that from this moment on, everything would be different. "His name," she said, "is Peter Houghton."

Alex's high heel twisted in a crack in the sidewalk, and she went down hard on one knee. Struggling upright again, she grabbed at the arm of a mother who was running past her. "The names of the wounded . . . where are they?"

"Posted at the hockey rink."

Alex hurried across the street, which had been blocked off to cars and was now a triage area for the medical personnel loading students into ambulances. When her shoes slowed her down—they were designed for an indoor courthouse, not running around outside—she reached down and stepped out of them, running in her stockings down the wet pavement.

The hockey rink, which was shared by both the Sterling High School team and the college players, was a five-minute walk from the school. Alex reached it in two minutes and found herself being pushed forward by a throng of parents all determined to see the handwritten lists that had been taped to the door panels, lists of the children who'd been taken to area hospitals. There was no indication of how badly they'd been hurt . . . or worse. Alex read the first three names: Whitaker Obermeyer. Kaitlyn Harvey. Matthew Royston.

Matt?

"No," a woman beside her said. She was petite, with the dark darting eyes of a bird and a froth of red hair. "No," she repeated, but this time, the tears had already begun.

Alex stared at her, unable to offer comfort, out of fear that grief might be contagious. She was suddenly shoved hard from the left and found herself now standing in front of the list of wounded who'd been taken to Dartmouth-Hitchcock Medical Center.

Alexis, Emma.

Horuka, Min.

Pryce, Brady.

Cormier, Josephine.

Alex would have fallen if not for the press of anxious parents on either side of her. "Excuse me," she murmured, giving up her place to another frantic mother. She struggled through the growing crowd. "Excuse me," Alex said again, words that were no longer polite discourse, but a plea for absolution.

"Captain," a desk sergeant said as Patrick walked into the station, and he slid his eyes toward the woman who was waiting across the room, coiled tight with purpose. "That's her."

Patrick turned. Peter Houghton's mother was tiny and looked nothing like her son. She had a pile of dark curls twisted on top of her head and secured with a pen. She wore scrubs and a pair of Merrell clogs. He wondered, briefly, if she was a doctor. He thought about the irony of that: *First, do no harm.*

She didn't look like a person who'd created a monster, although Patrick realized she might have been caught just as unaware by her son's actions as the rest of the community. "Mrs. Houghton?"

"I want to see my son."

"Unfortunately, you can't," Patrick replied. "He's being held in custody."

"He has a lawyer."

"Your son is seventeen—legally, an adult. That means that Peter's going to have to invoke his right to an attorney himself."

"But he might not know . . ." she said, her voice breaking. "He might not know that's what he needs to do."

Patrick knew that, in a different way, this woman was a victim of her son's actions, too. He had interrogated enough parents of minors to know that the last thing you ever wanted to do was burn a bridge. "Ma'am, we're doing our best to understand what happened today. And honestly, I hope you'll be willing to talk to me later—to help me figure out what Peter was thinking." He hesitated, and then added, "I'm very sorry."

He let himself into the inner sanctum of the police station with his keys and jogged up the stairs to the booking room with its adjacent lockup. Peter Houghton sat on the floor with his back to the bars, rocking slowly.

"Peter," Patrick said. "You all right?"

Slowly, the boy turned his head. He stared at Patrick. "You remember me?"

Peter nodded.

"How'd you like a cup of coffee or something?"

A hesitation, and then Peter nodded again.

Patrick summoned the sergeant to open Peter's cell and led him to the kitchen. He'd already arranged to have a camcorder running, so that if it came down to it, he could get Peter's verbal consent to his rights on tape and then get him to talk. Inside, he invited Peter to take a seat at the scarred table, and he poured two cups of coffee. He didn't ask Peter how he liked it—just added sugar and milk and set it in front of the boy.

Patrick sat down, too. He hadn't gotten a good look at the boy before—adrenaline will do that to your vision—but now he stared. Peter Houghton was slight, pale, with wire-rimmed glasses and freckles. One of his front teeth was crooked, and his Adam's apple looked fist-sized. His knuckles were knotty and chapped. He was crying quietly, and it might have been enough to engender sympathy had he not been wearing a T-shirt splattered with the blood of other students.

"You feel all right, Peter?" Patrick asked. "You hungry?"

The boy shook his head.

"Can I get you anything else?"

Peter put his head down on the table. "I want my mom," he whispered.

Patrick looked at the part in the boy's hair. Had he brushed it that morning, thinking, *Today's the day I'm going to kill ten students*? "I'd like to talk about what happened today. Would you be willing to do that?"

Peter didn't answer.

"If you explain it to me," Patrick urged, "maybe I can explain it to everyone else."

Peter lifted his face, crying in earnest now. Patrick knew this wasn't going to go anywhere; he sighed, pushing away from the table. "All right," he said. "Let's go."

Patrick led Peter back to the holding cell and watched him curl up on the floor on his side, facing the cement wall. He knelt behind the boy, one last-ditch attempt. "Help me help you," he said, but Peter just shook his head and continued to cry.

It wasn't until Patrick had stepped out of the cell and turned the key in the lock that he heard Peter speak again. "They started it," he whispered.

*   *   *

Dr. Guenther Frankenstein had worked as the state medical examiner for six years, which was exactly how long he'd held the Mr. Universe title in the early 1970s, before he traded in his barbells for a scalpel—or as he liked to put it, went from building bodies to taking them apart. His muscles were still formidable, and visible enough beneath his jacket to stop the onslaught of any monster jokes incurred by his last name. Patrick liked Guenther—how could you not admire a guy who could lift three times his body weight and yet also know, just by eyeballing a liver, roughly how many grams it would weigh?

Every now and then Patrick and Guenther would grab a few beers together, consuming enough alcohol for the former bodybuilder to tell him stories of women offering to oil him up before a competition or good anecdotes about Arnold, before he became political. Today, however, Patrick and Guenther did not joke around, and they did not talk about the past. They were overwhelmed by the present as they moved silently through the halls, cataloguing the dead.

Patrick met Guenther at the school after his abortive interview with Peter Houghton. The prosecutor had only shrugged when Patrick told her Peter hadn't been willing or able to talk. "We have hundreds of witnesses saying he killed ten people," Diana had said. "Arrest him."

Guenther crouched down beside the body of the sixth casualty. She had been shot in the girls' bathroom, and her body was sprawled facedown in front of the sinks. Patrick turned to the principal, Arthur McAllister, who'd agreed to accompany them for identification. "Kaitlyn Harvey," the principal said, his voice haunted. "Special-needs kid . . . sweet girl."

Guenther and Patrick looked at each other. The principal did not just identify the bodies; he also gave a little one-

or two-sentence eulogy each time. Patrick supposed that the man couldn't help himself—unlike Patrick and Guenther, he wasn't used to dealing with tragedy in the course of his normal occupation.

Patrick had tried to retrace Peter's footsteps, from the front hallway to the cafeteria (Victims 1 and 2: Courtney Ignatio and Maddie Shaw), to the stairwell outside it (Victim 3: Whit Obermeyer), to the boys' bathroom (Victim 4: Topher McPhee), through another hallway (Victim 5: Grace Murtaugh), into the girls' bathroom (Victim 6: Kaitlyn Harvey). Now, as he led the team upstairs, he took a left into the first classroom, trailing a smeared line of blood to a spot near the chalkboard where the body of the only adult victim lay . . . and beside him, a young man with his hand pressed tight over the bullet wound in the man's belly. "Ben?" McAllister said. "What are you still doing here?"

Patrick turned to the boy. "You're *not* an EMT?"

"I . . . no . . ."

"You told me you were an EMT!"

"I said I'd had medical training!"

"Ben's an Eagle Scout," the principal said.

"I couldn't leave Mr. McCabe. I . . . applied pressure, and it's working, see? The blood's stopped."

Guenther gently removed the boy's bloody hand from his teacher's stomach. "That's because he's gone, son."

Ben's face crumpled. "But I . . . I . . ."

"You did the best you could," Guenther assured him.

Patrick turned to the principal. "Why don't you take Ben outside . . . maybe let one of the doctors take a look at him?" *Shock*, he mouthed over the boy's head.

As they left the classroom, Ben grasped the principal's sleeve, leaving a bright red handprint behind. "Jesus," Patrick said, running a hand down his face.

Guenther stood up. "Come on. Let's just get this over with."

They walked toward the gymnasium, where Guenther certified the deaths of two more students—a black boy and a white one—and then into the locker room where Patrick had ultimately cornered Peter Houghton. Guenther examined the body of the boy Patrick had seen earlier, the kid in the hockey jersey whose cap had been blown off his head by a bullet. Meanwhile, Patrick walked into the abutting shower room and glanced out the window. The reporters were still there, but most of the wounded had been dealt with. There was only one waiting ambulance, instead of seven.

It had started to rain. By the next morning, the bloodstains on the pavement outside the school would be pale; this day might never have happened.

"This is interesting," Guenther said.

Patrick closed the window against the weather. "Why? Is he deader than the rest of them?"

"Yeah. He's the only victim that's been shot twice. Once in the gut, once in the head." Guenther looked at him. "How many guns did you find on the shooter?"

"One in his hand, one on the floor here, two in his backpack."

"Nothing like a little backup plan."

"Tell me about it," Patrick said. "Can you tell which bullet was fired first?"

"No. My educated guess, though, would be the one in the belly . . . since it was the slug to the brain that killed him." Guenther knelt beside the body. "Maybe he hated this kid most of all."

The door of the locker room flew open, revealing a street cop soaked by the sudden downpour. "Captain?" he said. "We just found the makings of another pipe bomb in Peter Houghton's car."

When Josie was younger, Alex had a recurring nightmare about being on a plane when it went into a nosedive. She could feel the spin of gravity, the pressure that held her back in her chair; she saw purses and coats and carry-on luggage burst out of the overhead compartments to fall into the aisle. *I have to get to my cell phone,* Alex had thought, intent on leaving Josie a message on the answering machine that she could carry around forever, digital proof that Alex loved her and was thinking of her at the end. But even after Alex had grabbed her phone from her purse and turned it on, it took too long. She'd hit the ground when the phone was still searching for a signal.

She'd awaken shaking and sweaty, even as she dismissed the dream: she rarely traveled apart from Josie; she certainly didn't take flights for her job. She'd throw back the covers and head to the bathroom and splash water on her face, but it didn't stop her from thinking: *I was too late.*

Now, as she sat in the quiet dark of a hospital room where her daughter was sleeping off the effects of a sedative given to her by the admitting doctor, Alex felt the same way.

This is what Alex had managed to learn: Josie had fainted during the shooting. She had a cut on her forehead decorated with a butterfly bandage, and a mild concussion. The doctors wanted to keep her overnight for observation, to be safe.

Safe had a whole new definition now.

Alex had also learned, from the unending news coverage, the names of the dead. One of whom was Matthew Royston.

Matt.

What if Josie had been with her boyfriend when he was shot?

Josie had been unconscious the whole time Alex had been here. She was small and still under the faded hospital sheets; the tie at the neck of her hospital johnny had come unraveled. From time to time, her right hand twitched. Alex reached out now and grasped it. *Wake up,* she thought. *Prove to me you're okay.*

What if Alex hadn't been late to work that morning? Might she have stayed at the kitchen table with Josie, talking about the things she imagined mothers and daughters discussed but that she never seemed to have the time to? What if she'd taken a better look at Josie when she hurried downstairs, told her to go back to bed and get some rest?

What if she'd taken Josie on a spur-of-the-moment trip to Punta Cana, San Diego, Fiji—all the places Alex dream-surfed on her computer in chambers and thought about visiting, but never did?

What if she'd been a prescient enough mother to keep her daughter home from school today?

There were, of course, hundreds of other parents who'd made the same honest mistake she had. But that was shallow comfort to Alex: none of their children were Josie. None of them, surely, had as much to lose as she did.

When this is over, Alex promised silently, *we will go to the rain forest, or the pyramids, or a beach as white as bone. We will eat grapes from the vine, we will swim with sea turtles, we will walk miles on cobblestone streets. We will laugh and talk and confess. We will.*

At the same time, a small voice in her head was scheduling this paradise. *After,* it said. *Because first, this trial will come to your courtroom.*

It was true: a case like this would be fast-tracked to the docket. Alex was the superior court judge for Grafton County, and would be for the next eight months. Although Josie had been at the scene of the crime, she wasn't technically a victim of the shooter. Had Josie been wounded, Alex would have automatically been removed from the case. But as it stood, there was no legal conflict in Alex's sitting as judge, as long as she could separate her personal feelings as the mother of a high school student from her professional feelings as a justice. This would be her first big trial as a superior court judge, the one that set a tone for the rest of her tenure on the bench.

Not that she was really thinking about that now.

Suddenly, Josie stirred. Alex watched consciousness pour into her, reach a high-water mark. "Where am I?"

Alex combed her fingers through her daughter's hair. "In the hospital."

"Why?"

Her hand stilled. "Do you remember anything about today?"

"Matt came over before school," Josie said, and then she pushed herself upright. "Was there, like, a car accident?"

Alex hesitated, unsure of what she was supposed to say. Wasn't Josie better off not knowing the truth? What if this was the way her mind was protecting her from whatever she'd witnessed?

"You're fine," Alex said carefully. "You weren't hurt."

Josie turned to her, relieved. "What about Matt?"

Lewis was getting a lawyer. Lacy held that nugget of information to her chest like a hot stone as she rocked back and forth on Peter's bed and waited for him to come home. *It's going to be all right*, Lewis had promised, although she did not understand how he could make so specious a state-

ment. *Clearly this is a mistake,* Lewis had said, but he
hadn't been down at the high school. He hadn't seen the
faces of the students, kids who would never really be kids
again.

There was a part of Lacy that wanted so badly to believe Lewis—to think that somehow, this broken thing
might be fixed. But there was another part of her that remembered him waking Peter at four in the morning to go
out and sit in a duck blind. Lewis had taught his son how
to hunt, never expecting that Peter might find a different
kind of prey. Lacy understood hunting as both a sport and
an evolutionary claim; she even knew how to make an excellent venison stew and teriyaki goose and enjoyed whatever meal Lewis's hobby put on the table. But right now,
she thought, *It is his fault,* because then it couldn't be
hers.

How could you change a boy's bedding every week
and feed him breakfast and drive him to the orthodontist
and not know him at all? She'd assumed that if Peter's answers were monosyllabic, it was just because of his age;
that any mother would have made the same assumption.
Lacy combed through her memories for some red flag,
some conversation she might have misread, something
overlooked, but all she could recall were a thousand ordinary moments.

A thousand ordinary moments that some mothers would
never get to have again with their own children.

Tears sprang to her eyes; she wiped them with the back
of her hand. *Don't think about them,* she silently scolded.
Right now you have to worry about yourself.

Had Peter been thinking that, too?

Swallowing, Lacy walked into her son's room. It was
dark, the bed neatly made just as Lacy had left it this morning, but now she saw the poster of a band called Death

Wish on the wall and wondered why a boy might hang it up. She opened the closet and saw the empty bottles and electrical tape and torn rags and everything else she had missed the first time around.

Suddenly, Lacy stopped. She could fix this herself. She could fix this for *both* of them. She ran downstairs to the kitchen and ripped three large black thirty-three-gallon trash bags free from their coil before hurrying back to Peter's room. She started in the closet, shoving packages of shoelaces, sugar, potassium nitrate fertilizer, and—my God, were these *pipes?*—into the first bag. She did not have a plan about what she would do with all these things, but she would get them out of her house.

When the doorbell rang, Lacy sighed with relief, expecting Lewis—although, if she'd been thinking clearly, she would have realized that Lewis would have simply let himself in. She abandoned her haul and went downstairs to find a policeman holding a slim blue folder. "Mrs. Houghton?" the officer said.

What could they possibly want? They already had her son.

"We've got a search warrant." He handed her the paperwork and pushed past her, followed by five other policemen. "Jackson and Walhorne, you head up to the boy's room. Rodriguez, the basement. Tewes and Gilchrist, start with the first floor, and everyone, let's make sure you cover the answering machines and all computer equipment . . ." Then he noticed Lacy still standing there, stricken. "Mrs. Houghton, you'll have to leave the premises."

The policeman escorted her to her own front hallway. Numb, Lacy followed. What would they think when they reached Peter's room and found that trash bag? Would they blame Peter? Or Lacy, for enabling him?

Did they already?

A rush of cold air hit Lacy in the face as the front door opened. "For how long?"

The officer shrugged. "Till we're done," he said, and he left her out in the cold.

Jordan McAfee had been an attorney for nearly twenty years and truly believed he had seen and heard it all, until now, when he and his wife, Selena, stood in front of the television set watching CNN's coverage of the school shooting at Sterling High. "It's like Columbine," Selena said. "In our backyard."

"Except right now," Jordan murmured, "there's someone to blame who's still alive." He glanced down at the baby in his wife's arms, a blue-eyed, coffee-colored mixture of his own WASP genes and Selena's never-ending limbs and ebony skin, and he reached for the remote to turn down the volume, just in case his son was taking any of this in subconsciously.

Jordan knew Sterling High. It was just down the street from his barber and two blocks away from the room over the bank he rented as his law office. He had represented a few students who'd been busted with pot in their glove compartments or who got caught drinking underage at the college in town. Selena, who was not only his wife but also his investigator, had gone into the school to talk to kids from time to time about a case.

They hadn't lived here very long. His son Thomas—the only good thing to come out of his lousy first marriage—graduated from high school in Salem Falls and was now a sophomore at Yale, where Jordan spent $40,000 a year to hear that he had narrowed down his career plans to becoming either a performance artist, an art historian, or a professional clown. Jordan had finally asked Selena to marry him, and after she'd gotten pregnant, they'd moved to Sterling—because the school district had such a good reputation.

Go figure.

When the telephone rang and Jordan—who didn't want to watch the coverage but couldn't tear his eyes away from it either—made no motion to answer it, Selena dumped the baby in his arms and reached for the receiver. "Hey," she said. "How's it going?"

Jordan glanced up and raised his brows.

Thomas, Selena mouthed. "Yeah, hang on, he's right here."

He took the phone from Selena. "What the hell is going on?" Thomas asked. "Sterling High's all over MSNBC.com."

"I don't know any more than you do," Jordan said. "It's pandemonium."

"I know some kids there. We competed against them in track and field. It's just—it's not *real*."

Jordan could still hear ambulance sirens in the distance. "It's real," he said. There was a click on the line—call-waiting. "Hang on, I have to take this."

"Is this Mr. McAfee?"

"Yes . . ."

"I, um, understand that you're an attorney. I got your name from Stuart McBride over at Sterling College . . ."

On the television, a list of the names of the known dead began to scroll, with yearbook pictures. "You know, I'm on the other line," Jordan said. "Could I take down your name and number, and get back to you?"

"I was wondering if you'd represent my son," the caller said. "He's the boy who . . . the one from the high school who . . . ." The voice stumbled, and then broke. "They say my son's the one who did it."

Jordan thought of the last time he'd represented a teenage boy. Like this one, Chris Harte had been found holding a smoking gun.

"Will you . . . will you take his case?"

Jordan forgot about Thomas, waiting. He forgot about Chris Harte and how the case had nearly turned him inside out. Instead he looked at Selena and the baby in her arms. Sam twisted, grabbing at her earring. This boy—the one who had walked into Sterling High this morning and committed a massacre—was someone's son. And in spite of a town that would be reeling for years, and media coverage that had already reached the point of saturation, he deserved a fair trial.

"Yes," Jordan said. "I will."

Finally—after the bomb squad had dismantled the pipe bomb in Peter Houghton's car; after one hundred and sixteen shell casings had been found scattered in the school from fired bullets; after the accident recon guys had begun to measure the evidence and the location of the bodies so that they could produce a scale diagram of the scene; after the crime techs had taken the first of hundreds of snapshots that they would put into indexed photobooks— Patrick called everyone together into the auditorium of the school and stood on the stage in the near darkness. "What we have is a massive amount of information," he told the crowd assembled before him. "There's going to be a lot of pressure on us to do this fast, and to do this right. I want everyone back here in twenty-four hours, so that we can see where we're at."

People began to disperse. At the next meeting, Patrick would be given the completed photobooks, all evidence not being sent to the lab, and all lab submissions. In twenty-four hours, he'd be buried so far underneath the avalanche he wouldn't know which way was up.

While the others headed back to various parts of the building to complete the work that would take them all night and the next day, Patrick walked out to his car. It had stopped raining. Patrick planned to go back to the station to review the evidence that had been seized from the Houghtons' home, and he wanted to talk to the parents, if they were still willing. But he found himself pointing his car instead toward the medical center, and he pulled into the parking lot. He walked into the emergency entrance and flashed his badge. "Look," he said to the nurse, "I know you had a lot of kids come through here today. But one of the first was a girl named Josie. I'm trying to find her."

The nurse fluttered her hands over her computer keyboard. "Josie who?"

"That's the thing," Patrick admitted. "I don't know."

The screen swam with a flurry of information, and the nurse tapped her finger against the glass. "Cormier. She's up on the fourth floor, Room 422."

Patrick thanked her and took the elevator upstairs. Cormier. The name sounded familiar, but he couldn't quite place it. It was common enough, he figured—maybe he'd read it in the paper or seen it on a television show. He slipped past the nurses' desk and followed the numbers down the hall. The door to Josie's room was ajar. The girl sat up in bed, wrapped in shadows, talking to a figure that stood beside her.

Patrick knocked softly and stepped into the room. Josie stared at him blankly; the woman beside her turned around.

Cormier, Patrick realized. *As in Judge Cormier*. He'd

been called to testify in her courtroom a few times before she became a superior court judge; he'd gone to her for warrants as a last resort—after all, she came from a public defender's background, which in Patrick's mind meant that even if she now was scrupulously fair, she *still* had once played for the other side.

"Your Honor," he said. "I didn't realize Josie was your daughter." He approached the bed. "How are you doing?"

Josie stared at him. "Do I know you?"

"I'm the one who carried you out—" He stopped as the judge put her hand on his arm and drew him out of Josie's range of hearing.

"She doesn't remember anything that happened," the judge whispered. "She thinks for some reason that she was in a car accident . . . and I . . ." Her voice trailed off. "I haven't been able to tell her the truth."

Patrick understood—when you loved someone, you didn't want to be the one who brought their world crashing down. "Would you like me to do it?"

The judge hesitated, and then nodded gratefully. Patrick faced Josie again. "You all right?"

"My head hurts. The doctors said I have a concussion and have to stay overnight." She looked up at him. "I guess I ought to thank you for rescuing me." Suddenly, a flicker of intention crossed her face. "Do *you* know what happened to Matt? The guy who was in the car with me?"

Patrick sat down on the edge of the hospital bed. "Josie," he said gently, "you weren't in a car accident. There was an incident at your school—a student came in and started shooting people."

Josie shook her head, trying to dislodge the words.

"Matt was one of the victims."

Her eyes filled with tears. "Is he okay?"

Patrick looked down at the soft waffle weave of the blanket between them. "I'm sorry."

"No," Josie said. "*No.* You're lying to me." She struck out at Patrick, clipping him across the face and chest. The judge rushed forward, trying to hold her daughter back, but Josie was wild—shrieking, crying, clawing, drawing the attention of the nursing staff down the hall. Two of them flew into the room on white wings, shooing out Patrick and Judge Cormier, while they administered a sedative to Josie.

In the hallway, Patrick leaned against the wall and closed his eyes. Jesus Christ. Was this what he'd have to put every one of his witnesses through? He was about to apologize to the judge for upsetting Josie when she turned on him just like her daughter had. "What the *hell* do you think you're doing, telling her about Matt!"

"You *asked* me to," Patrick bristled.

"To tell her about the *school*," the judge qualified. "Not to tell her her boyfriend's dead!"

"You know damn well Josie would have found out sooner or—"

"Later," the judge interrupted. "*Much* later."

The nurses appeared in the doorway. "She's sleeping now," one of them whispered. "We'll be back in to check on her."

They both waited until the nurses were out of hearing range. "Look," Patrick said tightly. "Today I saw kids who'd been shot in the head, kids who will never walk again, kids who died because they were in the wrong place at the wrong time. Your daughter . . . she's in shock . . . but she's one of the lucky ones."

His words hit her, a solid slap. For just a moment, when Patrick looked at the judge, she no longer seemed furious. Her gray eyes were heavy with all the scenarios that, thankfully, had not come to pass; her mouth softened with relief. And then, just as suddenly, her features smoothed, impassive. "I'm sorry. I'm not usually like this. It's just . . . been a really awful day."

Patrick tried, but he could see no trace left of the emotion that had, for a moment, broken her. *Seamless.* That's what she was.

"I know you were only trying to do your job," the judge said.

"I *would* like to talk to Josie . . . but that's not why I came. I'm here because she was the first one . . . well, I just needed to know she was all right." He offered Judge Cormier the smallest of smiles, the kind that can start a heart to breaking. "Take care of her," Patrick said, and then he turned and walked down the hall, aware of the heat of her gaze on his back, and how much it felt like the touch of a hand.

Twelve Years Before

On his first day of kindergarten, Peter Houghton woke up at 4:32 a.m. He padded into his parents' room and asked if it was time yet to take the school bus. For as long as he could remember, he'd watched his brother Joey get on the bus, and it was a mystery of dynamic proportion: the way the sun bounced off its snub yellow nose, the door that hinged like the jaw of a dragon, the dramatic sigh when it came to a stop. Peter had a Matchbox car that looked just like the bus Joey rode on twice a day—the same bus that now he was going to get to ride on, too.

His mother told him to go back to sleep until it was morning, but he couldn't. Instead, he got dressed in the special clothes his mother had bought for his first day of school and he lay back down in bed to wait. He was the first one downstairs for breakfast, and his mother made chocolate chip pancakes—his favorite. She kissed him on the cheek and took a picture of him sitting at the breakfast table, and then another one when he was dressed in his coat and had his empty knapsack on his back, like the shell of a turtle. "I can't believe my baby is going to school," his mother said.

Joey, who was in first grade this year, told him to stop acting stupid. "It's just school," he said. "Big deal."

Peter's mother finished buttoning his coat. "It was a big deal to you once, too," she said. Then she told Peter she had a surprise for him. She went into the kitchen and reappeared with a Superman lunch box. Superman was reaching forward, as if he were trying to break out of the metal. His whole body stuck out from the background the tiniest bit, like the letters on books blind people read. Peter liked thinking that even if he couldn't see, he would be able to tell that this was his lunch box. He took it from his mother and hugged her. He heard the thud of a piece of fruit rolling, the crinkle of wax paper, and he imagined the insides of his lunch, like mysterious organs.

They waited at the end of the driveway, and just as Peter had dreamed over and over, the yellow bus rose over the crest of the hill. "One more!" his mother called, and she took a picture of Peter with the bus groaning to a stop behind him. "Joey," she instructed, "take care of your brother." Then she kissed Peter on the forehead. "My big boy," she said, and her mouth pinched tight, the way it did when she was trying not to cry.

Suddenly Peter felt his stomach turn to ice. What if kindergarten was not as great as he'd imagined? What if his teacher looked like the witch on that TV program that gave him nightmares sometimes? What if he forgot which direction the letter E went and everyone made fun of him?

With hesitation, he climbed the steps of the school bus. The driver wore an army jacket and had two teeth missing in the front. "There's seats in back," he said, and Peter headed down the aisle, looking for Joey.

His brother was sitting next to a boy Peter didn't know. Joey glanced at him as he walked by, but didn't say anything.

"Peter!"

He turned and saw Josie patting the empty seat next to her. She had her dark hair in pigtails and was wearing a skirt, even though she hated skirts. "I saved it for you," Josie said.

He sat down next to her, feeling better already. He was riding inside a *bus*. And he was sitting next to his best friend in the whole world. "*Cool* lunch box," Josie said.

He held it up, to show her the way that you could make Superman look like he was moving if you wiggled it, and just then a hand reached across the aisle. A boy with ape arms and a backward baseball cap grabbed the lunch box out of Peter's grasp. "Hey, freak," he said, "you want to see Superman fly?"

Before Peter understood what the older boy was doing, he opened a window and hurled Peter's lunch box out of it. Peter stood up, craning his neck around to see out the rear emergency door. His lunch box burst open on the asphalt. His apple rolled across the dotted yellow line of the road and vanished beneath the tire of an oncoming car.

"Sit down!" the bus driver yelled.

Peter sank back into his seat. His face felt cold, but his ears were burning. He could hear the boy and his friends laughing, as loud as if it were happening in his own head. Then he felt Josie's hand slide into his. "I've got peanut butter," she whispered. "We can share."

Alex sat in the conference room at the jail, across from her newest client, Linus Froom. This morning, at 4:00 a.m., he'd dressed in black, pulled a ski mask over his head, and robbed an Irving gas station convenience store at gunpoint. When the police were called in after Linus ran off, they found a cell phone on the ground. It rang while the detective was sitting at his desk. "Dude," the caller said. "This is my cell phone. Do you have it?" The detective said yes, and asked where he'd lost it. "At the Irving station, man. I was there, like, a half hour ago." The detective suggested that they meet at the corner of Route 10 and Route 25A; he'd bring the cell phone.

Needless to say, Linus Froom showed up, and was arrested for robbery.

Alex looked at her client across the scarred table. Her daughter was at this moment having juice and cookies or story time or Advanced Crayoning or whatever else the first day of kindergarten consisted of, and *she* was stuck in a conference room at the county jail with a criminal too stupid to even be good at his craft. "It says here," Alex said, perusing the police report, "that there was some contention when Detective Chisholm read you your rights?"

Linus lifted his gaze. He was a kid—only nineteen—with acne and a unibrow. "He thought I was dumb as shit."

"He *said* this to you?"

"He asked me if I could read."

All cops did; they were supposed to have the perp follow along with the Miranda rights. "And your response, apparently, was, 'Hello, fucko, do I look like a moron?'"

Linus shrugged. "What was I *supposed* to say?"

Alex pinched the bridge of her nose. Her days in the public defender's office were an exhausting blur of moments like this: a great amount of energy and time expended on behalf of someone who—a week, a month, a year later—would wind up sitting across from her again. And yet, what else was she qualified to do? This was the world she had chosen to inhabit.

Her beeper went off. Glancing at the number, she silenced it. "Linus, I think we're going to have to plead this one out."

She left Linus in the hands of a detention officer and

ducked into the office of a secretary at the jail in order to borrow her phone. "Thank God," Alex said when the person picked up on the other end. "You saved me from jumping out a second-story window at the jail."

"You forgot, there are bars," Whit Hobart said, laughing. "I used to think maybe they'd been installed not to keep the prisoners in, but to prevent their public defenders from running away when they realize how bad their cases are."

Whit had been Alex's boss when she'd joined the NH public defender's office, but he had retired nine months ago. A legend in his own right, Whit had become the father she'd never had—one who, unlike her own, had praise for her instead of criticism. She wished Whit were here, now, instead of in some golf community on the seacoast. He'd take her out to lunch and tell her stories that made her realize every public defender had clients—and cases—like Linus. And then he'd somehow leave her with the bill and a renewed drive to get up and fight all over again.

"What are you doing up?" Alex said. "Early tee time?"

"Nah, damn gardener woke me with the leaf blower. What am I missing?"

"Nothing, really. Except the office isn't the same without you. There's a certain . . . *energy* missing."

"Energy? You're not becoming some New Age crystal-reading hack, are you, Al?"

Alex grinned. "No—"

"Good. Because that's why I'm calling: I've got a job for you."

"I already *have* a job. In fact, I have enough work for *two* jobs."

"Three district courts in the area are posting a vacancy in the *Bar News*. You really ought to put your name in, Alex."

"To be a judge?" She started to laugh. "Whit, what are you smoking these days?"

"You'd be good at it, Alex. You're a fine decision maker. You're even-tempered. You don't let your emotions get in the way of your work. You have the defense perspective, so you understand the litigants. And you've always been an excellent trial attorney." He hesitated. "Plus, it's not too often that New Hampshire has a Democratic female governor picking a judge."

"Thanks for the vote of confidence," Alex said, "but I am *so* not the right person for that job."

She knew, too, because her father had been a superior court justice. Alex could remember swinging around in his swivel chair, counting paper clips, running her thumbnail along the green felt surface of his spotless blotter to make a hatch-marked grid. She'd pick up the phone and talk to the dial tone. She'd pretend. And then inevitably her father would come in and berate her for disturbing a pencil or a file or—God forbid—himself.

On her belt, her beeper began to vibrate again. "Listen, I have to get to court. Maybe we can do lunch next week."

"Judges' hours are regular," Whit added. "What time does Josie get home from school?"

"Whit—"

"Think about it," he said, and then he hung up.

"Peter," his mother sighed, "how could you possibly lose it *again?*" She skirted around his father, who was pouring himself a cup of coffee, and fished through the dark bowels of the pantry for a brown paper lunch sack.

Peter hated those sacks. The banana never could quite fit in, and the sandwich *always* got crushed. But what else was he supposed to do?

"What did he lose?" his father asked.

"His lunch box. For the third time this month." His mother began to fill the brown bag—fruit and juice pack on the bottom, sandwich floating on top. She glanced at Peter, who was not eating his breakfast, but vivisecting his paper napkin with a knife. He had, so far, made the letters *H* and *T*. "If you procrastinate, you're going to miss the bus."

"You've got to start being responsible," his father said.

When his father spoke, Peter pictured the words like smoke. They clouded up the room for a moment, but before you knew it, they'd be gone.

"For God's sake, Lewis, he's five."

"I don't remember Joey losing his lunch box three times during the first month of school."

Peter sometimes watched his father playing soccer in the backyard with Joey. Their legs pumped like crazy pistons and gears—forward, backward, forward—as if they were doing a dance together with the ball caught between them. When Peter tried to join them, he got tangled up in his own frustration. The last time, he'd scored against himself by accident.

He looked over his shoulder at his parents. "I'm not Joey," he said, and even though nobody answered, he could hear the reply: *We know.*

"Attorney Cormier?" Alex glanced up to find a former client standing in front of her desk, beaming from ear to ear.

It took her a moment to place him. Teddy MacDougal or MacDonald, something like that. She remembered the charge: simple assault domestic violence. He and his wife had gotten drunk and gone after each other. Alex had gotten him acquitted.

"I got somethin' for ya," Teddy said.

"I hope you didn't buy me anything," she answered, and

she meant it—this was a man from the North Country who was so poor that the floor of his house was literally dirt and he stocked his freezer with the spoils of his own hunting. Alex was not a fan of hunting, but she understood that for some of her clients—like Teddy—it was not about sport, but survival. Which was exactly why a conviction for him would have been so devastating: it would have cost him his firearms.

"I didn't buy it. Promise." Teddy grinned. "It's in my truck. Come on out."

"Can't you bring it in here?"

"Oh, no. No, can't do that."

Oh, excellent, Alex thought. *What could he possibly have in his truck that he can't bring in?* She followed Teddy out to the parking lot and in the back of his pickup truck saw a huge, dead bear.

"This is for your freeza'," he said.

"Teddy, this is enormous. You could eat it all winter."

"Damn right. But I thoughta you."

"Thank you so much. I really appreciate it. But I don't, um, eat meat. And I wouldn't want it to go to waste." She touched his arm. "I really want you to have it."

Teddy squinted into the sun. "All right." He nodded at Alex, climbed into the cab of his truck, and bounced out of the parking lot as the bear thumped against the walls of the pickup bed.

"Alex!"

She turned to find her secretary standing in the doorway.

"A call from your daughter's school just came in," the secretary said. "Josie got sent to the principal's office."

Josie? In trouble at school? "For *what*?" Alex asked.

"She beat the crap out of a boy on the playground."

Alex started toward her car. "Tell them I'm on my way."

*   *   *

On the ride home, Alex stole glances at her daughter in the rearview mirror. Josie had gone to school this morning in a white cardigan and khaki pants; now that cardigan was streaked with dirt. There were twigs in her hair, which had fallen from its ponytail. The elbow of her sweater had a hole in it; her lip was still bleeding. And—here was the amazing thing—apparently, she'd fared better than the little boy she'd gone after.

"Come on," Alex said, leading Josie upstairs to the bathroom. There, she peeled off her daughter's shirt, washed her cuts, and covered them with Neosporin and Band-Aids. She sat down in front of Josie, on the bathmat that looked like it was made of Cookie Monster skin. "You want to talk about it?"

Josie's lower lip quivered, and she started to cry. "It's Peter," she said. "Drew picks on him all the time and Peter gets hurt, so today I wanted it to be the other way around."

"Aren't there teachers on the playground?"

"Aides."

"Well, you should have told them that Peter was getting teased. Beating up Drew only makes you just as bad as him in the first place."

"We *went* to the aides," Josie complained. "They told Drew and the other kids to leave Peter alone, but they never listen."

"So," Alex said, "you did what you thought was the best thing at the time?"

"Yeah. For Peter."

"Imagine if you *always* did that. Let's say you decided that you liked someone else's coat better than yours, so you took it."

"That would be stealing," Josie said.

"Exactly. *That's* why there are rules. You can't break the

rules, not even when it seems like everyone else is doing it. Because if you do—if we *all* do—then the whole world becomes a very scary place. One where coats get stolen and people get beat up on the playground. Instead of doing the *best* thing, we sometimes have to settle for the *rightest* thing."

"What's the difference?"

"The best thing is what *you* think should be done. The rightest thing is what *needs* to be done—when you think not just of you and how you feel, but also the extra stuff—who else is involved, and what's happened before, and what the rules say." She glanced at Josie. "Why didn't Peter fight?"

"He thought he'd get in trouble."

"I rest my case," Alex said.

Josie's eyelashes were spiked with tears. "Are you mad at me?"

Alex hesitated. "I'm angry at the aides for not paying attention when Peter was getting teased. And I'm not thrilled that you punched a boy in the nose. But I'm proud of you for wanting to defend your friend." She kissed Josie on the forehead. "Go get some clothes that don't have holes in them, Wonder Woman."

When Josie scrambled off into her bedroom, Alex remained sitting on the bathroom floor. It struck her that dispensing justice was really more about being present and engaged than anything else—unlike those aides on the playground, for example. You could be firm without being bossy; you could make it a point to know the rules; you could take all evidence into consideration before coming to a conclusion.

Being a good judge, Alex realized, was not all that different from being a good mother.

She stood up, went downstairs, and picked up the

phone. Whit answered on the third ring. "Okay," she said. "Tell me what I have to do."

The chair was too small beneath Lacy's bottom; her knees did not fit under the desk; the colors on the walls were too bright. The teacher who sat across from her was so young that Lacy wondered if she could go home and drink a glass of wine without breaking any laws. "Mrs. Houghton," the teacher said, "I wish I could give you a better explanation, but the fact is, some kids are simply magnets for teasing. Other children see a weakness, and they exploit it."

"What's Peter's weakness?" she asked.

The teacher smiled. "I don't see it as a weakness. He's sensitive, and he's sweet. But that means he's far less likely to be running around with the other boys playing police chase than he is to be coloring in a corner with Josie. The other children in the class notice."

Lacy remembered being in elementary school, not that much older than Peter, and raising chicks from an incubator. The six eggs had hatched, but one of the chicks was born with a gnarled leg. It was always the last to the feed tray and the water trough, and it was scrawnier and more tentative than its siblings. One day, while the class watched in horror, the maimed chick was pecked to death by the others.

"The behavior of these other boys is not being tolerated," the teacher assured Lacy. "When we see it, we immediately send the child to the principal." She opened her mouth as if she was about to say something, and then snapped it shut.

"What?"

The teacher looked down at the desk. "It's just that, unfortunately, that response can have the opposite effect. The boys identify Peter as the reason they're in trouble, and that perpetuates the cycle of violence."

Lacy felt her face growing hot. "What are you doing, personally, to make sure this doesn't happen again?"

She expected the teacher to talk about a time-out chair, or some retributive punishment that would be handed out if Peter was again taunted by the in crowd. But instead, the young woman said, "I'm showing Peter how to stand up for himself. If someone cuts him in the lunch line, or if he's teased, to say something in return instead of just accepting it."

Lacy blinked at her. "I . . . I can't believe I'm hearing this. So if he gets shoved, he's supposed to shove back? When his food gets knocked on the floor, he should reciprocate?"

"Of course not—"

"You're telling me that for Peter to feel safe in school, he's going to have to start acting like the boys who do this to him?"

"No, I'm telling you about the reality of grade school," the teacher corrected. "Look, Mrs. Houghton. I can tell you what you want to hear. I can say that Peter is a wonderful child, which he is. I can tell you that the school will teach tolerance and will discipline the boys who've been making Peter's life so miserable, and that this will be enough to stop it. But the sad fact is that if Peter wants it to end, he's going to have to be part of the solution."

Lacy looked down at her hands. They looked gargantuan on the surface of the tiny pupil's desk. "Thank you. For your honesty." She stood up carefully, because that is how it's best to move in a world where you no longer fit.

She let herself out of the kindergarten classroom. Peter was waiting on a small wooden bench beneath the cubbies in the hall. It was her job as Peter's mother to smooth the road in front of him so that he wouldn't falter. But what if she couldn't bulldoze on his behalf all the time? Is *that* what the teacher had been trying to tell her?

She squatted down in front of Peter and reached for his hands. "You know I love you, right?" Lacy said.

Peter nodded.

"You know I only want what's best for you."

"Yes," Peter said.

"I know about the lunch boxes. I know what's been going on with Drew. I heard about Josie punching him. I know the kinds of things he says to you." Lacy felt her eyes fill with tears. "The next time it happens, you have to stick up for yourself. You *have* to, Peter, or I . . . I'm going to have to punish you."

Life wasn't fair. Lacy had been passed over for promotions, no matter how hard she'd worked. She'd seen mothers who'd taken meticulous care of themselves deliver stillborns, while crack addicts had healthy infants. She'd seen fourteen-year-olds dying of ovarian cancer before they ever got a chance to really live. You couldn't fight the injustice of fate; you could only suffer it and hope that one day it might be different. But somehow, it was even more difficult to stomach on behalf of your child. It tore Lacy apart to have to be the one to pull back that curtain of innocence, so that Peter would see that no matter how much she loved him—no matter how much she had wanted this world to be perfect for him—it would always fall short.

Swallowing, she stared at Peter, trying to think of what she could do to spur him to self-defense, which punishment would make him change his behavior, even as it broke her heart to make him do just that. "If this happens again . . . no playdates with Josie for a month."

She closed her eyes at the ultimatum. It was not the way she liked to parent, but apparently her usual advice—be kind, be polite, be what you want others to be—had done Peter no good. If a threat might make Peter roar, so loud that Drew and all those other awful children slunk away with their tails between their legs, then Lacy would do it.

She brushed Peter's hair back from his face, watching the play of doubt cloud his features—and why *shouldn't* it? His mother had certainly never given him a directive like *this* before. "He's a bully. A jerk, in a tiny package. But he'll grow up to be a bigger jerk, and you—you're going to grow up to be someone incredible." Lacy smiled widely at her son. "One day, Peter, everyone's going to know your name."

There were two swings out on the playground, and sometimes you had to wait your turn for them. When that happened, Peter would cross his fingers and hope that he got the one that hadn't been swung around the top bar by a fifth grader, making it so that the seat was incredibly high off the ground and hard to get into. He was afraid he would fall off, trying to get on the swing, or, even more embarrassing, not even be able to hike himself up in the first place.

When he waited with Josie, she always took that swing. She pretended she liked it, but Peter realized she was only pretending she didn't know how much he *disliked* it.

Today at recess, they weren't swinging. Instead, they'd twisted the chains round and round until they were as knotted as a throat, and then they'd lift up their feet and go spinning. Peter would sometimes look back at the sky and imagine that he was flying.

When they stopped, his swing and Josie's staggered against each other and their feet got all tangled. She laughed, and lightly locked their ankles together so that they were connected, a human chain link.

He turned to her. "I want people to like me," he blurted out.

Josie tilted her head. "People *do* like you."

Peter split his feet, disengaging them. "I meant people," he said, "who aren't you."

The application to become a judge took Alex two full days to complete, and as she filled it out, a remarkable thing happened: she realized that she *did* actually want to be a judge. In spite of what she'd said to Whit, in spite of her earlier reservations, she was making the right decision for the right reasons.

When the Judicial Selection Commission called for an interview, they made it clear that such invitations were not extended to just anybody. That if Alex was being interviewed, she was being seriously considered for the position.

The job of the commission was to give the governor a short list of candidates. Judicial commission interviews were conducted at the old governor's mansion, Bridges House, in East Concord. They were staggered, and candidates entered through one entrance and left through another, presumably so that no one knew who else was up for the job.

The twelve members of the commission were lawyers, policemen, executive directors of victim's advocacy organizations. They stared so hard at Alex that she expected her face to burst into flames. It did not help, either, that she had been up half the night with Josie, who'd awakened from a nightmare about a boa constrictor and refused to go back to sleep. Alex didn't know who the other candidates were for this position, but she'd wager that they weren't single moms who'd had to poke the radiator vents with a yardstick at 3:00 a.m. to prove that there weren't any snakes hiding in the dark tunnels.

"I like the pace," she said carefully, replying to a question. There were answers she was expected to give, she knew. The trick was to somehow imbue the stock phrases and anticipated responses with part of her personality. "I like the pressure of making a quick decision. I'm strong on the rules of evidence. I've been in courtrooms with justices who don't do their homework in advance, and I know I won't function that way." She hesitated, looking around at the men and women, wondering if she should cultivate a persona like most of the other people who applied for judicial positions—and who'd come through the hallowed ranks of the prosecutorial office—or if she should be herself and allow the petticoat hem of her public defender background to peek out.

Oh, hell.

"I guess the reason I really want to be a judge is because I love the way a courtroom is an equal opportunity environment. When you come into it, for that brief amount of time, your case is the most important thing in the world, to everyone in that room. The system works for *you*. It doesn't matter who you are, or where you're from—your treatment will depend on the letter of the law, not on any socioeconomic variables."

One of the commission members looked down at her notes. "What do you think makes a good judge, Ms. Cormier?"

Alex felt a bead of sweat run down between her shoulder blades. "Being patient but firm. Being in control but not being arrogant. Knowing the rules of evidence and the rules of a courtroom." She paused. "This is probably not what you're used to hearing, but I think a good judge probably is a whiz at tangrams."

An older woman from a victim's advocacy group blinked. "I beg your pardon?"

"Tangrams. I'm a mom. My little girl, she's five. And there's this game she has where you're given a geometric outline of a figure—a boat, a train, a bird—and you somehow construct it from a set of puzzle pieces: triangles and parallelograms—some bigger than others. It's easy for a person with good spatial relations skills, because you really have to think outside the box. And being a judge is like that. You've got all of these competing factors—the parties involved, the victims, law enforcement, society, even *precedent*—and you somehow have to use them to solve the problem within a given framework."

In the uncomfortable silence that followed, Alex turned her head and caught a glimpse through a window of the next interviewee arriving through the entrance vestibule. She blinked, certain she'd seen wrong, but you did not forget the silvered curls that you'd once run your fingers through; you did not put out of your mind the geography of cheekbones and jaw you'd traced with your own lips. Logan Rourke—her trial advocacy professor; her old lover; her daughter's *father*—headed into the building and closed the door.

Apparently, he was a judicial candidate as well.

Alex drew in her breath, even more determined to win this position than she had been a moment ago. "Ms. Cormier?" the older woman said again, and Alex realized she'd missed her question the first time around.

"Yes. Sorry?"

"I asked how successful you are when you play tangrams."

Alex met her gaze. "Ma'am," she said, letting a broad smile escape, "I'm the New Hampshire State Champion."

At first, the numbers just looked fatter. But then they started to twist a little, and Peter had to either squinch up his face or get closer to see if it was a 3 or an 8. His teacher sent him to the nurse, who smelled like teabags and feet, and she made him look at a chart on the wall.

His new eyeglasses were light as a feather and had special lenses that wouldn't scratch even if he fell down and they went flying across a sandbox. The frames were made out of wire, too thin, in his opinion, to hold up the curved pieces of glass that made his eyes look like an owl's: oversized, bright, so blue.

When Peter got his glasses he was amazed. Suddenly, the blur in the distance coagulated into a farm with silos and fields and spots of cows. The letters on the red sign said STOP. There were tiny lines, like the creases on his knuckles, at the corners of his mother's eyes. All superheroes had accessories—Batman's belt, Superman's cape—this was his, and it gave him X-ray vision. He was so excited about having his new glasses that he slept with them.

It wasn't until he got to school the next day that he understood that with better vision came perfect hearing: *Four-eyes; blind as a bat.* His glasses were no longer a mark of distinction but only a scar, something else that made him different from everyone else. And that wasn't even the worst of it.

As the world came into focus, Peter realized how people looked when they glanced at him. As if he were the punch line to a joke.

And Peter, with his 20/20 vision, cast his eyes downward, so that he wouldn't see.

"We are subversive parents," Alex whispered to Lacy as they sat with their knees bent high as a grasshopper's at one of the undersize tables during Open School Day. She took the Cuisenaire rods used for math—bright colored unit strips of twos, threes, fours, fives—and fashioned them to spell a curse word.

"It's all fun and games until someone turns out to be

a judge," Lacy chided, and she scattered the word with her hand.

"Afraid I'm going to get you kicked out of kindergarten?" Alex laughed. "And as for the judge thing, that's about as much of a long shot as me winning the lottery."

"We'll see," Lacy said.

The teacher leaned down between them and handed each woman a small piece of paper. "Today I'm inviting all the parents to write down one word that best describes their child. Later, we'll make a love collage out of them."

Alex glanced at Lacy. "A *love* collage?"

"Stop being anti-kindergarten."

"I'm not. In fact, I think everything you need to know about the law you learn in kindergarten. You know: Don't hit. Don't take what's not yours. Don't kill people. Don't rape them."

"Oh, yeah, I remember that lesson. Right after snack time," Lacy said.

"You know what I mean. It's a social contract."

"What if you wound up on the bench and had to uphold a law you didn't believe in?"

"First off, that's a big *if*. And second, I'd do it. I'd feel horrible about it, but I'd do it," Alex said. "You don't want a judge with a personal agenda, believe me."

Lacy tore the edge of her paper into a fringe. "If you become the job, then when do you get to be *you*?"

Alex grinned and pushed the Cuisenaire rods into another four-letter word. "At kindergarten open houses, I guess."

Suddenly Josie appeared, rosy-cheeked and flushed. "Mommy," she said, tugging on Alex's hand as Peter climbed onto Lacy's lap. "We're all done."

They had been in the block corner, creating a surprise. Lacy and Alex stood up, letting themselves be led past the book rack and the stacks of tiny carpets and the science table with its rotting pumpkin experiment whose pitted skin and sunken flesh reminded Alex of the face of a prosecutor she knew. "This is our house," Josie announced, pushing open a block that served as the front door. "We're married."

Lacy nudged Alex. "I always wanted to get along with my in-laws."

Peter stood at a wooden stove, mixing imaginary food in a plastic pot. Josie put on an oversize lab coat. "Time to go to work. I'll be home for dinner."

"Okay," Peter said. "We're having meatballs."

"What's your job?" Alex asked Josie.

"I'm a judge. I send people to jail all day long and then I come home and eat pisghetti." She walked around the perimeter of the block house and reentered through the front door.

"Sit down," Peter said. "You're late again."

Lacy closed her eyes. "Is it just me, or is this like looking into a really unflattering mirror?"

They watched Josie and Peter put aside their plates and then move to another part of their block house, a smaller square within the square. They lay down inside it. "This is the bed," Josie explained.

The teacher came up behind Alex and Lacy. "They play house all the time," she said. "Isn't it sweet?"

Alex watched Peter curl up on his side. Josie spooned against him, wrapping her arm around his waist. She wondered how her daughter had ever formed an image of a couple like this in her mind, given that she'd never even seen her mother go out on a date.

She watched Lacy lean against the block cubby and write, on her small slip of paper, TENDER. That did describe Peter—he was tender, almost to the point of being raw. It

took someone like Josie—curled around him like a shell—
to protect him.

Alex reached for a pencil and smoothed out the piece of
paper. Adjectives tumbled through her mind—there were
so many for her daughter: *dynamic, loyal, bright, breathtak-
ing*—but she found herself forming different letters.

Mine, she wrote.

This time when the lunch box hit the pavement, it broke
wide across its hinges and the car behind the school bus
ran right over his tuna fish sandwich and his bag of Dori-
tos. The bus driver, as usual, didn't notice. The fifth-grade
boys were so good at doing this by now that the window
was opened and closed before you could even yell for
them to stop. Peter felt his eyes welling with tears as the
boys high-fived each other. He could hear his mother's
voice in his head—this was the moment where he was supposed to stick up for himself!—but his mother did not realize that would only make it worse.

"Oh, Peter," Josie sighed as he sat down again beside
her.

He stared down at his mittens. "I don't think I can go to
your house on Friday."

"How come?"

"Because my mom said she'll punish me if I lose my
lunch box again."

"That's not fair," Josie said.

Peter shrugged. "Nothing is."

No one was more surprised than Alex when the governor
of New Hampshire officially picked her from a short list
of three candidates for a district court judicial position.
Although it made sense that Jeanne Shaheen—a young,
Democratic female governor—would want to appoint a

young, Democratic female judge, Alex was still a little light-headed over the news when she went for her interview.

The governor was younger than Alex had expected, and prettier. *Which is exactly what most people will think about me if I'm on the bench*, she thought. She sat down and slipped her hands under her thighs to keep them from shaking.

"If I nominate you," the governor said, "is there anything I should know?"

"You mean skeletons in my closet?"

Shaheen nodded. What it really came down to, for a gubernatorial appointee, was whether or not that nominee would in some way reflect poorly on the governor herself. Shaheen was trying to cross her t's and dot her i's before making an official decision, and for that, Alex could only admire her. "Is anyone going to come to your Executive Council hearing and oppose your nomination?" the governor asked.

"That depends. Are you giving out furloughs at the state prison?"

Shaheen laughed. "I take it that's where your disgruntled clients have ended up."

"That's exactly why they're disgruntled."

The governor stood up and shook Alex's hand. "I think we'll get along well," she said.

Maine and New Hampshire were the only two states left in the country with an Executive Council—a group that acted as a direct check on the governor's power. For Alex, this meant that in the month between her nomination and her confirmation hearing, she had to do whatever she could to placate five Republican men before they put her through the wringer.

She called them weekly, asking if they had any questions they needed answered. She also had to arrange for witnesses to appear on her behalf at the confirmation hearing. After years in the public defender's office, this should have been simple, but the Executive Council did not want to hear from lawyers. They wanted to hear from the community where Alex worked and lived—from her first-grade teacher to a state trooper who liked her in spite of her allegiance to the Dark Side. The tricky part was that Alex had to call in all her favors to get these people to prepare and testify, but she also had to make it clear that if she did get confirmed as a judge, she could give them nothing in return.

And then, finally, it was Alex's turn to take the hot seat. She sat in the Executive Council office in the State House, fielding questions that ranged from *What was the last book you read?* to *Who has the burden of proof in abuse and neglect cases?* Most of the questions were substantive and academic, until she was thrown a curve.

Ms. Cormier, who has the right to judge someone else?

"Well," she said. "That depends on whether you're judging in a moral sense or a legal sense. Morally, no one has the right to judge anyone else. But legally, it's not a right—it's a responsibility."

Following up on that, what is your position on firearms?

Alex hesitated. She was not a fan of guns. She didn't let Josie watch anything on television that showed violence. She knew what happened when you put a gun in the hand of a troubled kid, or an angry husband, or a battered wife—she'd defended those clients too many times to dismiss that kind of catalytic reaction.

And yet.

She was in New Hampshire, a conservative state, in front of a group of Republicans who were terrified she would turn out to be a left-wing loose cannon. She would be presiding over communities where hunting was not only revered but necessary.

Alex took a sip of water. "Legally," she said, "I am pro-firearms."

"It's crazy," Alex said as she stood in Lacy's kitchen. "You go to these robe sites online, and the models are all linebackers with breasts. The public perception of a female judge is one that looks like Bea Arthur." She leaned into the hallway and yelled up the stairs. "Josie! I'm counting to ten and then we're leaving!"

"Are there choices?"

"Yeah, black . . . or black." Alex folded her arms. "You can get cotton and polyester or just polyester. You can get bell sleeves or gathered sleeves. They're all hideous. What I really want is something with a waist."

"Guess Vera Wang doesn't do judicial," Lacy said.

"Not quite." She stuck her head into the hallway again. "Josie! Now!"

Lacy put down the dish towel she had been using to dry a pan and followed Alex into the hall. "Peter! Josie's mother has to get home!" When there was no response from the children, Lacy headed upstairs. "They're probably hiding."

Alex followed her into Peter's bedroom, where Lacy threw open the closet doors and checked beneath the bed. From there, they checked the bathroom, Joey's room, and the master bedroom. It wasn't until they went downstairs again that they heard voices coming from the basement. "It's heavy," Josie said.

Then Peter: "Here. Like this."

Alex wound down the wooden stairway. Lacy's basement was a one-hundred-year-old root cellar with a dirt floor and

cobwebs strung like Christmas decorations. She homed in
on the whispers coming from a corner of the basement, and
there, behind a stack of boxes and a shelf full of home-
canned jelly, was Josie, holding a rifle.

"*Oh my God,*" Alex breathed, and Josie swung around,
pointing the barrel at her.

Lacy grabbed the gun and pulled it away. "Where did
you get this?" she demanded, and only then did Peter and
Josie seem to realize that something was wrong.

"Peter," Josie said. "He had a key."

"A key?" Alex cried. "To what?"

"The safe," Lacy murmured. "He must have seen Lewis
taking out a rifle when he went hunting last weekend."

"My daughter has been coming over to your house for
how long now, and you've got *guns* lying around?"

"They're not lying around," Lacy said. "They're in a
locked gun safe."

"Which your *five-year-old* can open!"

"Lewis keeps the bullets—"

"Where?" Alex demanded. "Or should I just ask Peter?"

Lacy turned to Peter. "You know better. What on earth
made you do this?"

"I just wanted to show it to her, Mom. She *asked.*"

Josie lifted a frightened face. "I did not."

Alex turned. "So now your son's *blaming* Josie—"

"Or *your* daughter's lying," Lacy countered.

They stared at each other, two friends who had separated along the fault lines of their children. Alex's face was
flushed. *What if,* she kept thinking. What if they'd been five
minutes later? What if Josie had been hurt, killed? On the
edges of this thought, another one ignited—the answers
she'd given the Executive Council weeks before. Who has
the right to judge someone else?

No one, she had said.

And yet, here she was doing it.

I am pro-firearms, she had told them.

Did that make her a hypocrite? Or was she only being a good mother?

Alex watched Lacy kneel beside her son and that was all it took to trip the switch: Josie's steadfast loyalty to Peter suddenly seemed to only be a weight dragging her down. Maybe it was best for Josie if she started making other friends. Friends who did not get her called to the principal's office and who placed rifles in her hand.

Alex anchored Josie to her side. "I think we ought to leave."

"Yes," Lacy agreed, her voice cool. "I think that would be best."

They were in the frozen-food aisle when Josie began her tantrum. "I don't like peas," she whined.

"You don't have to eat them." Alex opened up the freezer door, letting the cold air kiss her cheek as she reached for the Green Giant vegetables.

"I want Oreos."

"You're not getting Oreos. You already had animal crackers." Josie had been contentious for a week now, ever since the fiasco at Lacy's house. Alex knew she couldn't keep Josie from being with Peter at school during the day, but that didn't mean she had to cultivate the relationship by allowing Josie to invite him over to play afterward.

Alex hauled a vat of Poland Spring water into her cart, then a bottle of wine. On second thought, she reached for another. "Do you want chicken or hamburger for dinner?"

"I want tofurkey."

Alex started laughing. "Where did you hear about to-furkey?"

"Lacy made it for us for lunch. They're like hot dogs but they're better for you."

Alex stepped forward as her number was called at the meat counter. "Can I have a half pound of boneless chicken breasts?"

"How come you get what *you* want, but I never get what *I* want?" Josie accused.

"Believe me, you're not as deprived a child as you'd like to think you are."

"I want an apple," Josie announced.

Alex sighed. "Can we just please get through the grocery store without you saying *I want* again?"

Before Alex realized what her daughter was doing, Josie kicked out from the seat of the shopping cart, catching Alex hard in the middle. "I hate you!" Josie screamed. "You're the worst mom in the whole world!"

Alex was uncomfortably aware of the other shoppers looking at her—the old woman feeling melons, the grocery employee with his fists full of fresh broccoli. Why did kids always fall apart in venues where you would be duly measured for your actions? "Josie," she said, smiling through her teeth, "calm down."

"I wish you were like Peter's mother! I wish I could just go *live* with them."

Alex grasped her shoulders, hard enough to make Josie burst into tears. "You listen to me," she said in a heated undertone, and then she caught a distant whisper, and the word *judge*.

There had been an article in the local paper about her recent appointment to the district court; it ran with a photo. Alex had felt the spark of recognition when she passed people in the baking aisle and the cereal aisle: *Oh, that's her.* But right now, she also felt the checks and balances of their stares as they watched her with Josie, waiting for her to act—well—judiciously.

She relaxed her grasp. "I know you're tired," Alex said, loud enough for the rest of the entire store to hear. "I know you want to go home. But you have to behave when we're out in public."

Josie blinked through her tears, listening to the Voice of Reason and wondering what this alien creature had done with her real mother, who would have yelled right back at her and told her to cut it out.

A judge, Alex suddenly realized, doesn't get to be a judge only on the bench. She's still a judge when she goes out to a restaurant or dances at a party or wants to throttle her child in the middle of the produce aisle. Alex had been given a mantle to wear, without realizing that there was a catch: she would never be allowed to take it off.

If you spent your life concentrating on what everyone else thought of you, would you forget who you really were? What if the face you showed the world turned out to be a mask . . . with nothing beneath it?

Alex pushed the cart toward the checkout lines. By now, her raging child had turned into a contrite little girl again. She listened to Josie's diminishing hiccups. "There," she said, to comfort herself as much as her daughter. "Isn't that better?"

Alex's first day on the bench was spent in Keene. No one but her clerk would know officially that it was her first day—attorneys had heard she was new, but weren't sure when she quite started—and yet, she was terrified. She changed her outfit three times, even though no one would see it underneath her robe. She threw up twice before she left for the courthouse.

She knew how to get to chambers—after all, she'd tried

cases here on the other side of the bench a hundred times. The clerk was a thin man named Ishmael who remembered Alex from their previous meetings and hadn't particularly liked her—she'd cracked up after he introduced himself ("Call me Ishmael"). Today, however, he practically fell at her high-heeled feet. "Welcome, Your Honor," he said. "Here's your docket. I'll take you to your chambers, and we'll send a court officer in to get you when we're ready. Is there anything else I can do for you?"

"No," Alex said. "I'm all set."

He left her in chambers, which were freezing cold. She adjusted the thermostat and pulled her robe out of her briefcase to dress. There was an adjoining bathroom; Alex stepped inside to scrutinize herself. She looked fair. Commanding.

And maybe a little like a choirgirl.

She sat down at the desk and immediately thought of her father. *Look at me, Daddy*, she thought, although by now he was in a place where he couldn't hear her. She could remember dozens of cases he'd tried; he'd come home and tell her about them over dinner. What she couldn't remember were the moments when he wasn't a judge and was just her father.

Alex scanned the files she needed for that morning's run of arraignments. Then she looked at her watch. She still had forty-five minutes before court went into session; it was her own damn fault for being so nervous that she'd gotten here too early. She stood up, stretched. She could do cartwheels in this room, it was that big.

But she wouldn't, because judges didn't do that.

Tentatively, she opened the door to the hall, and immediately Ishmael materialized. "Your Honor? What can I do for you?"

"Coffee," Alex said. "That would be nice."

Ishmael jumped on this request so fast that Alex realized if she asked him to go out and buy a gift for Josie's birthday, he would have it wrapped and on her desk by noon. She followed him into the lounge, one shared by attorneys and other judges, and walked toward the coffeemaker. Immediately, a young attorney fell back. "You go right ahead, Your Honor," she said, giving up her place in line.

Alex reached for a paper cup. She'd have to remember to bring a mug to leave in chambers. Then again, since her position was a rotating one that would take her through Laconia, Concord, Keene, Nashua, Rochester, Milford, Jaffrey, Peterborough, Grafton, and Coos, depending on what day of the week it was, she'd have to find a lot of coffee mugs. She pushed down on the thermal coffee dispenser, only to have it whistle and hiss—empty. Without even thinking about it, she reached for a filter to make a fresh pot.

"Your Honor, you don't have to do that," the attorney said, clearly embarrassed on Alex's behalf. She took the filter out of her hand and started to make the coffee.

Alex stared at the lawyer. She wondered if anyone would ever call her Alex again, or if she should just have her name officially changed to Your Honor. She wondered if anyone would have the guts to tell her if she had toilet paper hanging off her shoe as she walked down the hall, or if she had spinach in her teeth. It was a strange feeling to be scrutinized so carefully and to know all the same that no one would ever dare to tell her to her face that something was wrong.

The lawyer brought her the maiden cup of fresh coffee. "I wasn't sure how you liked it, Your Honor," she said, offering sugar and creamer cups.

"This is fine," Alex said, but as she reached for the cup,

her bell sleeve caught the edge of the Styrofoam, and the coffee spilled.

Smooth, Alex, she thought.

"Oh, gosh," the lawyer said. "I'm sorry!"

Why are you *sorry,* Alex wondered, *when it was* my *fault?* The girl was already setting out napkins to clean up the mess, so Alex stripped off her gown to clean it. For one giddy moment she thought about not stopping there— disrobing completely, down to her bra and panties, and parading through the courthouse like the Emperor in the fairy tale. *Isn't my gown beautiful?* she'd say, and she would listen to everyone answer: *Oh, yes, Your Honor.*

She rinsed the sleeve off in the sink and wrung it dry. Then, still carrying her robe, she started back to chambers. But the thought of sitting there for another half hour, alone, was too depressing, so instead Alex began to wander the halls of the Keene courthouse. She took turns she'd never taken before and wound up at a basement door that led to a loading zone.

Outside, she found a woman dressed in the green jumpsuit of a groundskeeper, smoking a cigarette. The air was full of winter, and frost glittered on the asphalt like broken glass. Alex wrapped her arms around herself—it was quite possibly even colder out here than in chambers—and nodded at the stranger. "Hi," she said.

"Hey." The woman exhaled a stream of smoke. "I haven't seen you around here before. What's your name?"

"Alex."

"I'm Liz. I'm the whole property maintenance department." She grinned. "So where do you work in the courthouse?"

Alex fumbled in her pocket for a box of Tic Tacs—not that she wanted or needed a mint, but because she wanted to buy some time before this conversation came to a screeching halt. "Um," she said, "I'm the judge."

Immediately, Liz's face fell, and she stepped back, uncomfortable.

"You know, I hate telling you that, because it was so nice the way you just struck up a conversation with me. No one else around here will do that and it's . . . well, it's a little lonely." Alex hesitated. "Could you maybe forget that I'm the judge?"

Liz ground out the cigarette beneath her boot. "Depends."

Alex nodded. She turned the small plastic box of mints over in her palm; they rattled like music. "You want a Tic Tac?"

After a moment, Liz held out her hand. "Sure, Alex," she said, and she smiled.

Peter had taken to wandering his own home like a ghost. He was grounded, which had something to do with the fact that Josie didn't come over anymore, even though they used to see each other after school three or four times a week. Joey didn't want to play with him—he was always off at soccer practice or playing a computer game where you had to drive really fast around a racetrack that was bent like a paper clip—which meant that Peter, officially, had nothing to do.

One evening after dinner, he heard rustling in the basement. He hadn't been down there since his mother had found him with Josie and the gun, but now he was drawn like a moth to the light over his father's workbench. His father sat on a stool in front of it, holding the very gun that had gotten Peter into so much trouble.

"Aren't you supposed to be getting ready for bed?" his father asked.

"I'm not tired." He watched his father's hands run down the swan neck of the rifle.

"Pretty, isn't it? It's a Remington 721. A thirty-ought-six." Peter's father turned to him. "Want to help me clean it?"

Peter instinctively glanced toward the stairs, where his mother was washing dishes from dinner.

"The way I figure it, Peter, if you're so interested in guns, you need to learn how to respect them. Better safe than sorry, right? Even your mom can't argue with that." He cradled the gun in his lap. "A gun is a very, very dangerous thing, but what makes it so dangerous is that most people don't really understand how it works. And once you do, it's just a tool, like a hammer or a screwdriver, and it doesn't do anything unless you know how to pick it up and use it correctly. You understand?"

Peter didn't, but he wasn't about to tell his father. He was about to learn how to use a real rifle! None of those idiot kids in his class, the ones who were such jerks, could say that.

"First thing we have to do is open the bolt, like this, to make sure there aren't any bullets in it. Look in the magazine, right down there. See any?" Peter shook his head. "Now check again. You can never check too many times. Now, there's a little button under the receiver—just in front of the trigger guard—push that and you can remove the bolt completely."

Peter watched his father take off the big silver ratchet that attached the butt of the rifle to the barrel, just like that. He reached onto his workbench for a bottle of solvent—Hoppes #9, Peter read—and spilled a little bit on a rag. "There's nothing like hunting, Peter," his father said. "To be out in the woods when the rest of the world is still sleeping . . . to see that deer raise its head and stare right at you . . ." He held the rag away from him—the smell made Peter's head swim—and started to rub the bolt with it. "Here," Peter's father said. "Why don't you do this?"

Peter's jaw dropped—he was being told to hold the rifle, after what had happened with Josie? Maybe it was because his father was here to supervise, or maybe this was a trick and he was going to get punished for *wanting* to hold it again. Tentative, he reached for it—surprised, as he had been before, at how incredibly heavy it was. On Joey's computer game, Big Buck Hunter, the characters swung their rifles around as if they were feather-light.

It wasn't a trick. His father wanted him to help, for real. Peter watched him reach for another tin—gun oil—and dribble some onto a clean rag. "We wipe down the bolt and put a drop on the firing pin. . . . You want to know how a gun works, Peter? Come over here." He pointed out the firing pin, a teensy circle inside the circle of the bolt. "Inside the bolt, where you can't see it, there's a big spring. When you pull the trigger, it releases the spring, which hits this firing pin and pushes it out just the tiniest bit—" He held his thumb and forefinger apart just a fraction of an inch, for illustration. "That firing pin hits the center of a brass bullet . . . and dents a little silver button called the primer. The dent sets off the charge, which is gunpowder inside the brass casing. You've seen a bullet—how it gets thinner and thinner at the end? That skinny part holds the actual bullet, and when the gunpowder goes off, it creates pressure behind the bullet and pushes it from behind."

Peter's father took the bolt out of his hands, wiped it with oil, and set it aside. "Now look into the barrel." He pointed the gun as if he were going to shoot at a lightbulb on the ceiling. "What do you see?"

Peter peeked into the open barrel from behind. "It's like the noodles Mom makes for lunch."

"Yeah, I guess it is. Rotini? Is that what they're called?

The twists in the barrel are like a screw. As the bullet gets pushed out, these grooves make the bullet turn. Kind of like when you throw a football and put some spin on it."

Peter had tried to do that in the backyard with his father and Joey, but his hand was too small or the football was too big and when he tried to make a pass, mostly it just crashed at his own feet.

"If the bullet comes out spinning, it can fly straight without wobbling." His father began to fiddle with a long rod that had a loop of wire on the end. Sticking a patch into the loop, he dipped it in solvent. "The gunpowder leaves gunk inside the barrel, though," he said. "And that's what we have to clean off."

Peter watched his father jam the rod into the barrel, up and down, like he was churning butter. He put on a clean patch and ran it through the barrel again, and then another, until they didn't come out streaked black anymore. "When I was your age, my father showed me how to do this, too." He threw the patch out in the trash. "One day, you and I will go hunting."

Peter couldn't contain himself at the very thought of this. He—who couldn't throw a football or dribble a soccer ball or even swim very well—was going to go *hunting* with his father? He loved the thought of leaving Joey at home. He wondered how long he'd have to wait for this outing—how it would feel to be doing something with his father that was just *theirs*.

"Ah," his father said. "Now, look down the barrel again."

Peter grabbed the gun backward, looking down through the muzzle, the barrel of the gun pressed up against his face near his eye. "Jesus, Peter!" his father said, taking it out of his hands. "Not like that! You've got it backward!" He turned the gun so that the barrel was facing away from Peter. "Even though the bolt's way over there—and it's safe—you don't *ever* look down the muzzle of a rifle. You don't point a gun at something you don't want to kill."

Peter squinted, looking into the barrel the *right* way. It was blinding, silver, shiny. Perfect.

His father rubbed down the outside of the barrel with oil. "Now, pull the trigger."

Peter stared at him. Even *he* knew you didn't do that.

"It's safe," his father repeated. "It's what we need to do to reassemble the gun."

Peter hesitantly curled his finger around the half-moon of metal and pulled. It released a catch so that the bolt his father was holding slid into place.

He watched his father take the rifle back to the gun cabinet. "People who get upset about guns don't know them," his father said. "If you know them, you can handle them safely."

Peter watched his father lock up the gun case. He understood what his father was trying to say: The mystery of the rifle—the very thing that had sparked him to steal the key to the cabinet from his father's underwear drawer and show Josie—was no longer quite as compelling. Now that he'd seen it taken apart and put back together, he saw the firearm for what it was: a collection of fitted metal, the sum of its parts.

A gun was nothing, really, without a person behind it.

Whether or not you believe in fate comes down to one thing: who you blame when something goes wrong. Do you think it's your fault—that if you'd tried better, or worked harder, it wouldn't have happened? Or do you just chalk it up to circumstance?

I know people who'll hear about the people who died, and will say it was God's will. I know people who'll say it was bad luck. And then there's my personal favorite: They were just in the wrong place at the wrong time.

Then again, you could say the same thing about me, couldn't you?

The Day After

For Peter's sixth Christmas, he'd been given a fish. It was one of those Japanese fighting fish, a beta with a shredded tissue-thin tail that trailed like the gown of a movie star. Peter named it Wolverine and spent hours staring at its moonbeam scales, its sequin eye. But after a few days, he started to imagine what it would be like to have only a bowl to explore. He wondered if the fish hovered over the tendril of plastic plant each time it passed because there was something new and amazing he'd discovered about its shape and size, or because it was a way to count another lap.

Peter started waking up in the middle of the night to see if his fish ever slept, but no matter what time it was, Wolverine was swimming. He thought about what the fish saw: a magnified eyeball, rising like a sun through the thick glass bowl. He'd listen to Pastor Ron at church, talking about God seeing everything, and he wondered if that was what he was to Wolverine.

As he sat in a cell at the Grafton County jail, Peter tried to remember what had happened to his fish. It died, he supposed. He'd probably *watched* it to death.

He stared up at the camera in the corner of the cell,

which blinked at him impassively. They—whoever *they* were—wanted to make sure he didn't kill himself before he was publicly crucified. To this end, his cell didn't have a cot or a pillow or even a mat—just a hard bench, and that stupid camera.

Then again, maybe this was a good thing. As far as he could tell, he was alone in this little pod of single cells. He'd been terrified when the sheriff's car pulled up in front of the jail. He'd watched all the TV shows; he knew what happened in places like this. The whole time he was being processed, Peter had kept his mouth shut—not because he was so tough, but because he was afraid that if he opened it he would start to cry, and not remember how to stop.

There was the swordfight sound of metal being drawn across metal, and then footsteps. Peter stayed where he was, his hands locked between his knees, his shoulders hunched. He didn't want to look too eager; he didn't want to look pathetic. Invisibility, actually, was something he was pretty good at. He'd perfected it over the past twelve years.

A correctional officer stopped in front of his cell. "You've got a visitor," he said, and he opened the door.

Peter got up slowly. He looked up at the camera, and then followed the officer down a pitted gray hallway.

How hard would it be to get out of this jail? What if, like in all the video games, he could do some fancy kung fu move and deck this guard, and another, and another, until he was able to race out the door and suck in the air whose taste he'd already started to forget?

What if he had to *stay* here forever?

That was when he remembered what had happened to his fish. In a sweeping moment of animal rights and humanity, Peter had taken Wolverine and flushed him down the toilet. He figured that the plumbing emptied out into some big ocean, like the one his family had gone to last summer on a beach vacation, and that maybe Wolverine could find his way back to Japan and his other beta relatives. It was after Peter confided in his brother that Joey told him about sewers, and that instead of giving his pet freedom, Peter had killed it.

The officer stopped in front of a room whose door read PRIVATE CONFERENCE. He couldn't imagine who would visit him, except for his parents, and he didn't want to see them yet. They would ask him questions he couldn't answer—about how you could tuck a son into bed, and not recognize him the next morning. Maybe it would be easier to just go back to the camera in his cell, which stared but didn't pass judgment.

"Here you go," the officer said, and he opened the door.

Peter took a shuddering breath. He wondered what his fish had thought, expecting the cool blue of the sea, only to wind up swimming in shit.

Jordan walked into the Grafton County Jail and stopped at the check-in point. He had to sign in before he went to visit Peter Houghton and get a visitor's badge from the correctional officer on the other side of the Plexiglas divider. Jordan reached for the clipboard and scrawled his name, then pushed it through the tiny slot at the bottom of the plastic wall—but there was no one there to receive it. The two COs inside were huddled around a small black-and-white TV that was tuned, like every other television on the planet, to a news report about the shooting.

"Excuse me," Jordan said, but neither man turned.

"When the shooting began," the reporter was saying, "Ed McCabe peered out the door of his ninth-grade math classroom, putting himself between the gunman and his students."

The screen cut to a sobbing woman, identified in white block letters below her face as JOAN MCCABE, SISTER OF VIC-

TIM. "He cared about his kids," she wept. "He cared about them the whole seven years he'd taught at Sterling, and he cared about them during the last minute of his life."

Jordan shifted his weight. "Hello?"

"Just a second, buddy," one correctional officer said, waving an absent hand in his direction.

The reporter appeared again on the grainy screen, his hair blowing upward like a boat's sail in the light wind, the monotone brick of the school a wall behind him. "Fellow teachers remember Ed McCabe as a committed teacher who was always willing to go the extra mile to help a student, and as an avid outdoorsman who talked often in the faculty room about his dreams to hike through Alaska. A dream," the reporter said gravely, "that will never come to pass."

Jordan took the clipboard and shoved it through the slot in the Plexiglas, so that it clattered on the floor. Both correctional officers turned at once.

"I'm here to see my client," he said.

Lewis Houghton had never missed a lecture in the nineteen years he'd been a professor at Sterling College, until today. When Lacy had called he'd left in such a hurry that he hadn't even thought to put a sign on the lecture hall's door. He imagined students waiting for him to appear, waiting to take notes on the very words that came out of his mouth, as if the things he had to say were still beyond reproach.

What word, what platitude, what comment of his had led Peter to this?

What word, what platitude, what comment might have stopped him?

He and Lacy were sitting in their backyard, waiting for the police to leave the house. Well, they had left—or at least one of them—to broaden the search warrant, most likely. Lewis and Lacy had not been allowed into their own home for the duration of the search. For a while, they'd stood in the driveway, occasionally watching officers carry out bags and boxes full of things Lewis would have expected—computers, books from Peter's room—and things he hadn't—a tennis racket, a jumbo box of waterproof matches.

"What do we do?" Lacy murmured.

He shook his head, numb. For one of his journal articles on the value of happiness, he'd interviewed elderly folks who were suicidal. *What's left for us?* they'd said, and at the time, Lewis had not been able to understand that utter lack of hope. At the time, he couldn't imagine the world going so sour that you couldn't see the way to set it to rights.

"There's nothing we *can* do," Lewis replied, and he meant it. He watched an officer walk out holding a stack of Peter's old comic books.

When he'd first come home to find Lacy pacing the driveway, she'd flung herself into his arms. "Why," she had sobbed. "Why?"

There were a thousand questions in that one, but Lewis couldn't answer any of them. He'd held on to his wife as if she were driftwood in the middle of this flood, and then he had noticed the eyes of a neighbor across the street, peeking from a drawn curtain.

That's when they had moved to the backyard. They sat on the porch swing, surrounded by a thicket of bare branches and melting snow. Lewis sat perfectly still, his fingers and lips numb from cold, from shock.

"Do you think," Lacy whispered, "it's our fault?"

He stared at her, amazed at her bravery: she'd put into words what he hadn't allowed himself to even think. But what else was left to say between them? The shootings had happened; their son was involved. You couldn't argue the facts; you could only change the lens through which you looked at them.

Lewis bent his head. "I don't know." Where did you even begin to look at those statistics? Had it happened because Lacy had picked Peter up too much as a baby? Or because Lewis had pretended to laugh when Peter took a tumble, hoping that the toddler wouldn't cry if he didn't think there was anything to cry about? Should they have monitored more closely what he read, watched, listened to . . . or would smothering him have led to the same outcome? Or maybe it was the combination of Lacy and Lewis together. If a couple's children counted as a track record, then they had failed miserably.

Twice.

Lacy stared down at the intricate brickwork between her shoes. Lewis remembered laying this patio; he'd leveled the sand and set the brick himself. Peter had wanted to help, but Lewis hadn't let him. The bricks were too heavy. *You could get hurt*, he'd said.

If Lewis had been less protective—if Peter had felt true pain, might he have been less likely to inflict it?

"What was the name of Hitler's mother?" Lacy asked.

Lewis blinked at her. "What?"

"Was she awful?"

He put his arm around Lacy. "Don't do this to yourself," he murmured.

She buried her face in his shoulder. "Everyone else will."

For just a moment, Lewis let himself believe that everyone was mistaken—that Peter couldn't have been the shooter today. In a way, this was true—although there had been hundreds of witnesses, the boy they'd seen was not the same one Lewis had talked to last night before he went to bed. They'd had a conversation about Peter's car.

You know you have to get it inspected by the end of the month, Lewis had said.

Yeah, Peter had replied. *I already made an appointment.*

Had he been lying about that, too?

"The lawyer—"

"He said he'll call us," Lewis answered.

"Did you tell him Peter's allergic to shellfish? If they feed him any—"

"I told him," Lewis said, although he hadn't. He pictured Peter, sitting alone in a cell at a jail he'd driven by every summer, en route to the Haverhill Fairgrounds. He thought of Peter, calling home on the second night of sleepaway camp, begging to be picked up. He thought of his son, who was *still* his son, even if he had done something so horrible that Lewis could not close his eyes without imagining the worst; and then his ribs felt too tight and he couldn't draw in enough air.

"Lewis?" Lacy said, pulling away as he gasped. "Are you all right?"

He nodded, smiled, but he was choking on the truth.

"Mr. Houghton?"

They both glanced up to find a police officer standing in front of them.

"Sir, could you come with me for a second?"

Lacy stood up beside him, but he held her off with one hand. He didn't know where this cop was taking him, what he was about to be shown. He didn't want Lacy to see it if she didn't have to.

He followed the policeman into his own house, arrested for a moment by the white-gloved officers combing through his kitchen, his closet. As soon as they reached the basement door, he started to sweat. He knew where they were headed; it was something he had studiously avoided thinking about since he'd first gotten Lacy's call.

Another officer was standing in the basement, blocking Lewis's view. It was ten degrees colder down here, and yet Lewis was sweating. He mopped his forehead with his sleeve. "These rifles," the officer said. "They belong to you?"

Lewis swallowed. "Yes. I hunt."

"Can you tell us, Mr. Houghton, if all your firearms are here?" The officer stepped aside to reveal the glass-fronted gun cabinet.

Lewis felt his knees buckle. Three of his five hunting rifles were nestled inside the gun cabinet, like wallflowers at a dance. Two were missing.

Until this moment, he had not allowed himself to believe this horrible thing about Peter. Until this moment, it had been a devastating accident.

Now, Lewis started blaming himself.

He faced the officer, looking the man in the eye without giving any of his feelings away. An expression, Lewis realized, he'd learned from his own son. "No," he said. "They're not."

The first unwritten rule of defense law was to act like you knew everything, when in fact you knew absolutely nothing at all. You were facing an unknown client who may or may not have had a chance in hell of acquittal; the trick, however, was to remain simultaneously impassive and impressive. You had to immediately set the parameters of the relationship: *I am boss; you tell me only what I need to hear.*

Jordan had been in this situation a hundred times before—waiting, in a private conference room at this very jail, for his next meal ticket to arrive—and he truly believed he had seen it all, which is why he was stunned to find that Peter Houghton had the ability to surprise him. Given the magnitude of the shooting and the damage wrought, the terror on the faces Jordan had seen on the television screen—well, this skinny, freckled, four-eyed kid hardly seemed capable of such an act.

This was his first thought. His second was: *That'll work to my advantage.*

"Peter," he said. "I'm Jordan McAfee, and I'm a lawyer. I've been retained by your parents to represent you."

He waited for a response. "Have a seat," he said, but the boy remained standing. "Or don't," Jordan added. He put on his business mask and looked up at Peter. "You'll be arraigned tomorrow. You're not going to get bail. We'll have a chance to go over the charges in the morning, before you go into court." He gave Peter a moment to digest this information. "From here on in, you're not going through this alone. You've got me."

Was it Jordan's imagination, or had something flashed in Peter's eyes when he'd said those words? As quickly as it might have happened, it was gone; Peter stared down at the ground, expressionless.

"Well," Jordan said, getting to his feet. "Any questions?"

As he expected, there wasn't any response. Hell, for all of Peter's involvement in this little discussion, Jordan might as well have been chatting up one of the less fortunate victims of the shooting.

Maybe you are, he thought, and the voice in his head sounded too damn much like his wife's.

"All right, then. I'll see you tomorrow." He knocked on the door, summoning the correctional officer who would take Peter back to his cell, when suddenly the boy spoke.

"How many did I get?"

Jordan hesitated, his hand on the knob. He did not turn to face his client. "I'll see you tomorrow," he repeated.

Dr. Ervin Peabody lived across the river in Norwich, Vermont, and worked part-time at Sterling College's psychology program. Six years ago he had been one of seven coauthors of a published paper about school violence—an academic exercise he barely remembered. And yet, he'd been called by the NBC affiliate out of Burlington—a morning news show he sometimes watched over a bowl of cereal for the sheer glee of seeing how often the inept newscasters screwed up. *We're looking for someone who can talk about the shooting from a psychological standpoint,* the producer had said, and Ervin had replied, *I'm your man.*

"Warning signals," he said in response to the anchor's question. "Well, these young men pull away from others. They tend to be loners. They talk about hurting themselves, or others. They can't function in school, or are subjected to discipline there. They lack a connection with someone—anyone—who might make them feel important."

Ervin knew the network hadn't come to him for his expertise—only for solace. The rest of Sterling—the rest of the *world*—wanted to know that kids like Peter Houghton were recognizable, as if the potential to turn into a murderer overnight were a visible birthmark. "So there's a general profile of a school shooter," the anchor prodded.

Ervin Peabody looked into the camera. He knew the truth—that if you said these kids wore black or listened to odd music or were angry, you were discussing most of the male teenage population at some point during their adolescent years. He knew that if a deeply disturbed individual was intent on doing damage, he'd probably succeed. But he also knew that every eye in the Connecticut Valley was on him—maybe even in the whole Northeast—and that he was up for tenure at Sterling. A little prestige—a label of *expert*—couldn't hurt. "You could make that argument," he said.

*   *   *

Lewis was the one who settled the Houghton household for the night. He'd start in the kitchen and load the dishwasher. He'd lock the front door and turn off the lights. Then he'd head upstairs, where Lacy was usually already in bed, reading—if not out assisting at a birth—and he'd stop in his son's room. Tell him to shut off the computer and go to bed.

Tonight he found himself standing in front of Peter's room, looking at the mess wrought by the police during their search. He thought about righting the remaining books on the shelves, putting away the contents of the desk drawers that had been dumped onto the carpet. On second thought, he gently closed the door.

Lacy was not in the bedroom, or brushing her teeth. He hesitated, an ear cocked. There was chatter—it sounded like a furtive conversation—coming from the room directly below him.

He retraced his steps, drawing closer to the voices. Who would Lacy be talking to at nearly midnight?

The screen of the television glowed green and unearthly in the dark study. Lewis had forgotten there even *was* a television in that room, it was so infrequently used. He saw the CNN logo and familiar ticker tape of breaking news along the bottom. A thought occurred to him: that ticker tape hadn't existed until 9/11—until people were so scared that they needed to know, without any delay, the facts of the world they inhabited.

Lacy was kneeling on the carpet, her face turned up to the anchor's. "There is little word yet about how the man who was the shooter secured his weapons, or exactly what those weapons are . . ."

"Lacy," he said, swallowing. "Lacy, come to bed."

Lacy did not move, did not give any indication she'd heard him. Lewis passed her, trailing his hand over her shoulder as he went to shut off the television. "Preliminary reports are focusing on two pistols," the anchor confided, just before his image disappeared.

Lacy turned to him. Her eyes reminded him of the sky you see from airplanes: a boundless gray that could be anywhere, and nowhere, all at once. "They keep calling him a man," she said, "but he's only a boy."

"Lacy," he repeated, and she stood and moved into his arms, as if this were her invitation to the dance.

If you listen carefully in a hospital, you can hear the truth. Nurses whisper to one another over your still body when you are pretending to sleep; policemen trade secrets in the hallway; doctors enter your room with another patient's condition on their lips.

Josie had been making a mental list of the wounded. It seemed she could play six degrees of separation with any of the injured—when she had seen them last; when they had crossed her path; where they had been in proximity to her when they had been shot. There was Drew Girard, who'd grabbed Matt and Josie to tell them that Peter Houghton was shooting up the school. Emma, who'd been sitting three chairs away from Josie in the cafeteria. And Trey MacKenzie, a football player known for his house parties. John Eberhard, who had been eating Josie's French fries that morning. Min Horuka, an exchange student from Tokyo who'd gotten drunk last year out on the ropes course behind the track and then peed into the open window of the principal's car. Natalie Zlenko, who'd been in front of Josie in the cafeteria line. Coach Spears and Miss Ritolli, two former teachers of Josie's. Brady Pryce and Haley Weaver, the golden senior couple.

There were others that Josie knew only by name— Michael Beach, Steve Babourias, Natalie Phlug, Austin

Prokiov, Alyssa Carr, Jared Weiner, Richard Hicks, Jada Knight, Zoe Patterson—strangers with whom, now, she'd be linked forever.

It was harder to find out the names of the dead. They were whispered about even more quietly, as if their condition were contagious to the rest of the unfortunate souls just taking up space in the hospital beds. Josie had heard rumors: that Mr. McCabe had been killed, and Topher McPhee—the school pot dealer. To hoard crumbs of information, Josie tried to watch television, which was running twenty-four-hour Sterling High Shooting coverage, but inevitably her mother would come into the room and turn it off. All she had gleaned from her forbidden media forays was that there had been ten fatalities.

Matt was one.

Every time Josie thought about it, something happened to her body. She stopped breathing. All the words she knew congealed at the bottom of her throat, a boulder blocking the exit from a cave.

Thanks to the sedatives, so much of this seemed unreal—as if she were walking on the spongy floor of a dream—but the moment she thought of Matt, it became authentic and raw.

She would never kiss Matt again.

She would never hear him laugh.

She would never feel the print of his hand on her waist, or read a note he'd slipped through the furrows of her locker, or feel her heart beat into his hand when he unbuttoned her shirt.

She was only remembering the half of it, that she knew—as if the shooting had not only split her life into before and after, but also robbed her of certain skills: the ability to last an hour without puddling into tears; the ability to see the color red without feeling queasy; the ability to form a skeleton of the truth from the bare bones of memory. To remember the rest of it, given what had happened, would be nearly obscene.

So instead, Josie found herself veering drunkenly from the soft-focus moments with Matt to the macabre. She kept thinking of a line from *Romeo and Juliet* that had freaked her out when they'd studied the play in ninth grade: *With worms that are thy chambermaids.* Romeo had said it to Juliet's looks-like-dead body in the Capulet crypt. Ashes to ashes, dust to dust. But there were a whole bunch of steps in between that no one ever talked about, and when the nurses were gone in the middle of the night, Josie found herself wondering how long it took for flesh to peel from a skull; what happened to the jelly of eyes; whether Matt had already stopped looking like Matt. And then she'd wake up and find herself screaming, with a dozen doctors and nurses holding her down.

If you gave someone your heart and they died, did they take it with them? Did you spend the rest of forever with a hole inside you that couldn't be filled?

The door to her room opened and her mother stepped inside. "So," she said, with a fake smile so wide it divided her entire head like an equator. "You ready?"

It was only 7:00 a.m., but Josie had already been discharged. She nodded at her mother. Josie sort of hated her right now. She was acting all concerned and worried, but it was too much too late, as if it had taken this shooting for her to wake up to the fact that she had absolutely no relationship with Josie. She kept telling Josie she was here if Josie needed to talk, which was ridiculous. Even if Josie wanted to—which she *didn't*—her mother was the last person on earth she'd want to confide in. She wouldn't understand—no one would, except for the other kids lying in different rooms in this hospital. This hadn't been just some murder on the street somewhere, which would have been bad enough. This was the worst that could happen, in a place where Josie would have to return, whether she wanted to or not.

Josie was wearing different clothes than the ones she'd been brought here with, which had mysteriously disappeared. No one was admitting to anything, but Josie assumed they were covered with Matt's blood. In this, they had been right to throw them away: no matter how much bleach was used and how many washings were done, Josie knew she'd be able to see the stains.

Her head still ached from where she'd struck the floor when she fainted. She'd cut her forehead and narrowly avoided needing stitches, although the doctors had wanted to watch her overnight. (*For what?* Josie had wondered. *A stroke? A blood clot? Suicide?*) When Josie stood up, her mother was at her side immediately, an arm anchored around her for support. It reminded Josie of the way that she and Matt sometimes walked down the street in the summer, their hands filed into the back pockets of each other's jeans.

"Oh, Josie," her mother said, and that was how she realized she'd started to cry again. It happened so often, now, that Josie had lost the capacity to tell when it stopped and started. Her mother offered her a tissue. "You know what? You'll start feeling better when you get home. I promise."

Well, duh. Josie couldn't start feeling any *worse*.

But she managed a grimace, which might have been a smile if you weren't looking too closely, because she knew that's what her mother needed right now. She walked the fifteen steps to the door of her hospital room.

"You take care, sweetheart," one of the nurses said as Josie passed their pod of desks.

Another one—the one Josie had liked the best, who fed

her ice chips—smiled. "Don't come back and see us, you hear?"

Josie moved slowly toward the elevator, which seemed to get farther and farther away each time she glanced up. As she passed by one of the patient rooms she noticed a familiar name on the clipboard outside: HALEY WEAVER.

Haley was a senior, homecoming queen for the past two years. She and her boyfriend, Brady, were the Brangelina of Sterling High—roles Josie actually had believed she and Matt stood a good chance to inherit after Haley and Brady graduated. Even the wishful thinkers who pined after Brady for his smoky smile and sculpted body had to admit that there was a poetic justice to his dating Haley, the most beautiful girl in the school. With her waterfall of white-blond hair and her clear blue eyes, she had always reminded Josie of a magical fairy—the serene, heavenly creature that floats down to grant someone's wishes.

There were all sorts of stories that circulated about them: how Brady had given up football scholarships at colleges that didn't have art programs for Haley; how Haley had gotten a tattoo of Brady's initials in a place no one could see; how on their first date, he'd had rose petals spread on the passenger seat of his Honda. Josie, circulating in the same crowd as Haley, knew that most of this was bullshit. Haley herself had admitted, first, that it was a temporary tattoo, and second, that it wasn't rose petals, but a bouquet of lilacs he'd stolen from a neighbor's garden.

"Josie?" Haley whispered now, from inside the room. "Is that you?"

Josie felt her mother's hand on her arm, restraining her. But then Haley's parents, who were blocking a clear view of the bed, moved away.

The right half of Haley's face was swathed in bandages; her hair was shaved to the scalp above it. Her nose had been broken, and her one visible eye was completely blood-shot. Josie's mother drew in her breath silently.

She stepped inside and forced herself to smile.

"Josie," Haley said. "He killed them. Courtney and Maddie. And then he pointed the gun at me, but Brady stepped in front of it." A tear streaked down the cheek that wasn't bandaged. "You know how people are always saying they'd do that for you?"

Josie started shaking. She wanted to ask Haley a hundred questions, but her teeth were chattering so hard that she couldn't manage a single word. Haley grabbed on to her hand, and Josie startled. She wanted to pull away. She wanted to pretend she'd never seen Haley Weaver like this.

"If I ask you something," Haley said, "you'll be honest, won't you?"

Josie nodded.

"My face," she whispered. "It's ruined, isn't it?"

Josie looked Haley in the eye. "No," she said. "It's fine."

They both knew she wasn't telling the truth.

Josie said good-bye to Haley and her parents, grabbed on to her mother, and hurried even faster toward the elevators, even though every step felt like a thunderstorm behind her eyes. She suddenly remembered studying the brain in science class—how a steel rod had pierced a man's skull, and he opened up his mouth to speak Portuguese, a language he'd never studied. Maybe it would be like this, now, for Josie. Maybe her native tongue, from here on in, would be a string of lies.

By the time Patrick returned to Sterling High the next morning, the crime-scene detectives had turned the halls of the school into an enormous spiderweb. Based on where the victims had been found, string was taped up—a burst of lines radiating from one spot where Peter Houghton had paused long enough to fire shots before moving on. The lines of string crossed each other at points: a grid of panic, a graph of chaos.

He stood for a moment in the center of the commotion, watching the techs weave the string across the hallways and between banks of lockers and into doorways. He imagined what it would have been like to start running at the sound of the gunshots, to feel people pushing behind you like a tide, to know that you couldn't move faster than a speeding bullet. To realize too late you were trapped, a spider's prey.

Patrick picked his way through the web, careful not to disturb the work of the techs. He would use what they did to corroborate the stories of the witnesses. All 1,026 of them.

The breakfast broadcast of the three local network news stations was devoted to that morning's arraignment of Peter Houghton. Alex stood in front of the television in her bedroom, nursing her cup of coffee and staring at the backdrop behind the eager reporters: her former workplace, the district courthouse.

She'd settled Josie in her bedroom to sleep the dark, dreamless sleep of the sedated. To be perfectly honest, Alex needed this time alone, too. Who would have guessed that a woman who'd become a master at putting on a public face would find it so emotionally exhausting to hold herself together in front of her daughter?

She wanted to sit down and get drunk. She wanted to weep, her head buried in her hands, at her good fortune: her daughter was two doors away from her. Later, they would have breakfast together. How many parents in this town were waking up to realize this would never be true again?

Alex shut off the television. She didn't want to compromise her objectivity as the future judge on this case by listening to what the media had to say.

She knew there would be critics—people who said that because her daughter went to Sterling High School, Alex should be removed from the case. If Josie had been shot, she would have quickly agreed. If Josie had even still been *friendly* with Peter Houghton, Alex would have recused herself. But as it stood, Alex's judgment was compromised no more than that of any other justice who lived in the area, or who knew a child who attended the school, or who was the parent of a teenager. It happened all the time to North Country justices: someone you knew would inevitably wind up in your courtroom. When Alex was rotating as a district court judge, she'd faced defendants she'd known on a personal level: her mailman caught with pot in his car; a domestic disturbance between her mechanic and his wife. As long as the dispute didn't involve Alex personally, it was perfectly legal—in fact, *mandatory*—for her to try the case. In those scenarios, you simply took yourself out of the equation. You became the judge and nothing more. The shooting, as Alex saw it, was the same set of circumstances, ratcheted up a notch. In fact, she'd argue that in a case with the massive media coverage this one had, it would take someone with a defense background—like Alex's—to truly be impartial to the shooter. And the more she thought about it, the more firmly convinced Alex became that justice couldn't be done without her involvement, the more ludicrous it seemed to suggest she was not the best judge for the job.

She took another sip of her coffee and tiptoed from her bedroom to Josie's. But the door stood wide open, and her daughter was not inside.

"Josie?" Alex called, panicking. "Josie, are you all right?"

"Down here," Josie said, and Alex felt the knot inside

her unravel again. She walked downstairs to find Josie sitting at the kitchen table.

She was dressed in a skirt and tights and a black sweater. Her hair was still damp from a shower, and she had tried to cover the bandage on her forehead with a swath of bangs. She looked up at Alex. "Do I look all right?"

"For what?" Alex asked, dumbfounded. She couldn't be expecting to go to school, could she? The doctors had told Alex that Josie might never remember the shooting, but could she erase the fact that it had ever *happened* from her mind, too?

"The arraignment," Josie said.

"Sweetheart, there is no way you're going near that courthouse today."

"I have to."

"You're not going," Alex said flatly.

Josie looked as if she were unraveling at the seams. "Why not?"

Alex opened her mouth to answer, but couldn't. This wasn't logic; it was gut instinct: she didn't want her daughter to relive this experience. "Because I said so," she finally replied.

"That's not an answer," Josie accused.

"I know what the media will do if they see you at the courthouse today," Alex said. "I know that nothing's going to happen at that arraignment that's going to be a surprise to anyone. And I know that I don't want to let you out of my sight right now."

"Then come with me."

Alex shook her head. "I can't, Josie," she said softly. "This is going to be my case." She watched Josie pale, and realized that until that moment, Josie hadn't considered this. The trial, by default, would put an even thicker wall between them. As a judge, there would be information she couldn't share with her daughter, confidences she couldn't keep. While Josie was struggling to move past this tragedy, Alex would be knee-deep in it. Why had she put so much thought into judging this case, and so little into how it would affect her own daughter? Josie didn't give a damn if her mother was a fair judge right now. She only wanted—needed—a mother, and motherhood, unlike the law, was something that had never come easily to Alex.

Out of the blue, she thought of Lacy Houghton—a mother who was in a whole different level of hell right now—who would have simply taken Josie's hand and sat with her and somehow made it seem sympathetic, instead of contrived. But Alex, who had never been the June Cleaver type, had to reach back years to find some moment of connection, something she and Josie had done once before that might work again now to hold them together. "Why don't you go upstairs and change, and we'll make pancakes. You used to like that."

"Yeah, when I was *five* . . ."

"Chocolate chip cookies, then."

Josie blinked at Alex. "Are you on *crack?*"

Alex sounded ridiculous even to herself, but she was desperate to show Josie that she could and would take care of her, and that her job came second. She stood up, opening cabinets until she found a Scrabble game. "Well, then, how about this?" Alex said, holding out the box. "I bet you can't beat me."

Josie pushed past her. "You win," she said woodenly, and then she walked away.

The student who was being interviewed by the CBS affiliate out of Nashua remembered Peter Houghton from a ninth-grade English class. "We had to write a story with a first-person narrator, and we could pick anyone," the boy said. "Peter did the voice of John Hinckley. From the things he said, you think he's looking out from hell, but then at the end you find out it's heaven. It freaked out our teacher. She had the principal look at the paper and everything." The boy hesitated, scratching his thumb along the seam of his jeans. "Peter told them it was poetic license, and an unreliable narrator—which we'd been studying, also." He glanced up at the camera. "I think he got an A."

At the traffic light, Patrick fell asleep. He dreamed that he was running through the halls of the school, hearing gunshots, but every time he turned a corner he found himself hovering in midair—the floor having vanished beneath his feet.

At a honk, he snapped alert.

He waved in apology to the car that pulled up alongside him to pass and drove to the state crime lab, where the ballistics tests had been given priority. Like Patrick, these techs had been working around the clock.

His favorite—and most trusted—technician was a woman named Selma Abernathy, a grandmother of four who knew more about cutting-edge technology than any technogeek. She looked up when Patrick came into the lab and raised a brow. "You've been napping," she accused.

Patrick shook his head. "Scout's honor."

"You look too good for someone who's exhausted."

He grinned. "Selma, you've really got to get over your crush on me."

She pushed her glasses up on her nose. "Honey, I'm smart enough to fall for someone who doesn't make my life a pain in the ass. You want your results?"

Patrick followed her over to a table, on which were four guns: two pistols and two sawed-off shotguns. They were tagged: Gun A, Gun B—the two pistols; Gun C and Gun

D—the shotguns. He recognized the pistols—they were the ones found in the locker room—one held by Peter Houghton, the other one a short distance away on the tile floor. "First I tested for latent prints," Selma said, and she showed the results to Patrick. "Gun A had a print that matches your suspect. Guns C and D were clean. Gun B had a partial print on it that was inconclusive."

Selma nodded to the rear of the laboratory, where enormous barrels of water were used for test-firing the guns. She would have test-fired each weapon into the water, Patrick knew. When a bullet was fired, it spun through the barrel of a gun, which caused striations on the metal. As a result, you could tell, by looking at a bullet, exactly which gun it had been fired from. This would help Patrick piece together Peter Houghton's rampage: where he'd stopped to shoot, which weapon he'd used.

"Gun A was the one primarily used during the shooting, Guns C and D were left in the backpack retrieved at the crime scene. Which is actually a good thing, because they most likely would have done more damage. All of the bullets retrieved from the bodies of victims were fired from Gun A, the first pistol."

Patrick wondered where Peter Houghton had gotten his armory. And at the same time, he realized that it wasn't hard in Sterling to find someone who hunted or went target shooting at the site of an old dump in the woods.

"I know, from the gunpowder residue, that Gun B was fired. However, there hasn't been a bullet recovered yet that confirms this."

"They're still processing—"

"Let me finish," Selma said. "The other interesting thing about Gun B is that it jammed after that one discharge. When we examined it we found a double-feed of a bullet."

Patrick crossed his arms. "There's no print on the weapon?" he clarified.

"There's an inconclusive print on the trigger . . . probably smudged when your suspect dropped it, but I can't say that for certain."

Patrick nodded and pointed to Gun A. "This is the one he dropped, when I drew down on him in the locker room. So, presumably, it's the last one he fired."

Selma lifted a bullet with a pair of tweezers. "You're probably right. This was retrieved from Matthew Royston's brain," she said. "And the striations are consistent with a discharge from Gun A."

The boy in the locker room, the one who'd been found with Josie Cormier.

The only victim who'd been shot twice.

"What about the bullet in the kid's stomach?" Patrick asked.

Selma shook her head. "Went through clean. It could have been fired from either Gun A or Gun B, but we won't know until you bring me a slug."

Patrick stared at the weapons. "He'd used Gun A all over the rest of the school. I can't imagine what made him switch to the other pistol."

Selma glanced up at him; he noticed for the first time the dark circles under her eyes, the toll this overnight emergency had taken. "I can't imagine what made him use either of them in the first place."

Meredith Vieira stared gravely into the camera, having perfected the demeanor for a national tragedy. "Details continue to accumulate in the case of the Sterling shootings," she said. "For more, we go to Ann Curry at the news desk. Ann?"

The news anchor nodded. "Overnight, investigators

have learned that four weapons were brought into Sterling High School, although only two were actually used by the shooter. In addition, there is evidence that Peter Houghton, the suspect in the shootings, was an ardent fan of a hard-core punk band called Death Wish, often posting on fan websites and downloading lyrics onto his personal computer. Lyrics that, in retrospect, have some people wondering what kids should and should not be listening to."

The green screen behind her shoulder filled with text:

> *Black snow falling*
> *Stone corpse walking*
> *Bastards laughing*
> *Gonna blow them all away, on my Judgment Day.*
>
> *Bastards don't see*
> *The bloody beast in me*
> *The reaper rides for free*
> *Gonna blow them all away, on my Judgment Day.*

"The Death Wish song 'Judgment Day' includes a frightening foreshadowing of an event that became all too real in Sterling, New Hampshire, yesterday morning," Curry said. "Raven Napalm, lead singer for Death Wish, held a press conference late last night."

The footage cut to a man with a black Mohawk, gold eye shadow, and five pierced hoops through his lower lip, standing in front of a group of microphones. "We live in a country where American kids are dying because we're sending them overseas to kill people for oil. But when one sad, distraught child who doesn't see the beauty in life goes and wrongly acts on his rage by shooting up a school, people start pointing a finger at heavy metal music. The problem isn't with rock lyrics, it's with the fabric of this society itself."

Ann Curry's face filled the screen again. "We'll have more on the continuing coverage of the tragedy in Sterling as it unfolds. In national news, the Senate defeated the gun control bill last Wednesday, but Senator Roman Nelson suggests that it's not the last we've seen of that fight. He joins us today from South Dakota. Senator?"

Peter didn't think he'd slept at all last night, but all the same, he didn't hear the correctional officer coming toward his cell. He startled at the sound of the metal door scraping open.

"Here," the man said, and he tossed something at Peter. "Put it on."

He knew that he was going to court today; Jordan McAfee had told him so. He assumed that this was a suit or something. Didn't people always get to wear a suit in court, even if they were coming straight from jail? It was supposed to make them sympathetic. He thought he'd seen that on TV.

But it wasn't a suit. It was Kevlar, a bulletproof vest.

In the holding cell beneath the courthouse, Jordan found his client lying on his back on the floor, an arm shielding his eyes. Peter was wearing a bulletproof vest, an unspoken nod to the fact that everyone packing the courtroom that morning wanted to kill him. "Good morning," Jordan said, and Peter sat up.

"Or not," he murmured.

Jordan didn't respond. He leaned a little closer to the bars. "Here's the plan. You've been charged with ten counts of first-degree murder and nineteen counts of attempted first-degree murder. I'm going to waive the readings of the complaints—we'll go over them individually some other time. Right now we just have to go in there and enter not-guilty pleas. I don't want you to say a word. If you have any questions, you whisper them to me. You are, for all intents and purposes, mute for the next hour. Understand?"

Peter stared at him. "Perfectly," he said, sullen. But Jordan was looking at his client's hands.

They were shaking.

From the log of items removed from the bedroom of Peter Houghton:

1. Dell laptop computer.
2. Gaming CDs: Doom 3, Grand Theft Auto: Vice City.
3. Three posters from gun manufacturers.
4. Assorted lengths of pipe.
5. Books: *The Catcher in the Rye*, Salinger; *On War*, Clausewitz; graphic novels by Frank Miller and Neil Gaiman.
6. DVD—*Bowling for Columbine*.
7. Yearbook from Sterling Middle School, various faces circled in black marker. One circled face x'd out with words LET LIVE beneath picture. Girl identified in caption as Josie Cormier.

The girl spoke so softly that the microphone, hanging on a boom over her head like a piñata, had trouble picking up the unraveled threads of her voice. "Mrs. Edgar's classroom is right next to Mr. McCabe's, and sometimes we could hear them moving their chairs around or shouting out answers," she said. "But this time we heard screaming. Mrs. Edgar, she took her desk and shoved it up against the door and told us all to go to the far end of the classroom, near

the windows, and sit on the floor. The gunshots, they
sounded like popcorn. And then . . ." She stopped and
wiped her eyes. "And then there wasn't any more screaming."

Diana Leven hadn't expected the gunman to look so
young. Peter Houghton was shackled and chained, wearing
his orange jumpsuit and bulletproof vest, but he still had
the apple cheeks of a boy who hadn't come through the far
side of puberty yet, and she would have bet money he
didn't have to shave. The glasses, too, upset her. The defense would play that to the hilt, she was certain, claiming
some myopia that would have made sharpshooting an im-
possibility.

The four cameras that the district court judge had
agreed on to represent the networks—ABC, CBS, NBC,
and CNN—hummed to life like a barbershop quartet as
soon as the defendant was led into the room. Since it had
gotten so quiet in the room that you could hear the sound
of your own doubts, Peter turned immediately toward them.
Diana realized that his eyes were not all that different from
those of the cameras: dark, blind, empty behind the lenses.

Jordan McAfee—a lawyer Diana didn't like very much
on a personal level but grudgingly admitted was damn good
at his job—leaned toward his client the moment Peter
reached the defense table. The bailiff stood. "All rise," he
bellowed, "the Honorable Charles Albert presiding."

Judge Albert hustled into the courtroom, his robes whispering. "Be seated," he said. "Peter Houghton," he began,
turning to the defendant.

Jordan McAfee stood. "Your Honor, we waive the reading of the charges. We'd like to enter not-guilty pleas for all
of them, and we request that a probable cause hearing be
scheduled in ten days."

This wasn't a surprise to Diana—why would Jordan want the whole world to hear his client being indicted on ten separate counts of first-degree murder? The judge turned to her. "Ms. Leven, the statute requires that a defendant charged with first-degree murder—multiple counts, at that—be held without bail. I assume you have no problem with this."

Diana hid a smile. Judge Albert, God bless him, had managed to slip in the charges anyway. "That's correct, Your Honor."

The judge nodded. "Well then, Mr. Houghton. You're remanded back into custody."

The whole procedure had taken less than five minutes, and the public wouldn't be happy. They wanted blood; they wanted revenge. Diana watched Peter Houghton stumble between the hold of two sheriff's deputies and turn back to his lawyer one last time with a question on his lips that he didn't utter. Then the door closed behind him, and Diana gathered her briefcase and walked out of the courtroom to the cameras.

She stood in front of a thrust of microphones. "Peter Houghton was just arraigned on ten counts of first-degree murder and nineteen counts of attempted first-degree murder, and various accompanying charges involving illegal possession of explosives and firearms in this recent tragedy. The rules of professional responsibility prevent us from commenting on the evidence at this point, but the community can rest assured that we are prosecuting this case vigorously, that we have been working around the clock with our investigators to make sure that the evidence is collected, preserved, and appropriately handled so that this unspeakable tragedy will not go unanswered." She opened her mouth to continue but realized that there was another voice speaking, just across the hallway, and that reporters were defecting from her impromptu press conference to hear Jordan McAfee instead.

He stood sober and penitent, his hands in the pockets of his trousers, as he stared right at Diana. "I grieve with the community for its losses, and will represent my client to the fullest. Peter Houghton is a seventeen-year-old boy; he's very scared. And I ask you to please have respect for his family and to remember that this is a matter to be determined in court." Jordan hesitated, ever the showman, and then made eye contact with the crowd. "I ask you to remember that what you see is not always all it seems to be."

Diana smirked. The reporters—and the people all over the world who would be listening to Jordan's careful speech—would hear his little salvo at the end and believe that he had some fabulous truth up his sleeve—something that would prove his client was not a monster. Diana, however, knew better. She could translate legalese, because she spoke it fluently. When an attorney spun mysterious rhetoric like that, it was because he had nothing else he could use to defend his client.

At noon, the governor of New Hampshire held a press conference on the steps of the Capitol building in Concord. On his lapel he was wearing a loop of maroon and white ribbon, the school colors of Sterling High, which had sprouted up at gas station cash registers and Wal-Mart counters and were being sold for $1 each, the proceeds going to support the Sterling Victims Fund. One of his minions had driven twenty-seven miles to get one, because the governor planned to throw his hat into the Democratic primary in 2008 and knew this was a perfect media moment during which he could portray compassion at its strongest. Yes, he felt for the citizens of Sterling, and especially those poor parents of the dead, but there was also a calculated part of him that knew a man who could shepherd a state through one of the most tragic school shooting incidents in America would be seen as a strong leader. "Today, all of this country grieves with New Hampshire," he said. "Today, all of us feel the pain that Sterling feels. They are all our children."

He glanced up. "I've been up to Sterling, and I've spoken to the investigators who are working hard, round the clock, to understand what happened yesterday. I've spent time with some of the families of the victims, and at the hospital with the brave survivors. Part of our past and part of our future disappeared in this tragedy," the governor said as he looked solemnly into the cameras. "What we all need, now, is to focus on the future."

It took Josie less than a morning to learn the magic words: when she wanted her mother to leave her alone, when she was sick of her mother watching her like a hawk, all she had to do was say that she needed a nap. Then, her mother would back off, completely unaware of the fact that her whole face relaxed the minute Josie let her off the hook, and that only then could Josie recognize her.

Upstairs, in her room, Josie sat in the dark with her shades drawn and her hands folded in her lap. It was broad daylight, but you'd never know it. People had figured out all sorts of ways to make things seem different than they truly were. A room could be turned into an artificial night. Botox transformed people's faces into something they weren't. TiVo let you think you could freeze time, or at least reorder it to your own liking. An arraignment at a courthouse fit like a Band-Aid over a wound that really needed a tourniquet.

Fumbling in the dark, Josie reached underneath the frame of her bed for the plastic bag she'd stashed—her supply of sleeping pills. She was no better than any of the other stupid people in this world who thought if they pretended hard enough, they could make it so. She'd thought that death could be an answer, because she was too immature to realize it was the biggest question of all.

Yesterday, she hadn't known what patterns blood could make when it sprayed on a whitewashed wall. She hadn't understood that life left a person's lungs first, and their eyes last. She had pictured suicide as a final statement, a *fuck you* to the people who hadn't understood how hard it was for her to be the Josie they wanted her to be. She'd somehow thought that if she killed herself, she'd be able to watch everyone else's reaction; that she'd get the last laugh. Until yesterday, she hadn't really understood. Dead was dead. When you died, you did not get to come back and see what you were missing. You didn't get to apologize. You didn't get a second chance.

Death wasn't something you could control. In fact, it would always have the upper hand.

She ripped the plastic bag open into her palm and stuffed five of the pills into her mouth. She walked into the bathroom and ran the tap, stuck her head close to the faucet until the pills were swimming in the fishbowl of her bulging cheeks.

Swallow, she told herself.

But instead, Josie fell in front of the toilet and spit the pills out. She emptied the rest of the pills, still clutched in her fist. She flushed before she could think twice.

Her mother came upstairs because she heard the sobbing. It had seeped through the grout of the tile and the soffits and the plaster that made up the ceiling downstairs. It would, in fact, become as much of this household as the bricks and the mortar, although neither of the women realized it yet. Josie's mother burst into the bedroom and sank down beside her daughter in the attached bathroom. "What can I do, baby?" she whispered, running her hands up and down Josie's shoulders and back, as if the answer were a visible tattoo instead of a scar on the heart.

Yvette Harvey sat on a couch holding her daughter's eighth-grade graduation photo, taken two years, six months, and four days before she died. Kaitlyn's hair had grown out, but you could still see the easy lopsided smile, the moon face that was part and parcel of Down syndrome.

What would have happened if she hadn't chosen to mainstream Kaitlyn in middle school? If she'd sent her to a school for kids who had disabilities? Were those kids any less angry, less likely to have bred a killer?

The producer from *The Oprah Winfrey Show* handed back the stack of photographs that Yvette had given her. She hadn't known, before today, that there were levels of tragedy, that even if the Oprah show called you to ask you to tell your sad story, they would want to make sure it was sad enough before they let you speak on camera. Yvette hadn't planned to show her pain on television—in fact, her husband was so dead set against it he refused to be here when the producer came to call—but she was determined. She had been listening to the news. And now, she had something to say.

"Kaitlyn had a beautiful smile," the producer said gently.

"She does," Yvette replied, then shook her head. "*Did.*"

"Did she know Peter Houghton?"

"No. They weren't in the same grade; they wouldn't have had classes together. Kaitlyn's were in the learning center." She pushed her thumb into the edge of the silver portrait frame until it hurt. "All of these people who are going around saying that Peter Houghton had no friends—that

Peter Houghton was teased . . . that's not true," she said. "My daughter had no friends. My daughter was teased every single day. My daughter was the one who felt like she was on the fringe, because she was. Peter Houghton wasn't a misfit, like everyone wants to make him out to be. Peter Houghton was just evil."

Yvette looked down at the glass covering Kaitlyn's portrait. "The grief counselor from the police department told me Kaitlyn died first," she said. "She wanted me to know that Kaitie didn't know what was going on—that she didn't suffer."

"That must have been some consolation," the producer offered.

"It was. Until we all started talking to each other and realized that the grief counselor had told the same thing to every one of us with a dead child." Yvette glanced up, tears in her eyes. "The thing is, they couldn't all have been first."

In the days after the shooting, the families of the victims were showered with donations: money, casseroles, babysitting services, sympathy. Kaitlyn Harvey's father woke up one morning after a light, last springtime snow to find that his driveway had already been shoveled by a Samaritan. Courtney Ignatio's family became the beneficiaries of their local church, whose members signed up to provide food or cleaning services on a different day of the week, a rotating schedule that would take them through June. John Eberhard's mother was presented with a handicapped-accessible van, courtesy of Sterling Ford, to help her son adapt to life as a paraplegic. Everyone wounded at Sterling High received a letter from the president of the United States, crisp White House stationery commending them on their bravery.

The media—at first a wave as unwelcome as a

tsunami—became something ordinary on the streets of Sterling. After days of watching their high-heeled black boots sink into the soft mud of a New England March, they visited the local Farm-Way and bought Merrell clogs and muck boots. They stopped asking the front desk at the Sterling Inn why their cell phones didn't work and instead congregated in the parking lot of the Mobil station, the point of highest elevation in town, where they could get a minimal signal. They hovered in front of the police station and the courthouse and the local coffee shop, waiting for any crumb of information they could call their own.

Every day in Sterling, there was a different funeral.

Matthew Royston's memorial service was held in a church that wasn't large enough to hold the grief of its mourners. Classmates and parents and family friends packed into the pews, stood along the walls, spilled out the doors. A contingent of kids from Sterling High had come dressed in green T-shirts with the number 19 on the front—the same one that had graced Matt's hockey jersey.

Josie and her mother were sitting somewhere in the back, but that didn't keep Josie from feeling that everyone was staring at her. She wasn't sure if that was because they all knew she was Matt's girlfriend or because they could see right through her.

"Blessed are those who mourn," the pastor read, "for they will be comforted."

Josie shivered. Was she mourning? Did mourning feel like a hole in the middle of you that got wider and wider every time you tried to plug it up? Or was she incapable of mourning, because that meant remembering, which she couldn't do?

Her mother leaned closer. "We can leave. You just say the word."

It was hard enough not having a clue who *she* was, but here in the Afterward, she couldn't seem to recognize anyone else, either. People who had ignored her for her whole life suddenly knew her by name. Everyone's eyes got soft at the edges when they looked at her. And her mother was the most foreign of all—like one of those corporate addicts who has a near-death experience and becomes a tree-hugger. Josie had expected to have to fight her mother in order to attend Matt's funeral, but to Josie's surprise, her mother had suggested it. The stupid shrink Josie had to see now—probably for the rest of her life—kept talking about *closure*. Closure, apparently, meant that she was supposed to realize that losing *normal* was something you got over, like losing a soccer game or a favorite T-shirt. Closure also meant that her mother had morphed into a crazy, overcompensating emotive machine, one who kept asking her if she needed anything (how many cups of herbal tea could a person drink without liquefying?) and trying to act like an ordinary mother, or at least what she imagined an ordinary mother to be. *If you really want me to feel better,* Josie felt like saying, *go back to work.* Then they could pretend it was business as usual, and after all, her mother was the one who'd taught Josie how to pretend in the first place.

In the front of the church was a coffin. Josie knew it wasn't open; rumors had flown about that. It was hard to imagine that Matt was inside that lacquered black box. That he wasn't breathing; that his blood had been drained out and his veins were pumped full of chemicals instead.

"Friends, as we gather here to remember Matthew Carlton Royston, we are beneath the protective shelter of God's healing love," the pastor said. "We are free to pour out our grief, release our anger, face our emptiness, and know that God cares."

Last year, in ancient world history, they had learned about how the Egyptians prepared their dead. Matt—who studied only when Josie forced him to do it—had been truly fascinated. The way the brain was sucked out through the nose. The possessions that went into a tomb with a pharaoh. The pets that were buried beside him. Josie had been reading the chapter in the textbook out loud, her head cradled on Matt's lap. He'd stopped her by putting his hand on her forehead. "When I go," he said, "I'm going to take you with me."

The pastor looked out over the congregation. "The death of a loved one can shake us to our very foundations. When the person is so young and so full of potential and skill, the feelings of grief and loss can be even more overwhelming. At times such as this we turn to our friends and family for support, for a shoulder to cry on and for someone to walk that road of pain and anguish with us. We cannot have Matt back, but we can rest easy knowing that he's found the peace in death he was denied here on earth."

Matt didn't go to church. His parents did, and they tried to make him go, but Josie knew he hated it. He thought it was a waste of a Sunday, and that if God was at all worthy of hanging around with, he'd probably be out riding around with the top down on his Jeep or playing pickup pond hockey instead of sitting in a stuffy building doing responsive reading.

The pastor moved aside, and Matt's father stood up. Josie knew him, of course—he cracked the worst jokes, silly puns that were never funny. He'd played hockey at UVM until he blew out his knee, and he'd had high hopes for Matt. But overnight, he'd turned hunch-shouldered and sullen, like a husk that used to contain the whole of him. He stood up and talked about the first time he'd taken Matt out to skate, how he'd started out pulling him along on the end of a hockey stick and realized, not much later, that Matt wasn't holding on. In the front row, Matt's mother began crying. Loud, noisy sobs—the kind that splattered against the walls of the church like paint.

Before Josie realized what she was doing, she'd gotten to her feet. "Josie!" her mother whispered, fierce, beside her—in that instant a flicker of the mother she was accustomed to, the one who would never make a spectacle of herself. Josie was shaking so hard that her feet did not seem to touch the ground, not as she stepped into the aisle in the black dress she had borrowed from her mother, not as she moved toward Matt's coffin, magnetically drawn to a pole.

She could feel Matt's father's eyes on her, could hear the whispers of the congregation. She reached the casket, polished to such a gleam that she could see her own face reflected back at her, an imposter.

"Josie," Mr. Royston said, coming down from the podium to embrace her. "You all right?"

Josie's throat closed like a rosebud. How could this man, whose son was dead, be asking *her* that? She felt herself dissolving, and wondered if you could turn into a ghost without dying; if that part of it was only a technicality.

"Did you want to say something?" Mr. Royston offered. "About Matt?"

Before she knew what was happening, Matt's father had led her up to the podium. She was vaguely aware of her mother, who'd gotten out of her seat in the pew and was edging her way down toward the front of the church—to do what? Spirit her away? Stop her from making another mistake?

Josie stared out at a landscape of faces she recognized and did not really know at all. *She loved him*, they were all thinking. *She was with him when he died.* Her breath caught like a moth in the cage of her lungs.

But what would she say? The truth?

Josie felt her lips twist, her face crumple. She started to sob, so hard that the wooden floorboards of the church bowed and creaked; so hard that even in that sealed casket, Josie was sure Matt could hear her. "I'm sorry," she choked out—to him, to Mr. Royston, to anyone who would listen. "Oh, God. I'm so sorry."

She did not notice her mother climbing the steps to the podium, wrapping an arm around Josie, leading her behind the altar to a little vestibule used by the organist. She didn't protest when her mother handed her Kleenex and rubbed her back. She didn't even mind when her mother tucked her hair back behind her ears, the way she used to when Josie was so small, she could barely remember the gesture. "Everyone must think I'm an idiot," Josie said.

"No, they think you miss Matt." Her mother hesitated. "I know you believe this was your fault."

Josie's heart was pounding so hard, it moved the thin chiffon fabric of the dress.

"Sweetheart," her mother said, "you couldn't have saved him."

Josie reached for another tissue, and pretended that her mother understood.

Maximum security meant Peter did not have a roommate. He did not get recreation time. His food was brought to him three times a day in his cell. His reading material was restricted by the correctional officers. And because the staff still believed he might be suicidal, his room consisted of a toilet and a bench—no sheets, no mattress, nothing that might be fashioned into a means of checking out of this world.

There were four hundred and fifteen cinder blocks on the back wall of his cell; he'd counted. Twice. Since then, he'd taken the time to stare right at the camera that was watching him. Peter wondered who was at the other end of that camera. He pictured a bunch of COs clustered around a crummy TV monitor, poking each other and cracking up when Peter had to go to the bathroom. Or, in other words, yet another group of people who'd find a way to make fun of him.

The camera had a red light on it, a power indicator, and a single lens that shimmered like a rainbow. There was a rubber bumper around the lens that looked like an eyelid. It struck Peter that even if he *wasn't* suicidal, a few weeks of this and he would be.

It did not get dark in jail, just dim. That hardly mattered, since there was nothing to do but sleep anyway. Peter lay on the bench, wondering if you lost your hearing if you never had to use it; if the power of speech worked the same way. He remembered learning in one of his social studies classes that in the Old West, when Native Americans were thrown into jail, they sometimes dropped dead. The theory was that someone so used to the freedom of space couldn't handle the confinement, but Peter had another interpretation. When the only company you had was yourself, and when you didn't want to socialize, there was only one way to leave the room.

One of the COs had just come through, doing his security sweep—a heavy-booted run past the cells—when Peter heard it:

I know what you did.

Holy shit, Peter thought. I've already started to go crazy.

Everyone knows.

Peter swung his feet to the cement floor and stared at the camera, but it wasn't giving up any secrets.

The voice sounded like wind passing over snow—bleak,

a whisper. "To your right," it said, and Peter slowly got to his feet and walked to a corner of the cell.

"Who . . . who's there?" he said.

"It's about fucking time. I thought you were never going to stop wailing."

Peter tried to see through the bars, but couldn't. "You heard me crying?"

"Fucking baby," the voice said. "Grow the fuck up."

"Who are you?"

"You can call me Carnivore, like everyone else."

Peter swallowed. "What did you do?"

"Nothing they said I did," Carnivore answered. "How long?"

"How long what?"

"How long till your trial?"

Peter didn't know. It was the one question he had forgotten to ask Jordan McAfee, probably because he was afraid to hear the answer.

"Mine's next week," Carnivore said before Peter could reply.

The metal door of the cell felt like ice against his temple. "How long have you been here?" Peter asked.

"Ten months," Carnivore answered.

Peter imagined sitting in this cell for ten straight months. He thought about all the times he'd count those stupid cinder blocks, all the pisses that the guards would get to watch on their little television set.

"You killed kids, right? You know what happens in this jail to guys who kill kids?"

Peter didn't respond. He was roughly the same age as everyone at Sterling High; it wasn't like he'd gone into a nursery school. And it wasn't like he hadn't had a good reason.

He didn't want to talk about this anymore. "How come you didn't get bail?"

Carnivore scoffed. "Because they say I raped some waitress, and then stabbed her."

Did everyone in this jail think they were innocent? All this time Peter had spent lying on that bench, convincing himself that he was nothing like anyone else in the Grafton County Jail—and as it turned out, that was a lie.

Did he sound like this to Jordan?

"You still there?" Carnivore asked.

Peter lay back down on his bench without saying another word. He turned his face to the wall, and he pretended not to hear as the man next to him tried over and over to make a connection.

The first thing that struck Patrick, again, was how much younger Judge Cormier looked when she wasn't on the bench. She answered the door in jeans and a ponytail, wiping her hands on a dish towel. Josie stood just behind her, her face washed by the same vacant stare he'd seen a dozen times over, now, in other victims he'd interviewed. Josie was a vital piece in the puzzle, the only one who had seen Peter kill Matthew Royston. But unlike those victims, Josie had a mother who knew the intricacies of the legal system.

"Judge Cormier," he said. "Josie. Thanks for letting me come over."

The judge stared at him. "This is a waste of time. Josie doesn't remember anything."

"With all due respect, Judge, it's my job to hear that from Josie herself."

He steeled himself for an argument, but she stepped back to let him inside. Patrick let his eyes roam the foyer—the antique table with a spider plant spilling over its surface, the tasteful landscapes that hung on the walls. So this was how a judge lived. His own place was a pit stop, a haven of laundry and old newspapers and food long past its expiration date, where he'd go for a few hours between his stints at the office.

He turned to Josie. "How's the head?"

"It still hurts," she said, so softly that Patrick had to strain to hear her.

He turned to the judge again. "Is there a room where we could go talk for a few minutes?"

She led them into the kitchen, which looked like just the kind of kitchen Patrick sometimes thought about when he imagined where he should have been by now. There were cherry cabinets and lots of sun streaming through the bay window and a bowl of bananas on the counter. He sat down across from Josie, expecting the judge to pull up a chair beside her daughter, but to his surprise she remained standing. "If you need me," she said, "I'll be upstairs."

Josie looked up, pained. "Can't you just stay?"

For a moment, Patrick saw something light in the judge's eyes—want? regret?—but it vanished before he could put a name to it. "You know I can't," she said gently.

Patrick didn't have any kids of his own, but he was pretty damn sure that if one of his had come this close to dying, he'd have a hard time letting her out of his sight. He did not know exactly what was going on between the mother and daughter, but he knew better than to get in the middle of it.

"I'm sure Detective Ducharme will make this utterly painless," the judge said.

It was part wish, part warning. Patrick nodded at her. A good cop did whatever he could to protect and serve, but when it was someone you knew who was robbed or threatened or hurt, the stakes changed. You'd make a few more phone calls; you'd shuffle your responsibilities so that one took priority. Patrick had experienced that, to a greater degree, years ago with his friend Nina and her son. He didn't know Josie Cormier personally, but her mother was in the field of law enforcement—Christ, she was at its top level—and for this, her daughter deserved to be treated with kid gloves.

He watched Alex walk up the stairs, and then he took a pad and pencil out of his coat pocket. "So," he said. "How are you doing?"

"Look, you don't have to pretend you care."

"I'm not pretending," Patrick said.

"I don't even get why you're here. It's not like anything anyone says to you is going to make those kids less dead."

"That's true," Patrick agreed, "but before we can try Peter Houghton we need to know exactly what happened. And unfortunately, I wasn't there."

"Unfortunately?"

He looked down at the table. "I sometimes think it's easier to be the one who's been hurt than the one who couldn't stop it from happening."

"I was there," Josie said, shaken. "I couldn't stop it."

"Hey," Patrick said, "it's not your fault."

She looked up at him then, as if she so badly wished she could believe that, but knew he was wrong. And who was Patrick to tell her otherwise? Every time he envisioned his mad dash to Sterling High, he imagined what would have happened if he'd been at the school when the shooter first arrived. If he'd disarmed the kid before anyone was hurt.

"I don't remember anything about the shooting," Josie said.

"Do you remember being in the gym?"

Josie shook her head.

"How about running there with Matt?"

"No. I don't even remember getting up and going to school in the first place. It's like a blank spot in my head that I just skip over."

Patrick knew, from talking to the shrinks who'd been assigned to work with the victims, that this was perfectly normal. Amnesia was one way for the mind to protect itself from reliving something that would otherwise break you apart. In a way, he wished he could be as lucky as Josie, that he could make what he'd seen vanish.

"What about Peter Houghton? Did you know him?"

"Everyone knew who he was."

"What do you mean?"

Josie shrugged. "He got noticed."

"Because he was different from everyone else?"

Josie thought about this for a moment. "Because he didn't try to fit in."

"You were dating Matthew Royston?"

Immediately, tears welled in Josie's eyes. "He liked to be called Matt."

Patrick reached for a paper napkin and passed it to Josie. "I'm sorry about what happened to him, Josie."

She ducked her head. "Me too."

He waited for her to wipe her eyes, blow her nose. "Do you know why Peter might have disliked Matt?"

"People used to make fun of him," Josie said. "It wasn't just Matt."

Did you? Patrick thought. He'd looked at the yearbook confiscated from Peter's room—the circles around certain kids who became victims, and others who did not. There were many reasons for this—from the fact that Peter ran out of time to the truth that hunting down thirty people in a school of a thousand was more difficult than he'd imagined. But of all the targets Peter had marked in the yearbook, only Josie's photo had been crossed out, as if he'd

changed his mind. Only her face had words printed beneath it, in block letters: LET LIVE.

"Did you know him personally? Have any classes or anything with him?"

She looked up. "I used to work with him."

"Where?"

"The copy store downtown."

"Did you two get along?"

"Sometimes," Josie said. "Not always."

"Why not?"

"He lit a fire there once and I ratted him out. He lost his
job after that."

Patrick marked a note down on his pad. Why had Peter
made the decision to spare her when he had every reason to
hold a grudge?

"Before that," Patrick asked, "would you say you were
friends?"

Josie pleated the napkin she'd used to dry her tears into
a triangle, a smaller one, a smaller one still. "No," she said.
"We weren't."

The woman next to Lacy was wearing a checkered flannel
shirt, reeked of cigarettes, and was missing most of her
teeth. She took one look at Lacy's skirt and blouse. "Your
first time here?" she asked.

Lacy nodded. They were waiting in a long room, side by
side in a row of chairs. In front of their feet ran a red dividing line, and then a second set of chairs. Inmates and visi-
tors sat like mirror images, speaking in shorthand. The
woman beside Lacy smiled at her. "You get used to it," she
said.

One parent was allowed to visit Peter every two weeks,
for one hour. Lacy had come with a basket full of home-
baked muffins and cakes, magazines, books—anything she

could think of to help Peter. But the correctional officer who'd signed her in for visitation had confiscated the items. No baked goods. And no reading material, not until it was vetted by the jail staff.

A man with a shaved head and sleeves of tattoos up and down his arms headed toward Lacy. She shivered—was that a *swastika* inked onto his forehead? "Hi, Mom," he murmured, and Lacy watched the woman's eyes strip away the tattoos and the bare scalp and the orange jumpsuit to see a little boy catching tadpoles in a mudhole behind their house. *Everyone,* Lacy thought, *is somebody's son.*

She glanced away from their reunion and saw Peter being led into the visitation room. For a moment her heart caught—he looked too thin, and behind his glasses, his eyes were so empty—but then she tamped down whatever she was feeling and offered him a brilliant smile. She would pretend that it didn't bother her to see her son in a prison jumpsuit; that she hadn't had to sit in the car and fight a panic attack after pulling into the jail lot; that it was perfectly normal to be surrounded by drug dealers and rapists while you asked your son if he was getting enough to eat.

"Peter," she said, folding him into her arms. It took a moment, but he hugged her back. She pressed her face to his neck, the way she used to when he was a baby, and she thought she would devour him—but he did not smell like her son. For a moment she let herself entertain the pipe dream that this was all a mistake—*Peter's not in jail! This is someone else's unfortunate child!*—but then she realized what was different. The shampoo and deodorant he had to use here were not what he'd used at home; this Peter smelled sharper, coarser.

Suddenly there was a tap on her shoulder. "Ma'am," the correctional officer said, "you'll have to let go now."

If only it was that easy, Lacy thought.

They sat down on opposite sides of the red line.

"Are you all right?" she asked.

"I'm still here."

The way he said it—as if he'd totally expected otherwise by now—made Lacy shudder. She had a feeling he wasn't talking about being let out on bail, and the alternative—the idea of Peter killing himself—was something she could not hold in her head. She felt her throat funnel tight, and she found herself doing the one thing she'd promised herself she would not do: she started to cry. "Peter," she whispered. "*Why?*"

"Did the police come to the house?" Peter asked.

Lacy nodded—it seemed as if it had happened so long ago.

"Did they go to my room?"

"They had a warrant—"

"They took my things?" Peter exclaimed, the first emotion she'd seen from him. "You let them take my things?"

"What were you doing with those things?" she whispered. "Those bombs. The *guns . . . ?*"

"You wouldn't understand."

"Then make me, Peter," she said, broken. "*Make* me understand."

"I haven't been able to make you understand in seventeen years, Mom. Why should it be any different *now?*" His face twisted. "I don't even know why you bothered to come."

"To see you—"

"Then *look* at me," Peter cried. "Why won't you fucking *look* at me?"

He put his head in his hands, his narrow shoulders rounding with the sound of a sob.

It came down to this, Lacy realized: You stared at the

stranger in front of you and decided, categorically, that this was no longer your son. Or you made the decision to find whatever scraps of your child you still could in what he had become.

Was that even really a choice, if you were a mother?

People could argue that monsters weren't born, they were made. People could criticize her parenting skills, point to moments when Lacy had let Peter down by being too lax or too firm, too removed or too smothering. The town of Sterling would analyze to death what she had done to her son—but what about what she would do *for* him? It was easy to be proud of the kid who got straight A's and who made the winning basket—a kid the world already adored. But true character showed when you could find something to love in a child everyone else hated. What if the things she had or hadn't done for Peter were the wrong criteria for measurement? Wasn't it just as telling a mark of motherhood to see how, from this awful moment on, she behaved?

She reached across the red line until she could embrace Peter. She didn't care if it was allowed or not. The guards could come and pull her off him, but until that happened, Lacy was not planning to let her son go.

On the surveillance video taken from the cafeteria, students were carrying trays and doing homework and chatting when Peter entered the room holding a handgun. There was a discharge of bullets and a cacophony of screaming. A smoke alarm went off. When everyone started to run, he shot again, and this time two girls fell down. Other students ran right over them in an effort to get away.

When the only people left in the cafeteria were Peter and the victims, he walked through the rows of tables, surveying his handiwork. He passed by the boy he'd shot who lay in a puddle of blood on top of a book, but he stopped to pick up an iPod that had been left on the table and put the earphones in his ears before turning it off and setting it down again. He turned the page in an open notebook. And then he sat down at one untouched tray and placed the gun on it. He opened a box of Rice Krispies and poured them into a Styrofoam bowl. He added the contents of a milk container and ate all the cereal before standing up again, retrieving his pistol, and exiting the cafeteria.

It was the most chilling, deliberate thing Patrick had ever seen in his life.

He looked down at the bowl of ramen noodles he had cooked himself for dinner, and realized he'd lost his appetite. Setting it aside on a stack of old newspapers, he rewound the video and forced himself to watch it again.

When the phone rang, he picked it up, still distracted by the sight of Peter on his television screen. "Yeah."

"Well, hello to you, too," Nina Frost said.

He melted when he heard her voice; old habits died hard. "Sorry. I'm just in the middle of something."

"I can imagine. It's all over the news. How are you holding up?"

"Oh, you know," he said, when what he really meant was that he was not sleeping at night; that he saw the faces of the dead whenever he closed his eyes; that his mouth was full of the questions he was certain he'd forgotten to ask.

"Patrick," she said, because she was his oldest friend and because she knew him better than anyone, including himself, "don't blame yourself."

He bent his head. "It happened in my town. How *can't* I?"

"If you had a videophone, I'd be able to tell if you're wearing your hair shirt or your cape and boots," Nina said.

"It's not funny."

"No, it's not," she agreed. "But you must know it's a slam dunk at trial. You have, what? A thousand witnesses?"

"Something like that."

Nina grew quiet. Patrick did not have to explain to her—a woman who'd lived with regret as a constant companion—that convicting Peter Houghton was not enough. For Patrick to lay this to rest, he'd have to understand why Peter had done this in the first place.

So that he could keep it from happening again.

From an FBI investigatory report, published by special agents in charge of examining school shootings around the globe:

> Among school shooters, we have seen a similarity of family dynamics. Often the shooter will have a turbulent relationship with his parents, or will have parents who accept pathological behavior. There is a lack of intimacy within the family. There are no limits for television or computer use imposed on the shooter, and sometimes there is access to weapons.
>
> Within the school environment, we found a tendency toward detachment from the learning process on the part of the shooter. The school itself tended to tolerate disrespectful behavior, exhibited inequitable discipline and an inflexible culture—with certain stu-

dents enjoying prestige given to
them by teachers and staff.

Shooters are more likely to have
access to violent movies, television, and video games; to use drugs
and alcohol; to have a peer group
that exists outside of school and
supports their behavior.

In addition, prior to a violent
act, there is evidence of leakage—a
clue that something is coming.
These hints might take the form of
poems, writings, drawings, Internet
posts, or threats made in person or
in absentia.

In spite of the commonalities
described within, we caution the
use of this report to create a
checklist that might predict future
school shooters. In the hands of
the media, this might result in la-
beling many nonviolent students as
potentially lethal. In fact, a
great many adolescents who will
never commit violent acts will show
some of the traits on the list.

*   *   *

Lewis Houghton was a creature of habit. Every morning,
he woke up at 5:35 and went for a run on the treadmill in
the basement. He showered and he ate a bowl of cornflakes while he scanned the headlines in the paper. He
wore the same overcoat, no matter how cold or hot the
weather, and he parked in the same spot in the faculty lot.

He'd once tried to mathematically figure the effect of

routine on happiness, but there was an interesting twist to the calculation: The measure of joy brought by the familiar was amplified or reduced by the individual's resistance to change. Or—as Lacy would have said, *English, Lewis*—for every person like himself who liked the worn grooves of the familiar, there was another person who found it stifling. In those cases, the comfort quotient became a negative number, and doing what came habitually actually detracted from happiness.

It was that way, he supposed, for Lacy, who wandered around the house as if she'd never seen it before, who couldn't stand the thought of going back to her practice. *How can you expect me to think of someone else's child right now?* she had argued.

She kept insisting that they needed to *do* something, but Lewis didn't know what that was supposed to be. And because he couldn't comfort either his wife or his son, Lewis decided he was left to comfort himself. After sitting at home for five days after Peter's arraignment, one morning he woke up and packed his briefcase, ate his cornflakes, read the paper, and headed off to work.

He was thinking of the equation for happiness as he headed to the office. One of the tenets of his breakthrough—$H = R/E$, or *happiness equals reality divided by expectation*—was based on the universal truth that you always had some expectation for what was to come. In other words, E was always a real number, since you could not divide by zero. But recently, he wondered about the truth of that. Math could only take a man so far. In the middle of the night, when he was wide awake and staring up at the ceiling, knowing that his wife lay beside him pretending to be asleep and doing the very same thing, Lewis had come to believe that you might be conditioned to expect absolutely nothing from one's life. That way, when you lost your first son, you didn't grieve. When your second son was jailed for a massacre, you were not shattered. You *could* divide by zero; it felt like a canyon where your heart used to be.

As soon as he set foot on the campus, Lewis felt better. Here, he was not the father of the shooter and never had been. He was Lewis Houghton, professor of economics. Here, he was still at the top of his game; he didn't have to look at the body of his research and wonder at what point it had begun to unravel.

Lewis had just pulled a sheaf of papers out of his briefcase that morning when the chair of the econ department poked his head through the open doorway. Hugh Macquarie was a big man—*Huge Andhairy* is what the college students called him behind his back—who had taken over the position with gusto. "Houghton? What are you *doing* here?"

"Last I checked, the college was still paying me to work," Lewis said, trying to make a joke. He couldn't make jokes, never had been able to do so. His timing was off; he gave away punch lines by accident.

Hugh walked into the room. "My God, Lewis, I don't know what to say." He hesitated.

Lewis didn't blame Hugh. He barely knew what to say himself. There were Hallmark cards for bereavement, for loss of a beloved pet, for getting laid off from a job, but no one seemed to have the right words of comfort for someone whose son had just killed ten people.

"I thought about calling you at home. Lisa even wanted to bring a casserole or something. How's Lacy holding up?"

Lewis pushed his glasses higher on the bridge of his nose. "Oh," he said. "You know. We're trying to keep things as normal as possible."

When he said this, he pictured his life as a graph. Normal was a line that stretched on and on, teasing its way closer to an axis but never really reaching it.

Hugh sat down in the chair across from Lewis's desk— the same chair that was sometimes filled by a student who needed a tutorial in microeconomics. "Lewis, take some time off," he said.

"Thanks, Hugh. I appreciate that." Lewis glanced at an equation on the far blackboard that he'd been puzzling out. "Right now, though, I really need to be here. It keeps me from thinking about being *there*." Reaching for some chalk, Lewis began to print across the board, a long and lovely stream of numbers that calmed him inside.

He knew that there was a difference between something that makes you happy and something that doesn't make you unhappy. The trick was convincing yourself these were one and the same.

Hugh put his hand on Lewis's arm, stilling it mid-equation. "Maybe I said that wrong. We *need* you to take time off."

Lewis stared at him. "Oh. Um. I see," he said, although he didn't. If Lewis was willing to segregate his work life from his home life, why couldn't Sterling College do the same?

Unless.

Had that been his mistake in the first place? If you were uncertain in the decisions you made as a father, could you patch over your insecurities with the confidence you had as a professional? Or would the fix always be flimsy, a paper wall that couldn't bear weight?

"It's just for a bit," Hugh said. "It's what's best."

For whom? Lewis thought, but he remained silent until he heard Hugh close the door behind himself on his way out.

When the chairman was gone, Lewis lifted the chalk again. He stared at the equations until they melded together, and then he began to scrawl furiously, a composer with a symphony moving too fast for his fingers. Why hadn't he realized this before? Everyone knew that if you divided reality by expectation, you got a happiness quotient. But when you inverted the equation—expectation divided by reality—you didn't get the opposite of happiness. What you got, Lewis realized, was hope.

Pure logic: Assuming reality was constant, expectation had to be greater than reality to create optimism. On the other hand, a pessimist was someone with expectations lower than reality, a fraction of diminishing returns. The human condition meant that this number approached zero without reaching it—you never really completely gave up hope; it might come flooding back at any provocation.

Lewis stepped back from the blackboard, surveying his handiwork. Someone who was happy would have little need to hope for change. But, conversely, an optimistic person was that way because he wanted to believe in something better than his reality.

He started wondering if there were exceptions to the rule: if happy people might be hopeful, if the unhappy might have given up any anticipation that things might get better.

And that made Lewis think of his son.

He stood in front of the blackboard and started to cry, his hands and his sleeves covered in fine white chalk dust, as if he had become a ghost.

The office of the Geek Squad, as Patrick affectionately referred to the tech guys who hacked into hard drives to find proof of pornography and downloads from *The Anarchist*

Cookbook, was filled with computers. Not just the one seized from Peter Houghton's room, but also several from Sterling High, including the one from the secretary's main office and another batch from the library.

"He's good," said Orestes, a tech that Patrick would have sworn was not old enough to have graduated from high school himself. "We're not just talking HTML programming. Guy knew his shit."

He pulled up a few files from the bowels of Peter's computer, graphics files that didn't make much sense to Patrick until the tech typed a few buttons and suddenly a three-dimensional dragon appeared on the screen and breathed fire at them. "Wow," Patrick said.

"Yeah. From what I can tell, he actually made up a few computer games, even posted them for gamers on a couple of sites where you can do that and get feedback."

"Any message boards on those sites?"

"Dude, give me an iota of credit," Orestes said, and he clicked onto one he'd already flagged. "Peter went by the screen name DeathWish. They're a—"

"—band," Patrick finished. "I know."

"They're not *just* a band," Orestes said with reverence, his fingers flying over the keyboard. "They're the modern voice of the collective human conscience."

"Tell that to Tipper Gore."

"Who?"

Patrick laughed. "She was before your time, I guess."

"What did you used to listen to when you were a kid?"

"The cavemen, banging rocks together," Patrick said dryly.

The screen filled with a series of posts from DeathWish. Most of them were entries about how to enhance a certain graphic or reviews of other games that had been posted on the site. Two quoted lyrics from the band Death Wish.

"This is my personal favorite," Orestes said, and he scrolled down.

> From: DeathWish
> To: Hades1991
>   This town blows. This weekend there is a craft fes-
> tival where old bags come to show off the ticky tacky
> shit they made. They should call it a CRAP festival.
> I'm gonna hide in the bushes outside the church. Tar-
> get practice as they cross the street—ten points each!
> Yee ha!

Patrick leaned back in the chair. "Well, that doesn't prove anything."

"Yeah," Orestes said. "Craft festivals do kind of suck. But check this out." He swiveled in his own chair to reach another terminal, set up on a table. "He hacked into the school's secure computer system."

"To do what? Change his grades?"

"Nope. The program he wrote broke through the firewalls on the school system at 9:58 a.m."

"That's when the car bomb went off," Patrick murmured.

Orestes pivoted the monitor so that Patrick could see. "This was on every single screen on every single computer at the school."

Patrick stared at the purple background, the flaming red letters that scrolled like a marquee: READY OR NOT . . . HERE I COME.

Jordan was already sitting at the table of the conference room when Peter Houghton was brought in by a correctional officer. "Thanks," he said to the guard, his eyes on Peter, who immediately canvassed the room, his gaze lighting on the only window. Jordan had seen this over and over in prisoners he'd represented—an ordinary human could so quickly turn into a caged animal. Then again, it was a chicken-and-egg conundrum: were they animals because they were in jail . . . or were they in jail because they were animals?

"Have a seat," he said, and Peter remained standing.

Unfazed, Jordan started talking. "I want to lay out the ground rules, Peter," he said. "Everything I say to you is confidential. Everything you say to me is confidential. I can't tell anyone what you say. I *can* tell you, however, not to talk to the media or the police or anyone else for that matter. If anyone tries to contact you, you contact me immediately—call me collect. As your lawyer, I get to do the talking for you. From now on, I'm your best friend, your mother, your father, your priest. Are we clear on that?"

Peter glared at him. "Crystal."

"Good. So." Jordan pulled a legal pad out of his briefcase, a pencil. "I imagine you've got a few questions; we can start with those."

"I hate it here," Peter burst out. "I don't get why I have to stay here."

Most of Jordan's clients started out quiet and terrified in jail—which quickly gave way to anger and indignation. But at that moment Peter sounded like any other ordinary teenage kid—like Thomas had sounded at his age, when the world apparently revolved around him and Jordan just happened to be living on it as well. However, the lawyer in Jordan trumped the parent in him, and he started to wonder if Peter Houghton truly might *not* know why he was in jail. Jordan would be the first to tell you insanity defenses rarely worked and were grossly overrated, but maybe Peter could be passed off as the real deal—and that was the key to securing an acquittal. "What do you mean?" he pressed.

"They're the ones who did this to me, and now I'm the one who's being punished."

Jordan sat back and crossed his arms. Peter didn't feel remorse for what he'd done, that much was clear. In fact, he considered himself a victim.

And here was the remarkable thing about being a defense attorney: Jordan didn't really care. There was no room in his line of work for his own personal feelings. He had worked with the scum of the earth before—killers and rapists who fancied themselves martyrs. His job wasn't to believe them or to pass judgment. It was simply to do or say whatever he had to in order to get them free. In spite of what he'd just told Peter, he was not a clergyman or a shrink or a friend to a client. He was simply a spin doctor.

"Well," Jordan said evenly, "you need to understand the jail's position. To them, you're just a murderer."

"Then they're all hypocrites," Peter said. "If they saw a roach, they'd step on it, wouldn't they?"

"Is that how you'd describe what happened at the school?"

Peter flicked his eyes away. "Do you know that I'm not allowed to read magazines?" he said. "I can't even go into the exercise yard like everyone else."

"I'm not here to register your complaints."

"Why *are* you here?"

"To help you get out," Jordan said. "And if that's going to happen, then you need to talk to me."

Peter folded his arms across his chest and glanced from Jordan's collared shirt to his tie to his polished black shoes. "Why? You don't really give a shit about me."

Jordan stood up and stuffed his notebook into his briefcase. "You know what? You're right. I *don't* really give a shit about you. I'm just doing my job, because unlike you, I won't have the state paying my room and board for the rest of my life." He started for the door, but was called back by the sound of Peter's voice.

"Why is everyone so upset that those jerks are dead?"

Jordan turned slowly, making a mental note that kindness had not worked especially well with Peter, nor had the voice of authority. What had made him respond was pure and simple anger.

"I mean, people are crying over them . . . and they were assholes. Everyone's saying I ruined their lives, but no one seemed to care when *my* life was the one being ruined."

Jordan sat down on the edge of the table. "How?"

"Where do you want me to start," Peter answered, bitter. "In nursery school, when the teacher would bring out snacks, and one of them would pull out my chair so I'd fall down and everyone else would crack up? Or in second grade, when they held my head down in the toilet and they flushed it over and over, just because they knew they could? Or that time they beat me up on my way home from school and I needed stitches?"

Jordan picked up his pad and wrote STITCHES. "Who's *they?*"

"A whole bunch of kids," Peter said.

The ones you wanted to kill? Jordan thought, but he didn't ask. "Why do you think they targeted you?"

"Because they're dickheads? I don't know. They're like a pack. They have to make someone else feel like shit in order to feel good about themselves."

"What did you try to do to stop it?"

Peter snorted. "In case you haven't noticed, Sterling's not exactly a metropolis. Everyone knows everyone. You wind up in high school with the same kids who were in the sandbox in your preschool."

"Couldn't you stay out of their path?"

"I had to go to school," Peter said. "You'd be surprised how small it gets when you're there for eight hours every day."

"So did they do this outside of school, too?"

"When they could catch me," Peter said. "If I was by myself."

"How about harassment—phone calls, letters, threats?" Jordan asked.

"Online," Peter said. "They'd send me instant messages, saying I was a loser, things like that. And they took an email I wrote and spammed it out to the whole school . . . made it a joke . . ." He looked away, falling silent.

"Why?"

"It was . . ." He shook his head. "I don't want to talk about it."

Jordan made a note on his pad. "Did you ever tell anyone about what was going on? Parents? Teachers?"

"No one gives a crap," Peter said. "They tell you to ignore it. They say they'll be watching out to make sure it doesn't happen, but they never watch." He walked to the window and pressed his palms against the glass. "There was this kid in my first-grade class who had that disease, the one where your spine grows outside your body—"

"Spina bifida?"

"Yeah. She had a wheelchair and she couldn't sit up or anything, and before she came to class the teacher told us we had to treat her like she was just like us. The thing is, she wasn't like us, and we all knew it, and *she* knew it. So we were supposed to lie to her face?" Peter shook his head. "Everyone talks like it's all right to be different, but America's supposed to be this melting pot, and what the hell does that mean? If it's a melting pot, then you're really just trying to make everyone the same, aren't you?"

Jordan found himself thinking about his son Thomas's

transition to middle school. They'd moved from Bainbridge to Salem Falls, a small enough school system that the cliques had already developed thick cellular walls against outsiders. For a while, Thomas had been a chameleon—he'd come home from school and hole up in his room, emerging as a soccer player, a thespian, a "mathlete." It took him several sheddings of his own adolescent skin to find a group of friends who let him be whoever he wanted; and the rest of Thomas's high school career was a fairly peaceful one. But what if he *hadn't* found that group of friends? What if he'd continued peeling off layers of himself until there was nothing left at his core?

As if he could read Jordan's mind, Peter suddenly stared at him. "Do you have kids?"

Jordan did not talk about his personal life with clients. Their relationship existed in the confines of a court, and that was that. The few times in his career when this unwritten rule had been broken had nearly wrecked him personally and professionally. But he met Peter's gaze and said, "Two. A six-month-old baby and a son at Yale."

"Then you get it," Peter said. "Everyone wants their kid to grow up and go to Harvard or be a quarterback for the Patriots. No one ever looks at their baby and thinks, *Oh, I hope my kid grows up and becomes a freak. I hope he gets to school every day and prays he won't catch anyone's attention.* But you know what? Kids grow up like that every single day."

Jordan found himself at a loss for words. There was the finest line between unique and odd, between what made a child grow up to be as well adjusted as Thomas versus unstable, like Peter. Did every teenager have the capacity to fall on one side or the other of that tightrope, and could you identify a single moment that tipped the balance?

He suddenly thought of Sam this morning, when Jordan

was changing his diaper. The baby had grabbed hold of his own toes, fascinated to have located them, and immediately stuffed his foot into his mouth. *Look at that*, Selena had joked over his shoulder, *like father like son*. As Jordan had finished dressing Sam, he'd marveled at the mystery life must be for someone that young. Imagine a world that seemed so much bigger than you. Imagine waking up one morning and finding a piece of yourself you didn't even know existed.

When you don't fit in, you become superhuman. You can feel everyone else's eyes on you, stuck like Velcro. You can hear a whisper about you from a mile away. You can disappear, even when it looks like you're still standing right there. You can scream, and nobody hears a sound.

You become the mutant who fell into the vat of acid, the Joker who can't remove his mask, the bionic man who's missing all his limbs and none of his heart.

You are the thing that used to be normal, but that was so long ago, you can't even remember what it was like.

Six Years Before

Peter knew he was doomed, the first day of sixth grade, when his mother presented him with a gift over breakfast. "I know how much you wanted one," she said, and she waited for him to open the wrapping paper.

Inside was a three-ring binder with a graphic of Superman on the cover. And he *had* wanted one. Three years ago, when that was a cool thing to have.

He had managed a smile. "Thanks, Mom," he said, and she beamed at him, while he imagined all the ways carrying this totally stupid notebook would be used against him.

Josie, as usual, had come to his rescue. She told the school custodian that her bike handlebars were all screwed up and that she needed some duct tape to jury-rig it until she got home. In reality, she didn't bike to school—she walked with Peter, who lived a little farther out of town but picked her up along the way. Although they never saw each other outside of school—and hadn't in years, thanks to some blowout fight between his mother and hers that neither of them could really remember the details about—Josie still hung out with Peter. And thank God for that, because no one else really did. They sat together during lunch, they read each other's rough drafts in English, they were always each other's lab partners. Summers were always tough. They could email, and every now and then they saw each other at the town pond, but that was about it. And then, come September, they fell back in step as if they'd never missed a beat. That, Peter figured, was the very definition of a best friend.

Today, thanks to the Superman binder, they'd started off the year with a crisis. With Josie's help, he'd made a slip-cover of sorts from the tape and an old newspaper they stole from the science lab. He could take it off when he was home, she reasoned, so that his mother wouldn't be offended.

The sixth graders had lunch fourth period, when it was only 11:00 a.m., but by that point it felt like they hadn't eaten in months. Josie bought—her mother's cooking skills, she said, were limited to writing a check to the cafeteria ladies—and Peter stood beside her in the snaking line to pick up a carton of milk. His mother would have packed him a sandwich with the crusts cut off, a bag of carrot sticks, an organic fruit that might or might not be bruised.

Peter slid his binder onto the cafeteria tray, embarrassed even though it was still covered up by the newspaper. He popped a straw into his milk carton. "You know, it shouldn't make a difference what binder you've got," Josie said. "What do you care what they think?"

As they headed into the lunchroom, Drew Girard slammed into Peter. "Watch where you're going, retard," Drew said, but it was too late—Peter had already dropped his tray.

His milk spilled all over his splayed binder, melting the newspaper into a muddy clot and revealing the Superman graphic beneath it.

Drew started to laugh. "Are you wearing your Underoos, too, Houghton?"

"Shut up, Drew."

"Or what? Will you melt me with your X-ray vision?"

Mrs. McDonald, the art teacher who was patrolling the lunchroom—and who Josie swore she'd once caught sniffing glue in the supply closet—took a halfhearted step forward. By seventh grade, there were kids like Drew and Matt Royston who were taller than the teachers and had deep voices and were *shaving*; but there were also kids like Peter, who prayed every night that puberty would hit but hadn't seen any viable signs yet. "Peter, why don't you just go take a seat . . ." Mrs. McDonald sighed. "Drew will bring you another carton of milk."

Probably poisoned, Peter thought. He started mopping off his binder with a wad of napkins. Even after it dried, it would reek, now. Maybe he could tell his mother that he'd spilled his milk on it at lunch. It was the truth, after all, even if he'd had a little help doing it. And it just might be enough incentive for her to buy him a new, normal notebook, one like everyone else's.

Inside, Peter was grinning: Drew Girard had actually just done him a favor.

"Drew," the teacher said. "I meant *now*."

As Drew took a step toward the interior of the cafeteria toward the pyramid of milk cartons, Josie stuck out her foot surreptitiously so that he tripped, landing flat on his face. In the lunchroom, other kids started to laugh. That was the way this society worked: you were only at the bottom of the totem pole until you could find someone else to take your place. "Watch out for kryptonite," Josie whispered, just loud enough for Peter to hear.

*   *   *

The two best things about being a district court judge, in Alex's mind, were, first, being able to address people's problems and make them feel as if they are being listened to, and second, the intellectual challenge. You had so many factors to balance when you were making decisions: the victims, the police, law enforcement, society. And all of them had to be considered in the context of precedent.

The worst part of the job was that you couldn't give people what they really needed when they came to court: for a defendant—the sentencing that would really offer treatment, instead of a punishment. For a victim—an apology.

Today there was a girl standing in front of her who wasn't much older than Josie. She was wearing a NASCAR jacket and a black pleated skirt, and had blond hair and acne. Alex had seen kids like her, hanging out in parking lots after the Mall of New Hampshire was closed for the night, spinning 360s in their boyfriends' I-Rocs. She wondered what this girl would have been like if she'd grown up with a judge for a mother. She wondered if, at some point, this girl had played with stuffed animals underneath the kitchen table and read books beneath her covers with a flashlight when she was supposed to be going to bed. It never failed to amaze Alex how, with the brush of a hand, the track of someone's life might veer in a completely different direction.

The girl had been charged with receiving stolen property—a $500 gold necklace that her boyfriend gave her. Alex looked down at her from the bench. There was a reason it was up so high in a courtroom—it had nothing to do with logistics and everything to do with intimidation. "Are you knowingly, voluntarily, and intelligently waiving your rights? And you understand that by pleading guilty, you're admitting to the truth of the charge?"

The girl blinked. "I didn't know it was stolen. I thought it was a present from Hap."

"If you read the face of the complaint, it says you're charged with knowingly receiving this necklace, knowing it was stolen. If you didn't know it was stolen, you have the right to go to trial. You have the right to mount a defense. You have the right to have me appoint a lawyer to represent you because you are charged with a Class A misdemeanor and this is punishable by up to a year in jail and a $2,000 fine. You have a right to have the prosecution prove its case beyond a reasonable doubt. You have the right to see, hear, and question all the witnesses against you. You have the right to have me subpoena into court any evidence and/or witnesses in your favor. You have the right to appeal your decision to the Supreme Court, or the Superior Court for a jury trial *de novo* if I make an error of law or if you don't agree with my decision. By pleading guilty, you give up these rights."

The girl swallowed. "Well," she repeated. "I did pawn it."

"That's not the essence of the charge," Alex explained. "The essence of the charge is that you took that necklace even after you knew it was stolen."

"But I want to plead guilty," the girl said.

"You're telling me you didn't do what the charge said you did. You can't plead guilty to something you didn't do."

In the rear of the courtroom, a woman stood up. She looked like a poorly aged carbon copy of the defendant. "I told her to plead *not* guilty," the girl's mother said. "She came here today and she was going to do that, but then the prosecutor said she'd get a better deal if she said she was guilty."

The prosecutor sprung out of his chair like a jack-in-the-box. "I never said that, Your Honor. I told her what the deal on the table was, today, if she was pleading guilty, plain and simple. And that if she pled not guilty instead and went to trial, the deal was off the table and Your Honor would make the decision that you wanted to make."

Alex tried to imagine what it would be like to be this girl, completely overwhelmed by the massive stature of this legal system, unable to speak its language. She would look at the prosecutor and see Monty Hall. *Do you take the money? Or do you choose Door Number One—which might reveal a convertible, or might reveal a chicken?*

This girl had taken the money.

Alex motioned the prosecutor to approach the bench. "Do you have any evidence from your investigation to prove she knew it was stolen?"

"Yes, Your Honor." He produced the police report and handed it over. Alex scanned it—there was no way, given what she'd said to the cops and how they'd recorded it, that she hadn't known it was stolen.

Alex turned to the girl. "Based on the facts of the police report, coupled with the offer of proof, I find that there's a basis for your plea. There's enough evidence here to sub-stantiate the fact that you knew this necklace was stolen, and you took it anyway."

"I don't . . . I don't understand," the girl said.

"It means I'll take your plea, if you still want me to. But," Alex added, "first you have to tell me that you're guilty."

Alex watched the girl's mouth tighten and start to trem-ble. "Okay," she whispered. "I did it."

It was one of those incredibly beautiful autumn days, the kind when you drag your feet on the sidewalk in the morn-ing as you walk to school because you *cannot* believe you have to waste eight hours there. Josie was sitting in math class, staring at the blue of the sky—*cerulean*, that was a vocabulary word this week, and just saying it made Josie feel like her mouth was full of ice crystals. She could hear the seventh graders playing Capture the Flag in gym class in the recess yard, and the drone of the lawn mower as the custodian moved past their window. A piece of paper was dropped over her shoulder, into her lap. Josie unfolded it, read Peter's note.

> Why do we always have to solve for x? Why can't x do it himself and spare us the HELL!!!!!

She turned around, giving him a half-smile. Actually, she liked math. She loved knowing that if she worked hard enough, at the end there was going to be an answer that made sense.

She didn't fit in with the popular crowd at school because she was a straight-A student. Peter was different—he got B's and C's, and once a D. He didn't fit in either, but it wasn't because he was a brain. It was because he was Peter.

If there was a totem pole of unpopularity, Josie knew she still ranked relatively higher than some. Every now and then she wondered if she hung out with Peter because she enjoyed his company or because being with him made her feel better about herself.

While the class worked on the review sheet, Mrs. Rasmussin surfed the Internet. It was a schoolwide joke—who could catch her buying a pair of pants from Gap.com, or reading soap opera fansites. One kid swore he'd found her looking at porn one day when he went to her desk to ask a question.

Josie finished early, as usual, and looked up to see Mrs. Rasmussin at her computer . . . but there were tears streaming down her cheeks, in that strange way that happens when people do not even realize they are crying.

She stood up and walked out of the room without even saying a word to the class about being quiet in her absence.

The minute she left, Peter tapped on Josie's shoulder. "What's wrong with her?"

Before Josie could answer, Mrs. Rasmussin returned. Her face was as white as marble, and her lips were pressed together like a seam. "Class," she said, "something terrible has happened."

In the media center, where the middle school students had been herded, the principal told them what he knew: two planes had crashed into the World Trade Center. Another one had just crashed into the Pentagon. The south tower of the World Trade Center had collapsed.

The librarian had set up a television so that they could all watch the unfolding coverage. Even though they had been pulled out of class—usually a cause for celebration—it was so quiet in that library that Peter could hear his own heart pounding. He looked around the walls of the room, at the sky outside the windows. This school wasn't a safety zone. Nothing was, no matter what you'd been told.

Was this what it felt like to be at war?

Peter stared at the screen. People were sobbing and screaming in New York City, but you could barely see because of the dust and smoke in the air. There were fires everywhere, and the ululations of screaming fire engines and car alarms. It looked nothing like the New York Peter remembered the one time he'd vacationed there with his parents. They'd gone to the top of the Empire State Building and they were planning to have a fancy dinner at Windows on the World, but then Joey had gotten sick from eating too much popcorn and instead they'd headed back to the hotel.

Mrs. Rasmussin had left school for the day. Her brother was a bond trader in the World Trade Center.

Had been.

Josie was sitting next to Peter. Even with a few inches of space separating their chairs, he could feel her shaking. "Peter," she whispered, horrified, "there's people *jumping.*"

He couldn't see as well as she could, even with his glasses, but when he squinted he could tell Josie was right. It made his chest hurt to watch, as if his ribs were suddenly a size too small. What kind of person would *do* that?

He answered his own question: *The kind who doesn't see any other way out.*

"Do you think they could get us *here?*" Josie whispered.

Peter glanced at her. He wished he knew what to say to make her feel better, but the truth was, he didn't feel all that great himself and he didn't know if there were even any words in the English language to take away this kind of stunning shock, this understanding that the world isn't the place you thought it was.

He turned back to the screen so that he didn't have to answer Josie. More people leaped out of the windows of the north tower; then there was a massive roar as if the ground itself were opening its jaws. When the building collapsed, Peter let out the breath he'd been holding—relieved, because now he couldn't see anything at all.

The switchboards to the schools were completely jammed, and so parents fell into two categories: the ones who didn't want to scare their kids to death by showing up at school and shepherding them into a basement bunker, and those who wanted to ride out this tragedy with their children close at hand.

Lacy Houghton and Alex Cormier both fell into the latter category, and both arrived at the school simultaneously. They parked beside each other in the bus circle and got out of their cars, and only then recognized each other—they had not seen each other since the day Alex marched her daughter out of Lacy's basement, where the guns were kept. "Is Peter—" Alex began.

"I don't know. Josie?"

"I'm here to get her."

They went into the main office together, and were directed down the hall to the media center. "I can't believe they're letting them watch the news," Lacy said, running beside Alex.

"They're old enough to understand what's happening," Alex said.

Lacy shook her head. "*I'm* not old enough to understand what's happening."

The media center was spread with students—on chairs, on tables, sprawled on the floor. It took Alex a moment to realize what was so unnatural about the crowd: no one was making a sound. Even the teachers stood with their hands over their mouths, as if they were afraid to let out any of the emotion, because once the floodgates opened, everything else in their path would be swept away.

In the front of the room was a single television, and every eye was on it. Alex spotted Josie because she had stolen one of Alex's headbands—a leopard print. "Josie," she called, and her daughter whipped around, then nearly climbed over other kids in her effort to reach Alex.

Josie hit her like a hurricane, all emotion and fury, but Alex knew that somewhere inside was the eye of that storm. And then, like any force of nature, you had to brace yourself for another onslaught before things went back to normal. "Mommy," she sobbed. "Is it over?"

Alex didn't know what to say. As the parent, she was supposed to have all the answers, but she didn't. She was supposed to be able to keep her daughter safe, but she couldn't promise that either. She had to put on a brave face and tell Josie it was going to be fine, when she really didn't know that herself. Even driving here from court, she had been aware of the fragility of the roads beneath her wheels, of the divider of sky that could so easily be breached. She passed wells and thought about drinking-water contamination; she wondered how far away the closest nuclear power plant was.

And yet, she had spent years being the judge others expected her to be—someone cool and collected, someone who could reach conclusions without getting hysterical. She could certainly put on that demeanor for her daughter, too.

"We're fine," Alex said calmly. "It's over." She did not know that even as she spoke, a fourth plane was crashing into a field in Pennsylvania. She did not realize that her fierce grip on Josie contradicted her words.

Over Josie's shoulder Alex nodded to Lacy Houghton, who was leaving with her two sons in tow. With some shock she realized Peter was tall now, nearly as tall as a man.

How many years had it been since she'd seen him?

You could lose track of someone when you blinked, Alex realized. She vowed not to let that happen to her and her daughter. Because when it came down to it, being a judge didn't matter nearly as much as being a mother. When Alex's clerk had told her the news about the World Trade Center, her first thought had not been for her constituents . . . only for Josie.

For a few weeks, Alex held to her promises. She rearranged her docket so that she was home when Josie got there; she left legal briefs in the office instead of bringing them home to read on weekends; every night, over dinner, they *talked*—not just chatter, but real conversation: about why *To Kill a Mockingbird* might very well be the best book ever written; about how you could tell if you'd fallen in love; even about Josie's father. But then, one week, a particularly knotty case had her staying late at the office. And Josie started being able to sleep through the night again, instead of waking up screaming. Part of going back to normal meant erasing the boundaries of what was *abnormal*, and within a few months, the way Alex had felt on 9/11 was slowly forgotten, like a tide washing out a message she'd once scrawled on the sand.

Peter hated soccer, but he was on the middle school team. They had an anyone-can-play policy, so that even kids who might not normally make varsity or JV or—who was he kidding? the *team,* period—could join. It was this—plus his mother's belief that part of fitting in meant being in the crowd to begin with—that led him to a season of afternoon practices where he found himself doing passing drills and running after the ball more often than he returned it; and games twice a week where he warmed middle school soccer field benches all over Grafton County.

There was only one thing Peter hated more than soccer, and that was getting dressed for it. After school, he'd purposely find something to do at his locker, or a question to ask a teacher, so that he wound up in the locker room after most of his teammates were outside stretching and warming up. Then, in a corner section, Peter would strip without having to listen to anyone make fun of the way his chest sort of caved in at the bottom, or having the elastic of his boxers twisted to give him a wedgie. They called him Peter Homo, instead of Peter Houghton, and even when he was the only one in the locker room he could still hear the slap of their high-fives and the laughter that rolled toward him like an oil slick.

After practice, he usually was able to do something that ensured he would be the last one in the locker room—picking up the practice balls, asking the coach a question about an upcoming game, even retying his cleats. If he was really lucky, by the time he reached the showers, everyone else would already have left for home. But today, just as practice had ended, a thunderstorm had rolled in. The coach herded all the kids off the field and into the locker room.

Peter walked slowly into his corner bank of lockers. Several guys were already headed to the showers, towels wrapped around their waists. Drew, for one, and his friend Matt Royston. They were laughing as they walked, punching each other in the arms to see who could land the harder hit.

Peter turned his back to the other locker sections and skimmed off his uniform, then covered himself quickly with a towel. His heart was pounding. He could already imagine what everyone else saw when they looked at him, because he saw it, too, in the mirror: skin white as the belly of a fish; knobs sticking out of his spine and collarbones. Arms without a single rope of muscle.

The last thing Peter did was take off his glasses and put them on the shelf of his open locker. It made everything blissfully fuzzy.

He ducked his head and walked into the shower, pulling off his towel at the last possible minute. Matt and Drew were already soaping themselves up. Peter let the spray hit him in the forehead. He imagined being an adventurer on some wild white river, being pummeled by a waterfall as he was sucked into a vortex.

When he wiped his eyes and turned around, he could see the blurred edges of the bodies that were Matt and Drew. And the dark patch between their legs—pubic hair.

Peter didn't have any yet.

Matt suddenly twisted sideways. "Jesus Christ. Stop looking at my dick."

"Fucking fag," Drew said.

Peter immediately turned away. What if it turned out they were right? What if that was the reason his gaze had fallen right there at that moment? Worse, what if he got hard right now, which was happening more and more lately?

That would mean he was gay, wouldn't it?

"I wasn't looking at you," Peter blurted. "I can't see anything."

Drew's laughter bounced against the tile walls of the shower. "Maybe your dick's too small, Mattie."

Suddenly Matt had Peter by the throat. "I don't have my glasses on," Peter choked out. "That's why."

Matt let go, shoving Peter against the wall, then stalked out of the shower. He reached over and plucked Peter's towel from a hook, tossing it into the spray. It fell, soaked, to cover the central drain.

Peter picked it up and wrapped it around his waist. The cotton was sopping wet, and he was crying, but he thought maybe people couldn't tell because the rest of him was dripping, too. Everyone was staring.

When he was around Josie, he didn't feel anything—didn't want to kiss her or hold her hand or anything like that. He didn't think he felt those things about guys, either; but surely you had to be gay or straight. You couldn't be *neither*.

He hurried to the corner bank of lockers and found Matt standing in front of his. Peter squinted, trying to see what Matt was holding, and then he heard it: Matt took his glasses, slammed the locker door on them, and let the mangled frames drop to the floor. "Now you *can't* look at me," he said, and he walked away.

Peter knelt down on the floor, trying to pick up the broken pieces of glass. Because he couldn't see, he cut his hand. He sat, cross-legged, with the towel puddled in his lap. He brought his palm closer to his face, until everything was clear.

In her dream, Alex was walking down Main Street stark naked. She went into the bank and deposited a check. "Your Honor," the teller said, smiling. "Isn't it beautiful out today?"

Five minutes later, she went into the coffee shop and ordered a latte with skim milk. The barista was a girl with improbable purple hair and a straight piercing that went across the bridge of her nose at the level of her eyebrows; when Josie was little and they'd come here, Alex would have to tell her not to stare. "Would you like biscotti with that, Judge?" the barista asked.

She went into the bookstore, the pharmacy, and the gas station, and in each place, she could feel people staring at her. She knew she was naked. *They* knew she was naked. But no one said anything until she got to the post office. The postal clerk in Sterling was an old man who had been working there, probably, since the changeover from the Pony Express. He handed Alex a roll of stamps, and then furtively covered her hand with his own. "Ma'am, it might not be my place to say so . . ."

Alex lifted her gaze, waited.

The worry lines on the clerk's forehead smoothed. "But that's a beautiful dress you've got on, Your Honor," he said.

Her patient was screaming. Lacy could hear the girl sobbing all the way down the hall. She ran as fast as she could, turning the corner and entering the hospital room.

Kelly Gamboni was twenty-one years old, orphaned, and

had an IQ of 79. She had been gang-raped by three high school boys who were now awaiting trial at a juvy facility in Concord. Kelly lived at a group home for Catholics, so abortion was never an option. But now, an ER doctor had deemed it medically necessary to induce Kelly, at thirty-six weeks. She lay in the hospital bed with a nurse trying ineffectually to comfort her, as Kelly clutched a teddy bear. "Daddy," she cried, to a parent who had died years ago. "Take me home. Daddy, it hurts!"

The doctor walked into the room, and Lacy rounded on him.

"How dare you," she said. "This is my patient."

"Well, she was brought into the ER and became *mine*," the doctor countered.

Lacy looked at Kelly and then walked into the hall; it would do Kelly no good to have them fighting in front of her. "She came in complaining of wetting her underwear for two days. The exam was consistent with premature rupture of membranes," the doctor said. "She's afebrile and the fetal monitor tracing is reactive. It's completely reasonable to induce. *And* she signed off on the consent form."

"It may be reasonable, but it's not *advisable*. She's mentally retarded. She doesn't know what's happening to her right now; she's terrified. And she certainly doesn't have the ability to consent." Lacy turned on her heel. "I'm calling psych."

"Like hell you are," the doctor said, grabbing her arm.

"Let go of me!"

They were still screaming at each other five minutes later when the psych consult arrived. The boy who stood in front of Lacy looked to be about Joey's age. "You've got to be kidding," the doctor said, the first comment he'd made that she agreed with.

They both followed the shrink into Kelly's room. By

now, the girl was curled into a ball around her belly, whimpering. "She needs an epidural," Lacy muttered.

"It's not safe to give one at two centimeters," the doctor argued.

"I don't care. She needs one."

"Kelly?" the psychiatrist said, squatting down in front of her. "Do you know what a C-section is?"

"Uh-huh," Kelly groaned.

The psychiatrist stood up. "She's capable of consent, unless a court's ruled otherwise."

Lacy's jaw dropped. "That's *it*?"

"I have six other consults waiting for me," the psychiatrist snapped. "Sorry to disappoint you."

Lacy yelled after him. "I'm not the one you're disappointing!" She sank down beside Kelly and squeezed her hand. "It's okay. I'm going to take care of you." She winged a prayer to whoever might move the mountains that could be men's hearts. Then she lifted her face to the doctor's. "First do no harm," she said softly.

The doctor pinched the bridge of his nose. "I'll get her an epidural," he sighed; and only then did Lacy realize she had been holding her breath.

The last place Josie wanted to go was out to dinner with her mother, so that she could spend three hours watching maître d's and chefs and other guests suck up to her. This was *Josie's* birthday celebration, so she didn't really understand why she couldn't just demand take-out Chinese and a video. But her mother was insisting that it wouldn't be a celebration if they just stayed at home, and so here she was, trailing after her mother like a lady-in-waiting.

She'd been counting. There were four *Nice to see you, Your Honor*s. Three *Yes, Your Honor*s. Two *My pleasure, Your Honor*s. And one *For Your Honor, we have the best* *table in the house.* Sometimes Josie read about celebrities in *People* magazine who were always getting handouts from purse companies and shoe stores and free tickets to opening nights on Broadway and Yankee Stadium—when you got right down to it, her mother was a celebrity in the town of Sterling.

"I cannot believe," her mother said, "that I have a *twelve*-year-old."

"Is that my cue to say something like, you must have been a child prodigy?"

Her mother laughed. "Well, that would work."

"I'm going to be driving in three and a half years," Josie pointed out.

Her mother's fork clattered against the plate. "Thanks for *that.*"

The waiter came over to the table. "Your Honor," he said, setting a platter of caviar down in front of Josie's mother, "the chef would like you to have this appetizer with his compliments."

"That's so gross. Fish eggs?"

"Josie!" Her mother smiled stiffly at the waiter. "Please thank the chef."

She could feel her mother's eyes on her as she picked at her food. "What?" she challenged.

"Well, you sounded like a spoiled brat, that's all."

"Why? Because I don't like fish embryos sitting under my nose? *You* don't eat them either. *I* was at least being honest."

"And I was being discreet," her mother said. "Don't you think that the waiter is going to tell the chef that Judge Cormier's daughter is a piece of work?"

"Like I care?"

"*I* do. What you do reflects on me, and I have a reputation I have to protect."

"As what? A suck-up?"

"As someone who's above criticism both in and out of the courtroom."

Josie tilted her head to one side. "What if I did something bad?"

"Bad? How bad?"

"Let's say I was smoking pot," Josie said.

Her mother froze. "Is there something you want to tell me, Josie?"

"God, Mom, I'm not *doing* it. This is hypothetical."

"Because you know, now that you're in middle school, you're going to start coming across kids who do things that are dangerous—or just plain stupid—and I would hope you'd be—"

"—strong enough to know better than that," Josie finished, echoing her in a singsong. "Yeah. Got it. But what if, Mom? What if you came home and found me getting stoned in the living room? Would you turn me in?"

"What do you mean, turn you in?"

"Call the cops. Hand over my stash." Josie grinned. "Of hash."

"No," her mother said. "I would not report you."

Josie used to think, when she was younger, that she would grow up to look like her mother—fine-boned, dark-haired, light-eyed. The combination of elements were all there in her features, but as she'd gotten older, she started to look like someone else entirely—someone she had never met. Her father.

She wondered if her father—like Josie herself—could memorize things in a snap and picture them on the page just by closing his eyes. She wondered if her father sang off key and liked to watch scary movies. She wondered if he had the straight slash of eyebrows, so different from her mother's delicate arches.

She wondered, period.

"If you didn't report me because I'm your daughter," Josie said, "then you're not really being fair, are you?"

"I'd be acting like a parent, not a judge." Her mother reached across the table and put her hand on Josie's, which felt weird—her mother wasn't one of these touchy-feely types. "Josie, you can come to me, you know. If you need to talk, I'm there to listen. You're not going to get into legal trouble, no matter what you tell me—not if it's about you, not even if it's about your friends."

To be perfectly honest, Josie didn't have many of those. There was Peter, who she'd known forever—although Peter no longer came to her house and vice versa, they still hung out together in school, and he was the last person in the world Josie could ever imagine doing anything illegal. She knew that one of the reasons other girls excluded Josie was because she always stuck up for Peter, but she told herself that it didn't matter. She didn't really want to be surrounded by people who only cared about what happened on *One Life to Live* and who saved their babysitting money to go to The Limited; they seemed so fake sometimes that Josie thought if she poked one of them with a sharp pencil they'd burst like a balloon.

So what if she and Peter weren't popular? She was always telling Peter it didn't matter; she might as well start to believe it herself.

Josie pulled her hand away from her mother and pretended to be fascinated by her cream of asparagus soup. There was something about asparagus that she and Peter found hilarious. They'd done an experiment, once, to see how much you had to eat before your pee smelled weird, and it was less than two bites, swear to God.

"Stop using your Judge Voice," Josie said.

"My what?"

"Your Judge Voice. It's the one you use when you answer the phone. Or when you're out in public. Like now."

Her mother frowned. "That's crazy. It's the same voice I—"

The waiter glided over, as if he were skating across the dining room. "I don't mean to interrupt . . . is everything to your liking, Your Honor?"

Without missing a beat, her mother turned her face up to the waiter. "It's gorgeous," she said, and she smiled until he walked away. Then she turned to Josie. "It's the same voice I always use."

Josie looked at her, and then at the waiter's back. "Maybe it is," she said.

The other kid on the soccer team who would rather have been anywhere else was named Derek Markowitz. He'd introduced himself to Peter when they were sitting on the bench during a game against North Haverhill. "Who forced you to play?" Derek had asked, and Peter had told him his mother. "Mine too," Derek admitted. "She's a nutritionist and she's nuts about fitness."

At dinner, Peter would tell his parents that practice was going fine. He made up stories based on plays he'd seen other kids execute—athletic feats that he himself could never have done. He did this so that he could see his mother glance at Joey and say things like, "Guess there's more than one athlete in this family." When they came to cheer him on during games, and Peter never left the bench, he said it was because Coach played his favorites; and in a way, that was true.

Like Peter, Derek was just about the worst soccer player on the planet. He was so fair that his veins looked like a road map underneath his skin, and he had such pale hair that you had to search hard to find his eyebrows. Now, when they were at games, they sat next to each other on the bench. Peter liked him because he smuggled Snickers bars into practice and ate them when Coach wasn't looking, and because he knew how to tell a good joke: *Why did the ref stop the leper hockey game? There was a face-off in the corner. What's more fun than stapling Drew Girard to a wall? Ripping him off.* It got to the point where Peter actually was looking forward to soccer practice, just to hear what Derek had to say—although then Peter began to worry again if he liked Derek just because he was Derek, or because Peter was gay; and then he'd sit a little farther away, or tell himself that no matter what, he wouldn't look Derek in the eye for the whole practice, so that he didn't get the wrong idea.

They were sitting on the bench one Friday afternoon, watching everyone else play Rivendell. Sterling was expected to be able to kick their collective ass with their eyes closed (not that that was reason enough for the coach to put Peter or Derek in to actually play during a real league game). The score was climbing to something humiliating in the last minute of the final quarter—Sterling 24, Rivendell 2—and Derek was telling Peter another joke.

"A pirate walks into a bar with a parrot on his shoulder, a peg leg, and a steering wheel on his pants," Derek said. "The bartender says, 'Hey, you've got a steering wheel on your pants.' And the pirate goes, 'Arrrgh, I know. It's driving me nuts.'"

"Good game," the coach said, congratulating each of the players with a handshake. "Good game. Good game."

"You coming?" Derek asked, standing up.

"I'll meet you in there," Peter said, and as he leaned down to retie his cleats he saw a pair of lady's shoes stop in front of him—a pair he recognized, because he was always tripping over them in the mudroom.

"Hi, baby," his mother said, smiling down.

Peter choked. What middle school kid had Mommy come to pick him up right at the field, as if he were leaving nursery school and needed a hand crossing the street?

"Just give me a second, Peter," his mother said.

He glanced up long enough to see that the team had not gone into the locker room, as usual, but hung around to watch this latest humiliation. Just when he thought it couldn't get any worse, his mother marched up to the coach. "Coach Yarbrowski," she said. "Could I have a word?"

Kill me now, Peter thought.

"I'm Peter's mother. And I'm wondering why you don't play my son during the games."

"It's a matter of teamwork, Mrs. Houghton, and I'm just giving Peter the chance to come up to speed with some of the other—"

"It's halfway through the season, and my son has just as much right to play on this soccer team as any of the other boys."

"Mom," Peter interrupted, wishing that there were earthquakes in New Hampshire, that a ravine would open under her feet and swallow her mid-sentence. "Stop."

"It's all right, Peter. I'm taking care of it."

The coach pinched the bridge of his nose. "I'll put Peter in on Monday's game, Mrs. Houghton, but it isn't going to be pretty."

"It doesn't have to be pretty. It just has to be *fun.*" She turned around and smiled, clueless, at Peter. "Right?"

Peter could barely hear her. Shame was a shot that rang in his ears, broken only by the buzz of his teammates. His mother squatted down in front of him. He had never really understood what it meant to love someone and hate them at the same time, but now he was starting to get it. "Once he sees you on that field, you'll be playing first string." She patted his knee. "I'll wait for you in the parking lot."

The other players laughed as he pushed past them. "Mama's boy," they said. "Does she fight all your battles, homo?"

In the locker room, he sat down and pulled off his cleats. He had a hole in the toe of one sock, and he stared at it as if he were truly amazed by that fact, instead of because he was trying so hard not to cry.

He nearly jumped out of his skin when he felt someone sit down beside him. "Peter," Derek said. "You okay?"

Peter tried to say yes, but just couldn't get the lie through his throat.

"What's the difference between this team and a porcupine?" Derek asked.

Peter shook his head.

"A porcupine has pricks on the outside." Derek grinned. "See you Monday."

Courtney Ignatio was a spaghetti-strap girl. That's what Josie called that posse, for lack of a better term—the girls who wore belly-baring tanks and who, during the student-run recitals, made up dances to the songs "Bootylicious" and "Lady Marmalade." Courtney had been the first seventh grader to get a cell phone. It was pink, and sometimes it even rang in class, but teachers never got angry at her.

When she was paired with Courtney in social studies to make a timeline of the American Revolution, Josie had groaned—she was sure she'd be pulling all the weight. But Courtney had invited her over to work on the project, and Josie's mother told her that if she didn't go, she *would* be stuck doing all the work, so now she was sitting on Courtney's bed, eating chocolate chip cookies and organizing note cards.

"What?" Courtney said, standing in front of her with her hands on her hips.

"What *what?*"

"Why do you have that look on your face?"

Josie shrugged. "Your room. It's totally different than mine."

Courtney glanced around, as if seeing her bedroom for the first time. "Different how?"

Courtney had a wild purple shag rug and beaded lamps strung with gauzy silk scarves for atmosphere. An entire dresser top was dedicated to makeup. A poster of Johnny Depp hung on the back of her door, and a shelf sported a state-of-the-art stereo system. She had her own DVD player.

Josie's room, in comparison, was spartan. She had a bookshelf, a desk, a dresser, and a bed. Her comforter looked like an old-lady quilt, compared to Courtney's satin one. If Josie had any style at all, it was Early American Dork.

"Just different," Josie said.

"My mom's a decorator. She thinks this is what every teenage girl dreams of."

"*Do* you?"

Courtney shrugged. "I kind of think it looks like a bordello, but I don't want to ruin it for her. Let me just go get my binder, and we can start . . ."

When she left to go back downstairs, Josie found herself staring into the mirror. Drawn forward to the dresser with makeup on it, she found herself picking up tubes and bottles that were completely unfamiliar. Her mother rarely wore any makeup—maybe lipstick, but that was it. Josie lifted a mascara wand and unscrewed the cap, ran her finger over the black bristles. She uncapped a bottle of perfume and sniffed.

In the reflection of the mirror, she watched the girl who

looked just like her take a tube of lipstick—"Positively Hot!" the label read—and apply it. It put a bloom of color in her face; it brought her to life.

Was it really that easy to become someone else?

"*What* are you doing?"

Josie jumped at the sound of Courtney's voice. She watched in the mirror as Courtney came forward and took the lipstick out of her hands.

"I . . . I'm sorry," Josie stammered.

To her surprise, Courtney Ignatio grinned. "Actually," she said, "it suits you."

Joey got better grades than his younger brother; he was a better athlete than Peter. He was funnier; he had more common sense; he could draw more than a straight line; he was the one people gravitated toward at a party. There was only one thing, as far as Peter could tell (and he'd been counting), that Joey could not do, and that was stand the sight of blood.

When Joey was seven and his best friend went over the handlebars of his bike and opened a cut over his forehead, it was Joey who passed out. When a medical show was on television, he had to leave the room. Because of this, he'd never gone hunting with his father, although Lewis had promised his boys that as soon as they turned twelve, they were old enough to come out with him and learn how to shoot.

It seemed as if Peter had been waiting all fall for this weekend. He had been reading up on the rifle his father was going to let him use—a Winchester Model 94 lever action 30-30 that had been his father's, before the purchase of the bolt-action Remington 721 30.06 he used now to hunt deer. Now, at 4:30 in the morning, Peter could barely believe he was holding it in his hands, the safety carefully locked. He crept through the woods behind his father, his breath crystallizing in the air.

It had snowed last night—which was why the conditions were perfect for deer hunting. They'd been out yesterday to find fresh scrapes—spots on live trees where a buck had rubbed his antlers and returned to scrape over and over, marking its territory. Now it was just a matter of finding the same spot and checking for fresh tracks, to see if the buck had come through yet.

The world was different when there was no one in it. Peter tried to match his father's footsteps, setting his boot into the print left behind by his father. He pretended he was in the army, on a guerrilla mission. The enemy was right around the corner. At any moment now, he might be surprised into an exchange of fire.

"Peter," his father hissed over his shoulder. "Keep your rifle pointed up!"

They approached the ring of trees where they'd seen the rub. Today, the antler scrapes were fresh, the white flesh of the tree and the pale green strip of peeled bark chafed raw. Peter looked down at his feet. There were three sets of tracks—one much larger than the other two.

"He's already been through here," Peter's father murmured. "He's probably following the does." Deer in rut weren't as smart as usual—they were so focused on the does they were chasing, they forgot to avoid the humans who might be hunting them.

Peter and his father walked softly through the woods, following tracks toward the swamp. Suddenly, his father stuck out his hand—a signal to stop. Glancing up, Peter could see two does—one older, one a yearling. His father turned, mouthing, *Don't move.*

When the buck stepped out from behind the tree, Peter stopped breathing. It was massive, majestic. Its thick neck supported the weight of a six-point rack. Peter's father nod-ded imperceptibly at the gun. *Go ahead.*

Peter fumbled with the rifle, which felt thirty pounds heavier. He lifted it to his shoulder and got the deer in his sights. His pulse was pounding so hard that the gun kept shaking.

He could hear his father's instructions as if they were being whispered aloud even now: *Shoot underneath the front leg, low on the body. If you hit the heart, you'll kill it instantly. If you miss the heart, you'll get the lungs, so it will run for a hundred yards or so and then drop.*

Then the deer turned and looked at him, eyes trained on Peter's face.

Peter squeezed the trigger, sending the shot wide.

On purpose.

The three deer ducked in unison, unsure of where the danger was. Just as Peter wondered whether or not his father had noticed that he wimped out—or simply as-sumed Peter was a lousy shot—a second shot rang from his father's rifle. The does bolted away; the buck dropped like a stone.

Peter stood over the deer, watching blood pump from its heart. "I didn't mean to steal your shot," his father said, "but if you'd reloaded, they would have heard you and run."

"No," Peter said. He could not tear his eyes from the deer. "It's okay." Then he vomited into the scrub brush.

He could hear his father doing something behind him, but he wouldn't turn around. Instead Peter stared hard at a patch of snow that had already begun to melt. He felt his fa-ther approach. Peter could smell the blood on his hands, the disappointment.

Peter's father reached out, patting his shoulder. "Next time," he sighed.

*   *   *

Dolores Keating had transferred to the middle school this year in January. She was one of those kids that slipped by unnoticed—not too pretty, not too smart, not a trouble-maker. She sat in front of Peter in French class, her pony-tail bobbing up and down as she conjugated verbs out loud.

One day, as Peter was doing his best not to fall asleep to Madame's recitation of the verb *avoir*, he noticed that Do-lores was sitting in the middle of an ink stain. He thought that was pretty funny, given that she was wearing white pants, and then he realized that it wasn't ink at all.

"Dolores has her period!" he cried out loud, out of sheer shock. In a house full of males—with the exception of his mother, of course—menstruation was one of those great mysteries about women, like how do they put on mascara without poking out their eyes and how can they hook a bra behind themselves, without seeing what they're doing?

Everyone in the class turned, and Dolores's face went as scarlet as her pants. Madame ushered her into the hall, sug-gesting she go to the nurse. On the seat in front of Peter was a small red puddle of blood. Madame called the custodian, but by then, the class was out of control—whispers raging like a brush fire about how much blood there was, how Do-lores was now one of the girls that everyone knew had her period.

"Keating's bleeding," Peter said to the kid sitting next to him, whose eyes lit up.

"Keating's bleeding," the boy repeated, and the chant went around the room. *Keating's bleeding. Keating's bleed-ing.* Across the room, Peter caught Josie's eye—Josie, who'd started to wear makeup lately. She was singing along with the rest of them.

Belonging felt like helium; Peter felt himself swell in-side. He'd been the one to start this; by drawing a line around Dolores, he'd become part of the inner circle.

At lunch that day, he was sitting with Josie when Drew Girard and Matt Royston came over with their trays. "We heard that you saw it happen," Drew said, and they sat down so that Peter could tell them the details. He began embellishing—a teaspoon of blood became a cup; the stain on her white pants grew from a modest spot to a Rorschach blot of enormous proportion. They called over their friends—some who were kids on Peter's soccer team, yet hadn't spoken to him all year. "Tell them, too, it's hilarious," Matt said, and he smiled at Peter as if Peter were one of them.

Dolores stayed out of school. Peter knew that it wouldn't have made any difference if she was gone for a month or more—the memories of sixth graders were steel traps, and for the rest of her high school career, Dolores would always be remembered as the girl who got her period in French class and bled all over the seat.

The morning that she came back, she stepped off the bus and was immediately flanked by Drew and Matt. "For a *woman*," they said, drawing out the words, "you sure don't have any boobs." She pushed away from them, and Peter didn't see her again until French class.

Someone—he really didn't know who—had come up with a plan. Madame was always late to class; she had to come from the other end of the school. So before the bell rang, everyone would walk up to Dolores's desk and hand her a tampon they'd been given by Courtney Ignatio, who'd pilfered a box from her mother.

Drew was first. As he set the tampon on her desk he said, "I think you might have dropped this." Six tampons later, the bell still hadn't rung, and Madame wasn't in the room yet. Peter walked up, holding the wrapped tube in his fist, ready to drop it—and noticed Dolores was crying.

It wasn't loud, and it was barely even visible. But as

Peter reached out with the tampon, he suddenly realized that this was what it looked like from the other side, when *he* was being put through hell.

Peter crushed the tampon in his fist. "Stop," he said softly, and then he turned around to the next three students waiting in line to humiliate Dolores. "Just stop already."

"What's your problem, homo?" Drew asked.

"It's not funny anymore."

Maybe it was never funny. It was just that it hadn't been *him*, and that was good enough.

The boy behind him shoved Peter out of the way and flicked his tampon so that it bounced off Dolores's head, rolled underneath Peter's seat. And then it was Josie's turn.

She looked at Dolores, and then she looked at Peter. "Don't," he murmured.

Josie pressed her lips together and let the tampon roll from her outstretched fingers onto Dolores's desk. "Oops," she said, and when Matt Royston laughed, she went to stand beside him.

Peter was lying in wait. Although Josie hadn't been walking with him for a few weeks now, he knew what she was doing after school—usually strolling into town to get an iced tea with Courtney & Co. and then window-shopping. Sometimes he stood back at a distance and watched her the way you'd stare at a butterfly that you'd only known as a caterpillar, wondering how the hell change could be that dramatic.

He waited until she'd left the other girls, and then he followed her down the street that led to her house. When he caught up to her and grabbed her arm, she shrieked.

"God!" she said. "Peter, why don't you just scare me to death!"

He had worked out what he was going to ask her in his

mind, because words didn't come easily to him, and he knew that he had to practice them more than others would; but when he had Josie this close, after everything that had happened, every question felt like a slap. Instead, he sank onto the curb, spearing his hands through his hair. "Why?" he asked.

She sat down next to him, folding her arms over her knees. "I'm not doing it to hurt you."

"You're such a fake with them."

"I'm just not the way I am with you," Josie said.

"Like I said: fake."

"There's different kinds of real."

Peter scoffed. "If that's what those jerks are teaching you, it's bullshit."

"They're not teaching me anything," Josie argued. "I'm there because I *like* them. They're fun and funny and when I'm with them—" She broke off abruptly.

"*What?*" Peter prompted.

Josie looked him in the eye. "When I'm with them," she said, "people like *me*."

Peter guessed change *could* be that dramatic: in an instant, you could go from wanting to kill someone to wanting to kill yourself.

"I won't let them make fun of you anymore," Josie promised. "That's a silver lining, right?"

Peter didn't respond. This wasn't about him.

"I just . . . I just can't really hang out with you right now," Josie explained.

He lifted his face. "*Can't?*"

Josie stood up, backing away from him. "I'll see you around, Peter," she said, and she walked out of his life.

You can feel people staring; it's like heat that rises from the pavement during summer, like a poker in the small of your back. You don't have to hear a whisper, either, to know that it's about you.

I used to stand in front of the mirror in the bathroom to see what they were staring at. I wanted to know what made their heads turn, what it was about me that was so incredibly different. At first I couldn't tell. I mean, I was just me.

Then one day, when I looked in the mirror, I understood. I looked into my own eyes and I hated myself, maybe as much as all of them did.

That was the day I started to believe they might be right.

Ten Days After

Josie waited until she could no longer hear the television in her mother's bedroom—Leno, not Letterman—and then rolled onto her side to watch the LED acrobatics of the digital clock. When it was 2:00 a.m., she decided it was safe, and she pulled back her covers and got out of bed.

She knew how to sneak downstairs. She'd done it a couple of times before, meeting Matt outside in the backyard. One night, he'd texted her on her cell—*1/2 2 C U now*. She had gone out to him in her pajamas, and for a moment when he touched her she actually thought she would slip through his fingers.

There was only one landing where the floorboards creaked, and Josie knew enough to step over it. Downstairs, she rummaged through the stack of DVDs for the one she wanted—the one she didn't want to be caught viewing. Then she turned on the television, muting the sound so low she had to sit right on top of the screen and its built-in speakers to hear.

The first person shown was Courtney. She held up her hand, blocking whoever had been videotaping. She was laughing, though; her long hair falling over her features like a screen of silk. Offscreen, Brady Pryce's voice: *Give us something for* Girls Gone Wild, *Court.* The camera fuzzed out for a moment, and then there was a close-up of a birthday cake. HAPPY SWEET SIXTEEN, JOSIE. A run of faces, including Haley Weaver's, singing to her.

Josie paused the DVD. There was Courtney, and Haley, and Maddie, and John, and Drew. She touched her finger to each of their foreheads, getting a tiny electric shock each time.

At her birthday party, they'd had a barbecue at Storrs Pond. There were hot dogs and hamburgers and sweet corn. They had forgotten the ketchup and someone had to drive back into town to buy some at a mini-mart. Courtney's card had been signed BFF, best friends forever, even though Josie knew she'd written the same thing on Maddie's card a month earlier.

By the time the screen fuzzed out again and her own face came on, Josie was crying. She knew what was coming; she remembered this part. The camera panned back and there was Matt, his arms around her as she sat on his lap on the sand. He had taken off his shirt, and Josie remembered that his skin had been warm where it pressed up against hers.

How could you be so alive one moment, and then have everything stop—not just your heart and your lungs, but the way you smiled slowly, the left side of your mouth curling before the right; and the pitch of your voice; and the habit you had of tugging at your hair when you were doing your math homework?

I can't live without you, Matt used to say, and now Josie realized he wouldn't have to.

She couldn't stop sobbing, so Josie pushed her fist into her mouth to keep herself from making noise. She watched Matt on the screen the way you might study an animal you had never seen before, if you had to memorize it and tell the world later what you'd found. Matt's hand splayed across her bare stomach, grazed the edge of her bikini top. She watched herself push him away, blush. "Not here," her voice said, a funny voice, a voice that didn't sound like Josie to her own ears. You never did, when you heard yourself on tape.

"Then let's go somewhere else," Matt said.

Josie ruched up the edge of her pajama top, until she could reach underneath. She spread her own hand across her belly. She edged her thumb up, like Matt had, to the curve of her breast. She tried to pretend it was him.

He had given her a gold locket for that birthday, one she hadn't taken off since that day nearly six months ago. Josie was wearing it on the DVD. She remembered that when she'd looked at it in the mirror, Matt's thumbprint had been on the back, left behind after he clasped it around her neck. That had seemed so intimate, and for a few days, she had done everything she could to keep it from rubbing off.

On the night that Josie had met Matt out in her own backyard, beneath the moon, he'd laughed at her pajamas, printed all over with pictures of Nancy Drew. *What were you doing when I texted you?* he asked.

Sleeping. Why did you have to see me in the middle of the night?

To make sure you were dreaming about me, he said.

On the DVD, someone called out Matt's name. He turned, grinning. His teeth were wolf's teeth, Josie thought. Sharp, impossibly white. He stamped a kiss on Josie's mouth. "Be right back," he said.

Be right back.

She pressed Pause again, just as Matt stood up. Then she reached around her neck and ripped the locket off its thin gold chain. She unzipped one of the couch cushions and pushed the necklace deep inside the stuffing.

She turned off the television. She pretended that Matt would be suspended like that forever, inches away from Josie so that she could still reach out and grab him, even though she knew that the DVD would reset itself even before she left the room.

Lacy had known they were out of milk; that morning, as she and Lewis sat like zombies at the kitchen table, she had brought it up:

I hear it's going to rain again.

We're out of milk.

Have you heard from Peter's lawyer?

It devastated Lacy to know that she could not visit Peter again for another week—jail rules. It killed her to know Lewis hadn't been there to see him at *all* yet. How was she supposed to go through the motions of an ordinary day, knowing that her son was sitting in a cell less than twenty miles away?

There was a point where the events of your life became a tsunami; Lacy knew, because she'd been washed away once before by grief. When that happened, you would find yourself days later on unfamiliar ground, rootless. The only other choice you had was to move to higher ground while you still could.

Which is why Lacy found herself at a gas station buying a carton of milk, although all gut instinct told her to crawl under the covers and sleep. This was not as easy as it seemed: to get the milk, she had to first back out of her garage with reporters slapping the car windows and blocking her path. She had to elude the news van that followed her to the highway. As a result, she found herself paying for

the milk at a service station in Purmort, New Hampshire—
one she rarely frequented.

"That's $2.59," the cashier said.

Lacy opened her wallet and extracted three dollar bills.
Then she noticed the small, hand-lettered display at the
register. *Memorial Fund for the Victims of Sterling High*,
the sign read, and there was a coffee can to hold the donations.

She started shaking.

"I know," the cashier sympathized. "It's just tragic,
isn't it?"

Lacy's heart was pounding so fiercely she was certain
the clerk would hear it.

"You've got to wonder about the parents, don't you? I
mean, how could they *not* have known?"

Lacy nodded, afraid that even the sound of her voice
would ruin her anonymity. It was almost too easy to agree:
Had there ever been a more awful child? A worse mother?

It was simple to say that behind every terrible child
stood a terrible parent, but what about the ones who had
done the best they could? What about the ones, like Lacy,
who had loved unconditionally, protected ferociously, cher-
ished mightily—and still had raised a murderer?

I didn't know, Lacy wanted to say. *It's not my fault.*

But she stayed silent because—truth be told—she
wasn't quite sure she believed that.

Lacy emptied the contents of her wallet into the coffee
can, bills and coins. Numb, she walked out of the gas station, leaving the carton of milk on the counter.

She had nothing left inside. She'd given it all to her son.
And that was the greatest heartbreak of all—no matter how
spectacular we want our children to be, no matter how perfect we pretend they are, they are bound to disappoint. As it

turns out, kids are more like us than we think: damaged, through and through.

Ervin Peabody, the professor of psychiatry at the college, offered to run a grief session for the entire town of Sterling at the white clapboard church in its center. There was a tiny line item in the daily paper and purple flyers posted at the coffee shop and bank, but that was enough to spread the word. By the time the meeting convened at 7:00 p.m., cars were parked as far as a half mile away; people spilled through the open doors of the church onto the street. The press, which had come en masse to cover the meeting, was turned away by a battalion of Sterling policemen.

Selena pressed the baby closer against her chest as another wave of townspeople pushed past her. "Did you know it was going to be like this?" she whispered to Jordan.

He shook his head, eyes roaming over the crowd. He recognized some of the same people who'd come to the arraignment, but also a host of other faces that were new, and that wouldn't have been intimately connected to the high school: the elderly, the college kids, the couples with young babies. They had come because of the ripple effect, because one person's trauma is another's loss of innocence.

Ervin Peabody sat in the front of the room, beside the police chief and the principal of Sterling High. "Hello," he said, standing up. "We've called this session tonight because we're all still reeling. Nearly overnight, the landscape's changed around us. We may not have all the answers, but we thought it might be beneficial for us to start to talk about what's happened. And maybe more importantly, to listen to each other."

A man stood up in the second row, holding his jacket in his hands. "I moved here five years ago, because my wife and I wanted to get away from the craziness of New York

City. We were starting a family, and were looking for a place that was . . . well, just a little bit kinder and gentler. I mean, when you drive down the street in Sterling you get honked at by people who know you. You go to the bank and the teller remembers your name. There aren't places like that in America anymore, and now . . ." He broke off.

"And now Sterling's not one either," Ervin finished. "I know how difficult it can be when the image you've had of something doesn't match its reality; when the friend beside you turns into a monster."

"Monster?" Jordan whispered to Selena.

"Well, what is he *supposed* to say? That Peter was a time bomb? *That'll* make them all feel safe."

The psychiatrist looked out over the crowd. "I think that the very fact that you're all here tonight shows that Sterling hasn't changed. It may not ever be normal again, as we know it. . . . We're going to have to figure out a new kind of normal."

A woman raised her hand. "What about the high school? Are our kids going to have to go back inside there?"

Ervin glanced at the police chief, the principal. "It's still the site of an active investigation," the chief said.

"We're hoping to finish out the year in a different location," the principal added. "We're in talks with the superintendent's office in Lebanon, to see if we can use one of their empty schools."

Another woman's voice: "But they're going to have to go back sometime. My daughter's only ten, and she's terrified about walking into that high school, ever. She wakes up in the middle of the night screaming. She thinks there's someone with a gun there, waiting for her."

"Be happy she's able to have nightmares," a man replied. He was standing next to Jordan, his arms folded, his eyes a livid red. "Go in there every night, when she cries, and hold her and tell her you'll keep her safe. Lie to her, just like I did."

A murmur rolled through the church, like a ball of yarn being unraveled. *That's Mark Ignatio. The father of one of the dead.*

Just like that, a fault line opened up in Sterling—a ravine so deep and bleak that it would not be bridged for many years. There was already a difference in this town, between those who had lost children and those who still had them to worry about.

"Some of you knew my daughter Courtney," Mark said, pushing away from the wall. "Maybe she babysat for your kids. Or served you a burger at the Steak Shack in the summer. Maybe you'd recognize her by sight, because she was a beautiful, beautiful girl." He turned to the front of the stage. "You want to tell me how I'm supposed to figure out a new kind of normal, Doc? You wouldn't dare suggest that one day, it gets easier. That I'll be able to move past this. That I'll forget my daughter is lying in a grave, while some psychopath is still alive and well." Suddenly the man turned to Jordan. "How can you live with yourself?" he accused. "How the hell can you sleep at night, knowing you're *defending* that sonofabitch?"

Every eye in the room turned to Jordan. Beside him, he could feel Selena press Sam's face against her chest, shielding the baby. Jordan opened his mouth to speak, but couldn't find a single word.

The sound of boots coming up the aisle distracted him. Patrick Ducharme was headed straight for Mark Ignatio. "I can't imagine the pain you're feeling, Mark," Patrick said, his gaze locked on the grieving man's. "And I know you have every right to come here and be upset. But the way our country works, someone's innocent until they're proven guilty. Mr. McAfee's just doing his job." He clapped his hand on Mark's shoulder and lowered his voice. "Why don't you and I grab a cup of coffee?"

As Patrick led Mark Ignatio toward the exit, Jordan remembered what he had wanted to say. "I live here, too," he began.

Mark turned around. "Not for long."

Alex was not short for Alexandra, like most people assumed. Her father had simply given her the name of the son he would have preferred to have.

After Alex's mother had died of breast cancer when she was five, her father had raised her. He wasn't the kind of dad who showed her how to ride a bike or to skip stones—instead, he taught her the Latin words for things like *faucet* and *octopus* and *porcupine*; he explained to her the Bill of Rights. She used academics to get his attention: winning spelling bees and geography contests, netting a string of straight A's, getting into every college she applied to.

She wanted to be just like her father: the kind of man who walked down the street and had storekeepers nod to him in awe: *Good afternoon, Judge Cormier.* She wanted to hear the change in tone of a receptionist's voice when the woman heard it was Judge Cormier on the line.

If her father never held her on his lap, never kissed her good night, never told her he loved her—well, it was all part of the persona. From her father, Alex learned that everything could be distilled into facts. Comfort, parenting, love—all of these could be boiled down and explained, rather than experienced. And the law—well, the law supported her father's belief system. Any feelings you had in the context of a courtroom had an explanation. You were given permission to be emotional, in a logical setting. What you felt for your clients was not really what was in your own heart, or so you could pretend, so that no one ever got close enough to hurt you.

Alex's father had had a stroke when she was a second-year law student. She had sat on the edge of his hospital bed and told him she loved him.

"Oh, Alex," he'd sighed. "Let's not bother with that."

She hadn't cried at his funeral, because she knew that's what he would have wanted.

Had her own father wished, as she did now, that the basis of their relationship had been different? Had he eventually given up hoping, settling for teacher and student instead of parent and child? How long could you march along on a parallel track with your child before you lost any chance of intersecting her life?

She'd read countless websites about grief and its stages; she'd studied the aftermath of other school shootings. She could do research, but when she tried to connect with Josie, her daughter looked at her as if she'd never seen her before. At other times, Josie burst into tears. Alex didn't know how to combat either outcome. She felt incompetent—and then she'd remember that this wasn't about *her*, it was about *Josie*—and she'd feel even more like a failure.

The great irony hadn't escaped Alex: she was more like her father than he ever might have guessed. She felt comfortable in her courtroom, in a way she did not feel in the confines of her own home. She knew just what to say to a defendant who'd come in with his third DUI charge, but she couldn't sustain a five-minute conversation with her own child.

Ten days after the shooting at Sterling High, Alex went into Josie's bedroom. It was midafternoon and the curtains were shut tight; Josie was hidden in the cocoon she'd made of her bedcovers. Although her immediate instinct was to snap open the shades and let the sunlight in, Alex lay down on the bed instead. She wrapped her arms around the bundle that was her daughter. "When you were little," Alex said, "sometimes I'd come in here and sleep with you."

There was a shifting, and the sheets fell away from Josie's face. Her eyes were red-rimmed, her face swollen. "Why?"

She shrugged. "I was never a big fan of thunderstorms."

"How come I never woke up and found you here?"

"I always went back to my own bed. I was supposed to be the tough one. . . . I didn't want you to think I was scared of anything."

"Supermom," Josie whispered.

"But I'm scared of losing you," Alex said. "I'm scared it's already happened."

Josie stared at her for a moment. "I'm scared of losing me, too."

Alex sat up and tucked Josie's hair behind her ear. "Let's get out of here," she suggested.

Josie froze. "I don't want to go out."

"Sweetheart, it would be good for you. It's like physical therapy, but for the brain. Go through the motions, the pattern of your everyday life, and eventually you remember how to do it naturally."

"You don't understand . . ."

"If you don't try, Jo," she said, "then that means he wins."

Josie's head snapped up. Alex didn't have to tell her who *he* was. "Did you guess?" Alex heard herself asking.

"Guess what?"

"That he might do this?"

"Mom, I don't want to—"

"I keep thinking about him as a little boy," Alex said.

Josie shook her head. "That was a really long time ago," she murmured. "People change."

"I know. But sometimes I can still see him handing you that rifle—"

"We were little," Josie interrupted, her eyes filling with tears. "We were stupid." She pushed back the covers, in a sudden hurry. "I thought you wanted to go somewhere."

Alex looked at her. A lawyer would press the point. A mother, though, might not.

Minutes later, Josie was sitting in the passenger seat of the car beside Alex. She buckled the seat belt, then unlatched it, then secured it again. Alex watched her tug on the belt to make sure it would lock up.

She pointed out the obvious as they drove—that the first daffodils had pushed their brave heads through the snow on the median strip of Main Street; that the Sterling College crew team was training on the Connecticut River, the bows of their boats breaking through the residual ice. That the temperature gauge in the car said it was more than fifty degrees. Alex intentionally took the long route—the one that did not go past the school. Only once did Josie's head turn to look at the scenery, and that was when they passed the police station.

Alex pulled into a parking spot in front of the diner. The street was filled with lunchtime shoppers and busy pedestrians, carrying boxes to be mailed and talking on cell phones and glancing into store windows. To anyone who didn't know better, it was business as usual in Sterling. "So," Alex said, turning to Josie. "How are we doing?"

Josie looked down at her hands in her lap. "Okay."

"It's not as bad as you thought, is it?"

"Not yet."

"My daughter the optimist." Alex smiled at her. "You want to split a BLT and a salad?"

"You haven't even looked at a menu yet," Josie said, and they both got out of the car.

Suddenly a rusted Dodge Dart ran the light at the head of Main Street, backfiring as it sped away. "Idiot," Alex muttered, "I should get his plate number . . ." She broke off when she realized that Josie had vanished. "Josie!"

Then Alex saw her daughter, pressed against the sidewalk, where she'd flattened herself. Her face was white, her body trembling.

Alex knelt beside her. "It was a car. Just a car." She helped Josie to her knees. All around them, people were watching and pretending not to.

Alex shielded Josie from their view. She had failed again. For someone renowned for her good judgment, she suddenly seemed to be lacking any. She thought of something she'd read on the Internet—how sometimes, when it came to grief, you could take one step forward and then three steps back. She wondered why the Internet did not add that when someone you loved was hurting, it cut you right to the bone, too. "All right," Alex said, her arm anchored tight around Josie's shoulders. "Let's get you back home."

Patrick had taken to living, eating, and sleeping his case. At the station, he acted cool and in command—he was the point man, after all, for all those investigators—but at home, he questioned every move he made. On his refrigerator were the pictures of the dead; on his bathroom mirror he'd created a dry-erase marker timeline of Peter's day. He sat awake in the middle of the night, writing lists of questions: What was Peter doing at home before leaving for school? What else was on his computer? Where did he learn to shoot? How did he get guns? Where did the anger come from?

During the day, however, he plowed through the massive amount of information to be processed, and the even more massive amount of information to be gleaned. Now, Joan McCabe sat across from him. She had cried her way through the last box of Kleenex at the station, and was now wadding paper towels up in her fist. "I'm sorry," she said to Patrick. "I thought this would get easier the more I do it."

"I don't think that's how it works," he said gently. "I do appreciate you taking the time to speak to me about your brother."

Ed McCabe had been the only teacher killed in the shooting. His classroom had been at the top of the stairs, en route to the gymnasium; he'd had the bad fortune to come out and try to stop what was happening. According to school records, Peter had had McCabe as a math teacher in tenth grade. He'd gotten B's. No one else could remember his not getting along with McCabe that year; most of the other students hadn't even recalled Peter being in the class.

"There's really nothing else I can tell you," Joan said. "Maybe Philip remembers something."

"Your husband?"

Joan looked up at him. "No. That's Ed's partner."

Patrick leaned back in his chair. "Partner. As in—"

"Ed was gay," Joan said.

It might be something, but then again, it might not. For all Patrick knew, Ed McCabe—who'd been just a hapless victim a half hour ago—could have been the reason Peter started shooting.

"No one at the school knew," Joan said. "I think he was afraid of backlash. He told people in town that Philip was his old college roommate."

Another victim—one who was still alive—was Natalie Zlenko. She'd been shot in the side and had to have her liver resected. Patrick thought he remembered seeing her name listed as president of the GLAAD club at Sterling

High. She'd been one of the first people shot; McCabe had been one of the last.

Maybe Peter Houghton was homophobic.

Patrick handed Joan his card. "I'd really like to talk to Philip," he said.

Lacy Houghton set a teapot and a plate of celery in front of Selena. "I don't have any milk. I went to buy some, but . . ." Her voice trailed off, and Selena tried to fill in the blanks.

"I really appreciate you talking to me," Selena said. "Whatever you can tell me, we'll use to help Peter."

Lacy nodded. "Anything," she said. "Anything you want to know."

"Well, let's start with the easy stuff. Where was he born?"

"Right at Dartmouth-Hitchcock," Lacy said.

"Normal delivery?"

"Totally. No complications." She smiled a little. "I used to walk three miles every day when I was pregnant. Lewis thought I'd wind up delivering in someone's driveway."

"Did you nurse him? Was he a good eater?"

"I'm sorry, I don't see why . . ."

"Because we have to see if there might be a brain disorder," Selena said matter-of-factly. "An organic problem."

"Oh," Lacy said faintly. "Yes. I nursed him. He's always been healthy. A little smaller than other kids his age, but neither Lewis nor I are very big people."

"How was his social development as a child?"

"He didn't have a lot of friends," Lacy said. "Not like Joey."

"Joey?"

"Peter's older brother. Peter is a year younger, and much quieter. He got teased because of his size, and because he wasn't as good an athlete as Joey. . . ."

"What kind of relationship does Peter have with Joey?"

Lacy looked down at her knotted hands. "Joey died a year ago. He was killed in a car accident, by a drunk driver."

Selena stopped writing. "I'm so sorry."

"Yes," Lacy said. "Me, too."

Selena leaned back slightly in her chair. It was crazy, she knew, but just in case misfortune was contagious, she did not want to get too close. She thought of Sam, how she'd left him sleeping this morning in his crib. During the night he'd kicked off a sock; his toes were plump as early peas; it was all she could do not to taste his caramel skin. So much of the language of love was like that: you devoured someone with your eyes, you drank in the sight of him, you swallowed him whole. Love was sustenance, broken down and beating through your bloodstream.

She turned back to Lacy. "Did Peter get along with Joey?"

"Oh, Peter adored his big brother."

"He told you that?"

Lacy shrugged. "He didn't have to. He'd be at all of Joey's football games, and cheering just as loud as the rest of us. When he got to the high school, everyone expected great things of him, because he was Joey's little brother."

Which could be, Selena knew, just as much a source of frustration as it was of pride. "How did Peter react to Joey's death?"

"He was devastated, just like we were. He cried a lot. Spent time in his room."

"Did your relationship with Peter change after Joey died?"

"I think it got stronger," Lacy said. "I was so overwhelmed. Peter . . . he let us lean on him."

"Did he lean on anyone else? Have any intimate relationships?"

"You mean with girls?"

"Or boys," Selena said.

"He was still at that awkward age. I know he'd asked a few girls out, but I don't think anything ever came of it."

"How were Peter's grades?"

"He wasn't a straight-A student like his brother," Lacy said, "but he'd get B's and the occasional C. We always told him to just do the best he could."

"Did he have any learning disabilities?"

"No."

"What about outside of school? What did he like to do?" Selena asked.

"He'd listen to music. Play video games. Like any other teenager."

"Did you ever listen to his music, or play those games?"

Lacy let a smile ghost over her face. "I actively tried not to."

"Did you monitor his Internet use?"

"He was only supposed to be using it for school projects. We had long talks about chat rooms and how unsafe the Internet can be, but Peter had a good head on his shoulders. We—" She broke off, looking away. "We trusted him."

"Did you know what he was downloading?"

"No."

"What about weapons? Do you know where he got them from?"

Lacy took a deep breath. "Lewis hunts. He took Peter out with him once, but Peter didn't like it very much. The shotguns are always locked in a gun case—"

"And Peter knew where the key was."

"Yes," Lacy murmured.

"What about the pistols?"

"We've never had those in our house. I have no idea where they came from."

"Did you ever check his room? Under the bed, in the closets, that kind of thing?"

Lacy met her gaze. "We've always respected his privacy. I think it's important for a child to have his own space, and—" She pressed her lips shut.

"And?"

"And sometimes when you start looking," Lacy said softly, "you find things you don't really want to see."

Selena leaned forward, her elbows on her knees. "When did that happen, Lacy?"

Lacy walked to the window, drawing aside the curtain. "You would have had to know Joey to understand. He was a senior, an honors student, an athlete. And then, a week before graduation, he was killed." She let her hand trail the edge of the fabric. "Someone had to go through his room—pack it up, get rid of the things we didn't want to keep. It took me a while, but finally, I did it. I was going through his drawers when I found the drugs. Just a little powder, in a gum wrapper, and a spoon and a needle. I didn't know it was heroin until I looked it up on the Internet. I flushed it down the toilet and threw the hypodermic out at work." She turned toward Selena, her face red. "I can't believe I'm telling you this. I've never told anyone, not even Lewis. I didn't want him—or *anyone*—to think anything bad about Joey."

Lacy sat down on the couch again. "I didn't go into Peter's room on purpose, because I was afraid of what I'd find," she confessed. "I didn't know that it could be even worse."

"Did you ever interrupt him when he was in his room? Knock on the door, pop your head inside?"

"Sure. I'd come in to say good night."

"What was he usually doing?"

"He was on his computer," Lacy said. "Almost always."

"Didn't you see what was on the screen?"

"I don't know. He'd close the file."

"How did he act when you interrupted him unexpectedly? Did he seem upset? Annoyed? Guilty?"

"Why does it feel like you're judging him?" Lacy said. "Aren't you supposed to be on our side?"

Selena met her gaze steadily. "The only way I can thoroughly investigate this case is to ask you the facts, Mrs. Houghton. That's all I'm doing."

"He was like any other teenager," Lacy said. "He'd suffer while I kissed him good night. He didn't seem embarrassed. He didn't act like he was hiding anything from me. Is that what you want to know?"

Selena put down her pen. When the subject started getting defensive, it was time to end the interview. But Lacy was still talking, unprompted.

"I never thought there was any problem," she admitted. "I didn't know Peter was upset. I didn't know he wanted to kill himself. I didn't know any of those things." She began to cry. "All those families out there, I don't know what to say to them. I wish I could tell them that I lost someone, too. I just lost him a long time ago."

Selena folded her arms around the smaller woman. "It's not your fault," she said, words she knew Lacy Houghton needed to hear.

In a fit of high school irony, the principal of Sterling High had placed the Bible Study Club next door to the Gay and Lesbian Alliance. They met Tuesdays, at three-thirty, in Rooms 233 and 234 of the high school. Room 233 was, during the day, Ed McCabe's classroom. One member of the Bible Study Club was the daughter of a local minister, named Grace Murtaugh. She'd been killed in the hallway leading to the gymnasium, shot in front of a water fountain.

The leader of the Gay and Lesbian Alliance was still in the hospital: Natalie Zlenko, a yearbook photographer, had come out as a lesbian after her freshman year, when she'd wandered into the GLAAD meeting in Room 233 to see if there was anyone else on this planet like herself.

"We're not supposed to give out names." Natalie's voice was so faint that Patrick had to lean over the hospital bed to hear her. Natalie's mother hovered at his shoulder. When he'd come in to ask Natalie a few questions, she said that he'd better leave or else she'd call the police. He reminded her that he *was* the police.

"I'm not asking for names," Patrick said. "I'm just asking you to help me help a jury understand why this happened."

Natalie nodded. She closed her eyes.

"Peter Houghton," Patrick said. "Did he ever attend a meeting?"

"Once," Natalie said.

"Did he say or do anything that sticks in your mind?"

"He didn't say or do anything, period. He showed up the one time, and he never came back."

"Does that happen often?"

"Sometimes," Natalie said. "People wouldn't be ready to come out. And sometimes we got jerks who just wanted to know who was gay so that they could make life hell for us in school."

"In your opinion, did Peter fit into either one of these categories?"

She was silent for a long time, her eyes still closed. Patrick drew away, thinking that she'd fallen asleep. "Thanks," he said to her mother, just as Natalie spoke again.

"Peter was getting ragged on long before he ever showed up at that meeting," she said.

*   *   *

Jordan was on diaper detail while Selena interviewed Lacy Houghton, and Sam was appallingly bad at going to sleep on his own. However, a ten-minute ride in the car could knock the kid out like a prizefighter, so Jordan bundled the baby up and strapped him into the car seat. It wasn't until he put the Saab into reverse that he realized his wheel rims were grinding against the driveway; all four of his tires had been slashed.

"Fuck," Jordan said, as Sam started to wail again in the backseat. He plucked the baby out, carried him back inside, and tethered him into the Snugli that Selena wore around the house. Then he called the police to report the vandalism.

Jordan knew he was in trouble when the dispatch officer didn't ask him to spell his last name—he already knew it. "We'll get to it," the officer said. "But first we've got a squirrel up a tree that needs a hand climbing down." The line went dead.

Could you sue the cops for being unsympathetic bastards?

Through some miracle—pheromones of stress, probably—Sam fell asleep, but startled, bawling, when the doorbell rang. Jordan yanked the door open to find Selena outside. "You woke up the baby," he accused as she lifted Sam out of the carrier.

"Then you shouldn't have locked the door. Oh, hi, you sweet man," Selena cooed. "Has Daddy been a monster the whole time I've been gone?"

"Someone slashed my tires."

Selena glanced at him over the baby's head. "Well, you sure know how to win friends and influence people. Let me guess—the cops aren't exactly scrambling to take your report?"

"Not quite."

"Comes with the territory, I guess," Selena said. "You're the one who took this case."

"How about a little spousal understanding?"

Selena shrugged. "Wasn't in the vows I took. If you want to have a pity party, set the table for one."

Jordan ran a hand through his hair. "Well, did you at least get anything out of the mother? Like, for example, that Peter had a psychiatric diagnosis?"

She peeled off her jacket while juggling Sam in one hand and then the other, unbuttoned her blouse, and sat down on the couch to nurse. "No. But he did have a sibling."

"Really?"

"Yeah. A dead one, who—prior to being killed by a drunk driver—was the All-American Son."

Jordan sank down beside her. "I can use this . . ."

Selena rolled her eyes. "Just for once, could you not be a lawyer and focus instead on being a human? Jordan, this family was in so deep they didn't have a chance. The kid was a powder keg. The parents were dealing with their own grief and were asleep at the wheel. Peter had no one to turn to."

Jordan glanced up at her, a grin splitting his face. "Excellent," he said. "Our client's just become sympathetic."

One week after the school shooting at Sterling High, the Mount Lebanon School—a primary grade school that had become an administrative building when the population of students in Lebanon dipped—was outfitted to be the temporary home for high school kids to finish out their school year.

On the day that classes were beginning again, Josie's mother came into her bedroom. "You don't have to do this," she said. "You can take a few more weeks off, if you want."

There had been a flurry of phone calls, a pulse of panic that began a few days ago when each student received the written word that school would be starting again. *Are you going back? Are* you? There were rumors: whose mother wouldn't let them return; who was getting transferred to St. Mary's; who was going to take over Mr. McCabe's class. Josie had not called any of her friends. She was afraid to hear their answers.

Josie did not want to go back to school. She could not imagine having to walk down a hallway, even one not physically located at Sterling High. She didn't know how the superintendent and the principal expected everyone to act—and they would all be doing that: acting—because to feel anything real would be devastating. And yet there was another part of Josie that understood she had to go back to school; it was where she belonged. The other students at Sterling High were the only ones who really understood what it was like to wake up in the morning and crave those three seconds before you remembered your life wasn't what it used to be; who had forgotten how easy it was to trust that the ground beneath your feet was solid.

If you were drifting with a thousand other people, could you really still say you were lost?

"Josie?" her mother said, prompting.

"It's fine," she lied.

Her mother left, and Josie started to gather her books. She realized, suddenly, that she'd never taken her science test. Catalysts. She didn't remember anything about them anymore. Mrs. Duplessiers wouldn't be evil enough to hand out the test on their first day back, would she? It wasn't like time had stopped during these three weeks—it had changed completely.

The last morning she had gone to school, she hadn't been thinking of anything in particular. That test, maybe.

Matt. How much homework she'd have that night. Normal things, in other words. A normal day. There had been nothing to set it apart from any other morning at school; so how could Josie be sure that today wouldn't dissolve at the seams, too?

When Josie reached the kitchen, her mother was wearing a suit—work clothes. It took her by surprise. "You're going back *today?*" she asked.

Her mother turned, holding a spatula. "Oh," she answered, faltering. "I just figured that since you were . . . You can always reach me through the clerk, if there's a problem. I swear to God, Josie, I'll be there in less than ten minutes. . . ."

Josie sank into a chair and closed her eyes. Somehow, it didn't matter that Josie herself was leaving the house for the day—she'd still imagined her mother sitting home waiting for her, just in case. But that was stupid, wasn't it? It had never been like that, so why should now be any different?

Because, a voice whispered in Josie's head. *Everything else is.*

"I've rearranged my schedule so I'll be able to pick you up from school. And if there's any problem—"

"Yeah. Call the clerk. Whatever."

Her mother sat down across from her. "Honey, what did you expect?"

Josie glanced up. "Nothing. I stopped that a long time ago." She stood up. "You're burning your pancakes," she said, and she walked back upstairs to her bedroom.

She buried her face in her pillow. She didn't know what the hell was wrong with her. It was as if, *after,* there were two Josies—the little girl who kept hoping it might be a nightmare, might never have happened, and the realist who still hurt so badly she lashed out at anyone who got too close. The thing was, Josie didn't know which persona was going to take over at any given moment. Here was her mother, for God's sake, who couldn't boil water but was now attempting pancakes for Josie before she went back to school. When she was younger, she had imagined living in the kind of house where on the first day of school your mother had a whole spread of eggs and bacon and juice to start the day off right—instead of a lineup of cereal boxes and a paper napkin. Well, she'd gotten what she wished for, hadn't she? A mother who sat at her bedside when she was crying, a mother who had temporarily abandoned the job that defined her to hover over Josie instead. And what did Josie do? She pushed her away. She said, in all the spaces between her words, *You never cared about anything that happened in my life when nobody was watching, so don't think you can just start now.*

Suddenly, Josie heard the roar of an engine pulling into the driveway. *Matt,* she thought, before she could stop herself; and by then, every nerve in her body was stretched to the point of pain. Somehow, she hadn't really thought about how she would physically be transported to school—Matt had always picked her up en route. Her mother, of course, would have driven her. But Josie wondered why she hadn't worked through these logistics earlier. Because she was afraid to? Didn't *want* to?

From her bedroom window she watched Drew Girard get out of his battered Volvo. By the time she reached the front door to open it, her mother had come out of the kitchen, too. She held the smoke detector in her hand, popped off its plastic snap on the ceiling.

Drew stood in a shaft of sunlight, shading his eyes with his free hand. His other arm was still in a sling. "I should have called."

"That's okay," Josie said. She felt dizzy. She realized that, in the background, the birds had come back from wherever they went in the winter.

Drew looked from Josie to her mother. "I thought maybe, you know, you might need a ride."

Suddenly Matt was standing there with them; Josie could feel his fingers on her back.

"Thanks," her mother said, "but I'm going to take Josie in today."

The monster in Josie uncoiled. "I'd rather go with Drew," she said, grabbing her backpack off the newel post of the banister. "I'll see you at pickup." Without turning around to see her mother's face, Josie ran to the car, which gleamed like a sanctuary.

Inside, she waited for Drew to turn over the ignition and pull out of the driveway. "Are your parents like that?" Josie asked, closing her eyes as they sped down the street. "Like you can't breathe?"

Drew glanced at her. "Yeah."

"Have you talked to anyone?"

"Like the police?"

Josie shook her head. "Like us."

He downshifted. "I went over to the hospital to see John a couple of times," Drew said. "He couldn't remember my name. He can't remember the words for things like forks or hairbrushes or stairs. I kind of sat there and told him stupid things—who'd won the last few Bruins games, things like that—but the whole time I was wondering if he even knows he can't walk anymore." At a stoplight, Drew turned to her. "Why not me?"

"What?"

"How come we got to be the lucky ones?"

Josie didn't know what to say to that. She looked out the window, pretending to be fascinated by a dog that was pulling its owner, instead of the other way around.

Drew pulled into the parking lot of the Mount Lebanon School. Beside the building was a playground—this had been an elementary school, after all, and even once it became administrative, neighborhood kids would still come to use the monkey bars and the swings. In front of the school's main doors stood the principal and a line of parents, calling out the names of students and encouraging them as they walked inside.

"I have something for you," Drew said, and he reached behind his seat and held out a baseball cap—one Josie recognized. Whatever embroidery had once been on it had long since unraveled; the brim was frayed and curled tight as a fiddlehead. He handed it to Josie, who ran a finger gently along the inside seam.

"He left it in my car," Drew explained. "I was going to give it to his parents . . . after. But then I kind of thought you might want it instead."

Josie nodded, as tears rose along the watermark of her throat.

Drew bent his head against the wheel. It took Josie a moment to realize that he was crying, too.

She reached out and put her hand on his shoulder. "Thank you," Josie managed, and she settled Matt's baseball cap onto her head. She opened the passenger door and reached for her knapsack, but instead of heading toward the school she walked through the rusted gates onto the playground. She strode into the middle of the sandbox and stared at her shoe prints, wondered how much wind or weather it would take to make them disappear.

Twice Alex had excused herself from the courtroom to call Josie's cell, even though she knew Josie kept it turned off during classroom hours. The message she left both times was the same:

It's me. I just wanted to know how you were holding up.

Alex told her clerk, Eleanor, that if Josie called back, she was to be disturbed. No matter what.

She was relieved to be back at work, but had to force herself to pay attention to the case in front of her. There was a defendant on the stand who claimed to have no experience with the criminal justice system. "I don't understand the court process," the woman said, turning to Alex. "Can I go now?"

The prosecutor was in the middle of his cross-examination. "First, why don't you tell Judge Cormier about the last time you were in court."

The woman hesitated. "Maybe for a speeding ticket."

"What else?"

"I can't remember," she said.

"Aren't you on probation?" the prosecutor asked.

"Oh," the woman replied. "That."

"What are you on probation for?"

"I can't remember." She looked up at the ceiling, her brow wrinkling in thought. "It begins with an F. F . . . F . . . F . . . *felony!* That's it!"

The prosecutor sighed. "Didn't it have to do with a check?"

Alex looked at her watch, thinking that if she got this woman off the damn stand, she could see if Josie had called in yet. "How about *forgery*," she interrupted. "That starts with an F."

"So does *fraud*," the prosecutor pointed out.

The woman faced Alex blankly. "I can't remember."

"I'm calling a one-hour recess," Alex announced. "Court will resume at eleven a.m."

As soon as she was through the door that took her to her chambers, she stripped off her robes. They felt suffocating today, something that Alex didn't really understand—this was where she had always felt *comfortable*. Law was a set of rules she understood—a code of behavior where certain actions had certain consequences. She could not say the same of her personal life, where a school that was supposed to be safe turned into a slaughterhouse, where a daughter carved from her own body had become someone Alex no longer understood.

Okay, if she was going to be honest, that she'd *never* understood.

Frustrated, she stood up and walked into her clerk's office. Twice, before the trial began, she'd called on Eleanor for trivial things, hoping that instead of hearing "Yes, Your Honor," the clerk would let down her guard and ask Alex how she was doing, how Josie was doing. That for a half a moment, she wouldn't be a judge to someone, just another parent who'd had the scare of a lifetime.

"I need a cigarette," Alex said. "I'm going downstairs."

Eleanor glanced up. "All right, Your Honor."

Alex, she thought. *Alex Alex Alex.*

Outside, Alex sat down on the cement block near the loading zone and lit a cigarette. She drew in deeply, closed her eyes.

"Those'll kill you, you know."

"So will old age," Alex replied, and she turned around to see Patrick Ducharme.

He turned his face up to the sun, squinted. "I wouldn't have expected a judge to have vices."

"You probably think we sleep under the bench, too."

Patrick grinned. "Well, that would be just plain silly. There's not enough room for a mattress."

She held out the pack. "Be my guest."

"If you want to corrupt me, there are more interesting ways."

Alex felt her face flame. He hadn't just said that, had he? To a *judge*? "If you don't smoke, why'd you come out here?"

"To photosynthesize. When I'm stuck in court all day it ruins my feng shui."

"People don't have feng shui. Places do."

"Do you know that for a fact?"

Alex hesitated. "Well. No."

"There you go." He turned to her, and for the first time she noticed that he had a white streak in his hair, right at the widow's peak. "You're staring."

Alex immediately jerked her gaze away.

"It's all right," Patrick said, laughing. "It's albinism."

"Albinism?"

"Yeah, you know. Pale skin, white hair. It's recessive, so I got a skunk streak. I'm one gene away from looking like a rabbit." He faced her, sobering. "How's Josie?"

She considered putting up that Chinese wall, telling him she didn't want to talk about anything that could compromise her case. But Patrick Ducharme had done the one thing Alex had wished for—he'd treated her like a person instead of a public figure. "She went back to school," Alex confided.

"I know. I saw her."

"You . . . Were you there?"

Patrick shrugged. "Yeah. Just in case."

"Did anything happen?"

"No," he said. "It was . . . ordinary."

The word hung between them. Nothing was going to be ordinary again, and both of them knew it. You could patch up whatever was broken, but if you were the one who had fixed it, you'd always know in your heart where the fault lines lay.

"Hey," Patrick said, touching her shoulder. "Are you all right?"

She realized, mortified, that she was crying. Wiping her eyes, Alex moved out of his reach.

"There's nothing wrong with me," she said, daring Patrick to challenge her.

He opened his mouth as if he was about to speak, but then snapped it shut. "I'll leave you to your vices, then," he said, and walked back inside.

It wasn't until Alex was back in chambers that she realized the detective had used the plural. That he'd not only caught her smoking, but also lying.

There were new rules: All the doors except for the main entrance would be locked after school began, even though a shooter who was a student might already be inside. No backpacks were allowed in classrooms anymore, although a gun could be sneaked in under a coat or in a purse or even in a zippered three-ring binder. Everyone—students and staff—would get ID cards to wear around their necks. It was supposed to make everyone accountable, but Josie couldn't help but wonder if this way, next time, it would be easier to tell who'd been killed.

The principal got on the loudspeaker during homeroom and welcomed everyone back to Sterling High, even if it wasn't Sterling High. He suggested a moment of silence.

While other kids in her homeroom bowed their heads, Josie glanced around. She was not the only one who wasn't praying. Some kids were passing notes. A couple were listening to their iPods. A guy was copying someone else's math notes.

She wondered if they, like her, were afraid to honor the dead, because it made them feel more guilty.

Josie shifted, banging her knee against the desk. The desks and chairs that had been brought back to this makeshift school were for little children, not high school refugees. As a result, nobody fit. Josie's knees were bent up to her chin. Some kids couldn't even sit at the desks; they had to write with their binders on their laps.

I am Alice in Wonderland, Josie thought. *Watch me fall.*

Jordan waited for his client to sit down across from him in the conference room of the jail. "Tell me about your brother, Peter," he said.

He scrutinized Peter's face—saw the disappointment flash across it as he realized that Jordan had again unearthed something he'd hoped would stay hidden. "What about him?" Peter replied.

"You two get along?"

"I didn't kill him, if that's what you're asking."

"I wasn't." Jordan shrugged. "I'm just surprised you didn't mention him earlier."

Peter glared at him. "Like when? When I was supposed to shut up at the arraignment? Or after that, when you came here and told me you were going to do all the talking and I was going to listen?"

"What was he like?"

"Look. Joey's dead, which you obviously know. So I don't really get why talking about him is going to help me."

"What happened to him?" Jordan pressed.

Peter rubbed his thumbnail against the metal edging of the table. "He got his golden boy straight-A self rammed by a drunk driver."

"Hard to beat that," Jordan said carefully.

"What do you mean?"

"Well, your brother is the perfect kid, right? That's tough enough right there, but then he dies and turns into a saint."

Jordan had been playing devil's advocate, to see if Peter would take the bait, and sure enough the boy's face transformed. "You *can't* beat it," Peter said fiercely. "You *can't* measure up."

Jordan tapped his pencil on the edge of his briefcase. Had Peter's anger been born of jealousy or loneliness? Or was his massacre a way to turn attention to himself, finally, instead of Joey? How could he formulate a defense that Peter's act was one of desperation, not an attempt to one-up his brother's notoriety?

"Do you miss him?" Jordan asked.

Peter smirked. "My brother," he said, "my brother, the captain of the baseball team; my brother who placed first in the state in a French competition; my brother who was friends with the principal; my brother, my fabulous brother, used to drop me off a half mile away from the gates of the high school so that he didn't have to be seen driving all the way in with me."

"How come?"

"You don't exactly get any perks for hanging around with me, or haven't you noticed yet."

Jordan had a flash of his car tires, slashed to their metal haunches. "Joey wouldn't stick up for you if you were being bullied?"

"Are you kidding? Joey was the one to start it."

"How?"

Peter walked toward the window in the small room. A mottled flush rose up his neck, as if memory could be burned into the flesh. "He used to tell people I was adopted. That my mother was a crack whore, and that's why my brain was all fucked up. Sometimes he did it right in front of me, and when I'd get pissed off and whale on him he'd just laugh and knock me on my ass and then he'd look back to his friends, as if this was proof of everything he'd been saying in the first place. So, do I miss him?" Peter repeated, and he faced Jordan. "I'm glad he's dead."

Jordan wasn't often surprised, and yet Peter Houghton

had shocked him several times already. Peter was, simply, what a person would look like if you boiled down the most raw emotions and filtered them of any social contract. If you hurt, cry. If you rage, strike out.

If you hope, get ready for a disappointment.

"Peter," Jordan murmured, "did you mean to kill them?"

Immediately Jordan cursed himself—he'd just asked the one question a defense attorney is never supposed to ask, setting Peter up to admit to premeditation. But instead of answering, Peter threw a question back at him that had just as unsettling an answer. "Well," he said, "what would *you* have done?"

Jordan stuffed another bite of vanilla pudding into Sam's mouth and then licked the spoon himself.

"That's not for you," Selena said.

"It tastes good. Unlike that pea crap you make him eat."

"Excuse me for being a good mother." Selena took a wet washcloth and wiped down Sam's mouth, then applied the same treatment to Jordan, who squirmed away from her hand.

"I am totally screwed," he said. "I can't make Peter sympathetic over losing his brother, because he hated Joey. I don't even have a valid legal defense for him, unless I try for insanity, and it's going to be impossible to prove that with the mountain of evidence the prosecution's got for premeditation."

Selena turned to him. "You know what the problem is here, don't you?"

"What?"

"You think he's guilty."

"Well, for Christ's sake. So are ninety-nine percent of my clients, and it's never stopped me from getting acquittals before."

"Right. But deep down, you don't *want* Peter Houghton to get acquitted."

Jordan frowned. "That's crap."

"It's true crap. You're scared of someone like him."

"He's a kid—"

"—who freaks you out, just a little bit. Because he wasn't willing to sit down and let the world shit on him anymore, and that's not supposed to happen."

Jordan looked up at her. "Shooting ten students doesn't make you a hero, Selena."

"It does to the millions of other kids who wish they'd had the guts to do it," she said flatly.

"Excellent. You can be the leader of Peter Houghton's fan club."

"I don't condone what he did, Jordan, but I do see where he's coming from. You were born with six silver spoons up your ass. I mean, honestly, have you ever *not* been in the elite group? At school, or in court, or wherever? People know you, people look up to you. You're granted passage and you don't even realize that other people never get to walk that way."

Jordan folded his arms. "Are you about to do your African pride thing again? Because to tell you the truth—"

"You've never gone down the street and had someone cross it just because you're black. You've never had someone look at you with disgust because you're holding a baby and you forgot to put on your wedding ring. You want to do something about it—take action, scream at them, tell them they're idiots—but you can't. Being on the fringe is the most disempowering feeling, Jordan. You get so used to the world being a certain way, there seems to be no escape from it."

Jordan smirked. "You took that last part from my closing in the Katie Riccobono case."

"The battered wife?" Selena shrugged. "Well, even if I did, it fits."

Suddenly Jordan blinked. He stood up, grabbed his wife, and kissed her. "You are so *fucking* brilliant."

"I'm not going to argue, but *do* tell me why."

"Battered woman syndrome. It's a valid legal defense. Battered women get stuck in a world that slams them down; eventually they feel so constantly threatened that they take action, and truly believe they're protecting themselves—even if their husbands are fast asleep. That fits Peter Houghton, to a T."

"Far be it from me to point this out to you, Jordan," Selena said, "but Peter's not female, and he's not married."

"That's not the point. It's post-traumatic stress disorder. When these women go ballistic and shoot their husbands or slice off their dicks, they aren't thinking about the consequences . . . just about stopping the aggression. That's what Peter's been saying all along—he just wanted it to *stop*. And this is even better, because I don't have to fight the prosecutor's usual rebuttal about a grown woman being old enough to know what she's doing when she picks up the knife or the gun. Peter's a kid. By definition, he *doesn't* know what he's doing."

Monsters didn't grow out of nowhere; a housewife didn't turn into a murderer unless someone turned her into one. The Dr. Frankenstein, in her case, was a controlling husband. And in Peter's case, it was the whole of Sterling High School. Bullies kicked and teased and punched and pinched, all behaviors meant to force someone back where he belonged. It was at the hands of his tormentors that Peter learned how to fight back.

In the high chair, Sam started to fuss. Selena pulled him out and into her arms. "No one's ever done this," she said. "There is no bullied victim syndrome."

Jordan reached for Sam's jar of vanilla custard and scraped out the leftovers with his forefinger. "There is now," he said, and he savored the last of the sweet.

Patrick sat at his office computer in the dark, moving a cursor through the video game created by Peter Houghton.

You started by picking a character—one of three boys: the spelling bee champ, the math genius, the computer nerd. One was small and thin, with acne. One wore glasses. One was grossly overweight.

You did not come equipped with a weapon. Instead, you had to go to various rooms of the school and use your wits: the teachers' lounge had vodka, to make hand grenades. The boiler room had a bazooka. The science lab had burning acid. The English classroom had heavy books. The math room had compasses for stabbing and metal rulers for slicing. The computer room had wires, for garrotes. The wood shop had chain saws. The home arts class had blenders and knitting needles. The art room had a kiln. You could combine materials to make combo assault weapons: flaming bullets from the bazooka and vodka, acid daggers from the chemicals and compasses, snares from the computer wires and the heavy books.

Patrick maneuvered the cursor through hallways and up staircases, through locker rooms and into the janitor's office. It struck him, as he was turning virtual corners, that he'd walked this map before. It was the floor plan of Sterling High.

The object of the game was to aim for the jocks, the bullies, and the popular kids. Each was worth a certain amount of points. Kill two at once, you got triple the points. However, you could be wounded, too. You might be sucker-punched, slammed into a wall, shoved in a locker.

If you accrued 100,000 points, you got a shotgun. If you

reached 500,000 points, you received a machine gun. Cross a million, and you'd find yourself straddling a nuclear missile.

Patrick watched a virtual door fly open. *Freeze,* his speakers cried, and a phalanx of policemen in SWAT jackets stormed onto the screen. He positioned his hand on the arrow keys again, readying himself. Twice now, he'd gotten this far and had been killed or had killed himself—which meant losing.

This time, though, he raised his virtual machine gun and watched the officers fall in a spray of bright blood.

CONGRATULATIONS! YOU HAVE WON *HIDE-N-SHRIEK!* the screen read. DO YOU WANT TO PLAY AGAIN?

On the tenth day after the shooting at Sterling High, Jordan sat in his Saab in the parking lot of the district courthouse. As he'd expected, there were white news vans everywhere, their satellites pointed to the sky like the faces of sunflowers. He tapped his fingers on the steering wheel in time to the Wiggles CD, which was doing its effortless job of keeping Sam from throwing a fit in the backseat.

Selena had already slipped into the court undeterred— no one in the media would recognize her as anyone connected to this case. As she approached the car again, Jordan got out and took the piece of paper she offered him. "Great," he said.

"See you later." She bent down to unbuckle Sam from the car seat as Jordan headed into the courthouse. As soon as one reporter saw him, there was a domino effect—flashbulbs burst like a string of fireworks; microphones were thrust in front of him. He pushed them away with one outstretched arm, muttered "No comment," and hustled inside.

Peter had already been brought to the holding cell of

the sheriff's office, awaiting his appearance in court. He was pacing in a small circle, talking to himself, when Jordan was brought into the cell. "So today's the day," Peter said, a little nervous, a little breathless.

"Funny you should mention that," Jordan said. "Do you remember why we're here today?"

"Is this some kind of test?"

Jordan just stared at him.

"A probable cause hearing," Peter said. "That's what you told me last week."

"Well. What I didn't tell you is that we're going to waive it."

"Waive it?" Peter said. "What does that mean?"

"It means we fold before the hand's even played," Jordan replied. He handed Peter the piece of paper Selena had brought him in the car. "Sign it."

Peter shook his head. "I want a new lawyer."

"Anyone worth their salt is going to tell you the same thing—"

"What? To give up without even *trying?* You said—"

"I said I'd give you the best defense I can," Jordan interrupted. "There's already probable cause to believe that you committed a crime, since there are hundreds of witnesses claiming to have seen you shooting in the school that day. The issue isn't whether or not you did it, Peter, it's *why* you did it. Having a probable cause hearing today means they score a lot of points, and we score none—it would just be a way for the prosecution to release evidence to the media and the public before they get a chance to hear our side of the story." He thrust the paper at Peter again. "Sign it."

Peter met his gaze, fuming. Then he took the paper from Jordan, and a pen. "This *sucks,*" he said as he scrawled his signature.

"It would suck more if we did the probable cause hearing." Jordan took the paper and left the cell, heading out of the sheriff's office to give the waiver to the clerk. "I'll see you in there."

By the time he reached the courtroom, it was packed to the rafters. The media that had been allowed in stood in the back row, their cameras ready. Jordan sought out Selena— she was juggling Sam in the middle of the third row behind the prosecution's table. *So?* she asked, a shorthand lift of her brows.

Jordan nodded the slightest bit. *Done.*

The judge presiding was inconsequential to him: someone who would rubber-stamp this process and turn it over to the court where Jordan would have to put on his dog-and-pony show. The Honorable David Iannucci: what Jordan remembered about him was that he had hair plugs, and when you appeared before him you had to do your absolute best to keep your eyes trained on his ferret-face instead of on the seeded line of his scalp.

The clerk called Peter's case, and two bailiffs led him through a doorway. The gallery, which had been buzzing with quiet conversation, fell silent. Peter didn't look up as he entered; he continued to stare at the ground even as he was shuttled into place beside Jordan.

Judge Iannucci scanned the paper that had been set in front of him. "I see, Mr. Houghton, that you wish to waive your probable cause hearing."

At this news—as Jordan had expected—there was a collective sigh from the media, all of whom had been hoping for a spectacle.

"Do you understand that I would have had the obligation today to find whether or not there was probable cause to believe that you committed the acts for which you are charged, and that by waiving the probable cause hearing, you are not requiring me to find that probable cause; you will now be bound over to the grand jury, and I will bind this case over to the superior court?"

Peter turned to Jordan. "Was that English?"

"Say yes," Jordan answered.

"Yes," Peter repeated.

Judge Iannucci stared at him. "Yes, Your Honor," he corrected.

"Yes, Your *Honor.*" Peter turned to Jordan again and, under his breath, muttered, "This still sucks."

"You're excused," the judge said, and the bailiffs hefted Peter out of his seat again.

Jordan stood, giving way to the next defense attorney for the next case. He approached Diana Leven at the prosecutor's table, still organizing the files she never had a chance to use. "Well," she said, not bothering to look up at him. "I can't say that was a surprise."

"When are you going to send me discovery?" Jordan asked.

"I don't remember getting your letter requesting it yet." She pushed past him, hurrying up the aisle. Jordan made a mental note to get Selena to type something up and send it off to the prosecutor's office, a formality, but one that he knew Diana would uphold. In a case this big, the DA followed every rule to the letter, so that if the case ever went up on appeal, procedure would not be the downfall of the original verdict.

Just outside the double doors of the courtroom, he was waylaid by the Houghtons. "What the hell was that?" Lewis demanded. "Aren't we paying you to work in court?"

Jordan counted to five under his breath. "I spoke about this with my client, Peter. He gave me permission to waive the hearing."

"But you didn't say *anything,*" Lacy argued. "You didn't even give him a chance."

"Today's hearing wouldn't have benefited Peter. It would, however, have put your family under the microscope of every camera outside the courthouse today. That's going to happen anyway. Did you really want it to be sooner rather than later?" He looked from Lacy Houghton to her husband, and then back again. "I did you a favor," Jordan said, and he left them holding the truth between them, a stone that got heavier with every passing moment.

Patrick had been heading to the probable cause hearing for Peter Houghton when he received a cell phone call that sent him screaming in the opposite direction, to Smyth's Gun Shop in Plainfield. The owner of the store, a round little man with a tobacco-stained beard, was sitting outside on the curb, sobbing, when Patrick arrived. Beside him was a patrol officer, who jerked his chin in the direction of the open door.

Patrick sat down beside the owner. "I'm Detective Ducharme," he said. "Can you tell me what happened?"

The man shook his head. "It was so fast. She asked to see a pistol, a Smith and Wesson. Said she wanted to keep it in the house, for protection. She asked if I had any literature on that model, and when I turned my back to find some . . . she . . . ." He shook his head and went silent.

"Where did she get the bullets?" Patrick asked.

"I didn't sell them to her," the owner said. "She must have had them in her purse."

Patrick nodded. "You stay here with Officer Rodriguez. I might have some more questions."

Inside the gun shop, there was a spray of blood and brain matter on the right-hand wall. The medical examiner, Guenther Frankenstein, was already bent over the body, lying sideways on the floor. "How the hell did you get here so fast?" Patrick asked.

Guenther shrugged. "I was in town at a baseball card collectors' show."

Patrick squatted beside him. "You collect baseball cards?"

"Well, I can't very well collect livers, can I?" He glanced at Patrick. "We really have to stop meeting like this."

"I wish."

"Pretty self-explanatory," Guenther said. "She stuck the gun in her mouth and pulled the trigger."

Patrick noticed the purse on the glass counter. He rifled through it, finding a box of ammunition and the Wal-Mart receipt for them. Then he opened the woman's wallet to find her ID, just at the same time Guenther rolled the body over.

Even with the gunshot residue blackening her features, Patrick recognized her before he saw her name. He'd spoken to Yvette Harvey; he'd been the one to tell her that her only child—a daughter with Down syndrome—had not survived the shooting at Sterling High.

Indirectly, Patrick realized, Peter H_____

lena that he never should have taken this case, and then he wanted to drive with his family to the eighteen stingy miles of beach that New Hampshire was blessed with and jump fully clothed into the frigid Atlantic. Dying of hypothermia couldn't be any worse than the slow kill Diana Leven and the DA's office had in store for him in court.

Whatever small hope Jordan had kindled by discovering a valid defense—albeit one that had never been used before a judge—had been steadily eroded in the weeks following the hearing by the discovery that had arrived from the DA's office: stacks of paperwork, photos, and evidence. Given all this information, it was hard to imagine a jury caring *why* Peter had killed ten people—just that he *had.*

Jordan pinched the bridge of his nose. "You were collecting guns," he repeated. "I suppose you just happened to be storing them under your bed until you could get a nice glass display case."

"Don't you believe me?"

Peter shook his head. *"That's* a loaded question."

Had something happened here that Jordan didn't know about?

"Was she your girlfriend?"

Peter smiled, but it didn't reach his eyes. "No."

Jordan had been in Judge Cormier's district court a few times. He liked her. She was tough, but she was fair. In fact, she was the best judge Peter could have drawn for his case—the alternative superior court justice was Judge Wagner, who was a very old, prosecution-biased judge. Josie Cormier had not been a victim of the shooting, but that wasn't the only scenario that would compromise Judge Cormier as the justice for the trial. Suddenly Jordan was thinking of witness tampering, of the hundred things that could go wrong. He was wondering how he could find out what Josie Cormier knew about the shooting, without anyone else learning that he'd been looking into it.

He was wondering what she knew that might help Peter's case.

"Have you talked to her since you've been in here?" Jordan said.

"If I'd talked to her, would I be asking you if she was okay?"

"Well, *don't* talk to her," Jordan instructed. "Don't talk to anyone except me."

"That's like talking to a brick wall," Peter muttered.

"You know, I could rattle off a thousand things I'd rather be doing than sitting with you in a conference room that's as hot as hell."

Peter narrowed his eyes. "Then why don't you go do some of them? You don't listen to a word I say, anyway."

"I listen to every word, Peter. I listen to it, and then I think about the boxes of evidence the DA dropped at my door, all of which make you look like a cold-blooded killer.

I hear you tell me you were collecting guns, like you're some kind of Civil War buff."

Peter flinched. "Fine. You want to know if I was going to use the guns? Yeah, I was. I planned it. I ran through the whole thing in my head. I worked out the details, down to the last second. I was going to kill the person I hated the most. But then I didn't get to do it."

"Those ten people—"

"Just got in the way," Peter said.

"Then who were you trying to kill?"

On the opposite side of the room, the air conditioner suddenly choked to life. Peter turned away. "Me," he said.

One Year Before

I still don't think this is a good idea," Lewis said as he opened the back door of the van. The dog, Dozer, was lying on his side, fighting to breathe.

"You heard the vet," Lacy said, stroking the retriever's head. Good dog. They'd gotten him when Peter was three; now, at twelve, his kidneys had shut down. Keeping him alive with medications was only for their benefit, not his: it was too hard to imagine their house without the dog padding through its halls.

"I wasn't talking about putting him down," Lewis clarified. "I was talking about bringing everyone along."

The boys fell out of the back of the van like heavy stones. They squinted in the sunlight, hunched their shoulders. Their broad backs made Lacy think of oak trees that tapered to the ground; they both had the same habit of turning in their left foot when they walked. She wished they could have seen how very alike they were.

"I can't believe you dragged us here," Joey said.

Peter kicked at the gravel in the parking lot. "This sucks."

"Language," Lacy warned. "And as for all of us being

here, I cannot believe you'd be selfish enough to not want to say good-bye to a member of the family."

"We could have said good-bye at home," Joey muttered.

Lacy put her hands on her hips. "Death is a part of life. I'd want to be surrounded by people I love when it's my time, too." She waited for Lewis to haul Dozer into his arms, then closed the hatch of the door.

Lacy had requested the last appointment of the day, so that the doctor wouldn't be rushed. They sat alone in the waiting room, the dog draped like a blanket over Lewis's legs. Joey picked up a *Sports Illustrated* magazine from three years ago and started to read. Peter folded his arms and stared up at the ceiling.

"Let's all talk about our best Dozer memory," Lacy said.

Lewis sighed. "For God's sake . . ."

"This is lame," Joey added.

"For me," Lacy said, as if they hadn't even spoken, "it was when Dozer was a puppy, and I found him on the dining room table with his head stuck inside the turkey." She stroked the dog's head. "That was the year we had soup for Thanksgiving."

Joey slapped the magazine back on the end table and sighed.

Marcia, the vet's assistant, was a woman with a long braid that reached past her hips. Lacy had delivered her twin sons five years ago. "Hi, Lacy," she said, and she came right up and folded her in her arms. "You okay?"

The thing about death, Lacy knew, was that it robbed you of your vocabulary for comfort.

Marcia walked up to Dozer and rubbed him behind the ears. "Did you want to wait out here?"

"Yes," Joey mouthed toward Peter.

"We're all coming in," Lacy said firmly.

They followed Marcia into one of the treatment rooms

and settled Dozer on the examination table. He scrabbled for purchase, his claws clicking against the metal. "That's a good boy," Marcia said.

Lewis and the boys filed into the room, standing against the wall like a police lineup. When the vet walked in, bearing his hypodermic, they shrank back even further. "Would you like to help hold him?" the vet asked.

Lacy moved forward, nodding, and settled her arms around Marcia's.

"Well, Dozer, you put up a fine fight," the vet said. He turned to the boys. "He won't feel this."

"What *is* it?" Lewis asked, staring at the needle.

"A combination of chemicals that relax the muscles and terminate nerve transmission. And without nerve transmission, there's no thought, no feeling, no movement. It's a bit like drifting off to sleep." He felt around for a vein in the dog's leg, while Marcia kept Dozer steady. He injected the solution and rubbed Dozer's head.

The dog took a deeper breath, and then stopped moving. Marcia stepped away, leaving Dozer in Lacy's arms. "We'll give you a minute," she said, and she and the vet left the room.

Lacy was used to holding new life in her hands, not feeling it pass from the body in her arms. It was just another transition—pregnancy to birth, child to adult, life to death—but there was something about letting go of the family pet that was even more difficult, as if it were silly to have feelings this strong for something that wasn't human. As if admitting that you loved a dog—one that was always underfoot and scratching the leather and tracking mud into the house—as much as you loved your biological children were foolish.

And yet.

This was the dog who had stoically and silently allowed

three-year-old Peter to ride him like a horse around the yard. This was the dog who had barked the house down when Joey had fallen asleep on the couch while his dinner was cooking, until the entire oven was on fire. This was the dog who sat beneath the desk on Lacy's feet in the dead of winter as she answered email, sharing the heat of his pale, pinkened belly.

She bent over the dog's body and began to weep—quietly, at first, and then with loud sobs that made Joey turn away and Lewis wince.

"Do something," she heard Joey say, his voice thick and ropy.

She felt a hand on her shoulder and assumed it was Lewis, but then Peter began to speak. "When he was a puppy," Peter said. "The time we went to pick him out from the litter. All his brothers and sisters were trying to climb over the pen, and he was on the top of the stairs, and he looked at us and tripped and fell down them." Lacy raised her face and stared at him. "That's my best memory," Peter said.

Lacy had always considered herself lucky to have somehow received a child who was not the cookie-cutter American boy, one who was sensitive and emotional and so in tune with what others felt and thought. She let go of her fist-grip on the dog's fur and opened her arms so that Peter could move into them. Unlike Joey, who was already taller than her and more muscular than Lewis, Peter still fit into her embrace. Even that square span of his shoulder blades—so expansive underneath a cotton shirt—seemed more delicate underneath her hands. Unfinished and rough-hewn, a man still waiting to happen.

If only you could keep them that way: cast in amber, never growing up.

*   *   *

At every school concert and play in Josie's life, she'd had only one parent in the audience. Her mother—to her credit—had rearranged court dates so that she could watch Josie be plaque in the school dental hygiene play, or hear her five-note solo in the Christmas chorale. There were other kids who also had single parents—the ones who came from divorced families, for example—but Josie was the only person in the school who had never met her father. When she was little and her second-grade class was making necktie cards for Father's Day, she was relegated to sitting in the corner with the girl whose dad had died prematurely at age forty-two of cancer.

Like any curious kid, she'd asked her mother about this when she was growing up. Josie wanted to know why her parents weren't married anymore; she hadn't expected to hear that they were *never* married. "He wasn't the marrying type," she'd told Josie, and Josie hadn't understood why that also meant he wasn't the type to send a present for his daughter's birthday, or to invite her to his home for a week during the summer, or to even call to hear her voice.

This year, she was supposed to be taking biology, and she was already nervous about the unit on genetics. Josie didn't know if her father had brown eyes or blue ones; if he had curly hair or freckles or six toes. Her mother had shrugged off Josie's concerns. "Surely there's someone in your class who's adopted," she said. "You know fifty percent more about your background than they do."

This is what Josie had pieced together about her father:

His name was Logan Rourke. He'd been a teacher at the law school her mother had attended.

His hair had gone white prematurely, but—her mother assured her—in a cool, not creepy, way.

He was ten years older than her mother, which meant he was fifty.

He had long fingers and played the piano.

He couldn't whistle.

Not quite enough to fill a standard biography, if you asked Josie, not that anyone ever bothered to.

She was sitting in bio lab next to Courtney. Josie ordinarily would not have picked Courtney as a lab partner—she wasn't the brightest bulb in the chandelier—but that didn't seem to matter. Mrs. Aracort was the teacher-adviser to the cheerleaders, and Courtney was one of those. No matter how skimpy their lab reports turned out, they still always managed to get A's.

A dissected cat brain was sitting on the front desk next to Mrs. Aracort. It smelled of formaldehyde and looked like roadkill, which would have been bad enough, but in addition, last period had been lunchtime. ("That thing," Courtney had shuddered, "is going to make me even more bulimic.") Josie was trying not to look at it while she worked on her class project: each student had been given a wireless-enabled Dell laptop to surf the Net for examples of humane animal research. So far Josie had catalogued a primate study being done by an allergy pill manufacturer, where monkeys were made asthmatic and then cured, and another one that involved SIDS and puppies.

She hit a browser button by mistake and got a home page for *The Boston Globe*. Splashed across the screen was election coverage: the race between the incumbent district attorney and his challenger, the dean of students at Harvard Law School, a man named Logan Rourke.

Butterflies rose inside Josie's chest. There couldn't be more than one, could there? She squinted, leaning closer to the screen, but the photograph was grainy and there was a sunlight glare. "What's wrong with you?" Courtney whispered.

Josie shook her head and closed the cover of her laptop, as if it, too, could hold fast to this secret.

He never used a urinal. Even if Peter just had to pee, he didn't want to do it standing next to some gargantuan twelfth grader who might make a comment about, well, the fact that he was a puny ninth grader, particularly in his nether regions. Instead, he'd go into a stall and close the door for privacy.

He liked to read the bathroom walls. One of the stalls had a running series of knock-knock jokes. Others blurted the names of girls who gave blow jobs. There was one scribble that Peter found his eye veering toward repeatedly: TREY WILKINS IS A FAGGOT. He didn't know Trey Wilkins—didn't think he was even a student at Sterling High anymore—but Peter wondered if Trey had come into the bathroom and used the stalls to pee, too.

Peter had left English in the middle of a pop quiz on grammar. He truly didn't think that in the grand scheme of life, it was going to matter whether or not an adjective modified a noun or a verb or just dropped off the face of the earth, which is what he was sincerely hoping would happen before he had to go back to class. He had already done his business in the bathroom; now he was just wasting time. If he failed this quiz, it would be the second in a row. It wasn't even his parents' anger that Peter was worried about. It was the way they'd look at him, disappointed that he hadn't turned out more like Joey.

He heard the door of the bathroom open, and the busy slice of hallway noise that trailed on the heels of the two kids who entered. Peter ducked down, scanning beneath the stall door. Nikes. "I'm sweating like a pig," said one voice.

The second kid laughed. "That's because you're a lard-ass."

"Yeah, right. I could beat you on a basketball court with one hand tied behind my back."

Peter could hear a faucet running, water splashing.

"Hey, you're getting me soaked!"

"Aaaah, much better," the first voice said. "At least now I'm not sweating. Hey, check out my hair. I look like Alfalfa."

"Who?"

"What are you, retarded? The kid from the Little Rascals with the cowlick thing on the back of his head."

"Actually, you look like a total fag . . ."

"You know . . ." More laughter. "I *do* sort of look like Peter."

As soon as Peter heard his name, his heart thumped hard. He slid open the bolt in the stall door and stepped outside. Standing in front of the bank of sinks was a football player he knew only by sight, and his own brother. Joey's hair was dripping wet, standing up on the back of his head the way Peter's sometimes did, even when he tried to slick it down with his mother's hair gel.

Joey flicked a glance his way. "Get lost, freak," he ordered, and Peter hurried out of the bathroom, wondering if that was even possible when you'd been missing most of your life.

The two men standing in front of Alex's bench shared a duplex, but hated each other. Arliss Undergroot was a Sheetrock installer with tattoos up and down both arms, a shaved head, and enough piercings in his head to have set off the metal detectors at the courthouse. Rodney Eakes was a vegan bank teller with a prized record collection of original cast recordings from Broadway shows. Arliss lived downstairs, Rodney lived upstairs. A few months back, Rodney had brought home a bale of hay, planning to use it for mulching his organic garden, but he never got around to it and the hay bale remained on Arliss's porch. Arliss asked Rodney to get rid of the hay, but Rodney hadn't moved fast enough. So one night, Arliss and his girlfriend cut the twine and spread the hay out over the front lawn.

Rodney called the police, and they had actually arrested Arliss on the grounds of criminal mischief: legalspeak for destroying a bale of hay.

"Why are the taxpayers of New Hampshire shelling out money for a case like this to be tried in court?" Alex asked.

The police prosecutor shrugged. "The Chief asked me to pursue it," he said, but then he rolled his eyes.

He had already proven that Arliss had taken the bale of hay and spread it over the lawn—the burden of proof fulfilled. But a conviction in this case would mean Arliss would have a criminal record for the rest of his life.

He might have been a lousy neighbor, but he didn't deserve that.

Alex turned to the prosecutor. "How much did the victim pay for that bale of hay?"

"Four dollars, Your Honor."

Then she faced the defendant. "Do you have four dollars with you today?"

Arliss nodded.

"Good. Your case is filed without a finding conditional upon your paying the victim. Take four dollars out of your wallet and give it to the police officer over there, who will bring it to Mr. Eakes in the back of the courtroom." She glanced at her clerk. "We're taking a fifteen-minute recess."

In chambers, Alex stripped off her robe and grabbed a pack of cigarettes. She took the back stairs to the bottom floor of the building and lit up, inhaling deeply. There were days when she was proud of her job, and then there were others, like today, when she wondered why she even bothered.

She found Liz, the groundskeeper, raking the lawn in front of the courthouse. "I brought you a cigarette," Alex said.

"What's wrong?"

"How did you know something was wrong?"

"Because you've been working here for how many years, and you've never brought me a cigarette."

Alex leaned against the tree, watching leaves as bright as jewels catch in the tines of Liz's rake. "I just wasted three hours on a case that never should have made it to a courthouse. I have a splitting headache. *And* I ran out of toilet paper in the bathroom in chambers and had to call the clerk in to get me a roll from maintenance."

Liz glanced up at the tree as a gust of wind sent a new score of leaves onto the raked grass. "Alex," she said. "Can I ask you a question?"

"Sure."

"When was the last time you got laid?"

Alex turned, her mouth dropping open. "What does that have to—"

"Most people who go to work spend their time wondering how long till they get back home to do whatever it is they *really* want to do. For you, it's the other way around."

"That's not true. Josie and I—"

"What did you two do for fun this weekend?"

Alex plucked a leaf and shredded it. In the past three years, Josie's social calendar had become crammed with phone calls and sleepovers and packs of kids going to a movie or hanging out in someone's basement lair. This weekend, Josie had gone shopping with Haley Weaver, a junior who'd just gotten her driver's license. Alex had written two decisions and cleaned out the fruit and vegetable drawers in her refrigerator.

"I'm setting you up on a blind date," Liz said.

✢   ✢   ✢

There were a number of business establishments in Sterling that hired teenagers for after-school employment. After his first summer at QuikCopy, Peter had deduced that this was because the jobs mostly sucked, and they couldn't find anyone else to do them.

He was responsible for photocopying most of the course material for Sterling College, which professors brought in. He knew how to shrink a document down to one-thirty-second of its original size, and how to add toner. When customers paid, he liked to guess what size bill they were going to pull out of their wallets just by the way they dressed or wore their hair. College kids always used twenties. Moms with strollers whipped out a credit card. Professors used crumpled singles.

The reason he was working was because he needed a new computer with a better graphics card, so that he could do some of the gaming design he and Derek had been into lately. It never failed to amaze Peter how you could take a seemingly senseless string of commands and—magic!—it would become a knight or a sword or a castle on the screen. He liked the very concept: that something the ordinary person might dismiss as gibberish was actually vibrant and eye-catching, if you knew how to look at it.

Last week, when his boss said he'd hired another high school student, Peter had become so nervous that he actually had to lock himself in the bathroom for twenty minutes until he could act like it was no big deal. As stupid and boring as this job was, it was a haven. Peter was alone here most of the afternoon; he didn't have to worry about crossing paths with the cool kids.

But if Mr. Cargrew was hiring someone else from Sterling High, then that person knew who Peter was. And even if the kid wasn't part of the popular crowd, the copy center would no longer be a comfortable place. Peter would have to think twice about what he said or did, because otherwise, it would become fodder for rumors around school.

To Peter's great surprise, however, his co-worker turned out to be Josie Cormier.

She had walked in behind Mr. Cargrew. "This is Josie," he said, by way of introduction. "You two know each other?"

"Sort of," Josie had replied, as Peter answered, "Yeah."

"Peter will show you the ropes," Mr. Cargrew said, and then he left to go play golf.

Occasionally when Peter walked down the hall in school and he saw Josie with her new group of friends, he didn't recognize her. She dressed differently now—in jeans that showed off her flat belly and a rainbow of T-shirts layered one over the other. She wore makeup that made her eyes look enormous. And a little sad, he sometimes thought, but he doubted she knew that.

The last major conversation he'd had with Josie had been five years ago, when they were in sixth grade. He had been certain that the real Josie would come out of this fog of popularity and realize that the people she was hanging around with were about as scintillating as cardboard cutouts. He was sure that as soon as they started ripping on other people, she'd come back to Peter. *Oh my God*, she would say, and they'd laugh about her journey to the underworld. *What was I thinking?*

But Josie never came crawling back to him, and then he started to hang out with Derek from the soccer team, and by the time he was in seventh grade he found it really hard to believe that once, he and Josie had spent two weeks coming up with a secret handshake that no one else would ever be able to duplicate.

"So," Josie had said that first day, as if she'd never met him before, "what do we do?"

They had been working together for a week now. Well,

not *together*—it was more like they were doing a dance punctuated with the sighs and throaty grumbles of the copiers and the shrill ring of the telephone. Mostly, if they spoke, it was informational: *Do we have any more toner for the color copier? How much do I charge someone to receive a fax here?*

This afternoon, Peter was photocopying articles for a psychology course at the college. Every now and then, as the pages whipped through the automatic collating machine, he'd see brain scans of schizophrenics—bright pink circles at the frontal lobes that reproduced in shades of gray. "What's that word you use when you call something by its brand name instead of what it really is?"

Josie was stapling together another job. She shrugged.

"Like Xerox," Peter said. "Or Kleenex."

"Jell-O," Josie answered after a moment.

"Google."

Josie glanced up. "Band-Aid," she said.

"Q-tip."

She thought for a second, a grin spreading over her face. "FedEx. Wiffle ball."

Peter smiled. "Rollerblade. Frisbee."

"Crock-Pot."

"That's not—"

"Go look it up," Josie said. "Jacuzzi. Post-it."

"Magic Marker."

"Ping-Pong!"

By now they'd both stopped working. They were standing next to each other, laughing, when the bell over the door chimed.

Matt Royston walked into the store. He was wearing a Sterling hockey cap—even though the season wouldn't start for another month, everyone knew he would be tapped for varsity, even as a freshman. Peter—who'd been reveling in the miracle that here was Josie, again, like she used to be — watched her turn to Matt. Her cheeks pinkened; her eyes leaped like the brightest part of a flame. "What are *you* doing here?"

He leaned against the counter. "Is that how you treat all your customers?"

"Do you need something copied?"

Matt's mouth cocked up in a grin. "No way. I'm an original." He glanced around the store. "So this is where you work."

"No, I just come here for the free caviar and champagne," Josie joked.

Peter watched this exchange from behind the counter. He waited for Josie to tell Matt that she was in the middle of doing something, which might not necessarily be true, but they *had* been having a conversation. Sort of.

"When do you get off?" Matt asked.

"Five."

"Some of us are going over to Drew's tonight to hang out."

"Is that an invitation?" she said, and Peter noticed that when she smiled, really hard, she had a dimple he'd never noticed before. Or maybe she just hadn't smiled that way around him.

"Do you want it to be?" Matt answered.

Peter walked toward the counter. "We have to get back to work," he blurted out.

Matt's eyes flicked over Peter. "Stop looking at me, homo."

Josie moved so that her body was blocking Peter's view of Matt. "What time?"

"Seven."

"I'll see you over there," she said.

Matt rapped his hands against the counter. "Cool," he replied, and he walked out of the store.

"Saran Wrap," Peter said. "Vaseline."

Josie turned to him, confused. "What? Oh. Right." She picked up the materials she'd been stapling, stacked a few more packets on top of each other, aligned their edges.

Peter added paper to the machine that was working on his job. "Do you like him?" he asked.

"Matt? I guess."

"Not like that," Peter said. He pressed the Copy button, watched the machine begin to birth a hundred identical babies.

When Josie didn't answer, he went to stand next to her at the sorting table. He gathered a packet of papers in his hands and stapled it, then handed it to her. "What does it feel like?" he asked.

"What does *what* feel like?"

Peter thought for a moment. "Being at the top."

Josie reached across him for another packet of material and fed it into the stapler. She did three of these, and Peter was certain that she was going to ignore him, but then she spoke. "Like if you take one wrong step," she said, "you're going to fall."

When she said that, Peter could hear a note in her voice that was like a lullaby. He could vividly remember sitting on Josie's driveway in the heat of July, trying to make a fire with sawdust, sunlight, and his glasses. He could hear her yelling over her shoulder as they ran home from school, daring Peter to catch up. He saw a faint flush paint her face and realized that the Josie who used to be his friend was still there, trapped inside several cocoons, like one of those Russian nesting dolls that hides another and another, until you reach the one that fits snug in the palm of your hand.

If he could just somehow make her remember those things, too. Maybe being popular wasn't what had made Josie start hanging out with Matt and Company. Maybe it was just because she'd forgotten that she liked hanging out with Peter.

From the corner of his eye, he looked at Josie. She was biting her lower lip, concentrating hard on getting the staple straight. Peter wished he knew how to be as easy and natural as Matt, but all his life, he'd always seemed to laugh just a little too loud or too late; to be oblivious to the fact that he was the one being laughed at. He didn't know how to be anyone except who he'd always been, so he took a deep breath and told himself that not too long ago, that had been good enough for Josie anyway.

"Hey," he said. "Check this out." He walked into the adjoining office, the one where Mr. Cargrew kept a picture of his wife and kids and his computer, which was firmly off-limits and password-encoded.

Josie followed him and stood behind the chair as Peter sat down. He keyed a few strokes, and suddenly the screen opened up for access.

"How did you do that?" Josie asked.

Peter shrugged. "I've been playing around with computers a lot. I hacked into Cargrew's last week."

"I don't think we should—"

"Wait." Peter picked his way through the computer until he reached a well-hidden file of downloads and opened up the first porn site.

"Is that . . . a *dwarf*?" Josie murmured. "And a donkey?"

Peter tilted his head. "I thought it was a really big cat."

"Either way, it's totally gross." She shuddered. "Ugh. How am I going to take a paycheck from that guy's hand now?" Then she looked down at Peter. "What else can you do with that computer?"

"Anything," he bragged.

"Like . . . hack into other places? Schools and stuff?"

"Sure," Peter said, although he didn't really know about

that. He was just starting to learn about encryption and how to make wormholes through it.

"What about finding an address?"

"Piece of cake," Peter answered. "Whose?"

"Someone totally random," she said, and she leaned over him to type. He could smell her hair—apples—and felt the press of her shoulder against his. Peter closed his eyes, waiting for lightning to strike. Josie was pretty, and she was a girl, and yet . . . he felt nothing.

Was that because she was *too* familiar—like a sister?

Or because she wasn't a *he*?

Stop looking at me, homo.

He did not tell Josie this, but when he'd first found Mr. Cargrew's porn site, he'd found himself staring at the guys, not the girls. Did that mean he was attracted to them? Then again, he'd looked at the animals, too. Couldn't it just have been curiosity? Comparison, even, between the men and him?

What if it turned out that Matt—and everyone else—was right?

Josie clicked on the mouse a few times until the screen was filled with an article from *The Boston Globe*. "There," she said, pointing. "That guy."

Peter squinted at the caption. "Who's Logan Rourke?"

"Who cares," Josie said. "Someone who looks like he has an unlisted address, anyway."

He did, but then, Peter figured that anyone running for public office probably was smart enough to take their personal information out of the phone book. It took him ten minutes to figure out that Logan Rourke had worked for Harvard Law School, and another fifteen to hack into the human resources files there.

"Ta-da," Peter said. "He lives in Lincoln. Conant Road."

He looked over his shoulder and saw his smile spread,

contagious, over Josie's face. She stared at the screen for a long moment. "You *are* good," she said.

Economists, it was often said, knew the price of everything and the value of nothing. Lewis considered this as he opened up the enormous file on his office computer, the World Values Survey. Gathered by Norwegian social scientists, here was data collected from hundreds of thousands of people around the world—an endless array of details. Simple ones—like age, gender, birth order, weight, religion, marital status, number of children—and more complex accounts, like political views and religious affiliations. The survey had even considered time allocation: how long a person spent at work, how often he went to church, how many times a week he had sex and with how many partners.

What would have seemed tedious to most people was, to Lewis, like a roller-coaster ride. When you started to sort out the patterns in data this massive, you didn't know where you'd twist or turn, how steep the fall or how soaring the heights. He'd examined these numbers often enough to know that he'd be able to quickly crank out a paper for next week's conference. It didn't have to be perfect—the gathering was small, and his higher-ranking peers wouldn't be present. He could always take whatever he eked out now and polish it later for publication in an academic journal.

The focus of his paper involved putting a price on the variables of happiness. Everyone always said that money bought happiness, but how much? Did income have a direct or causal effect on happiness? Were happier people more successful in their jobs, or were they given a higher wage because they were happier people?

Happiness wasn't limited to one's income, either. Was marriage more valuable in America or Europe? Did sex matter? Why did churchgoers report higher levels of happiness than nonchurchgoers? Why did Scandinavians—who scored high on the happiness scale—have one of the highest suicide rates in the world?

As Lewis set about picking through the variables of the survey using multivariate regression analysis on STATA, he thought about the value he'd have put on the variables of his own happiness. What monetary compensation would have made up for not having a woman like Lacy in his life? For not getting a tenured position at Sterling College? For his health?

It didn't do the average person much good to know that marital status was associated with a 0.07 level increase in happiness (with a standard error of 0.02 percent). On the other hand, tell the Average Joe that being married had the same effect on overall happiness as an additional $100,000 a year, and it put things into perspective.

These were the findings he'd reached so far:

1. Higher income was associated with higher happiness, but in diminishing returns. For example, someone who made $50,000 reported being happier than the man with a salary of $25,000. But the incremental gain in happiness that came from getting a raise from $50K to $100K was much less.
2. In spite of material improvements, happiness is flat over time—relative income might be more important than absolute income gains.
3. Well-being was greatest among women, married people, the highly educated, and those whose parents didn't divorce.
4. Women's happiness was declining over time, possibly because they'd reached greater equality with men in the labor market.

5. Blacks in the U.S. were much less happy than whites, but their life satisfaction was on the upswing.

6. Calculations indicated that "reparation" for being unemployed would take $60,000 per year. "Reparation" for being black would take $30,000 per year. "Reparation" for being widowed or separated would take $100,000 per year.

There was a game Lewis used to play with himself, after the kids were born, when he was feeling so ridiculously lucky that surely tragedy was bound to strike. He'd lie in bed and force himself to choose what he was first willing to lose: his marriage, his job, a child. He would wonder how much a man could take before he reduced himself to nothing.

He closed the data window and stared at the screen saver on his computer. It was a picture taken when the kids were eight and ten, at a petting zoo in Connecticut. Joey had hoisted his brother up, piggyback, and they were grinning, with a striated pink sunset in the background. Moments later, a deer (deer on *steroids*, Lacy had said) had knocked Joey's feet out from beneath him and both boys had fallen and dissolved into tears . . . but that was not the way Lewis liked to recall it.

Happiness wasn't just what you reported; it was also how you chose to remember.

There was one other finding he'd catalogued: happiness was U-shaped. People were happiest when they were very young and very old. The trough came, roughly, when you hit your forties.

Or in other words, Lewis thought with relief, this is as bad as it gets.

*   *   *

Although Josie got A's in math and liked the subject, it was the one grade she had to fight for. Numbers did not come easily to her, although she could reason with logic and write an essay without breaking a sweat. In this, she supposed, she was like her mother.

Or possibly her father.

Mr. McCabe, their math teacher, was walking through the rows of desks, tossing a tennis ball against the ceiling and singing a bastardized Don McLean song:

> "Bye, bye, what's the value of pi
> Gotta fidget with the digits
> Till this class has gone by . . .
> Them ninth graders were workin' hard with a sigh
> Sayin', Mr. McCabe, come on, why?
> Oh Mr. McCabe, come on, why-y-y . . ."

Josie erased a coordinate from the graph paper in front of her. "We're not even using pi," one kid said.

The teacher whirled around and tossed the tennis ball so that it bounced on the boy's desk. "Andrew, I'm so glad to see you woke up in time to notice that."

"Does this count as a pop quiz?"

"No. Maybe I should go on TV," Mr. McCabe mused. "Is there a *Math Idol*?"

"God, I hope not," Matt muttered from the desk behind Josie. He poked her shoulder and she pushed her paper to the upper left corner of her desk, because she knew he could see the homework answers better there.

This week they were working on graphing. In addition to a bazillion assignments that made you take data and force it into bar graphs and charts, each student had had to create and present a graph of something near and dear to them. Mr. McCabe left ten minutes at the end of each class period for the presentation. Yesterday, Matt had shown off a graph of relative age of hockey players in the NHL. Josie, who was presenting hers tomorrow, had polled her friends to see if there was a ratio between the number of hours you spent doing your homework and your grade point average.

Today was Peter Houghton's turn. She had seen him carrying his graph into school, a rolled-up piece of poster board. "Well, look at that," Mr. McCabe said. "Turns out we are talking about pie. The *other* one, that is."

Peter's graph was a pie chart. It had been clearly shaded with colors, and computer labels identified each section. The title at the top of the chart said POPULARITY.

"Whenever you're ready, Peter," Mr. McCabe said.

Peter looked a little bit like he was going to pass out, but then, Peter always looked like that. Since Josie had started working at the copy shop, they'd been talking again, but— by unwritten rule—only outside of school. Inside was differ- ent: a fishbowl where anything you said and did was being watched by everyone else.

When they were kids, Peter had never seemed to notice when he was drawing attention just by being himself. Like when he'd decide to speak Martian during recess, for exam- ple. Josie supposed that the flip side of this, the optimistic angle, was that Peter never tried to be like anyone else. She couldn't lay claim to that herself.

Peter cleared his throat. "My graph is about status in this school. My statistical sample came from the twenty-four students in this class. You can see here"—he pointed at one wedge of the pie—"that a little less than a third of the class are popular."

Shaded violet—the color of popularity—were seven wedges, each sporting a different classmate's name. There was Matt, and Drew. A few girls who hung out at lunchtime with Josie. But the class clown was also lumped in that group, Josie noticed, and the new kid who'd transferred from Washington, D.C.

"Over here are the geeks," Peter said, and Josie could see the names of the class brain and the girl who played tuba in the marching band. "The largest group is what I call normal. And roughly five percent are outcasts."

Everyone had grown quiet. This was one of those moments, Josie realized, when the guidance counselors would get called in to give everyone a booster shot of tolerance for differences. She could see Mr. McCabe's brow furrow like origami as he tried to figure out how to turn Peter's presentation into an *After School Special* moment; she saw Drew and Matt grinning at each other; and most of all, she noticed Peter, who was blissfully unaware that all hell was about to break loose.

Mr. McCabe cleared his throat. "You know, Peter, maybe you and I should—"

Matt's hand shot up. "Mr. McCabe, I have a question."

"Matt—"

"No, seriously. I can't read that skinny piece of the pie chart. The orange one."

"Oh," Peter said. "That's a bridge. You know. A person who can fit into more than one category, or who hangs out with different kinds of people. Like Josie."

He turned to her, beaming, and Josie felt everyone's eyes on her—a hail of arrows. She curled over her desk like a midnight rose, letting her hair fall over her face. To be honest, she was used to being stared at—walk anywhere with Courtney and it was bound to happen—but there was a difference between people looking at you because they wanted to be like you, and people looking at you because your misfortune brought them one rung higher.

At the very least, kids would remember that once, Josie

had been an outcast who used to hang out with Peter. Or they'd assume that Peter had some weird crush on her, which was just *sick*, and she'd never hear the end of it. A murmur ran through the classroom like an electric shock. *Freak*, someone whispered, and Josie prayed prayed prayed that they were not talking about her.

Because there was a God, the bell rang.

"So, Josie," Drew said. "Are you the Tobin or the Golden Gate?"

Josie tried to stuff her books into her backpack, but they scattered to the ground, pages splayed. "London," John Eberhard snickered. "Look, she's falling down."

By now, someone in her math class had surely told someone else down the hall what had happened. Josie would hear laughter following her like a kite's tail for that whole day—maybe even longer.

She realized that someone was trying to help her pick up her books, and then—one beat later—that this someone was Peter. "Don't," Josie said, holding up a hand, a force field that stopped Peter in his tracks. "Don't ever talk to me again, all right?"

In the hallway, she turned corners blindly until she found the little alley that led to the wood shop. Josie had been so naïve, thinking that once she belonged, she was firmly entrenched. But *In* only existed because someone had drawn a line in the sand, so that everyone else was *Out*; and that line changed constantly. You might find yourself, through no fault of your own, suddenly standing on the wrong side.

What Peter hadn't graphed was how fragile popularity was. Here was the irony: she wasn't a bridge at all; she'd completely crossed over to become part of her group. She'd excluded other people to get to where she so badly wanted to be. Why would those kids ever welcome her back?

"Hey."

At the sound of Matt's voice, Josie drew in a sharp breath. "Just so you know, I'm not friends with him."

"Well, actually, he's right about you."

Josie blinked at him. She'd witnessed, firsthand, Matt's cruelty—how he'd shoot rubber bands at ESL students who didn't know the words to report him to the faculty; how he called one overweight girl the Walking Earthquake; how he'd hide a shy kid's math textbook in order to watch him freak out, thinking it was lost. It was funny then, because it hadn't been about Josie. But being the object of his humiliation felt like a slap. She'd thought, mistakenly, that hanging with the right crowd granted her immunity, but that turned out to be a joke. They'd cut you down anyway, as long as it made them seem funnier, cooler, different from you.

Seeing Matt with that grin on his face, as if he'd thought she was a total joke all along, hurt even more, because she'd considered him a friend. Well, to be honest, sometimes she wished for even more than that: when a fringe of hair fell over his eyes and his smile lit as slowly as a fuse, she went totally monosyllabic. But Matt had that effect on everyone—even Courtney, who'd gone out with him in sixth grade for two weeks.

"I never thought anything the homo said would be worth listening to, but bridges take you from one place to another," Matt said. "And that's what you do to me." He took Josie's hand, pressed it up against his chest.

His heart was beating so hard she could feel it, as if possibility were something you might cup in your palm. She looked up at him, keeping her eyes wide open as he leaned in to kiss her, so that she would not miss a single, startling moment. Josie could taste the heat of him like cinnamon candy, the kind that burned.

Finally, when Josie remembered that she had to breathe, she tore away from Matt. She had never been so aware of every inch of her skin; even the bits hidden under layers of T-shirt and sweater had come alive.

"Jesus," Matt said, backing away.

She panicked. Maybe he had just remembered he was kissing a girl who five minutes ago had been a social pariah. Or maybe she'd done something wrong during the kiss. It's not like there was a manual you could read so you'd know how to do it right.

"I guess I'm not very good at that," Josie stammered.

Matt raised his brows. "If you get much better . . . you might kill me."

Josie felt a smile start inside her like a candle flame. "Really?"

He nodded.

"That was my first kiss," she admitted.

When Matt touched her lower lip with his thumb, Josie could feel it everywhere—from her fingertips to her throat to the heat between her legs. "Well," he said. "It's not going to be your last."

Alex was getting ready in her bathroom when Josie wandered in, looking for a new razor. "What's that?" Josie had asked, scrutinizing Alex's face in the mirror as if it belonged to a stranger.

"Mascara?"

"Well, I know what it *is*," Josie said. "I meant, what's it doing on *you?*"

"Maybe I felt like wearing makeup."

Josie sank down onto the lip of the bathtub, grinning. "And maybe I'm the Queen of England. What is it . . . a new photo for some law review?" Suddenly, her eyebrows shot up. "You're not going on, like, a *date*, are you?"

"Not 'like' a date," Alex said, brushing on blush. "It's an honest-to-goodness one."

"Oh, my gosh. Tell me about him."

"I don't know anything. Liz set me up."

"Liz the custodian?"

"She's a groundskeeper," Alex said.

"Whatever. She must have told you something about this guy." Josie hesitated. "It is a *guy*, right?"

"Josie!"

"Well, it's been a really long time. The last date you went out on that I can remember was the man who wouldn't eat anything green."

"That wasn't the issue," Alex said. "It was that he wouldn't let *me* eat anything green."

Josie stood up and reached for a tube of lipstick. "This is a good color for you," she said, and she swept the tube over Alex's mouth.

Alex and Josie were exactly the same height; looking into her daughter's eyes, Alex could see a tiny reflection of herself. She wondered why she'd never done this with Josie: sat her down in the bathroom and played with eye shadow, painted her toenails, curled her hair. They were memories that every other mother of a daughter seemed to have; only now was Alex realizing that it had been up to her to create them.

"There," Josie said, turning Alex to look in the mirror. "What do you think?"

Alex was staring, but not at herself. Over her shoulder was Josie—and for the first time, Alex could really see a piece of herself in her daughter. It wasn't so much the shape of the face but the shine of it; not the color of the eyes but the dream caught like smoke in them. There was no amount of expensive makeup that would make her look the way her Josie did; that was simply what falling in love did to a person.

Could you be jealous of your own child?

"Well," Josie said, patting Alex's shoulders. "*I'd* ask you out for a second date."

The doorbell rang. "I'm not even dressed," Alex said, panicked.

"I'll stall him." Josie hurried down the stairs; as Alex shimmied into a black dress and heels, she could hear conversation stir, rise up the stairs.

Joe Urquhardt was a Canadian banker who'd been roommates with Liz's cousin in Toronto. He was, she had promised, a nice guy. Alex asked why, then, if he was so nice, he was still single.

How would you answer that question? Liz had asked, and Alex had to think for a moment.

I'm not that nice, she'd said.

She was pleasantly surprised to see that Joe was not troll-statured, that he had a head of wavy brown hair that did not seem to be attached by double-sided tape, and that he had teeth. He whistled when he saw Alex. "All rise," he said. "And by *all*, I do mean Mr. Happy."

The smile froze on Alex's face. "Would you excuse me for a moment?" she asked, and she dragged Josie into the kitchen. "Shoot me now."

"Okay, that was pretty awful. But at least he eats green food. I asked."

"What if you go out there and say I'm violently ill?" Alex said. "You and I can get take-out. Rent a movie or something."

Josie's smile faded. "But, Mom, I've already got plans." She peered out the doorway to where Joe was waiting. "I could tell Matt that—"

"No, no," Alex said, forcing a smile. "*One* of us ought to be having a good time."

She walked out of the kitchen and found Joe holding up

a candlestick, scrutinizing the bottom. "I'm very sorry, but something's come up."

"Tell me about it, babe," Joe said, leering.

"No, I mean that I can't go out tonight. There's a case," she lied. "I have to go back into court."

Maybe being from Canada was what kept Joe from understanding how incredibly unlikely it would be for court to be in session on a Saturday night. "Oh," he said. "Well, far be it from me to keep those wheels of justice from grinding. Some other time?"

Alex nodded, ushering him outside. She took off her heels and padded upstairs to change into her rattiest sweats. She would eat chocolate for dinner; she would watch chick flicks until she was completely sobbed out. As she passed the bathroom, she could hear the shower running—Josie getting ready for her own date.

For a moment Alex stood with her hand on the door, wondering whether Josie would welcome her if she went in and guided her in putting on her makeup, offered to style her hair—just as Josie had done for her. But for Josie, that was natural—she'd spent a lifetime grabbing moments of Alex's time, when Alex was busy preparing for something else. Somehow, Alex had assumed that time was infinite, that Josie would always be there waiting. She never guessed that she herself would one day be left behind.

In the end, Alex drew away from the bathroom door without knocking, too afraid she might hear Josie say she did not need her mother's help to even risk making that initial offer.

The one thing that had saved Josie from total social ruin in the wake of Peter's math presentation was her simultaneous anointing as Matt Royston's girlfriend. Unlike most of the other sophomores who were occasional couples—random hookups at parties, best-friend-with-benefits situations—she and Matt were an *item*. Matt walked her to her classes and often left her at the door with a kiss that everyone watched. Anyone stupid enough to mention Peter Houghton's name in conjunction with Josie's had to answer to him.

Everyone, that is, except for Peter himself. At work, he didn't seem to be able to pick up on the clues that Josie gave him—turning her back when he came into the room, ignoring him when he asked her a question. He finally cornered her in the supply room one afternoon. *How come you're acting like this?* he said.

Because when I was nice to you, you thought we were friends.

But we are *friends,* he replied.

Josie had faced him. You *don't get to decide that,* she said.

One afternoon at work, when Josie went out to the Dumpster with a load of trash, Peter was already there. It was his fifteen-minute break; usually he walked across the street and bought himself an apple juice, but today he was leaning over the metal lip of the Dumpster. "Move," she said, and she hefted the bags of garbage up and over.

As soon as they struck bottom, a shower of sparks rose. Almost immediately, fire climbed up the cardboard stacked inside the Dumpster; it roared against the metal. "Peter, get down from there," Josie yelled. Peter didn't move. The flames danced in front of his face, the heat distorted his features. "Peter, now!" She reached up, grabbing his arm, pulling him down to the pavement as something—toner? oil?—exploded inside the Dumpster.

"We have to call 911," Josie cried, and she scrambled to her feet.

The firemen arrived in minutes, spraying some noxious chemical into the Dumpster. Josie paged Mr. Cargrew, who'd been on the golf course. "Thank God you weren't hurt," he said to both of them.

"Josie saved me," Peter replied.

While Mr. Cargrew spoke to the firemen, she went back into the copy shop with Peter following. "I knew you'd save me," Peter said. "That's why I did it."

"Did *what?*" But Peter didn't have to answer, because Josie already knew why Peter had been up on the Dumpster when he should have been on break. She knew who'd tossed the match, the moment he heard her exiting the back door with bags of garbage.

Josie told herself, even as she pulled Mr. Cargrew aside, that she was only doing what any responsible employee would do: tell the boss who had tried to destroy his property. She did not admit that she was scared by what Peter had said, by the truth of it. And she pretended not to feel that small fanning in her chest—a smaller version of the fire that Peter had started—which she identified, for the very first time in her life, as revenge.

When Mr. Cargrew fired Peter, Josie didn't listen to the conversation. She felt his gaze on her—hot, accusing—as he left, but she focused her attention on a job from a local bank instead. As she stared at the papers coming out of the machine, she considered how strange it was to measure success by how closely each product resembled the one that had come before.

After school, Josie waited for Matt at the flagpole. He'd sneak up behind her and she'd pretend she didn't notice him coming, until he kissed her. People watched, and Josie loved that. In a way, she thought of her status as a secret identity: now, if she got straight A's or said she actually *liked* to read for fun, she wouldn't be thought of as a freak, simply because when people saw her, they noticed her popularity first. It was, she figured, a little like what her mother experienced wherever she went: when you were the judge, no other trait really mattered.

Sometimes she had nightmares in which Matt realized she was a fraud—that she wasn't beautiful; she wasn't cool; she wasn't anyone worthy of admiration. *What were we thinking?* she imagined her friends saying, and maybe for that reason, it was so hard even when she was awake to think of them as friends.

She and Matt had plans for this weekend—important plans that she could hardly keep to herself. As she sat on the stone steps leading up to the flagpole, waiting for him, she felt someone tap her on the shoulder. "You're late," she accused, grinning, and then she turned around to see Peter.

He looked just as shocked as she felt, even though he'd been the one to seek her out. In the months since Josie had gotten Peter fired from the copy shop, she had gone out of her way to avoid coming in contact with him—no easy feat, given that they were in math class together every day and passed in the halls numerous times. Josie would always make sure she had her nose in a book or her attention firmly focused on another conversation.

"Josie," he said, "can we talk for a minute?"

Students were streaming out of the school; she could feel their glances flick over her like a whip. Were they staring at her because of who she was, or because of who she was with?

"No," she said flatly.

"It's just . . . I really need Mr. Cargrew to give me my job back. I know it was a mistake, what I did. I thought maybe—maybe if you told him . . ." He broke off. "He likes you," Peter said.

Josie wanted to tell him to go away; that she didn't want to work with him again, much less be seen having a conversation with him. But something had happened during the months since Peter had set that Dumpster fire. The payback she'd thought he was due, after his math-class elegy to Josie, had burned in her chest every time she thought about it. And Josie had started to wonder if maybe Peter had gotten the wrong idea not because he was crazy, but because she'd led him to it. After all, when no one was around at the copy shop, they'd talked to each other, they'd laughed. He was an okay kid—just not someone you wanted to be associated with, necessarily, in public. But feeling that way was different than acting on it, right? She wasn't like Drew and Matt and John, who'd shove Peter into the wall when they walked by him in the halls, or who stole his brown-bag lunch and played monkey in the middle with it, until it ripped and the contents spilled onto the floor—was she?

She didn't want to talk to Mr. Cargrew. She didn't want Peter to think that she wanted to be his friend, that she even wanted to be his acquaintance.

But she didn't want to be like Matt either, whose comments to Peter sometimes made her feel sick inside.

Peter was sitting across from her, waiting for an answer, and then suddenly he wasn't. He tumbled down the stone steps as Matt stood over him. "Get away from my girlfriend, homo," Matt said. "Go find a nice little boy to play with."

Peter had landed facedown on the pavement. When he lifted his head, his lip was bleeding. He looked at Josie first, and to her surprise, he didn't seem upset or even angry—just truly, deeply tired. "Matt," Peter said, coming up on his knees. "Do you have a big dick?"

"Wouldn't *you* like to know," Matt said.

"Not really." Peter staggered to his feet. "I just wondered if it was long enough for you to go fuck yourself."

Josie felt the air charge between them the moment before Matt was on Peter like a hurricane, punching him in the face, wrestling him bodily to the ground. "You like this, don't you," Matt spat as he pinned Peter down.

Peter shook his head, tears streaming down his cheeks, streaking the blood. "Get . . . off . . ."

"I bet you wish you could," Matt sneered.

By now a crowd had gathered. Josie glanced around frantically, looking for a teacher, but it was after school and there were none around. "Stop," she cried, watching Peter squirm away as Matt went after him again. "Matt, just stop it."

He pulled his next punch and got to his feet, leaving Peter curled on his side like a fiddlehead. "You're right. Why waste my time," Matt said, and he started walking, waiting for Josie to fall into place beside him.

They were heading toward his car. Josie knew that they'd swing into town and grab a coffee before going back to her house. There, Josie would focus on her homework until it became impossible to ignore Matt rubbing her shoulders or kissing her neck, and then they'd make out until they heard her mother's car pulling into the garage.

There was still an unleashed fury to Matt; his fists were curled at his sides. Josie reached for one, unfurled his hand, threaded their fingers together. "Can I say something without making you mad?" she asked.

This was rhetorical, Josie knew: Matt was already angry. It was the flip side to the passion that made her feel as if she'd gone electric inside—just directed, negatively, at someone weak.

When he didn't answer, Josie forged ahead. "I don't get why you have to pick on Peter Houghton."

"The homo was the one who started it," Matt argued. "You heard what he said."

"Well, yeah," Josie said. "After you pushed him down the steps."

Matt stopped walking. "Since when did *you* become his guardian angel?"

He was staring in a way that cut her to the quick. Josie shivered. "I'm not," she said quickly, and she took a deep breath. "I just . . . I don't like the way you treat kids who aren't like us, all right? Just because you don't want to hang out with losers doesn't mean you have to torture them, does it?"

"Yeah, it does," Matt said. "Because if there isn't a *them*, there can't be an *us*." His eyes narrowed. "You should know that better than anyone."

Josie felt herself go numb. She didn't know whether Matt was bringing up Peter's little math chart, or worse, her history as Peter's friend in earlier grades—but she didn't want to find out, either. This was her biggest fear, after all: that the in crowd would realize she'd been out all the time.

She wouldn't tell Mr. Cargrew what Peter had said. She wouldn't even acknowledge him again, if he came up to her. And she wouldn't lie to herself, either, and pretend she was any less awful than Matt when he mocked Peter or beat him up. You did what you had to, to cement your place in the pecking order. And the best way to stay on top was to step on someone else to get there.

"So," Matt said, "are you coming with me?"

She wondered if Peter was still crying. If his nose was broken. If that was the worst of it.

"Yes," Josie said, and she followed Matt without looking back.

Lincoln, Massachusetts, was a suburb of Boston that had once been farmland and that now was a hodgepodge of massive homes with ridiculously high real estate values. Josie stared out the window at the scenery that might have been hers to grow up with, under different circumstances: the stone walls that snaked around properties, the "historic property" badges worn by houses that were nearly two hundred years old, the small ice cream stand that smelled like fresh milk. She wondered whether Logan Rourke would suggest that they take a ride down to the Dairy Joy and share a sundae. Maybe he would walk right up to the counter and order butter pecan without even having to ask her what her favorite flavor was; maybe that's what a father could spin out of instinct.

Matt was driving lazily, his wrist canted over the steering wheel. Just sixteen, he had his driver's license and was ready and willing to go anywhere—to get a quart of milk for his mother, to drop off the dry cleaning, to squire Josie home after school. For him, it wasn't the destination that was important, it was the journey—which was why Josie had asked him to take her to see her father.

Besides, it wasn't as if she had an alternative. She couldn't very well ask her mother to do it, given that her mother didn't even know Josie had been looking for Logan Rourke. She could have probably figured out how to take a bus to Boston, but reaching a home in the suburbs was more complicated than that. So in the end, she decided to tell Matt the whole truth—that she had never known her father, and that she'd found him in a newspaper, because he was running for public office.

Logan Rourke's driveway was not as grandiose as some of the others they'd passed, but it was immaculate. The lawn had been trimmed to a half inch; a spray of wildflowers craned their necks around the iron base of the mailbox. Hanging from a tree branch overhead was the house number: 59.

Josie felt the hair stand up on the back of her neck. When she'd been on the field hockey team last year, that had been her jersey number.

It was a *sign*.

Matt pulled into the driveway. There were two cars—a Lexus and a Jeep—and also a toddler's ride-on fire truck. Josie could not take her eyes off it. Somehow, she hadn't imagined that Logan Rourke might have *other* children. "You want me to come in with you?" Matt asked.

Josie shook her head. "I'm okay."

As she walked up to the front door, she began to wonder what on earth she'd been thinking. You couldn't just drop in on some guy who was a public figure, could you? Surely there would be a Secret Service agent or something; an attack dog.

As if she'd cued it, a bark rang out. Josie turned in the direction of the sound to find a tiny little Yorkie with a pink bow on its head making a beeline for her feet.

The front door opened. "Titania, leave the postman al—" Logan Rourke broke off when he noticed Josie standing in front of him. "You're not the postman."

He was taller than she'd imagined, and he looked just like he did in the *Globe*—white hair, Roman nose, rangy build. But his eyes were the same color as hers, so electric that Josie couldn't look away. She wondered if this had been her mother's downfall, too.

"You're Alex's daughter," he said.

"Well," Josie replied. "*And* yours."

Through the open doorway, Josie heard the shriek of a child still dizzy and delighted from being chased. A woman's voice: "Logan, who is it?"

He reached back and closed the door so that Josie couldn't see into his life any more. He looked incredibly uncomfortable, although in all fairness Josie imagined it was a little off-putting to be confronted by the daughter you'd abandoned before birth. "What are you doing here?"

Wasn't that obvious? "I wanted to meet you. I thought you might want to meet me."

He drew a deep breath. "This really isn't a good time."

Josie glanced back at the driveway, where Matt was still parked. "I can wait."

"Look . . . it's just that . . . I'm running for political office. Right now, this is a complication I can't afford—"

Josie tripped over that one word. She was a *complication*?

She watched Logan Rourke take out his wallet and peel three hundred-dollar bills away from the rest. "Here," he said, pushing it into her hand. "Will this do it?"

Josie tried to breathe, but someone had driven a stake through her chest. She realized that this was blood money; that her own father thought she'd come here to blackmail him.

"After the election," he said, "maybe we could have lunch."

The bills were crisp in her palm, the kind that had just come into circulation. Josie had a sudden memory of being little and accompanying her mother to the bank: how her mother would let her count the twenties to make sure the teller had gotten the withdrawal amount right; how fresh money always smelled of ink and good fortune.

Logan Rourke wasn't her father, not any more than the guy who'd taken their coins at the toll booth or any other stranger. You could share DNA with someone and still have nothing in common with them.

Josie realized, fleetingly, that she had already learned that lesson from her mother.

"Well," Logan Rourke said, and he started toward the

door again. He hesitated with his hand on the knob. "I . . . I don't know your name."

Josie swallowed. "Margaret," she said, so that she would be just as much of a lie to him as he was to her.

"Margaret, then," he answered, and he slipped back inside.

On the way to the car, Josie opened her fingers like a flower. She watched the bills fall to the ground near a plant that looked, like everything else here, as if it was thriving.

Honestly, the whole idea for the game came to Peter when he was asleep.

He'd created computer games before—Pong replicates, racing courses, and even one sci-fi scenario that let you play online with someone in another country if they logged onto the site—but this was the biggest idea he'd conceived of yet. It came about because, after one of Joey's football games, they'd stopped off at a pizza place where Peter had eaten way too much meatball and sausage pizza, and had been staring at an arcade game called DEER HUNT. You put in your quarter and shot your fake rifle at the bucks that poked their heads out from behind trees; if you hit a doe, you lost.

That night Peter dreamed about hunting with his father, but instead of going after deer, they were looking for real people.

He had awakened in a sweat, his hand cramped as if he'd been holding a gun.

It wouldn't be all that hard to create avatars—computerized personas. He'd done some experimenting, and even if the skin tone wasn't right and the graphics weren't perfect, he knew how to differentiate between races and hair color and build through programming language. It might be kind of cool to do a game where the prey was human.

But war games were old hat, and even gangs had been totally overdone, thanks to Grand Theft Auto. What he needed, Peter realized, was a new villain, one that other people would want to gun down, too. That was the joy of a video game: watching someone who deserved it getting his comeuppance.

He tried to think of other microcosms of the universe that might be battlegrounds: alien invasions, Wild West shootouts, spy missions. Then Peter thought about the front line he braved every day.

What if you took the prey . . . and made *them* the hunters?

Peter got out of bed and sat down at his desk, pulling his eighth-grade yearbook from the drawer where he'd banished it months ago. He'd create a computer game that was *Revenge of the Nerds*, but updated for the twenty-first century. A fantasy world where the balance of power was turned on its head, where the underdog finally got a chance to beat the bullies.

He took a marker and started to look through the yearbook, circling portraits.

Drew Girard.

Matt Royston.

John Eberhard.

Peter turned the page and stopped for a moment. Then he circled Josie Cormier's face, too.

"Can you stop here?" Josie said, when she really didn't think she was going to be able to spend another minute riding in the car and pretending that her meeting with her father had gone well. Matt had barely pulled over when she opened the door, flew through the high grass into the woods at the edge of the road.

She sank down on the carpet of pine needles and started

to cry. What she'd been expecting, she really couldn't say—except that this wasn't it. Unconditional acceptance, maybe. Curiosity, at the very least.

"Josie?" Matt said, coming up behind her. "You okay?"

She tried to say yes, but she was so sick of lying. She felt Matt's hand stroke her hair, and that only made her cry harder; tenderness cut as sharp as any knife. "He didn't give a shit about me."

"Then you shouldn't give a shit about him," Matt answered.

Josie glanced up at him. "It's not that simple."

He pulled her into his arms. "Aw, Jo."

Matt was the only one who'd ever given her a nickname. She couldn't remember her mother calling her anything silly, like Pumpkin or Ladybug, the way other parents did. When Matt called her Jo, it reminded her of *Little Women*, and although she was pretty sure Matt had never read the Alcott novel, secretly she was pleased to be associated with a character so strong and sure of herself.

"It's stupid. I don't even know why I'm crying. I just . . . I wanted him to *like* me."

"I'm crazy about you," Matt said. "Does that count?" He leaned forward and kissed her, right on the trail of her tears.

"It counts a lot."

She felt Matt's lips move from her cheek to her neck to the spot behind her ear that always made her feel like she was dissolving. She was a novice at fooling around, but Matt had coaxed her further and further each time they were alone. *It's your fault*, he'd say, and give her that smile. *If you weren't this hot, I'd be able to keep my hands off you.* That alone was an aphrodisiac to Josie. Her? *Hot?* And—just as Matt had promised every time—it *did* feel good to let him touch her everywhere, to let him taste her. Every incremental intimacy with Matt felt as if she were falling off a cliff—that loss of breath, those butterflies in her stomach. One step, and she'd be flying. It didn't occur to Josie, when she leaped, that she was just as likely to fall.

Now she felt his hands moving under her T-shirt, slipping beneath the lace of her bra. Her legs tangled with his; he rubbed up against her. When Matt tugged up her shirt, so that the cool air feathered over her skin, she snapped back to reality. "We can't do this," she whispered.

Matt's teeth scraped over her shoulder.

"We're parked on the side of the *road*."

He looked up at her, drugged, feverish. "But I want you," Matt said, like he had a dozen times.

This time, though, she glanced up.

I want you.

Josie could have stopped him, but she realized she did not intend to. He wanted her, and right now, that was what she most needed to hear.

There was a moment when Matt went still, wondering if the fact that she hadn't shoved his hands away meant what he thought it meant. She heard the rip of a foil condom packet—*How long had he been carrying that around?* Then he tore at his jeans and hiked up her skirt, as if he still expected her to change her mind. Josie felt Matt pulling aside the elastic of her underwear, the burn of his finger pushing inside her. This was nothing like the times before, when his touch had left a track like a comet over her skin; when she found herself aching after she told him she wanted to stop. Matt shifted his weight and came down on top of her again, only this time there was more burning, more pressure. "Ow," she whimpered, and Matt hesitated.

"I don't want to hurt you," he said.

She turned her head away. "Just do it," Josie said, and Matt pushed his hips flush against hers. It was the kind of pain that—even though she was expecting it—made her cry out.

Matt mistook that for passion. "I know, baby," he groaned. She could feel his heartbeat, but from the inside, and then he started to move faster, bucking against her like a fish released from a hook onto a dock.

Josie wanted to ask Matt whether it had hurt the first time he had done it, too. She wondered if it *always* would hurt. Maybe pain was the price everyone paid for love. She turned her face into Matt's shoulder and tried to understand why, even with him still inside of her, she felt empty.

"Peter," Mrs. Sandringham said at the end of English class. "Could I see you for a moment?"

At the sound of his teacher's summons, Peter sank down in his chair. He began to think of excuses he could give his parents when he came home with another failing grade.

He actually liked Mrs. Sandringham. She was only in her late twenties—you could actually look at her while she was prattling on about grammar and Shakespeare and imagine not so long ago, when she might have been slouched in a seat like any ordinary kid and wondering why the clock never seemed to move.

Peter waited until the rest of the class had cleared out before he approached the teacher's desk. "I just wanted to talk to you about your essay," Mrs. Sandringham said. "I haven't graded everyone's yet, but I did have a chance to look over yours and—"

"I can redo it," Peter blurted out.

Mrs. Sandringham raised her brows. "But Peter . . . I wanted to tell you that you're getting an A." She handed it to him; Peter stared at the bright red grade in the margin.

The assignment had been to write about a significant

event that had changed your life. Although it had happened only a week ago, Peter had written about getting fired for setting the fire in the Dumpster at work. In it, he didn't mention Josie Cormier at all.

Mrs. Sandringham had circled one sentence in his conclusion: *I've learned you will get caught, so you have to think things through before you act.*

The teacher reached out and put her hand on Peter's wrist. "You really *have* learned something from this incident," she said, and she smiled at him. "I'd trust you in a heartbeat."

Peter nodded and took the paper from the desk. He swam into the stream of students in the hallway, still holding it. He imagined what his mother would say if he came home with a paper that had a big fat A on it—if, for just once in his life, he did something everyone expected of Joey, and not Peter.

But that would have necessitated telling his mother about the Dumpster incident in the first place. Or admitting that he'd been fired at all, and now spent his afterschool hours at the library instead of at the copy center.

Peter crumpled up the essay and threw it into the first trash can that he passed.

As soon as Josie started spending her free time almost exclusively with Matt, Maddie Shaw had seamlessly slipped into the position of being Courtney's sidekick. In a way, she fit better than Josie ever had: if you were walking behind Courtney and Maddie, you wouldn't be able to tell who was who; Maddie had so closely cultivated the style and movement of Courtney that she'd elevated it from imitation to art.

Tonight they'd gathered at Maddie's house because her parents had gone to visit her older brother, a sophomore at

Syracuse. They weren't drinking—it was hockey season, and the players had to sign a contract with the coach—but Drew Girard had rented the uncut version of a teen sex comedy, and the guys were discussing who was hotter, Elisha Cuthbert or Shannon Elizabeth. "I wouldn't throw either of them out of bed," Drew said.

"What makes you think they'd get in in the first place?" John Eberhard laughed.

"My reputation reaches far and wide . . ."

Courtney smirked. "It's the *only* part of you that does."

"Aw, Court, you wish you knew that for sure."

"Or not . . ."

Josie was sitting on the floor with Maddie, trying to make a Ouija board work. They'd found it in the basement closet, along with Chutes and Ladders and Trivial Pursuit. Josie's fingertips rested lightly on the planchette. "Are you pushing it?"

"Swear to God, no," Maddie said. "Are you?"

Josie shook her head. She wondered what kind of ghost would come to hang out at a teenage party. Someone who'd died tragically, of course, and too young—in a car crash, maybe. "What's your name?" Josie said loudly.

The planchette swiveled to the letter A, and then B, and then stopped.

"Abe," Maddie announced. "It must be."

"Or Abby."

"Are you male or female?" Maddie asked.

The planchette slipped off the edge of the board entirely. Drew started to laugh. "Maybe it's gay."

"Takes one to know one," John said.

Matt yawned and stretched, his shirt riding up. Although Josie's back was to him, she could practically *sense* this, so attuned were their bodies. "As thrillingly fun as this has been, we're out of here. Jo, come on."

Josie watched the planchette spell out a word: N-O. "I'm not leaving," she said. "I'm having fun."

"Meow," Drew said. "Who's pussy-whipped?"

Since they'd started dating, Matt spent more time with Josie than with his friends. And although Matt had told her he'd much rather fool around with her than be in the company of fools, Josie knew it was still important to him to have the respect of Drew and John. But that didn't mean he had to treat her like a slave, did it?

"I said we're leaving," Matt repeated.

Josie glanced up at him. "And I said I'll come when I want to come."

Matt smiled at his friends, smug. "You never came in your life before you met me," he said.

Drew and John burst out laughing, and Josie felt herself flush with embarrassment. She stood, averting her eyes, and ran up the basement stairs.

In the entryway of Maddie's house she grabbed her jacket. When she heard footsteps behind her, Josie didn't even turn around. "I was having fun. So—"

She broke off with a small cry as Matt grabbed her arm hard and spun her around, pinning her up against the wall by her shoulders. "You're hurting me—"

"Don't ever do that to me again."

"You're the one who—"

"You made me look like an idiot," Matt said. "I told you it was time to go."

Bruises bloomed on her skin where he held her fast, as if she were a canvas and he was determined to leave his mark. She went limp beneath his hands: instinct, a surrender. "I . . . I'm sorry," she whispered.

The words were a key—Matt's grip relaxed. "Jo," he sighed, and he rested his forehead against hers. "I don't like sharing you. You can't blame me for that."

Josie shook her head, but she still didn't trust herself to speak.

"It's just that I love you so much."

She blinked. "You do?"

He hadn't said those words yet, and she hadn't said them either, even though she felt them, because if he didn't say them back then Josie was sure she'd simply evaporate on the spot from sheer humiliation. But here was Matt, saying he loved her, *first*.

"Isn't that obvious?" he said, and he took her hand, brought it to his lips, and kissed the knuckles so gently that Josie almost forgot all that had happened to get them to that moment.

"Kentucky Fried People," Peter said, mulling Derek's idea while they sat on the sidelines in gym class, as the teams for basketball were being picked. "I don't know . . . doesn't it seem a little . . ."

"Graphic?" Derek said. "Since when were you aiming for politically correct? See, imagine if you could go to the art room, if you had enough points, and use the kiln as a weapon."

Derek had been road testing Peter's new computer game, pointing out room for improvement and flaws in the design. They knew they had plenty of time for conversation, since they were bound to be the last kids chosen for teams.

Coach Spears had chosen Drew Girard and Matt Royston to be team captains—a huge surprise, *not*—they were varsity athletes, even as sophomores. "Look alive, people," Coach called out. "You want your captains to think you're hungry to play. You want them to think you're the next Michael Jordan."

Drew pointed to a boy in the back. "Noah."

Matt nodded to the kid who'd been sitting next to him. "Charlie."

Peter turned to Derek. "I heard that even though Michael Jordan's retired, he's still getting forty million dollars in endorsements."

"That means he makes $109,589 a day, for not working," Derek figured.

"Ash," Drew called out.

"Robbie," Matt said.

Peter leaned closer to Derek. "If he goes to see a movie, it'll cost him ten bucks, but he'll make $9,132 while he's there."

Derek grinned. "If he hard-boils an egg for five minutes, he'll make $380."

"Stu."

"Freddie."

"O-boy."

"Walt."

By now there were only three kids left to be picked for teams: Derek, Peter, and Royce, who had aggression issues and came complete with his own aide.

"Royce," Matt said.

"He makes $4,560.85 more than he would working at McDonald's," Derek added.

Drew scrutinized Peter and Derek. "He makes $2,283 watching a rerun of *Friends*," Peter said.

"If he wanted to save up for a new Maserati, it would take him a whole twenty-one hours," Derek said. "Damn, I wish I could play basketball."

"Derek," Drew picked.

Derek started to stand up. "Yeah," Peter said, "but even if Michael Jordan saved a hundred percent of his income for the next four hundred and fifty years, he still wouldn't have as much as Bill Gates has right this second."

"All right," Matt said, "I'll take the homo."

Peter shuffled toward the back of Matt's team. "You ought to be good at this game, Peter," Matt said, loud enough so that everyone else could hear. "Just keep your hands on the balls."

Peter leaned against a floor mat that had been strung on the wall, like the inside of an insane asylum. A rubber room, where all hell could break loose.

He sort of wished he was as sure of who he was as everyone else seemed to be.

"All right," Coach Spears said. "Let's play."

The first ice storm of the season arrived before Thanksgiving. It started after midnight, wind rattling the old bones of the house and pellets drumming the windows. The power went out, but Alex had been expecting that. She woke up with a start at the absolute silence that came with a loss of technology, and reached for the flashlight that she'd put next to her bed.

There were candles, too. Alex lit two candles and watched her shadow, larger than life, creep along the wall. She could remember nights like this when Josie was little, when they'd crawl into bed together and Josie would fall asleep crossing her fingers that there would not be school in the morning.

How come grown-ups never got that kind of holiday? Even if there wasn't school tomorrow—which there wouldn't be, if Alex was guessing correctly—even if the wind was still howling as if the earth were in pain and the ice was caked on her windshield wipers, Alex would be expected to show up in court. Yoga classes and basketball games and theater performances would be postponed, but no one ever canceled real life.

The door to the bedroom flew open. Josie stood there

in a wifebeater tank and a pair of boy's boxers—Alex had no idea where she'd gotten them, and prayed they didn't belong to Matt Royston. For a moment, Alex could barely reconcile this young woman with her curves and long hair with the daughter she still expected, a little girl with an unraveling braid, wearing Wonder Woman pajamas. She tossed back the covers on one side of the bed, an invitation.

Josie dove underneath them, yanking the blankets up to her chin. "It's freaky out there," she said. "It's like the sky's falling down."

"I'd be more worried about the roads."

"Do you think we'll have a snow day tomorrow?"

Alex smiled in the dark. Josie may have been older, but her priorities were still the same. "Most likely."

With a contented sigh, Josie flopped down on her pillow. "I wonder if Matt and I could go skiing somewhere."

"You're not leaving this house if the roads are bad."

"*You* will."

"I don't have a choice," Alex said.

Josie turned to her, her eyes reflecting the candlelight. "Everyone has a choice," she said. She came up on an elbow. "Can I ask you something?"

"Sure."

"Why didn't you marry Logan Rourke?"

Alex felt as if she'd been thrust out into the storm, naked; she was that unprepared for Josie's question. "Where did *this* come from?"

"What was it about him that wasn't good enough? You told me he was handsome and smart. And you had to love him, at least at one point . . ."

"Josie, this is ancient history—and it's stuff you shouldn't worry about, because it has nothing to do with you."

"It has *everything* to do with me," Josie said. "I'm half *him*."

Alex stared up at the ceiling. Maybe the sky *was* falling down; maybe that's what happened when you thought your smoke and mirrors would create a lasting illusion. "He was all of those things," Alex said quietly. "It wasn't him at all. It was me."

"And then there was the whole married part."

She sat up in bed. "How did you find out?"

"It's all over the papers, now that he's running for office. You don't have to be a rocket scientist."

"Did you call him?"

Josie looked her in the eye. "No."

There was a part of Alex that wished Josie *had* talked to him—to see whether he'd followed Alex's career, if he'd even asked about her. The act of leaving Logan, which had seemed so righteous on behalf of her unborn baby, now seemed selfish. Why hadn't she talked to Josie about this before?

Because she'd been protecting Logan. Josie may have grown up without knowing her father, but wasn't that better than learning he'd wanted you to be aborted? *One more lie*, Alex thought, *just a little one. Just to keep Josie from being hurt.* "He wouldn't leave his wife." Alex glanced sideways at Josie. "I couldn't make myself small enough to fit into the space he wanted me to fit into, in order to be part of his life. Does that make sense?"

"I guess."

Beneath the covers, Alex reached for Josie's hand. It was the kind of action that would have seemed forced, had it been in visible sight—something too openly emotional for either of them to lay claim to—but here, in the dark, with the world tunneling in around them, it seemed perfectly natural. "I'm sorry," she said.

"For what?"

"For not giving you the choice of having him around when you were growing up."

Josie shrugged and pulled her hand away. "You did the right thing."

"I don't know," Alex sighed. "The right thing sets you up to be incredibly lonely, sometimes." Suddenly she turned to Josie, stretching a bright smile on her face. "Why are we even talking about this? Unlike me, you're lucky in love, right?"

Just then, the power came back on. Downstairs, the microwave beeped to be reset; the light in the bathroom spilled yellow down the hallway. "I guess I'll go back to my own bed," Josie said.

"Oh. All right," Alex answered, when what she meant to say was that Josie was welcome to stay right where she was.

As Josie padded down the hallway, Alex reached over to reset her alarm clock. It blinked *12:00 12:00 12:00* in panicked LED, like Cinderella's red-flag reminder that fairy-tale endings are hard to come by.

To Peter's surprise, the bouncer at the Front Runner didn't even glance at his fake ID, so before he had time to think twice about the fact that he was actually, *finally* here, he was pushed inside.

He was hit in the face with a blast of smoke, and it took him a minute to adjust to the dim light. Music filled in all the spaces between people, techno-dance stuff that was so loud it made Peter's eardrums pulse. Two tall women were flanking the front door, checking out the new entrants. It took Peter a second glance to realize that one had the shadow of a beard on her face. *His* face. The other one looked more like a girl than most girls he'd ever seen, but then again, Peter had never seen a transvestite up close. Maybe they were perfectionists.

Men were standing in groups of two or three, except for the ones that perched like hawks on a balcony overlooking the dance floor. There were men in leather chaps, men kissing other men in the corners, men passing joints. Mirrors on every wall made the club look huge, its rooms endless.

It hadn't been hard to find out about the Front Runner, thanks to Internet chat rooms. Since Peter was still taking driver's ed, he had to take a bus to Manchester and then a taxi to the club's front door. He still wasn't sure why he was there—it was like an anthropology experiment, in his mind. See if he fit in with this society, instead of his own.

It wasn't that he wanted to fool around with a guy—not yet, anyway. He just wanted to know what it was like to be among guys who were gay, and totally okay with it. He wanted to know if they could look at him and know, instantly, that Peter belonged.

He stopped in front of a couple that was going at it in a dark corner. Seeing a guy kiss a guy was strange in real life. Sure, there were gay kisses on television shows—Big Moments that usually were controversial enough to get press, so that Peter knew when they were airing—and he'd sometimes watch them to see if he *felt* anything, watching them. But they were *acted*, just like regular hookups on TV shows . . . unlike the display in front of his eyes right now. He waited to see if his heart started pounding a little harder, if it made *sense* to him.

He didn't feel particularly excited, though. Curious, sure—did a beard scratch you when you were making out?—and not repulsed, but Peter couldn't say he felt with any great conviction that that was something he wanted to try, too.

The men broke away from each other, and one of them narrowed his eyes. "This ain't no peep show," he said, and he shoved Peter away.

Peter stumbled, falling against someone sitting at the bar. "Whoa," the man said, and then his eyes lit up. "What have we here?"

"Sorry . . ."

"Don't be." He was in his early twenties, with white-blond crew-cut hair and nicotine stains on his fingertips. "First time here?"

Peter turned to him. "How can you tell?"

"You've got that deer-in-the-headlights look." He stubbed out his cigarette and summoned the bartender, who, Peter noticed, looked like he'd walked out of the pages of a magazine. "Rico, get my young friend here a drink. What would you like?"

Peter swallowed. "Pepsi?"

The man's teeth flashed. "Yeah, right."

"I don't drink."

"Ah," he said. "Here, then."

He handed a pair of small tubes to Peter, and then took two for himself out of his pocket. There was no powder in them—just air. Peter watched him open the top, inhale deeply, then do the same with the second vial in his other nostril. Mimicking this, Peter felt his head spin, like the one time he'd drunk a six-pack when his parents had gone off to watch Joey play football. But unlike then, when he'd only wanted to fall asleep afterward, Peter now felt every cell of his body buzzing, wide awake.

"My name's Kurt," the man said, holding out his hand.

"Peter."

"Bottom or top?"

Peter shrugged, trying to look like he knew what the guy was talking about, when in fact he had no clue.

"My God," Kurt said, his jaw dropping. "New blood."

The bartender set a Pepsi down in front of Peter. "Leave him alone, Kurt. He's just a kid."

"Then maybe we should play a game," Kurt said. "You like pool?"

A game of pool Peter could *totally* handle. "That would be great."

He watched Kurt peel a twenty out of his wallet and leave it behind for Rico. "Keep the change," he said.

The poolroom was adjacent to the main part of the club, four tables that were already engaged in various stages of play. Peter sat down on a bench along the wall, studying people. Some were touching each other—an arm on the shoulder, a pat on the rear—but most were just acting like a bunch of guys. Like friends would.

Kurt took a handful of quarters out of his pocket and put them down on the lip of the table. Thinking that this was the pot they would be playing for, Peter pulled two crumpled dollars out of his jacket. "It's not a bet," Kurt laughed. "It's what you pay to play." He stood up as the group in front of them sank the last ball, and started feeding the quarters to the table, until it released a colorful torrent of stripes and solids.

Peter picked a cue off the wall and rubbed chalk over the tip. He wasn't great at pool, but he'd played a couple of times before, and he hadn't done anything totally stupid, like scratch and make the ball jump off the edge of the table. "So you're a betting man," Kurt said. "That could make this interesting."

"I'll put down five bucks," Peter said, hoping that made him sound older.

"I don't bet for money. How about if I win, I get to take

you home. And if you win, you get to take *me* home."

Peter didn't really see how he could win either way, since he didn't want to go home with Kurt and he sure as hell wasn't bringing Kurt home with him. He put the cue down on the edge of the table. "I guess I don't really feel like playing after all."

Kurt grabbed Peter's arm. His eyes were too bright in his face, like small, hot stars. "My quarters are already in there. It's all racked up. You wanted to play the game . . . that means you've got to finish it."

"Let me go," Peter said, his voice climbing higher on a ladder of panic.

Kurt smiled. "But we're just getting started."

Behind Peter, another man spoke. "I think you heard the boy." Peter turned around, still bound by Kurt, and saw Mr. McCabe, his math teacher.

It was one of those strange moments, like when you're at a movie theater and you see the lady who works at the post office, and you know you know her from somewhere, but without the PO boxes and scales and stamp machines around her, you cannot quite figure out who she is. Mr. McCabe was holding a beer and wearing a shirt made out of something silky. He put down the bottle and folded his arms. "Don't fuck with him, Kurt, or I'll call the cops and get you bounced out of here."

Kurt shrugged. "Whatever," he said, and he walked back into the smoky bar.

Peter looked down at the ground, waiting for Mr. McCabe to speak. He was sure that the teacher would call his parents, or rip up his ID in front of him, or ask him why he thought coming to a gay bar in downtown Manchester was a good idea.

Suddenly Peter realized he could have asked Mr. Mc-Cabe the same thing. As he lifted his gaze, he considered a mathematical principle that surely his teacher already knew: If two people have the same secret, it's not a secret anymore.

"You probably need a ride home," Mr. McCabe said.

Josie held her hand up to Matt's, a giant's paw.

"Look at how tiny you are, compared to me," Matt said. "It's amazing I don't kill you."

He shifted then, still hard inside her, so that she felt the bulk of his weight. Then he put his hand up to her throat.

"Because," he said, "I could."

He pressed just the slightest bit, pressure on her windpipe. Not enough to rob her of air, but certainly to scatter speech.

"Don't," Josie managed.

Matt stared down at her, puzzled. "Don't what?" he said, and when he started to move in her again, Josie was sure she had heard it all wrong.

For most of the hour-long ride from Manchester, the conversation between Peter and Mr. McCabe was as superficial as a dragonfly on the surface of a lake, darting around topics neither of them particularly cared about: hockey standings for the Bruins, the upcoming winter formal dance, what good colleges were looking for these days from applicants.

It was after they pulled off Route 89 at the exit for Sterling, and they were driving down dark back roads toward Peter's house, that Mr. McCabe even mentioned the reason they were both in the car. "About tonight," he began. "Not many people know about me in school. I haven't come out yet." The small rectangle of reflected light from the rearview mirror banded his eyes like a raccoon's.

"Why not?" Peter heard himself ask.

"It's not that I don't think the faculty would be support-ive . . . it's that I don't think it's any of their business. Right?"

Peter didn't know how to answer, and then realized that Mr. McCabe was not asking him for his opinion—just for directions. "Yeah," Peter said. "Turn here, and then it's the third house on the left."

Mr. McCabe pulled up in front of Peter's driveway, but didn't turn in. "I'm telling you this because I trust you, Peter. And because if you need someone to talk to, I want you to feel free to come to me."

Peter unbuckled his seat belt. "I'm not gay."

"All right," Mr. McCabe replied, but something in his eyes went soft at the edges.

"I'm not gay," Peter repeated more firmly, and he opened the car door and ran as fast as he could toward his house.

Josie shook up the bottle of OPI nail polish and looked at the sticker on the bottom. *I'm Not Really a Waitress Red.* "Who do you think comes up with these? Do you think it's a bunch of women who sit around a conference table?"

"No," Maddie said. "They're probably just old friends who get drunk once a year and write down all the flavors."

"It's not a flavor if you don't eat it," Emma pointed out.

Courtney rolled over, so that her hair tumbled over the side of the bed like a waterfall. "This is bogus," she an-nounced, although it was her house and her slumber party. "There's got to be something exciting to do."

"Let's call someone," Emma suggested.

Courtney considered this. "Like a prank?"

"We could order pizza and have it delivered to some-one," Maddie said.

"We did that last time with Drew," Courtney sighed, and

then she grinned and reached for the phone. "I've got something better."

She put on the speakerphone and dialed—a musical jingle that sounded awfully familiar to Josie. "Hello," a voice said gruffly on the other end.

"Matt," Courtney said, holding up a finger to her lips to keep everyone else quiet. "Hey."

"It's fucking three in the morning, Court."

"I know. I just . . . I've been wanting to tell you something for a really long time, and I don't know how to do it, because Josie's my friend and everything—"

Josie started to speak, to let Matt know he was being led into a trap, but Emma clapped her hand over Josie's mouth and pushed her back on the bed.

"I like you," Courtney said.

"I like you, too."

"No, I mean . . . I *like* you."

"Geez, Courtney. If I'd known that, I guess I would be having wild sex with you, except for the fact that I love Josie, and she's probably less than three feet away from you right now."

The silence shattered, laughter breaking it apart like glass. "God! How'd you know?" Courtney said.

"Because Josie tells me everything, including when she's sleeping over at your house. Now take me off speakerphone and let me say good night to her."

Courtney handed the receiver over. "Good answer," Josie said.

Matt's voice was smoky with sleep. "Did you doubt it?"

"No," Josie replied, smiling.

"Well, have fun. Just not as much fun as you'd be having with me."

She listened to Matt yawn. "Go to bed."

"Wish you were next to me," he said.

Josie turned her back on the other girls. "Me, too."

"Love you, Jo."

"I love you, too."

"And I," Courtney announced, "am going to throw up." She reached over and punched the disconnect button of the phone.

Josie tossed the receiver on the bed. "It was *your* idea to call him."

"You're just jealous," Emma said. "I wish I had someone who couldn't live without me."

"You're so lucky, Josie," Maddie agreed.

Josie opened the bottle of nail polish again, and a drop spilled off the brush to land on her thigh like a bead of blood. Any of her friends—well, maybe not Courtney, but most of them—would have killed to be in her position.

But would they die for it, a voice inside her whispered.

She looked up at Maddie and Emma and forced a smile. "Tell me about it," Josie said.

In December, Peter got a job in the school library. He was in charge of the audiovisual equipment, which meant that for an hour after school each day, he'd rewind microfilm and organize DVDs alphabetically. He'd bring the overhead projectors and TV/VCRs to classrooms, so that they were in place when the teachers who needed them arrived at school in the morning. He especially liked how nobody bothered him in the library. The cool kids wouldn't have been caught dead there after school; Peter was more likely to find the special-needs students, with their aides, working on assignments.

He'd gotten the job after helping Mrs. Wahl, the librarian, fix her ancient computer so that it stopped bluescreening on her. Now Peter was her favorite student at Sterling High. She let him lock up after she left for the day, and she made him his own key to the custodial elevator, so that he could transport equipment from one floor of the high school to another.

Peter's last job that day was moving a projector from a bio lab on the second floor back down to the AV room. He had stepped into the elevator and turned a key to close the door when someone called out, asking him to hold the door.

A moment later, Josie Cormier hobbled inside.

She was on crutches, sporting an AirCast. She glanced at Peter as the doors of the elevator closed, and then quickly down at the linoleum floor.

Although it had been months since she'd gotten him fired, Peter still felt a flash of anger when he saw Josie. He could practically hear Josie ticking off the seconds in her head until the elevator doors opened again. *Well, I'm not thrilled being stuck in here with you either,* he thought to himself, and just about then the elevator bobbled and screeched to a halt.

"What's wrong with it?" Josie punched at the first-floor button.

"That's not going to do anything," Peter said. He reached across her—noticing that she nearly lost her balance trying to lean back, as if he had a communicable disease—and pushed the red Emergency button.

Nothing happened.

"This sucks," Peter said. He stared up at the roof of the elevator. In movies, action heroes were always climbing through the air ducts into the elevator shaft, but even if he stood on top of the projector, he didn't see how he could get the hatch open without a screwdriver.

Josie punched at the button again. "Hello?!"

"No one's going to hear you," Peter said. "The teachers are all gone and the custodian watches *Oprah* from five until six in the basement." He glanced at her. "What are you doing here, anyway?"

"An independent study."

"What's that?"

She lifted a crutch. "It's what you do for credit when you can't play gym. What were *you* doing here?"

"I work here now," Peter said, and they both fell silent.

Logistically, Peter thought, they'd be found sooner or later. The custodian would probably discover them when he was moving his floor buffer upstairs, but if not, the longest they'd have to wait was morning when everyone arrived again. He smiled a little, thinking about what he could truthfully tell Derek: *Guess what, I slept with Josie Cormier.*

He opened an iBook and pressed a button, starting a PowerPoint presentation on the screen. Amoebas, blastospheres. Cell division. An embryo. Amazing to think that we all started out like that—microscopic, indistinguishable.

"How long before they find us?"

"I don't know."

"Won't the librarians notice if you don't come back?"

"My own *parents* wouldn't notice if I didn't come back."

"Oh, God . . . what if we run out of air?" Josie banged on the doors with a crutch. "Help!"

"We're not going to run out of air," Peter said.

"How do you know that?"

He didn't, not really. But what else was he going to say?

"I get freaked out in small spaces," Josie said. "I can't do this."

"You're claustrophobic?" He wondered how he hadn't known that about Josie. But then again, why should he? It wasn't as though he'd been such an active part of her life for the past six years.

"I think I'm going to throw up," Josie moaned.

"Oh, shit," Peter said. "Don't. Just close your eyes, then you won't even realize you're in an elevator."

Josie closed her eyes, but when she did, she swayed on her crutches.

"Hang on." Peter took her crutches away, so that she was balancing on one foot. Then he held on to her hands while she sank to the floor, extending her bad leg.

"How'd you get hurt?" he asked, nodding at the cast.

"I fell on some ice." She started to cry, and gasp—hyperventilate, Peter guessed, although he'd only seen the word written, not live. You were supposed to breathe into a paper bag, right? Peter searched the elevator for something that would suffice. There was a plastic bag with some documents in it on the AV trolley, but somehow putting that on your head didn't seem particularly brilliant. "Okay," he said, brainstorming, "let's do something to get your mind off where you are."

"Like what?"

"Maybe we should play a game," Peter suggested, and he heard the same words repeated in his head, Kurt's voice from the Front Runner. He shook his head to clear it. "Twenty Questions?"

Josie hesitated. "Animal, vegetable, or mineral?"

After six rounds of Twenty Questions, and an hour of geography, Peter was getting thirsty. He also had to pee, and that was really troubling him, because he didn't think he could last until morning and there was absolutely no way he was going to take a whiz with Josie watching. Josie had gotten quiet, but at least she'd stopped shaking. He thought she might be asleep.

Then she spoke. "Truth or dare," Josie said.

Peter turned toward her. "Truth."

"Do you hate me?"

He ducked his head. "Sometimes."

"You should," Josie said.

"Truth or dare?"

"Truth," Josie said.

"Do you hate *me*?"

"No."

"Then why," Peter asked, "do you act like you do?"

She shook her head. "I have to act the way people expect me to act. It's part of the whole . . . thing. If I don't . . ." She picked at the rubber brace of her crutch. "It's complicated. You wouldn't understand."

"Truth or dare," Peter said.

Josie grinned. "Dare."

"Lick the bottom of your own foot."

She started to laugh. "I can't even *walk* on the bottom of my own foot," she said, but she bent down and slipped off her loafer, stuck out her tongue. "Truth or dare?"

"Truth."

"Chicken," Josie said. "Have you ever been in love?"

Peter looked at Josie, and thought of how they had once tied a note with their addresses to a helium balloon and let it go in her backyard, certain it would reach Mars. Instead, they had received a letter from a widow who lived two blocks away. "Yeah," he said. "I think so."

Her eyes widened. "With who?"

"That wasn't the question. Truth or dare?"

"Truth," Josie said.

"What's the last lie you told?"

The smile faded from Josie's face. "When I told you I slipped on the ice. Matt and I were having a fight and he hit me."

"He *hit* you?"

"It wasn't like that. . . . I said something I shouldn't have, and when he—well, I lost my balance, anyway, and hurt my ankle."

"Josie—"

She ducked her head. "No one knows. You won't tell, will you?"

"No." Peter hesitated. "Why *didn't* you tell anyone?"

"That wasn't the question," Josie said, parroting him.

"I'm asking it now."

"Then I'll take a dare."

Peter curled his hands into fists at his sides. "Kiss me," he said.

She leaned toward him slowly, until her face was too close to be in focus. Her hair fell over Peter's shoulder like a curtain and her eyes closed. She smelled like autumn— like apple cider and slanting sun and the snap of the coming cold. He felt his heart scrambling, caught inside the confines of his own body.

Josie's lips landed just on the edge of his, almost his cheek and not quite his mouth. "I'm glad I wasn't stuck in here alone," she said shyly, and he tasted the words, sweet as mint on her breath.

Peter glanced down at his lap and prayed that Josie wouldn't notice that he was hard as a rock. He started to smile so wide that it hurt. It wasn't that he didn't like girls; it was that there was only one right one.

Just then there was a knock on the metal door. "Anyone in here?"

"Yes!" Josie cried, struggling to stand with her crutches. "Help!"

There was a bang and a hammering, the sound of a crowbar breaching a seam. The doors flew open, and Josie hurried out of the elevator. Matt Royston was waiting next to the janitor. "I got worried when you weren't home," he said, and pulled Josie into his embrace.

But you hit her, Peter thought, and then he remembered that he had made a promise to Josie. He listened to her whoop with surprise as Matt swept her into his arms, carrying her so that she wouldn't have to use her crutches.

Peter wheeled the iBook and projector back to the library and locked the AV room. It was late now, and he had to walk home, but he almost didn't mind. He decided that the first thing he'd do was erase the circle around Josie's portrait in his yearbook, take her characteristics off the roster of villains in his video game.

He was mentally reviewing the logistics of that, in terms of programming, when he finally reached home. It took Peter a moment to realize something wasn't right—the lights weren't on in the house, but the cars were there. "Hello?" he called out, wandering from the living room to the dining room to the kitchen. "Anyone here?"

He found his parents sitting in the dark at the kitchen table. His mother looked up, dazed. It was clear that she'd been crying.

Peter felt something warm break free in his chest. He'd told Josie his parents wouldn't notice his absence, but that wasn't true at all. Clearly, his parents had been *frantic.* "I'm fine," Peter told them. "Really."

His father stood up, blinking back tears, and hauled Peter into his arms. Peter couldn't remember the last time he'd been hugged like this. In spite of the fact that he wanted to seem cool, that he was sixteen years old, he melted against his father's frame and held on tightly. First Josie, and now this? It was turning out to be the best day of Peter's life.

"It's Joey," his father sobbed. "He's dead."

Ask a random kid today if she wants to be popular and she'll tell you no, even if the truth is that if she was in a desert dying of thirst and had the choice between a glass of water and instant popularity, she'd probably choose the latter. See, you can't admit to wanting it, because that makes you less cool. To be truly popular, it has to look like it's something you <u>are</u>, when in reality, it's what you <u>make</u> yourself.

I wonder if anyone works any harder at anything than kids do at being popular. I mean, even air-traffic controllers and the president of the United States take vacations, but look at your average high school student, and you'll see someone who's putting in time twenty-four hours a day, for the entire length of the school year.

So how do you crack that inner sanctum? Well, here's the catch: it's not up to you. What's important is what everyone else thinks of how you dress, what you eat for lunch, what shows you TiVo, what music is on your iPod.

I've always sort of wondered, though: If everyone else's opinion is what matters, then do you ever really have one of your own?

One Month After

Although the investigative report from Patrick Ducharme had been sitting on Diana's desk since ten
days post-shooting, the prosecutor hadn't given it a glance.
First she'd had a probable cause hearing to pull together,
then, she'd been in front of the grand jury, getting them to
hand down an indictment. Only now was she beginning to
sift through the analyses of fingerprints, ballistics, and
bloodstains, as well as all the original police reports.

She'd spent the morning poring over the logistics of the
shooting and mentally organizing her opening statement
along the same path of destruction Peter Houghton had
followed, tracking his movements from victim to victim.
The first to be shot was Zoe Patterson, on the school steps.
Alyssa Carr, Angela Phlug, Maddie Shaw. Courtney Ignatio. Haley Weaver and Brady Pryce. Lucia Ritolli, Grace
Murtaugh.

Drew Girard.

Matt Royston.

More.

Diana took off her glasses and rubbed her eyes. A book
of the dead, a map of the wounded. And those were only

the ones whose injuries had been serious enough to involve a hospital stay—there were scores of kids who had been treated and released, hundreds whose scars were buried too deep to see.

Diana did not have children—hell, in her position, the men she met were either felons, which was awful, or defense attorneys, which was worse. She did, however, have a three-year-old nephew, who'd been reprimanded in his nursery school for pointing his finger at a classmate and saying, "Bang, you're dead." When her sister called up indignant and spouting about the Bill of Rights, had Diana thought that her nephew was going to grow up to become a psychopath? Not for a moment. He was just a kid, playing around.

Had the Houghtons thought that, too?

Diana looked down at the list of names in front of her. Her job was to connect these dots, but what truly needed to be done was to draw a line long before this: the tipping point where Peter Houghton's mind had shifted, subtly, from *what if* to *when*.

Her eye fell on another list—one from the hospital. Cormier, Josie. According to the medical records, the girl—seventeen—had been admitted overnight for observation after a fainting spell, and had a laceration on the scalp. Her mother's signature was at the bottom of the consent form for blood tests—Alex Cormier.

It *couldn't* be.

Diana sat back in her chair. You'd never want to be the one to ask a judge to recuse herself. You might as well announce that you doubted her ability to be impartial, and since Diana would be in her court numerous times in the future, it just wasn't a smart career move. But Judge Cormier surely knew that she couldn't address this case fairly, not with a daughter who was a witness. Granted, Josie hadn't been shot, but she'd been *hurt* during the shooting. Judge Cormier would recuse herself, certainly. Which meant there was nothing to worry about.

Diana turned her attention back to the discovery spread across her desk, reading until the letters blurred on the page, until Josie Cormier was just another name.

On her way home from the courthouse, Alex passed the makeshift memorial that had been erected for the victims of Sterling High. There were ten white wooden crosses, even though one of the dead children—Justin Friedman— had been Jewish. The crosses were nowhere near the school, but instead on a stretch of Route 10 where there was only floodplain for the Connecticut River. In the days after the shooting, there might be any number of mourners standing by the crosses, adding to the individual piles of photos and Beanie Babies and bouquets.

Alex felt herself pulling her car off the road, onto the shoulder. She didn't know why she was stopping now, why she hadn't stopped before. Her heels sank into the spongy grass. She crossed her arms and stepped up to the markers.

They were in no particular order, and the name of each dead student was carved into the crosspiece of the wood. Most of the students Alex did not know, but Courtney Ignatio and Maddie Shaw had crosses beside each other. The flowers that had been left behind at the markers had wilted, their green tissue wrappers rotting into the ground. Alex knelt down, fingering a faded poem that was tacked to Courtney's memorial.

Courtney and Maddie had come for a sleepover several times. Alex remembered finding the girls in the kitchen, eating raw cookie dough instead of baking it, their bodies fluid as waves as they moved around each other. She could remember being jealous of them—to be so young, to know you hadn't yet made a mistake that would change your life. Now Alex flushed with chagrin: at least she had a life to be changed.

It was at Matt Royston's cross, however, that Alex started to cry. Propped against the white wooden base was a framed photograph, one that had been enclosed in a plastic bag to keep the elements from ruining it. There was Matt, his eyes bright, his arm hooked around Josie's neck.

Josie wasn't looking at the camera. She was staring at Matt, as if she couldn't see anything else.

Somehow, it seemed safer to fall apart here in front of a makeshift memorial than at home, where Josie might hear her crying. No matter how cool and collected she had been—for Josie's sake—the one person she could not fool was herself. She might pick up her daily routine like a missed stitch, she might tell herself that Josie was one of the lucky ones, but when she was alone in the shower, or caught in the interstitial space between waking and sleep, Alex would find herself shaking uncontrollably, the way you do when you've swerved to avoid an accident and have to pull to the side of the road to make sure you are really, truly all in one piece.

Life was what happened when all the *what-if*'s didn't, when what you dreamed or hoped or—in this case—feared might come to pass passed by instead. Alex had spent enough nights thinking of good fortune, of how it was thin as a veil, how seamlessly you might stream from one side to the other. This could easily have been Josie's cross she was kneeling before, Josie's memorial that hosted this photo. A twitch of the shooter's hand, a fallen footstep, a bullet's ricochet—and everything might have been different.

Alex got to her feet and took a fortifying breath. As she headed back to her car, she saw the narrow hole where an eleventh cross had been. After the ten had been erected, someone had added one with Peter Houghton's name on it. Night after night that extra cross had been taken down or vandalized. There had been editorials in the paper over it: Did Peter Houghton deserve a cross, when he was still very much alive? Was putting up a memorial for him a tragedy or a travesty? Eventually, whoever had carved Peter's cross decided to leave well enough alone and stopped replacing it every day.

As Alex slipped inside her car again, she wondered how—until she'd come here for herself—she had managed to forget that someone, at some point, considered Peter Houghton to be a victim, too.

Since That Day, as Lacy had taken to calling it, she'd delivered three babies. Each time, although the birth was uneventful and the delivery easy, something had gone wrong. Not for the mother, but for the midwife. When Lacy stepped into a delivery room, she felt poisonous, too negative to be the one to welcome another human being to this world. She had smiled her way through the births and had offered the new mothers the support and the medical care that they needed, but the moment she'd sent them on their way, cutting that last umbilical cord between hospital and home, Lacy knew she was giving them the wrong advice. Instead of easy platitudes like *Let them eat when they want to eat* and *You can't hold a baby too much*, she should have been telling them the truth: *This child you've been waiting for is not who you imagine him to be. You're strangers now; you'll be strangers years from now.*

Years ago, she used to lie in bed and imagine what her life would have been like had she not been a mother. She'd picture Joey bringing her a bouquet of dandelion weeds and clover; Peter falling asleep against her chest with the tail of her braid still clutched in his hand. She relived the clenching fist of labor pains, and the mantra she'd used to get through them: *When this is done, imagine what you'll have.* Motherhood had painted the colors of Lacy's world a bit brighter; had swelled her to the seams with the belief that her life could not possibly be more complete. What she hadn't realized was that sometimes when your vision was that sharp and true, it could cut you. That only if you'd felt such fullness could you really understand the ache of being empty.

She had not told her patients—God, she hadn't even told Lewis—but these days, when she lay in bed and imagined what her life would have been like had she not been a mother, she found herself sucking on one bitter word: *easier.*

Today Lacy was doing office visits; she'd gone through five patients and was about to move on to her sixth. *Janet Isinghoff*, she read, scanning the folder. Although she was another midwife's patient, the policy of the group was to have each woman see all of the midwives, since you never knew who'd be on call when you delivered.

Janet Isinghoff was thirty-three years old, primigravid, with a family history of diabetes. She had been hospitalized once before for appendicitis, had mild asthma, and was generally healthy. She was also standing in the door of the examination room, clutching her hospital johnny shut as she argued heatedly with Priscilla, the OB nurse.

"I don't care," Janet was saying. "If it comes down to that, I'll just go to a different hospital."

"But that's not the way our practice works," Priscilla explained.

Lacy smiled. "Anything I can do here?"

Priscilla turned, putting herself between Lacy and the patient. "It's nothing."

"Didn't sound like nothing," Lacy replied.

"I don't want my baby delivered by a woman whose son is a murderer," Janet burst out.

Lacy felt her feet root on the floor, her breath go so shallow that she might as well have fielded a blow. And hadn't she?

Priscilla turned crimson. "Mrs. Isinghoff, I think I can speak for the whole of the midwifery team when I say that Lacy is—"

"It's all right," Lacy murmured. "I understand."

By now the other nurses and midwives were staring; Lacy knew that they would rally to her defense—tell Janet Isinghoff to find herself another practice, explain that Lacy was one of the best and most seasoned midwives in New Hampshire. But that hardly mattered, really—it wasn't about Janet Isinghoff demanding to have another midwife deliver her child; it was that even after Janet had left, there would be another woman here tomorrow or the next day with the same uneasy request. Who would want the first hands touching her newborn to be the same hands that had held a murderer's when he crossed the street; that had brushed his hair off his forehead when he was sick; that had rocked him to sleep?

Lacy walked down the hall to the fire door and ran up four flights of stairs. Sometimes, when she'd had a particularly difficult day, Lacy would take refuge on the roof of the hospital. She'd lie on her back and stare up at the sky and pretend, with that view, she could be anywhere on earth.

A trial was just a formality—Peter would be found guilty. It didn't matter how she tried to convince herself—or Peter— otherwise; the fact was there between them at those horrible jail visits, immense and unmentionable. It reminded Lacy of running into someone you hadn't seen for a while, and finding her bald and missing her eyebrows: you knew she was in the throes of chemotherapy, but pretended you didn't, because it was easier that way for both of you.

What Lacy would have liked to say, if anyone had given her the podium on which to do it, was that Peter's actions were just as surprising to her—as *devastating* to her—as they were to anyone else. She'd lost her son, too, that day. Not just physically, to the correctional facility, but personally, because the boy she'd known had disappeared, swallowed by this beast she didn't recognize, capable of acts she could not conceive.

But what if Janet Isinghoff was right? What if it was something Lacy had said or done . . . or *not* said or done . . . that had brought Peter to that point? Could you hate your son for what he had done, and still love him for who he had been?

The door opened, and Lacy spun around. No one ever came up here, but, then again, she rarely left the floor this upset. It wasn't Priscilla, though, or one of her colleagues: Jordan McAfee stood on the threshold, a sheaf of papers in his hand. Lacy closed her eyes. "Perfect."

"Yes, that's what my wife tells me," he said, coming toward her with a wide smile on his face. "Or maybe it's just what I *wish* she'd tell me. . . . Your secretary told me you were probably up here, and— Lacy, are you all right?"

Lacy nodded, and then she shook her head. Jordan took her arm and led her to a folding chair that someone had carted all the way up to the roof. "Bad day?"

"You could say that," Lacy answered. She tried to keep Jordan from seeing her tears. It was stupid, she knew, but she didn't want Peter's attorney to think she was the kind of person who had to be treated with kid gloves. Then he might not tell her every blunt truth about Peter, and she wanted to hear that, no matter what.

"I needed you to sign some paperwork . . . but I can come back later . . ."

"No," Lacy said. "This is . . . fine." It was better than fine, she realized. It was sort of nice to be sitting next to someone who believed in Peter, even if she was paying him to do that. "Can I ask you a professional question?"

"Sure."

"Why is it so easy for people to point a finger at someone else?"

Jordan sank down across from her, on the ledge of the roof, which made Lacy nervous, but, again, she couldn't show it, because she didn't want Jordan to think she was fragile. "People need a scapegoat," he said. "It's human nature. That's the biggest hurdle we have to overcome as defense attorneys, because in spite of being innocent until proven guilty, the very act of an arrest makes people assume guilt. Do you know how many cops have un-arrested someone? I know, it's crazy—I mean, do you think they apologize profusely and make sure that person's family and friends and co-workers all know it was a big mistake, or do they just sort of say, 'My bad,' and take off?" He met her gaze. "I'm sure it's hard, reading the editorials that have already convicted Peter before the trial's even started, but—"

"It's not Peter," Lacy said quietly. "They're blaming me."

Jordan nodded, as if he'd expected this.

"He didn't do this because of how we raised him. He did it in spite of that," Lacy said. "You have a baby, don't you?"

"Yes. Sam."

"What if he turns out to be someone you never thought he'd be?"

"Lacy—"

"Like, what if Sam tells you he's gay?"

Jordan shrugged. "So what?"

"And if he decided to convert to Islam?"

"That's his choice."

"What if he became a suicide bomber?"

Jordan paused. "I really don't want to think about something like that, Lacy."

"No," she said, facing him. "Neither did I."

Philip O'Shea and Ed McCabe had been together for almost two years. Patrick stared at the photos on the fireplace mantel—the two men with their arms slung around each other, with a backdrop of the Canadian Rockies; a corn palace; the Eiffel Tower. "We liked to get away," Philip said as he brought out a glass of iced tea and handed it to Patrick. "Sometimes, for Ed, it was easier to get away than it was to stay here."

"Why was that?"

Philip shrugged. He was a tall, thin man with freckles that appeared when his face flushed with emotion. "Ed hadn't told everyone about . . . his lifestyle. And to be perfectly honest, keeping secrets in a small town is a bitch."

"Mr. O'Shea—"

"Philip. Please."

Patrick nodded. "I wonder if Ed ever mentioned Peter Houghton's name to you."

"He taught him, you know."

"Yeah. I meant . . . well, beyond that."

Philip led him to a screened porch, a set of wicker chairs. Every room he'd seen in the house looked like it had just been host to a magazine photo shoot: the pillows on the couches were tilted at a forty-five-degree angle; there were vases with glass beads in them; the plants were all lush and green. Patrick thought back to his own living room, where today he'd found a piece of toast stuffed between his sofa cushions that had what could really only be called penicillin growing on top of it by now. It might have been a ridiculous stereotype, but this home had Martha Stewart written all over it, whereas Patrick's looked more like a crack house.

"Ed talked to Peter," Philip said. "Or at least, he tried to."

"About what?"

"Being a bit of a lost soul, I think. Teens are always trying to fit in. If you don't fit into the popular crowd, you try the athletic crowd. If that doesn't work, you go to the drama crowd . . . or to the druggies," he said. "Ed thought that Peter might be trying out the gay and lesbian crowd."

"So Peter came to talk to Ed about being gay?"

"Oh, no. Ed sought *Peter* out. We all remember what it was like to be figuring out what was different about us, when we were his age. Worried to death that some other kid who was gay was going to come on to you and blow your cover."

"Do you think Peter might have been worried about Ed blowing his cover?"

"I sincerely doubt it, especially in Peter's case."

"Why?"

Philip smiled at Patrick. "You've heard of gaydar?"

Patrick felt himself coloring. It was like being in the presence of an African-American who made a racist joke, simply because he could. "I guess."

"Gay people don't come clearly marked—it's not like having a different color skin or a physical disability. You learn to pick up on mannerisms, or looks that last just a little too long. You get pretty good at figuring out if someone's gay, or just staring at you because *you* are."

Before he realized what he was doing, Patrick had leaned a little farther away from Philip, who started to laugh. "You can relax. Your vibe clearly says you bat for the other team." He looked up at Patrick. "And so does Peter Houghton."

"I don't understand . . ."

"Peter may have been confused about his sexuality, but it was crystal clear to Ed," Philip said. "That boy is straight."

Peter burst through the door of the conference room, bristling. "How come you haven't come to see me?"

Jordan looked up from the notes he was making on a pad. He noticed, absently, that Peter had put on some weight—and apparently some muscle. "I've been busy."

"Well, I'm stuck here all by myself."

"Yeah, and I'm busting my ass to make sure that isn't a permanent condition," Jordan replied. "Sit down."

Peter slumped into a chair, scowling. "What if I don't feel like talking to you today? Clearly, you don't always feel like talking to me."

"Peter, how about we drop the bullshit so I can do my job?"

"Like I care if you can do your job."

"Well, you should," Jordan said. "Seeing as *you're* the beneficiary." *At the end of this*, Jordan thought, *I will be either reviled or canonized.* "I want to talk about the explosives," he said. "Where would a person get something like that?"

"At www.boom.com," Peter answered.

Jordan just stared at him.

"Well, it's not all that far from the truth," Peter said. "I mean, *The Anarchist Cookbook* is online. So are about ten thousand recipes for Molotov cocktails."

"They didn't find a Molotov cocktail at the school. They found plastic explosives with a blasting cap and a timing device."

"Yeah," Peter said. "Well."

"Say I wanted to make a bomb with stuff I had lying around the house. What would I use?"

Peter shrugged. "Newspaper. Fertilizer—like Green

Thumb, the chemical stuff. Cotton. And some diesel fuel, but you'd probably have to get that at a gas station, so it wouldn't technically be in your house."

Jordan watched him count off the ingredients. There was a matter-of-factness to Peter's voice that was chilling, but even more unsettling was the tone threaded through his words: this was something Peter had been proud of.

"You've done this kind of thing before."

"The first time I built one, I just did it to see if I could." Peter's voice grew more animated. "I did some more after that. The kind you throw and run like hell."

"What made this one different?"

"The ingredients, for one. You have to get the potassium chlorate from bleach, which isn't easy, but it's kind of like doing a chemistry lab. My dad came into the kitchen when I was filtering out the crystals," Peter said. "That's what I told him I was doing—extra credit."

"Jesus."

"Anyway, after you've got that, all you need is Vaseline, which we keep under the bathroom sink, and the gas you'd find in a camp stove, and the kind of wax you use to can pickles. I was kind of freaked out about using a blasting cap," Peter said. "I mean, I'd never really done anything that *big* before. But you know, when I started to come up with the whole plan—"

"Stop," Jordan interrupted. "Just stop right there."

"You're the one who asked in the first place," Peter said, stung.

"But that's an answer I can't hear. My job is to get you acquitted, and I can't lie in front of the jury. On the other hand, I can't lie about the things I don't know. And right now, I can honestly say that you did not plan in advance what happened that day. I'd like to keep it that way, and if you have any sense of self-preservation, you should, too."

Peter walked to the window. The glass was fuzzy, scratched after all these years. *From what?* Jordan wondered. *Inmates clawing to get out?* Peter wouldn't be able to see that the snow had all melted by now; that the first crocuses had choked their way out of the soil. Maybe it was better that way.

"I've been going to church," Peter announced.

Jordan wasn't much for organized religion, but he didn't begrudge others their chosen comforts. "That's great."

"I'm doing it because they let me leave my cell to go to services," Peter said. "Not because I've found Jesus or anything."

"Okay." He wondered what this had to do with explosives or, for that matter, anything else regarding Peter's defense. Frankly, Jordan didn't have time to have a philosophical discussion with Peter about the nature of God—he had to meet Selena in two hours to go over potential defense witnesses—but something kept him from cutting Peter off.

Peter turned. "Do you believe in hell?"

"Yeah. It's full of defense attorneys. Just ask any prosecutor."

"No, seriously," Peter said. "I bet I'm headed there."

Jordan forced a smile. "I don't lay odds on bets I can't collect on."

"Father Moreno, he's the priest who leads the church services here? He says that if you accept Jesus and repent, you get excused . . . like religion is just some giant freebie hall pass that gets you out of anything and everything. But see, that can't be right . . . because Father Moreno also says that every life is worth something . . . and what about the ten kids who died?"

Jordan knew better, but he still heard himself asking Peter a question. "Why did you phrase it that way?"

"What way?"

"The ten kids who died. As if it was a natural progression."

Peter's brow wrinkled. "Because it was."

"How?"

"It's like those explosives, I guess. Once you light the fuse, either you destroy the bomb before it goes off . . . or the bomb destroys everything else."

Jordan stood up and took a step toward his client. "Who struck the match, Peter?"

Peter lifted his face. "Who *didn't?*"

Josie now thought of her friends as the ones who had been left behind. Haley Weaver had been sent to Boston for plastic surgery; John Eberhard was in some rehab place reading *Hop on Pop* and learning how to drink from a straw; Matt and Courtney and Maddie were gone forever. That left Josie and Drew and Emma and Brady: a posse that had dwindled to such a degree that you could barely call them a posse at all anymore.

They were in Emma's basement, watching a DVD. That was about the extent of their social life these days, because Drew and Brady were still in bandages and casts and besides, even if none of them wanted to say it out loud, going anywhere they used to go reminded them of who was missing.

Brady had brought the movie—Josie couldn't even remember the name, but it was one of those movies that had come out after *American Pie*, hoping to make the same killing at the box office by taking naked girls and daredevil guys and what Hollywood imagined teenage life to be like, and tossing them together like some sort of cosmic salad. Right now, a car chase filled the screen. The main character was screaming across a drawbridge that was slowly opening.

Josie knew he was going to make it across. First off, this was a comedy. Second, nobody had the guts to kill off the main character before the story was over. Third, her physics teacher had used this very movie to prove, scientifically, that given the speed of the car and the trajectory of the vectors, the actor could indeed jump the bridge—but only if the wind wasn't blowing.

Josie also knew that the person in the car wasn't real, wasn't even the actor playing the role, but a stuntman who had done this a thousand times. And yet, even as she watched the action unrolling on the television screen, she saw something entirely different: the car's fender, striking the far side of the open bridge. The twist of metal turning in midair, slapping against the water, sinking.

Grown-ups were always saying that teenagers drove too fast or got high or didn't use condoms because they thought they were invincible. But the truth was that at any moment, you could die. Brady could have a stroke on the football field, like those young college athletes who suddenly dropped dead. Emma could be hit by lightning. Drew might walk into an ordinary high school on an extraordinary day.

Josie stood up. "I need some air," she murmured, and she hurried up the basement stairs and out the front door of Emma's house. She sat down on the porch and looked at the sky, at two stars that were hitched at the elbows. You weren't invincible when you were a teenager. You were just stupid.

She heard the door open and close with a gasp. "Hey," Drew said, coming to sit beside her. "You okay?"

"I'm great." Josie pasted on a smile. It felt gummy, like wallpaper that hadn't been smoothed right. But she had gotten so good at this—faking it—that it was second nature.

Who would have thought that she'd inherited something from her mother after all?

Drew reached down for a blade of grass and began splitting it into hairs with his thumb. "I say the same thing when that bonehead school shrink calls me down to ask me how I'm doing."

"I didn't know he calls you down, too."

"I think he calls all of us who were, you know, close . . ."

He didn't finish his sentence: Close to the ones who didn't make it? Close to dying that day? Close to finishing ourselves off?

"Do you think anyone ever tells the shrink anything worthwhile?" Josie asked.

"Doubt it. He wasn't there that day. It's not like he really gets it."

"Does anyone?"

"You. Me. Those guys downstairs," Drew said. "Welcome to the club no one wants to join. You're a member for life."

Josie didn't mean to, but Drew's words and the stupid guy in the movie trying to jump the bridge and the way the stars were pricking at her skin, like inoculations for a terminal disease, suddenly made her start to cry. Drew reached around her, wrapping his one good arm around her, and she leaned into him. She closed her eyes and pressed her face into the flannel of his shirt. It felt so familiar, as if she'd come home to her own bed after years of circumnavigating the globe, to find that the mattress still somehow melted around the curve and weight of her. And yet—the fabric of the shirt didn't smell like it used to. The boy holding her wasn't quite the same size, the same shape, the same boy.

"I don't think I can do this," Josie whispered.

Immediately, Drew pulled away from her. His face was

flushed, and he could not look Josie in the eye. "I didn't mean it like that. You and Matt . . ." His voice went flat. "Well, I know you're still his."

Josie looked up at the sky. She nodded at him, as if that was what she had meant in the first place.

It all began when the service station left a message on the answering machine. Peter had missed his car inspection appointment. Did he want to reschedule?

Lewis had been alone in the house, retrieving that message. He had dialed the number before he even realized what he was doing, and thus it was no surprise to find himself actually keeping the rescheduled appointment. He got out of the car, handed his keys to the gas station attendant. "You can wait right inside," the man said. "There's coffee."

Lewis poured himself a cup, putting in three sugars and lots of milk, the way Peter would have fixed it. He sat down and instead of picking up a worn copy of *Newsweek*, he thumbed through *PC Gamer*.

One, he thought. *Two, three.*

On cue, the gas station attendant came into the waiting room. "Mr. Houghton," he said, "the car out there—it's not due for a state inspection until July."

"I know."

"But you . . . you made this appointment."

Lewis nodded. "I don't have that particular car with me right now."

It was impounded somewhere. Along with Peter's books and computer and journals and God only knew what else.

The attendant stared at him, the way you do when you realize the conversation you're having has veered from the rational. "Sir," he said, "we can't inspect a car that's not here."

"No," Lewis said. "Of course not." He put the magazine

back down on the coffee table, smoothed its wrinkled cover. Then he rubbed a hand over his forehead. "It's just . . . my son made this appointment," he said. "I wanted to keep it on his behalf."

The attendant nodded, slowly backing away. "Right . . . so, how about I just leave the car parked outside?"

"Just so you know," Lewis said softly, "he would have passed inspection."

Once, when Peter was young, Lacy had sent him to the same sleepaway camp that Joey had gone to and adored. It was somewhere across the river in Vermont, and campers water-skied on Lake Fairlee and took sailing lessons and did overnight canoe trips. Peter had called the first night, begging to be brought home. Although Lacy had been ready to start the car and drive to get him, Lewis had talked her out of it. *If he doesn't stick this out*, Lewis had said, *how will he ever know if he can?*

At the end of two weeks, when Lacy saw Peter again, there were changes in him. He was taller, and he'd put on weight. But there was also something different about his eyes—a light that had been burned to ash, somehow. When Peter looked at her, he seemed guarded, as if he understood that she was no longer an ally.

Now he was looking at her the same way even as she smiled at him, pretending that there was no glare from the fluorescent light over his head; that she could reach out and touch him instead of staring at him from the other side of the red line that had been drawn on the jail floor. "Do you know what I found in the attic yesterday? That dinosaur you used to love, the one that roared when you pulled its tail. I used to think you'd be carrying it down the aisle at your wedding . . ." Lacy broke off, realizing that there might never be a wedding for Peter, or any aisle outside of a prison walkway, for that matter. "Well," she said, turning up the wattage on her smile. "I put it on your bed."

Peter stared at her. "Okay."

"I think my favorite birthday party of yours was the dinosaur one, when we buried those plastic bones in the sandbox and you had to dig for them," Lacy said. "Remember?"

"I remember nobody showed up."

"Of course they did—"

"Five kids, maybe, whose moms had forced them to be there," Peter said. "God. I was six years old. Why are we even *talking* about this?"

Because I don't know what else to say, Lacy thought. She looked around the visitation room—there were only a handful of inmates, and the devoted few who still believed in them, caught on opposite sides of that red stripe. In reality, Lacy realized, this dividing line between her and Peter had been there for years. If you kept your chin up, you might even be able to convince yourself there was nothing separating you. It was only when you tried to cross it, like now, that you understood how real a barrier it could be. "Peter," Lacy blurted out, "I'm sorry I didn't pick you up at sleepaway camp, that time."

He looked at her as if she was crazy. "Um, thanks for that, but I got over it about a hundred years ago."

"I know. But I can still be sorry." She was sorry about a thousand things, suddenly: that she didn't pay more attention when Peter showed her some new programming skill; that she hadn't bought him another dog after Dozer died; that they did not go back to the Caribbean last winter vacation, because Lacy had wrongly assumed they had all the time in the world.

"Sorry doesn't change anything."

"It does for the person who's apologizing."

Peter groaned. "What the fuck is this? *Chicken Soup for the Kid Without a Soul?*"

Lacy flinched. "You don't have to swear in order to—"

"Fuck," Peter sang. "Fuck fuck fuck fuck fuck."

"I'm not going to sit here and take this—"

"Yes you are," Peter said. "You know why? Because if you walk out on me, it's just one more thing you've got to be sorry about."

Lacy was halfway out of her chair, but the truth in Peter's words weighted her back down into the seat. He knew her, it seemed, far better than she had ever known him.

"Ma," he said softly, his voice edging over that red line. "I didn't mean that."

She looked up at him, her throat thickening with tears. "I know, Peter."

"I'm glad you come here." He swallowed. "I mean, you're the only one."

"Your father—"

Peter snorted. "I don't know what he's been telling you, but I haven't seen him since that first time he came."

Lewis wasn't coming to see Peter? That was news to Lacy. Where did he go when he left the house, telling her that he was headed to the jail?

She imagined Peter, sitting in his cell every other week, waiting for a visit that did not come. Lacy forced a smile—she would get upset on her own time, not Peter's—and immediately changed the topic. "For the arraignment . . . I brought you a nice jacket to wear."

"Jordan says I don't need it. For the arraignment I just wear these clothes. I won't need the jacket until the trial." Peter smiled a little. "I hope you didn't cut the tags off yet."

"I didn't buy it. It's Joey's interview blazer."

Their eyes met. "Oh," Peter murmured. "So that's what you were doing in the attic."

There was silence as they both remembered Joey coming downstairs in the Brooks Brothers blazer Lacy had gotten him at Filene's Basement in Boston at deep discount. It had been purchased for college interviews; Joey had been setting them up at the time of the accident.

"Do you ever wish it was me who died," Peter asked, "instead of Joey?"

Lacy's heart fell like a stone. "Of course not."

"But then you'd still have Joey," Peter said. "And none of this would have happened."

She thought of Janet Isinghoff, the woman who had not wanted her as a midwife. Part of growing up was learning not to be quite that honest—learning when it was better to lie, rather than hurt someone with the truth. It was why Lacy came to these visits with a smile stretched like a Halloween mask over her face, when in reality, she wanted to break down sobbing every time she saw Peter being led into the visitation room by a correctional officer. It was why she was talking about camp and stuffed animals—the hallmarks of the son she remembered—instead of discovering who he had become. But Peter had never learned how to say one thing when he meant another. It was one of the reasons he'd been hurt so many times.

"It would be a happy ending," Peter said.

Lacy drew in a breath. "Not if you weren't here."

Peter looked at her for a long moment. "You're lying," he said—not angry, not accusing. Just as if he was stating the facts, in a way that she wasn't.

"I am not—"

"You can say it a million times, but that doesn't make it any more true." Peter smiled then, so guileless that Lacy felt it smart like a stripe from a whip. "You might be able to fool Dad, and the cops, and anyone else who'll listen," he said. "You just can't fool another liar."

By the time Diana reached the docket board to check which judge was sitting on the Houghton arraignment, Jordan McAfee was already standing there. Diana hated him on principle, because he hadn't ripped two pairs of stockings trying to get them on, because he wasn't having a bad hair day, because he didn't seem to be the least bit ruffled about the fact that half the town of Sterling was on the front steps of the courthouse, demanding blood. "Morning," he said, not even glancing at her.

Diana didn't answer. Instead, her mouth dropped open as she read the name of the judge sitting on the case. "I think there's a mistake," she said to the clerk.

The clerk glanced over her shoulder at the docket board. "Judge Cormier's sitting this morning."

"On the Houghton case? Are you *kidding* me?"

The clerk shook her head. "Nope."

"But her daughter—" Diana snapped her mouth shut, her thoughts reeling. "We need to have a chambers conference with the judge before the arraignment."

The moment the clerk was gone, Diana faced Jordan. "What the hell is Cormier thinking?"

It wasn't often that Jordan got to see Diana Leven sweat, and frankly, it was entertaining. To be honest, Jordan had been just as shocked to see Cormier's name on the docket board as the prosecutor had been, but he wasn't about to tell Diana. Not tipping his hand was the only advantage he had right now, because frankly, his case wasn't worth anything.

Diana frowned. "Didn't you expect her to—"

The clerk reappeared. Jordan got a kick out of Eleanor; she cut him slack in the superior courthouse and even laughed at the dumb-blonde jokes he saved for her, whereas most clerks had a terminal case of self-importance. "Her Honor will see you now," Eleanor said.

As Jordan followed the clerk into chambers, he leaned down and whispered the punch line he'd been getting at, before Leven so rudely interrupted his joke with her arrival. "So her husband looks at the box and says, 'Honey, it's not a puzzle . . . it's some Frosted Flakes!'"

Eleanor snickered, and Diana scowled. "What's that, some kind of code?"

"Yeah, Diana. It's secret defense attorney language for: *Whatever you do, don't tell the prosecutor what I'm saying.*"

"I wouldn't be surprised," Diana murmured, and then they were in chambers.

Judge Cormier was already in her robe, ready to start the arraignment. Her arms were folded; she was leaning against her desk. "All right, Counselors, we have a lot of people in the courtroom waiting. What's the problem?"

Diana glanced at Jordan, but he just raised his eyebrows. If she wanted to poke at the hornet's nest, that was just fine, but he'd be standing far away when it happened. Let Cormier hold a grudge against the prosecution, not the defense.

"Judge," Diana said hesitantly, "it's my understanding that your daughter was in the school at the time of the shooting. In fact, we've interviewed her."

Jordan had to give Cormier credit—she somehow managed to stare Diana down as if the prosecutor hadn't just presented a valid and disturbing fact, but had said something absolutely ludicrous instead. Like the punch line of a dumb-blonde joke, for example. "I'm quite aware of that," the judge said. "There were a thousand children in the school at the time of the shooting."

"Of course, Your Honor. I just . . . I wanted to ask before we got out there in front of everyone whether the court was planning to just handle the arraignment, or if you're planning to sit during the whole case?"

Jordan looked at Diana, wondering why she was so dead sure that Cormier shouldn't be sitting on this case. What did *she* know about Josie Cormier that he didn't?

"As I said, there were thousands of kids in that school. Some of their parents are police officers, some work here at the superior court. One even works in your office, Ms. Leven."

"Yes, Your Honor . . . but that particular attorney isn't handling this case."

The judge stared at her, calm. "Are you calling my daughter as a witness, Ms. Leven?"

Diana hesitated. "No, Your Honor."

"Well, I've read my daughter's statement, Counselor, and I don't see any reason that we can't proceed."

Jordan ran through what he knew so far:

Peter had asked about Josie's welfare.

Josie was present during the shooting.

Josie's yearbook photo, in the discovery, was the only one that had been marked with the words LET LIVE.

But according to her mother, whatever she told the police wouldn't affect the case. According to Diana, nothing Josie knew was important enough to make her a witness for the prosecution.

He dropped his gaze, his mind replaying these facts over and over like a loop of videotape.

One that just didn't make sense.

The former elementary school that was serving as the physical location for Sterling High did not have a cafeteria—little kids ate in their classrooms, at their desks. But somehow this was considered unhealthy for teenagers, so the library had been turned into a makeshift cafeteria. There were no books or shelves there anymore, but the carpet still had ABC's sprinkled into its weave, and a poster of the Cat in the Hat still hung beside the double doors.

Josie no longer sat with her friends in the cafeteria. It just didn't feel right—as if some critical mass were missing, and they were likely to be split apart like an atom under pressure. Instead, she sequestered herself in a corner of the library where there were carpeted risers, where she liked to imagine a teacher reading aloud to her kindergartners.

Today, when they'd arrived at school, the television cameras were already waiting. You had to walk right through them to get to the front door. They'd dribbled away over the past week—no doubt there was some tragedy somewhere else for these reporters to cover—but returned in full force to report on the arraignment. Josie had wondered how they were going to hightail it from the school all the way north to the courthouse in time. She wondered how many times in the course of her high school career they would come back. On the last day of school? At the anniversary of the shooting? At graduation? She imagined the *People* magazine article that would be written in a decade about the survivors of the Sterling High massacre—"Where Are They Now?" Would John Eberhard be playing hockey again, or even walking? Would Courtney's parents have moved out of Sterling? Where would Josie be?

And Peter?

Her mother was the judge at his trial. Even if she didn't talk about it with Josie—legally, she couldn't—it wasn't as if Josie didn't know. Josie was caught somewhere between utter relief, knowing her mom would be sitting on the case, and absolute terror. On the one hand, she knew her mother would start piecing together the events of that day, and that meant Josie wouldn't have to talk about it herself. On the other hand, once her mother did start piecing together the events of that day, what else would she figure out?

Drew walked into the library, tossing an orange up in the air and catching it repeatedly in his fist. He glanced around at the pods of students, settled in small groups on the carpet with their hot lunch trays balanced on their knees like the bows of crickets, and then spotted Josie. "What's up?" he asked, sitting down beside her.

"Not much."

"Did the jackals get you?"

He was talking about the television reporters. "I sort of ran past them."

"I wish they'd all just go fuck themselves," Drew said.

Josie leaned her head against the wall. "I wish it would all just go back to normal."

"Maybe after the trial." Drew turned to her. "Is it weird, you know, with your mom and all?"

"We don't talk about it. We don't talk about anything, really." She picked up her bottled water and took a sip, so that Drew wouldn't realize that her hand was shaking.

"He's not crazy."

"Who?"

"Peter Houghton. I saw his eyes that day. He knew exactly what the hell he was doing."

"Drew, shut up," Josie sighed.

"Well, it's true. Doesn't matter what some hotshot fucking lawyer says to try to get him off the hook."

"I think that's something the jury gets to decide, not you."

"Jesus Christ, Josie," he said. "Of all people, I wouldn't think you'd want to defend him."

"I'm not defending him. I'm just telling you how the legal system works."

"Well, thanks, Marcia Clark. But somehow you give less of a damn about that when you're the one with a slug being pulled out of your shoulder. Or when your best friend—or your *boyfriend*—is bleeding to death in front of—" He broke off abruptly as Josie fumbled her bottle of water, soaking herself and Drew.

"Sorry," she said, mopping up the mess with a napkin.

Drew sighed. "Me, too. I guess I'm a little freaked out, with the cameras and everything." He tore off a piece of the damp napkin and stuck it in his mouth, then tossed the spitball at the back of an overweight boy who carried the tuba in the school marching band.

Oh my God, Josie thought. *Nothing's changed at all.* Drew tore off another piece of napkin and rolled it in his palm. "*Stop* it," Josie said.

"What?" Drew shrugged. "You're the one who wanted to go back to normal."

There were four television cameras in the courtroom: ABC, NBC, CBS, and CNN; plus reporters from *Time, Newsweek, The New York Times, The Boston Globe,* and the Associated Press. The media had met with Alex last week in chambers, so that she could decide who would be represented in the courtroom while the others waited outside on the steps of the courthouse. She was aware of the tiny red lights on the cameras that indicated they were recording; of the scratch of pens on paper as the reporters wrote down her words verbatim. Peter Houghton had become infamous, and as a result of that, Alex would now have her fifteen minutes of fame. Maybe sixty, Alex thought. It would take her that long to simply read through all the charges.

"Mr. Houghton," Alex said, "you are charged with, on March 6, 2007, a count of first-degree murder, contrary to 631:1-A, in that you purposely caused the death of another, to wit, Courtney Ignatio. You are charged with, on March 6, 2007, a count of first-degree murder, contrary to 631:1-A, in that you purposely caused the death of another, to wit . . ." She glanced down at the name. "Matthew Royston."

The words were routine, something Alex could do in her sleep. But she focused on them, on keeping her voice measured and even, on giving weight to the name of each dead child. The gallery was packed full, and Alex could recognize the parents of these students, and some students themselves. One mother, a woman Alex did not know by sight or name, sat in the front row behind the defense table, clutching an 8 x 10 photo of a smiling girl.

Jordan McAfee sat beside his client, who was wearing an orange jail jumpsuit and shackles, and was doing everything he could to avoid looking at Alex as she read the charges.

"You are charged with, on March 6, 2007, a count of first-degree murder, contrary to 631:1-A, in that you purposely caused the death of another, to wit, Justin Friedman. . . .

"You are charged with, on March 6, 2007, a count of first-degree murder, contrary to 631:1-A, in that you purposely caused the death of another, to wit, Christopher McPhee. . . .

"You are charged with, on March 6, 2007, a count of first-degree murder, contrary to 631:1-A, in that you purposely caused the death of another, to wit, Grace Murtaugh. . . ."

The woman with the photo stood up as Alex was reciting the charges. She leaned over the bar, between Peter Houghton and his attorney, and smacked the photograph down so hard that the glass cracked. "Do you remember her?" the woman cried, her voice raw. "Do you remember Grace?"

McAfee whipped around. Peter ducked his head, keeping his eyes trained on the table in front of him.

Alex had had disruptive people in her courtroom before, but she could not remember them stealing her breath away. This mother's pain seemed to take up all the empty space in the gallery; heat the emotions of the other spectators to a boiling point.

Her hands began to tremble; she slipped them underneath the bench so that nobody could see. "Ma'am," Alex said. "I'm going to have to ask you to sit down . . ."

"Did you look her in the face when you shot her, you bastard?"

Did you? Alex thought.

"Your *Honor*," McAfee called.

Alex's ability to judge this case impartially had already been challenged by the prosecution. While she didn't have to justify her decisions to anyone, she'd just told the attorneys that she could easily separate her personal and her professional involvement in this case. She'd thought it would be a matter of seeing Josie not as her daughter, specifically, but as one of hundreds present during the shooting. She had not realized that it would actually come down to seeing herself not as a judge, but as another mother.

You can do this, she told herself. *Just remember why you're here.* "Bailiffs," Alex murmured, and the two beefy courtroom attendants grabbed the woman by the arms to escort her out of the courtroom.

"You'll burn in hell," the woman shouted as the television cameras followed her progress down the aisle.

Alex didn't. She kept her eyes on Peter Houghton, while his attorney's attention was distracted. "Mr. McAfee," she said.

"Yes, Your Honor?"

"Please ask your client to hold out his hand."

"I'm sorry, Judge, but I think there's already been enough prejudicial—"

"Do it, Counselor."

McAfee nodded at Peter, who lifted his shackled wrists and opened his fists. Winking in Peter's palm was a shard of broken glass from the picture frame. Blanching, the attorney reached for the glass. "Thank you, Your Honor," he muttered.

"Any time." Alex looked at the gallery and cleared her throat. "I trust there will be no more outbursts like that, or I'll be forced to close these proceedings to the public."

She continued reading the charges in a courtroom so quiet you could hear hearts break; you could hear hope fluttering to the rafters on the ceiling. "You are charged with, on March 6, 2007, a count of first-degree murder, contrary to 631:1-A, in that you purposely caused the death of another, to wit, Madeleine Shaw. You are charged with, on March 6, 2007, a count of first-degree murder, contrary to 631:1-A, in that you purposely caused the death of another, to wit, Edward McCabe.

"You are charged with attempted first-degree murder, contrary to 630:1-A and 629:1, in that you did commit an act in furtherance of the offense of first-degree murder, to wit, shooting at Emma Alexis.

"You are charged with possession of firearms on school grounds.

"Possession of explosive devices.

"Unlawful use of an explosive device.

"Receiving stolen goods, to wit, firearms."

By the time Alex had finished, her voice was hoarse. "Mr. McAfee," she said, "how does your client plead?"

"Not guilty to all counts, Your Honor."

A murmur spread virally through the courtroom, something that always happened in the wake of hearing that not-guilty plea, and that always seemed ridiculous to Alex— what was the defendant *supposed* to do? Say he was *guilty*?

"Given the nature of the charges, you are not entitled to bail as a matter of law. You are remanded to the custody of the sheriff."

Alex dismissed court and headed into chambers. Inside, with the door closed, she paced like an athlete coming off a brutal race. If there was anything she was sure of, it was her ability to judge fairly. But if it had been this hard at the arraignment, how would she function when the prosecution began to actually outline the events of that day?

"Eleanor," Alex said, pressing the intercom button for her clerk, "clear my schedule for two hours."

"But you—"

"Clear it," she snapped. She could still see the faces of those parents in the gallery. What they'd lost was written across their faces, a collective scar.

Alex stripped off her robe and headed down the back stairs to the parking lot. Instead of stopping for a cigarette, though, she got into her car. She drove straight to the elementary school and parked in the fire lane. There was one news van still in the teachers' parking lot, and Alex panicked, until she realized that the license plates were from New York; that the chance of someone recognizing her without her judicial robes on was unlikely.

The only person who had a right to ask Alex to recuse herself was Josie, but Alex knew that ultimately her daughter would understand. It was Alex's first big case in

superior court. It was modeling healthy behavior for Josie
herself, to get on with her life again. Alex tried to ignore
the last reason she was fighting to stay on this case—the
one that pricked like a thorn, like a splinter, rubbing raw
no matter which way she came at it: she had a better
chance of learning from the prosecution and the defense
what her daughter had endured than she ever would from
Josie herself.

She walked into the main office. "I need to pick up my
daughter," Alex said, and the school secretary pushed a
clipboard toward her, with information to be filled out. STU-
DENT, Alex read. TIME OUT. REASON. TIME IN.

Josie Cormier, she wrote. *10:45 a.m. Orthodontist.*

She could feel the secretary's eyes on her—clearly the
woman wanted to know why Judge Cormier was standing
in front of her desk instead of at the courthouse presiding
over the arraignment that they were all waiting to hear
about. "If you could just send Josie out to the car," Alex
said, and she walked out of the office.

Within five minutes, Josie opened the passenger door
and slid into the seat. "I don't have braces."

"I needed to think of an excuse fast," Alex answered. "It
was the first one to pop into my head."

"So why are you really here?"

Alex watched Josie turn up the volume of the vent. "Do
I need a reason to have lunch with my daughter?"

"It's, like, ten-thirty."

"Then we're playing hooky."

"What*ever,*" Josie said.

Alex pulled away from the curb. Josie was two feet away
from her, but they might as well have been on different
continents. Her daughter stared firmly out the window,
watching the world go by.

"Is it over?" Josie asked.

"The arraignment? Yes."

"Is that why you came here?"

How could Alex describe what it had felt like, seeing all of those nameless mothers and fathers in the gallery, without a child between them? If you lost your child, could you still even call yourself a parent?

What if you'd just been stupid enough to let her slip away?

Alex drove to the end of a road that overlooked the river. It was racing, the way it always did in the spring. If you didn't know better, if you were looking at a still photo, you might wish you could take a dip. You wouldn't realize, just by glancing, that the water would rob you of your breath; that you might be swept away.

"I wanted to see you," Alex confessed. "There were people in my courtroom today . . . people who probably wake up every day now wishing that they'd *done* this—left in the middle of the day to have lunch with their daughters, instead of telling themselves they could do it some other day." She turned to Josie. "Those people, they didn't get to have any other days."

Josie picked at a loose white thread, silent long enough for Alex to start mentally kicking herself. So much for her spontaneous foray into primal motherhood. Alex had been rattled by her own emotions during the arraignment; instead of telling herself she was being ridiculous, she'd acted on them. But this was exactly what happened, wasn't it, when you started to sift through the shifting sands of feelings, instead of just feeding facts hand over fist? The hell with putting your heart on your sleeve; it was likely to get ripped off.

"Hooky," Josie said quietly. "Not lunch."

Alex sat back, relieved. "What*ever*," she joked. She

waited until Josie met her gaze. "I want to talk to you about the case."

"I thought you couldn't."

"That's sort of what I wanted to talk about. Even if this was the biggest career opportunity in the world, I'd step down if I believed it was going to make things harder for you. You can still come to me anytime and ask me anything you want."

They both pretended, for a moment, that Josie did this on a regular basis, when in fact it had been years since she'd shared anything in confidence with Alex.

Josie's glance slanted toward her. "Even about the arraignment?"

"Even about the arraignment."

"What did Peter say in court?" Josie asked.

"Nothing. The lawyer does all the talking."

"What did he look like?"

Alex thought for a moment. She had, upon first seeing Peter in his jail jumpsuit, been amazed at how much he'd grown. Although she had seen him over the years—in the back of the classroom during school events, at the copy store where he and Josie had worked together briefly, even driving down Main Street—she still somehow had expected him to be the same little boy who'd played in kindergarten with Josie. Alex considered his orange scrubs, his rubber flip-flops, his shackles. "He looked like a defendant," she said.

"If he's convicted," Josie asked, "he'll never get out of prison, will he?"

Alex felt her heart squeeze. Josie was trying not to show it, but how could she not be afraid that something like this would happen again? Then again, how could Alex—as a judge—make a promise to convict Peter before he'd even been tried? Alex felt herself walking the high wire between personal responsibility and professional ethics, trying her damnedest not to fall. "You don't have to worry about that . . ."

"That's not an answer," Josie said.

"He'll most likely spend his life there, yes."

"If he was in prison, would people be allowed to talk to him?"

Suddenly, Alex couldn't follow Josie's line of logic. "Why? Do you *want* to talk to him?"

"I don't know."

"I can't imagine why you'd want to, after—"

"I used to be his friend," Josie said.

"You haven't been Peter's friend in years," Alex answered, but then the tumblers clicked, and she understood why her daughter, who was seemingly terrified about Peter's potential release from prison, might still want to communicate with him after his conviction: remorse. Maybe Josie believed that something she'd done—or hadn't—might have brought Peter to the point where he would have gone and shot his way through Sterling High.

If Alex didn't understand the concept of a guilty conscience, who would?

"Honey, there are people looking out for Peter—people whose *job* it is to look out for him. You don't have to be the one to do it." Alex smiled a little. "You just have to look out for yourself, all right?"

Josie looked away. "I have a test next period," she said. "Can we go back to school now?"

Alex drove in silence, because by that time it was too late to make the correction; to tell her daughter that there was someone looking out for her, too; that Josie was not in this alone.

*   *   *

At two in the morning, when Jordan had been bouncing a wailing, sick infant in his arms for five straight hours, he turned to Selena. "Remind me why we had a child?"

Selena was sitting at the kitchen table—well, no, actually she was sprawled across it, her head pillowed in her arms. "Because you wanted to pass along the finely tuned genetic blueprint of my bloodline."

"Frankly, I think all we're passing along is some viral crud."

Suddenly, Selena sat up. "Hey," she whispered. "He's asleep."

"Thank God. Get him off me."

"Like hell I will—that's the most comfortable he's been all day."

Jordan glowered at her and sank into the chair across from her, his hands still cupped around his sleeping son. "He's not the only one."

"Are we talking about your case again? Because to be honest, Jordan, I'm so damn tired that I need clues, here, if we're going to shift topics . . ."

"I just can't figure out why she hasn't recused herself. When the prosecution brought up her daughter, Cormier dismissed it . . . and more importantly, so did Leven."

Selena yawned and stood up. "You're looking a gift horse in the mouth, baby. Cormier's got to be a better judge for you than Wagner."

"But something's rubbing me the wrong way about this."

Selena smiled at him indulgently. "Got a little diaper rash, huh?"

"Even if her kid doesn't remember anything now, that doesn't mean she's not going to. And how is Cormier going to remain impartial, knowing that her daughter's boyfriend was blown away by my client while she stood there watching?"

"Well, you could make a motion to get her off the case," Selena said. "Or you could wait for Diana to do that instead."

Jordan glanced up at her.

"If I were you, I'd keep my mouth shut."

He reached out, snagging the sash of her robe so that it unraveled. "When do I ever keep my mouth shut?"

Selena laughed. "There's always a first time," she said.

Each tier in maximum security had four cells, six feet by eight feet. Inside the cell was a bunk bed and a toilet. It had taken Peter three days to be able to take a dump while the correctional officers were walking past, without his bowels seizing up, but—and this was how he knew he was getting used to being here—now he could probably crap on command.

At one end of the maximum-security catwalk was a small television. Because there was only room for one chair in front of the TV, the guy who'd been in the longest got to sit down. Everyone else stood behind him, like hoboes in a soup line, to watch. There were not a lot of programs the inmates could agree upon. Mostly it was MTV, although they always turned on Jerry Springer. Peter figured that was because no matter how much you'd screwed up in your life, you liked knowing that there were people out there even more stupid than you.

If anyone on the tier did something wrong—not even Peter, but for example an asshole like Satan Jones (Satan not being his real name; that was Gaylord, but if you mentioned it even in a whisper he'd go for your jugular), who had drawn a caricature of two of the COs doing the horizontal hora on the wall of his cell—everyone lost the television privilege for the week. Which left the other end of the catwalk to mosey on down toward: a shower with a plastic curtain, and the phone, where you could call collect for a dollar a minute, and every few seconds you'd hear *This call has originated at the Grafton County Department of Corrections*, just in case you had been lucky enough to forget.

Peter was doing sit-ups, which he hated. He hated all exercise, really. But the alternative was sitting around and getting soft enough for everyone to think they could pick on you, or going outside during his exercise hour. He went, a couple of times—not to shoot hoops or to jog or even make secret deals near the fence for the drugs or cigarettes that got smuggled into jail, but just to be outside and breathing in air that hadn't already been breathed by the other inmates in this place. Unfortunately, from the exercise yard you could see the river. You'd think that was a bonus, but in fact, it was the most awful tease. Sometimes the wind blew so that Peter could even smell it—the soil along the edge, the frigid water—and it nearly broke him to know that he couldn't just walk down there and take off his shoes and socks and wade in, swim, fucking *drown* himself if he wanted to. After that, he stopped going outdoors at all.

Peter finished his hundredth sit-up—the irony was that after a month, he was so much stronger that he could probably have kicked Matt Royston's and Drew Girard's asses simultaneously—and sat down on his bunk with the commissary form. Once a week, you got to go shopping for things like mouthwash and paper, with the prices jacked up ridiculously high. Peter remembered going to St. John one year with his family; in the grocery store, cornflakes cost, like, ten dollars, because they were such a rare commodity. It wasn't like shampoo was a rare commodity, but in jail, you were at the mercy of the administration, which meant they could charge $3.25 for a bottle of Pert, or $16 for a box fan. Your other alternative was to hope that an inmate who left for the state prison would will you his belongings, but to Peter, that felt a little like being a vulture.

"Houghton," a correctional officer said, his heavy boots ringing down the metal catwalk, "you've got mail."

Two envelopes zoomed into the cell and slid underneath Peter's bunk. He reached for them, scraping his fingernails against the cement floor. The first letter was from his mother, which he was almost expecting. Peter got mail from his mother at least three or four times a week. The letters were usually about stupid things like editorials in the local paper or how well her spider plants were doing. He'd thought, for a while, that she was writing in code—something he needed to know, something transcendent and inspirational—but then he started to realize that she was just writing to fill up space. That's when he stopped opening mail from his mother. He didn't feel bad about this, really. The reason his mother wrote to him, Peter knew, wasn't so that he'd read the letters. It was so that she could tell herself she'd written them.

He didn't really blame his parents for being clueless. First of all, he'd had plenty of practice with that particular condition. Second, the only people who understood him, really, were the ones who had been at the high school that day, and they weren't exactly jamming his mailbox with missives.

Peter tossed his mother's letter onto the floor again and stared at the address on the second envelope. He didn't recognize it; it wasn't from Sterling, or even New Hampshire, for that matter. Elena Battista, he read. Elena from Ridgewood, New Jersey.

He ripped open the envelope and scanned her note.

> *Peter,*
> *I feel like I already know you, because I've been following what happened at the high school. I'm in*

college now, but I think I know what it was like for
you . . . because it was like that for me. In fact, I'm
writing my thesis now on the effects of being bullied
at school. I know it's presumptuous to think that
you'd want to talk to someone like me . . . but I
think if I'd known someone like you when I was in
high school, my life would have been different, and
maybe it's never too late????

> Sincerely,
> Elena Battista

Peter tapped the ragged envelope against his thigh. Jordan had specifically told him he was to talk to nobody—that is, except his parents, and Jordan himself. But his parents were useless, and to be honest, it wasn't like Jordan had been holding up his end of the bargain, which involved being physically present often enough for Peter to get whatever was bugging him off his chest.

Besides. She was a *college* girl. It was kind of cool to think that a college girl wanted to talk to him; and it wasn't like he was going to tell her anything she didn't already know.

Peter reached for his commissary form again and checked off the box for a generic greeting card.

A trial could be split into halves: what happened the day of the event, which was the prosecution's baby; and everything that led up to it, which was what the defense had to present. To that end, Selena busied herself interviewing everyone who had come in contact with their client during the past seventeen years of his life. Two days after Peter's arraignment in superior court, Selena sat down with the principal of Sterling High in his modified elementary school office. Arthur McAllister had a sandy beard and a round belly and teeth that he didn't show when he smiled. He reminded Selena of one of those freaky talking bears that had come onto the market when she was a kid— Teddy Ruxpin—which made it all the more strange when he started answering her questions about anti-bullying policies at the high school. "It's not tolerated," McAllister said, although Selena had expected that party line. "We're completely on top of it."

"So, if a kid comes to you to complain about being picked on, what are the repercussions for the bully?"

"One of the things we've found, Selena—can I call you Selena?—is that if the administration intervenes, it makes it worse for the kid who's being bullied." He hesitated. "I know what people are saying about the shooting. How they're comparing it to Columbine and Paducah and the ones that came before them. But I truly believe that it wasn't bullying, per se, that led Peter to do what he did."

"What he allegedly did," Selena automatically corrected. "Do you keep records of bullying incidents?"

"If it escalates, and the kids are brought in to me, then yes."

"Was anyone ever brought to you for bullying Peter Houghton?"

McAllister stood up and pulled a file out of a cabinet. He began to leaf through it, and then stopped at a page. "Actually, *Peter* was brought in to see me twice this year. He was put into detention for fighting in the halls."

"Fighting?" Selena said. "Or fighting back?"

When Katie Riccobono had plunged a knife into her husband's chest while he was fast asleep—forty-six times— Jordan had called upon Dr. King Wah, a forensic psychiatrist who specialized in battered woman syndrome. It was a specific tangent of post-traumatic stress disorder, one that suggested a woman who'd been repeatedly victimized both mentally and physically might so constantly fear for her life that the line between reality and fantasy blurred, to the point where she felt threatened even when the threat was dormant, or in Joe Riccobono's case, as he lay sleeping off a three-day drinking spree.

King had won the case for them. In the years that had passed, he'd become one of the foremost experts on battered woman syndrome, and appeared routinely as a witness for the defense all over the country. His fees had skyrocketed; his time now came at a premium.

Jordan headed to King's Boston office without an appointment, figuring his charm could get him past whatever secretarial gatekeeper the good doctor employed, but he hadn't counted on a near-retirement-age dragon named Ruth. "The doctor's booking six months out," she said, not even bothering to look up at Jordan.

"But this is a personal call, not a professional one."

"And I care," Ruth said, in a tone that clearly suggested she didn't.

Jordan figured it wouldn't do any good to tell Ruth she was looking lovely today, or to grace her with a dumb-blonde joke, or even to play up his successful track record as a defense attorney. "It's a family emergency," he said.

"Your family is having a psychological emergency," Ruth repeated flatly.

"*Our* family," Jordan improvised. "I'm Dr. Wah's brother." When Ruth just stared at him, Jordan added, "Dr. Wah's *adopted* brother."

She raised one sharp eyebrow and pressed a button on her phone. A moment later, it rang. "Doctor," she said. "A man who claims to be your brother is here to see you." She hung up the receiver. "He says you can go right in."

Jordan opened the heavy mahogany door to find King

eating a sandwich, his feet crossed on top of his desk. "Jordan McAfee," he said, smiling. "I should have known. So tell me . . . how's Mom doing?"

"How the hell should I know, she always loved you best," Jordan joked, and he came forward to shake King's hand. "Thanks for seeing me."

"I had to find out who had enough chutzpah to say he was my brother."

" 'Chutzpah,' " Jordan repeated. "You learn that in Chinese school?"

"Yeah, Yiddish came right after Abacus 101." He gestured for Jordan to take a seat. "So how's it going?"

"Good," Jordan said. "I mean, maybe not as good as it's going for you. I can't turn on Court TV without seeing your face on the screen."

"It's been busy, that's for sure. I've only got ten minutes, in fact, before my next appointment."

"I know. That's why I took a chance that you'd see me— I want you to evaluate my client."

"Jordan, man, you know I would, but I'm booking nearly six months out for trial work."

"This one's different, King. It's multiple murder charges."

"Murders?" King said. "How many husbands did she kill?"

"None, and it's not a she. It's a boy. A *kid*. He was bullied for years, and then turned around and shot up Sterling High School."

King handed half of his tuna sandwich to Jordan. "All right, little brother," he said. "Let's talk over lunch."

Josie glanced from the serviceable gray tile floor to the cinder-block walls, from the iron bars that isolated Dispatch from the sitting area to the heavy door with its automatic lock. It was kind of like a jail, and she wondered if the policemen inside ever thought about that irony. But then, as soon as the image of jail popped into her head, Josie thought of Peter and began to panic again. "I don't want to be here," she said, turning to her mother.

"I know."

"Why does he even want to talk to me again? I already told him I can't remember anything."

They had received the letter in the mail; Detective Ducharme had "a few more questions" to ask her. To Josie, that meant he must know something now that he hadn't known the first time he questioned her. Her mother had explained that a second interview was just a way of making sure the prosecution had dotted their i's and crossed their t's; that it really didn't mean anything at all, but that she had to go to the station, all the same. God forbid Josie be the one to screw up the investigation.

"All you have to do is tell him, again, that you don't remember anything . . . and you'll be all done," her mother said, and she gently put her hand on Josie's knee, which had begun shaking.

What Josie wanted to do was stand up, burst through the double doors of the police station, and start running. She wanted to sprint through the parking lot and across the street, over the middle school playing fields and into the woods that edged the town pond, up the mountains that she could sometimes see from her bedroom window if the leaves had fallen from the trees, until she was as high as she could possibly go. And then . . .

And then maybe she'd just spread her arms and step off the edge of the world.

What if this was all a setup?

What if Detective Ducharme already knew . . . everything?

"Josie," a voice said. "Thanks so much for coming down here."

She glanced up to see the detective standing in front of them. Her mother got to her feet. Josie tried, honestly she did, but she couldn't find the courage to do it.

"Judge, I appreciate you bringing your daughter down here."

"Josie's very upset," her mother said. "She still can't remember anything about that day."

"I need to hear that from Josie herself." The detective knelt so that he could look into her eyes. He had, Josie realized, nice eyes. A little sad, like a basset hound's. It made her wonder what it would be like to hear all these stories from the wounded and the stunned; if you couldn't help but absorb them by osmosis. "I promise," he said gently. "This won't take long."

Josie started to imagine what it would feel like when the door to the conference room closed; how questions could build up like the pressure inside a champagne bottle. She wondered what hurt more: not remembering what had happened, no matter how hard you tried to will it to the front of your mind, or recalling every last, awful moment.

Out of the corner of her eye, Josie saw her mother sit back down. "Aren't you coming in with me?"

The last time the detective had talked to her, her mother had pulled the same excuse—she was the judge, she couldn't possibly sit in on the police interview. But then they'd had that conversation after the arraignment; her mother had gone out of her way to let Josie know that acting like a judge on this case would not be mutually exclusive to acting like a mother. Or in other words: Josie had been stupid enough to think that things between them might have started to change.

Her mother's mouth opened and closed, like a fish out of water. *Did I make you uncomfortable?* Josie thought, the words rising like welts in her mind. *Welcome to the club.*

"You want a cup of coffee?" the detective said, and then he shook his head. "Or a Coke. I don't know, do kids your age drink coffee yet, or am I dangling a vice right in front of you because I'm too stupid to know better?"

"I like coffee," Josie said. She avoided her mother's gaze as Detective Ducharme led her into the inner sanctum of the police station.

They went into a conference room and the detective poured her a mug of coffee. "Milk? Sugar?"

"Sugar," Josie said. She took two packets from the bowl and added them to the mug. Then she glanced around—at the Formica table, the fluorescent lights, the *normalness* of the room.

"What?"

"What *what*?" Josie said.

"What's the matter?"

"I was just thinking that this doesn't look like the kind of place where you'd beat a confession out of someone."

"Depends on whether you've got one to be beaten out of you," the detective said. When Josie blanched, he laughed. "I'm just joking. Honestly, the only time I beat confessions out of people is when I'm playing a cop on TV."

"*You* play a cop on TV?"

He sighed. "Never mind." He reached over to a tape recorder in the center of the table. "I'm going to record this, just like before . . . mostly because I'm too dumb to re-member it all correctly." The detective pressed the button and sat down across from Josie. "Do people tell you all the time that you look like your mom?"

"Um, never." She tilted her head. "Is that what you brought me down to ask me?"

He smiled. "No."

"I don't look like her, anyway."

"Sure you do. It's your eyes."

Josie looked down at the table. "Mine are a totally different color than hers."

"I wasn't talking about the color," the detective said. "Josie, tell me again what you saw the day of the shootings at Sterling High."

Underneath the table, Josie gripped her hands together. She dug the nails of one hand into the palm of the other, so that something hurt more than the words he was making her say. "I had a science test. I'd studied really late for it, and I was thinking about it when I woke up in the morning. That's all I know. I already told you, I can't even remember being in school that day."

"Do you remember what made you pass out in the locker room?"

Josie closed her eyes. She could picture the locker room—the tile floor, the gray lockers, the orphan sock stuffed in a corner of the shower. And then, everything went red as anger. Red as blood.

"No," Josie said, but tears had cut her voice into lace. "I don't even know why thinking about it makes me cry." She hated being seen like this; she hated *being* like this; most of all she hated not knowing when it would happen: a shift of the wind, a turn of the tide. Josie took the tissue the detective offered. "Please," she whispered, "can I just go now?"

There was a moment of hesitation, and Josie could feel the weight of the detective's pity falling over her like a net, one that only held on to her words, while the rest—the shame, the anger, the fear—seeped right through. "Sure, Josie," he said. "You can go."

Alex was pretending to read the Town of Sterling Annual Report when Josie suddenly burst out of the secured door into the police station's waiting area. She was crying hard, and Patrick Ducharme was nowhere in sight. *I'll kill him,* Alex thought rationally, calmly, *after I take care of my daughter.*

"Josie," she said, as Josie ran past her out of the building, toward the parking lot. Alex hurried after her, finally catching up to Josie in front of their car. She wrapped her arms around Josie's waist and felt her buckle. "Leave me alone," Josie sobbed.

"Josie, honey, what did he say to you? Talk to me."

"I can't talk to you! You don't understand. None of you understand." Josie backed away. "The people who do, they're all dead."

Alex hesitated, unsure of the right move. She could fold Josie tighter into an embrace and let her cry. Or she could make her see that no matter how upset she was, it was something she had the resources to handle. Sort of like an Allen charge, Alex realized—the instruction a judge would give to a jury that wasn't getting anywhere in its deliberations, which basically reminded them of their duty as American citizens, and assured them that they could and would come to a consensus.

It had always worked for her in court.

"I know this is hard, Josie, but you're stronger than you think, and—"

Josie shoved her hard, breaking away. "Stop talking to me like that!"

"Like what?"

"Like I'm some fucking witness or lawyer you're trying to impress!"

"Your Honor. Sorry to interrupt."

Alex wheeled around to find Patrick Ducharme standing two feet behind them, listening to every single word. Her cheeks reddened; this was exactly the kind of behavior you didn't put on public display when you were a judge.

He'd probably go back into the police station and send out a mass email to the entire force: *Guess what I just overheard.*

"Your daughter," he said. "She forgot her sweatshirt."

Pink and hooded, it was folded neatly over his arm. He handed it to Josie. But then, instead of backing away, he put his hand on her shoulder. "Don't worry, Josie," he said, meeting her gaze as if they were the only two people in this world. "We're going to make this okay."

Alex expected Josie to snap at him, too, but instead Josie went calm under his touch. She nodded, as if she believed this for the first time since the shooting had occurred.

Alex felt something rise inside her—relief, she realized, that her daughter had finally reached out for the slightest bit of hope. And regret, bitter as any almond, because she had not been the one to put the peace back into her daughter's face.

Josie wiped her eyes with the sleeve of her sweatshirt. "You all right?" Ducharme asked.

"I guess."

"Good." The detective nodded in Alex's direction. "Judge."

"Thank you," she murmured, as he turned and started back to the police station.

Alex heard the slam of the car door as Josie slipped into the passenger seat, but she watched Patrick Ducharme until he disappeared from sight. *I wish it had been me,* Alex thought, and she deliberately kept herself from filling in the rest of that sentence.

Like Peter, Derek Markowitz was a computer whiz. Like Peter, he hadn't been blessed with muscles and height or, for that matter, any gifts of puberty. He had hair that stuck up in small tufts, as if it had been planted. He wore his shirt tucked into his pants at all times, and he had never been popular.

Unlike Peter, he hadn't gone to school one day and killed ten people.

Selena sat at the Markowitzes' kitchen table, while Dee Dee Markowitz watched her like a hawk. She was there to interview Derek in the hope that he could be a witness for the defense—but to be perfectly honest, the information Derek had given her so far made him a much better candidate for the prosecution.

"What if it's all my fault?" Derek was saying. "I mean, I'm the only one who was given a clue. If I'd been listening harder, maybe I could have stopped him. I could have told someone else. But instead, I figured he was joking around."

"I don't think anyone would have done any differently in your situation," Selena said gently, and she meant it. "The Peter you knew wasn't the one who went to the school that day."

"Yeah," Derek said, and he nodded to himself.

"Are you about finished?" Dee Dee asked, stepping forward. "Derek's got a violin lesson."

"Almost, Mrs. Markowitz. I just wanted to ask Derek about the Peter he *did* know. How'd you two meet?"

"We were both on a soccer team together in sixth grade," Derek said, "and we both sucked."

"Derek!"

"Sorry, Mom, but it's true." He glanced up at Selena. "Then again, none of those jocks could write HTML code if their lives depended on it."

Selena smiled. "Yeah, well, count me in the ranks of the technologically impaired. So you two got to be friends while you were on the team?"

"We hung out on the bench, because we were never put in to play," Derek said. "But no, we weren't really friends until after that, when he stopped hanging out with Josie."

Selena fumbled her pen. "Josie?"

"Yeah, Josie Cormier. She goes to the school, too."

"And she's Peter's friend?"

"She used to be, like, the only kid he ever hung around with," Derek explained, "but then she became one of the cool kids, and she ditched him." He looked at Selena. "Peter didn't care, really. He said she'd turned into a bitch."

"Derek!"

"Sorry, Mom," he said. "But again, it's true."

"Would you excuse me?" Selena asked.

She walked out of the kitchen and into the bathroom, where she pulled her cell phone out of her pocket and dialed home. "It's me," she said when Jordan answered, and then she hesitated. "Why is it so quiet?"

"Sam's asleep."

"You didn't pop in another Wiggles video just to get your discovery read, did you?"

"Did you call specifically to accuse me of lousy parenting?"

"No," Selena said. "I called to tell you that Peter and Josie used to be best friends."

In maximum security, Peter was allowed only one real visitor a week, but certain people didn't count. For example, your lawyer could come and see you as many times as necessary. And—here's the crazy thing—so could reporters. All Peter had to do was sign a little release that said he was willingly making the choice to speak to the media, and Elena Battista was allowed to meet him.

She was hot. Peter noticed that right away. Instead of wearing some shapeless oversized sweater, she had dressed in a tight blouse with buttons. If he leaned forward, he could even see cleavage.

She had long, thick curly hair and doe-brown eyes, and Peter found it really hard to believe that she had ever been teased by anyone in high school. But she was sitting in front of him, that much was true, and she could barely look him in the eyes. "I can't believe this," she said, her toes coming right up to the red line that separated them. "I can't believe I'm actually meeting you."

Peter pretended he heard this all the time. "Yeah," he said. "It's cool that you drove up here."

"Oh, God, that was the least I could do," Elena said. Peter thought of stories he'd heard, of groupies who'd written to inmates and eventually married them in a prison ceremony. He thought of the correctional officer who'd brought Elena in, and wondered if he was telling everyone else that Peter Houghton had some hot girl visiting him.

"You don't mind if I take notes, do you?" Elena asked. "For my paper?"

"That's cool."

He watched her pull out a pencil and hold the cap in her mouth while she opened her notebook to a fresh page. "So, like I told you, I'm writing about the effects of bullying."

"How come?"

"Well, there were times when I was in high school that I thought I'd rather just kill myself than go back to class the next day, because it would be easier. I figured if I was thinking it, there had to be other people thinking it, too . . . and that's where I came up with the idea." She leaned forward—*cleavage alert*—and met Peter's eyes. "I'm hoping I can get it published in a psychology journal or something."

"That would be cool." He winced; God, how many times was he going to use the word *cool*? He probably sounded like a total retard.

"So, maybe you could start by telling me how often it used to happen. The bullying, I mean."

"Every day, I guess."

"What sorts of things did they do?"

"The usual," Peter said. "Stuffing me into a locker, throwing my books out the bus window." He gave her a litany he'd already given Jordan a thousand times: memories of being elbowed on his way up a staircase, moments where his glasses were ripped off and crushed, slurs pitched like fastballs.

Elena's eyes melted. "That must have been so hard for you."

Peter didn't know what to say. He wanted her to stay interested in his story, but not if it meant that she thought he was a total wimp. He shrugged, hoping that was a good enough response.

She stopped writing. "Peter, can I ask you something?"

"Sure."

"Even if it's kind of off topic?"

Peter nodded.

"Did you plan to kill them?"

She was leaning forward again, her lips parted, as if whatever Peter was about to say was some wafer, a communion host that she'd been waiting for her whole life. Peter could hear the footsteps of a guard walking past the doorway behind him, could practically taste Elena's breath through the receiver. He wanted to give her the right answer—sound dangerous enough for her to be intrigued, to want to come back.

He smiled, in a way that he hoped was sort of seductive. "Let's just say it needed to stop," Peter answered.

The magazines in Jordan's dentist's office had the shelf life of plutonium. They were so old that the celebrity bride on the cover now had two babies named for biblical characters, or pieces of fruit; that the president listed as Man of the Year had already left office. To that end, when he stumbled upon the latest issue of *Time* while awaiting his appointment for a filling, Jordan felt like he'd hit the mother lode.

HIGH SCHOOL: THE NEWEST FRONT LINE FOR BATTLE? the cover read, and there was a still image of Sterling High from a chopper, kids still streaming out of all the building's orifices. He absently leafed toward the article and its subsections, not expecting to see anything he didn't already know or hadn't already seen in the papers, but one piece caught his eye. "Inside the Mind of a Killer," he read, and he saw the much-used school picture of Peter from his eighth-grade yearbook.

Then he started to read.

"Goddamn," he said, and he got to his feet, starting for the door.

"Mr. McAfee," the secretary said, "the dentist is ready for you."

"I'll have to reschedule—"

"Well, you can't take our magazine . . ."

"Add it to my bill," Jordan snapped, and he hurried downstairs to his car. His cell phone rang just as he turned the key in the ignition—he completely expected it to be Diana Leven, gloating over her good fortune—but instead, it was Selena.

"Hey, are you done at the dentist? I need you to swing by CVS and grab some diapers on the way home. I ran out."

"I'm not coming home. I've got bigger problems right now."

"Honey," Selena said, "there *are* no bigger problems."

"I'll explain later," Jordan said, and he turned off his

phone, so that even if Diana called, she wouldn't be able to reach him.

He got to the jail in twenty-six minutes—a personal record—and stormed into the entryway. There, he plastered the magazine up to the plastic that separated him from the CO who was signing him in. "I need to bring this in when I see my client," Jordan said.

"Well, I'm sorry," the officer said, "but you can't take in anything that's got staples."

Frustrated, Jordan balanced the magazine against his leg and ripped out the binding staples. "Fine. Can I see my client *now?*"

He was brought to the same conference room he always used at the jail, and he paced while he waited for Peter to arrive. When he did, Jordan slammed the magazine down on the table, open to the article. "What the fuck were you thinking?"

Peter's mouth dropped open. "She . . . she never mentioned that she wrote for *Time!*" He scanned the pages. "I can't believe it," he murmured.

Jordan could feel all the blood in his body rushing to his head. Surely, this was how people had strokes. "Do you have any idea how serious the charges against you are? How awful your case is? How much evidence there is against you?" He smacked an open hand on the article. "Do you really think that this makes you look at all sympathetic?"

Peter scowled. "Well, thanks for the lecture. Maybe if you'd been here to deliver it a few weeks ago we wouldn't be having this discussion at all."

"Oh, that's priceless," Jordan said. "I don't come by often enough, so you decide to get back at me by talking to the media?"

"She wasn't the media. She was my friend."

"Guess what," Jordan said. "You don't get to have any friends."

"So what *else* is new?" Peter shot back.

Jordan opened his mouth to yell at Peter again, but couldn't. The truth of the statement struck him, as he remembered Selena's interview earlier this week with Derek Markowitz. Peter's buddies deserted him, or betrayed him, or spilled his secrets for a circulation of millions.

If he really wanted to do his job right, he couldn't just be an attorney to Peter. He had to be his confidant, and to date, all he'd done was string the kid along, just like everyone else in his life.

Jordan sat down next to Peter. "Look," he said quietly. "You can't do anything like this again. If anyone contacts you at all, for any reason, you need to tell me. And in return, I'll come to see you more often than I have been. Okay?"

Peter shrugged his agreement. For a long moment they both sat beside each other, silent, unsure of what came next.

"So now what?" Peter asked. "Do I have to talk about Joey again? Or prep for that psychiatric interview?"

Jordan hesitated. The only reason he'd come to see Peter was to tear into him for talking to a reporter; if not for that, he wouldn't have come to the jail at all. And he supposed he could ask Peter to recount his childhood or his school history or his feelings about being bullied, but somehow, that didn't seem right either. "Actually, I need some advice," he said. "My wife got me this computer game last Christmas, Agents of Stealth? The thing is, I can't make it past the first level without getting wiped out."

Peter glanced at him sideways. "Well, are you registering as a Droid or a Regal?"

Who the hell knew? He hadn't taken the CD out of its box. "A Droid."

"That's your first mistake. See, you can't enlist in the Pyrhphorus Legion—you need to get appointed to serve. The way to do that is by starting off in the Educatuary instead of the Mines. Understand?"

Jordan glanced down at the article, still spread on the table. His case had just grown immeasurably more difficult, but maybe that was offset by the fact that his relationship with his client had gotten easier. "Yeah," Jordan said. "I'm starting to."

"You're not going to like this," Eleanor said, handing a document to Alex.

"Why not?"

"It's a motion to recuse yourself from the Houghton case. The prosecution strongly requests a hearing."

A hearing meant that press would be present, the victims would be present, the families would be present. It meant that Alex would be under public scrutiny before this case could go any further. "Well, she's not getting one," Alex said dismissively.

The clerk hesitated. "I'd think twice about that."

Alex met her eyes. "You can leave now."

She waited for Eleanor to close the door behind herself, and then she closed her eyes. She didn't know what to do. It was true that she'd been more rattled during the arraignment than she'd anticipated. It was true, too, that the distance between herself and Josie could be measured by the very parameters of her role as judge. Yet because Alex had steadfastly assumed that she was infallible—because she'd been so sure that she could be a fair justice on this case—she'd gotten herself into a catch-22. It was one thing to recuse yourself before the proceedings started. But if she backed out now, it would make her seem flighty (at best) or inept (at worst). Neither one of those was an adjective she wanted associated with her judicial career.

If she didn't give Diana Leven the hearing she was requesting, it would look like Alex was hiding. Better to let them voice their positions and be a big girl. Alex pushed a button on her phone. "Eleanor," she said, "schedule it."

She speared her fingers through her hair and then smoothed it down again. What she needed was a cigarette. She rummaged in her desk drawers but turned up only an empty pack of Merits. "Shoot," she muttered, and then remembered her emergency pack, hidden in the trunk of her car. Grabbing her keys, Alex stood up and left chambers, hurrying down the back staircase to the parking lot.

She threw open the fire door and heard the sickening crunch as it hit flesh. "Oh my gosh," she cried, reaching for the man who'd doubled over in pain. "Are you all right?"

Patrick Ducharme straightened, wincing. "Your Honor," he said. "I've got to stop running into you. Literally."

She frowned. "You shouldn't have been standing next to a fire door."

"You shouldn't have been flinging it open. So where is it today?" Patrick asked.

"Where's what?"

"The fire?" He nodded at another cop, walking to a cruiser parked in the lot.

Alex took a step backward and folded her arms. "I believe we already had a conversation about, well, conversation."

"First of all, we're not talking about the case, unless there's some metaphorical thing going on that I don't know about. Second of all, your position on this case seems to be in doubt, at least if you believe the editorial in the *Sterling News* today."

"There's an editorial about me today?" Alex said, stunned. "What does it say?"

"Well, I'd tell you, but that would be talking about the case, wouldn't it?" He grinned and started to walk off.

"Hang on," Alex said, calling after the detective. When he turned, she glanced around to make sure that they were alone in the parking lot. "Can I ask you something? Off the record?"

He nodded slowly.

"Did Josie seem . . . I don't know . . . *all right* to you, when you talked to her the other day?"

The detective leaned against the brick wall of the court building. "You certainly know her better than I do."

"Well . . . sure," Alex said. "I just thought she might say something to you—as a stranger—that she wasn't willing to say to me." She looked down at the ground between them. "Sometimes it's easier that way."

She could feel Patrick's eyes on her, but she couldn't quite muster the courage to meet them. "Can I tell *you* something? Off the record?"

Alex nodded.

"Before I took this job, I used to work in Maine. And I had a case that wasn't just a case, if you know what I mean."

Alex did. She found herself listening in his voice for a note she hadn't heard before—a low one that resonated with anguish, like a tuning fork that never stopped its vibration. "There was a woman there who meant everything to me, and she had a little boy who meant everything to her. And when he was hurt, in a way a kid never should be, I moved heaven and earth to work that case, because I thought no one could possibly do a better job than I could. No one could possibly care more about the outcome." He looked directly at Alex. "I was so sure I could separate how I felt about what had happened from how I had to do my job."

Alex swallowed, dry as dust. "And did you?"

"No. Because when you love someone, no matter what you tell yourself, it stops being a job."

"What does it become?"

Patrick thought for a moment. "Revenge."

One morning, when Lewis had told Lacy he was headed to visit Peter at the jail, she got in her car and followed him. In the days since Peter had confessed that his father didn't come to see him, through the arraignment and afterward, Lacy had kept this secret hidden. She spoke less and less to Lewis, because she feared that once she opened her mouth, it would escape like a hurricane.

Lacy was careful to keep one car between hers and Lewis's. It made her think of a lifetime ago, when they had been dating, and she would follow Lewis to his apartment or he would follow her. They'd play games with each other, waving the rear windshield wiper like a dog wags its tail, flashing headlights in Morse code.

He drove north, as if he was going to the jail, and for a moment Lacy had a crisis of doubt: would Peter have lied to her, for some reason? She didn't think so. But then again, she hadn't thought Lewis would, either.

It started to rain just as they reached the green in Lyme Center. Lewis signaled and turned into a small parking lot with a bank, an artist's studio, a flower shop. She couldn't pull in behind him—he'd recognize her car right away—so instead she drove into the lot of the hardware store next door and parked behind the building.

Maybe he needs the ATM, Lacy thought, but she got out of her car and hid behind the oil tanks to watch Lewis enter a floral shop, and leave five minutes later with a bouquet of pink roses.

All the breath left her body. Was he having an affair? She had never considered the possibility that things could get even worse, that their small family unit could fracture further.

Lacy stumbled into her car and managed to follow Lewis. It was true, she had been obsessed with Peter's trial. And maybe she had been guilty of not listening to Lewis when he needed to talk, because nothing he had to say about economics seminars or publications or current events really seemed to matter anymore, not when her son was sitting in jail. But *Lewis?* She'd always imagined herself as the free spirit in their union; she'd seen him as the anchor. Security was a mirage; being tied down hardly counted when the other end of the rope had unraveled.

She wiped her eyes on her sleeve. Lewis would tell her, of course, that it was only sex, not love. That it didn't mean anything. He would say that there were all sorts of ways that people dealt with grief, with a hole in the heart.

Lewis put on his blinker again and turned right—this time, into a cemetery.

A slow burn started inside Lacy's chest. Well, this was just sick. Was this where he met her?

Lewis got out of the car, carrying his roses but no umbrella. The rain was coming down harder now, but Lacy was intent on seeing this through to the end. She stayed just far enough behind, following him to a newer section of the cemetery, the one with the freshest graves. There weren't even headstones yet; the plots looked like a patchwork: brown earth against the green of the clipped lawn.

At the first grave, Lewis knelt and placed a rose on the soil. Then he moved to another one, doing the same. And another, and another, until his hair was dripping into his face; until his shirt was soaked through; until he'd left behind ten flowers.

Lacy came up behind him as he was placing the last

rose. "I know you're there," he said, although he didn't turn around.

She could barely speak: the understanding that Lewis was not, in fact, cheating on her had been tempered by the knowledge of what he was actually spending his time doing these days. She couldn't tell if she was crying anymore, or if the sky was doing it for her. "How dare you come here," she accused, "and not visit your own son?"

He lifted his face to hers. "Do you know what chaos theory is?"

"I don't give a fuck about chaos theory, Lewis. I care about Peter. Which is more than I can say for—"

"There's this belief," he interrupted, "that you can explain only the last moment in time, linearly . . . but that everything leading up to it might have come from any series of events. So, you know, a kid skips a stone at the beach, and somewhere across the planet, a tsunami happens." Lewis stood up, his hands in his pockets. "I took him hunting, Lacy. I told him to stick with the sport, even if he didn't like it. I said a thousand things. What if one of them was what made Peter do this?"

He doubled over, sobbing. As Lacy reached for him, the rain drummed over her shoulders and back.

"We did the best we could," Lacy said.

"It wasn't good enough." Lewis jerked his head in the direction of the graves. "Look at this. *Look* at this."

Lacy did. Through the driving downpour, with her hair and clothes plastered to her, she took stock of the graveyard and saw the faces of the children who would still be alive, if her own son had never been born.

Lacy put her hand over her abdomen. The pain cut her in half, like a magician's trick, except she knew she would never really be put back together.

One of her sons had been doing drugs. The other was a murderer. Had she and Lewis been the wrong parents for the boys they'd had? Or should they never have been parents at all?

Children didn't make their own mistakes. They plunged into the pits they'd been led to by their parents. She and Lewis had truly believed they were headed the right way, but maybe they should have stopped to ask for directions. Maybe then they would never have had to watch Joey—and then Peter—take that one tragic step and free-fall.

Lacy remembered holding Joey's grades up against Peter's; telling Peter that maybe he should try out for soccer, because Joey had enjoyed it so much. Acceptance started at home, but so did intolerance. By the time Peter had been excluded at school, Lacy realized, he was used to feeling like an outcast in his own family.

Lacy squeezed her eyes shut. For the rest of her life, she'd be known as Peter Houghton's mother. At one point, that would have thrilled her—but you had to be careful what you wished for. Taking credit for what a child did well also meant accepting responsibility for what they did wrong. And to Lacy, that meant that instead of making reparations to these victims, she and Lewis needed to start closer to home—with Peter.

"He needs us," Lacy said. "More than ever."

Lewis shook his head. "I can't go to see Peter."

She drew away. "Why?"

"Because I still think, every day, of the drunk who crashed into Joey's car. I think of how much I wished he'd died instead of Joey; how he *deserved* to die. The parents of every one of these kids is thinking the same thing about Peter," Lewis said. "And Lacy . . . I don't blame a single one of them."

Lacy stepped back, shivering. Lewis wadded up the

paper cone that had held the flowers and stuffed it into his pocket. The rain fell between them like a curtain, making it impossible for them to see each other clearly.

Jordan waited at a pizza place near the jail for King Wah to arrive after his psychiatric interview with Peter. He was ten minutes late, and Jordan wasn't sure if that was a good thing or a bad thing.

King blew through the door on a gust of wind, his raincoat billowing out behind him. He slid into the booth where Jordan was sitting and picked up a slice of pizza on Jordan's plate. "You can do this," he pronounced, and he took a bite. "Psychologically, there isn't a significant difference between the treatment of a victim of bullying over time and the treatment of an adult female in battered woman syndrome. The bottom line for both is post-traumatic stress disorder." He put the crust back on Jordan's plate. "You know what Peter told me?"

Jordan thought about his client for a moment. "That it sucks being in jail?"

"Well, they all say that. He told me that he would rather have died than spend another day thinking about what could happen to him at school. Who does that sound like?"

"Katie Riccobono," Jordan said. "After she decided to give her husband a triple bypass with a steak knife."

"Katie Riccobono," King corrected, "poster child for battered woman syndrome."

"So Peter becomes the first example of bullied victim syndrome," Jordan said. "Be honest with me, King. You think a jury is going to identify with a syndrome that doesn't even really exist?"

"A jury's not made up of battered women, but they've been known to acquit them before. On the other hand, every single member of that jury will have been through high school." He reached for Jordan's Coke and took a sip. "Did you know that a single incident of bullying in childhood can be as traumatic to a person, over time, as a single incident of sexual abuse?"

"You gotta be kidding me."

"Think about it. The common denominator is being humiliated. What's the strongest memory you have from high school?"

Jordan had to think for a moment before any memory of high school even clouded its way into his mind, much less a salient one. Then he started to grin. "I was in Phys. Ed., and doing a fitness test. Part of it involved climbing a rope that was hung from the ceiling. In high school, I didn't have quite the massive physique I have now—"

King snorted. "Naturally."

"—so I was already worried about not making it to the top. As it turned out, that wasn't a problem. It was coming back down, because climbing up with the rope between my legs, I got a massive boner."

"There you go," King said. "Ask ten people, and half of them won't even be able to remember something concrete from high school—they've blocked it out. The other half will recall an incredibly painful or embarrassing moment. They stick like glue."

"That is incredibly depressing," Jordan pointed out.

"Well, most of us grow up and realize that in the grand scheme of life, these incidents are a tiny part of the puzzle."

"And the ones who don't?"

King glanced at Jordan. "They turn out like Peter."

The reason Alex was in Josie's closet in the first place was because Josie had borrowed her black skirt and never returned it, and Alex needed it tonight. She was meeting someone for dinner—Whit Hobart—her former boss, who'd retired from the public defender's office. After today's hearing, where the prosecution had made its motion to have her recused, she needed some advice.

She'd found the skirt, but she'd also found a trove of treasures. Alex sat on the floor with a box open in her lap. The fringe of Josie's old jazz costume, from lessons she'd taken when she was six or seven, fell into her palm like a whisper. The silk was cool to the touch. It was puddled on top of a faux fur tiger costume that Josie had worn one Halloween and kept for dress-up—Alex's first and last foray into sewing. Halfway through, she'd given up and soldered the fabric together with a hot glue gun. Alex had planned to take Josie trick-or-treating that year, but she'd been a public defender at the time, and one of her clients had been arrested again. Josie had gone out with the neighbor and her children; and that night, when Alex finally got home, Josie had spilled her pillowcase of candy on the bed. *You can take half,* Josie told her, *because you missed all the fun.*

She thumbed through the atlas Josie had made in first grade, coloring every continent and then laminating the pages; she read her report cards. She found a hair elastic and looped it around her wrist. At the bottom of the box was a note, written in the loopy script of a little girl: *Deer Mom I love you a lot XOXO.*

Alex let her fingers trace the letters. She wondered why Josie still had this in her possession; why it had never been given to its addressee. Had Josie been waiting, and forgotten? Had she been angry at Alex for something and decided not to give it at all?

Alex stood, then carefully put the box back where she'd found it. She folded the black skirt over her arm and headed toward her own bedroom. Most parents, she knew, went through their child's things in search of condoms and baggies of pot, to try to catch them in the act. For Alex, it was different. For Alex, going through Josie's possessions was a way of holding on to everything she'd missed.

The sad truth about being single was that Patrick couldn't justify going to all the bother to cook for himself. He ate most of his meals standing over the sink, so what was the point of making a mess with dozens of pots and pans and fresh ingredients? It wasn't as if he was going to turn to himself and say, *Patrick, great recipe, where'd you find it?*

He had it down to a science, really. Monday was pizza night. Tuesday, Subway. Wednesday was Chinese; Thursday, soup; and Friday, he got a burger at the bar where he usually grabbed a beer before heading home. Weekends were for leftovers, and there were always plenty. Sometimes, it got downright lonely ordering (was there any sadder phrase in the English language than *Pupu platter for one?*), but for the most part, his routine had netted him a collection of friends. Sal at the pizza place gave him garlic knots for free, because he was a regular. The Subway guy, whose name Patrick didn't know, would point at him and grin. "Hearty-Italian-turkey-cheese-mayo-olives-extra-pickles-salt-and-pepper," he'd call out, the verbal equivalent of their secret handshake.

This being a Wednesday, he was at the Golden Dragon, waiting for his take-out order to be filled. He watched May ferry it into the kitchen (where on earth did someone buy a wok that big, he always wondered) and turned his attention to the television over the bar, where the Sox game was just beginning. A woman was sitting alone, tearing a fringe around the edge of a cocktail napkin as she waited for the bartender to bring her her drink.

She had her back to him, but Patrick was a detective, and there were certain things he could figure out just from this side of her. Like the fact that she had a great ass, for one, and that her hair needed to be taken out of that librarian's bun so that it could wave around her shoulders. He watched the bartender (a Korean named Spike, which always struck Patrick as funny after the first Tsingtao) opening up a bottle of pinot noir, and he filed away this information, too: she was classy. Nothing with a little paper umbrella in it, not for her.

He sidled up behind the woman and handed Spike a twenty. "My treat," Patrick said.

She turned, and for a fraction of a second, Patrick stood rooted to the spot, wondering how this mystery woman could possibly have Judge Cormier's face.

It reminded Patrick of being in high school and seeing a friend's mom from a distance across a parking lot and automatically checking her out as a Potential Hot Babe until he realized who it actually was. The judge plucked the twenty-dollar bill out of Spike's hand and gave it back to Patrick. "You can't buy me a drink," she said, and she pulled some cash out of her pocketbook and handed it to the bartender.

Patrick sat down on the stool beside her. "Well, then," he said. "You can buy *me* one."

"I don't think so." She glanced around the restaurant. "I really don't think we ought to be seen talking."

"The only witnesses are the koi in the pond by the cash register. I think you're safe," Patrick said. "Besides, we're just talking. We're not talking about the case. You *do* still remember how to make conversation outside a courtroom, don't you?"

She picked up her glass of wine. "What are you doing here, anyway?"

Patrick lowered his voice. "I'm running a drug bust on the Chinese mafia. They import raw opium in the sugar packets."

Her eyes widened. "Honestly?"

"No. And would I tell you if it *were* true?" He smiled. "I'm just waiting for my take-out order. What about you?"

"I'm waiting for someone."

He didn't realize, until she'd said it, that he'd been enjoying her company. He got a kick out of flustering her, which, truthfully, wasn't really all that hard. Judge Cormier reminded him of the Great and Powerful Oz: all bluster and bells and whistles, but when you pulled back the curtain, she was just an ordinary woman.

Who happened to have a great ass.

He felt heat rise to his face. "Happy family," Patrick said.

"Excuse me?"

"That's what I ordered. I was just trying to help you out with that casual conversation thing again."

"You only got one dish? No one goes to a Chinese restaurant and only gets one dish."

"Well, not all of us have growing kids at home."

She traced the lip of her wineglass with one finger. "You don't have any?"

"Never married."

"Why not?"

Patrick shook his head, smiling faintly. "I'm not getting into that."

"Boy," the judge said. "She must have done a job on you."

His jaw dropped open. Was he really that easy to read?

"Guess you haven't cornered the market on those amazing detective skills," she said, laughing. "Except we call it women's intuition."

"Yeah, that'll get you your gold shield in no time." He glanced at her ringless hand. "Why aren't *you* married?"

The judge repeated his own answer. "I'm not getting into that."

She sipped her wine in silence for a moment, and Patrick tapped his fingers on the wood of the bar. "She was already married," he admitted.

The judge set her glass down, empty. "So was he," she confessed, and when Patrick turned to her, she looked him right in the eye.

Hers were the pale gray that made you think of nightfall and silver bullets and the edge of winter. The color that filled the sky before it was torn in half by lightning.

Patrick had never noticed this before, and suddenly he realized why. "You're not wearing glasses."

"I sure am glad to know Sterling's got someone as sharp as you protecting and serving them."

"You usually wear glasses."

"Only when I'm working. I need them to read."

And when I usually see you, you're working.

That was why he hadn't noticed before that Alex Cormier was attractive: before this, when they crossed paths, she was in full buttoned-up judge mode. She had not been curled over the bar like a hothouse flower. She had not been quite so . . . human.

"Alex!" The voice came from behind them. The man was spiffy, in a good suit and wingtips, with just enough gray hair at his temples to look distinguished. He had lawyer written all over him. He was no doubt rich and divorced; the kind of guy who would sit up at night and talk about penal code before making love; the kind of guy who slept on his side of the bed instead of with his arms wrapped so tight around her that even after falling asleep, they stayed tangled.

Jesus Christ, Patrick thought, looking down at the ground. *Where did that come from?*

What did he care who Alex Cormier dated, even if the guy was practically old enough to be her father?

"Whit," she said, "I'm so glad you could come." She kissed him on the cheek and then, still holding his hand, turned to Patrick. "Whit, this is Detective Patrick Ducharme. Patrick, Whit Hobart."

The man had a good handshake, which only pissed Patrick off even more. Patrick waited to see what else the judge was going to say about him by way of introduction. But then, what options did she have? Patrick wasn't an old friend. He wasn't someone she'd met sitting at the bar. She couldn't even say that they were both involved with the Houghton trial, because in that case, he shouldn't have been talking to her.

Which, Patrick realized, is what she'd been trying to tell him all along.

May appeared from the kitchen, holding a paper bag folded and neatly stapled. "Here you go, Pat," she said. "We see you next week, okay?"

He could feel the judge staring. "Happy family," she said, offering a consolation prize, the smallest of smiles.

"Nice seeing you, Your Honor," Patrick said politely. He threw the door of the restaurant open so hard that it banged on its hinges against the outside wall. He was halfway to his car when he realized he wasn't even really hungry anymore.

The lead story on the local news at 11:00 p.m. was the hearing at the superior court to get Judge Cormier removed from the case. Jordan and Selena sat in bed in the dark, each with a bowl of cereal balanced on their stomachs, watching the tearful mother of a paraplegic girl cry into the television camera. "No one's speaking for our children," she said. "If this case gets messed up because of some legal snafu . . . well, they aren't strong enough to go through it twice."

"Neither's Peter," Jordan pointed out.

Selena put down her spoon. "Cormier's gonna sit on that case if she has to crawl her way to the bench."

"Well, I can't very well get someone to gilhooly her kneecaps, can I?"

"Let's look at the bright side," Selena said. "Nothing in Josie's statement can hurt Peter."

"My God, you're right." Jordan sat up so quickly that he sloshed milk onto the quilt. He set his bowl on the nightstand. "It's brilliant."

"What is?"

"Diana's not calling Josie as a witness for the prosecution, because she's got nothing they can use. But there's nothing to stop *me* from calling her as a witness for the defense."

"Are you kidding? You're going to put the *judge's* daughter on your witness list?"

"Why not? She used to be Peter's friend. He's got precious few of them. It's all in good faith."

"You wouldn't really—"

"Nah, I'm sure I'll never use her. But the prosecutor doesn't need to know that." He grinned at Diana. "And incidentally . . . neither does the judge."

Selena set her bowl aside, too. "If you put Josie on your witness list . . . Cormier *has* to step down."

"Exactly."

Selena reached forward, bracketing his face with her palms to plant a kiss on his lips. "You're *awfully* good."

"What was that?"

"You heard me the first time."

"I know," Jordan grinned, "but I wouldn't mind hearing it again."

The quilt slipped down as he wrapped his arms around her. "Greedy li'l thing, aren't you," Selena murmured.

"Isn't that what made you fall in love with me?"

Selena laughed. "Well, it wasn't your charm and grace, honey."

Jordan leaned over her, kissing Selena until—he hoped—she had forgotten she was in the throes of making fun of him. "Let's have another baby," he whispered.

"I'm still nursing the first one!"

"Then let's *practice* having another one."

There was no one in the world quite like his wife, Jordan thought—statuesque and stunning, smarter than he was (not that he'd ever admit it to her face), and so perfectly attuned to him that he nearly had to concede his skepticism and believe that psychics truly did walk among us. He buried his face in the spot he loved best on Selena: the part where the nape of her neck ran into her shoulder, where her skin was the color of maple syrup and tasted even sweeter.

"Jordan?" she said. "Do you ever worry about our kids? I mean . . . you know. Doing what you do . . . and seeing what we see?"

He rolled onto his back. "Well," he said. "That certainly killed the moment."

"I'm serious."

Jordan sighed. "Of course I think about it. I worry about Thomas. And Sam. And whoever else might come along." He came up on an elbow so that he could find her eyes in the dark. "But then I figure that's the reason we had them."

"How so?"

He looked over Selena's shoulder, to the blinking green eye of the baby monitor. "Maybe," Jordan said, "they're the ones who'll change the world."

Whit hadn't really made up Alex's mind for her; that had already been done when she met him for dinner. But he'd been the salve she needed for her wounds, the justification she was afraid to give herself. *You'll get another big case, eventually*, he had said. *You won't get back this moment with Josie.*

She walked into chambers briskly, mostly because she knew that this was the easy part. Divorcing herself from the case, writing the motion to recuse herself—that was not nearly as terrifying as what would happen tomorrow, when she was no longer the judge on the Houghton case.

When, instead, she had to be a mother.

Eleanor was nowhere to be found, but she'd left Alex the paperwork on her desk. She sat down and scanned it.

Jordan McAfee, who yesterday hadn't even opened his mouth at the hearing, was noticing up his intention to call Josie as a witness.

She felt a fire spark in her belly. It was an emotion Alex didn't even have words for—the animal instinct that came when you realized someone you love has been taken hostage.

McAfee had committed the grievous sin of dragging Josie into this, and Alex's mind spiraled wildly as she wondered what she could do to get him fired, or even disbarred. Come to think of it, she didn't even really care if retribution came within the confines of the law or outside it. But suddenly, Alex stilled. It wasn't Jordan McAfee she'd chase to the ends of the earth—it was Josie. She'd do anything to keep her daughter from being hurt again.

Maybe she should thank Jordan McAfee for making her realize that she already had the raw material in her to be a good mother, after all.

Alex sat down at her laptop and began to type. Her heart was hammering as she walked out to the clerk's desk and handed the sheet of paper to Eleanor; but that was normal, wasn't it, when you were about to leap off a cliff?

"You need to call Judge Wagner," Alex said.

※   ※   ※

It wasn't Patrick who needed the search warrant. But when he heard another officer talking about swinging by the courthouse, he interceded. "I'm headed out that way," he'd said. "I'll do it for you."

In truth, he hadn't been heading toward the courthouse, at least not until he'd volunteered. And he wasn't such a Samaritan that he'd drive forty miles out of the goodness of his heart. Patrick wanted to go there for one reason only: it was another excuse to see Alex Cormier.

He pulled into an empty spot and got out of his car, immediately spotting her Honda. This was a good thing; for all he knew, she might not even have been in court today. But then he did a double take as he realized that someone was in the car . . . and that that someone was the judge.

She wasn't moving, just staring out the windshield. The wipers were on, but it wasn't raining. It looked like she didn't even realize she was crying.

He felt that same uneasy sway in the pit of his stomach that usually came when he'd reached a crime scene and saw a victim's tears. *I'm too late*, he thought. *Again.*

Patrick approached the car, but the judge must not have seen him coming. When he knocked on the window, she jumped a foot and hurriedly wiped her eyes. He mimed for her to roll down the window. "Everything okay?" he asked.

"I'm fine."

"You don't *look* fine."

"Then stop looking," she snapped.

He hooked his fingers over the curl of the car door. "Listen. You want to go somewhere and talk? I'll buy you coffee."

The judge sighed. "You *can't* buy me coffee."

"Well, we can still get some." He stood up and walked

around to the passenger door, opened it, slid into the seat beside her.

"You're on duty," she pointed out.

"I'm taking my lunch break."

"At ten in the morning?"

He reached across the console to the keys, dangling in the ignition, and started the car. "Head out of the parking lot and take a left, all right?"

"Or what?"

"For God's sake, don't you know better than to argue with someone who's wearing a Glock?"

She looked at him for a long moment. "You couldn't possibly be carjacking me," the judge said, but she started driving, as he'd asked.

"Remind me to arrest myself later," Patrick said.

Alex had been raised by her father to give everything her best shot, and apparently, that included falling off the deep end. Why not recuse herself from the biggest trial of her career, ask for administrative leave, and go out for coffee with the detective on the case all in one fell swoop?

Then again, she told herself, if she hadn't gone out with Patrick Ducharme, she would never have known that the Golden Dragon Chinese restaurant opened for business at 10:00 a.m.

If she hadn't gone out with him, she would have had to drive home and start her life over.

Everyone at the restaurant seemed to know the detective and didn't mind him going into the kitchen to get Alex her cup of coffee. "What you saw back there," Alex said hesitantly. "You won't . . ."

"Tell anyone you were having a little breakdown in your car?"

She looked down at the mug he set in front of her, not

even really knowing how to respond. In her experience, the moment you showed you were weak in front of someone, they'd use it against you. "It's hard to be a judge sometimes. People expect you to act like one, even when you've got the flu and feel like crawling up into a ball and dying, or cursing out the cashier who shortchanged you on purpose. There's not a lot of room for mistakes."

"Your secret's safe," Patrick said. "I won't tell anyone in the law enforcement community that you've actually got emotions."

Alex took a sip of the coffee, then looked up at him. "Sugar?"

Patrick folded his arms on the bar and leaned toward her. "Darling?" At her expression, he started to laugh, and then handed her the bowl. "Honestly, it's no big deal. We all have lousy days at work."

"Do *you* sit in your car and cry?"

"Not recently, but I have been known to overturn evidence lockers during fits of frustration." He poured milk into a creamer and set it down. "You know, it's not mutually exclusive."

"What's not?"

"Being a judge and being human."

Alex added the milk to her mug. "Tell that to everyone who wants me to recuse myself."

"Isn't this the part where you tell me we can't talk about the case?"

"Yes," Alex said. "Except I'm not on the case anymore. As of noon, it'll be public knowledge."

He sobered. "Is that why you were upset?"

"No. I'd already made the decision to leave the case. But then I got word that Josie's on the witness list for the defense."

"Why?" Patrick said. "She doesn't remember anything. What could she possibly say?"

"I don't know." Alex glanced up. "But what if it's my fault? What if the lawyer only did that to get me off the case because I was too stubborn to recuse myself when the issue was first raised?" To her great shame, she realized she was starting to cry again, and she stared down at the bar in the hope that Patrick would not notice. "What if she has to get up in front of everyone in court and relive that whole day?" Patrick passed her a cocktail napkin, and she wiped her eyes. "I'm sorry. I'm not usually like this."

"Any mother whose daughter came that close to dying has a right to fall apart at the seams," Patrick said. "Look. I've talked to Josie twice. I know her statement back and forth. It doesn't matter if McAfee puts her on the stand—there's nothing she can say that's going to hurt her. The silver lining is that now you don't have to worry about a conflict of interest. Josie needs a good mother right now more than she needs a good judge."

Alex smiled ruefully. "What a shame she's stuck with me instead."

"Come on."

"It's true. My whole life with Josie has been a series of disconnects."

"Well," Patrick pointed out, "that presumes that at one point, you were connected."

"Neither of us remembers back that far. *You've* had better conversations with Josie than I have lately." Alex stared into the mug of coffee. "Everything I say to Josie comes out wrong. She looks at me like I'm from another planet. Like I have no right to act like a concerned parent now because I wasn't acting like one before it happened."

"Why weren't you?"

"I was working. Hard," Alex said.

"Lots of parents work hard—"

"But I'm *good* at being a judge. And lousy at being a mother." Alex covered her mouth with her hand, but it was too late to take back the truth, which coiled on the bar in front of her, poisonous. What had she been thinking, confessing that to someone when she could barely admit it to herself? She might as well have drawn a bull's-eye on her Achilles' heel.

"Maybe you should try talking to Josie the way you talk to the people who come into your court, then," Patrick suggested.

"She hates it when I act like a lawyer. Besides, I hardly talk in court. Mostly, I listen."

"Well, Your Honor," Patrick said. "That might work, too."

Once, when Josie had been a baby, Alex let her out of her sight long enough for Josie to climb up on a stool. From across the room, Alex watched in terror as Josie's slight weight upset the balance. She couldn't get there fast enough to keep Josie from falling; she didn't want to yell out, because she was afraid that if she startled Josie, that would make her fall, too. So Alex had stood, waiting for an accident to happen.

But instead, Josie managed to perch herself on the stool; to stand up on its little disc seat; to reach the light switch she'd been heading for all along. Alex watched her flick the lights on and off, watched her face split with a smile every time she realized that her actions could transform the world.

"Since we're not in court," she said hesitantly, "I'd like it if you called me Alex."

Patrick smiled. "And I'd like it if you called me Your Majesty King Kamehameha."

Alex couldn't help herself; she laughed.

"But if that's too hard to remember, Patrick would be fine." He reached for the coffeepot and poured some into her mug. "Free refills," he said.

She watched him add sugar and cream, in the same quantities that she'd used for her first cup. He was a detective; his job was to notice details. But Alex thought that probably wasn't what made him such a good cop. It was that he had the capacity to use force, like any other police officer—but instead, he'd trap you with kindness.

That, Alex knew, was always more deadly.

It wasn't something he'd put on his résumé, but Jordan was especially gifted at cutting the rug to Wiggles songs. His personal favorite was "Hot Potato," but the one that really got Sam jazzed up was "Fruit Salad." While Selena was upstairs taking a hot bath, Jordan put on the DVD—she was opposed to bombarding Sam with media, and didn't want him to be able to spell D-O-R-O-T-H-Y, as in Dinosaur, before he could even write his own name. Selena always wanted Jordan to be doing something else with the baby, like memorizing Shakespeare or solving differential equations—but Jordan was a big believer in letting the television do its job in turning one's brain into porridge . . . at least long enough to get one good, silly tango session out of it.

Babies were always just the right weight, so that when you finally put them down, you felt like something was missing. "Fruit salad . . . yummy yummy!" Jordan crooned, whirling around until Sam opened his mouth and let a peal of giggles ribbon out.

The doorbell rang, and Jordan sashayed himself and his tiny partner through the entryway to answer it. Harmonizing—sort of—with Jeff, Murray, Greg, and Anthony in the background, Jordan opened the door. "Let's make some fruit salad today," he sang, and then he saw who was standing on his porch. "Judge Cormier!"

"Sorry to interrupt."

He already knew that she'd recused herself from the case—that happy announcement had been passed down this afternoon. "No, that's fine. Come on . . . in." Jordan glanced back at the trail of toys that he and Sam had left in their wake (he had to clean those up before Selena came back downstairs, too). Kicking as many as he could behind the couch, he led the judge into his living room and switched off the DVD.

"This must be your son."

"Yeah." Jordan looked down at the baby, who was in the process of deciding whether or not to throw a fit now that the music had been turned off. "Sam."

She reached out, letting Sam curl his hand around her forefinger. Sam could charm the pants off Hitler, probably, but seeing him only seemed to make Judge Cormier more agitated. "Why did you put my daughter on your witness list?"

Ah.

"Because," Jordan said, "Josie and Peter used to be friends, and I may need her as a character witness."

"They were friends ten years ago. Be honest. You did this to get me off the case."

Jordan hefted Sam higher on his hip. "Your Honor, with all due respect, I'm not going to allow anyone to try this case for me. Especially not a judge who isn't even involved in it anymore."

He watched something flare behind her eyes. "Of course not," she said tightly, and then she turned on her heel and walked out.

*   *   *

Ask a random kid today if she wants to be popular and she'll tell you no, even if the truth is that if she was in a desert dying of thirst and had the choice between a glass of water and instant popularity, she'd probably choose the latter.

As soon as she heard the knock, Josie took her notebook and shoved it between the mattress and the box spring, which had to be the world's lamest hiding spot.

Her mother stepped inside the bedroom, and for a second, Josie couldn't put her finger on what wasn't quite right. Then she figured it out: it wasn't dark out yet. Usually by the time her mother got home from court, it was dinnertime—but now it was only 3:45; Josie had barely gotten home from school.

"I have to talk to you," her mother said, sitting down beside her on the comforter. "I took myself off the case today."

Josie stared at her. In her whole life, she'd never known her mother to back down from any legal challenge; plus, hadn't they just had a conversation about the fact that she *wasn't* recusing herself?

She felt that sick sinking that came when the teacher called on her and she hadn't been paying attention. What had her mother found out that she hadn't known days ago?

"What happened?" Josie asked, and she hoped her mother wasn't paying attention enough to hear the way her voice was jumping all over the place.

"Well, that's the other thing I need to talk to you about," her mother said. "The defense put you on their witness list. They may ask you to go to court."

"*What?*" Josie cried, and for just one moment, everything stopped: her breath, her heart, her courage. "I can't go to court, Mom," she said. "Don't make me. Please . . ."

Her mother reached out for her, which was a good thing, because Josie was certain that at any second, she was going to simply vanish. *Sublimation,* she thought, *the act of going from solid to vapor.* And then she realized that this term was one she'd studied for the science test she'd never had because of everything else that had happened.

"I've been talking to the detective, and I know you don't remember anything. The only reason you're even on that list is because you used to be friends with Peter a long, long time ago."

Josie drew back. "Do you swear that I won't have to go to court?"

Her mother hesitated. "Honey, I can't—"

"You have to!"

"What if we go talk to the defense attorney?" her mother said.

"What good would that do?"

"Well, if he sees how upset this is making you, he might think twice about using you as a witness at all."

Josie lay down on her bed. For a few moments, her mother stroked her hair. Josie thought she heard her whisper *I'm sorry,* and then she got up and closed the door behind her.

"Matt," Josie whispered, as if he could hear her; as if he could answer.

Matt. She drew in his name like oxygen and imagined it breaking into a thousand tiny pieces, funneling into her red blood cells, beating through her heart.

Peter snapped a pencil in half and stuck the eraser end into his corn bread. "Happy birthday to me," he sang under his breath. He didn't finish the song; what was the point when you already knew where it was heading?

"Hey, Houghton," a correctional officer said, "we got a present for you."

Standing behind him was a kid not much older than Peter. He was rocking back and forth on the balls of his feet and he had snot running down his nose. The officer led him into the cell. "Make sure you share your cake," the officer said.

Peter sat down on the lower bunk, just to let this kid know exactly who was in charge. The boy stood with his arms crossed tight around the blanket he'd been given, staring down at the ground. He reached up and pushed his glasses up his nose, and that's when Peter realized there was something, well, *wrong* with him. He had that glassy-eyed, gum-lipped look of a special-needs kid.

Peter realized why they'd stuck the kid in his cell instead of anyone else's: they figured Peter would be least likely to fuck with him.

He felt his hands ball into fists. "Hey, you," Peter said.

The boy swiveled his head toward Peter. "I have a dog," he said. "Do you have a dog?"

Peter pictured the correctional officers watching this comedy through their little video hookups, expecting Peter to put up with this shit.

Expecting something of him, period.

He reached forward and plucked the glasses off the kid's nose. They were Coke-bottle-thick, with black plastic frames. The boy started to shriek, grabbing at his own face. His scream sounded like an air horn.

Peter put the glasses down on the floor and stomped on them, but in his rubber flip-flops that didn't do much damage. So he picked them up and smashed them into the bars of the cell until the glass shattered.

By then the officers had arrived to pull Peter away

from the kid, not that he was touching him anyway. They handcuffed him as the other inmates cheered him on. He was dragged down the hall to the superintendent's office.

He sat hunched in a chair, with a guard watching him breathe, until the superintendent came in. "What was that all about, Peter?"

"It's my birthday," Peter said. "I just wanted to be alone for it."

The funny thing, he realized, was that before the shooting, he'd believed that the best thing in the world was being left alone, so nobody could tell him he didn't fit in. But as it turned out—not that he was about to tell the superintendent this—he didn't much like himself, either.

The superintendent started to talk about disciplinary action; how this could affect him in the event of a conviction, what few privileges were left to be taken away. Peter deliberately tuned him out.

He thought instead of how angry the rest of the pod would be when this incident cost them television for a week.

He thought of Jordan's bullied victim syndrome and wondered if he believed it; if anyone would.

He thought of how nobody who saw him in jail—not his mother, not his lawyer—ever said what they should: that Peter would be imprisoned forever, that he'd die in a cell that looked just like this one.

He thought of how he would rather end his life with a bullet.

He thought of how at night, you could hear the wings of bats beating in the cement corners of the jail, and screams. No one was stupid enough to cry.

*　　　*　　　*

At 9:00 a.m. on Saturday, when Jordan opened the door, he was still wearing pajama bottoms. "You've got to be kidding," he said.

Judge Cormier pasted on a smile. "I'm really sorry we got off on the wrong foot," she said. "But you know how it is when it's your child who's in trouble . . . you just can't think straight." She stood arm in arm with the mini-me standing beside her. *Josie Cormier*, Jordan thought, scrutinizing the girl who was shaking like an aspen leaf. She had chestnut hair that hit her shoulders, and blue eyes that wouldn't meet his.

"Josie is really scared," the judge said. "I wondered if we could sit down for a minute . . . maybe you could put her at ease about being a witness. Hear whether or not what she knows will even help your case."

"Jordan? Who is it?"

He turned around to find Selena standing in the entryway, holding on to Sam. She was wearing *flannel* pajamas, which might or might not have been one step more formal.

"Judge Cormier was wondering if we could talk to Josie about her testimony," he said pointedly, trying desperately to telegraph to Selena that he was in deep trouble—since they all knew, with the exception perhaps of Josie, that the only reason he'd noticed up his intent to use her was to get Cormier off the case.

Jordan turned toward the judge again. "You see, I'm not really at that stage of planning yet."

"Surely you have some idea of what you're after if you call her as a witness . . . or you wouldn't have put her on the list," Alex pointed out.

"Why don't you ring my secretary, and make an appointment—"

"I was thinking of now," Judge Cormier said. "Please. I'm not here as a judge. Just as a mother."

Selena stepped forward. "You come right on in," she said, using her free arm to circle Josie's shoulders. "You must be Josie, right? This here's Sam."

Josie smiled shyly at the baby. "Hi, Sam."

"Baby, why don't you get the judge some coffee or juice?"

Jordan stared at his wife, wondering what the hell she was up to now. "Right. Why don't you come on in?"

Thankfully, the house looked nothing like it had the first time Cormier had showed up unannounced: there were no dishes in the sink; no papers cluttered the tables; toys were mysteriously missing. What could Jordan say— his wife was a neat freak. He pulled out one of the chairs at the kitchen table and offered it to Josie, then did the same for the judge. "How do you take your coffee?" he asked.

"Oh, we're fine," she said. She reached under the table for her daughter's hand.

"Sam and I, we're just going into the living room to play," Selena said.

"Why don't you stay?" He gave her a measured glance, one that begged her not to leave him alone to be eviscerated.

"You don't need us distracting you," Selena said, and she took the baby away.

Jordan sat down heavily across from the Cormiers. He was good at thinking on his feet; surely he could suffer through this. "Well," he said, "it really isn't anything to be scared of at all. I was just going to ask you some basic questions about your friendship with Peter."

"We're not friends," Josie said.

"Yes, I know that. But you used to be. I'm interested in the first time you met him."

Josie glanced at Alex. "Around nursery school, or maybe before."

"Okay. Did you play at your house? His?"

"Both."

"Did you have other friends who used to hang out with you?"

"Not really," Josie said.

Alex listened, but she couldn't help tuning a lawyer's ear to McAfee's questions. *He's got nothing,* she thought. *This is nothing.*

"When did you two stop hanging around?"

"Sixth grade," Josie answered. "We just kind of started liking different things."

"Did you have any contact with Peter after that?"

Josie shifted in her chair. "Only in the halls and stuff."

"You worked with him, too, right?"

Josie looked at her mother again. "Not for very long."

Both mother and daughter stared at him, anticipatory—which was awfully funny, because Jordan was making this all up as he went. "What about the relationship between Matt and Peter?"

"They didn't have one," Josie said, but her cheeks went pink.

"Did Matt do anything to Peter that might have been upsetting?"

"Maybe."

"Can you be more specific?"

She shook her head, her lips pressed tightly together.

"When was the last time you saw Matt and Peter together?"

"I don't remember," Josie whispered.

"Did they fight?"

Tears clouded her eyes. "I don't know." She turned to her

mother and then slowly sank her head down to the table, her face pressed into the curve of her own arm.

"Honey, why don't you go wait in the other room?" the judge said evenly.

They both watched Josie sit down on a chair in the living room, wiping her eyes, hunching forward to watch the baby playing on the floor.

"Look," Judge Cormier sighed. "I'm off the case. I know that's why you put her on the witness list, even if you'd never actually intended to call her. But I'm not questioning that right now. I'm talking to you parent to parent. If I give you an affidavit signed by Josie saying she doesn't remember anything, would you think twice about putting her on the stand?"

Jordan glanced into the living room. Selena had coaxed Josie onto the floor with her. She was pushing a toy plane toward Sam's feet. When he burst out with the sheer belly laugh that only a baby has, Josie smiled the tiniest bit, too. Selena caught his gaze, raised her brows in a question.

He'd gotten what he wanted: Cormier's recusal. He could be generous enough to do this for her.

"All right," he told the judge. "Get me the affidavit."

"When they say to scald the milk," Josie said, scrubbing another Brillo pad against the blackened bottom of the pot, "I don't think they mean like this."

Her mother picked up a dish towel. "Well, how was I supposed to know?"

"Maybe we should start with something easier than pudding," Josie suggested.

"Like?"

She smiled. "Toast?"

Now that her mother was home during the day, she was

restless. To that end, she'd taken up cooking—which was a good idea only if you happened to work for the fire department and needed job security. Even when her mother followed the recipe, it didn't turn out the way it was supposed to, and then inevitably Josie would press her for details and find out she'd used baking powder instead of baking soda, or whole wheat flour instead of cornmeal (We *didn't have any*, she complained).

At first, Josie had suggested nightly culinary classes out of self-preservation—she really didn't know what to say when her mother plunked a charred brick of meatloaf down with the same dramatic reverence that might have been given to the Holy Grail. As it turned out, though, it was sort of fun. When her mother wasn't acting like she knew it all (because she *so* totally didn't, when it came to cooking), she actually was pretty amusing to hang out with. It was cool, too, for Josie to feel as if she had control over a situation—any situation, even if it happened to be making chocolate pudding, or scrubbing its final remains from the bottom of a saucepan.

Tonight, they'd made pizza—which Josie had counted as a success, until her mother had tried to slide the pizza out of the oven and it had folded, halfway, on the coils inside, which meant they had to make grilled cheese as a default dinner. They had salad out of a bag—something her mother couldn't screw up, Josie figured, even if she worked hard at it. But now, thanks to the pudding disaster, there wasn't any dessert.

"How did you get to be Julia Child, anyway?" her mother asked.

"Julia Child's dead."

"Nigella Lawson, then."

Josie shrugged and turned off the water; stripped off the yellow plastic gloves. "I kind of got sick of soup," she said.

"Didn't I tell you not to turn on the oven when I wasn't home?"

"Yeah, but I didn't listen to you."

Once, when Josie was in fifth grade, the students had had to build a bridge out of popsicle sticks. The idea was to craft a design that could withstand the most pressure. She could remember riding in the car across the Connecticut River, and studying the arches and struts and supports of the real bridges, trying her best to copy them. At the end of the unit, two engineers from the Army Corps came in with a machine specially designed to put weight and torque on each bridge, to see to which child's was the strongest.

The parents were invited in for the testing. Josie's mother had been in court, the only mother not present that day. Or so she'd remembered until now, when Josie realized that her mother *had* been there, for the last ten minutes. She might have missed Josie's bridge test—during which the sticks splintered and groaned, and then burst apart in catastrophic failure—but she'd been there in time to help Josie pick up the pieces.

The pot was sparkling, silver. The milk carton was half full. "We could start over," Josie suggested.

When there was no answer, Josie turned around. "I'd like that," her mother answered quietly, but by that time, neither one of them was talking about cooking.

There was a knock at the door, and that connection between them—evanescent as a butterfly that lands on your hand—broke. "Are you expecting someone?" Josie's mother asked.

She wasn't, but she went to answer it anyway. When Josie opened the door, she found the detective who'd interviewed her standing there.

Didn't detectives show up at your door only when you were in serious trouble?

Breathe, Josie, she told herself, and she noticed he was holding a bottle of wine just as her mother came out to see what was going on.

"Oh," her mother said. "Patrick."

Patrick?

Josie turned and realized her mother was *blushing.*

He held out the bottle of wine. "Since this seems to be a bone of contention between us . . ."

"You know what?" Josie said, uncomfortable. "I'm just, um, going to go study." She'd leave it to her mother to figure out how she was going to do that, since she'd finished her homework before dinner.

She flew up the stairs, pounding extra hard with her feet so that she wouldn't hear what her mother was saying. In her room, she turned the music on her CD player up to its loudest level, threw herself onto her bed, and stared up at the ceiling.

Josie had a midnight curfew, not that she was using it at all now. But before, the bargain went like this: Matt would get Josie home by midnight; in return, Josie's mother would disappear like smoke the moment they entered the house, retreating upstairs so that she and Matt could fool around in the living room. She had no idea *what* her mother's rationale for this was—unless it was that it was safer for Josie to be doing this in her own living room than in a car or under the bleachers. She could remember how they'd come together in the dark, their bodies fusing and their silence measured. Realizing that at any moment her mom might come down for a drink of water or an aspirin only made it that much more exciting.

At three or four in the morning, when her eyes were blurry and her chin rubbed raw by beard stubble, Josie would kiss Matt good night at the front door. She'd watch his taillights disappear like the glow of a dying cigarette.

She'd tiptoe upstairs, past her mother's bedroom, thinking: *You don't know me at all.*

"If I won't let you buy me a drink," Alex said, "then what makes you think I'd take a bottle of wine from you?"

Patrick grinned. "I'm not giving it to you. I'm going to open it, and you might just choose to borrow some."

As he said this, he was walking into the house, as if he already knew the way. He stepped into the kitchen, sniffed twice—it still smelled of the ashes of pizza crust and incinerated milk—and began to randomly open and close drawers until he found a corkscrew.

Alex folded her arms, not because she was cold, but because she could not remember feeling this light inside, as if her body housed a second solar system. She watched Patrick remove two wineglasses from a cabinet and pour.

"To being a civilian," he said, toasting.

The wine was rich and full; like velvet; like autumn. Alex closed her eyes. She would have liked to hold on to this moment, drag it wider and fuller, until it covered up so many others that had come before.

"So, how is it?" Patrick asked. "Being unemployed?"

She thought for a moment. "I made a grilled cheese sandwich today without burning the pan."

"I hope you framed it."

"Nah, I left that to the prosecution." She smiled at her own little inside joke, and then felt it dissolve on the tails of her thoughts as she imagined Diana Leven's face. "Do you ever feel guilty?" Alex asked.

"Why?"

"Because for a half a second, you've almost forgotten everything that happened."

Patrick put down his wineglass. "Sometimes, when I'm going through the evidence and I see a fingerprint or a photo or a shoe that belonged to one of the kids who died, I take a little more time to look at it. It's crazy, but it seems like someone ought to, so that they're remembered an extra minute or two." He looked up at her. "When someone dies, their lives aren't the ones that stop at that moment, you know?"

Alex lifted her glass of wine and drained it. "Tell me how you found her."

"Who?"

"Josie. That day."

Patrick met her gaze, and Alex knew he was weighing her right to know what her daughter had experienced against his wish to save her from a truth that would cut her to the quick. "She was in the locker room," he began quietly. "And I thought . . . I thought she was dead, too, because she was covered in blood, facedown next to Matt Royston. But then she moved and—" His voice broke. "It was the most beautiful thing I'd ever seen."

"You know you're a hero, don't you?"

Patrick shook his head. "I'm a coward. The only reason I ran into that building was because if I didn't, I'd have nightmares for the rest of my life."

Alex shivered. "I have nightmares, and I wasn't even there."

He took away her wineglass and studied her palm, as if he were going to read her the line of her life. "Maybe you should try not sleeping," Patrick said.

His skin smelled of evergreen and spearmint, this close. Alex could feel her heart pounding through the tips of her fingers. She imagined he could feel it, too.

She didn't know what was going to happen next—what was supposed to happen next—but it would be random, unpredictable, uncomfortable. She was getting ready to push away from him when Patrick's hands anchored her in place. "Stop being such a judge, Alex," he whispered, and he kissed her.

When feeling came back, in a storm of color and force and sensation, the most you could do was hold on to the person beside you and hope you could weather it. Alex closed her eyes and expected the worst—but it wasn't a bad thing; it was just a different thing. A messier one, a more complicated one. She hesitated, and then she kissed Patrick back, willing to concede that you might have to lose control before you could find what you'd been missing.

The Month Before

When you love someone, there's a pattern to the way you come together. You might not even realize it, but your bodies are choreographed: a touch on the hip, a stroke of the hair. A staccato kiss, break away, a longer one, his hand slipping under your shirt. It's a routine, but not in the boring sense of the word. It's just the way you've learned to fit, and it's why, when you've been with one guy for a long time, your teeth do not scrape together when you kiss; you do not bump noses or elbows.

Matt and Josie had a pattern. When they started making out, he'd lean in and look at her as if he couldn't possibly see any other part of the world. It was hypnotism, she realized, because after a while she sort of felt that way, too. Then he'd kiss her, so slowly that there was hardly pressure on her mouth, until she was the one pushing against him for more. He worked his way down her body, from mouth to neck, from neck to breasts, and then his fingers would do a search-and-rescue mission below the waistband of her jeans. The whole thing lasted about ten minutes, and then Matt would roll off her and take the condom out of his wallet so they could have sex.

Not that Josie minded any of it. If she was going to be honest, she liked the pattern. It felt like a roller coaster—going up that hill, *knowing* what was coming next on track and knowing, too, that she couldn't do anything to stop it.

They were in her living room, in the dark, with the television on for background noise. Matt had already peeled off her clothes, and now he was leaning over her like a tidal wave, pulling down his boxers. He sprang free and settled between Josie's legs.

"Hey," she said, as he tried to push into her. "Aren't you forgetting something?"

"Aw, Jo. Just once, I don't want there to be anything between us."

His words could melt her just as surely as his kiss or his touch; she already knew that by now. She hated that rubbery smell that permeated the air the moment he ripped open the Trojan packet and stayed on his hands until they were finished. And God, did anything feel better than having Matt inside her? Josie shifted just a little, felt her body adjust to him, and her legs trembled.

When Josie had gotten her period at thirteen, her mother had not given her the typical heart-to-heart mother/daughter chat. Instead, she handed Josie a book on probability and statistics. "Every time you have sex, you can get pregnant or you can not get pregnant," her mother said. "That's fifty-fifty. So don't fool yourself into thinking that if you only do it once without protection, the odds are in your favor."

Josie pushed at Matt. "I don't think we should do this," she whispered.

"Have sex?"

"Have sex without . . . you know. Anything."

He was disappointed, Josie could tell by the way his face froze for just a moment. But he pulled out and fished for his wallet, found a condom. Josie took it out of his hand, tore open the package, helped him put it on. "One day," she began, and then he kissed her, and Josie forgot what she was going to say.

Lacy had started spreading corn on the lawn back in November to help the deer through the winter. There were plenty of locals who frowned upon artificially giving the deer a helping hand during the winter—mostly the same people whose gardens were wrecked by those surviving deer in the summer—but for Lacy, there was karma involved. As long as Lewis insisted on hunting, she was going to do what little she could to cancel out his actions.

She put on her heavy boots—there was still enough snow on the ground to merit it, although it had gotten warm enough for the sap to start flowing, which meant that at least in theory, spring was coming. As soon as Lacy walked outside, she could smell the maple syrup refining in the neighbor's sugar house, like candy crystals in the air. She carried the bucket of feed corn to the swing set in the backyard—a wooden structure that the boys had played on when they were small, and that Lewis had never quite gotten around to dismantling.

"Hey, Mom."

Lacy turned to find Peter standing nearby, his hands dug deep into the pockets of his jeans. He was wearing a T-shirt and a down vest, and she imagined he had to be freezing. "Hi, sweetie," she said. "What's going on?"

She could probably count on one hand the number of times Peter had come out of his room lately, much less outside. It was part of puberty, she knew, for adolescents to hole up in burrows and do whatever it was they did behind closed doors. In Peter's case, it involved the computer. He was online constantly—not for web surfing as much as programming, and how could she fault that kind of passion?

"Nothing. What are you doing?"

"Same thing I've done all winter."

"Really?"

She looked up at him. Against the beauty of the brisk outdoors, Peter seemed wildly out of place. His features were too delicate to match the craggy line of mountains in the backdrop behind him; his skin seemed nearly as white as the snow. He didn't fit, and Lacy realized that most of the time when she saw Peter somewhere, she could make the same observation.

"Here," Lacy said, handing him the bucket. "Help."

Peter took the bucket and began to toss handfuls of corn on the ground. "Can I ask you something?"

"Sure."

"Is it true that you were the one who asked out Dad?"

Lacy grinned. "Well, if I hadn't, I would have probably had to wait around forever. Your father is many things, but perceptive isn't one of them."

She had met Lewis at a pro-choice rally. Although Lacy would be the first to tell you that there was no greater gift than having a baby, she was a realist—she'd sent home enough mothers who were too young or too poor or too overburdened to know that the odds of that child having a good life were slim. She had gone with a friend to a march at the statehouse in Concord and stood on the steps with a sisterhood of women who held up signs: I'M PRO-CHOICE AND I VOTE . . . AGAINST ABORTION? DON'T HAVE ONE. She had looked around the crowd that day and realized that there was one lone man—well-dressed in a suit and tie, right in the thick of the protesters. Lacy had been fascinated by him—as a protester, he was completely cast against type. *Wow,* Lacy had said, working her way toward him. *What a day.*

Tell me about it.

Have you ever been here before? Lacy had asked.

My first time, Lewis said.

Mine, too.

They had gotten separated as a new influx of marchers came up the stone steps. A paper had blown off the stack that Lewis was carrying, but by the time Lacy could grab it, he'd been swallowed by the crowd. It was the cover page to something bigger; she knew by the staple holes at the top, and it had a title that nearly put her to sleep: "The allocation of public education resources in New Hampshire: a critical analysis." But there was also an author's name: Lewis Houghton, Sterling College Dept. of Economics.

When she called to tell Lewis that she had his paper, he said that he didn't need it. He could print out another copy. *Yes,* Lacy had said, *but I have to bring this one back to you.*

Why?

So you can explain it to me over dinner.

It wasn't until they'd gone out for sushi that Lacy learned the reason Lewis had been at the statehouse had nothing to do with attending a pro-choice rally, but only because he had a scheduled appointment with the governor.

"But how did you tell him?" Peter asked. "That you liked him, you know, like *that?*"

"As I recall, I grabbed him after our third date and kissed him. Then again, that may have been to shut him up because he was going on and on about free trade." She glanced back over her shoulder, and suddenly the questions all made sense. "Peter," she said, a smile breaking over her. "Is there someone you like?"

Peter didn't even have to answer—his face turned crimson.

"Do I get to know her name?"

"No," Peter said emphatically.

"Well, it doesn't matter." She looped her arm through Peter's. "Gosh, I envy you. There's nothing that compares to those first few months when all you can think of is each other. I mean, love in any form is pretty fabulous . . . but falling in love . . . well."

"It's not like that," Peter said. "I mean, it's kind of one-sided."

"I bet she's just as nervous as you are."

He grimaced. "Mom. She barely even registers my existence. I'm not . . . I don't hang out with the kind of people she hangs out with."

Lacy looked at her son. "Well," she said. "Then your first order of business is to change that."

"How?"

"Find ways to connect with her. Maybe in places where you know her friends won't be around. And try to show her the side of you that she doesn't normally see."

"Like what?"

"The inside." Lacy tapped Peter's chest. "If you tell her how you feel, I think you might be surprised at the reaction."

Peter ducked his head and kicked at a hummock of snow. Then he glanced up at her shyly. "Really?"

Lacy nodded. "It worked for *me*."

"Okay," Peter said. "Thanks."

She watched him trudge back up the hill to the house, and then she turned her attention back to the deer. Lacy would have to feed them until the snow melted. Once you started taking care of them, you had to follow through, or they just wouldn't make it.

They were on the floor of the living room and they were nearly naked. Josie could taste beer on Matt's breath, but she must have tasted like that, too. They'd both drunk a few at Drew's—not enough to get wasted, just buzzed, enough so that Matt's hands seemed to be all over her at once, so that his skin set fire to hers.

She'd been floating along pleasantly in a haze of the familiar. Yes, Matt had kissed her—one short one, then a longer, hungry kiss, as his hand worked open the clasp on her bra. She lay lazy, spread beneath him like a feast, as he pulled off her jeans. But then, instead of doing what usually came next, Matt reared over her again. He kissed her so hard that it hurt. "Mmmph," she said, pushing at him.

"Relax," Matt murmured, and then he sank his teeth into her shoulder. He pinned her hands over her head and ground his hips against hers. She could feel his erection, hot against her stomach.

It wasn't the way it normally was, but Josie had to admit that it was exciting. She couldn't remember ever feeling so heavy, as if her heart were beating between her legs. She clawed at Matt's back to bring him closer.

"Yeah," he groaned, and he pushed her thighs apart. And then suddenly Matt was inside her, pumping so hard that she scooted backward on the carpet, burning the backs of her legs.

"Wait," Josie said, trying to roll away beneath him, but he clamped his hand over her mouth and drove harder and harder until Josie felt him come.

Semen, sticky and hot, pooled on the carpet beneath her. Matt framed her face with his hands. "Jesus, Josie," he whispered, and she realized that he was in tears. "I love you so goddamn much."

Josie turned her face away. "I love you, too."

She lay in his arms for ten minutes and then said she was tired and needed to go to sleep. After she kissed Matt good-bye at the front door, she went into the kitchen and took the rug cleaner out from underneath the sink. She scrubbed it into the wet spot on the carpet, prayed it would not leave a stain.

*   *   *

```
# include <stdio.h>
main ( )
{
    int time;
    for (time=0; time<infinity (1) ; time ++)
    { printf ("I love you|n"); }
}
```

Peter highlighted the text on his computer screen and deleted it. Although he thought it would be pretty cool to open an email and automatically have an I LOVE YOU message written over and over on the screen, he could see where someone else—someone who didn't give a crap about C++—would think it was just downright strange.

He'd decided on an email because that way if she blew him off, he could suffer the embarrassment in private. The problem was, his mother had said to show what was inside him and he wasn't very good when it came to words.

He thought about how sometimes, when he saw her, it was just a part of her: her arm resting on the passenger window of the car, her hair blowing out its window. He thought about how many times he'd fantasized about being the one at the wheel.

My journey was pointless, he wrote. *Until I took a YOU-turn.*

Groaning, Peter deleted that, too. It made him sound like a Hallmark card writer, or even worse, one that Hallmark wouldn't even hire.

He thought about what he wished he could say to her, if he had the guts, and poised his hands over the keyboard.

I know you don't think of me.

And you certainly would never picture us together.

But probably peanut butter was just peanut butter for a long time, before someone ever thought of pairing it up with jelly. And there was salt, but it started to taste better when there was pepper. And what's the point of butter without bread?

(Why are all these examples FOODS!?!?!??)

Anyway, by myself, I'm nothing special. But with you, I think I could be.

He agonized about the ending.

Your friend, Peter Houghton

Well, technically that wasn't true.

Sincerely, Peter Houghton

That *was* true, but it was still sort of lame. Of course, there was the obvious:

Love, Peter Houghton

He typed it in, read it over once. And then, before he could stop himself, he pushed the Enter button and sent his heart across the Ethernet to Josie Cormier.

Courtney Ignatio was so freaking bored.

Josie was her friend and all, but there was, like, *nothing* to do. They'd already watched three Paul Walker movies on DVD, checked the *Lost* website for the bio on the hot guy who played Sawyer, and read all the *Cosmos* that hadn't been recycled, but there was no HBO, nothing chocolate in the fridge, and no party at Sterling College to sneak into. This was Courtney's second night at the Cormier household, thanks to her brainiac older brother, who had dragged her parents on a whirlwind tour of Ivy League colleges on the East Coast. Courtney plopped a stuffed hippo on her stomach and frowned into its button eyes. She'd already tried to get details out of Josie last night about Matt—important things, like how big a dick he had and if he had a clue how to use it—but Josie had gone all Hilary Duff on her and acted like she'd never heard the word *sex* before.

Josie was in the bathroom taking a shower; Courtney could still hear the water running. She rolled to her side and scrutinized a framed photograph of Josie and Matt. It would have been easy to hate Josie, because Matt was the über-boyfriend—always glancing around at a party to make sure he hadn't gotten too far away from Josie; calling her up to say good night, even when he'd just dropped her off a half hour before (yes, Courtney had been privy to a display of that very thing just last night). Unlike most of the guys on the hockey team—several of whom Courtney had dated—Matt honestly seemed to prefer Josie's company to anyone else's. But there was something about Josie that kept Courtney from being jealous. It was the way her expression slipped every now and then, like a colored contact lens, so you could see what was actually underneath. Josie might have been one-half of Sterling High School's Most Faithful Couple, but it almost seemed like the biggest reason she clung to that label was because that was the only reason she knew who she was.

You've got mail.

The automaton on Josie's computer spoke; until then, Courtney hadn't realized that they'd left the computer running, much less online. She settled down at the desk, wiggling the mouse so that the screen came back into focus. Maybe Matt was writing some kind of cyberporn. It would be fun to screw around with him a little and pretend that she was Josie.

The return address, though, wasn't one that Courtney recognized—she and Josie, after all, had nearly identical Buddy Lists. There was no subject. Courtney clicked on the link, assuming it was some kind of junk mail: enlarge your penis in thirty days; refinance your home; real deals on printer ribbon cartridges.

The email opened, and Courtney started to read.

"Oh my God," she murmured. "This is too fucking good."

She swiped the body of the email and forwarded it to *RTWING90@yahoo.com.*

Drew, she typed. *Spam this out to the whole wide world.*

The door to the bathroom opened, and Josie came back into the bedroom wearing a bathrobe, a towel wrapped around her head. Courtney closed the server window. "Good-bye," the automaton said.

"What's up?" Josie asked.

Courtney turned around in the chair, smiling. "Just checking my mail," she said.

Josie couldn't sleep; her mind was tumbling like a spring stream. This was exactly the sort of problem she wished she could talk about with someone—but who? Her mother? Yeah, *right.* Matt was out of the question. And Courtney—or any other girlfriend she had—well, she was afraid that if she spoke her worst fears out loud, maybe that would be enough for them to come true.

Josie waited until she heard Courtney's even breathing. She crept out of bed and into the bathroom. She closed the door and pulled down her pajama pants.

Nothing.

Her period was three days late.

On Tuesday afternoon, Josie sat on a couch in Matt's basement, writing a social studies essay for him about the historical abuse of power in America while he and Drew lifted free weights.

"There are a million things you could talk about," Josie said. "Watergate. Abu Ghraib. Kent State."

Matt strained beneath the weight of a barbell as Drew spotted him. "Whatever's easiest, Jo," he said.

"Come on, you pussy," Drew said. "At this rate they're going to demote you to JV."

Matt grinned and fully extended his arms. "Let's see *you* bench this," he grunted. Josie watched the play of his muscles, imagined them strong enough to do that and also tender enough to hold her. He sat up, wiping his forehead and the back of the weight bench, so that Drew could take his turn.

"I could do something on the Patriot Act," Josie suggested, biting down on the end of the pencil.

"I'm just looking out for your own best interests, dude," Drew said. "I mean, if you're not going to bulk up for Coach, do it for Josie."

She glanced up. "Drew, were you born an idiot, or did that evolve?"

"I *intelligently designed*," he joked. "All I'm saying is that Matt better watch out, now that he's got some competition."

"What are you *talking* about?" Josie looked at him as if he were crazy, but secretly, she was panicking. It didn't really matter whether or not Josie had shown attention to someone else; it only mattered whether Matt *thought* so.

"It was a *joke*, Josie," Drew said, lying down on the bench and curling his fists around the metal bar.

Matt laughed. "Yeah, that's a good description of Peter Houghton."

"Are you going to fuck with him?"

"Hopefully," Matt said. "I just haven't decided how yet."

"Maybe you need some poetic inspiration to come up with a suitable plan," Drew said. "Hey, Jo, grab my binder. The email's right in the pocket in the front."

Josie reached across the couch for Drew's backpack and rummaged through his books. She pulled out a folded piece of paper and opened it to find her own email address right at the top, the whole student body of Sterling High as the destination address.

Where had this come from? And why hadn't she ever *seen* it?

"Read it," Drew said, lifting the weights.

Josie hesitated. "'I know you don't think of me. And you certainly would never picture us together.'"

The words felt like stones in her throat. She stopped speaking, but that didn't matter, because Drew and Matt were reciting the email word for word.

"'By myself, I'm nothing special,'" Matt said.

"'But with you . . . I think . . . '" Drew convulsed, laughing, the weights falling hard back into their cradle. "Fuck, I can't do this when I'm cracking up."

Matt sank down on the couch beside Josie and slipped his arm around her, his thumb grazing her breast. She shifted, because she didn't want Drew to see, but Matt did, and shifted with her. "You inspire poetry," he said, smiling. "Bad poetry, but even Helen of Troy probably started with, like, a limerick, right?"

Josie's face reddened. She could not believe that Peter had written these things to her, that he'd *ever* think she might be receptive to them. She couldn't believe that the whole school knew that Peter Houghton liked her. She couldn't afford for them to think that she felt anything for him.

Even sorry.

More devastating was the fact someone had decided to make her the fool. It was not a surprise that someone had gotten into her email account—they all knew each other's passwords; it could have been any of the girls, or even Matt himself. But what would make her friends do something like this, something so totally humiliating?

Josie already knew the answer. This group of kids—they weren't her friends. Popular kids didn't really *have* friends; they had alliances. You were safe only as long as you hid your trust—at any moment someone might make you the laughingstock, because then they knew no one was laughing at *them*.

Josie was smarting, but she also knew part of the prank was a test to see how she reacted. If she turned around and accused her friends of hacking into her email and invading her privacy, she was doomed. Above all else, she wasn't supposed to show emotion. She was so socially above Peter Houghton that an email like this wasn't mortifying, but hilarious.

In other words: Laugh, don't cry.

"What a total loser," Josie said, as if it didn't bother her at all; as if she found this just as funny as Drew and Matt did. She balled up the email and tossed it behind the couch. Her hands were shaking.

Matt lay his head down in her lap, still sweaty. "What did I officially decide to write about?"

"Native Americans," Josie replied absently. "How the government broke treaties and took away their land."

It was, she realized, something she could sympathize with: that rootlessness, the understanding that you were never going to feel at home.

Drew sat up, straddling the weight bench. "Hey, how do I get myself a girl who can boost my GPA?"

"Ask Peter Houghton," Matt answered, grinning. "He's the lovemeister."

As Drew snickered, Matt reached for Josie's hand, the one holding the pencil. He kissed the knuckles. "You're too good to me," he said.

The lockers in Sterling High were staggered, one row on top and one row on the bottom, which meant that if you happened to be a lower locker you had to suffer getting your books and coat and stuff while someone else was practically standing on your head. Peter's locker was not only on the bottom row, it was also in a corner—which meant that he could never quite make himself small enough to get what he needed.

Peter had five minutes to get from class to class, but he was the first one into the halls when the bell rang. It was a carefully calculated plan: if he left as soon as possible, he'd be in the hallways during the biggest crush of traffic, and therefore was less likely to be singled out by one of the cool kids. He walked with his head ducked, his eyes on the floor, until he reached his locker.

He was kneeling in front of it, trading his math book for his social studies text, when a pair of black wedge heels stopped beside him. He glanced up the patterned stockings to the tweed miniskirt and asymmetrical sweater and long waterfall of blond hair. Courtney Ignatio was standing with her arms crossed, as if Peter had already taken up too much of her time, when he wasn't even the one who'd stopped *her* in the first place.

"Get up," she said. "I'm not going to be late for class."

Peter stood and closed his locker. He didn't want Courtney to see that inside, he had taped a picture of himself and Josie from when they were little. He'd had to climb up into the attic where his mother kept her old photo albums, since she'd gone digital two years ago, and now all they had were CDs. In the photo, he and Josie were sitting on the edge of a sandbox at nursery school. Josie's hand was on Peter's shoulder. That was the part he liked the best.

"Look, the last thing I want to do is stand here and be

seen talking to you, but Josie's my friend, which is why I volunteered to do this in the first place." Courtney looked down the hall, to make sure no one was coming. "She likes you."

Peter just stared at her.

"I mean she *likes* you, you retard. She's totally over Matt; she just doesn't want to ditch him until she knows for sure that you're serious about her." Courtney glanced at Peter. "I told her it's social suicide, but I guess that's what people do for love."

Peter felt all the blood rush to his head, an ocean in his ears. "Why should I believe you?"

Courtney tossed her hair. "I don't give a damn if you do or you don't. I'm just telling you what she said. What you do with it is up to you."

She walked down the hallway and disappeared around a corner just as the bell rang. Peter was going to be late now; he hated being late, because then you could feel everyone's eyes on you when you walked into class, like a thousand crows pecking at your skin.

But that hardly mattered, not in the grand scheme of things.

The best item the cafeteria served was Tater Tots, soaked in grease. You could practically feel the waist of your jeans getting snugger and your face breaking out—and yet, when the cafeteria lady held out her massive spoonful, Josie couldn't resist. She sometimes wondered: If they were as nutritious as broccoli, would she want them so much? Would they taste this good if they weren't so bad for you?

Most of Josie's friends only drank diet soda for their meals; getting anything substantial and carbohydrate-based practically labeled you as either a whale or a bulimic. Usually, Josie limited herself to three Tater Tots, and then gave the rest to the guys to devour. But today, she'd practically been salivating for the past two classes just *thinking* about Tater Tots, and she couldn't stop taking just one more. If it wasn't pickles and ice cream, did it still qualify as a *craving*?

Courtney leaned across the table and swept her finger through the grease that lined the Tater Tot tray. "Gross," she said. "How come gas is so expensive, when there's enough oil on these babies to fill Drew's pickup truck?"

"Different kind of oil, Einstein," Drew said. "Did you really think you were pumping out Crisco at the Mobil station?"

Josie bent down to unzip her backpack. She had packed herself an apple; it had to be in here somewhere. She rummaged through loose papers and makeup, so focused on her search that she didn't realize the banter between Drew and Courtney—or anyone else, for that matter—had fallen silent.

Peter Houghton was standing next to their table, holding a brown bag in one hand and an open milk carton in the other. "Hi, Josie," he said, as if she might be listening, as if she weren't dying a thousand kinds of death in that one second. "I thought you might like to join me for lunch."

The word *mortified* sounded like you'd gone to granite, like you couldn't move to save your soul. Josie imagined how years from now, students would point to the frozen gargoyle that used to be her, still rooted to the plastic cafeteria chair, and say, *Oh, right, I heard about what happened to her.*

Josie heard a rustling behind her, but she couldn't have moved at that moment if her life depended on it. She looked up at Peter, wishing there were some kind of secret language where what you said was not what you meant, and the listener would automatically know you were speaking that tongue. "Um," Josie began. "I . . ."

"She'd love to," Courtney said. "When hell freezes over."

The entire table dissolved into a fizz of laughter, an inside joke that Peter didn't understand. "What's in the bag?" Drew asked. "Peanut butter and jelly?"

"Salt and pepper?" Courtney chimed in.

"Bread and butter?"

The smile on Peter's face wilted as he realized how deep a pit he'd fallen into, and how many people had dug it. He glanced from Drew to Courtney to Emma and then back at Josie—and when he did, she had to look away, so that nobody—including Peter—would see how much it hurt her to hurt him; to realize that—in spite of what Peter had believed about her—she was no different from anyone else.

"I think Josie should at least get to sample the merchandise," Matt said, and when he spoke she realized that he was no longer sitting beside her. He was standing, in fact, behind Peter; and in one smooth stroke he hooked his thumbs into the loops of Peter's pants and yanked them down to his ankles.

Peter's skin was moon-white under the harsh fluorescent lamps of the cafeteria, his penis a tiny spiral shell on a sparse nest of pubic hair. He immediately covered his genitals with his lunch bag, and as he did, he dropped his milk carton. It spilled on the floor between his feet.

"Hey, look at that," Drew said. "Premature ejaculation."

The entire cafeteria began to spin like a carousel—bright lights and harlequin colors. Josie could hear laughter, and she tried to match her own to it. Mr. Isles, a Spanish teacher who had no neck, hurried over to Peter as he was pulling up his pants. He grabbed Matt with one arm and Peter with the other. "Are you two done," he barked, "or do we need to go see the principal?"

Peter fled, but by that time, everyone in the cafeteria was reliving the glorious moment of his pantsing. Drew high-fived Matt. "Dude, that was the best fucking lunch entertainment I've ever seen."

Josie reached into her backpack, pretending to search for that apple, but she wasn't hungry anymore. She just didn't want to see them all right now; to let them see her.

Peter Houghton's lunch bag was beside her foot, where he'd dropped it when he ran away. She glanced inside. A sandwich, maybe turkey. A bag of pretzels. Carrots, which had been peeled and cut into even strips by someone who cared about him.

Josie slipped the brown bag into her knapsack, telling herself that she'd find Peter and give it back to him, or leave it near his locker, when she knew she would do neither. Instead, she would carry it around until it started to reek, until she had to throw it out and could pretend it was that easy to get rid of.

Peter burst out of the cafeteria and careened down the narrow hallways like a pinball until he finally reached his locker. He fell to his knees and rested his head against the cold metal. How could he have been so stupid, trusting Courtney, thinking Josie might give a rat's ass about him, thinking he was someone she could fall for?

He banged his head until it hurt, then blindly dialed the numbers on his locker. It swung open, and he reached inside for the photo of himself and Josie. He crushed it into his palm and walked down the hall again.

On the way, he was stopped by a teacher. Mr. McCabe was frowning at him, putting a hand on his shoulder, when surely he could see that Peter couldn't bear to be touched, that it felt like a hundred needles were going through his skin. "Peter," Mr. McCabe said, "are you all right?"

"Bathroom," Peter ground out, and he pushed away, hurrying down the hallway.

He locked himself inside a stall and threw the picture of himself and Josie into the toilet bowl. Then he unzipped his fly and urinated on top of it. "Fuck you," he whispered, and then he said it loud enough to rattle the walls of the stall. "Fuck you *all*."

The minute Josie's mother left the room, Josie plucked the thermometer out of her mouth and held it up against the lightbulb of her nightstand lamp. She squinted to read the tiny numbers, and then stuck it back into her mouth as she heard her mother's footsteps. "Hunh," her mother said, holding the thermometer up to the window to better read it. "I guess you *are* sick."

Josie gave what she hoped was a convincing moan and rolled over.

"You sure you're going to be all right here, alone?"

"Yeah."

"You can call me if you need me. I can recess court and come back home."

"Okay."

She sat down on the bed and kissed her forehead. "You want juice? Soup?"

Josie shook her head. "I think I just need to go back to sleep." She closed her eyes so that her mother would get the message.

She waited until she heard the car drive away, and even then she stayed in bed for an extra ten minutes to make sure she was alone. Then Josie got out of bed and booted up her computer. She Googled *abortifacient*—the word she'd looked up yesterday, the one that meant *something that terminates a pregnancy.*

Josie had been thinking about this. It wasn't that she didn't want a baby; it wasn't even that she didn't want Matt's baby. All she knew for certain was that she didn't want to have to make that decision yet.

If she told her mother, her mom would curse and scream and then find a way to take her to Planned Parenthood or the doctor's office. To be honest, it wasn't even the cursing and screaming that worried Josie. It was realizing that—had her own mother done this, seventeen years ago—Josie wouldn't even be alive to be having this problem.

Josie had toyed with contacting her father again, which would have taken an enormous helping of humility. He hadn't wanted Josie born, so theoretically, he'd probably go out of his way to help her have an abortion.

But.

There was something about going to a doctor, or a clinic, or even to a parent, that she couldn't quite swallow. It seemed so . . . deliberate.

So before she reached that point, Josie had chosen to do a bit of research. She couldn't risk being caught on a computer at school looking these things up, so she'd decided to play hooky. She sank into the desk chair, one leg folded beneath her, and marveled as she received nearly 99,000 hits.

Some she already knew: the old wives' tales about sticking a knitting needle up inside her, or drinking laxatives or castor oil. Some she'd never imagined: douching with potassium, swallowing gingerroot, eating unripe pineapple. And then there were the herbs: oil infusions of calamus, mugwort, sage, and wintergreen; cocktails made out of black cohosh and pennyroyal. Josie wondered where you even got these things—it wasn't like they were in the aisle next to the aspirin at CVS.

Herbal remedies, the website said, worked 40–45 percent of the time. Which, she supposed, was at least a start.

She leaned closer, reading.

Don't start herbal treatment after the sixth week of pregnancy.

Keep in mind these are not reliable ways to end pregnancy.

Drink the teas day and night, so you don't ruin the progress you made during the day.

Catch the blood and add water to dilute it, and look at the clots and tissue to make sure the placenta has passed.

Josie grimaced.

Use ½ to 1 teaspoon of the dried herb per cup of water, 3–4 times a day. Don't confuse tansy with tansy ragwort, which has been fatal to cows that have eaten it growing nearby.

Then she found something that looked less, well, medieval: vitamin C. Surely that couldn't be too bad for her? Josie clicked on the link. *Ascorbic acid, eight grams, for five days. Menstruation should begin on the sixth or seventh day.*

Josie got up from her computer and went into her mother's medicine cabinet. There was a big white bottle of vitamin C, along with smaller ones of acidophilus, vitamin B12, and calcium supplements.

She opened the bottle and hesitated. The other warning that the websites all gave was to make sure you had reason to subject your body to these herbs before you started.

Josie padded back into her room and opened her backpack. Inside, still in its plastic bag from the pharmacy, was the pregnancy test she'd bought yesterday before she came home from school.

She read the directions twice. How could anyone pee on a stick for that long? With a frown, she sat down and went to the bathroom, holding the small wand between her legs. Then she set it into its little holder and washed her hands.

Josie sat on the lip of the bathtub and watched the control line turn blue. And then, slowly, she watched the second, perpendicular line appear: a plus sign, a positive, a cross to bear.

When the snow blower ran out of gas in the middle of the driveway, Peter went to the spare can they kept in the garage, only to discover it was empty. He tipped it over, watched a single drop strike the ground between his sneakers.

He usually had to be asked, like, six times to go out and clear the paths that led to the front and back doors, but today he'd turned to the chore without any badgering from his parents. He wanted—no, scratch that—he *needed* to get out there so that his feet could move at the same pace as his mind. But when he squinted against the lowering sun, he could still see a scroll of images on the backs of his eyelids: the cold air striking his ass as Matt Royston pulled his pants down, the milk splattering on his sneakers, Josie's gaze sliding away.

Peter trudged down the driveway toward the home of his neighbor across the street. Mr. Weatherhall was a retired cop, and his house looked it. There was a big flagpole in the middle of the front yard; in the summertime the grass was trimmed like a crew cut; there were never any leaves on the lawn in the fall. Peter used to wonder if Weatherhall came out in the middle of the night to rake them.

As far as Peter knew, Mr. Weatherhall now passed his time watching the Game Show Network and doing his militaristic gardening in sandals with black socks. Because he didn't let his grass grow longer than a half inch, he usually had a spare gallon of gas lying around; Peter had borrowed it on his dad's behalf other times for the lawn mower or the snow blower.

Peter rang the doorbell—which played "Hail to the Chief"—and Mr. Weatherhall answered. "Son," he said, although he knew Peter's name and had for years. "How are you doing?"

"Fine, Mr. Weatherhall. But I was wondering if you had any gas I could borrow for the snow blower. Well, gas I could *use*. I mean, I can't really give it back."

"Come on in, come on in." He held the door open for Peter, who walked into the house. It smelled of cigars and cat food. A bowl of Fritos was set next to his La-Z-Boy; on the television, Vanna White flipped a vowel. "Great Expectations," Mr. Weatherhall shouted at the contestants as he passed. "What are you, morons?"

He led Peter into the kitchen. "You wait here. The basement's not fit for company." Which, Peter realized, probably meant there was a dust mote on a shelf.

He leaned against the counter, his hands splayed on the Formica. Peter liked Mr. Weatherhall, because even when he was trying to be gruff, you could tell that he just really missed being a policeman and had no one else to practice on. When Peter was younger, Joey and his friends had always tried to screw around with Weatherhall, by piling snow at the end of his plowed driveway or letting their dogs take a dump on the manicured lawn. He could remember when Joey was around eleven and had egged Weatherhall's house on Halloween. He and his friends had been caught in the act. Weatherhall dragged them into the house for a "scared straight" chat. *The guy's a fruitcake*, Joey had told him. *He keeps a gun in his flour canister.*

Peter cocked an ear toward the stairwell that led down to

the basement. He could still hear Mr. Weatherhall puttering around down there, getting the gas can.

He sidled closer to the sink, where there were four stainless steel canisters. SODA, read the tiny one, and then in increasing size: BROWN SUGAR. SUGAR. FLOUR. Peter gingerly opened up the flour canister.

A puff of white powder flew into his face.

He coughed and shook his head. It figured; Joey had been lying.

Idly, Peter opened up the sugar canister beside it and found himself staring down at a 9-millimeter semiautomatic.

It was a Glock 17—probably the same one Mr. Weatherhall had carried as a policeman. Peter knew this because he knew about guns—he'd grown up with them. But there was a difference between a hunting rifle or a shotgun and this neat and compact weapon. His father said that anyone who wasn't in active law enforcement and kept a handgun was an idiot; it was more likely to do damage than protect you. The problem with a handgun was that the muzzle was so short that you forgot about holding it away from you for safety's sake; aiming was as simple and nonchalant as pointing your finger.

Peter touched it. Cold; smooth. Mesmerizing. He brushed the trigger, cupping his hand around the gun; that slight, sleek weight.

Footsteps.

Peter jammed the cover back on the canister and whipped around, folding his arms in front of himself. Mr. Weatherhall appeared at the top of the stairs, cradling a red gas can. "All set," he said. "Bring it back full."

"I will," Peter replied. He left the kitchen and did not look in the general direction of the canister, although it was what he wanted to do, more than anything.

After school, Matt arrived with chicken soup from a local restaurant and comic books. "What are you doing out of bed?" he asked.

"You rang the doorbell," Josie said. "I had to answer it, didn't I?"

He fussed over her as if she had mono or cancer, not just a virus, which is what she'd told him when he called her on his cell from school that morning. Tucking her back into bed, he settled her with the soup in her lap. "This is supposed to cure, like, anything, right?"

"What about the comics?"

Matt shrugged. "My mom used to get those for me when I was little and stayed home sick. I don't know. They always sort of made me feel better."

As he sat down beside her on the bed, Josie picked up one of the comics. Why was Wonder Woman always so bodacious? If you were a 38DD, would you honestly go leaping off buildings and fighting crime without a good jogging bra?

Thinking of that reminded Josie that she could barely put on her own bra these days, her breasts were so tender. And that made her recall the pregnancy test that she'd wrapped up in paper towels and thrown away outside in the garbage can so her mother wouldn't find it.

"Drew's planning a shindig this Friday night," Matt said. "His parents are going to Foxwoods for the weekend." Matt frowned. "I hope you're feeling better by then, so you can go. What do you think you've got, anyway?"

She turned to him and took a deep breath. "It's what I don't have. My period. I'm two weeks late. I took a pregnancy test today."

"He's already talked to some guy at Sterling College

about buying a couple of kegs from a frat. I'm telling you, this party will be off the hook."

"Did you *hear* me?"

Matt smiled at her the way you'd indulge a child who just told you the sky is falling. "I think you're overreacting."

"It was positive."

"Stress can do that."

Josie's jaw dropped. "And what if it's not stress? What if it's, you know, *real?*"

"Then we're in it together." Matt leaned forward and kissed her forehead. "Baby," he said, "you could never get rid of me."

A few days later, when it snowed, Peter deliberately drained the snow blower of its gas, and then walked across the street to Mr. Weatherhall's house.

"Don't tell me you ran out again," he said as he opened the door.

"I guess my dad didn't get around to filling up our spare tank yet," Peter replied.

"Gotta make time," Mr. Weatherhall said, but he was already moving into his house, leaving the door wide so Peter could follow. "Gotta stick to a schedule, that's how it's done."

As they passed the television, Peter glanced at the cast of the *Match Game.* "Big Bertha is so big," Gene Rayburn was saying, "that instead of skydiving with a parachute, she uses a *blank.*"

The moment Mr. Weatherhall disappeared downstairs, Peter opened the sugar canister on the kitchen counter. The gun was still inside. Peter reached for it and reminded himself to breathe.

He covered the canister and put it back exactly where it

had been. Then he took the gun and jammed it, nose first, into the waistband of his jeans. His down jacket billowed over the front, so you couldn't see a bulge at all.

He gingerly slid open the silverware drawer, peeked in the cabinets. It was when he ran his hand along the dusty top of the refrigerator that he felt the smooth body of a second handgun.

"You know, it's wise to keep a spare tank . . ." Mr. Weatherhall's voice floated from the bottom of the basement stairs, accompanied by the percussion of his footsteps. Peter let go of the gun, snapped his hands back to his sides.

He was sweating by the time Mr. Weatherhall walked into the kitchen. "You all right?" he asked, peering at Peter. "You look a little white around the gills."

"I stayed up late doing homework. Thanks for the gas. Again."

"You tell your dad I'm not bailing him out next time," Mr. Weatherhall said, and he waved Peter off from the porch.

Peter waited until Mr. Weatherhall had closed the door, and then he started to run, kicking up snow in his wake. He left the gas can next to the snow blower and burst into his house. He locked his bedroom door, took the gun from his pants, and sat down.

It was black and heavy, crafted out of alloyed steel. What was really surprising was how fake the Glock looked—like a kid's toy gun—although Peter supposed he ought to be marveling instead at how realistic the toy guns actually were. He racked the slide and released it. He ejected the magazine.

He closed his eyes and held the gun up to his head. "Bang," he whispered.

Then he set the gun on his bed and pulled off one of his

pillowcases. He wrapped the Glock inside it, rolling it up like a bandage. He slipped the gun between his mattress and his box spring and lay down.

It would be like that fairy tale, the one with the princess who could feel a bean or a pea or whatever. Except Peter wasn't a prince, and the lump wouldn't keep him up at night.

In fact, it might make him sleep better.

In Josie's dream, she was standing in the most beautiful tepee. The walls were made of buttery deerskin, sewed tight with golden thread. Stories had been painted all around her in shades of red, ochre, violet, and blue—tales of hunts and loves and losses. Rich buffalo skins were piled high for cushions; coals glowed like rubies in the firepit. When she looked up, she could see stars falling through the smoke hole.

Suddenly Josie realized that her feet were sliding; worse, that there was no way to stop this. She glanced down and saw only sky; wondered whether she'd been silly enough to believe she could walk among the clouds, or if the ground beneath her feet had disappeared when she looked away.

She started to fall. She could feel herself tumbling head over heels; felt the skirt she was wearing balloon and the wind rush between her legs. She didn't want to open her eyes, but she couldn't help peeking: the ground was rushing up at an alarming pace, postage-stamp squares of green and brown and blue that grew larger, more detailed, more realistic.

There was her school. Her house. The roof over her bedroom. Josie felt herself hurtle toward it and she steeled herself for the inevitable crash. But you never hit the ground in your dreams; you never get to see yourself die.

Instead, Josie felt herself splash, her clothes billowing like the sails of a jellyfish as she treaded warm water.

She woke up, breathless, and realized that she still felt wet. She sat up, lifted up the covers, and saw the pool of blood beneath her.

After three positive pregnancy tests, after her period was three weeks late—she was miscarrying.

Thankgodthankgodthankgod. Josie buried her face in the sheets and started to cry.

Lewis was sitting at the kitchen table on Saturday morning, reading the latest issue of *The Economist* and methodically working his way through a whole-wheat waffle, when the phone rang. He glanced at Lacy, who—beside the sink— was technically closer to it, but she held up her hands, dripping with water and soap. "Could you . . . ?"

He stood up and answered it. "Hello?"

"Mr. Houghton?"

"Speaking," Lewis said.

"This is Tony, from Burnside's. Your hollow-point bullets are in."

Burnside's was a gun shop; Lewis went there in the fall for his Hoppe's solvent and his ammunition; once or twice he'd been lucky enough to bring a deer in to be weighed. But it was February; deer season was over now. "I didn't order those," Lewis said. "There must be some mistake."

He hung up the phone and sat down again in front of his waffle. Lacy lifted a large frying pan out of the sink and set it on the drainer to dry. "Who was that?"

Lewis turned the page in his magazine. "Wrong number," he said.

Matt had a hockey game in Exeter. Josie went to his home games, but rarely the ones where the team traveled.

Today, though, she had asked her mother to borrow the car and drove to the seacoast, leaving early enough to be able to catch him in the locker room beforehand. She poked her head inside the visiting team's locker room and was immediately hit with the reek of all the equipment. Matt stood with his back to her, wearing his chest protector and his padded pants and his skates. He hadn't yet pulled on his jersey.

Some of the other guys noticed her first. "Hey, Royston," a senior said. "I think your fan club president's arrived."

Matt didn't like it when she showed up before a game. Afterward: well, that was mandatory—he needed someone to celebrate his win. But he'd made it very clear that he didn't have time for Josie when he was getting ready; that he'd only get shit from the guys if she clung that closely; that Coach wanted the team to be alone to focus on their game. Still, she thought that this might be an exception.

A shadow passed over his face as his team started catcalls.

Matt, you need help putting on your jock?

Hey, quick, get the guy a bigger stick . . .

"Yeah," Matt shot back as he walked across the rubber mats toward Josie. "You just wish you had someone who could suck the chrome off a hood ornament."

Josie felt her cheeks flame as the entire locker room burst into laughter at her expense, and the rude comments shifted focus from *Matt* to *her*. Grasping her by the arm, Matt pulled Josie outside.

"I told you not to interrupt me before a game," he said.

"I know. But it was important . . ."

"*This* is important," Matt corrected, gesturing around the rink.

"I'm fine," Josie blurted out.

"Good."

She stared at him. "No, Matt. I mean . . . I'm *fine*. You were right."

As he realized what Josie was really trying to tell him, he put his arms around her waist and lifted her off the ground. His gear caught like armor between them as he kissed her. It made Josie think of knights heading off to battle; of the girls they left behind. "Don't you forget it," Matt said, and he grinned.

PART TWO

When you begin a journey of revenge,
start by digging two graves:
one for your enemy, and one for yourself.

—CHINESE PROVERB

Sterling isn't the inner city. You don't find crack dealers on Main Street, or households below the poverty level. The crime rate is virtually nonexistent.

That's why people are still so shell-shocked.

They ask, <u>How could this happen here?</u>

Well. How could it <u>not</u> happen here?

All it takes is a troubled kid with access to guns.

You don't have to go to an inner city to find someone who meets those criteria. You only have to open your eyes. The next likely candidate might be upstairs, or sprawled in front of your TV right now. But hey, you just go right on pretending it won't happen here. Tell yourself that you're immune because of where you live or who you are.

It's easier that way, isn't it?

Five Months After

You can tell a lot about people by their habits. For example, Jordan had come across potential jurors who religiously took their cups of coffee to their computers and read the entire *New York Times* online. There were others whose welcome screen on AOL didn't even include news updates, because they found it too depressing. There were rural people who owned televisions but only got a grainy public broadcasting station because they couldn't afford the money it would take to bring cable lines up their dirt road; and there were others who had bought elaborate satellite systems so that they could catch Japanese soaps or Sister Mary Margaret's Prayer Hour at three in the morning. There were those who watched CNN, and those who watched FOX News.

It was the sixth hour of individual voir dire, the process by which the jury for Peter's trial would be selected. This involved long days in the courtroom with Diana Leven and Judge Wagner, as the pool of jurors dribbled one by one into the witness seat to be asked a variety of questions by the defense and the prosecution. The goal was to find twelve folks, plus an alternate, who weren't personally affected by

the shooting; a jury that could commit to a long trial if necessary, instead of worrying about their home business or
who was taking care of their toddlers. A group of people
who had not been living and breathing the news about this
trial for the past five months—or, as Jordan was affectionately starting to think of them: the blessed few that had
been living under a rock.

It was August, and for the past week the temperatures
had climbed to nearly a hundred degrees during the day.
To make matters worse, the air-conditioning in the courtroom was on the fritz, and Judge Wagner smelled like
mothballs and feet when he sweated.

Jordan had already taken off his jacket and loosened the
top button of his shirt beneath his tie. Even Diana—who
he secretly believed had to be some kind of Stepford
robot—ha̶_ _ _ _ _ _ _ twisted her hair up and jammed a pencil into
the bun to sec̶_ _ _ _ _ _ _ure it. "What are we up to?" Judge Wagner
asked.

"Juror number six m̶_ _ _ _ _ _ _ _ _ _illion seven hundred and thirty
thousand," Jordan murmured.

"Juror number eighty-eight," the _ _ _ _ _ _ clerk announced.

It was a man this time, wearing kh_ _ _ _ _ _aki pants and a short-
sleeved shirt. He had thinning hair, boa̶_ _ _ _ _ _ shoes, and a wedding band. Jordan noted all of this on his pad.

Diana stood up and introduced herself, then began asking her litany of questions. The answers would dete_ _ _ _rmine if
a potential juror could be dismissed for cause—if the_ _ _ _y had
a kid, for example, who'd been killed at Sterling Hig̶_ _ _ _ _ _ _and
couldn't be impartial. If not, Diana could choose to _ _ _ _ _ _ _ _
one of her peremptory strikes. Both she and Jordan had fi_ _ _
teen opportunities to dismiss a potential juror out of gut instinct. So far, Diana had used one of hers against a short,
bald, quiet software developer. Jordan had dismissed a former Navy SEAL.

"What do you do for work, Mr. Alstrop?" Diana asked.

"I'm an architect."

"You're married?"

"For twenty years, this October."

"Do you have any children?"

"Two, a fourteen-year-old boy and a nineteen-year-old girl."

"Do they go to public high school?"

"Well, my son does. My daughter's in college. Princeton," he said proudly.

"Do you know anything about this case?"

Saying he did, Jordan knew, wouldn't exclude him. It was what he believed or didn't believe, in spite of what the media had said.

"Well, only what I read in the papers," Alstrop said, and Jordan closed his eyes.

"Do you read a certain newspaper daily?"

"I used to get the *Union Leader*," he said, "but the editorials drove me crazy. I try to read the main section of *The New York Times* now, at least."

Jordan considered this. The *Union Leader* was a notoriously conservative paper, *The New York Times* a liberal one.

"What about television?" Diana asked. "Any shows you particularly like?"

You probably didn't want a juror who watched ten hours of Court TV per day. You also didn't want the guy who savored Pee-wee Herman marathons.

"*60 Minutes*," Alstrop replied. "And *The Simpsons*."

Now *that*, Jordan thought, was a normal guy. He got to his feet as Diana turned the questioning over to him. "What do you remember reading about this case?" he asked.

Alstrop shrugged. "There was a shooting at the high school and one of the students was charged."

"Did you know any of the students?"

"No."

"Do you know anyone who works at Sterling High?"
Alstrop shook his head. "No."

"Have you talked to anyone involved in this case?"

"No."

Jordan walked up to the witness stand. "There's a rule in this state that says you can take a right on red, if you stop first at the red light. You familiar with it?"

"Sure," Alstrop said.

"What if the judge told you that you can't turn right on red—that you must stay stopped until the light goes green again, even if there's a sign in front of you that specifically says RIGHT TURN ON RED. What would you do?"

Alstrop looked at Judge Wagner. "I guess I'd do what he said."

Jordan smiled to himself. He didn't give a damn about Alstrop's driving habits—that setup and question was a way to weed out the people who couldn't see past convention. There would be information in this trial that wasn't necessarily intuitive, and he needed people on a jury who were open-minded enough to understand that rules weren't always what you thought they were, who could listen to the new regulations and follow them accordingly.

When he finished his questioning, he and Diana walked toward the bench. "Is there any reason to dismiss this juror for cause?" Judge Wagner asked.

"No, Your Honor," Diana said, and Jordan shook his head.

"So?"

Diana nodded. Jordan glanced at the man, still sitting on the witness stand. "This one works for me," he said.

When Alex woke up, she pretended not to. Instead, she kept her eyes nearly closed so that she could stare at the man sprawled on the other side of her bed. This relationship—four months old now—was still a mystery to her, as much as the constellation of freckles on Patrick's shoulders, the valley of his spine, the startling contrast of his black hair against a white sheet. It seemed that he had invaded her life by osmosis: she'd find his shirt mixed in with her laundry; she'd smell his shampoo on her pillowcase; she would pick up the phone, thinking to call him, and he'd already be on the line. Alex had been single for so long; she was practical, resolute, and set in her ways (oh, who was she kidding . . . those were all just euphemisms for what she *really* was: stubborn)—she would have guessed that this sudden attack on her privacy would be unnerving. Instead, though, she found herself feeling disoriented when Patrick wasn't around, like the sailor who's just landed after months at sea and who still feels the ocean rolling beneath him even when it isn't there.

"I can feel you staring, you know," Patrick murmured. A lazy smile heated his face, but his eyes were still shut.

Alex leaned over, slipping her hand under the covers. "*What* can you feel?"

"What *can't* I?" Striking quick as lightning, he grabbed her wrist and pulled her underneath him. His eyes, still softened by sleep, were a crisp blue that made Alex think of glaciers and northern seas. He kissed her, and she vined around him.

Then suddenly her eyes snapped open. "Oh, shit," she said.

"That wasn't really what I was going for . . ."

"Do you know what time it is?"

They had drawn the shades in her bedroom because of a full moon last night. But by now, the sun was streaming through the thinnest crack at the bottom of the windowsill.

Alex could hear Josie banging pots and pans downstairs in the kitchen.

Patrick reached over Alex for the wristwatch he'd left on her nightstand. "Oh, shit," he repeated, and he threw back the covers. "I'm an hour late for work already."

He grabbed his boxers as Alex jumped out of bed and reached for her robe. "What about Josie?"

It wasn't that they had been hiding their relationship from Josie—Patrick often dropped by after work or for dinner or to hang out in the evenings. A few times, Alex had tried to talk to Josie about him, to see what she thought of the whole miracle of her mother dating again, but Josie did whatever it took to avoid having that conversation. Alex wasn't sure herself where this was all going, but she did know that she and Josie had been a unit for so long that adding Patrick to the mix meant Josie became the loner—and right now, Alex was determined to keep that from happening. She was making up for lost time, really, thinking of Josie before she thought of anything else. To that end, if Patrick spent the night, she made sure he left before Josie could wake up to find him there.

Except today, when it was a lazy summer Thursday and nearly ten o'clock.

"Maybe this is a good time to tell her," Patrick suggested.

"Tell her what?"

"That we're . . ." He looked at her.

Alex stared at him. She couldn't finish his sentence; she didn't really know the answer herself. She never expected that this was the way she and Patrick would have this conversation. Was she with Patrick because he was good at that—rescuing the underdog who needed it? When this trial was over, would he move on? Would she?

"We're together," Patrick said decisively.

Alex turned her back to him and yanked shut the tie of her robe. That wasn't, to paraphrase Patrick earlier, what she had been going for. But then again, how would he know that? If he asked her right now what she wanted out of this relationship . . . well, she knew: she wanted love. She wanted to have someone to come home to. She wanted to dream about a vacation they'd take when they were sixty and know he'd be there the day she stepped onto the plane. But she'd never admit any of this to him. What if she did, and he just looked at her blankly? What if it was too soon to think about things like this?

If he asked her right now, she wouldn't answer, because answering was the surest way to get your heart handed back to you.

Alex rummaged underneath the bed, searching for her slippers. Instead, she located Patrick's belt and tossed it to him. Maybe the reason she hadn't openly told Josie she was sleeping with Patrick had nothing to do with protecting Josie, and everything to do with protecting herself.

Patrick threaded the belt through his jeans. "It doesn't have to be a state secret," he said. "You are allowed to . . . you know."

Alex glanced at him. "Have sex?"

"I was trying to come up with something a little less blunt," Patrick admitted.

"I'm also allowed to keep things private," Alex pointed out.

"Guess I ought to get back the deposit on the billboard, then."

"That might be a good idea."

"I suppose I could just get you jewelry instead."

Alex looked down at the carpet so that Patrick couldn't see her trying to pick apart that sentence, find the commitment strung between the words.

God, was it *always* this frustrating when you weren't the one running the show?

"Mom," Josie yelled up the stairs, "I've got pancakes ready, if you want some."

"Look," Patrick sighed. "We can still keep Josie from finding out. All you have to do is distract her while I sneak out."

She nodded. "I'll try to keep her in the kitchen. You . . ." She glanced at Patrick. "Just hurry." As Alex started out of the room, Patrick grabbed her hand and yanked.

"Hey," he said. "Good-bye." He leaned down and kissed her.

"Mom, they're getting cold!"

"See you later," Alex said, pushing away.

She hurried downstairs and found Josie eating a plate of blueberry pancakes. "Those smell so good . . . I can't believe I slept this late," Alex began, and then she realized that there were three place settings at the kitchen table.

Josie folded her arms. "So how does he take his coffee?"

Alex sank into a chair across from her. "You weren't supposed to find out."

"A. I am a big girl. B. Then the brilliant detective shouldn't have left his car in the driveway."

Alex picked at a thread on the place mat. "No milk, two sugars."

"Well," Josie said. "Guess I'll know for next time."

"How do you feel about that?" Alex asked quietly.

"Getting him coffee?"

"No. The *next time* part."

Josie poked at a fat blueberry on the top of her pancake. "It's not really something I get to choose, is it?"

"Yes," Alex said. "Because if you're not all right with this, Josie, then I'll stop seeing him."

"You like him?" Josie asked, staring down at her plate.

"Yeah."

"And he likes you?"

"I think so."

Josie lifted her gaze. "Then you shouldn't worry about what anyone else thinks."

"I worry about what *you* think," Alex said. "I don't want you to feel like you're any less important to me because of him."

"Just be responsible," Josie answered, with a slow smile. "Every time you have sex, you can get pregnant or you can not get pregnant. That's fifty-fifty."

Alex raised her brows. "Wow. I didn't even think you were listening when I gave that speech."

Josie pressed her finger against a spot of maple syrup that had fallen onto the table, her eyes trained on the wood. "So, do you . . . like . . . *love* him?"

The words seemed bruised, tender. "No," Alex said quickly, because if she could convince Josie, then she surely could convince herself that what she felt for Patrick had everything to do with passion and nothing to do with . . . well . . . *that*. "It's only been a few months."

"I don't think there's a grace period," Josie said.

Alex decided that the best road to take through this minefield was the one that would keep both Josie and herself from being hurt: pretend this was nothing, a fling, a fancy. "I wouldn't know what being in love felt like if it hit me in the face," she said lightly.

"It's not like on TV, like everything's perfect all of a sudden." Josie's voice shrank until it was barely a thought. "It's more like, once it happens, you spend all your time realizing how much can go wrong."

Alex looked up at her, frozen. "Oh, Josie."

"Anyway."

"I didn't mean to make you—"

"Let's just drop it, okay?" Josie forced a smile. "He's not bad-looking, you know, for someone that old."

"He's a year younger than I am," Alex pointed out.

"My mother, the cradle robber." Josie picked up the plate of pancakes and passed it. "These are getting cold."

Alex took the plate. "Thank you," she said, but she held Josie's gaze just long enough for her daughter to realize what Alex was really grateful for.

Just then Patrick came creeping down the stairs. At the landing, he turned to give Alex a thumbs-up sign. "Patrick," she called out. "Josie's made us some pancakes."

Selena knew the party line—you were supposed to say that there was no difference between boys and girls—but she also knew if you asked any mom or nursery school teacher, they'd tell you differently, off the record. This morning, she sat on a park bench watching Sam negotiate a sandbox with a group of fellow toddlers. Two little girls were pretending to bake pizzas made out of sand and pebbles. The boy beside Sam was trying to demolish a dump truck by smashing it repeatedly into the sandbox's wooden frame. *No difference*, Selena thought. *Yeah, right.*

She watched with interest as Sam turned from the boy beside him and started to copy the girls, sifting sand into a bucket to make a cake.

Selena grinned, hoping that this was some small clue that her son would grow up to act against stereotype and do whatever he was most comfortable doing. But did it work that way? Could you look at a child and see who he'd become? Sometimes when she studied Sam, she could glimpse the adult he'd be one day—it was there in his eyes, the shell of the man he would grow to inhabit. But it was more than physical attributes you could sometimes puzzle out. Would these little girls become stay-at-home Betty

Crocker moms, or business entrepreneurs like Mrs. Fields? Would the little boy's destructive behavior bloom into drug addiction or alcoholism? Had Peter Houghton shoved playmates or stomped on crickets or done something else as a child that might have predicted his future as a killer?

The boy in the sandbox put down the truck and moved on to digging, seemingly to China. Sam abandoned his baking to reach for the plastic vehicle, and then he lost his balance and fell down, smacking his knee on the wooden frame.

Selena was out of her seat in a shot, ready to scoop up her son before he started to bawl. But Sam glanced around at the other kids, as if realizing he had an audience. And although his little face furrowed and reddened, a raisin of pain, he didn't cry.

It was easier for girls. They could say *This hurts,* or *I don't like how this feels,* and have the complaint be socially acceptable. Boys, though, didn't speak that language. They didn't learn it as children and they didn't manage to pick it up as adults, either. Selena remembered last summer, when Jordan had gone fishing with an old friend whose wife had just filed for divorce. *What did you talk about?* she asked when Jordan came home.

Nothing, Jordan had said. *We were fishing.*

This had made no sense to Selena; they'd been gone for six hours. How could you sit beside someone in a small boat for that long and not have a heart-to-heart about how he was doing; if he was holding up in the wake of this crisis; if he worried about the rest of his life.

She looked at Sam, who now had the dump truck in his hand and was rolling it across his former pizza. Change could come that quickly, Selena knew. She thought of how Sam would wrap his tiny arms around her and kiss her; how he'd come running to her if she held out her arms. But sooner or later he'd realize that his friends didn't hold their mothers' hands when they crossed the street; that they didn't bake pizzas and cakes in the sandbox, instead they built cities and dug caverns. One day—in middle school, or even earlier—Sam would start to hole himself up in his room. He would shy away from her touch. He would grunt his responses, act tough, be a man.

Maybe it was our own damn fault that men turned out the way they did, Selena thought. Maybe empathy, like any unused muscle, simply atrophied.

Josie told her mother that she had gotten a summer job volunteering with the school system to tutor middle and elementary school kids in math. She talked about Angie, whose parents had split up during the school year and who had failed algebra as an indirect consequence. She described Joseph, a leukemia patient who'd missed school for treatment and had the hardest time understanding fractions. Every day at dinner, her mother would ask her about work, and Josie would have a story. The problem was, it was just that—a fiction. Joseph and Angie didn't exist; and for that matter, neither did Josie's tutoring job.

This morning, like every morning, Josie left the house. She got on the Advance Transit bus and said hello to Rita, the driver who'd been on this route all summer. When the other passengers got off at the stop that was closest to the school, Josie stayed in her seat. She didn't get up, in fact, until the very last stop—the one that was a mile south of the Whispering Pines Cemetery.

She liked it there. At the cemetery, she didn't run into anyone she didn't feel like talking to. She didn't have to speak at all if she wasn't in the mood. Josie walked up the winding trail, which was so familiar to her by now that she could tell, with her eyes closed, when the pavement was going to make a dip and when it would veer left. She knew that the violently blue hydrangea bush was halfway to Matt's grave; that you could smell honeysuckle when you were only steps away from it.

By now, there was a headstone, a pristine block of white marble with Matt's name carefully carved. Grass had started to grow. Josie sat down on the raised hummock of dirt, which was warm, as if the sun had been seeping into the earth and holding that heat in wait for her. She reached into her backpack and took out a bottle of water, a peanut butter sandwich, a bag of saltines.

"Can you believe school's starting in a week?" she said to Matt, because sometimes she did that. It wasn't like she expected him to answer; it just felt better talking to him after so many months of *not* talking. "They're not opening the real school yet, though. They said maybe by Thanksgiving, when the construction's done."

What they were actually doing to the school was a mystery—Josie had driven by enough to know that the front hallway and library had been torn down, as had the cafeteria. She wondered if the administration was naïve enough to think that if they got rid of the scene of the crime, the students could be fooled into thinking it had never happened.

She'd read somewhere that ghosts didn't just hang around physical locations—that sometimes, a *person* could be haunted. Josie hadn't really considered herself big on the paranormal, but this she believed. There were some memories, she knew, you could run from forever and never shake.

Josie lay down, her hair spread over the newborn grass. "Do you like having me here?" she whispered. "Or would you tell me to get lost, if you were the one who could talk?"

She didn't want to hear the answer. She didn't even really want to think about it. So she opened her eyes as wide as she could and stared into the sky, until the brilliant blue burned the backs of her eyes.

Lacy stood in the men's department at Filene's, touching her hands to the bristled tweeds and hallowed blue and puckered seersucker fabrics of the sports jackets. She'd driven two hours to Boston so that she would have the best choices to outfit Peter for his trial. Brooks Brothers, Hugo Boss, Calvin Klein, Ermenegildo Zegna. They had been made in Italy, France, Britain, California. She peeked at a price tag, sucked in her breath, and then realized she did not care. This would most likely be the last time she would ever buy clothes for her son.

Lacy moved systematically through the department. She picked up boxer shorts made of the finest Egyptian cotton, a packet of Ralph Lauren white tees, cashmere socks. She found khaki trousers — 30 x 30. She plucked a button-down oxford shirt off a rack, because Peter had always hated having his collar peek out from a crewneck sweater. She chose a blue blazer, as Jordan had instructed. *We want him dressed as if you're sending him to Phillips Exeter*, he had said.

She remembered how, when Peter was around eleven, he'd developed an aversion to buttons. You'd think it would be easy to get around something like that, but it eliminated most pants. Lacy could remember driving to the ends of the earth to find elastic-waist flannel plaid pajama pants that might double for daily wear. She remembered seeing kids wearing pajama bottoms to school as recently as last year and wondering if Peter had started the trend, or simply been slightly out of sync.

Even after Lacy had gathered what she needed, she continued to walk through the men's department. She touched a rainbow of silk handkerchiefs that melted over her fingers, choosing one that was the color of Peter's eyes. She rifled through leather belts—black, brown, stippled, alligator—and neckties printed with dots, with fleurs-de-lis, with stripes. She picked up a bathrobe that was so soft it nearly brought her to tears, shearling slippers, a cherry-red bathing suit. She shopped until the weight in her arms was as heavy as a child.

"Oh, let me help you with those," a saleswoman said, taking some of the items from her arms and carrying them to the counter. She began to fold them, one by one. "I know how it feels," she said, smiling sympathetically. "When my son went away, I thought I was going to die."

Lacy stared at her. Was it possible that she wasn't the only woman who had gone through something as awful as this? Once you had, like this salesperson, would you be able to pick others out of a crowd, as if there were a secret society of those mothers whose children cut them to the quick?

"You think it's forever," the woman said, "but believe me, once they come home for Christmas break or summer vacation and start eating you out of house and home again, you'll be wishing college was year-round."

Lacy's face froze. "Right," she said. "College."

"I've got a girl at the University of New Hampshire, and my son's at Rochester," the saleswoman said.

"Harvard. That's where my son's going."

They had talked about it once—Peter liked the computer science department at Stanford better, and Lacy had joked around, saying she'd throw away any brochures from colleges west of the Mississippi, because they were so far away.

The state prison was sixty miles south, in Concord.

"Harvard," the saleswoman said. "He must be a smart one."

"He is," Lacy said, and she continued to tell this woman

about Peter's fictional transition to college, until the lie did not taste like licorice on her tongue; until she could nearly believe it herself.

Just after three o'clock, Josie rolled over onto her belly, spread her arms wide, and pressed her face into the grass. It looked like she was trying to hold on to the ground, which, she supposed, wasn't all that far from the truth. She breathed in deeply—usually, she smelled nothing but weeds and soil, but every now and then when it had just rained, she got the barest scent of ice and Pert shampoo, as if Matt were still himself just under that surface.

She gathered the wrapper from her sandwich and her empty water bottle and put them into her backpack, then headed down the winding path to the cemetery gates. There was a car blocking the entrance—only twice this summer had Josie been present when a funeral procession came, and it had made her a little sick to her stomach. She started to walk faster, in the hope that she would be long gone and sitting on her Advance Transit bus before the service began—and then she realized that the car blocking the gates was not a hearse, not even black for that matter. It was the same car that had been parked in their driveway this morning, and Patrick was leaning against it with his arms crossed.

"What are you doing here?" Josie asked.

"I could ask you the same thing."

She shrugged. "It's a free country."

Josie didn't really have anything against Patrick Ducharme himself. He just made her nervous, on so many counts. She couldn't look at him without thinking of That Day. But now she had to, because he also was her mother's lover (how weird was it to say *that*?) and in a way, that was even more upsetting. Her mother was on cloud nine, falling in love, while Josie had to sneak off to a graveyard to visit *her* boyfriend.

Patrick pushed himself off the car and took a step toward her. "Your mother thinks you're teaching long division right now."

"Did she tell you to stalk me?" Josie said.

"I prefer *surveillance*," Patrick corrected.

Josie snorted. She didn't want to sound like such a snot, but she couldn't help it. Sarcasm was like a force field; once she turned it off, he might be able to see that she was *this* close to falling to pieces.

"Your mother doesn't know I'm here," Patrick said. "I wanted to talk to you."

"I'm going to miss my bus."

"Then I'll drive you wherever you want to go," he said, exasperated. "You know, when I'm doing my job, I spend a lot of time wishing I could turn back the clock—get to the rape victim before it happened, stake out the house before the thief comes by. I know what it's like to feel like nothing you do or say is ever going to make things better. And I know what it's like to wake up in the middle of the night replaying one moment over and over so vividly that you might as well be living it again. In fact, I bet you and I replay the same moment."

Josie swallowed. In all these months, out of all the well-meaning conversations she'd had with doctors and psychiatrists and even other kids from the school, no one had captured, so succinctly, what it felt like to be her. But she couldn't let Patrick know that—couldn't admit to her weakness, even though she had the feeling that he could spot it all the same. "Don't pretend we have anything in common," Josie said.

"But we do," Patrick replied. "Your mother." He looked Josie in the eye. "I like her. A lot. And I'd like to know that you're okay with that."

Josie felt her throat closing. She tried to remember Matt saying that he liked her; she wondered if anyone would ever say it again. "My mother's a big girl. She can make her own decisions about who she f—"

"Don't," Patrick interrupted.

"Don't *what*."

"Don't say something you're going to wish you hadn't."

Josie stepped back, her eyes glittering. "If you think that buddying up to me is going to win her over, you're wrong. You're better off with flowers and chocolate. She couldn't care less about me."

"That's not true."

"You haven't exactly been around long enough to know, have you?"

"Josie," Patrick said, "she's crazy about you."

Josie felt herself choke on the truth, even harder to speak than it was to swallow. "But not as crazy as she is about you. She's happy. She's happy and I . . . I know I should be happy for her . . ."

"But you're here," Patrick said, gesturing at the cemetery. "And you're alone."

Josie nodded and burst into tears. She turned away, embarrassed, and then felt Patrick fold his arms around her. He didn't say anything, and for that one moment, she even liked him—any word at all, even a well-meaning one, would have taken up the space where her hurt needed to be. He just let her cry until finally it all stopped, and Josie rested for a moment against his shoulder, wondering if this was only the eye of the storm or its endpoint.

"I'm a bitch," she whispered. "I'm jealous."

"I think she'd understand."

Josie drew away from him and wiped her eyes. "Are you going to tell her I come here?"

"No."

She glanced up at him, surprised. She would have thought that he'd take her mother's side.

"You're wrong, you know," Patrick said.

"About what?"

"Being alone."

Josie glanced up the hill. You couldn't see Matt's grave from the gates, but it was still there—just like everything else about That Day. "Ghosts don't count."

Patrick smiled. "Mothers do."

What Lewis hated the most was the sound of the metal doors slamming. It hardly mattered that, thirty minutes from now, he'd be able to leave the jail. What was important was that the inmates couldn't. And that one of those inmates was the same boy he'd taught to ride a bike without training wheels; the same boy whose nursery school paperweight was still sitting on Lewis's desk; the same boy he'd watched take his very first breath.

He knew it would be a shock for Peter to see him—how many months had he told himself that this would be the week he got up the courage to see his son in jail, only to find another errand to run or paper to study? But, as a correctional officer opened up a door and led Peter into the visitation room, Lewis realized that he'd underestimated what a shock it would be for *him* to see *Peter*.

He was bigger. Maybe not taller, but broader—his shoulders filled out his shirt; his arms had thickened with muscle. His skin was translucent, almost blue under this unnatural light. His hands didn't stop moving—they were twitching at his sides and then, when he sat down, on the sides of the chair.

"Well," Peter said. "What do you know."

Lewis had rehearsed six or seven speeches, explanations of why he had not been able to bring himself to see his son, but when he saw Peter sitting there, only two words rose to his lips. "I'm sorry."

Peter's mouth tightened. "For what? Blowing me off for six months?"

"I was thinking," Lewis admitted, "more like eighteen years."

Peter sat back in his chair, staring at Lewis. He forced himself to return the stare. Could Peter grant him absolution, even if Lewis still wasn't entirely sure he could return the favor?

Rubbing a hand down his face, Peter shook his head. Then he started to smile. Lewis felt his bones loosen, his muscles relax. Until this moment, he hadn't really known what to expect from Peter. He could reason with himself all he wanted and assert that an apology would always be accepted; he could remind himself that *he* was the parent here, the one in charge—but all of that was extremely hard to remember when you were sitting in a visiting room at a jail, with a woman on your left who was trying to play footsie with her lover across that forbidden red line, and a man on your right who was cursing a blue streak.

The smile on Peter's face hardened, twisted into a sneer. "Fuck you," he spat out. "Fuck you for coming here. You don't give a shit about me. You don't want to tell me you're sorry. You just want to hear yourself *say* it. You're here for yourself, not me."

Lewis's head felt as if it were filled with stones. He bent forward, the stalk of his neck unable to bear the weight anymore, until he could rest his forehead in his hands. "I can't do anything, Peter," he whispered. "I can't work, I can't eat. I can't sleep." Then he lifted his face. "The new students,

"*Or.* I hate that word. It's two letters long and stuffed to the gills with reasonable doubt—"

She broke off as there was a knock at the door, and her secretary stuck her head inside. "Your two o'clock's here."

Diana turned to him. "I'm preparing Drew Girard for testifying. Why don't you stay for this one?"

Patrick moved to a chair on the side of the room to give Drew the spot across from the prosecutor. The boy entered with a soft knock. "Ms. Leven?"

Diana came around her desk. "Drew. Thanks for coming in." She gestured at Patrick. "You remember Detective Ducharme?"

Drew nodded at him. Patrick surveyed the boy's pressed pants, his collared shirt, his manners on display. This was not the cocky, big-man-on-campus hockey star, as he had been painted by students during Patrick's investigations, but then again, Drew had watched his best friend get killed; he'd been shot himself in the shoulder. Whatever world he had lorded over was gone now.

"Drew," Diana said, "we brought you in here because you got a subpoena, and that means you're going to be testifying sometime next week. We'll let you know when, for sure, as we get closer . . . but for now, I wanted to make sure you weren't nervous about going to court. Today, we'll go over some of the things you'll be asked, and how the procedure works. If you have any questions, we can cover those as well. Okay?"

"Yes, ma'am."

Patrick leaned forward. "How's the shoulder?"

Drew swiveled to face him, unconsciously flexing that body part. "I still have to do physical therapy and stuff, but it's a lot better. Except . . ." His voice trailed off.

"Except what?" Diana asked.

"I'll miss hockey season this whole year."

Diana met Patrick's eye; this was sympathy for a witness. "Do you think you'll be able to play again, eventually?"

Drew flushed. "The doctors say no, but I think they're wrong." He hesitated. "I'm a senior this year, and I was sort of counting on an athletic scholarship for college."

There was an uncomfortable silence, as no one acknowledged either Drew's courage or the truth. "So, Drew," Diana said. "When we get into court, I'll start by asking your name, where you live, if you were in school that day."

"Okay."

"Let's try it out a bit, all right? When you got to school that morning, what was your first class?"

Drew sat up a little straighter. "American History."

"And second period?"

"English."

"Where did you go after English class?"

"I had third period free, and most people with free periods hang out in the caf."

"Is that where you went?"

"Yeah."

"Was anyone with you?" Diana continued.

"I went down by myself, but when I got there, I hung out with a bunch of people." He looked at Patrick. "Friends."

"How long were you in the cafeteria?"

"I don't know, a half hour, maybe?"

Diana nodded. "What happened then?"

Drew looked down at his pants and drew his thumb along the crease. Patrick noticed that his hand was shaking. "We were all just, you know, talking . . . and then I heard this really big boom."

"Could you tell where the sound was coming from?"

"No. I didn't know what it was."

"Did you see anything?"

"No."

"So," Diana asked, "what did you do when you heard it?"

"I made a joke," Drew said. "I said it was probably the school lunch, igniting or something. *Oh, finally, that radioactive mac and cheese.*"

"Did you stay in the cafeteria after the boom?"

"Yeah."

"And then?"

Drew looked down at his hands. "There was this sound like firecrackers. Before anyone could figure out what it was, Peter came into the cafeteria. He was carrying a knapsack and holding a gun, and he started shooting."

Diana held up her hand. "I'm going to stop you there for a moment, Drew. . . . When you're on the stand, and you say that, I'll ask you to look at the defendant and identify him for the record. Got it?"

"Yes."

Patrick realized that he was not just seeing the shooting the way he'd have seen any other crime. He wasn't even visualizing it playing out as a prequel to the chilling cafeteria videotape he'd watched. He was imagining Josie—one of Drew's friends—sitting at a long table, hearing those firecrackers, not imagining in the least what came next.

"How long have you known Peter?" Diana asked.

"We both grew up in Sterling. We've been in the same school, like, forever."

"Were you friends?" Drew shook his head. "Enemies?"

"No," he said. "Not really enemies."

"Ever have any problems with him?"

Drew glanced up. "No."

"Did you ever bully him?"

"No, ma'am," he said.

Patrick felt his hands curl into fists. He knew, from interviewing hundreds of kids, that Drew Girard had stuffed

Peter Houghton into lockers; had tripped him while he was walking down the stairs; had thrown spitballs into his hair. None of that condoned what Peter had done . . . but still. There was a kid rotting in jail; there were ten people decomposing in graves; there were dozens in rehab and corrective surgery; there were hundreds—like Josie—who still could not get through the day without bursting into tears; there were parents—like Alex—who trusted Diana to get justice done on their behalf. And this little asshole was lying through his teeth.

Diana looked up from her notes and stared at Drew. "So if you get asked under oath whether you've ever picked on Peter, what's your answer going to be?"

Drew looked up at her, the bravado fading just enough for Patrick to realize he was scared to death that they knew something more than they were admitting to him. Diana glanced at Patrick and threw down her pen. That was all the invitation he needed—he was out of his chair in an instant, his hand grabbing Drew Girard's throat. "Listen, you little fuck," Patrick said, "don't screw this up. We know what you did to Peter Houghton. We know you were sitting front and center. There are ten dead victims, and eighteen more who are never going to have the lives they thought they would, and there are so many families in this community that are never going to stop grieving that I can't even count them. I don't know what your game plan is here— if you want to play the choirboy to protect your reputation, or if you're just scared to tell the truth—but believe me, if you get on that witness stand and you lie about your actions in the past, I will make sure you wind up in jail for obstruction of justice."

He let go of Drew and turned away, staring out the window in Diana's office. He had no authority to arrest Drew for anything—even if the kid did perjure himself—much less send him to jail, but Drew would never know that. And maybe it was enough to scare him into behaving. Taking a deep breath, Patrick bent down and picked up the pen Diana had dropped and handed it to her.

"Let me ask you again, Drew," she said smoothly. "Did you ever bully Peter Houghton?"

Drew glanced at Patrick and swallowed. Then he opened his mouth and started to speak.

"It's barbecued lasagna," Alex announced after Patrick and Josie had each taken their first bite. "What do you think?"

"I didn't know you could barbecue lasagna," Josie said slowly. She began to peel the noodles back from the cheese, as if she were scalping it.

"How's that work, exactly?" Patrick asked, reaching for the pitcher of water to refill his glass.

"It was regular lasagna. But some of the insides spilled out into the oven, and there was all this smoke . . . and I was going to start over, but then I sort of realized that I was only adding an extra, charcoal sort of flavor into the mix." She beamed. "Ingenious, right? I mean, I looked in all the cookbooks, Josie, and it's never been done before, as far as I can tell."

"Go figure," Patrick said, and he coughed into his napkin.

"I actually *like* cooking," Alex said. "I like taking a recipe and, you know, going off on a tangent to see what happens."

"Recipes are kind of like laws," Patrick replied. "You might want to try to stick to them, before you commit a felony . . ."

"I'm not hungry," Josie said suddenly. She pushed her plate away, stood up, and ran upstairs.

"The trial starts tomorrow," Alex said, by way of explanation. She went after Josie, not even excusing herself first,

because she knew Patrick would understand. Josie had
slammed the door shut and turned up her music; it would
do no good to knock. Alex turned the knob and stepped inside, reaching to the stereo to turn down the volume.

Josie lay on her bed facedown, the pillow over her head.
When Alex sat down on the mattress beside her, she didn't
move. "You want to talk about it?" Alex asked.

"No," Josie said, her voice muffled.

Alex reached out and yanked the pillow off her head.
"Try."

"It's just—God, Mom—what's wrong with me? It's like
the world's started spinning again for everyone else, but I
can't even get back on the carousel. Even you two—you
both must be thinking like crazy about the trial, too—but
here you are, laughing and smiling like you can put what
happened and what's *going* to happen out of your head,
when I can't *not* think about it every waking second." Josie
looked up at Alex, her eyes filling with tears. "Everyone's
moved on. Everyone but me."

Alex put her hand on Josie's arm and rubbed it. She
could remember delighting in the sheer physical proof of
Josie after she was born—that somehow, out of nothing,
she'd created this tiny, warm, squirming, flawless creature.
She'd spend hours on her bed with Josie beside her, touching her baby's skin, her seed-pearl toes, the pulse of her
fontanel. "Once," Alex said, "when I was working as a public defender, a guy in the office threw a Fourth of July party
for all the lawyers and their families. I took you, even
though you were only about three years old. There were
fireworks, and I looked away for a second to see them, and
when I turned back you were gone. I started to scream, and
someone noticed you—lying at the bottom of the pool."

Josie sat up, riveted by a story she had never heard before.

"I dove in and dragged you out and gave you mouth-to-mouth, and you spit up. I couldn't even speak, I was so scared. But you came back fighting and furious at me. You told me you'd been looking for mermaids, and I interrupted you."

Tucking her knees up under her chin, Josie smiled a little. "Really?"

Alex nodded. "I said that next time, you had to take me with you."

"*Was* there a next time?"

"Well, you tell me," Alex said, and she hesitated. "You don't need water to feel like you're drowning, do you?"

When Josie shook her head, the tears spilled over. She shifted, fitting herself into her mother's arms.

This, Patrick knew, was his downfall. For the second time in his life, he was growing so close to a woman and her child that he forgot he might not really be part of their family. He looked around the table at the detritus of Alex's awful dinner and started clearing the untouched plates.

The barbecued lasagna had congealed in its serving dish, a blackened brick. He piled the dishes in the sink and began to run warm water, then picked up a sponge and started to scrub.

"Oh my gosh," Alex said behind him. "You really *are* the perfect man."

Patrick turned, his hands still soapy. "Far from it." He reached for a dish towel. "Is Josie—"

"She's fine. She'll be fine. Or at least we're both going to keep saying that until it's true."

"I'm sorry, Alex."

"Who isn't?" She straddled a kitchen chair and rested her cheek on its spine. "I'm going to the trial tomorrow."

"I wouldn't have expected any less."

"Do you really think McAfee can get him acquitted?"

Patrick folded the dish towel beside the sink and walked toward Alex. He knelt in front of her chair. "Alex," he said, "that kid walked into the school like he was executing a battle plan. He started in the parking lot and set off a bomb to cause a distraction. He went around to the front of the school and took out a kid on the steps. He went into the cafeteria, shot at a bunch of kids, murdered some of them—and then he sat down and had a bowl of fucking *cereal* before he continued his killing spree. I don't see how, presented with that kind of evidence, a jury could dismiss the charges."

Alex stared at him. "Tell me something . . . why was Josie lucky?"

"Because she's alive."

"No, I mean, *why* is she alive? She was in the cafeteria and the locker room. She saw people die all around her. Why didn't Peter shoot *her*?"

"I don't know. Things happen that I don't understand all the time. Some of them—well, they're like the shooting. And some of them . . ." He covered Alex's hand with his own where it gripped the chair rail. "Some of them aren't."

Alex looked up at him, and Patrick was reminded again of how finding her—*being* with her—was like that first crocus you saw in the snow. Just when you assumed winter would last forever, this unexpected beauty could take you by surprise—and if you did not take your eyes off it, if you kept your focus, the rest of the snow would somehow melt.

"If I ask you something, will you be honest with me?" Alex asked.

Patrick nodded.

"My lasagna wasn't very good, was it?"

He smiled at her through the slats of the chair. "Don't give up your day job," he said.

In the middle of the night, when Josie could still not get to sleep, she slipped outside and lay down on the front lawn. She stared up at the sky, which clung so low by this time of the night that she could feel stars pricking her face. Out here, without her bedroom closing in around her, it was almost possible to believe that whatever problems she had were tiny, in the grand scheme of the universe.

Tomorrow, Peter Houghton was going to be tried for ten murders. Even the thought of it—of that last murder—made Josie sick to her stomach. She could not go watch the trial, as much as she wanted to, because she was on a stupid witness list. Instead, she was sequestered, which was a fancy word for being kept clueless.

Josie took a deep breath and thought about a social studies class she'd taken in middle school where they'd learned that someone—Eskimos, maybe?—believed stars were holes in the sky where people who'd died could peek through at you. It was supposed to be comforting, but Josie had always found it a little creepy, as if it meant she was being spied on.

It also made her think of a really dumb joke about a guy walking past a mental institution with a high fence, who hears the patients chanting *Ten! Ten! Ten!* and goes to peek through a hole in the fence to see what's going on . . . only to get poked in the eye with a stick and hear the patients chant *Eleven! Eleven! Eleven!*

Matt had told her that joke.

Maybe she'd even laughed.

Here's what the Eskimos don't tell you: Those people on the other side, they have to go out of their way to watch you. But you can see *them* any old time. All you have to do is close your eyes.

*   *   *

On the morning of her son's murder trial, Lacy picked a black skirt out of her closet, along with a black blouse and black stockings. She dressed like she was headed to a funeral, but maybe that wasn't so far off the mark. She ripped three pairs of hose because her hands were shaking, and finally decided to go without. By the end of the day her shoes would rub blisters on her feet, and Lacy thought maybe this was a good thing; maybe she could concentrate instead on a pain that made perfect sense.

She did not know where Lewis was; if he was even going to the trial today. They hadn't really spoken since the day she had tracked him to the graveyard, and he had taken to sleeping in Joey's bedroom. Neither one of them went into Peter's.

But this morning, she forced herself to turn left instead of right at the landing, and she opened the door of Peter's bedroom. After the police had come, she had put it back in some semblance of order, telling herself that she didn't want Peter to come home to a place that had been ransacked. There were still gaping holes—the desk looked naked without its computer, the bookshelves half empty. She walked up to one and pulled down a paperback. *The Picture of Dorian Gray*, by Oscar Wilde. Peter had been reading it for English class when he was arrested. She wondered if he'd had the time to finish.

Dorian Gray had a portrait that grew old and evil while he remained young and innocent-looking. Maybe the quiet, reserved mother who would testify for her son had a portrait somewhere that was ravaged with guilt, twisted with pain. Maybe the woman in that picture was allowed to cry and scream, to break down, to grab her son's shoulders and say *What have you done?*

She startled at the sound of someone opening the door. Lewis stood on the threshold, wearing the suit that he kept for conferences and college graduations. He was holding a blue silk tie in his hand and did not speak.

Lacy took the tie out of Lewis's hand and walked behind him. She noosed it around his neck, gently pulled the knot into place, and flipped down the collar. As she did, Lewis reached for her hand and didn't let go.

There weren't words, really, for moments like this—when you realized that you'd lost one child and the other was slipping out of your reach. Still holding Lacy's hand, Lewis led her out of Peter's room. He closed the door behind them.

At 6:00 a.m., when Jordan crept downstairs to read through his notes in preparation for the trial, he found a single place setting at the table: a bowl, a spoon, and a box of Cocoa Krispies—the meal he always used to kick off a battle. Grinning—Selena must have gotten up in the middle of the night to do this, since they'd headed up to bed together last night—he sat down and poured himself a healthy serving, then went into the fridge for the milk.

A Post-it note had been stuck to the carton. GOOD LUCK.

Just as Jordan sat down to eat, the telephone rang. He grabbed it—Selena and the baby were still asleep. "Hello?"

"Dad?"

"Thomas," he said. "What are you doing up at this hour?"

"Well, um, I sort of didn't go to bed yet."

Jordan smiled. "Ah, to be young and collegiate again."

"Anyway, I just called to wish you luck. It starts today, right?"

He looked down at his cereal and suddenly remembered the footage taken by the cafeteria video camera at Sterling High: Peter sitting down, just like this, to have a bowl of cereal, dead students flanking him. Jordan pushed the bowl away. "Yes," he said. "It does."

*   *   *

The correctional officer opened up Peter's cell and handed him a stack of folded clothes. "Time for the ball, Cinderella," he said.

Peter waited until he left. He knew his mother had bought these for him; she'd even left the tags on so that he could see they hadn't come from Joey's closet. They were preppy, the kind of clothes he imagined were worn to polo matches—not that he'd ever actually been to one to see.

Peter stripped out of his jumpsuit and pulled on the boxer shorts, the socks. He sat down on his bunk to pull up his trousers, which were a little tight at the waist. He buttoned the shirt wrong the first time and had to do it over. He didn't know how to do his tie right. He rolled it up and stuffed it into his pocket so that Jordan could help him.

There wasn't a mirror in his cell, but Peter imagined he looked ordinary now. If you beamed him from this jail into a crowded New York street or into the stands of a football game, people probably wouldn't glance twice at him; wouldn't realize that underneath all that washed wool and Egyptian cotton was someone they'd never imagine. Or in other words, after all this, nothing had changed.

He was about to leave the cell when he realized he had not been given a bulletproof vest, as he had for the arraignment. It probably wasn't because he was any less hated now; more likely, it had been an oversight. He started to ask the guard about it, but then snapped his mouth shut.

Maybe, for the first time in his life, Peter had gotten lucky.

Alex dressed like she was going to work, which she was, except not as a judge. She wondered what it would be like to sit in court in the role of civilian. She wondered if the grieving mother from the arraignment would be there.

She knew it was going to be hard to listen to this trial, and to understand all over again how close she had come to losing Josie. Alex was through pretending that she was listening only because it was her job; she was listening because she had to. One day Josie would remember and would need someone to hold her upright; and since Alex hadn't been there the first time to protect Josie, she'd bear witness now.

She hurried downstairs and found Josie sitting at the kitchen table, dressed in a skirt and blouse. "I'm going," she announced.

It was déjà vu—this was exactly what had happened the day of Peter's arraignment, except that seemed so long ago, and she and Josie had both been very different people back then. Today, she was on the defense's witness list, but she hadn't been served with a subpoena, which meant that she didn't actually have to be in the courthouse at all during the trial.

"I know I can't go in, but Patrick's sequestered, too, isn't he?"

The last time Josie had asked to go to court, Alex had flatly refused. This time, though, she sat down across from Josie. "Do you have any idea what it's going to be like? There are going to be cameras, lots of them. And kids in wheelchairs. And angry parents. And Peter."

Josie's gaze fell into her lap like a stone. "You're trying to keep me from going again."

"No, I'm trying to keep you from getting hurt."

"I *didn't* get hurt," Josie said. "That's why I have to go."

Five months ago, Alex had made this decision for her daughter. Now she knew that Josie deserved to speak for herself. "I'll meet you in the car," she said calmly. She held this mask until Josie closed the door behind herself, and then bolted upstairs to the bathroom and got sick.

She was afraid that reliving the shooting, even from a distance, would rattle Josie past the point of recovery. But mostly she worried that for the second time, she would be powerless to keep her daughter from being hurt.

Alex rested her forehead against the cool porcelain lip of the bathtub. Then, standing, she brushed her teeth and splashed her face with water. She hurried to the car, where her daughter was already waiting.

Because the sitter was late, Jordan and Selena found themselves fighting the crowd on the courtroom steps. Selena had been expecting it—and still wasn't entirely prepared for the hordes of reporters, the television vans, the spectators holding up their camera phones to capture a snapshot of the melee.

Jordan was playing the villain today—the vast majority of the onlookers were from Sterling, and since Peter would be transported to the court via underground tunnel, Jordan was their fall guy. "How do you sleep at night?" a woman shouted as Jordan hurried up the steps past her. Another held up a sign: *There's still a death penalty in NH.*

"Ooh boy," Jordan said under his breath. "This is gonna be a fun one."

"You'll be fine," Selena replied.

But he had stopped moving. There was a man standing on the steps holding up a piece of posterboard with two large mounted photos—one of a girl, one of a pretty woman. Kaitlyn Harvey, Selena realized, recognizing the face. And her mother. At the top of the display were two words: NINETEEN MINUTES.

Jordan met the man's gaze. Selena knew what he was thinking—that this could be him, that he had just as much to lose. "I'm sorry," Jordan murmured, and Selena looped her arm through his and pulled him up the stairs again.

There was a different crowd up here, though. They wore startling yellow shirts with BVA printed across the chest, and they were chanting: "Peter, you are not alone. Peter, you are not alone."

Jordan leaned closer to her. "What the fuck is this?"

"The Bullied Victims of America."

"You must be joking," Jordan said. "They exist?"

"You better believe it," Selena said.

Jordan started to smile for the first time since they'd started driving to court. "And you found them for us?"

Selena squeezed his arm. "You can thank me later," she said.

His client looked like he was going to faint. Jordan nodded at the deputy who let him into the holding cell where Peter was being kept at the courthouse, and then sat down. "Breathe," he commanded.

Peter nodded and filled up his lungs. He was shaking. Jordan had expected this, had seen it at the start of every trial he'd ever been a part of. Even the most hardened criminal suddenly panicked when he realized that this was the day his life was on the line. "I've got something for you," Jordan said, and he took a pair of glasses out of his pocket.

They were thick and tortoiseshell, Coke-bottle glasses, very different from the thin wire ones Peter usually wore. "I don't," Peter said, and then his voice cracked. "I don't need new ones."

"Well, take them anyway."

"Why?"

"Because everyone will notice these on your face," Jordan said. "I want you to look like someone who could never in a million years see well enough to shoot ten people."

Peter's hands curled around the metal edge of the bench. "Jordan? What's going to happen to me?"

There were some clients you had to lie to, just so that they'd get through the trial. But at this point, Jordan thought he owed Peter the truth. "I don't know, Peter. You haven't got a great case, because of all the evidence against you. The likelihood of you being acquitted is slim, but I'm still going to do whatever I can for you. Okay?" Peter nodded. "All I want you to do is try to be quiet out there. Look pathetic."

Peter bowed his head, his face contorting. *Yes, just like that*, Jordan thought, and then he realized that Peter had started to cry.

Jordan walked toward the front of the cell. This, too, was a familiar moment for him as a defense attorney. Jordan usually allowed his client to have this final breakdown in private before they went into the courtroom. It was none of his business, and to be honest, Jordan was all about business. But he could hear Peter sobbing behind him; and in that sad song was one note that reached right down into Jordan. Before he could think better of it, he had turned around and was sitting on the bench again. He wrapped an arm around Peter, felt the boy relax against him. "It's going to be okay," he said, and he hoped he was not lying.

Diana Leven surveyed the packed gallery, then asked a bailiff to turn off the lights. She pushed the button on her laptop, beginning her PowerPoint presentation.

The screen beside Judge Wagner filled with an image of Sterling High School. There was a blue sky in the background and some cotton-candy clouds. A flag snapped in the wind. Three school buses were lined up like a caravan in the front circle. Diana let this picture stand alone, in silence, for fifteen seconds.

The courtroom grew so quiet you could hear the hum of the transcriptionist's laptop.

Oh, God, Jordan thought. *I have to sit through this for the next three weeks.*

"This is what Sterling High School looked like on March 6, 2007. It was 7:50 a.m., and school had just started. Courtney Ignatio was in chemistry class, taking a quiz. Whit Obermeyer was in the main office getting a late pass, because he'd had car trouble that morning. Grace Murtaugh was leaving the nurse's office, where she'd taken some Tylenol for a headache. Matt Royston was in history class with his best friend, Drew Girard. Ed McCabe was writing homework on the blackboard for the math classes he taught. There was nothing to suggest to any of these people or any other members of the Sterling High School community at 7:50 a.m. on March sixth that this was anything other than a typical school day."

Diana clicked a button, and a new photo appeared: Ed McCabe, lying on the floor with his intestines spilling out of his stomach as a sobbing student pressed both hands against the gaping wound. "This is what Sterling High School looked like at 10:19 a.m. on March 6, 2007. Ed McCabe never got to give his homework assignment to his math class, because nineteen minutes earlier, Peter Houghton, a seventeen-year-old junior at Sterling High School, burst through the doors with a knapsack that contained four guns—two sawed-off shotguns, as well as two fully loaded, semiautomatic 9-millimeter pistols."

Jordan felt a tug on his arm. "Jordan," Peter whispered.

"Not now."

"But I'm going to be sick . . ."

"Swallow it," Jordan ordered.

Diana flicked back to the previous slide, the picture-perfect image of Sterling High. "I told you, ladies and gentlemen, that none of the people in Sterling High School had any inclination this would be something other than a typical school day. But one person *did* know that it was going to be different." She walked toward the defense table and pointed directly at Peter, who stared steadfastly down at his lap. "On the morning of March 6, 2007, Peter Houghton started his day by loading a blue knapsack with four guns and the makings of a bomb, plus enough ammunition to potentially kill one hundred and ninety-eight people. The evidence will show that when he arrived at the school, he set up this bomb in Matt Royston's car to divert attention away from himself. While it exploded, he walked up the front steps of the school and shot Zoe Patterson. Then, in the hallway, he shot Alyssa Carr. He made his way to the cafeteria and shot Angela Phlug and Maddie Shaw—his first casualty—and Courtney Ignatio. As students started running away, he shot Haley Weaver and Brady Pryce, Natalie Zlenko, Emma Alexis, Jada Knight, and Richard Hicks. Then, as the wounded were sobbing and dying all around him, do you know what Peter Houghton did? He sat down in the cafeteria and he had a bowl of Rice Krispies."

Diana let this information sink in. "When he finished, he picked up his gun and left the cafeteria, shooting Jared Weiner, Whit Obermeyer, and Grace Murtaugh in the hall, and Lucia Ritolli—a French teacher trying to shepherd her students to safety. He stopped off in the boys' bathroom and shot Steven Babourias, Min Horuka, and Topher McPhee; and then went into the girls' bathroom and shot Kaitlyn Harvey. He continued upstairs and shot Ed McCabe, the math teacher, John Eberhard, and Trey MacKenzie before reaching the gym and firing at Austin Prokiov, Coach Dusty Spears, Noah James, Justin Friedman, and Drew Girard. Finally, in the locker room, the defendant shot Matthew Royston twice—once in the stomach, and again in the head. You might remember that name—it's the owner of the car that Peter Houghton bombed at the very beginning of his rampage."

Diana faced the jury. "This entire spree lasted nineteen minutes in the life of Peter Houghton, but the evidence will show that its effects will last forever. And there's a lot of evidence, ladies and gentlemen. There are a lot of witnesses, and there's a lot of testimony to come . . . but by the end of this trial, you will be convinced beyond a reasonable doubt that Peter Houghton purposefully and knowingly, with premeditation, caused the deaths of ten people and attempted to cause the deaths of nineteen others at Sterling High School."

She walked toward Peter. "In nineteen minutes, you can mow the front lawn, color your hair, watch a third of a hockey game. You can bake scones or get a tooth filled by a dentist. You can fold laundry for a family of five. Or, as Peter Houghton knows . . . in nineteen minutes, you can bring the world to a screeching halt."

Jordan walked toward the jury, his hands in his pockets. "Ms. Leven told you that on the morning of March 6, 2007, Peter Houghton walked into Sterling High School with a knapsack full of loaded weapons, and he shot a lot of people. Well, she's right. The evidence is going to show that, and we don't dispute it. We know that it's a tragedy for both the people who died and those who will live with the aftermath. But here's what Ms. Leven *didn't* tell you: when Peter walked into Sterling High School that morning, he had no intention of becoming a mass murderer. He walked in intending to defend himself from the abuse he'd suffered for twelve straight years.

"On Peter's first day of school," Jordan continued, "his mother put him on the kindergarten bus with a brand-new Superman lunch box. By the end of the ride to the school, that lunch box had been thrown out the window. Now, all of us have childhood memories of other kids teasing us or being cruel, and most of us are able to shake that off, but Peter Houghton's life wasn't one where these things happened occasionally. From that very first day in kindergarten, Peter experienced a daily barrage of taunting, tormenting, threatening, and bullying. This child has been stuffed into lockers, had his head shoved into toilets, been tripped and punched and kicked. He has had a private email spammed out to an entire school. He's had his pants pulled down in the middle of the cafeteria. Peter's reality was a world where, no matter what he did—no matter how small and insignificant he made himself—he was still always the victim. And as a result, he started to turn to an alternate world: one created by himself in the safety of HTML code. Peter set up his own website, created video games, and filled them with the kind of people he wished were surrounding him."

Jordan ran his hand along the railing of the jury box. "One of the witnesses you're going to hear from is Dr. King Wah. He's a forensic psychiatrist who's examined Peter and has spoken with him. He's going to explain to you that Peter was suffering from an illness called post-traumatic stress disorder. It's a complicated medical diagnosis, but it's a real one—and children who have it can't distinguish between an immediate threat and a distant threat. Even though you and I might be able to walk down the hall and spy a bully who's paying no attention to us, Peter would see that same person and his heart rate would speed up . . . his body would sidle a little closer to the wall . . . because Peter was sure he'd be noticed, threatened, beaten, and hurt. Dr. Wah will not only tell you about studies that have been done on children like Peter, he'll tell you how Peter was directly affected by the years and years of torment at the hands of the Sterling High School community."

Jordan faced the jurors again. "Do you remember earlier this week, when we were talking to you about whether you'd be an appropriate juror to sit on this case? One of the things I asked each and every one of you during that process was whether you understood that you needed to listen to the evidence in the courtroom and apply the law as the judge instructs you. As much as we learned from civics class in eighth grade or *Law & Order* on Wednesday-night TV . . . until you're here listening to the evidence and hearing the instructions of the court, you don't know what the rules really are."

He held the gaze of each juror in turn. "For example, when most people hear the term *self-defense*, they assume it means that someone is holding up a gun, or a knife to the throat—that there's an immediate physical threat. But in this case, self-defense may not mean what you think. And what the evidence will show, ladies and gentlemen, is that the person who walked into Sterling High and fired all those shots was not a premeditated, cold-blooded killer, as the prosecution wants you to believe." Jordan walked behind the defense table and put his hands on Peter's shoulders. "He was a very scared boy who had asked for protection . . . and had never received it."

Zoe Patterson kept biting her nails, even though her mother had told her not to do that; even though a zillion pairs of eyes and (holy cow) television cameras were focused on her as she sat on the witness stand. "What did you have after French class?" the prosecutor asked. She'd already gone through her name, address, and the beginning of that horrible day.

"Math, with Mr. McCabe."

"Did you go to class?"

"Yes."

"And what time did that class start?"

"Nine-forty," Zoe said.

"Did you see Peter Houghton at all before math class?"

She couldn't help it, she let her glance slide toward Peter sitting at the defense table. Here was the weird thing—she had been a freshman last year and didn't know him at all. And even now, even after he'd *shot* her, if she'd walked down a street and passed him, she didn't think she would have recognized him.

"No," Zoe said.

"Anything unusual happen at math class?"

"No."

"Did you stay for the entire period?"

"No," Zoe said. "I had an orthodontist appointment at ten-fifteen, so I left a little before ten to sign out in the office and wait for my mom."

"Where was she going to meet you?"

"On the front steps. She was just going to drive up."

"Did you sign out of school?"

"Yes."

"Did you go to the front steps?"

"Yes."

"Was anyone else out there?"

"No. Class was in session."

She watched the prosecutor pull out a big overhead photograph of the school and the parking lot, the way it used to be. Zoe had driven by the construction, and now there was a big fence around the entire area. "Can you show me where you were standing?" Zoe pointed. "Let the record show that the witness pointed to the front steps of Sterling High," Ms. Leven said. "Now, what happened while you were standing and waiting for your mother?"

"There was an explosion."

"Did you know where it came from?"

"Somewhere behind the school," Zoe said, and she glanced at that big poster again, as if it might even now just detonate.

"What happened next?"

Zoe rubbed her hand over her leg. "He . . . he came around the side of the school and started to come up the steps . . ."

"By 'he,' do you mean the defendant, Peter Houghton?"

Zoe nodded, swallowing. "He came up the steps and I looked at him and he . . . he pointed a gun and shot me." She was blinking too fast now, trying not to cry.

"Where did he shoot you, Zoe?" the prosecutor asked gently.

"In the leg."

"Did Peter say anything to you before he shot you?"

"No."

"Did you know who he was at that point in time?"

Zoe shook her head. "No."

"Did you recognize his face?"

"Yes, from around school and all . . ."

Ms. Leven turned her back to the jury and gave Zoe a little wink, which made her feel better. "What kind of gun was he using, Zoe? Was it a small gun he held in one hand, or a big gun that he carried with two hands?"

"A small gun."

"How many times did he shoot?"

"One."

"Did he say anything after he shot you?"

"I don't remember," Zoe said.

"What did you do?"

"I wanted to get away from him, but my leg felt like it

was on fire. I tried to run but I couldn't do it—I just sort of crumpled and fell down the stairs, and then I couldn't move my arm either."

"What did the defendant do?"

"He went into the school."

"Did you see which way he went?"

"No."

"How's your leg now?" the prosecutor asked.

"I still need a cane," Zoe said. "I got an infection because the bullet blew fabric from my jeans into my leg. The tendon's attached to the scar tissue, and that's still really sensitive. The doctors don't know if they want to do another surgery, because it might do more damage."

"Zoe, were you on a sports team last year?"

"Soccer," she said, and she looked down at her leg. "Today they start practice for the season."

Ms. Leven turned to the judge. "Nothing further," she said. "Zoe, Mr. McAfee might have a few questions for you."

The other lawyer stood up. Zoe was nervous about this part, because even though she'd gotten to rehearse with the prosecutor, she had no idea what Peter's attorney would ask. It was like any other exam; she wanted to have the right answers. "When Peter was holding the gun, he was about three feet away from you?" the lawyer asked.

"Yes."

"He didn't look like he was running right toward you, did he?"

"I guess not."

"He looked like he was just trying to run up the stairs, right?"

"Yeah."

"And you were just waiting on the stairs, correct?"

"Yes."

"So it's fair to say that you were in the wrong place at the wrong time?"

"Objection," Ms. Leven said.

The judge—a big man with a mane of white hair who sort of scared Zoe—shook his head. "Overruled."

"No further questions," the lawyer said, and then Ms. Leven rose again. "After Peter went inside," she asked, "what did you do?"

"I started screaming for help." Zoe looked into the gallery, trying to find her mother. If she looked at her mother, then she could say what she had to say next, because it was already over and that was what you had to keep remembering, no matter how much it felt like it wasn't. "At first nobody came," Zoe murmured. "And then . . . then *everybody* did."

Michael Beach had seen Zoe Patterson leaving the room where the witnesses were sequestered. It was a weird collection of kids—everyone from losers like himself to popular kids like Brady Pryce. Even stranger, no one seemed to be inclined to break into their usual pods—the geeks in one corner, the jocks in another, and so on. Instead, they'd all just sat down next to each other at the one long conference table. Emma Alexis—who was one of the cool, beautiful girls—was now paralyzed from the waist down, and she rolled her wheelchair up right beside Michael. She'd asked him if she could have half of his glazed donut.

"When Peter first came into the gym," the prosecutor asked, "what did he do?"

"Wave a gun around," Michael said.

"Could you see what kind of gun it was?"

"Well, like a smallish one."

"A handgun?"

"Yes."

"Did he say anything?"

Michael glanced at the defense table. "He said 'All you jocks, front and center.'"

"What happened?"

"A kid started to run toward him, like he was going to take him down."

"Who was that?"

"Noah James. He's—he *was*—a senior. Peter shot him, and he just collapsed."

"Then what happened?" the prosecutor asked.

Michael took a deep breath. "Peter said, 'Who's next?' and my friend Justin grabbed me and started dragging me to the door."

"How long had you and Justin been friends?"

"Since third grade," Michael said.

"And then?"

"Peter must have seen something moving, so he turned around and he just started to shoot."

"Did he hit you?"

Michael shook his head and pressed his lips together.

"Michael," the prosecutor said gently, "who *did* he hit?"

"Justin got in front of me when the shooting started. And then he . . . he fell down. There was blood everywhere and I was trying to stop it, like they do on TV, by pushing on his stomach. I wasn't paying any attention to anything anymore, except Justin, and then all of a sudden I felt a gun press up against my head."

"What happened?"

"I closed my eyes," Michael said. "I thought he was going to kill me."

"And then?"

"I heard this noise, and when I opened my eyes, he was pulling out the thing that had all the bullets in it and jamming in another one."

The prosecutor walked up to a table and held up a gun clip. Just seeing it in her hand made Michael shudder. "Is this what went into the gun?" she asked.

"Yes."

"What happened after that?"

"He didn't shoot me," Michael said. "Three people ran across the gym, and he followed them into the locker room."

"And Justin?"

"I watched it," Michael whispered. "I watched his face while he died."

It was the first thing he saw in the morning when he awakened, and the last thing he saw before he went to bed: that moment where the shine in Justin's eyes just dulled. When the life left a person, it wasn't by degrees. It was instant, like someone pulling down a shade on a window.

The prosecutor came closer. "Michael," she said, "you all right?"

He nodded.

"Were you and Justin jocks?"

"Not even close," he admitted.

"Were you part of the popular crowd?"

"No."

"Had you and Justin ever been bullied by anyone in school?"

Michael glanced, for the first time, at Peter Houghton. "Who hasn't?" he said.

As Lacy waited for her turn to speak on Peter's behalf, she thought back to the first time she realized she could hate her own child.

Lewis had a bigwig economist from London coming to dinner, and in preparation, Lacy had taken the day off work to clean. Although she had no doubts about her prowess as a midwife, the nature of her work meant that toilets didn't get cleaned on a regular basis; that dust bunnies bloomed beneath the furniture. Usually, she didn't care—she thought a house that was lived in was preferential to one that was sterile—unless company was coming over; then pride kicked in. So that morning, she'd gotten up, made breakfast, and had already dusted the living room by the time Peter—a sophomore, then—threw himself angrily into a chair at the kitchen table. "I have no clean underwear," he fumed, although the rule in the house was that when his laundry bin filled, he had to do his own wash— there was so little that Lacy ever asked him to do, she didn't think this one task was unreasonable. Lacy had suggested that he borrow some from his father, but Peter was disgusted by that, and she decided to let him figure it out on his own. She had enough on her plate.

She usually let Peter's room stand in utter pigsty disarray, but as she passed by that morning, she noticed his laundry bin. Well, she was already home working, and he was at school. She could do this one thing for him. By the time Peter got home that day, Lacy had not only vacuumed and scrubbed the floors, cooked a four-course meal, and cleaned the kitchen—she had also washed, dried, and folded three loads of Peter's laundry. They were piled on the bed, clean clothing that covered the entire six-foot span of the mattress, segregated into pants, shirts, undershorts. All he had to do was set them into his closet, his drawers.

Peter arrived, sullen and moody, and immediately hurried upstairs to his room and his computer—the place he spent most of his time. Lacy—arm deep in the toilet, at that point, scouring—waited for him to notice what she'd done for him. But instead, she heard him groan. "*God!* I'm supposed to put all this away?" Then he slammed his bedroom door so loud that the house shook around her.

Suddenly, Lacy couldn't see straight. She had—of her own volition—done something nice for her son—her ridiculously *spoiled* son—and this was how he acted in return? She rinsed off the scrubbing gloves and left them in the sink. Then she stomped upstairs to Peter's room and threw open the door. "*What* is your problem?"

Peter glared at her. "What's *your* problem? Look at this mess."

Something inside Lacy had snapped like a filament, igniting her. "Mess?" she repeated. "I cleaned *up* the mess. You want to see a mess?" She reached past Peter, knocking over a pile of neatly folded T-shirts. She grabbed his boxer shorts and threw them on the floor. She shoved his pants off the bed, hurled them at his computer, so that his tower of CD-ROMs fell over and the silver disks scattered. "I hate you!" Peter yelled, and without missing a beat, Lacy yelled back, "I hate you, too!" Only then did she realize that she and Peter were now the same height; that she was arguing with a child who stood eye-level with her.

She backed out of Peter's room, and he slammed the door behind her. Almost immediately, Lacy burst into tears. She hadn't meant it—of course she hadn't. She loved Peter. She just, at that moment, hated what he'd said; what he'd done. When she knocked, he wouldn't answer. "Peter," she said. "Peter, I'm sorry I said that."

She held her ear to the door, but there was no sound coming from the inside. Lacy had gone back downstairs and finished cleaning the bathroom. She had moved like a zombie through dinner, making conversation with the economist without really knowing what she was saying. Peter had not joined them. She did not see him, in fact, until the next morning, when Lacy went to wake him up and found his room already empty—and spotless. The clothes had been refolded and placed in their drawers. The bed was made. The CDs organized again, in their tower.

Peter was sitting at the kitchen table, eating a bowl of cereal, when Lacy went downstairs. He did not meet her eyes, and she did not meet his—the ground between them was still too tender for that. But she poured him a glass of juice and set it on the table. He said thank you.

They never spoke of what they'd said to each other, and Lacy had vowed to herself that no matter how frustrating it got, being the parent of a teenage boy, no matter how selfish and self-centered Peter became, she would never again let herself reach a point where she truly, viscerally hated her own son.

But as the victims of Sterling High told their stories in a courtroom just down the hall from where Lacy sat, she hoped that she wasn't too late.

At first, Peter didn't recognize her. The girl who was being led up the ramp by a nurse—the girl whose hair had been cropped to fit underneath bandages and whose face was twisted with scar tissue and bone that had been broken and carved away—settled herself inside the witness box in a way that reminded him of fish being introduced to a new tank. They'd swim around the perimeter gingerly, as if they knew they had to assess the dangers of this new place before they could even begin to function.

"Can you state your name for the record?" the prosecutor asked.

"Haley," the girl said softly. "Haley Weaver."

"Last year, you were a senior at Sterling High?"

Her mouth rounded, flattened. The pink scar that curved like the seam on a baseball over her temple grew darker, an angry red. "Yes," she said. She closed her eyes, and a tear slid down her hollow cheek. "I was the homecoming queen." She bent forward, rocking slightly as she cried.

Peter's chest hurt, as if it were going to explode. He thought maybe he would just die on the spot and save everyone the trouble of going through this. He was afraid to look up, because if he did he would have to see Haley Weaver again.

Once, when he was little, he'd been playing with a Nerf football in his parents' bedroom and he knocked over an antique perfume bottle that had belonged to his great-grandmother. It was made out of glass and it broke into pieces. His mother told him she knew it was an accident, and she'd glued it back together. She kept it on her dresser, and every time he passed by he saw the lines. For years, he'd thought that might have been worse than being punished in the first place.

"Let's take a short recess," Judge Wagner said, and Peter let his head sink down to the defense table, a weight too heavy to bear.

The witnesses were sequestered by side, prosecution in one room and defense in another. The policemen had their own room, too. Witnesses were not supposed to see each other, but nobody really noticed if you left to go to the cafeteria to get a cup of coffee or a donut, and Josie had taken to leaving for hours at a time. It was there that she'd run into Haley, who'd been drinking orange juice through a straw. Brady was with her, holding the cup so she could reach it.

They'd been happy to see Josie, but she was glad when they left. It hurt, physically, to have to smile at Haley and pretend that you weren't staring at the pits and gullies of her face. She'd told Josie that she had already had three operations with a plastic surgeon in New York City who had donated his services.

Brady never let go of her hand; sometimes he ran his fingers through her hair. It made Josie want to cry, because she knew that when he looked at Haley, he was still able to see her in a way that no one else would again.

There were others there, too, that Josie hadn't seen since the shooting. Teachers, like Ms. Ritolli and Coach Spears, who came over to say hello. The DJ who ran the radio station at the school, the honors student with the really bad acne. They all cycled through the cafeteria while she sat and nursed a cup of coffee.

She glanced up when Drew flung himself into a chair across from her. "How come you're not in the room with the rest of us?"

"I'm on the defense's list." Or, as she was sure everyone in the other room thought of it, the traitors' side.

"Oh," Drew said, as if he understood, although Josie was sure he didn't. "You ready for this?"

"I don't have to be ready. They're not actually going to call me."

"Then why are you here?"

Before she could answer, Drew waved, and then she realized John Eberhard had arrived. "Dude," Drew said, and John headed toward them. He walked with a limp, she noticed, but he was walking. He leaned down to high-five Drew and when he did, Josie could see the pucker in his scalp where the bullet had entered his head.

"Where have you been?" Drew asked, making room for John to sit down beside him. "I thought I'd see you around this summer, for sure."

He nodded at them. "I'm . . . John."

Drew's smile faded like paint.

"This . . . is . . ."

"This is fucking unbelievable," Drew murmured.

"He can hear you," Josie snapped, and she crouched down in front of John. "Hi, John. I'm Josie."

"*Jooooz.*"

"Right. Josie."

"I'm . . . John," he said.

John Eberhard had played goalie on the all-star state hockey team since his freshman year. Whenever the team won, the coach had always credited John's reflexes.

"*Shoooo,*" he said, and he shuffled his foot.

Josie looked down at the undone Velcro strap of John's sneaker. "There you go," she said, fixing it for him.

Suddenly she could not stand being here, seeing this. "I've got to get back," Josie said, standing up. As she walked away, blindly turning the corner, she crashed into someone. "Sorry," she murmured, and then heard Patrick's voice.

"Josie? You all right?"

She shrugged, and then she shook her head.

"That makes two of us."

Patrick was holding a cup of coffee and a donut. "I know," he said. "I'm a walking cliché. You want it?" He held the pastry out to her, and she took it, even though she wasn't hungry. "You coming or going?"

"Coming," she lied, before she even realized she was doing it.

"Then keep me company for a few minutes." He led her to a table across the room from Drew and John; she could feel them looking at her, wondering why she might be hanging out with a cop. "I hate the waiting part," Patrick said.

"At least you're not nervous about testifying."

"Sure I am."

"Don't you do this all the time?"

Patrick nodded. "But that doesn't make it any easier to get up in front of a room full of people. I don't know how your mom does it."

"So what do you do to get over the stage fright? Imagine the judge in his underwear?"

"Well, not *this* judge," Patrick said, and then, realizing what he'd just implied, he blushed deep red.

"That's probably a good thing," Josie said.

Patrick reached for the donut and took a bite, then handed it back to her. "I just try to tell myself, when I get out there, that I can't get into trouble telling the truth. Then I let Diana do all the work." He took a sip of his coffee. "You need anything? A drink? More food?"

"I'm okay."

"Then I'll walk you back. Come on."

The room for the defense's witnesses was tiny, because there were so few of them. An Asian man Josie had never seen before was sitting with his back to her, typing away at a laptop. There was a woman inside who hadn't been there when Josie left, but Josie couldn't see her face.

Patrick paused in front of the door. "How do you think it's going in court?" she asked.

He hesitated. "It's going."

She slipped past the bailiff who was babysitting them, heading toward the window seat where she'd been curled before, reading. But at the last minute she sat down at the table in the middle of the room. The woman already seated there had her hands folded in front of her and was staring at absolutely nothing.

"Mrs. Houghton," Josie murmured.

Peter's mother turned. "Josie?" She squinted, as if that might bring Josie into better focus.

"I'm so sorry," Josie whispered.

Mrs. Houghton nodded. "Well," she said, and then she just stopped, as if the sentence were no more than a cliff to jump from.

"How are you doing?" Josie immediately wished she could take back her question—how did she *think* Peter's mother was doing, for God's sake? She was probably using all of her self-control right now to keep from dissolving into foam, blowing off into the atmosphere. Which, Josie realized, meant they had something in common.

"I wouldn't have expected to see you here," Mrs. Houghton said softly.

By *here* she didn't mean the courthouse; she meant this room. With the other meager witnesses who had been tapped to stick up for Peter.

Josie cleared her throat, to make way for the words she hadn't said for years, the words she still would have been afraid to use in front of nearly anyone else, for fear of the echo. "He's my friend," she said.

"We started running," Drew said. "It was like this mass exodus. I just wanted to get as far away from the cafeteria as I could, so I headed for the gym. Two of my friends had heard the shots, but they didn't know where they were coming from, so I grabbed them and told them to follow me."

"Who were they?" Leven asked.

"Matt Royston," Drew said. "And Josie Cormier."

At the sound of her daughter's name being spoken aloud, Alex shivered. It made it so . . . real. So *immediate*. Drew had located Alex in the gallery, and was staring right at her when he said Josie's name.

"Where did you go?"

"We figured if we could get to the locker room, we could climb out the window onto the maple tree and we'd be safe."

"Did you get to the locker room?"

"Josie and Matt did," Drew said. "But I got shot."

Alex listened as the prosecutor walked Drew through the extent of his injuries and how they had effectively ended his hockey career. Then she faced him squarely. "Did you know Peter before the day of the shooting?"

"Yes."

"How?"

"We were in the same grade. Everyone knows everyone."

"Were you friends?" Leven asked.

Alex glanced across the aisle at Lewis Houghton. He was sitting directly behind his son, his eyes fixed straight on the bench. Alex had a flash of him, years ago, opening the front door when she'd gone to pick Josie up from a playdate. *Here come da judge,* he'd said, and he laughed at his own joke.

Were you friends?

"No," Drew said.

"Did you have any problems with him?"

Drew hesitated. "No."

"Did you ever get in an argument with him?" Leven asked.

"We probably had a few words," Drew said.

"Did you ever make fun of him?"

"Sometimes. We were just kidding around."

"Did you ever physically attack him?"

"When we were younger, I might have pushed him around a little bit."

Alex looked at Lewis Houghton. His eyes were squeezed shut.

"Have you done that since you've been in high school?"

"Yes," Drew admitted.

"Did you ever threaten Peter with a weapon?"

"No."

"Did you ever threaten to kill him?"

"No . . . we were, you know. Just being kids."

"Thank you." She sat down, and Alex watched Jordan McAfee rise.

He was a good lawyer—better than she would have given him credit for. He put on a fine show—whispering with Peter, putting his hand on the boy's arm when he got upset, taking copious notes on the direct examination and sharing them with his client. He was humanizing Peter, in spite of the fact that the prosecution was making him out to be a monster, in spite of the fact that the defense hadn't even yet begun to have their turn.

"You had no problems with Peter," McAfee repeated.

"No."

"But he had problems with you, didn't he?"

Drew didn't respond.

"Mr. Girard, you're going to have to speak up," Judge Wagner said.

"Sometimes," Drew conceded.

"Have you ever stuck your elbow in Peter's chest?"

Drew's gaze slid sideways. "Maybe. By accident."

"Ah, yes. It's always easy to find yourself sticking out an elbow when you least expect to . . ."

"Objection—"

McAfee smiled. "In fact, it wasn't an accident, was it, Mr. Girard?"

At the prosecutor's table, Diana Leven raised her pen and dropped it on the floor. The noise made Drew glance over, and a muscle flexed in his jaw. "We were just joking around," he said.

"Ever shove Peter into a locker?"

"Maybe."

"Just joking around?" McAfee said.

"Yeah."

"Okay," he continued. "Did you ever trip him?"

"I guess."

"Wait . . . let me guess . . . joke, right?"

Drew glowered. "Yes."

"Actually, you've been doing this sort of stuff as a joke to Peter since you were little kids, right?"

"We just never were friends," Drew said. "He wasn't like us."

"Who's us?" McAfee asked.

Drew shrugged. "Matt Royston, Josie Cormier, John Eberhard, Courtney Ignatio. Kids like that. We had all hung out together for years."

"Did Peter know everyone in that group?"

"It's a small school, sure."

"Does Peter know Josie Cormier?"

In the gallery, Alex drew in her breath.

"Yes."

"Did you ever see Peter talking to Josie?"

"I don't know."

"Well, a month or so before the shooting, when you all were together in the cafeteria, Peter came over to speak to Josie. Can you tell us about that?"

Alex leaned forward on her chair. She could feel eyes on her, hot as the sun in a desert. She realized, from the direction, that now Lewis Houghton was staring at *her*.

"I don't know what they were talking about."

"But you were there, right?"

"Yes."

"And Josie's a friend of yours? Not one of the people who hung out with Peter?"

"Yeah," Drew said. "She's one of us."

"Do you remember how that conversation in the cafeteria ended?" McAfee asked.

Drew looked down at the ground.

"Let me help you, Mr. Girard. It ended with Matt Royston walking behind Peter and pulling his pants down while he was trying to speak to Josie Cormier. Does that sound about right?"

"Yes."

"The cafeteria was packed with kids that day, wasn't it?"

"Yeah."

"And Matt didn't just pull down Peter's pants . . . he pulled down his underwear too, correct?"

Drew's mouth twitched. "Yeah."

"And you saw all of this."

"Yes."

McAfee turned to the jury. "Let me guess," he said. "Joke, right?"

The courtroom had gone utterly silent. Drew was glaring at Diana Leven, subliminally begging to be dragged off the witness stand, Alex assumed. This was the first person, other than Peter, who had been offered up for sacrifice.

Jordan McAfee walked back to the table where Peter sat and picked up a piece of paper. "Do you remember what day Peter was pantsed, Mr. Girard?"

"No."

"Let me show you, then, Defense Exhibit One. Do you recognize this?"

He handed the piece of paper to Drew, who took it and shrugged.

"This is a piece of email that you received on February third, two days before Peter was pantsed in the Sterling High School cafeteria. Can you tell us who sent it to you?"

"Courtney Ignatio."

"Was it a letter that had been written to her?"

"No," Drew said. "It had been written to Josie."

"By whom?" McAfee pressed.

"Peter."

"What did he say?"

"It was about Josie. And how he was into her."

"You mean romantically."

"I guess," Drew said.

"What did you do with that email?"

Drew looked up. "I spammed it out to the student body."

"Let me get this straight," McAfee said. "You took a very private note that didn't belong to you, a piece of paper with Peter's deepest, most secret feelings, and you forwarded this to every kid at your school?"

Drew was silent.

Jordan McAfee slapped the email down on the railing in front of him. "Well, Drew?" he said. "Was it a good joke?"

Drew Girard was sweating so much that he couldn't believe all those people weren't pointing at him. He could feel the perspiration running between his shoulder blades and making looped circles beneath his arms. And why not? That bitch of a prosecutor had left him in the hot seat. She'd let him get skewered by this dickwad attorney, so that now, for the rest of his life, everyone would think he was an asshole when he—like every other kid in Sterling High—had just been having a little fun.

He stood up, ready to bolt out of the courtroom and possibly run all the way to the town boundary of Sterling— but Diana Leven was walking toward him. "Mr. Girard," she said, "I'm not quite finished."

He sank back into his seat, deflated.

"Have you ever called anyone other than Peter Houghton names?"

"Yes," he said warily.

"It's what guys do, right?"

"Sometimes."

"Did anyone you ever called names ever shoot you?"

"No."

"Ever seen anyone other than Peter Houghton be pantsed?"

"Sure," Drew said.

"Did any of those other kids who were pantsed ever shoot you?"

"No."

"Ever spammed anyone else's email out as a joke?"

"Once or twice."

Diana folded her arms. "Any of those folks ever shoot you?"

"No, ma'am," he said.

She headed back to her seat. "Nothing further."

Dusty Spears understood kids like Drew Girard, because he had once been one. The way he saw it, bullies either were good enough to get football scholarships to Big Ten schools, where they could make the business connections to play on golf courses for the rest of their lives, or they busted their knees and wound up teaching gym at the middle school.

He was wearing a collared shirt and tie, and that pissed him off, because his neck still looked like it had when he was a tight end at Sterling in '88, even if his abs didn't. "Peter wasn't a real athlete," he said to the prosecutor. "I never really saw him outside of class."

"Did you ever see Peter getting picked on by other kids?"

Dusty shrugged. "The usual locker room stuff, I guess."

"Did you intervene?"

"I probably told the kids to knock it off. But it's part of growing up, right?"

"Did you ever hear of Peter threatening anyone else?"

"Objection," said Jordan McAfee. "That's a hypothetical question."

"Sustained," the judge replied.

"If you had heard that, would you have intervened?"

"Objection!"

"Sustained. *Again.*"

The prosecutor didn't miss a beat. "But Peter didn't ask for help, did he?"

"No."

She sat back down, and Houghton's lawyer stood up. He was one of those smarmy guys that rubbed Dusty the wrong way—probably had been a kid who could barely field a ball, but smirked when you tried to teach him how, as if he already knew he'd be making twice as much money as Dusty one day, anyway. "Is there a bullying policy in place at Sterling High?"

"We don't allow it."

"Ah," McAfee said dryly. "Well, that's refreshing to hear. So let's say you witness bullying on an almost daily basis in a locker room right under your nose . . . according to the policy, what are you supposed to do?"

Dusty stared at him. "It's in the policy. Obviously I don't have it right in front of me."

"Luckily, I do," McAfee said. "Let me show you what's been marked as Defense Exhibit Two. Is this the bullying policy for Sterling High School?"

Reaching out, Dusty took a look at the printed page. "Yes."

"You get this in your teacher handbook every year in August, correct?"

"Yes."

"And this is the most recent version, for the academic year of 2006–2007?"

"I assume so," Dusty said.

"Mr. Spears, I want you to go through that policy very carefully—all two pages—and show me where it tells you what to do if you, as a teacher, witness bullying."

Dusty sighed and began to scan the papers. Usually, when he got the handbook, he shoved it in a drawer with his take-out menus. He knew the important things: don't miss an in-service day; submit curriculum changes to the department heads; refrain from being alone in a room with a female student. "It says right here," he said, reading, "that the Sterling School Board is committed to providing a learning and working environment that ensures the personal safety of its members. Physical or verbal threats, harassment, hazing, bullying, verbal abuse, and intimidation will not be tolerated." Glancing up, Dusty said, "Does that answer your question?"

"No, actually, it doesn't. What are you, as a teacher, supposed to do if a student bullies another student?"

Dusty read further. There was a definition of hazing, of bullying, of verbal abuse. There was mention of a teacher or school administrator being reported to, if the behavior had been witnessed by another student. But there was no set of rules, no chain of events to be set in motion by the teacher or administrator himself.

"I can't find it in here," he said.

"Thank you, Mr. Spears," McAfee replied. "That'll be all."

It would have been simple for Jordan McAfee to notice up his intent to call Derek Markowitz to testify, as he was one of the only character witnesses Peter Houghton had, in terms of friends. But Diana knew he had value for the prosecution because of what he had seen and heard—not because of his loyalties. She'd seen plenty of friends rat each other out over the years she'd been in this business.

"So, Derek," Diana said, trying to make him comfortable, "you were Peter's friend."

She watched him lock eyes with Peter and try to smile. "Yes."

"Did you two hang out after school sometimes?"

"Yes."

"What sort of things did you like to do?"

"We were both really into computers. Sometimes we'd play video games, and then we started to learn programming so we could create a few of our own."

"Did Peter ever write any video games without you?" Diana asked.

"Sure."

"What happened when he finished?"

"We'd play them. But there are also websites where you can upload your game and have other people rate them for you."

Derek looked up just then and noticed the television cameras in the back of the room. His jaw dropped, and he froze.

"Derek," Diana said. "Derek?" She waited for him to focus on her. "Let me hand you a CD-ROM. It's marked State's Exhibit 302. . . . Can you tell me what it is?"

"That's Peter's most recent game."

"What's it called?"

"Hide-n-Shriek."

"What's it about?"

"It's one of those games where you go around shooting the bad guys."

"Who are the bad guys in this game?" Diana asked.

Derek darted a glance at Peter again. "They're jocks."

"Where does the game take place?"

"In a school," Derek said.

From the corner of her eye, Diana could see Jordan shifting in his chair. "Derek, were you in school the morning of March 6, 2007?"

"Yeah."

"What was your first-period class that morning?"

"Honors Trig."

"How about second period?" Diana asked.

"English."

"Then where did you go?"

"I had gym third period, but my asthma was pretty bad, so I had a doctor's note to excuse me from class. Since I finished my work early in English, I asked Mrs. Eccles if I could go to my car to get it."

Diana nodded. "Where was your car parked?"

"In the student parking lot, behind the school."

"Can you show me on this diagram which door you used to leave the school at the end of second period?" Derek reached toward the easel and pointed to one of the rear doors of the school. "What did you see when you went outside?"

"Uh, a lot of cars."

"Any people?"

"Yes," Derek said. "Peter. It looked like he was getting something out of the backseat of his car."

"What did you do?"

"I went over to say hi. I asked him why he was late to school, and he stood up and looked at me in a weird way."

"Weird? What do you mean?"

Derek shook his head. "I don't know. Like he didn't know who I was for a second."

"Did he say anything to you?"

"He said, 'Go home. Something's about to happen.'"

"Did you think that was unusual?"

"Well, it was a little bit *Twilight Zone* . . ."

"Had Peter ever said anything like that to you before?"

"Yes," Derek said quietly.

"When?"

Jordan objected, as Diana had expected, and Judge Wagner overruled it, as she'd hoped. "A few weeks before,"

Derek said, "the first time we were playing Hide-n-Shriek."

"What did he say?" Derek looked down and mumbled a response. "Derek," Diana said, coming closer, "I have to ask you to speak up."

"He said, 'When this really happens, it's going to be awesome.'"

A hum rose in the gallery, like a swarm of bees. "Did you know what he meant by that?"

"I thought . . . I thought he was kidding," Derek said.

"The day of the shooting when you found Peter in the parking lot, did you see what he was doing in the car?"

"No . . ." Derek broke off, clearing his throat. "I just sort of laughed off what he said and told him I had to go to class."

"What happened next?"

"I went back into the school through the same door and walked to the office to get my gym note signed by Mrs. Whyte, the secretary. She was talking to another girl, who was signing out of school for an orthodontist appointment."

"And then?" Diana asked.

"Once she left, Mrs. Whyte and I heard an explosion."

"Did you see where it was coming from?"

"No."

"What happened after that?"

"I looked at the computer screen on Mrs. Whyte's desk," Derek said. "It was scrolling, like, a message."

"What did it say?"

"*Ready or not . . . here I come.*" Derek swallowed. "We heard these little pops, like lots of champagne bottles, and Mrs. Whyte grabbed me and dragged me into the principal's office."

"Was there a computer in that office?"

"Yes."

"What was on the screen?"

"Ready or not . . . here I come."

"How long were you in the office?"

"I don't know. Ten, twenty minutes. Mrs. Whyte tried to call the police, but she couldn't. There was something wrong with the phone."

Diana faced the bench. "Judge, at this time, the prosecution would like to move State's Exhibit 303 in full, and we ask that it be published to the jury." She watched the deputy wheel out a television monitor with a computer attached, so that the CD-ROM could be inserted.

HIDE-N-SHRIEK, the screen proclaimed. CHOOSE YOUR FIRST WEAPON!

A 3-D animated boy wearing horn-rimmed glasses and a golf shirt crossed the screen and looked down over an array of crossbows, Uzis, AK-47s, and biological weapons. He reached for one, and then with his other hand, he loaded up on ammunition. There was a close-up of his face: freckles; braces; fever in his eyes.

Then the screen went blue and started scrolling.

Ready or not, it read. *Here I come.*

Derek liked Mr. McAfee. He wasn't much to look at, but he had the hottest babe of a wife. Plus, he was probably the only other person in Sterling High who wasn't related to Peter and still felt sorry for him.

"Derek," the lawyer said, "you've been friends with Peter since sixth grade, right?"

"Yes."

"You spent a lot of time with him both in and outside school."

"Yeah."

"Did you ever see Peter getting picked on by other kids?"

"All the time," Derek said. "They'd call us fags and homos. They'd give us wedgies. When we walked down the hall, they'd trip us or slam us into lockers. Things like that."

"Did you ever talk to a teacher about this?"

"I used to, but that just made it worse. I got creamed for being a tattletale."

"Did you and Peter ever talk about getting picked on?"

Derek shook his head. "No. It was kind of nice to have someone around who just *got* it, you know?"

"How often was this happening . . . once a week?"

He snorted. "More like once a *day*."

"Just you and Peter?"

"No, there are others."

"Who did most of the bullying?"

"The jocks," Derek said. "Matt Royston, Drew Girard, John Eberhard . . ."

"Any girls participate in the bullying?"

"Yeah, the ones who looked at us like we were bugs on a windshield," Derek said. "Courtney Ignatio, Emma Alexis, Josie Cormier, Maddie Shaw."

"So what do you do when someone's slamming you into a locker?" Mr. McAfee asked.

"You can't fight back, because you're not as strong as they are, and you can't stop it . . . so you just kind of wait it out."

"Would it be fair to say that this group you named—Matt and Drew and Courtney and Emma and the rest—went after one person more than any others?"

"Yes," Derek said. "Peter."

Derek watched Peter's attorney sit back down next to him, and then the lady lawyer rose and started speaking again. "Derek, you said you were bullied, too."

"Yeah."

"You never helped Peter put together a pipe bomb to blow up someone's car, did you?"

"No."

"You never helped Peter hack into the phone lines and computers at Sterling High, so that once the shooting started, no one could call for help, did you?"

"No," Derek said.

"You never stole guns and hoarded them in your bedroom, did you?"

"No."

The prosecutor took a step closer. "You never put together a plan, like Peter, to go through the school, systematically killing the people who had hurt you the most, did you, Derek?"

Derek turned to Peter, so that he could look him square in the eye when he answered. "No," he said. "But sometimes I wish I had."

From time to time, over the course of her career as a midwife, Lacy had run into a former patient at the grocery store or the bank or on a bike trail. They'd present their babies—now three, seven, fifteen years old. *Look at what a great job you did,* they'd sometimes say, as if bringing the child into the world had anything to do with who he became.

She did not know quite what to feel when confronted with Josie Cormier. They'd spent the day playing hangman—the irony of which, given her son's fate, wasn't lost on her. Lacy had known Josie as a newborn, but also as a little girl and as a playmate for Peter. Because of this, there had been a point where she had viscerally hated Josie in a way that even Peter never seemed to, for being cruel enough to leave her son behind. Josie may not have initiated the teasing that Peter suffered over his middle and high school years, but she didn't intervene either, and in Lacy's book, that had made her equally responsible.

As it turned out, though, Josie Cormier had grown into a stunning young woman, one who was quiet and thoughtful and not at all like the vacuous, material girls who trolled the Mall of New Hampshire or encompassed the social elite of Sterling High—girls Lacy had always likened to black widow spiders, looking for someone they could destroy. Lacy had been surprised when Josie had peppered her with polite questions about Peter: Was he nervous about the trial? Was it hard, being in jail? Did he get picked on there? *You should send him a letter,* Lacy had suggested to her. *I'm sure he'd like to hear from you.*

But Josie had let her glance slide away, and that was when Lacy realized that Josie had not really been interested in Peter; she had only been trying to be kind to Lacy.

When court recessed for the day, the witnesses were told they could go home, provided they did not watch the news or read the papers or speak about the case. Lacy excused herself to go to the bathroom while she waited for Lewis, who'd be fighting the crush of reporters that would surely be packing the lobby outside the courtroom. She had just come out of the stall and was washing her hands when Alex Cormier stepped inside.

The racket in the hallway rode in on her heels, then cut off abruptly as the door shut. Their eyes met in the long mirror over the bank of sinks. "Lacy," Alex murmured.

Lacy straightened and reached for a paper towel to dry her hands. She didn't know what to say to Alex Cormier. She could barely even imagine that at one point, she'd had *anything* to say to her.

There was a spider plant in Lacy's midwifery office that had been dying by degrees, until the secretary moved a stack of books that had been blocking a window. She had forgotten to move the plant, though, and half the shoots started straining toward the light, growing in an unlikely sideways direction that seemed to defy gravity. Lacy and Alex were like that plant: Alex had moved off on a different course, and Lacy—well, she hadn't. She'd withered up, wilted, gotten tangled in her own best intentions.

"I'm sorry," Alex said. "I'm sorry you have to go through this."

"I'm sorry, too," Lacy replied.

Alex looked like she was going to speak again, but she didn't, and Lacy had run out of conversation. She started out of the bathroom to find Lewis, but Alex called her back. "Lacy," she said. "I remember."

Lacy turned around to face her.

"He used to like the peanut butter on the top half of the bread and the marshmallow fluff on the bottom." Alex smiled a little. "And he had the longest eyelashes I'd ever seen on a little boy. He could find anything I'd dropped—an earring, a contact lens, a straight pin—before it got lost permanently."

She took a step toward Lacy. "Something still exists as long as there's someone around to remember it, right?"

Lacy stared at Alex through her tears. "Thank you," she whispered, and left before she broke down completely in front of a woman—a stranger, really—who could do what Lacy couldn't: hold on to the past as if it was something to be treasured, instead of combing it for clues of failure.

"Josie," her mother said as they were driving home. "They read an email today in court. One that Peter had written to you."

Josie faced her, stricken. She should have realized this would come out at the trial; how had she been so stupid? "I didn't know Courtney had sent it out. I didn't even *see* it until after everyone else had."

"It must have been embarrassing," Alex said.

"Well, *yeah*. The whole school knew he had a crush on me."

Her mother glanced at her. "I meant for *Peter*."

Josie thought about Lacy Houghton. Ten years had passed, but Josie had still been surprised by how thin Peter's mom had gotten; how her hair was nearly all gray. She wondered if grief could make time run faster, like a glitch in a clock. It was incredibly depressing, since Josie remembered Peter's mother as someone who never wore a wristwatch, someone who didn't care about the mess if the end result was worthy. When Josie was little and they played over at Peter's, Lacy would make cookies from whatever was left in her cabinet—oatmeal and wheat germ and gummy bears and marshmallows; carob and cornstarch and puffed rice. She once dumped a load of sand in the basement during the winter so that they could make castles. She let them draw on the bread of their sandwiches with food coloring and milk, so that even lunch was a masterpiece. Josie had liked being at Peter's house; it was what she'd always imagined a *family* felt like.

Now she looked out the window. "You think this is all my fault, don't you?"

"No—"

"Is that what the lawyers said today? That the shooting happened because I didn't like Peter . . . the way he liked me?"

"No. The lawyers didn't say that at all. Mostly the defense talked about how Peter got teased. How he didn't have many friends." Her mother stopped at a red light and turned, her wrist resting lightly on the steering wheel. "Why did you stop hanging around with Peter, anyway?"

Being unpopular was a communicable disease. Josie could remember Peter in elementary school, fashioning the tinfoil from his lunch sandwich into a beanie with antennae, and wearing it around the playground to try to pick up radio transmissions from aliens. He hadn't realized that people were making fun of him. He never had.

She had a sudden flash of him standing in the cafeteria, a statue with his hands trying to cover his groin, his pants pooled around his ankles. She remembered Matt's comment afterward: *Objects in mirror are* way *smaller than they appear.*

Maybe Peter *had* finally understood what people thought of him.

"I didn't want to be treated like him," Josie said, answering her mother, when what she really meant was, *I wasn't brave enough.*

Going back to jail was like devolution. You had to relinquish the trappings of humanity—your shoes, your suit and tie—and bend over to be strip-searched, probed with a rubber glove by one of the guards. You were given another prison jumpsuit, and flip-flops that were too wide for your feet, so that you looked just like everyone else again and couldn't pretend to yourself that you were better than them.

Peter lay down on the bunk with his arm flung over his eyes. The inmate beside him, a guy awaiting trial for the rape of a sixty-six-year-old woman, asked him how it had gone in court, but he didn't answer. That was the only freedom he had left, pretty much, and he wanted to keep the truth to himself: that when he'd been put in his cell, he'd actually felt relieved to be back (*could he say it?*) home.

Here, no one was staring at him as if he were a growth on a petri dish. No one really looked at him at all.

Here, no one talked about him as if he were an animal.

Here, no one blamed him, because they were all in the same boat.

Jail wasn't all that different from public school, really. The correctional officers were just like the teachers—their job was to keep everyone in place, to feed them, and to make sure nobody got seriously hurt. Beyond that, you were left to your own devices. And like school, jail was an artificial society, with its own hierarchy and rules. If you did any work, it was pointless—cleaning the toilets every morning or pushing a library cart around minimum security wasn't really that different from writing an essay on the definition of *civitas* or memorizing prime numbers—you weren't going to be using them daily in your real life. And as with high school, the only way to get through jail was to stick it out and do your time.

Not to mention: Peter wasn't popular in jail, either.

He thought about the witnesses that Diana Leven had marched or dragged or wheeled to the stand today. Jordan had explained that it was all about sympathy; that the prosecution wanted to present all these ruined lives before they turned to the hard-core evidence; that he would soon have a chance to show how *Peter's* life had been ruined, too. Peter hardly even cared about that. He'd been more amazed, after seeing those students again, at how little had changed.

Peter stared up at the woven springs of the upper bunk, blinking fast. Then he rolled toward the wall and stuffed the corner of his pillowcase into his mouth, so no one would be able to hear him cry.

Even though John Eberhard couldn't call him a fag anymore, much less speak . . .

Even though Drew Girard would never be the jock that he had been . . .

Even though Haley Weaver wasn't a knockout . . .

They were all still part of a group Peter could not, and would never, fit into.

6:30 A.M., The Day Of

"Peter. Peter?!"

He rolled over to see his father standing on the threshold of his bedroom.

"Are you up?"

Did it *look* like he was up? Peter grunted and rolled onto his back. He closed his eyes again for a moment and ran through his day. *Englishfrenchmathhistorychem.* One big long run-on sentence, one class bleeding into the next.

He sat up, spearing his hands through his hair so that it stood on end. Downstairs, he could hear his father putting away pots and pans from the dishwasher, like some techno-symphony. He'd get his travel mug, pour some coffee, and leave Peter to his own devices.

Peter's pajama bottoms dragged underneath his heels as he shuffled from the bed to his desk and sat down on the chair. He logged onto the Internet, because he wanted to see if anyone out there had given him more feedback on Hide-n-Shriek. If it was as good as he thought it was, he was going to enter it in some kind of amateur competition. There were kids like him all over the country—all over the *world*—who would easily pay $39.99 to play a video game where history was rewritten by the losers. Peter imagined how rich he could get off licensing fees. Maybe he could ditch college, like Bill Gates. Maybe one day people would be calling him, pretending that they used to be his friend.

He squinted, and then reached for his glasses, which he kept next to the keyboard. But because it was freaking six-thirty in the morning, when no one should be expected to have much coordination, he dropped his eyeglass case right on the function keys.

The screen logging him onto the Net minimized, and instead, his Recycle Bin contents opened on the screen.

```
I know you don't think of me.
And you certainly would never picture us together.
```

Peter felt his head start to swim. He punched a finger against the Delete button, but nothing happened.

```
Anyway, by myself, I'm nothing special. But with
you, I think I could be.
```

He tried to restart the computer, but it was frozen. He couldn't breathe; he couldn't move. He couldn't do anything but stare at his own stupidity, right there in black and white.

His chest hurt, and he thought maybe he was having a heart attack, or maybe that was just what it felt like when the muscle turned to stone. With jerky movements, Peter leaned down for the cord of his power strip and instead smacked his head on the side of the desk. It brought tears to his eyes, or that's what he told himself.

He pulled the plug, so that the monitor went black.

Then he sat back down and realized it hadn't made a

difference. He could still see those words, as clear as day, written across the screen. He could feel the give of the keys under his fingers:

```
Love, Peter.
```

He could hear them all laughing.

Peter glanced at his computer again. His mother always said that if something bad happened, you could look at it as a failure, or you could look at it as a chance to head in another direction.

Maybe this had been a sign.

Peter's breathing was shallow as he emptied his school backpack of textbooks and three-ring binders, his calculator and pencils and crumpled tests he'd gotten back. Reaching beneath his mattress, he felt for the two pistols he'd been saving, just in case.

When I was little I used to pour salt on slugs. I liked watching them dissolve before my eyes. Cruelty is always sort of fun until you realize that something's getting hurt.

It would be one thing to be a loser if it meant no one paid attention to you, but in school, it means you're actively sought out. You're the slug, and they're holding all the salt. And they haven't developed a conscience.

There's a word we learned in social studies: schadenfreude. It's when you enjoy watching someone else suffer. The real question, though, is why? I think part of it is just self-preservation. And part of it is because a group always feels more like a group when it's banded together against an enemy. It doesn't matter if that enemy has never done anything to hurt you—you just have to pretend you hate someone even more than you hate yourself.

You know why salt works on slugs? Because it dissolves in the water that's part of a slug's skin, so the water inside its body starts to flow out. The slug dehydrates. This works with snails, too. And with leeches. And with people like me.

With any creature, really, too thin-skinned to stand up for itself.

Five Months After

For four hours on the witness stand, Patrick relived the worst day of his life. The signal that had come through on the radio as he was driving; the stream of students running out of the school, as if it were hemorrhaging; the slip of his shoes in an oily pool of blood as he ran through the corridors. The ceiling, falling down around him. The screams for help. The memories that imprinted on his mind but didn't register until later: a boy dying in the arms of his friend beneath the basketball hoop in the gym; the sixteen kids who were found crammed into a custodial closet three hours after the arrest, because they hadn't known that the threat was over; the licorice smell of the Sharpie markers used to write numbers on the foreheads of the wounded, so that they could be identified later.

That first night, when the only people left in the school were the crime techs, Patrick had walked through the classrooms and the hallways. He felt, sometimes, like the keeper of memories—the one who had to facilitate that invisible transition between the way it used to be and the way it would be from now on. He'd stepped over bloodstains to enter rooms where students had huddled with teachers, waiting to be rescued, their jackets still draped over chairs as if they were about to return at any moment. There were bullet holes chewed into the lockers; yet in the library, some student had both the time and inclination to arrange the media specialist's Gumby and Pokey figures into a compromising position. The fire sprinklers made a sea out of one corridor, but the walls were still plastered with bright posters advertising a spring dance.

Diana Leven held up a videocassette, the state's exhibit number 522. "Can you identify this, Detective?"

"Yes, I took it from the main office of Sterling High. It showed footage from a camera posted in the cafeteria on March 6, 2007."

"Is there an accurate representation on that tape?"

"Yes."

"When was the last time you watched it?"

"The day before this trial started."

"Has it been altered in any way?"

"No."

Diana walked toward the judge. "I ask that this tape be published to the jury," she said, and the same television unit that had been wheeled out earlier in the trial was brought back by a deputy.

The recording was grainy, but still intelligible. In the upper right-hand corner were the lunch ladies, slopping food onto plastic trays as students came through the line one by one, like drops through an intravenous tube. There were tables full of students—Patrick's eye gravitated toward a central one, where Josie was sitting with her boyfriend.

He was eating her French fries.

From the left-hand door, a boy entered. He was wearing a blue knapsack, and although you could not see his face, he had the same slight build and stoop to his shoulders that someone who knew Peter Houghton would recognize. He dipped beneath the range of the camera. A shot rang out as a girl slumped backward off one of the cafeteria chairs, a bloodstain flowering on her white shirt.

Someone screamed, and then everyone was yelling, and there were more shots. Peter reappeared on camera, holding a gun. Students started stampeding, hiding underneath the tables. The soda machine, freckled with bullets, fizzed and sprayed all over the floor. Some students crumpled where they were shot, others who were wounded tried to crawl away. One girl who'd fallen was trampled by the rest of the students and finally lay still. When the only people left in the cafeteria were either dead or wounded, Peter turned in a circle. He moved down an aisle, pausing here and there. He walked up to the table beside Josie's and put his gun down. He opened an untouched box of cereal still on a cafeteria tray, poured the cereal into a plastic bowl, and added milk from a carton. He swallowed five spoonfuls before he stopped eating, took a new clip out of his backpack, loaded it into his gun, and left the cafeteria.

Diana reached beneath the defense table and pulled out a small plastic bag and handed it to Patrick. "Do you recognize this, Detective Ducharme?"

The Rice Krispies box. "Yes."

"Where did you find it?"

"In the cafeteria," he said. "Sitting on the same table you just saw in the video."

Patrick let himself look at Alex, sitting in the gallery. Until now, he couldn't—he didn't think he'd be able to do his job well, if he was worrying about how this information and level of detail were affecting her. Now, glancing at her, he could see how pale she'd gotten, how stiff she was in her chair. It took all of his self-control not to walk away from Diana, hop the bar, and kneel down beside her. *It's all right*, he wanted to say. *It's almost over.*

"Detective," Diana said, "when you cornered the defendant in the locker room, what was he holding?"

"A handgun."

"Did you see any other weapons around him?"

"Yes, a second handgun, around ten feet away."

Diana lifted up a picture that had been enlarged. "Do you recognize this?"

"It's the locker room where Peter Houghton was apprehended." He pointed to a gun on the floor near the lockers, and then another a short distance away. "This is the weapon he dropped, Gun A," Patrick said, "and this one, Gun B, is the other one that was on the floor."

About ten feet past that, on the same linear path, was the body of Matt Royston. A wide pool of blood spread beneath his hip, and the top half of his head was missing.

There were gasps from the jury, but Patrick wasn't paying attention. He was staring right at Alex, who was not looking at Matt's body but at the spot beside it—a streak of blood from Josie's forehead, where she had been found.

Life was a series of ifs—a very different outcome if you'd only played the lottery last night; if you had picked a different college; if you had invested in stocks instead of bonds; if you had not been taking your kindergartner to his first day of school the morning of 9/11. If just one teacher had stopped a kid, once, from tormenting Peter in the hall. If Peter had put the gun in his mouth, instead of pointing it at someone else. If Josie had been standing in front of Matt, she might have been the one buried in the cemetery. If Patrick had been a second later, she still might have been shot. If he hadn't been the detective on this case, he would not have met Alex.

"Detective, did you collect these weapons?"

"Yes."

"Were they tested for fingerprints?"

"Yes, by the state crime lab."

"Did the lab find any fingerprints of value on Gun A?"

"Yes, one, on the grip."

"Where did they obtain the fingerprints of Peter Houghton?"

"From the station, when we booked him."

He walked the jury through the mechanics of fingerprint testing—the comparison of ten loci, the similarity in ridges and whorls, the computer program that verified the prints as a match.

"Did the lab compare the fingerprint on Gun A to any other person's fingerprints?" Diana asked.

"Yes, Matt Royston's. They were obtained from his body."

"When the lab collected the print off the gun's grip and compared it to Matt Royston's fingerprints, were they able to determine whether or not there was a match?"

"There was no match."

"And when the lab compared it to Peter Houghton's fingerprints, were they able to determine whether or not there was a match?"

"Yes," Patrick said. "There was."

Diana nodded. "What about on Gun B? Any prints?"

"Just a partial one, on the trigger. Nothing of value."

"What does that mean, exactly?"

Patrick turned to the jury. "A print of value in fingerprint typing is one that can be compared to another known print and either excluded or included as a match to that print. People leave fingerprints on items they touch all the time, but not necessarily ones we can use. They might be smudged or too incomplete to be considered forensically valuable."

"So, Detective, you don't know for a fact who left the fingerprint on Gun B."

"No."

"But it *could* have been Peter Houghton?"

"Yes."

"Do you have any evidence that anyone else at Sterling High School was carrying a weapon that day?"

"No."

"How many weapons were eventually found in the locker room?"

"Four," Patrick said. "One handgun with the defendant, one on the floor, and two sawed-off shotguns in a knapsack."

"In addition to processing the weapons found in the locker room for fingerprints, did the lab do any other forensic testing on them?"

"Yes, a ballistics test."

"Can you explain that?"

"Well," Patrick said, "you shoot the gun into water, basically. Every bullet that comes out of a gun has markings on it that are put in place when a bullet twists its way through the barrel of the gun. That means you can type each bullet to a gun that has been fired by test-firing a gun to see what a bullet would look like once fired from it, and then matching up bullets that have been retrieved. You can also tell whether a gun has ever been fired at all by examining residue within the barrel."

"Did you test all four weapons?"

"Yes."

"And what were the results of your tests?"

"Only two of the four guns were actually fired," Patrick said. "The handguns, A and B. Of the bullets that we found, all were determined to have come from Gun A. Gun B, when we retrieved it, had been jammed with a double feed. That means two bullets had entered the chamber at the same time, which keeps the gun from properly functioning. When the trigger was pulled, it locked up."

"But you said Gun B was fired."

"At least once." Patrick looked up at Diana. "The bullet has not been recovered to date."

Diana Leven led Patrick meticulously through the discovery of ten dead students and nineteen wounded ones. He started with the moment that he walked out of Sterling High with Josie Cormier in his arms and placed her in an ambulance, and ended with the last body being moved to the medical examiner's morgue; then the judge adjourned court for the day.

After he got off the stand, Patrick talked with Diana for a moment about what would happen tomorrow. The double doors of the courtroom were open, and through them, Patrick could see reporters sucking the stories out of any angry parent who was willing to give an interview. He recognized the mother of a girl—Jada Knight—who'd been shot in the back while she was running from the cafeteria. "My daughter won't go to school this year until eleven o'clock, because she can't handle being there when third period starts," the woman said. "Everything scares her. This has ruined her whole life; why should Peter Houghton's punishment be any less?"

He had no desire to run the media gauntlet, and as the only witness for the day, he was bound to be mobbed. So instead, Patrick sat down on the wooden railing that separated the court professionals from the gallery.

"Hey."

He turned at the sound of Alex's voice. "What are you still doing here?" He would have assumed she was upstairs, springing Josie out of the sequestered witness room, as she had done yesterday.

"I could ask you the same thing."

Patrick nodded toward the doorway. "I wasn't in the mood to do battle."

Alex came closer, until she was standing between his legs, and wrapped her arms around him. She buried her face against his neck, and when she took a deep, rattling breath, Patrick felt it in his own chest. "You could have fooled me," she said.

Jordan McAfee was not having a good day. The baby had spit up on him on his way out the door. He had been ten minutes late for court because the goddamn media were multiplying like jackrabbits and there were no parking spots, and Judge Wagner had reprimanded him for his tardiness. Add to this the fact that for whatever reason, Peter had stopped communicating with Jordan except for the odd grunt, and that his first order of the morning would be to cross-examine the knight in shining armor who'd rushed into the school to confront the evil shooter—well, being a defense attorney didn't get much more fabulous than this.

"Detective," he said, approaching Patrick Ducharme on the witness stand, "after you finished with the medical examiner, you went back to the police department?"

"Yes."

"You were holding Peter there, weren't you?"

"Yes."

"In a jail cell . . . with bars and a lock on it?"

"It's a holding cell," Ducharme corrected.

"Had Peter been charged with any crime yet?"

"No."

"He wasn't actually charged with anything until the following morning, is that right?"

"That's correct."

"Where did he stay that night?"

"At the Grafton County Jail."

"Detective, did you speak to my client at all?" Jordan asked.

"Yes, I did."

"What did you ask him?"

The detective folded his arms. "If he wanted some coffee."

"Did he take you up on the offer?"

"Yes."

"Did you ask him at all about the incident at the school?"

"I asked him what had happened," Ducharme said.

"How did Peter respond?"

The detective frowned. "He said he wanted his mother."

"Did he start crying?"

"Yes."

"In fact, he didn't stop crying, not the whole time you tried to question him, isn't that true?"

"Yes, it is."

"Did you ask him any other questions, Detective?"

"No."

Jordan stepped forward. "You didn't bother to, because my client was in no shape to be going through an interview."

"I didn't ask him any more questions," Ducharme said evenly. "I have no idea what kind of shape he was in."

"So you took a kid—a seventeen-year-old kid, who was crying for his mother—back to your holding cell?"

"Yes. But I told him I wanted to help him."

Jordan glanced at the jury and let that statement sink in for a moment. "What was Peter's response?"

"He looked at me," the detective answered, "and he said, 'They started it.'"

*   *   *

Curtis Uppergate had been a forensic psychiatrist for twenty-five years. He held degrees from three Ivy League medical schools and had a CV thick enough to serve as a doorstop. He was lily-white, but wore his shoulder-length gray hair cornrowed, and had come to court in a dashiki. Diana nearly expected him to call her *Sista* when she questioned him.

"What's your field of expertise, Doctor?"

"I work with violent teenagers. I assess them on behalf of the court to determine the nature of their mental illnesses, if any, and figure out an appropriate treatment plan. I also advise the court as to what their state of mind may have been at the time a crime has been committed. I worked with the FBI to create their profiles of school shooters, and to examine parallels between cases at Thurston High, Paducah, Rocori, and Columbine."

"When did you first become involved in this case?"

"Last April."

"Did you review Peter Houghton's records?"

"Yes," Uppergate said. "I reviewed all the records I received from you, Ms. Leven—extensive school and medical records, police reports, interviews done by Detective Ducharme."

"What, in particular, were you looking for?"

"Evidence of mental illness," he said. "Physical explanations for the behavior. A psychosocial construct that might resemble those of other perpetrators of school violence."

Diana glanced at the jury; their eyes were glazing over. "As a result of your work, did you reach any conclusion with a reasonable degree of medical certainty as to Peter Houghton's mental state on March 6, 2007?"

"Yes," Uppergate said, and he faced the jury, speaking slowly and clearly. "Peter Houghton was not suffering from any mental illness at the time he started shooting at Sterling High School."

"Can you tell us how you reached that conclusion?"

"The definition of sanity implies being in touch with the reality of what you are doing at the time you do it. There's evidence that Peter had been planning this attack for a while—from stockpiling ammunition and guns, to making lists of targeted victims, to rehearsing his Armageddon through a self-designed video game. The shooting was not a departure for Peter—it was something he had been considering all along, with great premeditation."

"Are there other examples of Peter's premeditation?"

"When he first reached the school and saw a friend in the parking lot, he tried to warn him off, for safety. He lit a pipe bomb in a car before going into the school, to serve as a diversion so that he could enter unimpeded with his guns. He concealed weapons that were preloaded. He targeted areas in the school where he himself had been victimized. These are not the acts of someone who doesn't know what he's doing—they're the hallmarks of a rational, angry—perhaps suffering, but certainly not delusional—young man."

Diana paced in front of the witness stand. "Doctor, were you able to compare information from past school shootings to this one, in order to support your conclusion that the defendant was sane and responsible for his actions?"

Uppergate flipped his braids over his shoulder. "None of the shooters from Columbine, Paducah, Thurston, or Rocori had status. It's not that they're loners, but in their minds, they perceive that they are not members of the group to the same degree as anyone else in that group. Peter was on the soccer team, for example, but was one of two students never put in to play. He was bright, but his grades didn't reflect that. He had a romantic interest, but that interest went unreturned. The only venue where he did feel comfortable was in a world of his own creation—computer games where Peter was not only comfortable . . . he was God."

"Does that mean he was living in a fantasy world on March sixth?"

"Absolutely not. If he had been, he wouldn't have been planning his attack as rationally and methodically."

Diana turned. "There's been some evidence, Doctor, that Peter was the subject of bullying in school. Have you reviewed that information?"

"Yes, I have."

"Has your research told you anything about the effect of bullying on kids like Peter?"

"In every single school shooting case," Uppergate said, "the bullying card gets played. It's the bullying, allegedly, that makes the school shooter snap one day and fight back with violence. However, in every other case—and this one, in my opinion—the bullying seems exaggerated by the shooter. The teasing isn't significantly worse for the shooter than it is for anyone else at the school."

"Then why shoot?"

"It becomes a public way to take control of a situation in which they usually feel powerless," Curtis Uppergate said. "Which, again, means it's something they've been planning for a while."

"Your witness," Diana said.

Jordan stood up and approached Dr. Uppergate. "When did you first meet Peter?"

"Well. We haven't officially been introduced."

"But you're a psychiatrist?"

"Last time I checked," Uppergate said.

"I thought the field of psychiatry was based on gaining a rapport with your client and getting to know what he thinks about the world and how he processes it."

"That's part of it."

"That's an incredibly *important* part of it, isn't it?" Jordan asked.

"Yes."

"Would you write a prescription for Peter today?"

"No."

"Because you'd have to physically meet with him before you decided whether he was an appropriate candidate for that medicine, correct?"

"Yes."

"Doctor, did you get a chance to talk to the school shooter from Thurston High?"

"Yes, I did," Uppergate said.

"What about the boy from Paducah?"

"Yes."

"Rocori?"

"Yes."

"Not Columbine . . ."

"I'm a psychiatrist, Mr. McAfee," Uppergate said. "Not a medium. However, I did speak at length to the families of the two boys. I read their diaries and examined their videos."

"Doctor," Jordan asked, "did you ever once speak directly to Peter Houghton?"

Curtis Uppergate hesitated. "No," he said. "I did not."

Jordan sat down, and Diana faced the judge. "Your Honor," she said. "The prosecution rests."

"Here," Jordan said, tossing Peter half a sandwich as he entered the holding cell. "Or are you on a hunger strike, too?"

Peter glared at him, but unwrapped the sandwich and took a bite. "I don't like turkey."

"I don't really care." He leaned against the cement wall

of the holding cell. "You want to tell me who peed in your Cheerios today?"

"Do you have any idea what it's like to sit in that room and listen to all these people talk about me like I'm not there? Like I can't even hear what they're *saying* about me?"

"That's the way the game's played," Jordan said. "Now, it's our turn."

Peter stood up and walked to the front of the cell. "Is that what this is to you? Some game?"

Jordan closed his eyes, counting to ten for patience. "Of course not."

"How much money do you get paid?" Peter asked.

"That's not your—"

"How much?"

"Ask your parents," Jordan said flatly.

"You get paid whether I win or lose, right?"

Jordan hesitated, and then nodded.

"So you don't really give a shit what the outcome is, do you?"

It struck Jordan, with some wonder, that Peter had the chops to be an excellent defense attorney. That sort of circular reasoning—the kind that left the person being grilled hung out to dry—was exactly what you aimed for in a courtroom.

"What?" Peter accused. "Now you're laughing at me, too?"

"No. I was just thinking you'd be a good lawyer."

Peter sank down again. "Great. Maybe the state prison offers that degree along with a GED."

Jordan reached for the sandwich in Peter's hand and took a bite. "Let's just wait and see how it goes," he said.

A jury was always impressed by King Wah's record, and Jordan knew it. He'd interviewed over five hundred subjects. He'd been an expert witness at 248 trials, not including this one. He had written more papers than any other forensic psychiatrist with a specialty in post-traumatic stress disorder. And—here was the beautiful part—he'd taught three seminars that had been attended by the prosecution's witness, Dr. Curtis Uppergate.

"Dr. Wah," Jordan began, "when did you first begin to work on this case?"

"I was contacted by you, Mr. McAfee, in June. I agreed to meet with Peter at that time."

"Did you?"

"Yes, for over ten hours of interviews. I also sat down and read the police reports, the medical and school records of both Peter and his older brother. I met with his parents. I then sent him to be examined by my colleague, Dr. Lawrence Ghertz, who is a pediatric neuropsychiatrist."

"What does a pediatric neuropsychiatrist do?"

"Studies organic causes for mental symptomology and disorder in children."

"What did Dr. Ghertz do?"

"He took several MRI scans of Peter's brain," King said. "Dr. Ghertz uses brain scans to show that there are structural changes in the adolescent brain that not only explain the timing of some major mental illnesses like schizophrenia and bipolar disorder, but also give biological reasons for some of the wild conduct that parents usually attribute to raging hormones. That's not to say that there aren't raging hormones in adolescents, but there's also a paucity of the cognitive controls that are necessary for mature behavior."

Jordan turned to the jury. "Did you get that? Because I'm lost . . ."

King grinned. "Layman's terms? You can tell a lot about a kid by looking at his brain. There might actually be a physiological reason why, when you tell your seventeen-year-old to put the milk back in the fridge, he nods and then completely ignores you."

"Did you send Peter to Dr. Ghertz because you thought he was bipolar or schizophrenic?"

"No. But part of my responsibility involves ruling those causes out before I begin to look at other reasons for his behavior."

"Did Dr. Ghertz send you a report detailing his findings?"

"Yes."

"Can you show us?" Jordan lifted up a diagram of a brain that he'd already entered as evidence, and handed it to King.

"Dr. Ghertz said that Peter's brain looked very similar to a typical adolescent brain in that the prefrontal cortex was not as developed as you'd find in a mature adult brain."

"Whoa," Jordan said. "You're losing me again."

"The prefrontal cortex is right here, behind the forehead. It's sort of like the president of the brain, in charge of calculated, rational thought. It's also the last part of the brain to mature, which is why teenagers often get into so much trouble." Then he pointed to a tiny spot on the diagram, centrally located. "This is called the amygdala. Since a teenager's decision-making center isn't completely turned on yet, they rely on this little piece of the brain instead. This is the impulsive epicenter of the brain—the one that houses feelings like fear and anger and gut instinct. Or in other words—the part of the brain that corresponds to 'Because my friends thought it was a good idea, too.'"

Most of the jury chuckled, and Jordan caught Peter's eye. He wasn't slumped in the chair anymore; he was sitting up, listening carefully. "It's fascinating, really," King said, "because a twenty-year-old might be physiologically capable of making an informed decision . . . but a seventeen-year-old won't be."

"Did Dr. Ghertz perform any other psychological tests?"

"Yes. He did a second MRI, one that was performed while Peter was working on a simple task. Peter was given photographs of faces and asked to identify the emotions reflected on them. Unlike a test group of adults who got most of those assessments correct, Peter tended to make errors. In particular, he identified fearful expressions as angry, confused, or sad. The MRI scan showed that while he was focused on this task, it was the amygdala that was doing the work . . . not the prefrontal cortex."

"What can you infer from that, Dr. Wah?"

"Well, Peter's capacity for rational, planned, premeditated thought is still in its developmental stages. Physiologically, he just can't do it yet."

Jordan watched the jurors' response to this statement. "Dr. Wah, you said you met with Peter as well?"

"Yes, at the correctional facility, for ten one-hour sessions."

"Where did you meet with him?"

"In a conference room. I explained who I was, and that I was working with his attorney," King said.

"Was Peter reluctant to speak to you?"

"No." The psychiatrist paused. "He seemed to enjoy the company."

"Did anything strike you about him, at first?"

"He seemed unemotional. Not crying, or smiling, or laughing, or showing hostility. In the business, we call it flat affect."

"What did you two talk about?"

King looked at Peter and smiled. "The Red Sox," he said. "And his family."

"What did he tell you?"

"That Boston deserved another pennant. Which—as a Yankees fan myself—was enough to call into question his capacity for rational thought."

Jordan grinned. "What did he say about his family?"

"He explained that he lived with his mother and father, and that his older brother Joey had been killed by a drunk driver about a year earlier. Joey had been a year older than Peter. We also talked about things he liked to do—mostly centered on programming and computers—and about his childhood."

"What did he tell you about that?" Jordan asked.

"Most of Peter's childhood memories involved situations where he was victimized either by other children or by adults whom he'd perceived as being able to help him, yet didn't. He described everything from physical threats—*Get out of my way* or *I'm going to punch your lights out*; to physical actions—doing nothing more than walking down a hallway and being slammed up against the wall because he happened to get too close to someone walking past him; to emotional taunts—like being called *homo* or *queer*."

"Did he tell you when this bullying started?"

"The first day of kindergarten. He got on the bus, was tripped as he walked down the aisle, and had his Superman lunch box thrown onto the highway. It continued up to shortly before the shooting, when he suffered public humiliation after his romantic interest in a classmate was revealed."

"Doctor," Jordan said, "didn't Peter ask for help?"

"Yes, but even when it was given, the result backfired. Once, for example, after being shoved by a boy at school, Peter charged him. This was seen by a teacher, who brought both boys to the principal's office for detention. In Peter's mind, he'd defended himself, and yet he was being punished as well." King relaxed on the stand. "More recent memories were colored by Peter's brother's death and his inability to live up to the same standards his brother had set as a student and a son."

"Did Peter talk about his parents?"

"Yes. Peter loved his parents, but didn't feel he could rely on them for protection."

"Protection from what?"

"Troubles in school, feelings he was having, suicide ideation."

Jordan turned toward the jury. "Based on your discussions with Peter, and Dr. Ghertz's findings, were you able to diagnose Peter's state of mind on March 6, 2007, with a reasonable degree of medical certainty?"

"Yes. Peter was suffering from post-traumatic stress disorder."

"Can you explain what that is?"

King nodded. "It's a psychiatric disorder that can occur following an experience in which a person is oppressed or victimized. For example, we've all heard of soldiers who come home from war and can't adjust to the world because of PTSD. People who suffer from PTSD often relive the experience through nightmares, have difficulty sleeping, feel detached. In extreme cases, after exposure to serious trauma, they might exhibit hallucinations or dissociation."

"Are you saying that Peter was hallucinating on the morning of March sixth?"

"No. I believe that he was in a dissociative state."

"What's that?"

"It's when you're physically present, but mentally removed," King explained. "When you can separate your feelings about an event from the knowledge of it."

Jordan knit his brows together. "Hang on, Doctor. Do you mean that a person in a dissociative state could drive a car?"

"Absolutely."

"And set up a pipe bomb?"

"Yes."

"And load weapons?"

"Yes."

"And fire those weapons?"

"Sure."

"And all that time, that person wouldn't know what he was doing?"

"Yes, Mr. McAfee," King said. "That's exactly right."

"In your opinion, when did Peter slip into this dissociative state?"

"During our interviews, Peter explained that the morning of March sixth, he got up early and went to check a website for feedback on his video game. By accident, he pulled up an old file on his computer—the email he had sent to Josie Cormier, detailing his feelings for her. It was the same email that, weeks before, had been sent to the entire school, and that had preceded an even greater humiliation, when his pants were pulled down in the cafeteria. After he saw that email, he said, he can't really remember the rest of what happened."

"I pull up old files by accident on my computer all the time," Jordan said, "but I don't go into a dissociative state."

"The computer had always been a safe haven for Peter. It was the vehicle he used to create a world that was comfortable for him, peopled by characters who appreciated him and whom he had control over, as he didn't in real life. Having this one secure zone suddenly become yet another place where humiliation occurred is what triggered the break."

Jordan crossed his arms, playing devil's advocate. "I don't know . . . we're talking about an email here. Is it really fair to compare bullying to the trauma seen by war veterans in Iraq, or survivors from 9/11?"

"The thing that's important to remember about PTSD is that a traumatic event affects different people differently. For example, for some, a violent rape might trigger PTSD. For others, a brief groping might trigger it. It doesn't matter if the traumatic event is war, or a terrorist attack, or sexual assault, or bullying—what counts is where the subject is starting from, emotionally."

King turned to the jury. "You might have heard, for example, of battered woman syndrome. It doesn't make sense, on the outside, when a woman—even one who's been victimized for years—kills her husband when he's fast asleep."

"Objection," Diana said. "Does anyone see a battered woman on trial?"

"I'll allow it," Judge Wagner replied.

"Even when a battered woman is not immediately under physical threat, she psychologically believes she is, thanks to a chronic, escalating pattern of violence that's caused her to suffer from PTSD. It's living in this constant state of fear that something's going to happen, that it's going to keep happening, which leads her to pick up the gun at that moment, even though her husband is snoring. To her, he is *still* an immediate threat," King said. "A child who is suffering from PTSD, like Peter, is terrified that the bully is going to kill him eventually. Even if the bully is not at that moment shoving him into a locker or punching him, it could happen at any second. And so, like the battered wife, he takes action even when—to you and me—nothing seems to warrant the attack."

"Wouldn't someone notice this sort of irrational fear?" Jordan asked.

"Probably not. A child who suffers from PTSD has made unsuccessful attempts to get help, and as the victimization continues, he stops asking for it. He withdraws socially, because he's never quite sure when interaction is going to lead to another incident of bullying. He probably thinks of killing himself. He escapes into a fantasy world, where he can call the shots. However, he starts retreating there so often that it gets harder and harder to separate that from reality. During the actual incidents of bullying, a child with PTSD might retreat into an altered state of consciousness—a dissociation from reality to keep him from feeling pain or humiliation while the incident occurs. That's exactly what I think happened to Peter on March sixth."

"Even though none of the kids who'd bullied him were present in his bedroom when that email appeared?"

"Correct. Peter had spent his entire life being beaten and taunted and threatened, to the point where he believed he would be killed by those same kids if he didn't do something. The email triggered a dissociative state, and when he went to Sterling High and fired shots, he was completely unaware of what he was doing."

"How long can a dissociative state last?"

"It depends. Peter could have been dissociating for several hours."

"*Hours?*" Jordan repeated.

"Absolutely. There's no point during the shootings that illustrates to me conscious awareness of his actions."

Jordan glanced at the prosecutor. "We all saw a video where Peter sat down after firing shots in the cafeteria and ate a bowl of cereal. Is that meaningful to your diagnosis?"

"Yes. In fact, I can't think of clearer proof that Peter was still dissociating at that moment. You've got a boy who is completely unaware of the fact that he's surrounded by classmates he'd either killed, wounded, or sent fleeing. He sits down and takes the time to calmly pour a bowl of Rice Krispies, unaffected by the carnage around him."

"What about the fact that many of the children Peter

fired at were not part of what could commonly be called the 'popular crowd'? That there were special-needs children and scholars and even a teacher who became his victims?"

"Again," the psychiatrist said, "we're not talking about rational behavior. Peter wasn't calculating his actions; at the moment he was shooting, he had separated himself from the reality of the situation. Anyone Peter encountered during those nineteen minutes was a potential threat."

"In your opinion, when did Peter's dissociative state end?" Jordan asked.

"When Peter was in custody, speaking to Detective Ducharme. That's when he started reacting normally, given the horror of the situation. He began to cry and ask for his mother—which indicates both a recognition of his surroundings and an appropriate, childlike response."

Jordan leaned against the rail of the jury box. "There's been some evidence in this case, Doctor, that Peter wasn't the only child in the school who was bullied. So why did he react this way to it?"

"Well, as I said, different people have different responses to stress. In Peter's case, I saw an extreme emotional vulnerability, which, in fact, was the reason he was teased. Peter didn't play by the codes of boys. He wasn't a big athlete. He wasn't tough. He was sensitive. And difference is not always respected—particularly when you're a teenager. Adolescence is about fitting in, not standing out."

"How does a child who is emotionally vulnerable wind up one day carrying four guns into a school and shooting twenty-nine people?"

"Part of it is the PTSD—Peter's response to chronic victimization. But a big part of it, too, is the society that created both Peter and those bullies. Peter's response is one enforced by the world he lives in. He sees violent video games selling off the shelves at stores; he listens to music that glorifies murder and rape. He watches his tormentors shove him, strike him, push him, demean him. He lives in a state, Mr. McAfee, whose license plate reads 'Live Free or Die.'" King shook his head. "All Peter did, one morning, was turn into the person he'd been expected to be all along."

Nobody knew this, but once, Josie had broken up with Matt Royston.

They had been going out for nearly a year when Matt picked her up one Saturday night. An upperclassman on the football team—someone Brady knew—was having a party at his house. *You up for it?* Matt had asked, even though he'd already been driving there when he asked her.

The house had been pulsing like a carnival by the time they arrived, cars parked on the curb and the sidewalk and the lawn. Through the upstairs windows, Josie could see people dancing; as they walked up the driveway, a girl was throwing up in the bushes.

Matt didn't let go of her hand. They twined through wall-to-wall bodies, embroidering their path to the kitchen, where the keg was set up, and then back to the dining room, where the table had been tipped on its side to create a bigger dance floor. The kids they passed were not only from Sterling High, but other towns, too. Some had the red-rimmed, loose-jawed stare that came from smoking pot. Guys and girls sniffed at each other, circling for sex.

She didn't know anyone, but that wasn't important, because she was with Matt. They pressed closer, in the heat of a hundred other bodies. Matt slid his leg between hers while the music beat like blood, and she lifted up her arms to fit herself against him.

Everything had gone wrong when she went to use the bathroom. First, Matt had wanted to follow her—he said it wasn't safe for her to be alone. She finally convinced him it would take all of thirty seconds, but as she started off, a tall boy wearing a Green Day shirt and a hoop earring turned too quickly and spilled his beer on her. *Oh, shit,* he'd said.

It's okay. Josie had a tissue in her pocket; she took it out and started to blot her blouse dry.

Let me, the boy said, and he took the napkin from her. At the same time they both realized how ridiculous it was trying to soak up that much liquid with a tiny square of Kleenex. He started laughing, and then she did, and his hand was still lightly resting on her shoulder when Matt came up and punched him in the face.

What are you doing! Josie had screamed. The boy was out cold on the floor, and other people were trying to get out of the way but stay close enough to see the fight. Matt grabbed her wrist so hard that she thought it was going to snap. He dragged her out of the house and into the car, where she sat in stony silence.

He was just trying to help, Josie said.

Matt put the car into reverse and lurched backward. *You want to stay? You want to be a slut?*

He'd started to drive like a lunatic—running red lights, taking corners on two wheels, doubling the speed limit. She told him to slow down three times, and then she just closed her eyes and hoped it would be over soon.

When Matt had screeched to a stop in front of her house, she turned to him, unusually calm. *I don't want to go out with you anymore,* she had said, and she got out of the car. His voice trailed her to the front door: *Good. Why would I want to go out with a fucking whore, anyway?*

She had managed to slip by her mother, feigning a headache. In the bathroom, she'd stared at herself in the mirror, trying to figure out who this girl was who had suddenly grown such a backbone, and why she still felt like crying. She'd lain in her bed for an hour, tears leaking from the corners of her eyes, wondering why—if *she'd* been the one to end it—she felt so miserable.

When the phone rang after three in the morning, Josie grabbed it and hung it up again, so that when her mother picked up, she would assume it had been a wrong number. She held her breath for a few seconds, and then lifted the receiver and punched in *69. She knew, even before she saw the familiar string of numbers, that it was Matt.

Josie, he had said, when she called back. *Were you lying?*

About what?

Loving me?

She had pressed her face into the pillow. *No*, she whispered.

I can't live without you, Matt had said, and then she heard something that sounded like a bottle of pills being shaken.

Josie had frozen. *What are you doing?*

What do you care?

Her mind had started racing. She had her driver's permit, but couldn't take the car out herself, and not after dark. She lived too far away from Matt to run there. *Don't move*, she said. *Just . . . don't do anything.*

Downstairs in the garage, she'd found a bicycle she hadn't ridden since she was in middle school, and she pedaled the four miles to Matt's house. By the time she got there, it had been raining; her hair and her clothes were glued to her skin. The light was still on in Matt's bedroom, which was on the first floor. Josie knocked on the window, and he opened it so that she could crawl inside.

On his desk was a bottle of Tylenol and another one, open, of Jim Beam. Josie faced him. *Did you—*

But Matt wrapped his arms around her. He smelled of

liquor. *You told me not to. I'd do anything for you.* Then he had pulled back from her. *Would you do anything for me?*

Anything, she vowed.

Matt had gathered her into his arms. *Tell me you didn't mean it.*

She felt a cage coming down around her; too late she realized that Matt had her trapped by the heart. And like any unwitting animal that was well and truly caught, Josie could escape only by leaving a piece of herself behind.

I'm so sorry, Josie had said at least a thousand times that night, because it was all her fault.

"Dr. Wah," Diana said, "how much were you paid for your work on this case?"

"My fee is two thousand dollars per day."

"Would it be fair to say that one of the most important components of diagnosing the defendant was the time you spent interviewing him?"

"Absolutely."

"During the course of those ten hours, you were relying on him to be truthful with you in his recollection of events, right?"

"Yes."

"You'd have no way of knowing if he *wasn't* being truthful, would you?"

"I've been doing this for some time, Ms. Leven," the psychiatrist said. "I've interviewed enough people to know when someone's trying to put one over on me."

"Part of what you use in determining whether or not a teen is putting one over on you is taking a look at the circumstances they're in, correct?"

"Sure."

"And the circumstances in which you found Peter included being locked up in jail for multiple first-degree murders?"

"That's right."

"So, basically," Diana said, "Peter had a huge incentive to find a way out."

"Or, Ms. Leven," Dr. Wah countered, "you could also say he had nothing left to lose by telling the truth."

Diana pressed her lips together; a yes or no answer would have done just fine. "You said that part of your diagnosis of PTSD came from the fact that the defendant was attempting to get help, and couldn't. Was this based on information he gave you during your interviews?"

"Yes, corroborated by his parents, and some of the teachers who testified for you, Ms. Leven."

"You also said that part of your diagnosis of PTSD was illustrated by Peter's retreat into a fantasy world, correct?"

"Yes."

"And you based that on the computer games that Peter told you about during your interviews?"

"Correct."

"Isn't it true that when you sent Peter to Dr. Ghertz, you told him he was going to have some brain scans done?"

"Yes."

"Couldn't Peter have told Dr. Ghertz that a smiling face looked angry, if he thought it would help you out with a diagnosis?"

"I suppose it would be possible . . ."

"You also said, Doctor, that reading an email the morning of March sixth is what put Peter into a dissociative state, one strong enough to last through Peter's entire killing spree at Sterling High—"

"Objection—"

"Sustained," the judge said.

"Did you base that conclusion on anything other than what Peter Houghton told you — Peter, who was sitting in a jail cell, charged with ten murders and nineteen attempted murders?"

King Wah shook his head. "No, but any other psychiatrist would have done the same."

Diana just raised a brow. "Any psychiatrist who stood to make two thousand bucks a day," she said, and even before Jordan objected she withdrew her remark. "You said that Peter was suffering from suicide ideation."

"Yes."

"So he wanted to kill himself?"

"Yes. That's very common for patients with PTSD."

"Detective Ducharme has testified that there were one hundred sixteen bullet casings found in the high school that morning. Another thirty unspent rounds were found on Peter's person, and another fifty-two unspent rounds were found in the backpack he was carrying, along with two guns he didn't use. So, do the math for me, Doctor. How many bullets are we talking about?"

"One hundred and ninety-eight."

Diana faced him. "In a span of nineteen minutes, Peter had two hundred chances to kill himself, instead of every other student he encountered at Sterling High. Is that right, Doctor?"

"Yes. But there is an extremely fine line between a suicide and a homicide. Many depressed people who have made the decision to shoot themselves choose, at the last moment, to shoot someone else instead."

Diana frowned. "I thought Peter was in a dissociated state," she said. "I thought he was incapable of making choices."

"He was. He was pulling the trigger without any thought of consequence or knowledge of what he was doing."

"Either that, or it was a tissue-paper line he felt like crossing, right?"

Jordan stood up. "Objection. She's bullying my witness."

"Oh, for God's sake, Jordan," Diana snapped, "you can't use your defense on *me*."

"Counselors," the judge warned.

"You also testified, Doctor, that this dissociative state of Peter's ended when Detective Ducharme began to ask him questions at the police station, correct?"

"Yes."

"Would it be fair to say that you based this assumption on the fact that at that moment, Peter started to respond in an appropriate manner, given the situation he was in?"

"Yes."

"Then how do you explain how, hours earlier, when three officers pointed a gun at Peter and told him to drop his weapon, he was able to do what they asked?"

Dr. Wah hesitated. "Well."

"Isn't that an appropriate response, when three policemen have their weapons drawn and pointed at you?"

"He put the gun down," the psychiatrist said, "because even on a subliminal level, he understood that otherwise, he was going to be shot."

"But Doctor," Diana said. "I thought you told us that Peter *wanted* to die."

She sat back down, satisfied that Jordan could do nothing on redirect that would damage the headway she'd made. "Dr. Wah," he said, "you spent a lot of time with Peter, didn't you?"

"Unlike some doctors in my field," he said pointedly, "I actually believe in meeting the client you're going to be talking about in court."

"Why is this important?"

"To build a rapport," the psychiatrist said. "To foster a relationship between doctor and patient."

"Would you take everything a patient told you at face value?"

"Certainly not, especially under these circumstances."

"In fact, there are many ways to corroborate a client's story, aren't there?"

"Of course. In Peter's case, I spoke with his parents. There were instances in the school records where bullying was mentioned—although there was no response from the administration. The police package I received supported Peter's statement about his email being sent out to several hundred members of the school community."

"Did you find any corroborative points that helped you diagnose the dissociative state Peter went into on March sixth?" Jordan asked.

"Yes. Although the police investigation stated that Peter had created a list of target victims, there were far more people shot who were not on the list . . . who were, in fact, students he didn't even know by name."

"Why is that important?"

"Because it tells me that at the time he was shooting, he wasn't targeting individual students. He was merely going through the motions."

"Thank you, Doctor," Jordan said, and he nodded to Diana.

She looked at the psychiatrist. "Peter told you he had been humiliated in the cafeteria," she said. "Did he mention any other specific places?"

"The playground. The school bus. The boys' bathroom and the locker room."

"When Peter started shooting at Sterling High, did he go into the principal's office?"

"Not that I'm aware of."

"How about the library?"

"No."

"The staff lounge?"

Dr. Wah shook his head. "No."

"The art studio?"

"I don't believe so."

"In fact, Peter went from the cafeteria, to the bathrooms, to the gym, to the locker room. He went methodically from one venue where he'd been bullied to the next, right?"

"It seems so."

"You said he was going through the motions, Doctor," Diana said. "But wouldn't you call that a plan?"

When Peter got back to the jail that night, the detention officer who took him to his cell handed him a letter. "You missed mail call," he said, and Peter couldn't speak, so unaccustomed was he to that concentrated a dose of kindness.

He sat down with his back to the wall on the lower bunk and surveyed the envelope. He was a little nervous, now, about mail—he had been since Jordan reamed him for talking to that reporter. But this envelope wasn't typed, like that one had been. This letter was handwritten, with little puffy circles floating over the i's like clouds.

He ripped it open and unfolded the letter inside. It smelled like oranges.

> *Dear Peter,*
> *You don't know me by name, but I was number 9. That's how I left the school, with a big magic marker label on my forehead. You tried to kill me.*
> *I am not at your trial, so don't try to find me in the crowd. I couldn't stand being in that town any-*

more, so my parents moved a month ago. I start school in a week here in Minnesota, and already people have heard about me. They only know me as a victim from Sterling High. I don't have interests, I don't have a personality, I don't even have a history, except the one you gave me.

I had a 4.0 average but I don't care very much about grades anymore. What's the point. I used to have all these dreams, but now I don't know if I'll go to college, since I still can't sleep through the night. I can't deal with people who sneak up behind me either, or doors that slam really loud, or fireworks. I've been in therapy long enough to tell you one thing: I'm never going to set foot in Sterling again.

You shot me in the back. The doctors said I was lucky—that if I'd sneezed or turned to look at you I would be in a wheelchair now. Instead, I just have to deal with the people who stare when I forget and put on a tank top—anyone can see the scars from the bullet and the chest tubes and the stitches. I don't care—they used to stare at the zits on my face; now they just have another place to focus their attention.

I've thought about you a lot. I think you should go to jail. It's fair, and this wasn't, and there's a kind of balance in that.

I was in your French class, did you know that? I sat in the row by the window, second from the back. You always seemed sort of mysterious, and I liked your smile.

I would have liked to be your friend.

Sincerely,
Angela Phlug

Peter folded the letter and slipped it inside his pillow-case. Ten minutes later, he took it out again. He read it all night long, over and over, until the sun rose; until he did not need to see the words to recite it by heart.

Lacy had dressed for her son. Although it was nearly eighty-five degrees outside, she was wearing a sweater she had dug out of a box in the attic, a pink angora one that Peter had liked to stroke like a kitten when he was tiny. Around her wrist was a bracelet Peter had made her in fourth grade by rolling up tiny bits of magazines into splashy colored beads. She had on a gray patterned skirt that Peter had laughed at once, saying it looked like a computer's motherboard, and wasn't that sort of fitting. And her hair was braided neatly, because she remembered how the tail had brushed Peter's face the last time she'd kissed him good night.

She'd made a promise to herself. No matter how hard this got, no matter how much she had to sob her way through the questions, she would not take her eyes off Peter. He would be, she decided, like the pictures of white beaches that birthing mothers sometimes brought in as a focal point. His face would force her to concentrate, even though her pulse was skittish and her heart was off a beat; she would show Peter that there was still someone stead-fastly watching over him.

As Jordan McAfee called her to the stand, the strangest thing happened. She walked in with the bailiff, but instead of marching toward the tiny wooden balcony where the wit-ness was to sit, her body moved of its own accord in the other direction. Diana Leven knew where she was heading before Lacy did herself—she stood up to object, but then decided against it. Lacy's step was quick, her arms flat at her sides, until she was positioned in front of the defense table. She knelt down beside Peter, so that his face was the only thing she could see in her range of vision. Then she reached out with her left hand and she touched his face.

His skin was still as smooth as a child's, warm to the touch. When she cupped his cheek, his lashes fanned over her thumb. She had visited her son weekly in the jail, but there had always been a line between them. This—the feeling of him underneath her own hands, vital and real—was the kind of gift you had to take out of its box every now and then, hold aloft, marvel at, so you didn't forget that it was still in your possession. Lacy remembered the moment Peter had first been placed in her arms, still slick with vernix and blood, his raw, red mouth round with a newborn's cry, his arms and legs splayed in this suddenly infinite space. Leaning forward, she did now the same thing she'd done the first time she'd met her son: closed her eyes, winged a prayer, and kissed his forehead.

A bailiff touched her shoulder. "Ma'am," he began.

Lacy shrugged him off and got to her feet. She walked to the witness box and unhooked the latch of the gate, let herself inside.

Jordan McAfee approached her, holding a box of Kleenex. He turned his back so that the jury could not see him speaking. "You okay?" he whispered. Lacy nodded, faced Peter, and offered up a smile like a sacrifice.

"Can you state your name for the record?" Jordan asked.

"Lacy Houghton."

"Where do you live?"

"1616 Goldenrod Lane, Sterling, New Hampshire."

"Who lives with you?"

"My husband, Lewis," Lacy said. "And my son, Peter."

"Do you have any other children, Ms. Houghton?"

"I had a son, Joseph, but he was killed by a drunk driver last year."

"Can you tell us," Jordan McAfee said, "when you first

became aware that something had happened at Sterling High School on March sixth?"

"I was on call overnight at the hospital. I'm a midwife. After I had finished delivering a baby that morning. I went out to the nurses' station, and they were all gathered around the radio. There had been an explosion at the high school."

"What did you do when you heard?"

"I told someone to cover for me, and I drove to the school. I needed to make sure that Peter was all right."

"How did Peter usually get to school?"

"He drove," Lacy said. "He has a car."

"Ms. Houghton, tell me about your relationship with Peter."

Lacy smiled. "He's my baby. I had two sons, but Peter was the one who was always quieter, more sensitive. He always needed a little more encouragement."

"Were you two close when he was growing up?"

"Absolutely."

"How was Peter's relationship with his brother?"

"It was fine . . ."

"And his father?"

Lacy hesitated. She could feel Lewis in the room as surely as if he were beside her, and she thought about him walking in the rain through the cemetery. "I think that Lewis had a tighter bond with Joey, while Peter and I have more in common."

"Did Peter ever tell you about the problems he had with other kids?"

"Yes."

"Objection," the prosecutor said. "Hearsay."

"I'm going to overrule it for now," the judge answered. "But be careful where you're going, Mr. McAfee."

Jordan turned to her again. "Why do you think Peter had problems with those kids?"

"He'd get picked on because he wasn't like them. He wasn't very athletic. He didn't like to play cops and robbers. He was artistic and creative and thoughtful, and kids made fun of him for that."

"What did you do?"

"I tried," Lacy admitted, "to toughen him up." As she spoke she directed her words at Peter, and hoped he could read it as an apology. "What does any mother do when she sees her child being teased by someone else? I told Peter I loved him; that kids like that didn't know anything. I told him that he was amazing and compassionate and kind and smart, all the things we want adults to be. I knew that all the attributes he was teased for, at age five, were going to work in his favor by the time he was thirty-five . . . but I couldn't get him there overnight. You can't fast-forward your child's life, no matter how much you want to."

"When did Peter start high school, Ms. Houghton?"

"In the fall of 2004."

"Was Peter still being picked on there?"

"Worse than ever," Lacy said. "I even asked his brother to keep an eye out for him."

Jordan walked toward her. "Tell me about Joey."

"Everybody liked Joey. He was smart, an excellent athlete. He could relate just as easily to adults as he could to kids his own age. He . . . well, he cut a swath through that school."

"You must have been very proud of him."

"I was. But I think that because of Joey, teachers and students had a certain sort of idea in mind for a Houghton boy, before Peter even arrived. And when he did get there, and people realized he wasn't like Joey, it only made things worse for him." She watched Peter's face transform as she spoke, like the change of a season. Why hadn't she taken the time before, when she had it, to tell Peter that she understood? That she knew Joey had cast such a wide shadow, it was hard to find the sunlight?

"How old was Peter when Joey died?"

"It was at the end of his sophomore year."

"That must have been devastating for the family," Jordan said.

"It was."

"What did you do to help Peter deal with his grief?"

Lacy glanced down at her lap. "I wasn't in any shape to help Peter. I had a very hard time helping myself."

"What about your husband? Was he a resource for Peter then?"

"I think we were both just trying to make it through one day at a time. . . . If anything, Peter was the one who was holding the family together."

"Mrs. Houghton, did Peter ever say that he wanted to hurt people at school?"

Lacy's throat tightened. "No."

"Was there ever anything in Peter's personality that led you to believe he was capable of an act like this?"

"When you look into your baby's eyes," Lacy said softly, "you see everything you hope they *can* be . . . not everything you wish they won't become."

"Did you ever find any plans or notes to indicate that Peter was plotting this event?"

A tear coursed down her cheek. "No."

Jordan softened his voice. "Did you look, Mrs. Houghton?"

She thought back to the moment she'd cleared out Joey's desk; how she'd stood over the toilet and flushed the drugs she'd found hidden in his drawer. "No," Lacy confessed. "I didn't. I thought I was helping him. After Joey died, all I wanted to do was keep Peter close. I didn't want to invade his privacy; I didn't want to fight with him; I didn't want anyone else to ever hurt him. I just wanted him to be a child forever." She glanced up, crying harder now. "But you can't do that, if you're a parent. Because part of your job is letting them grow up."

There was a clatter in the gallery as a man in the back stood up, nearly upending a television camera. Lacy had never seen him before. He had thinning black hair and a mustache; his eyes were on fire. "Guess what," he spat out. "My daughter Maddie is never going to grow up." He pointed at a woman beside him, and then further forward on a bench. "Neither is her daughter. Or his son. You goddamned bitch. If you'd done *your* job better, I could still be doing *my* job."

The judge began to smack his gavel. "Sir," he said. "Sir, I have to ask you to—"

"Your son's a monster. He's a fucking monster," the man yelled, as two bailiffs reached his seat and grabbed him by the upper arms, dragging him out of the courtroom.

Once, Lacy had been present at the birth of an infant that was missing half its heart. The family had known that their child would not live; they chose to carry through with the pregnancy, in the hope that they could have a few brief moments on this earth with her before she was gone for good. Lacy had stood in a corner of the room as the parents held their daughter. She didn't study their faces; she just *couldn't*. Instead, she focused on the medical needs of that newborn. She watched it, still and frost-blue, move one tiny fist in slow motion, like an astronaut navigating space. Then, one by one, her fingers unfurled and she let go.

Lacy thought of those miniature fingers, of slipping away. She turned to Peter. *I'm so sorry*, she mouthed silently. Then she covered her face with her hands and sobbed.

* * *

Once the judge had called for a recess and the jury had filed out, Jordan moved toward the bench. "Judge, the defense asks to be heard," he said. "We'd like to move for a mistrial."

Even with his back to her, he could feel Diana rolling her eyes. "How convenient."

"Well, Mr. McAfee," the judge said, "on what grounds?"

The grounds that I've got absolutely nothing better to salvage my case, Jordan thought. "Your Honor, there's been an incredibly emotional outburst from the father of a victim in front of the jury. There's no way that kind of speech can be ignored, and there's no instruction you can give them that will unring that bell."

"Is that all, Counselor?"

"No," Jordan said. "Prior to this, the jury may not have known that family members of the victims were sitting in the gallery. Now they do—and they also know that every move they make is being watched by those same people. That's a tremendous amount of pressure to put on a jury in a case that's already extremely emotional and highly publicized. How are they supposed to put aside the expectations of these family members and do their jobs fairly and impartially?"

"Are you kidding?" Diana said. "Who did the jury *think* was in the gallery? Vagrants? Of course it's full of people who were affected by the shootings. That's why they're here."

Judge Wagner glanced up. "Mr. McAfee, I'm not declaring a mistrial. I understand your concern, but I think I can address it with an instruction to the jurors to disregard any sort of emotional outburst from the gallery. Everyone involved in this case understands that emotions are running high, and that people may not always be able to control themselves. However, I'll also issue a cautionary instruction to the gallery to restrain themselves, or I will close the courtroom to observers."

Jordan sucked in his breath. "Please do note my exception, Your Honor."

"Of course, Mr. McAfee," he said. "See you in fifteen minutes."

As the judge exited for chambers, Jordan headed back to the defense table, trying to divine some sort of magic that would save Peter. The truth was, no matter what King Wah had said, no matter how clear the explanation of PTSD, no matter if the jury completely empathized with Peter—Jordan had forgotten one salient point: they would always feel sorrier for the victims.

Diana smiled at him on her way out of the courtroom. "Nice try," she said.

Selena's favorite room in the courthouse was tucked near the janitor's closet and filled with old maps. She had no idea what they were doing in a courthouse instead of a library, but she liked to hide up there sometimes when she got tired of watching Jordan strut around in front of the bench. She'd come here a few times during the trial to nurse Sam on the days they didn't have a sitter to watch him.

Now she led Lacy into her haven and sat her down in front of a world map that had the southern hemisphere as its center. Australia was purple, New Zealand green. It was Selena's favorite. She liked the red dragons painted into the seas, and the fierce storm clouds in the corners. She liked the calligraphed compass, drawn for direction. She liked thinking that the world might look completely different from another angle.

Lacy Houghton had not stopped crying, and Selena knew she had to—or the cross-examination was going to be a disaster. She sat down beside Lacy. "Can I get you something? Soup? Coffee?"

Lacy shook her head and wiped her nose with a tissue. "I can't do anything to save him."

"That's Jordan's job," Selena said, although to be frank, she couldn't imagine a scenario for Peter that did not involve serious jail time. She racked her brain, trying to think of what else she could say or do to calm Lacy down, just as Sam reached up and yanked on one of her braids.

Bingo.

"Lacy," Selena said. "Do you mind holding him while I look for something in my bag?"

Lacy lifted her gaze. "You . . . you don't mind?"

Selena shook her head and transferred the baby to her lap. Sam stared up at Lacy, diligently trying to fit his fist in his mouth. "Gah," he said.

A smile ghosted across Lacy's face. "Little man," she whispered, and she shifted the baby so that she could hold him more firmly.

"Excuse me?"

Selena turned to see the door crack open and Alex Cormier's face peek inside. She immediately stood up. "Your Honor, you can't come in—"

"Let her," Lacy said.

Selena stepped back as the judge walked into the room and sat down beside Lacy. She put a Styrofoam cup on the table and reached out, smiling a little as Sam grabbed onto her pinky finger and tugged on it. "The coffee here is awful, but I brought you some anyway."

"Thanks."

Selena moved gingerly behind the stacks of maps until she was standing behind the two women, watching them with the same stunned curiosity she'd have shown if a lioness cozied up to an impala instead of eating it.

"You did well in there," the judge said.

Lacy shook her head. "I didn't do well enough."

"She won't ask you much on cross, if anything."

Lacy lifted the baby to her chest and stroked his back. "I don't think I can go back in there," she said, her voice hitching.

"You can, and you will," the judge said. "Because Peter needs you to."

"They hate him. They hate *me*."

Judge Cormier put her hand on Lacy's shoulder. "Not everyone," she said. "When we go back, I'm going to be sitting in the front row. You don't have to look at the prosecutor. You just look at me."

Selena's jaw dropped. Often, with fragile witnesses or young children, they'd plant a person as a focal point to make testifying less scary. To make them feel that out of that whole crowd of people, they had at least one friend.

Sam found his thumb and started to suck on it, falling asleep against Lacy's chest. Selena watched Alex reach out, stroke the dark marabou tufts of her son's hair. "Everyone thinks you make mistakes when you're young," the judge said to Lacy. "But I don't think we make any fewer when we're grown up."

As Jordan walked into the holding cell where Peter was being kept, he was already doing damage control. "It's not going to hurt us," he announced. "The judge is going to give the jury instructions to disregard that whole outburst."

Peter sat on the metal bench, his head in his hands.

"Peter," Jordan said. "Did you hear me? I know it looked bad, and I know it was upsetting, but legally, it isn't going to affect your—"

"I need to tell her why I did it," Peter interrupted.

"Your mother?" Jordan said. "You can't. She's still sequestered." He hesitated. "Look, as soon as I can get you to talk to her, I—"

"No. I mean, I have to tell everyone."

Jordan looked at his client. Peter was dry-eyed; his fists rested on the bench. When he lifted his gaze, it wasn't the terrified face of the child he'd sat beside in court on the first day of the trial. It was someone who had grown up, overnight.

"We're getting out your side of the story," Jordan said. "You just have to be patient. I know this is hard to believe, but it's going to come together. We're doing the best we can."

"*We're* not," Peter said. "*You* are." He stood up, walking closer to Jordan. "You promised. You said it was *our* turn. But when you said that, you meant *your* turn, didn't you? You never intended for me to get up there and tell everyone what really happened."

"Did you see what they did to your mother?" Jordan argued. "Do you have any idea what's going to happen to you if you get up there and sit in that witness box?"

In that instant, something in Peter broke: not his anger, and not his hidden fear, but that last spider-thread of hope. Jordan thought of the testimony Michael Beach had given, about how it looked when the life left a person's face. You did not have to witness someone dying to see that.

"Jordan," Peter said. "If I'm going to spend the rest of my life in jail, I want them to hear my side of the story."

Jordan opened his mouth, intending to tell his client absolutely fucking not, he would not be taking the stand and ruining the tower of cards Jordan had created in the hope of an acquittal. But who was he kidding? Certainly not Peter.

He took a deep breath. "All right," he said. "Tell me what you're going to say."

Diana Leven didn't have any questions for Lacy Houghton, which—Jordan knew—was most likely a blessing. In addition to the fact that there wasn't anything the prosecutor could ask her that hadn't been covered better by Maddie Shaw's father, he hadn't known how much more stress Lacy could take without being rendered incomprehensible on the stand. As she was escorted from the courtroom, the judge looked up from his file. "Your next witness, Mr. McAfee?"

Jordan inhaled deeply. "The defense calls Peter Houghton."

Behind him, there was a flurry of activity. Rustling, as reporters dug fresh pens out of their pockets and turned to a fresh page on their pads. Murmurs, as the families of the victims traced Peter's steps to the witness stand. He could see Selena off to one side, her eyes wide at this unplanned development.

Peter sat down and stared only at Jordan, just as he'd told him to. *Good boy,* he thought. "Are you Peter Houghton?"

"Yes," Peter said, but he wasn't close enough to the microphone for it to carry. He leaned forward and repeated the word. *"Yes,"* he said, and this time, an unholy screech from the PA system rang through the courtroom speakers.

"What grade are you in, Peter?"

"I was a junior when I got arrested."

"How old are you now?"

"Eighteen."

Jordan walked toward the jury box. "Peter, are you the person who went to Sterling High School the morning of March 6, 2007, and shot and killed ten people?"

"Yes."

"And wounded nineteen others?"

"Yes."

"And caused damage to countless other people, and to a great deal of property?"

"I know," Peter said.

"You're not denying that today, are you?"

"No."

"Can you tell the jury," Jordan asked, "why you did it?"

Peter looked into his eyes. "They started it."

"Who?"

"The bullies. The jocks. The ones who called me a freak my whole life."

"Do you remember their names?"

"There are so many of them," Peter said.

"Can you tell us why you felt you had to resort to violence?"

Jordan had told Peter that whatever he did, he could not get angry. That he had to stay calm and collected while he spoke, or his testimony would backfire on him — even more than Jordan already expected. "I tried to do what my mom wanted me to do," Peter explained. "I tried to be like them, but that didn't work out."

"What do you mean by that?"

"I tried out for soccer, but never got any time on the field. Once, I helped some kids play a practical joke on a teacher by moving his car from the parking lot into the gym. . . . I got detention, but the other kids didn't, because they were on the basketball team and had a game on Saturday."

"But, Peter," Jordan said, "why *this?*"

Peter wet his lips. "It wasn't supposed to end this way."

"Did you plan to kill all those people?"

They had rehearsed this in the holding cell. All Peter had to say was what he'd said before, when Jordan had coached him. *No. No I didn't.*

Peter looked down at his hands. "When I did it in the game," he said quietly, "I won."

Jordan froze. Peter had broken from the script, and now Jordan couldn't find his line. He only knew that the curtain was going to close before he finished. Scrambling, he replayed Peter's response in his mind: it wasn't *all* bad. It made him sound depressed, like a loner.

You can salvage this, Jordan thought to himself.

He walked up to Peter, trying desperately to communicate that he needed focus here; he needed Peter to play along with him. He needed to show the jury that this boy had chosen to stand before them in order to show remorse. "Do you understand now that there weren't any winners that day, Peter?"

Jordan saw something shine in Peter's eyes. A tiny flame, one that had been rekindled—optimism. Jordan had done his job too well: after five months of telling Peter that he could get him acquitted, that he had a strategy, that he knew what he was doing . . . Peter, goddammit, had picked this moment to finally believe him.

"The game's not over yet, right?" Peter said, and he smiled hopefully at Jordan.

As two of the jurors turned away, Jordan fought for composure. He walked back to the defense table, cursing under his breath. This had always been Peter's downfall, hadn't it? He had no idea what he looked like or sounded like to the ordinary observer, the person who didn't know that Peter wasn't actively trying to sound like a homicidal killer, but instead trying to share a private joke with one of his only friends.

"Mr. McAfee," the judge said. "Do you have any further questions?"

He had a thousand: *How could you do this to me? How could you do this to yourself? How can I make this jury understand that you didn't mean that the way it sounded?* He shook his head, puzzling through his course of action, and the judge took that for an answer.

"Ms. Leven?" he said.

Jordan's head snapped up. *Wait*, he wanted to say. *Wait, I was still thinking.* He held his breath. If Diana asked Peter anything—even what his middle name was—then he'd have a chance to redirect. And surely, then, he could leave the jury with a different impression of Peter.

Diana riffled through the notes she'd been taking, and then she turned them facedown on the table. "The state has no questions, Your Honor," she said.

Judge Wagner summoned a bailiff. "Take Mr. Houghton back to his seat. We'll adjourn court for the weekend."

As soon as the jury was dismissed, the courtroom erupted in a roar of questions. Reporters swam up the stream of onlookers toward the bar, hoping to corral Jordan for a quote. He grabbed his briefcase and hurried out the back door, the one through which the bailiffs were taking Peter.

"Hold it," he called out. He jogged closer to the men, who stood with Peter between them, his hands cuffed. "I have to talk to my client about Monday."

The bailiffs looked at each other, and then at Jordan. "Two minutes," they said, but they didn't step away. If Jordan wanted to talk to Peter, this was the only circumstance in which he was going to do it.

Peter's face was flushed, beaming. "Did I do a good job?"

Jordan hesitated, fishing for a string of words. "Did you say what you wanted to say?"

"Yeah."

"Then you did a really good job," Jordan said.

He stood in the hallway and watched the bailiffs lead Peter away. Just before he turned the corner, Peter lifted his conjoined hands, a wave. Jordan nodded, his hands in his pockets.

He slipped out of the jail through a rear door and

walked past three media vans with satellite dishes perched on the top like enormous white birds. Through the back window of each van, Jordan could see the producers editing video for the evening news. His face was on every television monitor.

He passed the last van and heard, through the open window, Peter's voice. *The game's not over yet.*

Jordan hiked his briefcase over his shoulder and walked a little faster. "Oh, yes it is," he said.

Selena had made her husband what he referred to as the Executioner's Meal, the same thing she served him each night before a closing argument: roast goose, as in, *Your goose is cooked.* With Sam already in bed, she slipped a plate in front of Jordan and then sat down across from him. "I don't even really know what to say," she admitted.

Jordan pushed the food away. "I'm not ready for this yet."

"What are you talking about?"

"I can't end the case with *that.*"

"Baby," Selena pointed out, "after today, you couldn't save this case with an entire squad of firefighters."

"I can't just give up. I told Peter he had a chance." He turned his anguished face up to Selena's. "I was the one who let him get up on the stand, even though I knew better. There's got to be something I can do . . . something I can say so that Peter's testimony isn't the last one the jury's left with."

Selena sighed and reached for the dinner plate. She took Jordan's knife and fork and cut herself a piece, dipped it in cherry sauce. "This is some damn fine goose, Jordan," she said. "You don't know what you're missing."

"The witness list," Jordan said, standing up and rummaging through a stack of papers on the other end of the dining room table. "There's got to be someone we haven't called who can help us." He scanned the names. "Who's Louise Herrman?"

"Peter's third-grade teacher," Selena said, her mouth full.

"Why the hell is she on the witness list?"

"She called us," Selena said. "She told us that if we needed her, she'd be willing to testify that he was a good boy in third grade."

"Well, that's not going to work. I need someone recent." He sighed. "There's nobody else here . . ." Flipping to the second page, he saw a single, final name typed. "Except Josie Cormier," Jordan said slowly.

Selena put down her fork. "You're calling Alex's daughter?"

"Since when do you call Judge Cormier *Alex*?"

"The girl doesn't remember anything."

"Well, I'm completely screwed. Maybe she remembers something now. Let's bring her in and see if she'll talk."

Selena sifted through the piles of papers that covered the serving table, the fireplace mantel, the top of Sam's walker. "Here's her statement," she said, handing it to Jordan.

The first page was the affidavit that Judge Cormier had brought him—the one that said Jordan wouldn't put Josie on the stand because she didn't know anything. The second was the most recent interview the girl had given to Patrick Ducharme. "They've been friends since kindergarten."

"*Were* friends."

"I don't care. Diana's already laid the groundwork here—Peter had a crush on Josie; he killed her boyfriend. If we can get her to say something nice about him—maybe even to show that she forgives him—it will carry weight with the jury." He stood up. "I'm going back to the courthouse," he said. "I need a subpoena."

*   *   *

When the doorbell rang on Saturday morning, Josie was still in her pajamas. She'd slept like the dead, which wasn't surprising, because she hadn't managed to sleep well all week. Her dreams were full of highways that carried only wheelchairs; of combination locks with no numbers; of beauty queens without faces.

She was the only person left sitting in the sequestered witness room, which meant that this was nearly over; that soon, she'd be able to breathe again.

Josie opened the door to find the tall, stunning African-American woman who was married to Jordan McAfee smiling at her, holding out a piece of paper. "I need to give you this, Josie," she said. "Is your mom home?"

Josie took the folded blue note. Maybe it was like a cast party for the end of the trial. That would be kind of cool. She called for her mother over her shoulder. Alex appeared with Patrick trailing behind.

"Oh," Selena said, blinking.

Unflappable, her mother folded her arms. "What's going on?"

"Judge, I'm sorry to bother you on a Saturday, but my husband was wondering if Josie might be free to speak to him today."

"Why?"

"Because he's subpoenaed Josie to testify on Monday."

The room started to spin. "Testify?" Josie repeated.

Her mother stepped forward, and from the look on her face, she probably would have done serious damage if Patrick hadn't wrapped an arm around her waist to hold her back. He plucked the blue paper out of Josie's hand and scanned it.

"I can't go to court," Josie murmured.

Her mother shook her head. "You have a signed affidavit

from Josie stating that she doesn't remember anything—"

"I know you're upset. But the reality is, Jordan's calling Josie on Monday, and we'd rather talk to her about her testimony beforehand than have her come in cold. It's better for us, and it's better for Josie." She hesitated. "You can do it the hard way, Judge, or you can do it this way."

Josie's mother clenched her jaw. "Two o'clock," she gritted out, and she slammed the door in Selena's face.

"You *promised*," Josie cried. "You promised me I didn't have to get up there and testify. You said I wouldn't have to do this!"

Her mother grabbed her by the shoulders. "Honey, I know this is scary. I know you don't want to be there. But nothing you say is going to help him. It's going to be very short and painless." She glanced at Patrick. "Why the hell is he doing this?"

"Because his case is in the toilet," Patrick said. "He wants Josie to save it."

That was all it took: Josie burst into tears.

Jordan opened the door of his office, carrying Sam like a football in his arms. It was two o'clock on the dot, and Josie Cormier and her mother had arrived. Judge Cormier looked about as inviting as a sheer cliff wall; by contrast, her daughter was shaking like a leaf. "Thanks for coming," he said, pasting an enormous, friendly smile on his face. Above all else, he wanted Josie to feel at ease.

Neither of the women said a word.

"I'm sorry about this," Jordan said, gesturing toward Sam. "My wife was supposed to be here by now to get the baby so that we could talk, but a logging truck overturned on Route 10." He stretched his smile wider. "It should only be a minute."

He gestured toward the couch and chairs in his office,

offering a seat. There were cookies on the table, and a pitcher of water. "Please have something to eat, or drink."

"No," the judge said.

Jordan sat down, bouncing the baby on his knee. "Right."

He stared at the clock, amazed at how very long sixty seconds could be when you wanted them to pass quickly, and then suddenly the door flew open and Selena ran inside. "Sorry, sorry," she said, flustered, reaching for the baby. As she did, the diaper bag fell off her shoulder, skittering across the floor to land in front of Josie.

Josie stood up, staring at Selena's fallen backpack. She backed away, stumbling over her mother's legs and the side of the couch. "No," she whimpered, and she curled into a ball in the corner, covering her head with her hands as she started to cry. The noise set Sam off shrieking, and Selena pressed him up against her shoulder as Jordan watched, speechless.

Judge Cormier crouched beside her daughter. "Josie, what's the matter. Josie? What's going on?"

The girl rocked back and forth, sobbing. She glanced up at her mother. "I remember," she whispered. "More than I said I did."

The judge's mouth dropped open, and Jordan used her shock to seize the moment. "*What* do you remember?" he asked, kneeling beside Josie.

Judge Cormier pushed him out of the way and helped Josie to her feet. She sat her down on the couch and poured her a glass of water from the pitcher on the table. "It's okay," the judge murmured.

Josie took a shuddering breath. "The backpack," she said, jerking her chin toward the one on the floor. "It fell off Peter's shoulder, like that one did. The zipper was open, and . . . and a gun fell out. Matt grabbed it." Her face contorted. "He fired at Peter, but he missed. And Peter . . . and he . . ." She closed her eyes. "That's when Peter shot him."

Jordan caught Selena's eye. Peter's defense hinged on PTSD—how one event might trigger another; how a person who was traumatized might be unable to recall anything about the event at all. How someone like Josie might watch a diaper bag fall and instead see what had happened in the locker room months earlier: Peter, with a gun pointing at him—a real and present threat, a bully about to kill him.

Or, in other words, what Jordan had been saying all along.

"It's a mess," Jordan said to Selena after the Cormiers had gone home. "And that works for me."

Selena hadn't left with the baby; Sam was now asleep in an empty filing cabinet drawer. She and Jordan sat at the table where, less than an hour ago, Josie had confessed that she'd recently started to remember bits and pieces of the shooting but hadn't told anyone, out of fear of having to go to court and talk about it. That when the diaper bag had fallen, it had all come flooding back, full-force.

"If I'd found this out before the trial started, I would have taken it to Diana and used it tactically," Jordan said. "But since the jury's already sitting, maybe I can do something even better."

"Nothing like an eleventh-hour Hail Mary pass," Selena said.

"Let's assume we put Josie on the stand to say all this in court. All of a sudden, those ten deaths aren't what they seemed to be. No one knew the real story behind this one, and that calls into question everything else the prosecution's told the jury about the shootings. In other words, if the state didn't know this, what else don't they know?"

"And," Selena pointed out, "it highlights what King Wah said. Here was one of the kids who'd tormented Peter, holding a gun on him, just like he'd figured all along would happen." She hesitated. "Granted, Peter was the one who brought in the gun . . ."

"That's irrelevant," Jordan said. "I don't have to have all the answers." He kissed Selena square on the mouth. "I just need to make sure that the state doesn't either."

Alex sat on the bench, watching a ragged crew of college students playing Ultimate Frisbee as if they had no idea that the world had split at its seams. Beside her, Josie hugged her knees to her chest. "Why didn't you tell me?" Alex asked.

Josie lifted her face. "I couldn't. You were the judge on the case."

Alex felt a stab beneath her breastbone. "But even after I recused myself, Josie . . . when we went to see Jordan, and you said you didn't remember anything . . . That's why I had you swear the affidavit."

"I thought that's what you *wanted* me to do," Josie said. "You told me if I signed it, I wouldn't have to be a witness . . . and I didn't want to go to court. I didn't want to see Peter again."

One of the college players leaped and missed the Frisbee. It sailed toward Alex, landing in a scuffle of dust at her feet. "Sorry," the boy called, waving.

Alex picked it up and sent it soaring. The wind lifted the Frisbee and carried it higher, a stain against a perfectly blue sky.

"Mommy," Josie said, although she had not called Alex that for years. "What's going to happen to me?"

She didn't know. Not as a judge, not as a lawyer, not as a mother. The only thing she could do was offer good counsel and hope it withstood what was yet to come. "From here on out," Alex told Josie, "all you have to do is tell the truth."

Patrick had been called into a domestic-violence hostage negotiation down in Cornish and did not reach Sterling until it was nearly midnight. Instead of heading to his own house, he went to Alex's—it felt more like home, anyway. He'd tried to call her several times today to see what had happened with Jordan McAfee, but he couldn't get cell phone service where he was.

He found her sitting in the dark on the living room sofa, and sank down beside her. For a moment, he stared at the wall, just like Alex. "What are we doing?" he whispered.

She faced him, and that's when he realized she had been crying. He blamed himself—*You should have tried harder to call, you should have come home earlier.* "What's wrong?"

"I screwed up, Patrick," Alex said. "I thought I was helping her. I thought I knew what I was doing. As it turned out, I didn't know anything at all."

"Josie?" he asked, trying to fit together the pieces. "Where is she?"

"Asleep. I gave her a sleeping pill."

"You want to talk about it?"

"We saw Jordan McAfee today, and Josie told him . . . she told him that she remembered something about the shooting. In fact, she remembered everything."

Patrick whistled softly. "So she was *lying?*"

"I don't know. I think she was scared." Alex glanced up at Patrick. "That's not all. According to Josie, Matt shot at Peter first."

"*What?*"

"The knapsack Peter was carrying fell down in front of

Matt, and he got hold of one of the guns. He shot, but he missed."

Patrick rubbed a hand down his face. Diana Leven was *not* going to be happy.

"What's going to happen to Josie?" Alex said. "The best-case scenario is that she gets on the stand and the entire town hates her for testifying on Peter's behalf. The worst-case scenario is that she commits perjury on the stand and gets charged with it."

Patrick's mind was racing. "You can't worry about this. It's out of your hands. Besides, Josie will be fine. She's a survivor."

He leaned down and kissed her, softly, his mouth rounding over words he couldn't yet tell her, and promises he was afraid to make. He kissed her until he felt the tightness go out of her spine. "You ought to go take one of those sleeping pills," he whispered.

Alex tilted her head. "You're not staying?"

"Can't. I've still got work to do."

"You came all the way over here to tell me you're leaving?"

Patrick looked at her, wishing he could explain what he had to do. "I'll see you later, Alex," he said.

Alex had confided in him, but as a judge, she would know that Patrick could not keep her secret. On Monday morning, when Patrick saw the prosecutor, he'd have to tell Diana what he now knew about Matt Royston firing the first shot in the locker room. Legally, he was obligated to disclose this new wrinkle. However, technically, he had all day Sunday to do with that information whatever he liked.

If Patrick could find evidence to back up Josie's allegations, then it would soften the blow for her on the stand—

and make him a hero in Alex's eyes. But there was another part of him that wanted to search the locker room again for another reason. Patrick knew he had personally combed that small space for evidence, that no other bullet had been found. And if Matt *had* shot first at Peter, there should have been one.

He hadn't wanted to say this to Alex, but Josie had lied to them once. There was no reason she couldn't be doing it again.

At six in the morning, Sterling High School was a sleeping giant. Patrick unlocked the front door and moved through the corridors in the dark. They had been professionally cleaned, but that didn't stop him from seeing, in the beam of his flashlight, the spots where bullets had broken windows and blood had stained the floor. He moved quickly, the heels of his boots echoing, as he pushed aside blue construction tarps and avoided stacks of lumber.

Patrick opened the double doors of the gym and squeaked his way across the Morse-coded markings on the polyurethaned boards. He flicked a bank of switches and the gym flooded with light. The last time he'd been in here, there had been emergency blankets lying on the floor, corresponding to the numbers that had been inked on the foreheads of Noah James and Michael Beach and Justin Friedman and Dusty Spears and Austin Prokiov. There had been crime-scene techs crawling on their hands and knees, taking photographs of chips in the cement block, digging bullets out of the backboard of the basketball hoop.

He had spent hours at the police station, his first stop after leaving Alex's house, scrutinizing the enlarged fingerprint that had been on Gun B. An inconclusive one; one that he'd assumed, lazily, to be Peter's. But what if it was Matt's? Was there any way to prove that Royston had held the gun, as Josie claimed? Patrick had studied the prints taken from Matt's dead body and held them up every which way against the partial print, until the lines and ridges blurred even more than they should have.

If he was going to find proof, it was going to have to be in the school itself.

The locker room looked exactly like the photo he'd used during his testimony earlier this week, except that the bodies, of course, had been removed. Unlike the corridors and classrooms of the school, the locker room hadn't been cleaned or patched. The small area held too much damage—not physical, but psychological—and the administration had unanimously agreed to tear it down, along with the rest of the gym and the cafeteria, later this month.

The locker room was a rectangle. The door that led into it, from the gym, was in the middle of one long wall. A wooden bench sat directly opposite, and a line of metal lockers. In the far left corner of the locker room was a small doorway that opened into a communal shower stall. In this corner, Matt's body had been found, with Josie lying beside him; thirty feet away in the far right corner of the locker room, Peter had been crouching. The blue backpack had fallen just to the left of the doorway.

If Patrick believed Josie, then Peter had come running into the locker room, where Josie and Matt had gone to hide. Presumably, he was holding Gun A. He dropped his backpack, and Matt—who would have been standing in the middle of the room, close enough to reach it—grabbed Gun B. Matt shot at Peter—the bullet that had never been found, the one that proved Gun B was fired at all—and missed. When he tried to shoot again, the gun jammed. At that moment, Peter shot him, twice.

The problem was, Matt's body had been found at least fifteen feet away from the backpack where he'd grabbed the gun.

Why would Matt have backed up, and *then* shot at Peter? It didn't make sense. It was possible that Peter's shots had sent Matt's body recoiling, but basic physics told Patrick that a shot fired from where Peter was standing would still not have landed Matt where he'd been found. In addition, there had been no blood-spatter pattern to suggest that Matt had been standing anywhere near the backpack when he was hit by Peter. He'd pretty much dropped where he'd been shot.

Patrick walked toward the wall where he'd apprehended Peter. He started at the upper corner and methodically ran his fingers over every divot and niche, over the edges of the lockers and inside them, around the bend of the perpendicular walls. He crawled beneath the wooden bench and scrutinized the underside. He held his flashlight up to the ceiling. In such close quarters, any bullet fired by Matt should have made enough serious damage to be noticeable, and yet, there was absolutely no evidence that any gun had been fired—successfully—in Peter's direction.

Patrick walked to the opposite corner of the locker room. There was still a dark bloodstain on the floor, and a dried boot print. He stepped over the stain and into the shower stall, repeating the same meticulous investigation of the tiled wall that would have been behind Matt.

If he found that missing bullet here, where Matt's body had been found, then Matt clearly hadn't been the one to fire Gun B—it would have been Peter wielding that weapon, as well as Gun A. Or in other words: Josie would have been lying to Jordan McAfee.

It was easy work, because the tile was white, pristine. There were no cracks or flakes, no chips, nothing that would suggest a bullet had gone through Matt's stomach and struck the shower wall.

Patrick turned around, looking in places that didn't

make sense: the top of the shower, the ceiling, the drain. He took off his shoes and socks and shuffled along the shower floor.

It was when he'd just scraped his little toe along the line of the drain that he felt it.

Patrick got down on his hands and knees and felt along the edge of the metal. There was a long, raw scuff on the tile that bordered the drainage grate. It would have easily gone unnoticed because of its location—techs who saw it had probably assumed it was grout. He rubbed it with his finger and then peered with a flashlight into the drain. If the bullet had slipped through, it was long gone—and yet, the drainage holes were tiny enough that this shouldn't have been possible.

Opening a locker, Patrick ripped a tiny square of mirror off with his hands and set it face-up on the floor of the shower, just where the scuff mark was. Then he turned off the lights and took out a laser pointer. He stood where Peter had been apprehended and pointed the beam at the mirror, watched it bounce onto the far wall of the showers, where no bullet had left a mark.

Circling around, he continued to point the beam until it ricocheted up—right through the center of a small window that served as ventilation. He knelt, marking the spot where he stood with a pencil from his pocket. Then he dug out his cell phone. "Diana," he said when the prosecutor answered. "Don't let that trial start tomorrow."

"I know it's unusual," Diana said in court the next morning, "and that we have a jury sitting here, but I have to ask for a recess until my detective gets here. He's investigating something new on the case . . . possibly something exculpatory."

"Have you called him?" Judge Wagner asked.

"Several times." Patrick was not answering his phone. If he was, then she could have told him directly how much she wanted to kill him.

"I have to object, Your Honor," Jordan said. "We're ready to go forward. I'm sure that Ms. Leven will give me that exculpatory information, if and when it ever arrives, but I'm willing at this point to take my chances. And since we're all here at the bench, I'd like to add that I have a witness who's prepared to testify right now."

"What witness?" Diana said. "You don't have anyone else to call."

He smiled at her. "Judge Cormier's daughter."

Alex sat outside the courtroom, holding tight to Josie's hand. "This is going to be over before you know it."

The great irony here, Alex knew, was that months ago when she'd fought so hard to be the judge on this case, it was because she felt more at ease offering legal comfort to her daughter than emotional comfort. Well, here she was, and Josie was about to testify in the arena Alex knew better than anyone else, and she still didn't have any grand judicial advice that could help her.

It *would* be scary. It *would* be painful. And all Alex could do was watch her suffer.

A bailiff came out to them. "Judge," he said. "If your daughter's ready?"

Alex squeezed Josie's hand. "Just tell them what you know," she said, and she stood up to take a seat in the courtroom.

"Mom?" Josie called after her, and Alex turned. "What if what you know isn't what people want to hear?"

Alex tried to smile. "Tell the truth," she said. "You can't lose."

✳　　✳　　✳

To comply with discovery rules, Jordan handed Diana a synopsis of Josie's testimony as she was walking up to the stand. "When did you get this?" the prosecutor whispered.

"This weekend. Sorry," he said, although he really wasn't. He walked toward Josie, who looked small and pale. Her hair had been gathered into a neat ponytail, and her hands were folded in her lap. She was studiously avoiding anyone's gaze by focusing on the grain of the wood on the rail of the witness stand.

"Can you state your name?"

"Josie Cormier."

"Where do you live, Josie?"

"45 East Prescott Street, in Sterling."

"How old are you?"

"I'm seventeen," she said.

Jordan took a step closer, so that only she would be able to hear him. "See?" he murmured. "Piece of cake." He winked at her, and he thought she might even have smiled back the tiniest bit.

"Where were you on the morning of March 6, 2007?"

"I was at school."

"What class did you have first period?"

"English," Josie said softly.

"What about second period?"

"Math."

"Third period?"

"I had a study."

"Where did you spend it?"

"With my boyfriend," she said. "Matt Royston." She looked sideways, blinking too fast.

"Where were you and Matt during third period?"

"We left the cafeteria. We were going to his locker, before the next class."

"What happened then?"

Josie looked into her lap. "There was a lot of noise. And people started running. People were screaming about guns, about someone with a gun. A friend of ours, Drew Girard, told us it was Peter."

She glanced up then, and her eyes locked on Peter's. For a long moment, she just stared at him, and then she closed her eyes and turned away.

"Did you know what was going on?"

"No."

"Did you see anyone shooting?"

"No."

"Where did you go?"

"To the gym. We ran across it, toward the locker room. I knew he was coming closer, because I kept hearing gunshots."

"Who was with you when you went into the locker room?"

"I thought Drew and Matt, but when I turned around, I realized that Drew wasn't there. He'd been shot."

"Did you see Drew getting shot?"

Josie shook her head. "No."

"Did you see Peter before you got into the locker room?"

"No." Her face crumpled, and she wiped at her eyes.

"Josie," Jordan said, "what happened next?"

Get down," Matt hissed, and he shoved Josie so that she fell behind the wooden bench.

It wasn't a good place to hide, but then, nowhere in the locker room was a good place to hide. Matt's plan had been to climb out the window in the shower, and he'd even opened it up, but then they'd heard the shots in the gym and realized they didn't have time to drag the bench over and climb through. They'd boxed themselves in, literally.

She curled herself into a ball and Matt crouched down in front of her. Her heart thundered against his back, and she kept forgetting to breathe.

He reached behind him until he found her hand. "If anything happens, Jo," he whispered, "I loved you."

Josie started to cry. She was going to die; they were all going to die. She thought of a hundred things she hadn't done yet that she so badly wanted to do: go to Australia, swim with dolphins. Learn all the words to "Bohemian Rhapsody." Graduate.

Get married.

She wiped her face against the back of Matt's shirt, and

then the locker room burst open. Peter stumbled inside, his eyes wild, holding a handgun. His left sneaker was untied, Josie noticed, and then she couldn't believe she noticed. He lifted his gun at Matt, and she couldn't help it; she screamed.

Maybe it was the noise; maybe it was her voice. It startled Peter, and he dropped his backpack. It slid off his shoulder, and as it did, another gun fell out of an open pocket.

It skittered across the floor, landing just behind Josie's left foot.

Do you know how there are moments when the world moves so slowly you can feel your bones shifting, your mind tumbling? When you think that no matter what happens to you for the rest of your life, you will remember every last detail of that one minute forever? Josie watched her hand stretch back, watched her fingers curl around the cold black butt of the gun. Fumbling it, she staggered upright, pointing the gun at Peter.

Matt backed away toward the showers, under Josie's cover. Peter held his gun steady, still pointing it at Matt, even though Josie was closer. "Josie," he said. "Let me finish this."

"Shoot him, Josie," Matt said. "Fucking shoot him."

Peter pulled back the slide of the gun so that a bullet from the clip would cycle into place. Watching him carefully, Josie mimicked his actions.

She remembered being in nursery school with Peter—how other boys would pick up sticks or rocks and run around yelling *Hands up*. What had she and Peter used the sticks for? She couldn't recall.

"Josie, for Christ's sake!" Matt was sweating, his eyes wide. "Are you fucking stupid?"

"Don't talk to her like that," Peter cried.

"Shut up, asshole," Matt said. "You think she's going to save you?" He turned to Josie. "What are you waiting for? *Shoot.*"

So she did.

As the gun fired, it ripped two stripes of her skin from the base of her thumb. Her hands jerked upward, numb, humming. The blood was black on Matt's gray T-shirt. He stood for a moment, shocked, his hand over the wound in his stomach. She saw his mouth close around her name, but she couldn't hear it, her ears were ringing so loudly. *Josie?* and then he fell to the floor.

Josie's hand started shaking violently; she wasn't surprised when the gun just fell out of it, as singularly repelled by her grasp as it had been glued to it moments before. "Matt," she cried, running toward him. She pressed her hands against the blood, because that's what you were supposed to do, wasn't it, but he writhed and screamed in agony. Blood began to bubble out of his mouth, trailing down his neck. "Do something," she sobbed, turning to Peter. "Help me."

Peter walked closer, lifted the gun he was holding, and shot Matt in the head.

Horrified, she scrambled backward, away from them both. That *wasn't* what she'd meant; that *couldn't* have been what she meant.

She stared at Peter, and she realized that in that one moment, when she hadn't been thinking, she knew exactly what he'd felt as he moved through the school with his backpack and his guns. Every kid in this school played a role: jock, brain, beauty, freak. All Peter had done was what they all secretly dreamed of: be someone, even for just nineteen minutes, who nobody else was allowed to judge.

"Don't tell," Peter whispered, and Josie realized he was offering her a way out—a deal sealed in blood, a partnership of silence: *I won't share your secrets, if you don't share mine.*

Josie nodded slowly, and then her world went black.

I think a person's life is supposed to be like a DVD. You can see the version everyone else sees, or you can choose the director's cut—the way he wanted you to see it, before everything else got in the way.

There are menus, probably, so that you can start at the good spots and not have to relive the bad ones. You can measure your life by the number of scenes you've survived, or the minutes you've been stuck there.

Probably, though, life is more like one of those dumb video surveillance tapes. Grainy, no matter how hard you stare at it. And looped: the same thing, over and over.

Five Months After

Alex pushed past the people in the gallery who had erupted in confusion in the wake of Josie's confession. Somewhere in this crowd of people were the Roystons, who had just heard that their son had been shot by her daughter, but she could not think of that right now. She could only see Josie, trapped on that witness stand, while Alex struggled to get past the bar. She was a judge, dammit; she should have been allowed to go there, but two bailiffs were firmly holding her back.

Wagner was smacking his gavel, although nobody gave a damn. "We'll take a fifteen-minute recess," he ordered, and as another bailiff hauled Peter through a rear door, the judge turned to Josie. "Young lady," he said, "you are still under oath."

Alex watched Josie being taken through another door, and she called out after her. A moment later, Eleanor was at her side. The clerk took Alex's arm. "Judge, come with me. You're not safe out here right now."

For the first time she could actively remember, Alex allowed herself to be led.

✳   ✳   ✳

Patrick arrived in the courtroom just as it exploded. He saw Josie on the stand, crying desperately; he saw Judge Wagner fighting for control—but most of all, he saw Alex single-mindedly trying to get to her daughter.

He would have drawn his gun right then and there to help her do it.

By the time he fought his way down the central aisle of the courtroom, Alex was gone. He caught a glimpse of her as she slipped into a room behind the bench, and he hurdled the bar to follow her but felt someone grab his sleeve. Annoyed, he glanced down to see Diana Leven.

"What the hell is going on?" he asked.

"You first."

He sighed. "I spent the night at Sterling High, trying to check Josie's statement. It didn't make sense—if Matt had fired at Peter, there should have been physical evidence of destruction in the wall behind him. I assumed that she was lying again—that Peter had been the one to shoot Matt unprovoked. Once I figured out where that first bullet hit, I used a laser to see where it could have ricocheted—and then I understood why we didn't find it the first time around." Digging in his coat, he extracted an evidence bag with a slug inside. "The fire department helped me dig it out of a maple tree outside the window in the shower stall. I drove it straight to the lab for testing—and stood over them all night with a whip until they agreed to do the work on the spot. Not only was the bullet fired from Gun B, it's got blood and tissue on it that types to Matt Royston. The thing is, when you reverse the angle of that bullet—when you stand in the tree and ricochet the laser off the tile where it struck, to see where the shot originated from— you don't get anywhere close to where Peter was standing. It was—"

The prosecutor sighed wearily. "Josie just confessed to shooting Matt Royston."

"Well," Patrick said, handing the evidence bag to Diana, "she's finally telling the truth."

Jordan leaned against the bars of the holding cell. "Did you *forget* to tell me about this?"

"No," Peter said.

He turned. "You know, if you'd mentioned this at the beginning, your case could have had a very different outcome."

Peter was lying on the bench in the cell, his hands behind his head. To Jordan's shock, he was smiling. "She was my friend again," Peter explained. "You don't break a promise to a friend."

Alex sat in the dark of the conference room where defendants were usually brought during breaks, and realized that her daughter now would qualify. There would be another trial, and this time Josie would be at the center of it.

"Why?" she asked.

She could make out the silver edge of Josie's profile. "Because you told me to tell the truth."

"What *is* the truth?"

"I loved Matt. And I hated him. I hated *myself* for loving him, but if I wasn't with him, I wasn't anyone anymore."

"I don't understand . . ."

"How *could* you? You're *perfect*." Josie shook her head. "The rest of us, we're all like Peter. Some of us just do a better job of hiding it. What's the difference between spending your life trying to be invisible, or pretending to be the person you think everyone wants you to be? Either way, you're faking."

Alex thought of all the parties she'd ever gone to where the first question she was asked was *What do you do?* as if that were enough to define you. Nobody ever asked you who you really were, because that changed. You might be a judge or a mother or a dreamer. You might be a loner or a visionary or a pessimist. You might be the victim, and you might be the bully. You could be the parent, and also the child. You might wound one day and heal the next.

I'm not *perfect*, Alex thought, and maybe that was the first step toward becoming that way.

"What's going to happen to me?" Josie asked, the same question she'd asked a day ago, when Alex thought herself qualified to give answers.

"What's going to happen to *us*," Alex corrected.

A smile chased over Josie's face, gone almost as quickly as it had come. "I asked you first."

The door to the conference room opened, spilling light from the corridor, silhouetting whatever came next. Alex reached for her daughter's hand and took a deep breath. "Let's go see," she said.

Peter was convicted of eight first-degree murders and two second-degree murders. The jury decided that in the case of Matt Royston and Courtney Ignatio, he had not been acting with premeditation and deliberation. He'd been provoked.

After the verdict was handed down, Jordan met with Peter in the holding cell. He'd be brought back to the jail only until the sentencing hearing; then he would be transferred to the state prison in Concord. Serving out eight consecutive murder sentences, he would not leave it alive.

"You okay?" Jordan asked, putting his hand on Peter's shoulder.

"Yeah." He shrugged. "I sort of knew it was going to happen."

"But they *heard* you. That's why they came back with manslaughter for two of the counts."

"I guess I should say thanks for trying." He smiled crookedly at Jordan. "Have a good life."

"I'll come see you, if I get down to Concord," Jordan said.

He looked at Peter. In the six months since this case had fallen into his lap, his client had grown up. Peter was as tall as Jordan now. He probably weighed a little more. He had a deeper voice, a shadow of beard on his jaw. Jordan marveled that he hadn't noticed these things until now.

"Well," Jordan said. "I'm sorry it didn't work out the way I'd hoped."

"Me, too."

Peter held out his hand, and Jordan embraced him instead. "Take care."

He started out of the cell, and then Peter called him back. He was holding out the eyeglasses Jordan had brought him for the trial. "These are yours," Peter said.

"Hang on to them. You have more use for them."

Peter tucked the glasses into the front pocket of Jordan's jacket. "I kind of like knowing you're taking care of them," he said. "And there isn't all that much I really want to see."

Jordan nodded. He walked out of the holding cell and said good-bye to the deputies. Then he headed toward the lobby, where Selena was waiting.

As he approached her, he put on Peter's glasses. "What's up with those?" she asked.

"I kind of like them."

"You have perfect vision," Selena pointed out.

Jordan considered the way the lenses made the world curve in at the ends, so that he had to move more gingerly through it. "Not always," he said.

*   *   *

In the weeks after the trial, Lewis began fooling around with numbers. He'd done some preliminary research and entered it into STATA to see what kinds of patterns emerged. And—here was the interesting thing—it had absolutely nothing to do with happiness. Instead, he'd started looking at the communities where school shootings had occurred in the past and spinning them out to the present, to see how a single act of violence might affect economic stability. Or in other words—once the world was pulled out from beneath your feet, did you ever get to stand on firm ground again?

He was teaching again at Sterling College—basic microeconomics. Classes had only just begun in late September, and Lewis found himself slipping easily into the lecture circuit. When he was talking about Keynesian models and widgets and competition, it was routine—so effortless that he could almost make himself believe this was any other freshman survey course he'd taught in the past, before Peter had been convicted.

Lewis taught by walking up and down the aisles—a necessary evil, now that the campus had gone WiFi and students would play online poker or IM each other while he lectured—which was how he happened to come across the kids in the back. Two football players were taking turns squeezing a sports-top water bottle so that the stream arced upward and sprayed onto the back of another kid's neck. The boy, two rows forward, kept turning around to see who was squirting water at him, but by then, the jocks were looking up at the graphs on the screen in the front of the hall, their faces as smooth as choirboys'.

"Now," Lewis said, not missing a beat, "who can tell me what happens if you set the price above point A on the graph?" He plucked the water bottle out of the hands of one of the jocks. "Thank you, Mr. Graves. I was getting thirsty."

The boy two rows ahead raised his hand like an arrow, and Lewis nodded at him. "No one would want to buy the widget for that much money," he said. "So demand would fall, and that means the price would have to drop, or they'd wind up with a whole boatload of extras in the warehouse."

"Excellent," Lewis said, and he glanced up at the clock. "All right, guys, on Monday we'll be covering the next chapter in Mankiw. And don't be surprised if there's a surprise quiz."

"If you told us, it's not a surprise," a girl pointed out.

Lewis smiled. "Oops."

He stood by the chair of the boy who'd given the right answer. He was stuffing his notebook into his backpack, which was already so crammed with papers that the zipper wouldn't close. His hair was too long, and his T-shirt had a picture of Einstein's face on it. "Nice work today."

"Thanks." The boy shifted from one foot to the other; Lewis could tell that he wasn't quite sure what to say next. He thrust out his hand. "Um, nice to meet you. I mean, you've already met us all, but not, like, personally."

"Right. What's your name again?"

"Peter. Peter Granford."

Lewis opened up his mouth to speak, but then just shook his head.

"What?" The boy ducked his head. "You just, uh, looked like you were going to say something important."

Lewis looked at this namesake, at the way he stood with his shoulders rounded, as if he did not deserve so much space in this world. He felt that familiar pain that fell like a hammer on his breastbone whenever he thought of Peter, of a life that would be lost to prison. He wished he'd taken more time to look at Peter when Peter was right in front of his eyes, because now he would be forced to compensate with imperfect memories or—even worse—to find his son in the faces of strangers.

Lewis reached deep inside and unraveled the smile that he saved for moments like this, when there was absolutely nothing to be happy about. "It *was* important," he said. "You remind me of someone I used to know."

It took Lacy three weeks to gather the courage to enter Peter's bedroom. Now that the verdict had been handed down—now that they knew Peter would never be coming home again—there was no reason to keep it as she had for the past five months: a shrine, a haven for optimism.

She sat down on Peter's bed and brought his pillow to her face. It still smelled like him, and she wondered how long it would take for that to dissipate. She glanced around at the scattered books on his shelves—the ones that the police had not taken. She opened his nightstand drawer and fingered the silky tassel of a bookmark, the metal teeth of a lockjawed stapler. The empty belly of a television remote control, missing its batteries. A magnifying glass. An old pack of Pokémon cards, a magic trick, a portable hard drive on a keychain.

Lacy took the box she'd brought up from the basement and placed each item inside. Here was the crime scene: look at what was left behind and try to re-create the boy.

She folded his quilt, and then his sheets, and then pulled the pillowcase free. She suddenly recalled a dinner conversation where Lewis had told her that for $10,000, you could flatten a house with a wrecking ball. Imagine how much less it took to destroy something than it did to build it in the first place: in less than an hour, this room would look as if Peter had never lived here at all.

When it was all a neat pile, Lacy sat back down on the

bed and looked around at the stark walls, the paint a little brighter in the spots where posters had been. She touched the piped seam of Peter's mattress and wondered how long she would continue to think of it as Peter's.

Love was supposed to move mountains, to make the world go round, to be all you need, but it fell apart at the details. It couldn't save a single child—not the ones who'd gone to Sterling High that day, expecting the normal; not Josie Cormier; certainly not Peter. So what was the recipe? Was it love, mixed with something else for good measure? Luck? Hope? Forgiveness?

She remembered, suddenly, what Alex Cormier had said to her during the trial: *Something still exists as long as there's someone around to remember it.*

Everyone would remember Peter for nineteen minutes of his life, but what about the other nine million? Lacy would have to be the keeper of those, because it was the only way for that part of Peter to stay alive. For every recollection of him that involved a bullet or a scream, she would have a hundred others: of a little boy splashing in a pond, or riding a bicycle for the first time, or waving from the top of a jungle gym. Of a kiss good night, or a crayoned Mother's Day card, or a voice off-key in the shower. She would string them together—the moments when her child had been just like other people's. She would wear them, precious pearls, every day of her life; because if she lost them, then the boy she had loved and raised and known would really be gone.

Lacy began to stretch the sheets over the bed again. She settled the quilt, tucked the corners, fluffed the pillow. She set the books back on the shelves and the toys and tools and knickknacks back in the nightstand. Last, she unrolled the long tongues of the posters and put them back up on the walls. She was careful to place the thumbtacks in the same original holes. That way, she wouldn't be doing any more damage.

Exactly one month after he was convicted, when the lights were dimmed and the detention officers made a final sweep of the catwalk, Peter reached down and tugged off his right sock. He turned on his side in the lower bunk, so that he was facing the wall. He fed the sock into his mouth, stuffing it as far back as it would go.

When it got hard to breathe, he fell into a dream. He was still eighteen, but it was the first day of kindergarten. He was carrying his backpack and his Superman lunch box. The orange school bus pulled up and, with a sigh, split open its gaping jaws. Peter climbed the steps and faced the back of the bus, but this time, he was the only student on it. He walked down the aisle to the very end, near the emergency exit. He put his lunch box down beside him and glanced out the rear window. It was so bright he thought the sun itself must be chasing them down the highway.

"Almost there," a voice said, and Peter turned around to look at the driver. But just as there had been no passengers, there was no one at the wheel.

Here was the amazing thing: in his dream, Peter wasn't scared. He knew, somehow, that he was headed exactly where he'd wanted to go.

March 6, 2008

You might not have recognized Sterling High. There was a new green metal roof, fresh grass growing out front, and a glass atrium that rose two stories at the rear of the school. A plaque on the bricks by the front door read: A SAFE HARBOR.

Later today, there would be a ceremony to honor the memories of those who'd died here a year ago, but because Patrick had been involved in the new security protocols for the school, he'd been able to sneak Alex in for an advance viewing.

Inside, there were no lockers—just open cubbies, so that nothing was hidden from view. Students were in class; only a few teachers moved through the lobby. They wore IDs around their necks, as did the kids. Alex had not really understood this—the threat was always from the inside, not the outside—but Patrick said that it made people feel secure, and that was half the battle.

Her cell phone rang. Patrick sighed. "I thought you told them—"

"I did," Alex said. She flipped it open, and the secretary for the Grafton County public defender's office began reeling off a litany of crises. "Stop," she said, interrupting. "Remember? I'm missing in action for the day."

She had resigned her judicial appointment. Josie had been charged as an accessory to second-degree murder and accepted a plea of manslaughter, with five years served. After that, every time Alex had a child in her courtroom charged with a felony, she couldn't be impartial. As a judge, weighing the evidence had taken precedence; but as a mother, it was not the facts that mattered—only the feelings. Going back to her roots as a public defender seemed not only natural but comfortable. She understood, firsthand, what her clients were feeling. She visited them when she went to visit her daughter at the women's penitentiary. Defendants liked her because she wasn't condescending and because she told them the truth about their chances: what you saw of Alex Cormier was what you got.

Patrick led her to the spot that had once housed the back staircase at Sterling High. Instead, now, there was an enormous glass atrium that covered the spot where the gymnasium and locker room had been. Outside, you could see the playing fields, where a gym class was now in the thick of a soccer game, taking advantage of the early spring and the melted snow. Inside, there were wooden tables set up, with stools where students could meet or have a snack or read. A few kids were there now, studying for a geometry test. Their whispers rose like smoke to the ceiling: *complementary . . . supplementary . . . intersection . . . endpoint.*

To one side of the atrium, in front of the glass wall, were ten chairs. Unlike the rest of the seats in the atrium, these had backs and were painted white. You had to look closely to see that they had been bolted to the floor, instead of having been dragged over by students and left behind. They were not lined up in a row; they were not evenly spaced.

They did not have names or placards on them, but everyone knew why they were there.

She felt Patrick come up behind her and slide his arm around her waist. "It's almost time," he said, and she nodded.

As she reached for one of the empty stools and started to drag it closer to the glass wall, Patrick took it from her. "For God's sake, Patrick," she muttered. "I'm pregnant, not terminal."

That had been a surprise, too. The baby was due at the end of May. Alex tried not to think about it as a replacement for the daughter who would still be in jail for the next four years; she imagined instead that maybe this would be the one who rescued them all.

Patrick sank down beside her on a stool as Alex looked at her watch: 10:02 a.m.

She took a deep breath. "It doesn't look the same anymore."

"I know," Patrick said.

"Do you think that's a good thing?"

He thought for a moment. "I think it's a necessary thing," he said.

She noticed that the maple tree, the one that had grown outside the window of the second-story locker room, had not been cut down during the construction of the atrium. From where she was sitting, you couldn't see the hole that had been carved out of it to retrieve a bullet. The tree was enormous, with a thick gnarled trunk and twisted limbs. It had probably been here long before the high school ever was, maybe even before Sterling was settled.

10:09.

She felt Patrick's hand slip into her lap as she watched the soccer game. The teams seemed grossly mismatched, the kids who had already hit puberty playing against those who were still slight and small. Alex watched a striker charge a defenseman for the other team, leaving the smaller boy trampled as the ball hurtled high into the net.

All that, Alex thought, *and nothing's changed*. She glanced at her watch again: 10:13.

The last few minutes, of course, were the hardest. Alex found herself standing, her hands pressed flat against the glass. She felt the baby kick inside her, answering back to the darker hook of her heart. 10:16. 10:17.

The striker returned to the spot where the defenseman had fallen and reached out his hand to help the slighter boy stand. They walked back to center field, talking about something Alex couldn't hear.

It was 10:19.

She happened to glance at the maple tree again. The sap was still running. A few weeks from now, there would be a reddish hue on the branches. Then buds. A burst of first leaves.

Alex took Patrick's hand. They walked out of the atrium in silence, down the corridors, past the rows of cubbies. They crossed the lobby and threshold of the front door, retracing the steps they'd taken.